SONG OF MYSELF

A Gay Man's Odyssey of Self-Discovery

Arnie Kantrowitz

SENTINEL

VOICES

ISBN: 978-1629672700
Library of Congress Control Number: *Pending*

Cover Design: Tatiana Fernandez
Interior Layout: Brian Schwartz

v24-0328

ACKNOWLEDGMENTS

I would like to thank the following people for background information they provided through conversations, books, articles, and research notes: Allan Berube, John D'Emilio, Bruce Eves, Cathy Kent Fein, Randy Forrester, Jim Foster, Brad Gooch, Aoki Hirotsugu, Jonathan Ned Katz, Donald Knutson, Lawrence Mass, M.D., Ron Petty, John Preston, Cecil Rees, Marc Rubin, Vito Russo, Henry A. Sauerwein, Charley Shively, and Tom Steele.

Partial support for this project was made by a Creative Incentive Award from the Professional Staff Congress-City University of New York, and by a grant from the Helene Wurlitzer Foundation of New Mexico, Henry A. Sauerwein, Director.

In memory of my parents
Jean Zabarsky Kantrowitz Michaels
1924-1971
Morris Kantrowitz
1910-1986

In memory of
Irene Kask Pink
1940-1988

In memory of
All my friends who died of AIDS

For Larry Mass
with love

I celebrate myself, and sing myself,
And what I assume you shall assume,
For every atom belonging to me as good belongs to you.

—Walt Whitman,
"Song of Myself"

Many will say it is a dream, and will not follow my inferences;
but I confidently expect a time when there will be seen, running
like a half-hid warp through all the myriad audible and visible
worldly interests of America, threads of manly friendship, fond
and loving, pure and sweet, strong and life-long, carried to degrees
hitherto unknown—not only giving tone to individual character,
and making it unprecedentedly emotional, muscular, heroic, and
refined, but having the deepest relation to general politics. I say
democracy infers such loving comradeship, as its most inevitable
twin or counterpart, without which it will be incomplete, in vain,
and incapable of perpetuating itself.

—Walt Whitman,
"Song of Myself"

Not for a moment, Walt Whitman, lovely old man,
Have I failed to see your beard full of butterflies . . .

—Federico Garcia Lorca,
"Ode to Walt Whitman"

Good morning, America, how are you?
Say, don't you know me? I'm your native son.

—Steve Goodman,
"City of New Orleans"

TABLE OF CONTENTS

INTRODUCTION 13

EDITOR'S NOTE 17

PROLOGUE 19

PART I - DANIEL DELL BLAKE 21

PART II - DAN BLAKE 93

PART III - DANNY BLAKE 139

PART IV - DELL BLAKE 195

PART V - DELLA BLAKE 285

PART VI - D. D. BLAKE 355

PART VII - DANIEL DELL BLAKE 417

EPILOGUE 441

INTRODUCTION

by Lawrence D. Mass

Falling in love with Arnie Kantrowitz forty-three years ago, I inherited his extended family of Gay Liberation pioneers as my own—Vito Russo, the legendary gay and AIDS activist and author of *The Celluloid Closet*, and the likewise legendary Jim Owles, who initiated and led the struggle for gay civil rights legislation in New York City finally achieved fifteen years later, in 1987.

Talk about Gay Pride. I was living with three of the greatest figures of the post-Stonewall Gay Liberation Movement. I had found my family and my home.

As I read Arnie's novel, I kept thinking how true to life it was for him and us.

Song of Myself is the narrative of one gay man's odyssey of self-discovery through twentieth-century USA—a saga of sex, romance, love, adventure, history, humanity, heart, humor, and hope in times of brutal discrimination, oppression, and persecution.

The protagonist and narrator, Daniel Dell Blake, grows up in small-town America during the Depression and World War II years with no idea who he is, what tribe he belongs to, where and what to call home, who are his people. But, early on, he is given a touchstone to self-understanding that sets the trajectory of the rest of his life—Walt Whitman's *Leaves of Grass*. Whitman's texts, incorporated throughout the novel, provide ongoing illumination into character and motivation, as well as the true nature, the gay heart and soul, of Walt Whitman.

Because of Whitman's status as America's greatest poet, and though it is now more widely accepted that Whitman was homosexual, there continues to be great resistance to openly and clearly acknowledging that Whitman was gay, especially in today's reactionary climate of homophobia and book-banning. Bringing Walt Whitman out of the closet was Arnie's lifelong cause as teacher and activist. It's a quest that infuses every aspect of *Song of Myself*.

Although Arnie discussed his novel with me as he was writing it, I don't recall any capstone statements or spelled-out revelations of intention that aren't already easily discernible in the text. As a writer, as he was otherwise by nature in real life, Arnie was startlingly honest and direct. The same is true of his protagonist and narrator. Arnie wanted to write a fictional version of his own story, of a boy coming of age in pre-liberation America whose muse, in life and writing, is Walt Whitman.

What I intuit to be the deeper subtext and value of Arnie's novel, a context Arnie himself never articulated as such, was this issue of pre-liberation gay people as children, students eager to learn and understand, but without clear role models or guideposts, wandering in adult lands insistent on ignorance and intolerance, without a sense of social acknowledgment, respect, or inclusivity of themselves—ourselves—as real people.

For indeed there was none. We were always in search of home, identity, history, and integrity.

In this sense, *Song of Myself* can seem of a piece with the 1939 movie *The Wizard of Oz*, an icon of gay sensibility and experience released the same year as another of Arnie's favorite movies, *Goodbye, Mr. Chips*, based on the 1934 novella by James Hilton about a teacher beloved by his pupils.

Arnie himself spent more than forty years as a teacher at the College of Staten Island, CUNY, where he established a pioneering Gay Studies course. Like Mr. Chips, he was beloved by his students, many of whom were heterosexual, as he was more widely by his family and community. At the end of his semesters, he'd return home with handfuls of letters, testimonials of appreciation from his students. This "good-teacher sensibility" (with plenty of examples of bad teachers) is everywhere apparent in *Song of Myself*.

The experience of writing the novel, as observed by me, was like many other things in Arnie's life, including the ever-mounting demands of his worsening health. Arnie suffered from all the advanced major complications of diabetes, for which he was frequently hospitalized.

His writing was something he needed to do and wanted to do and that others kept urging him to do, and that he did with skill, purpose, and success, but which he found difficult to get down to the discipline of doing. He used to quote his closest friend, Vito Russo, about how he had to beat himself up to get to the typewriter.

Fortunately for us, Arnie managed to complete a draft of *Song of Myself* that he worked on for a decade and that his agent was able to submit to publishers. When it did not find a home, Arnie, still teaching full-time, put it aside.

Arnie Kantrowitz was inspired and inspiring, and though he could display remarkable grit, he was constitutionally vulnerable and wasn't self-important or personally ambitious. No matter how many times I would bring it up, no matter how gently and tactfully, Arnie, increasingly and eventually legally blind from his diabetes, not only didn't return to the novel, he didn't return to his writing at all.

Among his papers, which are being collected by the New York Public Library, fortunately not only was there a complete manuscript of *Song of Myself*, but also a collection of Arnie's poems. So private was Arnie about his poetry, that no one, including me, knew it existed. That collection hopefully will likewise be posthumously published.

When I began working with editor Patrick Merla on preparing *Song of Myself* for publication, I did so with commitment to gay history, culture, and literature. Arnie is a revered gay activist who is known for writing the Stonewall Classic, *Under The Rainbow: Growing Up Gay*, as an early officer of Gay Activists Alliance and of the Gay and Lesbian Alliance Against Defamation (GLAAD).

What wasn't forefront in my thinking when I embarked on this journey was how trenchant this novel would be for gay life in these rapidly devolving, reactionary times. Indeed, it is all too contemporary.

Daniel Dell Blake's story resonates for all of us today. *Song of Myself* offers alternative possibilities for its ending. That sense of not knowing what the future holds seems especially true today, when conflicts around "truth," stupidity, ignorance, and meanness once again seize us at every turn.

I'm grateful to Patrick Merla for his editorial guidance. Thanks also for their support to Arnie's friends and colleagues at College of Staten Island, Maryann Feola, Judith Stelboum, and Matt Brim; to production coordinator Brian Schwartz and cover designer Tatiana Fernandez; to Lavelle Porter for his work on Walt Whitman and race; to Michael Rubin for his help with Japanese words and phrases; and to Michele Karlsberg, Bill Goldstein, Jaime Manrique, and David Bergman.

New York City
January 26, 2024

EDITOR'S NOTE

by Patrick Merla

Although Arnie Kantrowitz and I were not in frequent touch, I considered him a friend. I esteemed Arnie for his activism, integrity, knowledge, and place in gay history, both as a figure and witness. Arnie's memoir, *Under the Rainbow: Growing Up Gay*, was a formative book for me; I actually apartment-sat at the address on Spring Street mentioned in it, during my itinerant days taking care of other people's houses. And I consider Arnie's short biography of Walt Whitman an important text.

So I felt honored and pleased when Larry Mass asked me to work with him to bring Arnie's novel into print.

As Larry writes in his introduction, "*Song of Myself* is the narrative of one gay man's odyssey of self-discovery through twentieth-century USA—a saga of sex, romance, love, adventure, history, humanity, heart, humor, and hope in times of brutal discrimination, oppression, and persecution." Early on the narrator, Daniel Dell Blake, is given a copy of *Leaves of Grass* and Whitman becomes a sort of spiritual mentor, with Danny repeatedly seeking—and finding—personal meaning in Whitman's texts, citing them liberally throughout the book.

Daniel Dell Blake is a Gay Everyman who experiences personally or at close hand almost everything a member of a sexual minority could go through during the years 1924 to 1987. (In a way this reminds me of John Boyne's *The Heart's Invisible Furies*, which does something similar for a gay Irishman during the years 1945 through 2015; Arnie completed his own novel in 1992.) If this sounds didactic, *Song of Myself* itself is not. The adventures, mishaps, tragedies, and joys of Arnie's vivid characters are continually engaging, and sometimes quite moving.

The book's success is due in part to Arnie's rooting Danny's story in key historical events and places. (At one point, Danny meets Arnie at a political gathering.) Arnie's credentials as a scholar serve him well here. The depth of his research—in a period before the Internet and Google—yields rich results. A few anachronisms have been silently corrected.

Given that Arnie is no longer with us, the decision was made to simply copy edit the novel rather than do even minimal line editing. Similarly with dialogue: Characters are delineated in part by how they talk; today Arnie would have worked with a sensitivity reader, impossible now. We hope this will not be a drawback for most readers. The subtitle was added by Larry Mass.

Danny states that the title page of his treasured edition of *Leaves of Grass* is dated 1892—making it Whitman's final text. All quotes were verified by referring to the online Walt Whitman Archive (whitmanarchive.org), which includes reproductions of pages from the 1892 publication; or from comparable contemporary sources if they are not on the Whitman Archive site.

New York City
March 12, 2024

PROLOGUE

This book is not what it was supposed to be, but then neither am I. I first set out to write about Walt Whitman, whose work I've loved since I was a boy. The title *Song of Myself* was supposed to refer to him, but after spending many years futilely trying to make sense of the life he led a century before my time, I finally realized that I had to make sense of my own life first, so the *Myself* in the title will have to be me, Dell Blake. I hope you won't be disappointed.

The life I was originally expected to lead was a dull one, confined to the small town of Elysium, New York, where I was born. But somehow my years have been spread all across the American continent (along with an ill-fated sojourn in a hell of a paradise known as the South Pacific), and I've managed to have more than my share of exotic adventures. Without even trying, I have been an outrage to my family, my church, and my nation, but never to myself or to those I love. To society I'm some kind of alien weed growing in the wrong soil, but to my mind, I'm the natural vegetation of the American landscape—not the artificial, evenly manicured kind of grass that's found in overly cultivated yards, but a wilder sort of crabgrass that defies the best efforts of the gardeners to eradicate it because it's sturdy and can take root anywhere.

I know that anybody who puts his life into a book is going to be called an egotist. Walt was called worse than that for writing *Leaves of Grass*. But I've never been especially worried about what other people think, and I see no reason to start now. I'm recording my story because it's interesting, not because I'm an exceptional person. "Who holds this book holds a man," Walt would have said, but let's face it: Who holds this book holds a book. You can turn yourself inside out and examine yourself minutely and be as honest as you know how, and render your story in the most exquisite phrases imaginable, but you can't make more than an approximation of a real human being out of words. You can only make a book, and that's accomplishment enough.

It's a little embarrassing for a man of sixty-three to be still formulating the structure of his life, but I have a reason. I am about to inherit a twelve-year-old son, and no matter what kind of man he grows up to be, I hope he will be able to benefit from my experience. His father, the man I love, is in the next room, dying, and I have agreed to take his place when he is gone. I am not called "husband" or "wife," "mother" or "father" in this family, but I am some of each. I am not even a "longtime companion," having been present for less than two years. What I am is loved, respected, and trusted, and that is sufficient for me. Although there have been many kinds of men in my life, these two are the most important of all, and so here is how I want to dedicate my autobiography:

To Alexander, my son,
and to the memory of his first father, Aaron,
with love and thanks.

This is the second chance I will have at being a parent, and I am all the more grateful for it because I failed miserably at it the first time, many years ago. The problems of fatherhood are something of a tradition in my family, my own father having been a miserable wretch at the job, like his father before him. I need an antacid to look back at some parts of my past because, like most people my age, I find that the longer my memory grows, the sharper it gets. I'm not sure what I had for breakfast this morning, but I can recall the scenes of more than half a century ago as if I were right there, living through them all over again.

When I lived in Elysium as a boy in the 1920s, I was blond and wide-eyed and apple-cheeked and full of spunk. Now in the late 1980s, my hair is gray, my face looks rutted with travel, my skin sags and flutters, and my energy, like a hired relative, takes occasional days off without notice. Even the luster in my eyes is beginning to grow dimmer. But I'm sure that's an indication of having seen so much and not a sign that my enthusiasm has diminished. In the end, it doesn't matter what I may look like. What matters is whether I am ready for the task that lies before me.

Daniel Dell Blake

PART I
DANIEL DELL BLAKE

There was a child went forth every day,
And the first object he look'd upon, that object he became,
And that object became part of him for the day or a certain
    part of the day,
Or for many years or stretching cycles of years.

—Walt Whitman,
"There Was a Child Went Forth"

CHAPTER ONE

"All flesh is as grass, and all the glory of man as the flower of grass." My father read from his Bible as I tried to stifle a yawn. He peered at me, over the top of the book, which he held in his hands like a weapon. Clearing his throat, he continued. "The grass withereth and the flower thereof falleth away: But the word of the Lord endureth forever." I, meanwhile, was imagining how I'd look in Theda Bara's dark eye makeup. I'd seen a picture of her in an old movie poster at the general store. I'd never been to a movie yet, but I planned to see one as soon as I could get to Syracuse on my own. I knew I was going to love it. My father closed the book with a solid thump and looked at me. "Is that clear, Daniel?"

"Yeth, Father," I said, hoping he wouldn't start carrying on about my lisp again. If I said the passage wasn't clear, I knew I was in for a twenty-minute lecture on the virtue of minding God's words, which still wouldn't make them any clearer. If he got worked up about my lisp, I was afraid he would end up hitting me and calling me names. I chose the safest course and hoped for the best.

"Good, then tell me what it means."

"It meanth . . . uh . . . I'm not sure I can thay."

"Daniel, were you paying attention?"

"Yeth, Father."

"Then what does the passage tell you?"

"It tellith me that the grath dieth young."

"Is that all?"

"And we die young too?" I was guessing, but something like that was usually the message of what my father read, so I knew I couldn't be too far off the mark.

"Amen," he said. "And therefore you must not be . . . ?"

I riffled through the answers I knew he was probably looking for: Proud? Slothful? Greedy? It had to be one of the sins that caused grief to Jesus and shut Him out of your life. Those were his favorites. "Vain," I guessed.

"That's right, boy. Sometimes you surprise me. I was sure you were dreaming about something else."

That shows you how well my father knew me. Bible reading was the only communication we had, aside from his assigning me chores. My childhood wasn't as bad as some, but it was a little short on nurture.

Since there was no breast handy when I was a baby, if I nursed on anything it was probably an apple. I was raised in an apple orchard, and Mrs. Varner, our housekeeper, had all she could do to keep up with the supply. She made applesauce and apple pie, Apple Brown Betty and apple fritters, apple pandowdy, baked apples, apple cake, apple cider, and in between she served just plain raw apples from the root cellar. I suppose I liked apples in the beginning, and I spent many a childhood afternoon sitting in the attic window with one of them in my hand and a good book in the other, but eventually I couldn't look an apple in the cheek without wanting to throw up. And that goes for all those songs, too—"(I'll Be With You) In Apple Blossom Time" and "Don't Sit Under the Apple Tree (With Anyone Else But Me)" and "Cherry Pink and Apple Blossom White." They all nauseate me. Johnny Appleseed is no hero of mine.

Aside from the apple trees, I didn't have much in the way of company in my early years. Mrs. Warner was a thin, tight-lipped, bony-cheeked widow with straggly hair that refused to stay tucked in its knot at the back of her head. She worked hard for my father and didn't have much to talk about aside from cooking and cleaning and God. She must have been a real masochist. The more God abused her, the more she loved Him. First He made one of her legs considerably shorter than the other, so she had to wear a heavy, built-up shoe as she limped through her life. Then He let her marry one of the poorest men in the valley, who beat her up regularly and blessed her with four sickly children. Finally, He took all her family away in a fire, and left her a thankless job with my father to spin out the rest of her miserable days. The only thing she could do in response to all this mistreatment was thank God and praise His name between scrubbing floors and ironing shirts and cooking those damned apples. I figure she was afraid to look ungrateful for fear that worse would be done to her, which is as good a reason for piety as any. I always wondered if she had committed some extravagant sin like murder or failing to honor her parents and had accepted her lot as a just punishment. But I wasn't about to ask her anything so personal and unleash one of her cautionary sermons about pleasing the Lord. I was only too glad to keep out of her misbegotten way.

My father was even worse company. I can't quite say I lived with him. We just slept in the same house. He was a bald, skinny man with stone gray eyes and a chiseled gray face composed of hard planes and angles. He spent most of his time by himself. "Keeping his own counsel" he called it. "Psychotic" is my word for it. His happiest mood was sullenness, and from there his emotions ran the gamut from disgust to anger to mind-your-own-damned-business: a real friendly sort of guy. I suppose I shouldn't be so harsh on the old man. He couldn't help what life made him any more than anybody else can, even if he did bring most of his own misery on himself.

Like Mrs. Warner, he talked about God a lot, but I never got the feeling that he really meant it. It was hard to tell with him. His version of enthusiasm was anyone else's idea of sarcasm. He never had that special light that some people get in their eyes when they talk about God, but he sure was a stickler for the rules in the Bible, which didn't include the use of such civilities as "please" or "thank you." So he usually communicated with a jerk of his head or a grunt or just a stone glare, unless he had something critical to say. I was glad he preferred the company of his apples to my own and Mrs. Warner's. He treated us both with contempt, and we did our best to ignore him.

I never knew my mother. My father wouldn't discuss her, except to tell me she was dead. I didn't even know what she looked like. There were no pictures of her in the house. There were no pictures of anything worth looking at, just the same blue Maxfield Parrish prints that almost every living room in town sported and no one paid any attention to. They probably grew on the walls like fungus in our part of the state. Wondering if my mother had been the one to pick them out from some tacky catalogue, I tried to find some other clue to who she had been. She wasn't buried in the family plot with the other relatives. She didn't seem to be anywhere. Finally, while rummaging in an attic drawer, I found my birth certificate, which announced that Daniel Dell Blake had been born on June 28, 1924. The "Dell" was news to me. I had only known myself as Daniel Blake until then. My father's name was written in his usual dark and angular hand: "John Ezra Blake." My mother's name looked carefully inscribed, in strong, elegant strokes: "Helen Dell Blake." I studied the signature for an hour, looking for some inkling of the woman who had held the pen. She was short, or maybe tall fat—no, slim, and beautiful: at least beautiful. But the only thing I ever knew about her was that she knew how to sign her name clearly.

We lived a couple of miles outside of Elysium, New York, which in the 1920s was little more than a general store with a post office inside, a two-room schoolhouse, and a small white church. A few dozen Victorian-style clapboard houses were strung along four or five wide, shady streets, most with elaborate gingerbread cutouts framing their spacious front porches, so the people who sat quietly sipping their lemonades there on silent summer afternoons looked like yellowed photographs from the nineteenth century waiting for somebody to come along and dust them.

On Sundays my father drove Mrs. Warner and me into town in his battered pickup truck, and we sat through the endless sermons delivered by Reverend Friendly, a cherubic-looking man who droned on monotonously for what seemed like hours without raising or lowering his pitch even slightly, so that staying awake was truly a service to God, at least as far as I was concerned. I think even Jesus would have nodded off. His wife played a small organ (no pun intended), and their five children sat right beneath the pulpit, where their father could watch them being bored and be sure that they didn't squirm in front of the congregation.

My father saw himself as God's warden. Whenever my head began to droop—which was pretty often—I got his sharp elbow in my ribs, and on the Sundays when the good Reverend was especially dull, my side became black-and-blue. Mrs. Warner sat on the other side of my father, lapping it all up, or maybe praying for a little mercy—I couldn't tell which. It was the high point of her wretched week. For all our disconnectedness, the three of us probably looked like a model family, lined up in our pew. I learned early that appearances are deceiving.

I suppose Mrs. Warner did her lackluster best, but if anyone was my spiritual parent during childhood, it was Martha. "Martha" was no more than a single name without identification or dates, surrounded by a simple circle carved on a plain white slab of granite at the edge of the family plot in the graveyard which abutted our orchard. Some of my earliest companions were in that graveyard. (Don't worry, I'm not a necrophiliac. But I did develop a special feeling for the dead very early in my life because, however silent they were, at least they didn't have the limitations of the living.)

Martha could have been anyone. I guessed immediately that she was my mother, but Mrs. Varner assured me that she was not and cautioned that I'd better not ask my father about Martha if I wanted to avoid a scene. So I made up my own stories about her and adjusted them from time to time to suit my changing moods. Sometimes she became a princess who'd been exiled from her exotic country for loving the wrong man, lived out her life in lonely anonymity on the road, and died in the snow at our doorstep. At other times she was a demented distant cousin who had been driven to insanity by the cruel coldness of her relatives and had died in a madhouse far away, in such degradation that her name was an embarrassment to the family. Sometimes she wasn't even a person at all, but a beloved lapdog belonging to some doting great aunt I never knew. I could always trust Martha to be whoever I needed her to be, and I told her all my childhood secrets and woes.

The other family gravestones had more explicit information on them. There were over two dozen of them: "Dear Wife Abigail Emerson Blake, 1835-1886"; and "James Blake, Six Years Olde, Crushed by Tree, 1860"; and the most timeworn, "Ezra Blake, 1721-1770, When thif you fee, remember me / The image of what ye fhall be." I had no idea what "thif" and "fee" and "fhall" meant unless they were misspellings, so I imagined that Great-Great-Grandpa Ezra might have had a lisp like mine, and I felt a special connection to him until I was years older and knew something about the eighteenth-century alphabet—and then I found the old boy kind of witty, especially compared to his miserable descendent, my father. I tried to imagine little James and Dear Wife Abigail and the two Johns, John Noah and John Jeremiah. But mostly I imagined Martha, who for me was the star of the cemetery.

My father rarely came out to the graveyard, which was just beyond a far corner of the orchard and shielded by apple trees. So I made it my special refuge whenever I wanted to get away from him, at least during the good weather. In the winter I had no choice, because snowstorms covered the ground from Thanksgiving to Easter and, like it or not, I was stuck in the house, where I was left to my own devices as long as I didn't make too much noise. My father stayed in his room a lot, and Mrs. Warner spent most of her time in the kitchen. So I lived inside my own head, in a land populated with pretend companions. I really wanted a doll to play with, but I knew that was out of the question; so I scoured the attic and found a faded old red braided-silk tassel with a large button top intended for disguising picture hooks where they protruded from the molding near the ceiling. It was an elegance scorned by my father, and I have no idea where it came from, but I pretended it was a doll and spent many hours crooning to it and putting it carefully to bed in a drawer where it was safe from the grown-ups. I named it Eve after the biblical character my father railed against most, calling her "evil temptress" and "the mother of sin," although I never understood what someone in his line of work could possibly have against anyone for sharing an apple.

One snowy day as I hung around the house, I noticed that the door to Mrs. Warner's room was ajar. Peering inside, I saw that no one was there. I assumed that she was probably down in the kitchen as usual, so I decided to explore. Her extra pair of special shoes stood neatly under the bed. The left one was built up with a thick sole and a high heel. My curiosity got the better of me, and I took off my own shoes and tried them on. I walked as quietly as I could on the threadbare carpet that covered the floor, enjoying the feeling of being so off balance.

I don't know what possessed me then, but I went to her closet where her wardrobe of drab dresses hung. They were nothing like the glamorous, short, beaded flapper dresses I'd seen in magazines. The colors were dark and the materials serviceable. They were all cut similarly, with long sleeves and prudent necklines. I chose a maroon one, slipped it on over my clothes, and hobbled over to the plain framed mirror, to see what I had wrought. The hem gathered in a ridiculous puddle around my feet, although when Mrs. Warner wore it, it came down only to her ankles. I cradled my imitation doll in my arms against the sagging pleated bodice and crooned, "Sleep, baby Eve, sleep," feeling at the same time soothingly maternal and thrilled with the danger of being caught at a game I was sure was forbidden, even though it had never been discussed. I thought I heard a sharp intake of someone's breath, almost a gasp, in the hall just outside the room, and I turned quickly to see if someone were there. I was almost sure I saw a sudden motion, as if someone were hastily withdrawing from the doorway. It had to be Mrs. Warner! I stood motionless for a minute or two to try to hear a sound, but there was none. Then I moved like a whirlwind to rid myself of the absurd dress and shoes. I replaced them carefully where I had found them and fled from the room, holding Eve by the knob that I pretended was her head.

I found Mrs. Warner was downstairs in the kitchen, but she didn't look up when I walked noisily in behind her. The usual silence was observed at the supper table, and I wasn't about to ask any damning questions. So I tried to annul the memory of that scene and did all I could not to arouse any further suspicion.

April turned the branches of the apple trees red, and I would run out to the orchards daily to check them for the first buds of spring, which meant liberation from the house. When they blossomed into miraculous white clouds in May, I was in paradise, far away from the drabness of winter. One year when the blossoms had just fallen and covered the ground like a layer of fragrant snow, I danced gleefully among the trees, sprinkling handfuls of petals behind me, imagining myself a satyr, minus the pipes, celebrating the rites of Bacchus. I was so lost in my reverie that I didn't hear my father approach until it was too late, and when I turned and found myself looking at the consternation in his gray face, I said placatingly, "Ithn't it a lovely day?"

He slapped me and said, "Don't use that word. It isn't manly. And stop that damnable lisping before I take you to have your tongue trimmed. You sound disgusting, like a lizzie." Of course I didn't ask him what a "lizzie" was. Somehow I knew it had something to do with being sissified, and I didn't want to have my frail masculinity challenged. So I determined that I would avoid saying the letter "s" as much as possible, which caused me to resort to some pretty convoluted phrasing—and that probably had the benefit of sharpening my awareness of words. I didn't say "lovely" again for a long time, at least not when my father was around, and I always checked to be sure I was alone before I let myself act the way I felt. But the next spring when I tried to dance among the apple blossoms, it just wasn't fun anymore, so I gave it up.

In the summer, when the trees were a rich shade of green, I would stay out after supper until dusk, just to be by myself. Before I went indoors, I used to say good night to each thing in the landscape—to the grass and rocks, the trees and the apples, the clouds and the stars—one by one. There was so much magic in it that it took me half an hour to get ready to go in, and by then, if I was lucky, my father would be asleep. On the way in, I used to catch fireflies in my cupped hands, trying to capture their glow for myself. Once I brought a glass jar with holes punched in its metal lid and caught seventeen of them and put them inside. The jar glowed with a beautiful, frail light almost constantly. I left the jar of fireflies behind Martha's stone and said good night to it as well, but when I came back the next day, all the fireflies were dead, and I promised myself never to kill anything else again if I could help it.

In the fall, the leaves in the orchard turned bright yellow-orange, and the apples hung in heavy clusters that filled the air for miles with their scent. In late August the William Tells were ready, and in early October the McIntoshes and then the Cortlands, each kind in its turn. But I was not there to enjoy them once I started school.

The one-room schoolhouse on the edge of town was run by Miss Standish, who seemed as stern as my father. She taught about twenty students a year, ranging from kindergarten to eighth grade, and she terrorized the smallest and largest of her charges with the same ease. Even the thirteen-year-olds, who were ready for the trip to Valley High School, withered under her stern glances. Her solid black hair was done up in a large bun that protruded from the nape of her neck like Olive Oyl's and was balanced by her large nose, on which was perched a pince-nez which fell off several times an hour, whenever she raised her eyebrows. She never failed to catch the falling eyeglasses with her free hand before they tautened the long black ribbon by which they were suspended from her neck, and she never missed a word while performing this feat. The apples I occasionally brought her were received as her due, with a cool-but-courteous "Thank you, Daniel." But if her glance ever warmed slightly, I couldn't see it.

She kept us constantly busy naming the chief exports of South America, multiplying fractions, or making endless lines of ovals with our scratchy straight pens, which we cleaned with chamois pen wipers, trying to avoid points off for the inevitable inkblots that marred the perfect pages she demanded. Her favorite form of torture was memorization. I can still hear the dutiful voices reciting her favorite, "O Captain! My Captain!":

> But O heart! heart! heart!
>   O the bleeding drops of red,
>   Where on the deck my Captain lies,
>   Fallen cold and dead.

Miss Standish acted as if it was a passage from the Bible or something, the way she insisted on perfection in our recitations. But I had a hard enough time not giggling when it was my turn, because instead of the death of Abraham Lincoln, I kept thinking of a valentine gone rotten. She said its author, Walt Whitman, was a great man, but it took a little more reading to convince me.

Miss Standish lived in the town with another spinster, Miss Betsy Binder, who was the part-time librarian in a small room attached to the schoolhouse. She was the opposite of Miss Standish. Her face always had a believably

sweet expression. Her dresses were patterned with tiny flowerets, and she
always kept a large cameo brooch at her throat, unlike Miss Standish, who
wore tailored suits with ankle-length skirts and a small, grim bow tie. Miss
Binder wore her hair in a Marcel wave instead of a bun, but she had a pince-
nez just like Miss Standish's, except that Miss Binder's spectacles never fell
off in public. Maybe she never needed to raise her eyebrows because she
was too innocent or too tolerant to be easily shocked. I don't know how
they got along on the tiny salaries the town could afford to pay them.
Possibly they had some private means of support. But few had much to
spare during the Great Depression, so their genteel poverty was not much
different from most people's.

Once I discovered the library, Miss Binder became the mother of my
secret world. She introduced me to the Brothers Grimm and Hans Christian
Andersen, with whom I fell in love immediately. I used to read their fairy
tales out by Martha's stone in the graveyard, because I knew my father would
never approve of such frivolous readings. He stuck to the Bible and the Sears
Roebuck catalogue while I liked "The Red Shoes" and "The Ugly Duckling."
But most of all I liked "The Little Mermaid" for its wistful story of hopeless
lovers from separate worlds.

It was Miss Binder who helped me to get over my lisp. When I asked for
her help, she responded with patient training, and taught me that I could
keep my tongue behind my teeth when I had to say "s." As soon as I had
practiced enough, I found that I didn't have to watch every word in order
to avoid the sound of "s," and I felt as if my speech had been unchained.

"I will be eternally grateful," I told her.

"A simple 'thank you' will suffice, Daniel," she said with a smile.

"Yes, if you say so, 'thank you' will suffice," I said, relishing all the "s"
sounds.

"There's no need to show off your new skill," she said, "but I am proud
of you." And she hugged me so closely that I could smell the faint traces of
her bath soap.

I loved Miss Binder, so I spent as much time in her library as I could and
brought her apples whenever possible. Unlike Miss Standish, she always
responded with a thank you and a hug, and soon she began to invite me to
her home, where she and Miss Standish and I had little tea parties. Their
parlor wasn't very different from ours. Like most places in town, it looked
as if the main effort in decorating was not to appear too individual.
Nevertheless, it was my idea of a great place to be. It was papered with a
faded floral pattern on which hung a picture—but not the usual blue
Maxfield Parrish. Their picture was a photograph of two large white flowers,
nestled against each other like lovers and lit in some miraculous way that
made them seem to glow with an almost erotic invitation to enter their deep,
mysterious centers. I had never seen a photograph framed as art before, only

the usual cluster of uncle and grandma portraits that most of the neighbors set out in small armies on tables covered with fringed cloths. I thought those flowers were the most beautiful thing in town, but I was equally drawn to a small pink marble sculpture that stood on its own separate wall shelf. It looked vaguely like two men wrestling, but that was probably my imagination. It was a convoluted jumble of curves and angles that might have been anything. I loved to trace my fingertips along its cool stone swells and creases. Carved into its base was the sculptor's signature: Chester Lane Stewart. "This is a gift from a former pupil," Miss Standish explained. "He's an artist now." In the middle of the room there was a worn settee with a carved wood frame and a lace antimacassar pinned to its back, facing two plump armchairs done up in the same accessories. All of them had doilies carefully placed at the ends of their arms, attempting to hide the worn patches. The Misses Standish and Binder sat in the armchairs, and I perched in the middle of the settee. I liked to imagine that the floor lamp with the fringed dome shade was a dancer that would take off and whirl about the room when I wasn't looking. But nothing that exciting could ever have happened in Elysium, New York, and it always stood there like a weary sentinel, waiting for the excitement to begin. The center of the floor was covered by a round, braided rag rug on which sat a small table with a blue china tea service and a plate of plain, round butter cookies.

"I hope you like these, Daniel," Miss Standish said. "Miss Binder baked them herself."

"Yes," I said, afraid that the crumbs from the one in my mouth would betray me and spill out over my chin. "I like them very much. You're a wonderful baker, Miss Binder."

"Don't talk with your mouth full, Daniel," Miss Standish cautioned. "It isn't polite."

"Hush, Myra," interceded Miss Binder. "He means well. Let him enjoy himself. We're not in school now." To my amazement, Miss Standish sputtered slightly, but did not demur. I got the distinct impression that Miss Binder was the boss at home, and Miss Standish's toughness was saved for the classroom. I was never quite as frightened of her again, but I was never disobedient either.

"Do you have any friends outside of school, Daniel?" Miss Binder continued.

"No, ma'am, there's nobody my age near enough to our farm. I like some of the kids in school, but most of the time I keep my own counsel." I hoped Miss Standish was impressed with my adult phrase, but she didn't lose her pince-nez over it.

"Sounds serious," Miss Binder said. "You must be lonely."

"I'm not lonely right now," I answered, bringing a faint smile even to Miss Standish's lips.

After that I visited the two women as often as they allowed me to, which was about once a month or so. Miss Standish still kept her distance, but she did seem a tiny bit softer at home than she did at school. Miss Binder, on the other hand, grew warmer and warmer. She always had something new for me to read. I progressed from fairy tales to animal stories to the Hardy Boys adventures to Horatio Alger's books. She was always one step ahead of my eager imagination, as if she knew my fantasy life better than I did myself.

Eventually I was confiding my childhood hopes and fears to her, hungry for someone to hear them, which she did with a sympathetic ear, not at all shocked, even when I told her I thought I was different from the other boys. They were busy with more manly occupations than the reading of fairy tales and stories, at least according to my father, who was beginning to grumble that I was becoming a bookworm and a sissy.

"Don't you worry about it, Daniel," Miss Binder consoled me. "There is a place for everyone in God's world."

When I was about twelve, my body began to change, and for the first time I didn't feel comfortable asking Miss Binder for advice. I was appalled by my first straggly pubic hairs, but the first time I had an erection, I was quite impressed with myself. I knew a thing or two about sex from seeing the local barnyard animals at play, but there were still lots of unexplained mysteries. My first orgasm happened in my sleep. I dreamed that my father came to my room wearing his long winter underwear, which I knew he changed no more often than once a week, even though he slept in it. He sat on my bed and held me close, so that I could smell the accumulated odors of his body that had settled into the begrimed cloth, and I was embarrassed because I was getting aroused. Then he kissed me on the lips, and that's when I woke up to find my nightclothes dripping with semen. I washed my pajamas myself and hid them in the attic to dry, not wanting to offend Mrs. Warner, who, despite having borne four children, seemed not to acknowledge that she possessed a body. The next few nights were spent guiltily trying to concentrate on my father before I fell asleep, hoping that I would have the same dream and the same exciting sensations. I didn't know how else to make it happen, until I found out at school that fall. What better place was there to learn the facts of life?

The only other boy my age in the schoolhouse was Adam Witherspoon. Adam was nobody's idea of a dreamboat. He was gawky and pimply, with a nose that looked like it belonged on somebody else's face. We were friendly enough, but we had never visited outside of school, since he lived on a farm a few miles from ours, which was too far to walk without a specific purpose. I figured that he might know what I was trying to learn, so I decided to keep my eye on him and if I thought he knew anything, I would give him a reason to visit me.

One day I arrived early at school and went out back to the privy, where I found the door locked from inside. I waited for my turn, but instead of the usual disgusting noises, I heard hard breathing and moaning and grunting. Finally there was a little cry and then a long, deep sigh. I don't know what told me, but I knew I was on the trail of what I was looking for.

When the door finally opened, Adam Witherspoon emerged. He had a weird look on his face when he saw me standing there. "Daniel, what are you doing here so early?" he said, sounding embarrassed.

"Spying," I said, just to kid him, but he didn't think it was very funny.

"Minding your own business would be a better idea," he said. "Then I guess I shouldn't tell you about the white goo all over your pants," I countered. There wasn't any, but it was a lucky guess. He turned all red and looked down at his pants in a panic. When he didn't find anything there, he gave me a disgusted look and walked off. I watched his trousers slide across his buns as he walked toward the school, and I wondered what it would be like to touch his body. I was so eager that even Frankenstein's monster would have held some appeal for me at that point.

During recess, Adam was standing by himself, staring at a yellow roadster which was parked near the schoolyard. A well-developed man's backside covered by work pants was all that could be seen of a mechanic whose torso was hidden under the hood. If I had had a camera, I would have begun my career in photography right there. I was so enthusiastic that it didn't even occur to me that Adam might be more interested in the car than in the buttocks it was framing.

"That's nice, isn't it?" I said, tiptoeing up behind him.

"Are you practicing to be a sneak or what?" he said, startled.

"What do you want me to do, knock? There isn't any door here, you know." I looked toward the car. "I wish he'd take me for a spin."

"Don't you know whose car that is?" he said, not understanding what I really wanted. "It's Chester Stewart's. Isn't it swell?"

"It sure is," I said. At that moment the mechanic stood up and wiped his forearm across his brow. His wavy auburn hair glinted in the sun as he glanced our way, and I could see that beneath the dirty workman's coveralls there was a clean, handsome gentleman. Then my mind registered the name I had just heard, and I remembered the sculpture in Miss Binder's parlor. "Do you mean Chester Lane Stewart?"

"Ayuh," he replied with the twang native to upstate New York. "I wish I had all the money that Chester inherited when his father died last year. I'd buy seven cars, one for each day of the week."

"What colors would they be?"

"Any colors. What a stupid question. It's what's under the hood that counts."

Noticing that the auburn-haired man had returned to his work, I said suggestively, "I'd like to see what's under the hood right now."

"You're weird," Adam said, and wrestled me to the ground. I let him get on top of me without too much struggle, and he sat on my chest, not knowing what to do next. My groin started to stir from the contact, and I could see his was swelling too.

"I'll show you mine if you'll show me yours," I said, hoping he wouldn't hit me.

"Who wants to see your old weenie? It's probably no bigger than this!" He thrust his pinky in front of my face.

"It is, too—but I don't know if it's any bigger than anybody else's. How big is yours?"

"Big enough," he said.

I seized my chance. "Does white stuff come out of the end?"

"I thought you knew so much about it," he said. "You talked pretty smart this morning."

Just then Miss Standish intervened. "Adam! Daniel! Get up from there this instant! I won't have you boys fighting on school property. You'll both write in your notebooks one hundred times, 'I must not fight in the schoolyard.' Now march!"

When we stood up to brush ourselves off, I could see that we both had erections tenting the fronts of our trousers. We immediately hid them by holding our books in front of ourselves. "Meet me after school," Adam said.

As we walked past Miss Standish's scowl and into the schoolhouse, I turned for a last look toward the yellow roadster. The auburn-haired man had emerged again and was looking after us with a curious smile on his face. I have never forgotten that moment. It was the handsomest face and the most appealing smile I have ever seen in my life.

After school, Adam took the bus home with me and we went into my father's orchard, where we compared erections under the apple trees. My first reaction was horror. They were different! Where he had a loose fold of skin encircling the head of his, I had nothing.

"How did you grow that extra piece?" I asked.

"I was born with it. All boys are."

"Then where's mine?" I inquired. I was embarrassed and tried to hide myself.

He took my hands away from my crotch.

"You've been cut," he said. "Circumcised."

"What's that mean?" I asked. "Who did it?"

"It means the doctor cut off your foreskin when you were born, to keep it clean. How does it feel?"

"How do I know? I don't remember what it felt like to have one."

"Mine feels good when I slide it," he said. "Hey, look at this!" He stuck his fingers under the rim and stretched it out into a kind of square, framing the round head. It looked kind of scary, as if it could rip, and I felt myself growing squeamish. But he seemed to be enjoying himself, and my distaste soon turned to jealousy, so I continued my comparison. They were about the same length, give or take half an inch, but his was skinnier and had a bigger head. Mine was better-looking, I decided. But a good deal of research since then has proved it to be a pretty average model.

I was average-looking all around, not too tall or short, not too fat or thin or handsome or ugly—just average. And that was fine with me, because I never felt quite like everybody else inside, and I was glad my appearance didn't give that fact away. I had sandy blond hair, which Mrs. Warner cut in bangs straight across my forehead; gray eyes; a straight, slightly upturned nose that, unlike Adam's, looked pretty good right where it was; and a firm, square chin that I presumed was my mother's gift because my father's was pointed.

Adam was something like a stork, with a long beak and a gangly walk, but his looks didn't matter to me as much as what he could teach me about what he held in his hand.

"Show me how the cream comes out," I said.

"Okay, but I think you're supposed to save it for your wife. It might be a sin or something if you do it to yourself. But I did it a few times anyway, and it feels real good—kind of high, like when you drink hard liquor."

"I see," I said, although I had never tasted anything harder than cider in my life. I had felt a little dizzy after drinking it once, and I guessed that was what Adam meant, but I wasn't about to show him all my ignorance in one day. "Let me see you do it."

He started, and then I imitated him, and it felt great once the rhythm got going, each of us pumping at his own rate. And then the cream spurted from his, and mine followed suit, spurting all over the ground, and we watched it sink into the soil.

"Let's do it again," I said. "I liked that."

"You have to wait a few minutes," he told me. "It takes a while to build up."

"I have to go in pretty soon. Can we try this again sometime?"

"I guess so." He didn't seem as enthusiastic about it as I was.

"Do you think it's weird or anything? I mean, two boys doing it together?"

"I don't see why, but it might be," he said. "I just don't know."

"Who can we ask?"

"Nobody. You'd better not talk about this, Daniel. We could get into a lot of trouble."

"Don't worry. Who would I tell?" I assured him, picking a couple of nearly ripe apples from a tree and handing him one. I knew I was disobeying my father's injunction to eat only those apples that had already been picked, but I didn't care. We sat there and ate them together without saying anything else. Then he picked up his schoolbooks and started home. "See you," he called over his shoulder.

"Ayuh," I said.

An hour later I had a bellyache, and I wondered if it was some sort of punishment—not for eating an unripe apple, but for what I'd done. Then I decided that I couldn't be held responsible for disobeying rules no one had ever told me about, and I thought about Adam's foreskin and played with myself until I had another orgasm.

There were some questions I just had to have the answers to, I decided, and there were no choices about who could provide them. At dinner that night, I broke the customary silence and addressed my father. "Are you circumcised?" I asked.

He nearly swallowed his spoon. "What business could that be of yours?"

"I don't have a foreskin like the other boys."

"Too bad for you, isn't it?"

"I thought you were so pious. If God put it there, why did you have it removed?"

"Your mother did it," he said, returning to his beef stew, and I knew that was the end of the conversation. He had never once mentioned her in two consecutive sentences. This was as major a piece of my mother's puzzle as any I had yet retrieved, but there was no way to pursue it. I looked at him for some sign that he might relent, but he met my glance with his cold, stone eyes, and I faded back into silence while Mrs. Warner brought in the applesauce.

Adam and I met secretly half a dozen times during the next year. We taught each other whatever we could, which wasn't much. We didn't know what two men could do together, and he wasn't willing to try out the exotic ideas I worked so hard at dreaming up, so we eventually got pretty bored. I played with myself pretty often, and on two or three of those occasions I borrowed my father's long johns from the hamper and put them on because their aroma was arousing, even if their owner's personality was not.

By the end of the school year, I had graduated from Miss Standish's school. There was a small ceremony, but my father didn't come because he was busy pruning his trees.

When I first got to Valley High School, I told everyone my name was "Dell Blake," hoping to add a little elegance to my drab identity. But when they called me, I didn't answer, so I soon settled for "Danny." Adam and I played together one or two times after we began classes at our new school, but we soon drifted into different circles of friends. It wasn't long before he started dating Sally Wayne, whose breasts were a school legend. It was a bigger world with more kinds of people, so I hoped I'd meet somebody to take his place, but even though I was as sociable as I could be, I had no really close friends at first. I was popular enough in a general sort of way, but I was always being careful not to let anyone know how much the senior football players aroused me—or the local farmhands, or the English teacher, or the school janitor. I kept my lust to myself, and I imagine that my guardedness didn't encourage others to be on more intimate terms with me.

I ordinarily wouldn't have said anything when the yellow roadster drove past the lunchtime crowd on the school's front lawn, and somebody near me whispered, "There goes that Chester Stewart. I hear he's a real cornholer."

Although I'd never heard the word before, I instinctively guessed that "cornholer" meant something sexual, and I grew excited, remembering Chester's appealing smile. But I managed to play innocent in spite of myself and asked, "Why, because he drives a yellow car?"

"Don't be a jerk. There's something queer about him. As far as anybody knows he's never had a girlfriend around here. He calls himself an artist, and he makes weird statues," was the answer.

Someone else added, "My father's on the town council, and he says Chester wants to put up a statue full of strange shapes and half-naked people. He says I should keep away from men like that."

"Like what?"

"I'm not sure. Artists, I guess."

"Do you know anything about artists?" I asked. "Are they all queer?"

"I don't know," he answered. "I never met one."

"Neither did I," was my answer. But right then and there I decided that, one way or another, I would meet Chester Stewart.

CHAPTER TWO

I convinced my father to take me to the next town meeting on the grounds that I should know something about local affairs. It was the first overt interest I had ever shown in politics, so I suppose he thought it was a good idea, but he certainly didn't pat me on the head about it. Of course I found most of the meeting stultifying. Financing the paving of dirt roads has never been high on my list of hot conversation topics. But Chester had no trouble holding my interest.

He stood out among the drab farmers like a lily in a wheat field. It wasn't that he was a showy dresser. His clothes did have a more citified cut and a richer fabric and color, but they were simple and dignified. Still, there was obviously something special about his person that had nothing to do with money or clothes. People didn't part before him like the Red Sea before Moses or anything like that, but somehow there was always a little extra space around him, whether he was walking, standing, or sitting still. His yellow roadster was the only flashy thing about him, and in the parking field behind the church there was a little space around it too, as if the battered pickup trucks and square black sedans were afraid to come too close.

We were sitting a few rows behind him, and I didn't hear one word of the proceedings because I was so busy staring at the back of his head. I had been reading about animal magnetism, and I was trying to exercise my will power to make him turn around, so I could look at his face. I wanted to drink in his beauty. I wanted to do things I didn't even dare think about, except that they started with some heavy kissing. I was so busy concentrating that I actually started to sink down in my seat, which earned me a jab in the ribs from my father's elbow. "Sit up straight and pay attention," he warned. "I didn't bring you here to lollygag." Dear old Dad, always such a sensitive soul. But my efforts hadn't been in vain. In the middle of the discussion about the feasibility of building a spur from the nearest railroad line, Chester turned around and stared straight at me for a moment—or at least so I fancied. He might have been just trying to figure out how crowded the place was, but I took the credit anyway.

He looked more earnest than seductive, but I fell madly in love nonetheless. His auburn hair was neatly combed into waves that set off his bright green eyes. He had a startlingly straight nose, beneath which he wore a small, closely trimmed mustache like Clark Cable's. His lips were thin, but they seemed sensuous to me, and his firm jaw promised strength of character. When he finally rose to speak and put forward his proposal for his gift to the town of a monument honoring the valley's original settlers, I knew I was committed to him for life. His voice was mellow and his manner decisive but unassuming. He had a kind of self-confidence that was unlike any I had yet encountered. It seemed born of self-knowledge rather than ignorance. If there was any way possible, I wanted to be just like him when I grew up.

"I just want to do something to show my appreciation for our valley's heritage," Chester said. "This town has been very good to my family, and I'd like to erect a monument that will commemorate our forefathers for future generations."

"How about opening a factory to draw industrial workers? We could use some new blood around here," offered Sam Winston, who was always talking about selling his land to build houses on.

"Not to mention the money they'd spend," added the owner of the general store. I could see we were in for a really artistic discussion.

I raised my hand, stirring up some amusement among the elders for my youthful presumption and some embarrassed harrumphing from my father, along with a warning jab from his elbow, which I paid no mind. When I was called on, I said, "In school, we learned that art is an important part of civilization. A culture is remembered for its art when its people are all dead, but who remembers how much they spent at the general store? I think we should look at Mr. Stewart's design before we say anything more, so at least we'll know what we're discussing."

My father didn't hit me in public, either because he didn't want to make a fool out of himself in front of the whole town or because he didn't know what I was talking about, but he did tell me to hush. "What do you know about this town's needs, boy? Have a little respect," he whispered. The owner of the general store had never been especially nice to me, so I didn't much care what he thought, but he was one of my father's friends—if you can call half a dozen clipped sentences a week any kind of friendship. So I held my tongue.

Chester looked at me gratefully, and before there was any further discussion, he unrolled his drawing of something I couldn't quite figure out. I thought he was holding it upside down. I certainly couldn't see any of the half-naked people my schoolmate's father had warned him about. If I wasn't sure what it was in spite of my good intentions, the others were altogether mystified. Some of them even started to snicker. Nobody said anything for a full three minutes, until Sam Winston said, with a falsely gentle manner that barely hid his contempt, "Can you tell us what that's supposed to be, son?"

Chester looked only mildly insulted, but he didn't drop his good will for an instant. "It's an abstract sculpture," he said. "Nothing is representational—that is, it isn't supposed to look like what it stands for. It's supposed to be symbolic, to suggest the feeling we have for the subject. For example, this section represents the Indians whose land it was before our forefathers arrived and the closeness they had to nature." He pointed to a collection of cones that could have been tepees, with what looked like clusters of arrows sticking out of them. "And this section represents the agriculture of our region," he continued, pointing to a smooth inverted cone, out of which was spilling an assortment of shapes that might have been pumpkins or apples, and some corn, or maybe cucumbers. "And here we have a symbol of Henry Hudson, who first explored this region in his ship the *Half Moon*," he said, pointing at a large semicircle at the bottom. "And of the minutemen who fought in the Revolution," he added, indicating what might have been a row of raised arms or rifles, or maybe just stick-figure torsos of some kind. I have to confess I was as baffled as the others, but at least I didn't join in the general laughter. The discussion was brought to a swift close when the council voted to thank Mr. Stewart very much, but asked if maybe they could have a new fire truck instead. Chester didn't lose his dignity for a moment. He said he'd think about the fire truck, and returned to his seat.

After the meeting was over, I was the first one out. My father was busy talking to some of his cronies, and I stood under the elm tree in front of the church. When Chester passed by, I gave him my brightest smile, and he stuck out his hand and said, "Thanks for the support. I needed a friend. I thought I was doing the town a favor, and they made me feel like Daniel in the lion's den."

"That's how I felt in there, too. But my name really is Daniel—Daniel Blake."

"Oh, so you're John Blake's boy?"

I nodded.

"You seem to be interested in art."

"Well . . . I like pictures. I draw a little, but I'm not very good at it. Not like you. Mostly I read books."

"I read a lot too. Around here that makes us both oddballs. The only book these people read is the Bible, but I bet you've gone further than that. What do you read? No, let me guess. I bet you like Robert Louis Stevenson and Jules Verne and that sort of thing. Those were the writers I loved when I was your age. How old are you anyway?"

I was a little overwhelmed with all the questions, but I was thrilled at his attention and the feeling of not being alone anymore. "I'm fifteen—almost sixteen," I stretched it. "And you're right. I do like *Dr. Jekyll and Mr. Hyde* and *Twenty Thousand Leagues Under the Sea* and Jules Verne, too. *The Time*

Machine is one of my favorites. I don't usually talk to anybody about them though, except Miss Binder in the library."

"She's an old friend of mine too," he said. "But I haven't seen her in quite a while. I've been busy. I spend a lot of time down in the city."

"New York City? Wow! I've never been there."

"You'd like it."

"What's it like?"

"It's exciting."

We stopped for a minute, almost out of breath. Then I asked, "Did you do the sculpture in Miss Binder's parlor?"

"The pink marble one? Yes. I'd almost forgotten about that. It was quite a while back. It was nice of you to notice it."

I blushed. "I like it a lot."

"Gee, thanks. You're a good kid. Tell me the truth. Did you like the sketch I did for the monument?"

I was embarrassed, and it took me a minute to answer. "Ayuh . . . well, I guess I really didn't know what it was at first. But sure I liked it—after you explained it, that is."

"Well, that's honest, at least. I guess it takes a little learning to understand these things. It's an acquired taste, like eating snails. But abstract art is all the rage back in the city, and in Europe it's old hat already."

"Do people really eat snails?" I asked.

"Only in the better restaurants." We both laughed. Then he said, "I've got to be going now, Daniel. Thanks again for speaking up in there."

"Any time," I answered. "I hope we meet again soon."

He gave me an amused look and walked off toward his car. I went to look for my father's truck in the parking field and found he had already gone. He'd pulled that trick before, when I'd lingered too long after church saying good-bye to Miss Binder. So I started the long walk home, planning to daydream about Chester to pass the time.

I had only gone a short way up the road when the yellow roadster pulled up alongside me. Chester said, "What's the matter? No ride home? You live out at Orphean Hill, don't you? Hop in. I'm going that way anyhow."

I couldn't get into that car fast enough, but I was careful not to rip the handle off the door. I didn't want to damage anything. It was the most elegant car I'd ever seen, and I felt like a princess sitting next to her prince in a royal coach.

"Gee, this is a swell car," I offered. Then I felt like a fool. "I bet you're tired of hearing stuff like that. Your city friends must be much more interesting."

"Just be yourself, Daniel. You're doing fine," he said graciously.

"What kind of people live in New York City?" I inquired, trying my best to relax.

"All kinds. That's what's so great about it. There are rich and poor, colored and white, straight business types and gay bohemians . . ."

"What's a bohemian?" I asked. I didn't pick up on the "gay." It just meant "cheerful" to me then.

"Oh, somebody who's an individualist, usually an artistic type. They wear unusual clothes and think unusual thoughts."

"Are you a bohemian? I know you're artistic."

"Well, maybe in a minor sort of way. I'm pretty much an individual. But most bohemians don't have as much money as I do. When you're well-heeled and act strange, they call you eccentric instead of bohemian. It gets rather complicated. But who cares what they call you, as long as you're having a good time?"

That was a wonderful philosophy, I thought, but maybe only the rich could afford to adopt it. "I'd like to be a bohemian," I said. "I sure get bored around here. Everybody's so much the same as everybody else. Except me. I'm different."

"How so?"

"I'm not sure if I can say. Nobody else around here likes to sit alone in the cemetery and read books the way I do. All of the other guys at school are interested in baseball, and they can't wait to start dating. I don't think I'm going to date anybody. The girls at school are so boring. I'd rather be by myself."

"You'd rather not date anybody at all? Or you'd rather not date the people you're supposed to date?"

"Ayuh, that's it. But I don't know who I do want to date. Well, maybe I do, but . . ."

"But what?"

"I don't know, exactly."

"I won't push you," he said gently, "but I have a feeling I know what you're talking about. I was just as confused as you are when I was your age. I wanted to be with my best friend, Albert, but Albert wanted to be with his girlfriend, Betty, and I didn't have a girlfriend. Or want one. I wanted Albert."

"That's something like it," I said. "But I don't have any best friend." I was pretty scared. I had never talked to anybody about this before. But he had as much as confessed to me, and if I couldn't talk to him, then whom could I talk to?

As if he could read my mind, he said, "You can talk to Miss Binder about this, you know."

"Oh? What does she know? I mean, she's nice and all that, but, well, she's a spinster. What does she know about love?"

"So it's love we're talking about, eh?"

I'm sure I blushed the color of a ripe McIntosh. I couldn't answer.

"Do you trust me, Daniel?"

I nodded.

"Go to Miss Binder. She's a smart old bird. She knows more than you think. And maybe we'll have another chance to talk, too. Just remember one thing, Danny. You're not as alone as you think."

We were pulling into the yard in front of our house at that point, and my father was standing there next to his truck with his usual disapproving expression. He had hoped the long walk home would be a good lesson for me, and instead here I was being delivered in a grand chariot.

"Good afternoon, Mr. Blake," Chester said, almost jauntily. "You forgot someone back at the church, so I thought I'd deliver him."

"Much obliged," my father said without a trace of gratitude. I knew my father just hated being obligated to people, especially rich young upstarts in fancy yellow cars, but I didn't care what he thought. I was beaming with love, and my protector was beside me. Any civilized father would have invited Chester in for a glass of apple juice, but I didn't expect civility. I was just relieved that there were no open insults.

Once Chester had gone, my father gave me one of his lectures about knowing my place and not burdening others. But I only listened with half an ear. I was too busy trying to memorize the shape of Chester's knuckles when his hand had gripped the steering wheel. I didn't want to forget a single thing. I had just experienced the most exciting half hour of my life.

From then on I had something to live for. I thought of Chester day and night. I doodled his name in my notebook in algebra class instead of listening to the teacher, and I flunked a test in solving equations. I looked longingly out of the school bus window, hoping to catch a glimpse of the yellow roadster. I mooned over the lyrics from popular songs. At least I knew I had the ability to love someone, I consoled myself. But he didn't know it. How could I tell him? No movie heroine suffered more than I did. No character in the most romantic tale was more in love. I was Juliet, Guinevere, Lois Lane—no, make that Jimmy Olsen. I'd always thought he had a crush on Superman. I pictured Chester flying around in tight blue underwear, with his red cape flowing behind him and me cradled in his arms. Within days I knew I was a major case, and I thought I'd burst if I didn't have somebody to talk to.

I went to see Miss Binder at the start of the next week. It only took half an hour of hemming and hawing before I came out with the simple truth.

"I think I'm in love."

"That's nice, Daniel. I'm happy for you."

"But I think I'm in love with . . . a man."

"I hope he's someone nice," she said, without averting her gaze.

"You mean you're not surprised? You don't think it's disgusting or anything?"

44

"No to both questions. Let's just say I have a special instinct for these matters. I was pretty sure about you, but it's always better to let people discover such things for themselves. Who's the lucky young man?"

"He says he's a friend of yours—Chester Stewart, the one who did the pink sculpture in your parlor."

"I should have guessed. Chester is a darling boy, but isn't he a good deal older than you?"

"Miss Binder, if I'm in love with someone who's the wrong sex, what's the difference if he's the wrong age too?"

"Get that word 'wrong' out of your mind, Daniel. There is nothing wrong with being in love—ever. It's just that Chester is so worldly. He goes to the city and knows sophisticated people. That could create problems for you."

"That's what I'm afraid of. I don't know how to tell him about my feelings. What could he find interesting in somebody like me? He might laugh or something."

"I'm sure he wouldn't do that, Daniel. And if he did, then he wouldn't be deserving of your love in the first place. Why don't you do a favor for both of you and break the news to him gently? Give him some time. I know you're impatient. Young lovers always are. But if there's really something there, a little time won't hurt it. It might even help."

"I guess you're right. You really know a lot, Miss Binder. I didn't think you'd understand so much about love. I mean, without a man of your own . . . Oh God, I'm sorry. I didn't mean to be unkind, especially after you've been so nice to me."

"It's all right, Daniel. You didn't mean any disrespect. But let's not talk about me. Let's just say I have my ways of knowing. I am a librarian, you know. Speaking of which, there's a book I've been saving for you, and I couldn't imagine a more appropriate time to give it to you."

She went upstairs and came back with a book in her hand. She held it as she held all books, with a special reverence and care that I admired her for. It was a dark green volume, whose spine was tooled in gold leaf in an ornate art nouveau design scrolled around its title. *Leaves of Grass* by Walt Whitman.

"This is a very special book," she said. "It's one I bought for you myself. It was going to be your grade school graduation present, but when the time came, I decided you weren't ready yet, and I was waiting for your high school graduation. After what you told me today, I think you're ready now. I know you haven't read much poetry yet, but I think you'll like this because it speaks so directly. I'm not going to tell you which poems to read. Why don't you just skim through it and decide for yourself what parts you like best?"

I opened it gingerly, trying to show as much respect in handling it as Miss Binder had. The title page was simple but impressively lettered, and it was dated 1892. The frontispiece opposite it showed a photograph of a wise-looking man with a flowing white beard. His eyes captured mine immediately. I couldn't tell from the black-and-white picture if they were gray or blue, but they had a special light that made them seem alive, as if he were there with me in the room, regardless of who I was or when I lived, as if he were my friend and knew all my secrets and didn't mind them at all.

"Wow," I said. "Is this the man who wrote 'O Captain! My Captain!'?"

"Ayuh," answered Miss Binder. "But I would call that the least of his accomplishments. Why don't you read something?"

I flipped the pages and sampled a line or two from several poems, but when I came to these lines, I read further, reciting aloud.

> "We two boys together clinging,
> One the other never leaving,
> Up and down the roads going, North and South excursions
>   making,
> Power enjoying, elbows stretching, fingers clutching,
> Arm'd and fearless, eating, drinking, sleeping, loving,
> No law less than ourselves owning . . ."

And I fell in love for the second time that week.

I carried *Leaves of Grass* with me wherever I went after that. In fact, I still have the same volume. During my boyhood it was always in my schoolbag or under my arm. I read it in bits and snatches, a poem from this section and a poem from that. I found poems about love and war and death and time and the universe. Some of the lines seemed especially beautiful, even if there were parts I couldn't yet understand. Do you know how it is when you come upon something that just rings true, as if you were reading what you've thought yourself but haven't yet put into words? Maybe it was just Whitman's poetic genius, but he seemed to understand the world from the same vantage point I did. He and I were soul mates of some kind. What was important to him was important to me. We asked the same questions, only he had some of the answers. Maybe I would have arrived at the same ideas myself without his help, but I'll never know that. I trusted Walt's wisdom right from the beginning.

I loved to read *Leaves of Grass* out by Martha's stone, and sometimes I would stop reading in order to look at the grass growing all around me and speculate on the new meanings with which Walt had endowed it for me:

> A child said *What is the grass?* fetching it to me with full hands;
> How could I answer the child? I do not know what it is any
>   more than he.

> I guess it must be the flag of my disposition, out of hopeful
>   green stuff woven.

> Or I guess it is the handkerchief of the Lord . . .

Bearing the owner's name someway in the corners, that we
    may see and remark, and say *Whose?*

Or I guess the grass is itself a child . . .

And now it seems to me the beautiful uncut hair of graves.

Tenderly will I use you curling grass,
It may be you transpire from the breasts of young men,
It may be if I had known them I would have loved them . . .

When a particularly loving passage made me think about Chester, I
would get an erection and stop reading to masturbate, which was my other
favorite activity, and I would feel secretly clean and good.

On rainy days, I carried the book around the house with me, reading in
one corner or another, wherever the light was best. One day my father came
out of his room unexpectedly to question Mrs. Warner about some
household expenses. I scarcely bothered to look up, not wanting to be
interrupted.

"What's that, boy? You still readin' them fairy books? You're gettin' too
old for that. Give it here."

"This is not a children's book. It's poetry, and it's none of your business."

He slapped my face sharply. "Keep a civil tongue in your head when you
talk to me, boy. That's one of the Commandments." He snatched the book
from my grasp.

I wanted to cry, more in frustration than in pain, but I wouldn't give him
the satisfaction. So, ignoring the wet weather, I went out to sit near Martha's
stone, but by then I was more sad than indignant. The cool drizzle calmed
me. I imagined the ghost of Martha putting her wraith's arms around me in
comfort, and I listened as hard as I could to the soughing wind for some
sound of encouragement. But of course I was alone.

When I returned to the house, my father was waiting for me. "You know
that this is the Devil's book, don't you?" he asked.

"No, I thought it was Miss Binder's. She gave it to me."

"Think you've got a right to be sassy, eh? You and your librarian and her
so-called friend, too. Well we'll see about that. You all have some answerin'
to do. Do you know what it says in here? Listen to this: 'I am for those who
believe in loose delights—I share the midnight orgies of young men.' This
book is full of smut! It's unnatural! It's a perversion of nature!"

He ranted on for much of the evening, and I sat there and put up with
it—not because I wanted to hear what he had to say, but because I didn't
want to let that book out of my sight. The old fool might have tried to burn
it. Finally, when he had spent his wrath for the day and fallen asleep, I
sneaked into his room and took the book from his dresser where he had left

it, and I hid it carefully away with my birth certificate in the attic, where he would never think to look.

Mrs. Warner couldn't help but hear all the commotion, and she invited me into the kitchen for a cup of hot cider to calm me down. "You know I don't like to mix in your affairs, Daniel. I don't say much, but I do know what's going on around here. I'd have to be blind not to. If you're not careful with yourself, something terrible's going to happen. We all have desires that must be tamed. We're all sinners. God punished me for my sins. That's why I fear Him now, and it's not too late for you to do the same. Don't give in to the Devil, Daniel. That book is just a trap to lead you to hell. Don't you want to spend eternity with Jesus? You don't have to give in to temptation. You can follow the right road. It doesn't matter what you think you are. It matters what you do. Beat back those awful desires, and you'll be a better person for it. Then God will give you His love instead of His wrath. You know I'm right, Daniel. Now kneel here with me and pray. Come on."

That was the most Mrs. Warner had said to me at one time, and I was impressed with her concern, if not with her message. I was too embarrassed to dispute the issue with her, so I knelt down beside her while she began to pray.

"Oh God, help this boy to see Your true will. Make his desires Your desires. Remove this awful temptation from his path and make him righteous in Your name, so he can fulfill his duties in this, Your world, as a man and a father. Close his eyes to evil books and his ears to evil people . . ."

I couldn't take any more. She meant well, but I didn't want to hear the people I loved called evil. I didn't want to end up like her, with my head bowed and my mouth shut and fear in my eyes. If there were problems in my path, I'd face them, but at least it would still be my own chosen path and not someone else's. I stood up and walked out and left her kneeling there. The pitiful sound of her praying followed me up the stairs.

I fell asleep almost immediately, but a short while later I awoke with a start from a vivid nightmare:

I could hear Mrs. Warner's footsteps dragging up the stairs. She was moving slowly, as if she were uncertain of herself. She stood in the doorway of my room, watching me as I lay on my bed, waiting. There was a strange electricity between us. She slowly crossed the floor and stood beside the bed. Then she sat down beside me and said, "Daniel, you know what God wants, don't you?"

I remained silent.

"God wants me to save you. To show you the way."

I didn't move an inch.

"You know that Jesus loves you, don't you?"

I didn't respond. She put the palm of her left hand gently to my cheek. With her right hand she clasped mine and brought it to her bosom, her face raised and her eyes tightly closed, as if she were in silent communion with God. I imagined my hand slipping inside her dress and past her undergarments. I imagined how her small soft breast would feel in my hand, its rigid nipple pressed against my palm.

I imagined her leaning toward me to kiss me, even though she hadn't moved.

Suddenly I pulled my hand from her bodice. "You can't make me do it!" I screamed. "You'll never make me be what you want!" I sprang from the bed and ran through the door and downstairs. I didn't stop until I had reached Martha's stone.

That's when I woke up, shuddering. It took another hour before I could fall asleep again.

From then on, for as long as I lived in that house, I had the feeling that Mrs. Warner was watching me from a careful distance and waiting for some violent doom to descend upon me. But she never mentioned the subject again.

The next morning was Sunday, and I hoped that my father would forget about Walt Whitman in the bustle of getting ready for church. But as soon as he was awake, he came to my room and said, "Where is the book?"

I swallowed my fear and stared at him with a level gaze and didn't answer.

"Where is it?" he repeated. "Remember, 'Thou shalt not steal.' "

If there was a thief in the room, it certainly wasn't me, but I remained silent.

"I see you have more than one lesson to learn," he said grimly, and he left me in my room, locking the door behind him. I did without breakfast that morning.

When he and Mrs. Warner were ready to leave for church, he came and unlocked the door. "Get in the truck," he said.

He didn't mention the missing book. Not a word passed between us as we rode to town. Only at the end of the service did I know the depth of his rage. We were recovering from Reverend Friendly's droning dissertation on "Purity of Thought," and we had all seated ourselves after caterwauling our way through "He Walks With Me" when the good minister announced, among other community excitements, that Miss Binder was planning a library exhibit of books on the Bible.

As was customary, all eyes turned to whichever member of the congregation was mentioned by name. The Misses Binder and Standish sat side by side, looking like bookends. Just as they shopped together and made visits together, they always attended church together. Their attendance was frequent, but slightly irregular. I'd say they missed not one more Sunday morning than decency allowed.

Miss Binder was nodding and smiling politely, like the newsreels I had seen of Queen Mary on the balcony of Buckingham Palace, until my father jumped to his feet and started yelling.

"That woman's got no right even touching our Bible, let alone showing it to our children! She does the Devil's work! She gave my boy a book full of unnatural lusts and perversions! Self-abuse! Men together with men! Sex! It's disgusting! And that's not all. She's one of 'em herself, her and her schoolmarm friend over there. You all know it. You just won't say it. But now their vice is reachin' our young. They aren't friends or house mates. They aren't spinsters either. They're lovers! Female sodomites! Spawn of the Devil! And they're after my boy! They're tryin' to turn him into some kind of sissy, and I won't let them!"

I wanted to crawl under the pew with shame. Miss Standish's pince-nez fell off immediately. But this was the first time I'd ever seen her fail to catch it. It swung wildly on its ribbon as she rose to her feet. "You have no right…" she sputtered. But her courage failed her, and the tyrant of the schoolroom crumpled softly into her seat.

Miss Binder took over. Her pince-nez had not fallen off. "It's all right, Myra," she said. "Mr. Blake, this is not the first time that you have launched such a crusade. Are you planning to make a career of it?" She amazed me. Her sweet gentility was backed up by a strength I hadn't suspected in her. "As for the book I gave your son, it is widely known to be America's finest book of poems. Thank God this country is broader than your mind."

But my father wasn't about to be intimidated. "Your kind should be hounded out of this country! You aren't a fit woman to be sittin' in this church! And the same goes for your partner in sin. She's not the kind of person we want schoolin' our children. God alone knows what terrible things she's taught them!"

Reverend Friendly interrupted from the height of his pulpit. "You've said your piece, John, and I'm sure we all want to consider it carefully. If we act in haste, we will surely repent at leisure. Services are over now, and I think it's time for everyone to be going. This is not an appropriate subject to discuss in the house of God." He had abandoned his usual droning and sounded tense. "Enjoy your Sunday dinners, everybody, and between now and next Sunday, think on what Our Lord said about casting the first stone."

The crowd filed out silently, but the air was thick with tension. Most people probably wanted to get their children out of earshot before discussing such a horrible topic. Few lingered to see Miss Binder and Miss Standish walk out the front door—side by side, their arms linked in mutual support, their chins held high, and their eyes fixed straight ahead. I went out after them and followed them toward their house, ignoring the sound of my father's voice calling my name.

I walked some paces behind them, afraid to catch up to them because I could hear that Miss Standish was crying, and I knew she wouldn't like me to see that. Finally, a few yards away from their small front porch, I cleared my throat as loudly as I could. They both squared their shoulders suddenly, as if to deflect a blow from behind. When they turned, I could see Miss Standish's pince-nez still dangling from the end of its ribbon. Otherwise, except for her reddened eyes, to all outward appearances she had regained her composure.

"I just wanted to apologize for what my father said back there. I didn't want you to think I was on his side. I don't care if you are what he said. I wouldn't betray you. I love you both."

Miss Binder answered, "We know that, Daniel. We know who you are. It's not your fault, and you mustn't worry about it. We are quite capable of defending ourselves. You have enough worries of your own, living with someone as cruel and obsessed as your father."

"I'll be okay," I said, not at all sure that I would. "Miss Binder, I just wanted to tell you I thought you were wonderful back there. But what did you mean when you said that this wasn't the first time my father had done such a thing?"

"I'm sorry, Daniel, but I am not at liberty to answer that. Why don't you ask your father?"

"Fat chance he'd ever tell me anything," I said. "Besides, I don't think I ever want to talk to him again."

"You don't mean that," said Miss Standish. "Whatever his opinions are, he's still your father. You need each other." She sounded much softer than I had ever heard her in the classroom, or even in her own parlor. "You'd better go home now, Daniel. We have a lot of plans to make."

"Yes, Miss Standish," I said, falling back into my grade school pupil's voice. "But one last thing, Miss Binder: I still have the book. I won't let him have it. I wanted you to know that."

"I'm glad, Daniel. You must cherish it. You'll need it for comfort." She sounded weary.

"Maybe Reverend Friendly will be on your side. I'm sure he can help you!" I hated to leave them in such despair.

"No, Daniel, I don't think so. He's no crusader. He has his own position to consider. He's the one who asked me to keep the book off the open shelf. But don't you worry. We'll manage just fine."

"Isn't there something I can do?"

"Thank you, no. You've already done enough by coming here."

"Good luck, then," I said. "Let me know if there's some way I can help."

I walked off into the sunny afternoon, not sure where I was going until I was all the way past the other side of town and the sun was beginning to set. Then I realized that Chester's house was in that part of the valley, and I was determined to find it.

CHAPTER THREE

I t was well after dark by the time I found the Stewart estate. Chester lived in a big brick house with a wooden studio connected to it. The studio's windows were uncovered, and by standing on a large rock I could look into them. I could see several large abstract sculptures faintly gleaming in the moonlight. One of them might have been the monument he had proposed for the town, but I couldn't be sure in the dimness. All I could be sure of was that Chester wasn't inside.

The big house looked mostly dark. What if Chester weren't home? I wasn't even sure what time it was. What if he were asleep for the night? I was afraid just to walk up to the front door and ring the bell. What could I say? That I was running away and wanted to live there? That I was in love with him and had just dropped by to mention it? That he must come rushing to Miss Binder's rescue? I don't know what I had been thinking about all the time I had been walking there, but I had no plan of action. So I walked around the house looking for something to stand on, so I could peep in one of the windows and maybe get a fix on the situation. Before I found a perch, however, I heard voices.

"Then this makes an end of it," said one. It wasn't Chester's voice, but it sounded familiar.

"I'm really sorry," said the second voice, which was Chester's. "Even if I've only been in the area part of the time, it's been a good three years."

"But frightening," the first voice said. "At least we won't have to hide anymore."

Hidden by shadows, I edged my way behind some shrubbery until I was near the back porch where the voices were coming from. In the moonlight I could see Chester wearing a silken bathrobe, and Reverend Friendly, looking around very nervously.

"It's all right," said Chester. "There's no way anyone can see us here, unless old Blake has planted spies in the bushes." He kissed the good Reverend on the lips.

"I'll sure miss this," Reverend Friendly said, reaching his hand into the opening of Chester's robe and leaving it there.

"I'll miss you too, Franklin," said Chester.

"But you do agree it's for the best? You do understand?"

"Why take chances? It's the best thing."

"There won't be any trouble?"

"Don't worry, Franklin. It's my secret, too—at least in this valley," Chester said. "I think I'll be spending even more of my time down in the city from now on."

"Good-bye, then, Chester."

"Good-bye."

Reverend Friendly looked back several times as he walked toward his car. Poor old guy. I guess I should have felt sorry for him, but I was too busy being shocked to think of his feelings.

I waited at least five minutes after he had gone before I knocked on Chester's back door. He answered, still wearing his robe. He looked more beautiful than ever.

"Who's out there?"

"It's Daniel, Mr. Stewart."

"Daniel? Oh, come in, Daniel. Call me Chester, okay?"

"I hope you don't mind my coming here . . . Chester."

"Of course not, but how did you get here? I didn't hear any car."

"I walked."

"All the way from home?"

"From town."

"I see."

I looked around the room. It was filled with art deco furniture, which made it like no other home I'd been in. There were oriental rugs, and several of Chester's smaller sculptures were on display. The walls were adorned with strange-looking paintings and photographs signed with names like Picasso and Man Ray, names which meant nothing to me then. I hadn't known what it would look like, but I had expected my prince to have a palace and I certainly wasn't disappointed.

"I just couldn't go home," I said. "Not after what my father did in church."

"Yes, I heard."

"From Reverend Friendly?"

"How did you know?"

"I saw him leave."

"From the road?"

"From the back door. I was the spy in the bushes you were talking about. I'm sorry. I was afraid to knock, and when you came out, I just hid. I didn't know if you'd want to see me or if you'd even remember me, but I didn't know where else to go. I won't tell anybody what I saw. I promise."

"Reverend Friendly says your father's hopping mad, and he's accusing Miss Binder of hiding you. You'll have to go home for her sake."

"I don't want to get her into any more trouble. But do I have to go back tonight?"

"I guess it can wait till morning. They're probably all asleep by now, and I'm not much in the mood for a drive this late. It's been a pretty rough day for all of us. You can stay in the guest room if you like."

I would rather have shared his room, but I didn't know how to tell him that, so I just nodded. He gave me some chocolate milk and graham crackers, and then he tucked me into the biggest bed I had ever slept in, surrounded by a handsome room done in shades of green. But try though I might, I couldn't keep my eyes closed. I listened to the sounds he made as he prepared to go to sleep down the hall. I thought the water in the bathroom sink was luckier than I because it could touch his face. When the door to his room closed, I envied the knob because he held it in his hand. And when I heard his bedsprings creak in welcome, I wanted so badly to be lying there with him that it was too much to bear. I waited for what must have been an hour, afraid to move. Then I got up and tiptoed down the hall to the one closed door. His breathing was measured, so I knew he was asleep. I opened the door as softly as I could and stood there in his room, watching while he slept. I felt like some sort of guardian angel. Finally I was so sleepy I could hardly stand up. But I still didn't want to go back to the room where I belonged. So I eased myself slowly into the other half of his wide bed and fell asleep, smiling because I was thinking of the most romantic lines I knew from Walt Whitman:

> For the one I love most lay sleeping by me under the same
> cover in the cool night,
> In the stillness, in the autumn moonbeams, his face was
> inclined toward me,
> And his arm lay lightly around my breast—and that night I
> was happy.

In the morning, I opened my eyes to find his face above mine, looking down at me. He seemed more perplexed than angry.

"Why did you come here?" he said.

"I couldn't sleep. I was afraid."

"No, I mean why did you come to this house?"

"I didn't know where else to go. I've been thinking about you since that day we met. I . . . I don't know what's happening to me. I think I love you!" I started to cry.

He took me in his arms until I had calmed down. Then he said, "Let's have some breakfast before we continue this conversation, okay?"

I nodded, grateful for the respite. The world looked a little brighter over the flapjacks and bacon which were brought out on a silver tray and served efficiently by a man called Boris, who was the only butler I'd ever seen. Boris acted as if nothing were out of the ordinary as he went about his chores. Chester watched me, seeming to enjoy the gusto with which I ate. When I realized why he was smiling, I explained that, except for the graham crackers he had given me, I hadn't eaten anything the day before. And he asked Boris to bring a second helping. When the dishes were finally cleared, we sat across the empty table.

"I have to explain some things to you," he said. "It isn't always easy to be what we are. The world doesn't make it easy for men who are different."

"But if you love somebody . . ."

"That's wonderful. But you don't even know me."

"I know as much as I need to."

"Then let's say I don't know you."

"What do you want to know?"

"Daniel, I don't even think you know very much about yourself yet. Why, you're only fifteen."

"Almost sixteen."

"And I'm twenty-two."

"Six years isn't so much."

"At our age it is."

"Reverend Friendly must be more than six years older than you."

"I thought we weren't going to mention that again. Yes, Franklin is much older than I am."

"Are you in love with him? Is that why you don't want me?"

"I didn't say I don't want you. I think you're very attractive. I like you very much. I might even grow to love you someday. But I don't want to lead you into a life you may not be ready for. Your feelings might be different when you're old enough to choose for yourself. As for Franklin and I, we were . . . um . . . let's call it 'companions.' There aren't too many men of our persuasion around here, and we sort of needed each other."

"But he's a married man with five children."

"That's just what I mean. There's a lot you don't know about this life. Being married has nothing to do with it. Lots of men who like men also like women. Sometimes they get married as a cover."

"But a minister!"

"Let's not judge other people now. Your father does enough of that. Do you want to be like him?"

"I'm sorry."

"Anyway, Reverend Friendly and I did get . . . um . . . physical together. We had sex, but we were never in love. We were just a convenience for each other."

"Like me and Adam Witherspoon," I murmured.

"Who?"

"A guy from school who taught me some things about my body."

"So you're not a virgin?"

"We never actually touched each other. I saved myself for you."

"You did not. You just met me."

"Well, I saved myself for the right man, and I think you're him."

"I think you're jumping the gun a bit. Listen, I'm going to be spending more of my time down in the city. I can be myself down there, where people aren't so nosy. Maybe when I'm far away, things will look different. Maybe after some time passes, we'll get to know each other better. There's plenty of time to make decisions. Meanwhile, you've got some growing up to do, and maybe I do, too. It's best if I take you back to your father for now."

"Won't I ever see you?"

"You can come down to the city and visit me sometime if you like—and if your father agrees."

"Golly, that would be wonderful," I said, my eyes shining. All my dreams weren't coming true, but they weren't dead either. At least I could hope.

When we arrived at the farm, Chester parked his car and came to the door with me. My father was standing just inside, with an ugly frown on his face.

"Where've you been?" he snapped. "I was fixin' to get the police out lookin' for you."

"I walked all the way to Chester's . . . Mr. Stewart's house. I was upset about what you did to Miss Binder in church yesterday."

"Never you mind. She'll get no more than what's comin' to her, and her partner will, too. If it was up to me, we'd ride 'em both out of town on a rail—tarred and feathered, like in the old days. It looks like Friendly's goin' easy on 'em, but we'll get 'em out of here one way or the other. There's a meetin' Wednesday night to decide." He turned his attention to Chester. "What're you doin' here, Stewart?"

"I just brought Daniel back. He needed some time to think, and he stayed at my house last night. We've already had breakfast."

"Wait a minute. Is somethin' funny goin' on around here? Why should a rich man like you be drivin' my kid around all the time? I'm not stupid, you know."

"Nothing funny is going on. Something tragic is going on."

"Don't think I don't know that you're a little strange yourself, Stewart, you with your fancy ways. Why do you people plague my life? What's your connection to my Daniel?

"Now, Mr. Blake, there's no need to work yourself up. You're letting your imagination run away with you. I assure you nothing has happened between Daniel and me. We talked. That was all."

"Well, nothin' had better happen either. You think you're a powerful man, but just because you hold the mortgage on my land don't mean you own me. I don't care who you are. If you lay one sinful hand on my boy, I'll have you in prison for unnatural acts. You keep away from him."

"Now you listen, Blake!" Chester's face was red. "I broke no law concerning this boy, and I don't intend to. You and your witch-hunters won't have that to pin on me. When Daniel's eighteen years old, he can be responsible for himself, but in the meantime I plan to keep in touch, to make sure he's all right. There's no law against that. And if I hear that you're beating him, I won't need to foreclose your mortgage or call in the law. I'll take it out of your hide myself, and that's a promise!"

My father sputtered and glowered at Chester, who said, "Good-bye, Daniel. Let me know if you need any help." He tucked a small card, smartly printed with his name and New York City address, into my shirt pocket. Then he turned on his heel and walked off. He rode his yellow car gallantly down the road, and I stood there watching it disappear. I couldn't have loved anyone better than I loved him at that moment.

Two days later, I learned that Miss Binder and Miss Standish had quietly left town. A new schoolmarm would be found by the following fall, and the little library was closed until further notice. There was no one to discuss this with but Chester, I thought. Then I learned that he too had already gone. So I kept it to myself.

I turned to my high school career with new interest. Aside from *Leaves of Grass* it was all I had to keep me going during the years of my captivity. I was determined that I would leave home on my eighteenth birthday, which fell right after graduation day. I was equally determined that I would spend that night in Chester Stewart's arms. I fixed the date of my freedom in my mind: June 28, 1942.

Until then Chester and I exchanged letters. Mine were full of boyish love. I worked hard over each one, revising it several times so I could sound enthusiastic without seeming overly eager, but I'm embarrassed at the thought of anyone reading them now. Chester's letters were full of warmth and encouragement. For many years I kept a packet of them tucked away with a romantic purple ribbon around it. One of them read:

September 15, 1939

Dear Daniel,

Terrible things are happening in the world, and it is good to know that you are safely tucked away in our peaceful valley. Now that the monster Hitler has invaded Poland, who knows how long anyone in this world will be safe?

I am very busy sculpting. I feel as if there's an endless amount to learn, but I love it. I hope your education is proceeding as well.

Lots of things are happening here—plays, parties, and so on—but I don't want to interrupt my work with too much fun. I hope you're not as strict with yourself as I am. Now is the time you should be enjoying yourself. I envy you the opportunity, and you must make the best of it. As I say, who knows how much more of a chance any of us will have for good times with the world going up in blazes?

Take care of yourself, Daniel. I can't say why, but you are very important to me. I know we will see each other again before too long. I'll be traveling up your way next year sometime for sure. Meanwhile, keep in touch.

Your Friend,
Chester

As long as my heart remained loyal to Chester, I saw no reason not to take advantage of whatever opportunities for sexual experience I found, especially since they were so rare. I told myself that I was learning the ropes so I wouldn't disappoint Chester when we were finally together, but who was I kidding? I was as horny as a toad, and I was ready to do unspeakable things for any man who even glanced my way.

I no longer had anything to do with Adam Witherspoon. He and Sally Wayne were always together now, and if they passed me, Adam would nod his head, but not say hello. Maybe he didn't want to encourage me, or maybe I was becoming too obvious to be seen with. I wasn't especially effeminate or anything, but my motions were a little too lithe, my vocabulary was a touch too elegant, and my eyes helplessly followed every high school Adonis who walked by. I didn't make many friends among the rowdy, high-spirited adolescent guys, but I loved to look at them. Once in a while I would catch one of them returning my admiring gaze with a menacing glare, and two or three times I had to use my wits to make a quick exit in order to avoid being battered by someone twice my size.

The best-looking of the local golden boys was Bruno Todd, captain of the baseball team. He was in two of my classes: English and Physical Education. Bruno was the star of the gym class, but he was flunking English. I was getting A's in English. The teacher, Mr. DeVito, always called on me. But in gym I was a catastrophe, always the last to finish calisthenics and always the one who missed the ball in the outfield and earned the scorn of the team.

My real physical education occurred in the locker room, where I had to change fast enough so that my pants were up before my penis was, and that didn't leave much time to look. All the guys surreptitiously checked out one another's equipment, but for most of them it was no more than a casual scientific comparison while for me it was more like my life's work. Luckily

Bruno's locker was right next to mine, so I could watch his muscles ripple across his back when he bent down to lower his shorts, and I timed my own changing so that I could be sure to catch the brief revelation of his genitals, which were big and hairy and stood comparison with a bull's. I was always sorry to see them disappear into his loose one-piece underwear as he began to button up the front, and I envied the flimsy white cotton that contained them for the rest of the day. I thought of them when I followed him down the corridors, watching the little wrinkle of material wag back and forth above the cleft in his buttocks as he took each step.

Apparently my scrutiny hadn't gone unnoticed. I found that out one day in the locker room when Bruno turned to me and looked me right in the eye while he used his crumpled woolen sweat socks to wipe under his balls, slowly and deliberately, as if he were displaying himself for my inspection. I was genuinely shocked, and I was sure I must be misinterpreting his intentions. But I kept glancing around, to be sure there was no one else in sight. I struggled to keep my eyes above his waist, but of course I finally failed. For a moment I stared right at his display with awe. Then I regained my senses.

"Bruno, put that away before somebody sees you," I said between clenched teeth.

He snickered. "I got nothing to be ashamed of," he said.

"I didn't say you should be ashamed," I muttered.

"And what are you hiding down there, kiddo?" he asked with a leer as he gestured with his chin toward the erection I had just stuffed into my pants.

"Nothing," I said. I could feel my cheeks blazing.

"I can see that," he said with a laugh. Then, as he started to get dressed, he changed the subject. "Listen, did you finish the English homework?"

"Sure," I said.

"Do you really understand that stuff?"

"Of course. I like it."

"I don't know how anybody could like that stuff. I can't make head or tail out of it. Uh . . . do you mind if I copy your homework?"

"Bruno, that's cheating! You can't learn anything that way."

"I don't want to learn anything. I just want to pass. Please?"

"No."

"I'll be your best friend." He advanced and put his muscular arm around my shoulder protectively. I shriveled, knowing that he was mocking me, and I said nothing.

He stepped back. "Will you help me with my homework then?" he asked, making a big show of adjusting his pants as if his genitals were too large to be confined.

I nodded silently.

"Come to my house after school," he said. "My folks are away."

At the end of the day, the school bus took us to his stop, which was less than an hour's walk from my own. Over a few beers, which Bruno produced from his father's supply in the cellar, we spent three-quarters of an hour on Walt Whitman's poem "The Wound Dresser," which was more pleasure than work for me:

> . . . I thread my way through the hospitals,
> The hurt and wounded I pacify with soothing hand,
> I sit by the restless all the dark night, some are so young,
> Some suffer so much, I recall the experience sweet and sad,
> (Many a soldier's loving arms about this neck have cross'd
>   and rested,
> Many a soldier's kiss dwells on these bearded lips.)

"What is this guy, some kind of nurse?" asked Bruno.

"Ayuh. During the Civil War he worked in a hospital."

"They say we'll be dragged into the war in Europe soon, the way we were the last time. Are you gonna join up?"

"I'd rather do what Whitman did—be a nurse. I'd rather heal wounds than cause them."

"Typical sissy talk. It takes a real man to fight a war. What's all this stuff about kissin' bearded lips? Is this guy some kind of cornholer or somethin'?"

"What's important is his compassion for the wounded, the way he loves them."

"Yeah, that's what I mean. He loves them. Is that why you're helping me with the homework? Is it because you're compassionate? Or is it because you love me?"

"Well, I really love someone else, but he's away now." I was usually very careful with my pronouns, but I felt there wasn't much point in trying to hide now.

Bruno stretched his arms above his head as if he were tired, but it was clear that he was just showing off his well-built torso. Then he slid his hand into the top of his pants as if to adjust himself, and when he was done he left his hand where it was.

"You do want me to pay you for helping me, don't you?"

"What do you mean?" I said, even though I knew there was little point in playing innocent at this stage of the game.

"You know damned well what I mean. I saw the way you looked at me. I don't care who you think you're in love with. You want to suck on my peter, don't you?"

"Let's just say I need the practice."

"You can't suck it unless you love me," he said tauntingly.

I didn't answer. Instead, I felt myself gritting my teeth.

He stood up and got my arm in a hammerlock. "Now say you love me."

"Ow! Okay, I love you, I love you."

"Now you can have what you want." He unbuttoned his fly. "Do you want it?"

"Yes," I whispered throatily. "I want it."

I let him put his organ in my mouth, and I began to suck on it, but as it hardened, it grew so big that I began to gag. Bruno laughed and kept right on going. So I learned to loosen my throat and let him invade it, even though it made my eyes tear. I couldn't catch my breath until I learned to adjust it to his pumping rhythm. When I got the hang of it, I eventually grew excited enough to become careless. He cuffed the side of my face and said, "Watch your damned teeth." I made sure to touch him only with my lips after that, and concentrated on pleasing him without any consideration for my own satisfaction. But I didn't care; I was getting what I needed. When I was finished, he pulled me up from my knees and held me by the front of my shirt.

"Okay, sucker, now you're going to write my book report for me. I need it by tomorrow morning."

"The hell I will," I said angrily. "I already spent an hour helping you do your work, and you spent five minutes paying me back. Writing the book report will take me another hour. That's not fair."

"Who says it has to be fair? Meet me at lunch hour with that report," he said, "or I'll tell the guys on the baseball team what you just did. Then you'll have more homework than you can handle!"

"Okay," I said, defeated.

"Good, you can go now. See you tomorrow."

As I got to the door, he called after me, "Do you still love me?" And he laughed a very sour laugh.

The next day at lunch hour when I gave him his book report, he didn't even say thank you. We handed in our papers in English class, and I thought that would put an end to it. But at the end of the week, when we were in English again and Mr. DeVito had returned our papers, Bruno expressed his gratitude for the B+ I had earned him by fishing his equipment out of his pants and playing with it underneath his desk until it got hard. The way the rows were arranged, I was the only one who could see what was going on. He flashed a raised eyebrow and a broad smirk when he saw that he had my attention. Then he pursed his lips in my direction as if offering me a kiss. I flushed a red as deep as the orchard in autumn, and forced myself to look away.

After class, Mr. DeVito asked to talk to me. "Daniel, is anything wrong?" he asked.

"What do you mean, Mr. DeVito?" I asked.

"Well, I don't know how to put this delicately, but I noticed a sudden change in another student's work. It's gone from being mindless to being sensitive and well-expressed, much like your own. Do you know what I mean?"

"No, sir."

"You don't know what I'm talking about?"

"No, sir. I really don't."

"Okay, we'll drop it. But there's something else I have to say. I couldn't help but notice you squirming and blushing in the middle of class today. I didn't say anything about it because I didn't want to embarrass you. What's going on?"

I didn't answer, except by lowering my eyes.

"Daniel, I know a lot more than you think about young men like you. Is there something . . . ah . . . of a physical nature happening to you?"

I blushed.

"Daniel, I'm not as blind as some others may be about the truth. I can tell that you're . . . let's call it an 'exceptional' kind of person. I just want you to know that it's fine to be whoever you are—as long as you're discreet, that is. You know, you're not the only person in the world who's different."

I looked at him with shining eyes. How could he know so much about me? Maybe he was like me and was trying to let me know as carefully as possible. Maybe he was even interested in me. He wasn't a bad-looking man, even if he did wear horn-rimmed glasses. He was in his early twenties and had broad features and thick, wavy brown hair. In fact, I had found him rather sexy during the first weeks of the course, but I had decided to ignore those feelings so I could concentrate on my classwork. I tried to smile. Maybe here was a man I could look up to and love. Then I felt immediately guilty about being unfaithful to Chester. What I was thinking about wasn't a casual encounter, and if I pursued it any further, I wouldn't be worthy of Chester's love.

Mr. DeVito had no way of knowing what was racing through my mind, but he could see he had struck a chord in me, so he continued. "Daniel, I'm making some wild guesses here, and I may be way off base, but let me give you some advice. Don't let anybody take advantage of you or bully you. You deserve better than that. You're worth more than any dumb bully. You are a sensitive, talented boy, and you have a bright future ahead of you. But you mustn't waste your skills. Save them for yourself. You'll need them."

"I understand, Mr. DeVito."

"Are you sure?"

I nodded. "I'll take care of it. Thanks for the advice."

"Okay, Daniel. Just remember, if you ever need a friend, that's what I'm here for."

"Thank you. You'll never know how much I appreciate this," I said.

The next time a book report was assigned, Bruno said, "Have it ready for me tomorrow."

"No," I said.

"What do you mean 'No'?" he asked, surprised.

"What does it sound like I mean?"

"I'll let you suck on my lollipop. You'd like that, wouldn't you?"

"No. I've had enough of that."

"Listen, creep," he said menacingly. "I'm not somebody you can brush off just like that."

"Oh no?" I said, and turned and walked away.

Two days later, he made good on his threat. After gym class, when I was taking a shower, Bruno stood in the doorway, blocking my exit. Lewis Elliot and another friend of his, Bob Martin, stood behind him.

"You know, I flunked my latest book report," Bruno said.

"I'm sorry to hear it," I replied.

"It's your fault, creep."

I was getting really nervous, but I held my ground. "Why should it be my fault? You're the one who flunked."

"I told Lewis and Bob all about it, smart-ass. You kept saying you wanted to suck my prick, and you got me so angry that I couldn't do my work. Now I'm gonna show you what I think of creeps like you." He gestured to the two boys behind him. "Hold him, boys."

Lewis and Bob stepped into the shower and grabbed my arms, oblivious to the water soaking their shorts. Bruno took his cock out of his shorts and aimed it at me. I struggled, but Lewis and Bob held tight. Bruno was silent for a moment, but then with a small grunt he let go, and his urine cascaded all over me, mixing with the water of the shower, which mercifully washed it right off.

"Careful," said Lewis. "I don't want to get any on me. It's disgusting."

"It won't kill you," Bruno said, aiming his stream right into my face. I squeezed my eyes closed.

"That's enough," said Bob, evidently not too happy to be participating in this scene. "You said you wouldn't hurt him."

"I lied," Bruno said, and he punched me in the eye.

The other two boys let go of me then, and I crumpled to the cool floor of the shower stall. "That's it," Lewis said to Bruno. "You said it was only a joke. We don't want to get into any trouble. We're getting out of here."

"It's okay," said Bruno, "I'm finished." Before he left, he spat in my face and said, "So long, sucker." I could feel his spittle land on my forehead and slide down my nose. Finally it washed away in the shower stream. When I opened my eyes, the three of them were gone. Only then did I allow myself to feel humiliated and cry. But in spite of my wounds, I knew I'd stood my ground and won.

I explained away my black eye by saying I had been hit with a baseball. Bruno gave me no more trouble after that. In the gym we simply kept our distance, and when he sat next to me in English, he didn't speak to me.

Mr. DeVito asked after me, with a look of deep concern in his eyes. "What happened?"

"I took care of that little problem you mentioned to me."

"Are you all right?"

"I'm fine, better than ever."

Mr. DeVito looked relieved.

I kept mostly to myself, stopping often in the library to read. I tried to find something that would explain my experience to me, but I didn't know what to look up. I knew I wouldn't find "cornholing" in the catalogue, and there was no listing for "homosexual," a word I'd overheard some boys in the lunchroom snickering about. Finally I asked Mr. DeVito. He scratched his head for a moment and said, "The only thing I can think of is the Krafft-Ebing book."

I had to get special permission to take *Psychopathia Sexualis* out of the library, but it was no help. All the specific words were rendered in medical Latin, and what I could decipher made me feel like some kind of distasteful bug being examined through a sterile microscope. Instead, I decided to read about Natty Bumppo and Huckleberry Finn. I loved stories that took me to other times and places. With their help, even if I were trapped in Elysium for the duration, at least I could be free in my imagination.

That's why when the school drama club put on an operetta, I was one of the first ones on line for a ticket. I don't remember the name of it. It was something like *The Gypsy Princess*. It took place in tzarist Russia and was full of saccharine songs and preposterous costumes made of white satin and gold braid. As tacky as it was, it seemed like a dream to me. I had never been to a live theater production before. Of course I was turned on by the handsome young prince, but it was the gypsy girl he loved who really caught my attention. It wasn't just that she was pretty, which she was, but she had some special quality that made her stand out among the others, some force of personality that made her seem like a real person beyond all the scenery and costumes and artificial dialogue. When I saw her in the cafeteria a few days later, I went up to her to say hello.

"I really enjoyed your performance the other night," I said.

"Thanks," she said.

"I guess you're tired of people telling you that all the time."

"I'm not famous enough to be a snob yet."

"You really looked like a star up there."

"Good stage lighting," she said, and we laughed. "But my singing voice could be better."

"No, it was fine," I said. "You really put it across."

"My first true fan," she said, batting her eyelashes and folding her hands at her breasts with her elbows jutting out like a silent movie heroine's. "Pray tell, kind sir," she said ingenuously, "What be thy name?"

I almost let myself be seduced into fake elegance by the formal language, but I caught myself in time. "My name is Dell Blake . . . I mean, everyone calls me Danny—Danny Blake."

"I'm Kelly Barrett."

"I know, from the theater program."

"Aha, my reputation precedes me."

"You're sure you're not a snob?"

"Are you sure you're not just trying to make a date?"

"Scout's honor. I don't date."

"Me neither."

"What do you do with your spare time? Got any hobbies?" I asked. I was amazed at how relaxed I felt with her.

"Nope. No paper dolls, no knitting sweaters, no baking cookies. Sometimes I help out my mom in the diner where she works. How about you? I bet you put model cars together."

"No. I just read a lot, and I write and draw a little. Nothing much."

"What do you read?"

"Novels mostly. But I like some poetry, too. Walt Whitman especially."

"I've read some of his stuff. It's nice."

"I think we're going to be friends," I said.

Kelly and I palled around together from then on. She was easier to talk to than any of the guys I had met, and she seemed to understand me. She was also pretty unhappy at home. Her mother was a waitress, who brought home strange men several times a week. Kelly said she didn't mind what her mother did because it was her own business, but she got crawly when the men gave her lecherous looks. Some of them tried to act a little too fatherly, but her mother pretended not to notice.

I didn't tell her everything about myself, not at first. But after a few months, when we knew we could trust each other, we started to confide our deeper secrets. She wasn't quite a virgin, she told me. She had tried sex once, with Lewis Elliot, Bruno's buddy, just to see what it was like, and she didn't think it was so terrific. After that all the guys tried to pressure her into sex, and she just wasn't interested, at least not with them. I started to visit her house after school. We had it to ourselves when her mother was at work, which was most of the time. We would eat cookies and talk and try out the latest dance steps to her mother's Glenn Miller records. Soon we held hands and even put our arms around each other, just as pals of course.

One afternoon, without any planning, we found ourselves embracing, and in short order we were kissing with what seemed like a desperate passion. And then we were in bed, naked. I grazed her breasts with my fingertips timidly, afraid I would hurt her, but she assured me it felt fine. Her nipples rose at my touch, and my penis rose at hers. But I found it difficult to look at her crotch, which seemed somehow obscene to me, as if I were looking at a face without a nose. Then she spread her legs and showed me the mouth that was inside there, and I entered it, fully erect, and tried to do what came naturally, thrusting and pumping with all the artistry I could muster. But no matter how hard I tried, I couldn't reach a climax. Finally she said, "You're hurting me. I don't think I was wet enough."

I pulled out, thoroughly depressed, and rolled over, so I didn't have to look her in the eye.

"It's all right," she said. "Maybe we were just meant to be friends."

"Maybe I'd be better off dead," I whined. "If you were really my friend, you'd stick a knife in me now and get it over with."

"If you were really my friend, you wouldn't ask such a thing. How could I live with myself after that?"

"Never mind," I said. "Maybe it's best if I leave. I hope I didn't ruin our friendship. I'm not much of a man, am I?"

"You're a terrific man," she said. "There's more to being a man than sex. Stay and talk to me. You're not the only one with problems. Some of the responsibility is mine, too. I'm afraid I don't have very much interest in having a man do that to me. It's all that Bruno Todd's fault. When I wouldn't give in to him the way I did with Lewis, Bruno wrote my name on the boys' room wall. A friend of mine told me it says I sucked him. Can you beat that? What a rat! I wouldn't even go near his filthy thing. Now I have a reputation as the school tramp. It isn't fair."

"I did," I said.

"Did what?"

"Went near Bruno's filthy thing. It wasn't so filthy, actually, but he made me do his homework for him. He said he'd tell everyone if I didn't. I got rid of him eventually, but I can't help myself. I like to have sex with men. Do you think I'm disgusting?"

"Only for doing it with Bruno. Listen, Danny. I don't care if you like to have sex with boys. It's none of my business, unless you want it to be. I'm your friend. The truth is, I might like to do it with women instead of men, but I haven't had a chance to try it out. Do you know where there's a girl who might be interested?"

"I wish I did. The only women I know who were accused of having a love affair had to leave our town. It's a pity. One of them was very nice to me. But I guess they were too old for you anyway."

"Well, keep your eyes open. Meanwhile, let's figure out how to get back at Bruno. I didn't mind having a slightly bad reputation at first. I thought it would be a good cover for my real interests. But my little smoke screen is turning into a forest fire, and I want to get even."

"What can we do?"

"First I want to see what Bruno wrote on the wall. Somebody told me it's in the second floor boys' room. Will you take me there after school?"

"Are you kidding? You can't go in there! It's for boys only."

"Don't tell me you're scared."

"I'm scared."

"All the more reason to do it!"

"You're right."

The next afternoon I took her up to the second floor, and she waited outside while I checked to make sure there was no one in the boys' room. Then we both waited until the hall was clear, and in a flash she was in the white-tiled forbidden zone, staring at the urinals.

"So that's how boys pee," she said. "I always heard they stood up. Girls have to sit down."

"This isn't a biology classroom," I said. "Let's find the thing and get out of here."

In the stall farthest from the entrance door we found it, right above the toilet, surrounded by slogans like "Judge Crater, call your office!" and crude sexual drawings. It read, "Slut Kelly sucks Bruno."

"Maybe it was his idea of a compliment," I offered.

"Then let's leave him one in return," she said, taking out her lipstick. "I hate makeup. My mother said I could wear it after school, but I have a better use for it." She covered over part of it and added some words, so that it read, "Cute Boys suck Bruno." Under it she wrote, "Kelly was here!"

"Thanks for calling me cute!" I said, and we both collapsed in giggles.

At that moment the door opened, and we heard footsteps heading toward the urinals. We hadn't expected that, since classes were over for the day. We froze where we were, hoping that whoever it was would go about his business and leave. But at the sound of water striking porcelain, Kelly muffled a giggle, and I couldn't help but join her. As soon as the splashing stopped, the footsteps came our way. And there stood the vice principal, Mr. Townsend, with an angry look on his face.

We each served a month of detention, during which we were supposed to stay after school an hour a day and contemplate our sins in silence. Instead we passed notes to each other, hatching a simple plot to finish our revenge, which required just the right wording. Finally we settled on this: "Beware of Bruno Todd, Sex Maniac!" Kelly used the remainder of her lipstick to write it in the last stall of the second floor girls' room. She had such a sense of symmetry, that Kelly.

That spring Kelly said she had a surprise for me. She introduced me to George Grimes, who was in her history class. He wasn't gorgeous, but he was decent-looking enough, with brown curly hair and dark, wistful eyes. It took me about four minutes of conversation to figure out that George was like me, at least in his sexual tastes, so we included him in our group. But liking sex with men was more painful for George than it was for me, and he was pretty sour about the whole thing. We tried it together two or three times, but there wasn't much fun in it. The type he went in for was more like Bruno Todd. In George's eyes, if a man was eager for sex with him then he wasn't a real man, and George didn't want him. I told him that was a good way to be a permanent virgin, and he pouted for three days.

I did everything I could to comfort him. I even showed him a supportive passage from *Leaves of Grass*:

> O my Body! I dare not desert the likes of you in other men
> and women, nor the likes of the parts of you.

"Terrific," said George. "Now we have a poet. That ought to be a big help in finding a man."

"It's better than not having a poet," I said, a little hurt at the rebuff, more for Walt's sake than for my own.

Kelly and I practiced the jitterbug during free period, but George preferred to sit by himself and think up excuses for being unhappy. We were getting pretty tired of his eternal blues, but we stuck together because we needed one another. For all we knew we were the only people like us in the whole student body.

Finally, near the end of the school year, Kelly and I had a bright idea at about the same time. We told George to see Bruno Todd, and we gave him a note of introduction, which said, "Dear Bruno, This is George. He'd like to help you with your homework, at the usual fee." I signed it.

George didn't want to take it at first, but the promise of Bruno's manly charms was more than he could resist, so he braved the potential humiliation and went to see Bruno at his house.

A few days later, I asked him how it had gone. "Bruno's wonderful," he said. "I'm really in love. Thanks, Danny. You're a real friend."

"Look at it this way," Kelly said. "If they're together, at least they'll save two other people a lot of grief."

I spent my spare time that year trying to write poetry. It seems pretty juvenile now, but I had to start somewhere. I made it sound as much as possible like my idol's, so maybe it wasn't too original. But it was heartfelt. Here's a sample that I saved:

The Apple Orchard

> I sing the roots and branches.
> I sing the blossoms and the fruit.
> I sing the song of manly companions
> Waiting beneath the boughs for love.

O youth, I said, belong to me.
Give me your joys beneath the apple boughs.
Give me knowledge, pleasure, growth.
Give me life between my lips.

The apples answer with ripeness.
And gorgeous Death is in the breeze.
Together we wait to be plucked by your hand
And eaten by your hungry lips, O Youth.

Let's not evaluate it, okay? We're all entitled to a little immaturity when we start out.

Over the summer, my attention moved to other matters. Hitler's troops were swallowing Europe, and the Japanese held much of the Far East. War was in the air, and we were all afraid of what it would do to our lives. I returned to school as a senior and found it a more serious place. People were talking about the possibility of air raids and surprise attacks, even though there was nothing of military value in our area, and whatever fun there was had a desperate feeling to it. Finishing school was as much a matter of patriotic duty as personal accomplishment, so I buckled down to hard work. But in October Chester Stewart returned, and it was hard to think about the future with anything but hope.

CHAPTER FOUR

"I'm just here for a short while to take care of some business, but I'm really glad for the chance to see you," Chester said as we walked across his lawn. Our breath frosted the air for the first time that year, but I felt warm inside.

"I thought you'd forgotten about me," I said.

"Quite the opposite, I've thought about you a great deal. You must know that from reading my letters."

"I was afraid you were just being kind, out of pity."

"I don't pity you."

"You must have a lot of friends in the city, a lot of opportunities."

"You mean for sex? I do take advantage of an occasional opportunity, but most of the time I'm too busy to worry about it. You must be suffering up here. Chances for sex are few and far between."

"I've tried it a couple of times. It's not so great."

"Maybe once you get used to it."

"Maybe with someone I love . . ."

"Brazen little hussy, aren't you? Well, I'm eager too, but I think the best thing would be to stick to our original bargain. We'll respect ourselves more for it. If we choose to be together after you're eighteen, at least it will be a fully informed decision, not a matter of desperation. After that, I'll raise hell if you so much as look at someone else. But until then you can do your worst."

"Around here, my worst is nothing for you to worry about."

"I was pretty sure of that," he said, smiling. "Anyway, in a few months you can visit me, and then you'll see for yourself just how it is in New York."

It didn't matter that he soon left for the city again. I had something to look forward to. I hadn't been fooling myself. What existed between us was real! I couldn't believe my luck. Chester was so worldly, so sophisticated— at least by my standards. What could he see in a little hick like me? Whatever it was, his interest thrilled me, and I was determined to make myself worthy of it.

Most of my sex life continued to happen anywhere I was alone—in my bedroom, out at Martha's stone, in the stalls of the boys' room at school. Whenever I had a few minutes for myself, I reached inside my pants for pleasure, often three or four times a day. I was insatiable. I even worried about going blind or growing hair on my palms, but I took comfort in knowing that even as eminent a personage as Walt Whitman had written about my favorite exercise, and I assumed he spoke from personal experience:

> The torment, the irritable tide that will not be at rest . . .
> The young man that wakes deep at night, the hot hand
>   seeking to repress what would master him,
> The mystic amorous night, the strange half-welcome pangs,
>   visions, sweats,
> The pulse pounding through palms and trembling encircling
>   fingers, the young man all color'd, red, ashamed, angry;
> The souse upon me of my lover the sea, as I lie willing and
>   naked . . .

It was as if someone understood my most secret longings in a way that no living person did. I could share myself with Walt in ways that made me feel even closer to him than I did to Chester, but that didn't lessen my desire to touch the flesh of the man I loved.

Kelly envied my love for Chester, but not as a competitor, only because she had similar dreams of her own. Our friendship deepened as we hatched plot after plot to find her a willing woman, but to no avail. At least I knew of a few men who shared my interests. What Kelly was looking for was altogether invisible. George Grimes, on the other hand, was doing Bruno's homework regularly, and he lorded it over both of us because we had only phantasms and long-distance lovers to pursue.

I didn't see Chester again until the following summer, when he invited me to visit him in New York City. I wasn't worried about getting permission to go. My father had given up trying to control me. I was respectful in the house and did what I pleased outside, and he did his best to ignore my comings and goings altogether. I simply informed him that I was going to the city and that nothing would stop me, assuring him that Chester had no intentions of breaking his promise or violating the law. Of course if I had anything to say about it, Chester would violate the law on the very first night, but that was none of my father's business.

Seeing Chester waiting for my train to pull up to the platform at Grand Central Terminal was enough to give me an erection. Even here he stood out from the crowd with that extra little space around him. His body looked lean and desirable underneath his full-cut summer clothes, but despite the animal sexuality I sensed, he still looked elegant, as if he didn't know how to sweat and never had a wrinkle in his slacks. I was ashamed of my cardboard suitcase full of rumpled shirts.

I had to wait an extra minute before getting off the train because I didn't want to embarrass us both with the bulge in my pants, and I had to restrain myself from throwing my arms around him for the same reason. We ended up shaking hands like business acquaintances.

As glad as I was to see him, New York drew my attention away as soon as we left the station. That first time I saw it, it was a city without flaws. Its colors made it look more alive than it did in the black-and-white movies I had seen. I craned my neck in all directions and stared shamelessly at everyone and everything, my mouth agape. I had never seen so many people in one place. I thought there might be some kind of emergency because everyone was rushing so fast. The buildings reached upward without end. And the store windows! I had no idea there were so many kinds of things to buy. I don't think I closed my mouth for the entire cab ride to Chester's apartment.

He had the top two floors of a five-story building in Greenwich Village. The neighboring buildings were only three stories high, so his apartment stood apart from its surroundings, which gave him a good view of Washington Square. But there was far less space for living and working than his house and studio near Elysium had afforded him. Here he worked in one large room with a skylight. There was one other room on the top floor, which he used as his bedroom. The lower floor was divided into a small kitchen, a large living room, and a library, which was easily transformed into a second bedroom. The whole place was decorated in quiet good taste, full of things that the folks back home had never seen: Bauhaus chairs and art deco lamps and streamlined automatic appliances. But in spite of the splendor, I felt confined.

"Actually, it's a great deal of space compared to some city apartments," Chester assured me. "And there's a little terrace off the studio if you feel you have to get outside. It's quite a bit like being in Paris, if you squint."

"Paris, France?" I said in awe. "Have you been there?"

"Twice, before the war," he said, and a faraway look glistened in his eyes. "I hate to think of what it's like there now, with Hitler's troops running things. It was so beautiful. All the buildings are cream-colored, and the sunlight makes them seem to glow. Maybe someday the Nazis will be kicked out and I'll be able to take you there. It's fun showing the world to someone who's never seen it."

"You've done so many things," I said, "and I have no experience. I don't know how to behave, and I don't even have the right kind of clothes. I'm afraid I'll embarrass you in front of your friends. I'm a hopeless hick."

"You should think more of yourself," he said. "I do. Remember we all have to start somewhere. I was once a hick myself. Just be yourself and stop worrying. You behave perfectly well. And tomorrow I'll take you shopping for some clothes, so you won't have to feel out of place. Okay?"

"You're awfully good to me."

"Let's just say I enjoy sharing."

That night I took my chance and, as I had two years before, I entered his bedroom while he was asleep. This time, my entrance woke him. He looked glad to see me, but he was firm. "There are only eleven months to go now," he said. "I want you just as much as you want me, but could we trust any other promises we made if we broke our first one?"

"Why not?" I said. "I'm old enough to know what I want. I won't change my mind in eleven months. I didn't change it in the last two years."

"Well, maybe I am being too strict, but I still want to save the main course for next June. I guess I'm old-fashioned. I believe that if you work hard for something, it's worth more to you in the end. It's more exciting that way. How about this? We'll kiss good morning and good night, but nothing further, promise? That way we'll have something to look forward to."

"I guess I'll have to settle for what I can get," I said. "You're a hard man to bargain with."

"Never mind how hard I am," he answered. "Kiss me good night and go back to your bed."

I was very obedient, but I was a hard man too, and an excited one. Before I fell asleep, I masturbated three times to thoughts of Chester: Chester in his underwear, Chester naked, Chester waiting in his bed. It was the only way I could tire myself out enough to sleep.

By the time we had finished shopping the next day, I looked like a fashionable man about town. I was glad I wouldn't feel conspicuous as I met new people, and I was just as glad I'd have proof to show my friends back home when I described the wonders of New York's department stores to them. But as we entered our last store, Saks Fifth Avenue, I forgot all about the choosing of shirts and ties and shoes. I thought I was seeing a ghost! There, behind the men's sweater counter, looking efficient and totally in charge of her domain, stood my grade school teacher Miss Standish, her pince-nez perched tidily in place.

"Did you know about this?" I asked Chester.

He nodded.

I ran up to the counter. "Miss Standish, remember me? It's Daniel from Elysium!"

"Of course I remember you, Daniel. You've changed quite a bit in the last two years."

"You haven't, Miss Standish. You look just the same."

She knit her brows. "Thank you for the compliment, Daniel, but I feel considerably different now. Being in charge of sweaters is a good deal less demanding than being in charge of students." She paused for a moment, then continued. "I don't mean to sound ungrateful. I don't know what would have become of me without Chester's help in finding me this job."

I could have sworn she was softer, gentler than she used to be. In a strange way I felt not only pity for her, but love, although I was sure that the thought of either would have offended her sense of dignity. So I kept up formal appearances, as she had taught me to do.

"And Miss Binder?" I asked. "Is she all right?"

"I was saving that for last, Danny," Chester said. "Come with me."

We said good-bye to Miss Standish and we rode on top of a double-decker bus down Fifth Avenue, past the most glamorous people I could imagine, to the Fifth Avenue library. We passed between the stone lions that guarded the steps and went upstairs to the main reading room, where we found Miss Binder with a pile of books in her arms. Tears sprang to her eyes when she saw us, and she put down the books and gave me a big hug.

"I'm so glad to see you, Daniel. I've thought about you often. Thank you for bringing him, Chester."

"My pleasure," said Chester, endearing himself to me even more, if that were possible.

"Do you still have the copy of *Leaves of Grass* that I gave you?" Miss Binder asked.

"It's back at Chester's apartment. I read it every day. I can never thank you enough for it. But what a terrible price you had to pay for giving it to me. I feel that the whole thing was my fault."

"Nonsense," she said. "Things have worked out for the best. Life in the city has its compensations as well as its challenges. Did you see Miss Standish?"

I nodded.

"Actually we're quite content. We've made the best of things, and we're doing nicely. We have a sunny apartment and lots of interesting friends, some of them from back home."

I thought I saw Chester give her a warning look, and she changed the subject. Later, when I asked him why, he said it was just my imagination.

We saw Miss Binder and Miss Standish for lunch later in the week, and on another day we all went for a walk in Central Park. At last I felt at peace about the grief I had caused them. But I had little time to dwell on the past. Most of my time in New York was spent enjoying a kaleidoscope of new wonders.

Chester and I saw Gertrude Lawrence in *Lady in the Dark* and we had dinner at the Plaza Hotel. We rode on the Staten Island ferry and visited the Statue of Liberty. We went to the top of the Empire State Building and we toured the Metropolitan Museum of Art. We ate lunch in Chinatown and walked across the Brooklyn Bridge. One of my favorite expeditions was to a small gallery on the northern fringe of Greenwich Village, where Chester showed me one of his sculptures for sale. I was so proud of him, I thought I'd burst.

"And what about you?" he asked, one morning after breakfast. "Are you still writing poems?" I had mailed him a few of my efforts and his letters had always been full of praise and encouragement.

"Yes, but they're probably not very good. I can't tell for sure. I'm too shy to show them to anyone."

"Did you bring any with you?"

"Yes."

"Afraid to leave them with your father?"

"I thought I might work on them some more on the train, but I was too busy watching the scenery."

"Show them to me."

I showed him my latest works.

I watched nervously as he read through them all thoughtfully. When he was finished, he pulled one of them out, saying, "They're all very good, at least as far as I can tell, but this is the one I like best." He read it aloud, and I listened with a very special pleasure as I heard his clear voice pronounce my words.

I Am a Tree

by Daniel Dell Blake

I am a tree.
I come from the earth.
I reach toward the sky.
I am old, old, old.
I do not know what it means to die.

My wooden limbs bear trays of fruit.
    I am food.
I shake my leaves in agreement with the wind.
    I am music.
Blossoms and colored leaves bedeck me.
    I am beauty.
Birds and squirrels and caterpillars abide in me.
    I am home.
I generate seeds.
    I am the future.

I stand long and long, *imperturbe,*
waiting for your pleasure.
Burn me:
    I am fuel.
Carve me:
    I am art.

Cut me into planks:
   I will be your coffin.

Embrace me.
Put your arms about me.
Stop for a while and stand with me.
   I am your lover.

I reach toward the earth.
I turn from the sky.
I am old, old, old.
I do not know what it means to die.

"I like the way it sounds," Chester commented after a moment's reflection. "It seems very sensitive to nature and very true. Of course I don't know much about poetry. I'm only a sculptor, not a professor. What does that word '*imperturbe*' mean?"

"I was afraid you'd ask that. It's one of Walt Whitman's words. I can't find it in the dictionary, but I'm sure it means something like 'serene.' I was just experimenting with short lines and new words. I don't know if it's real poetry or not."

"Would you like an expert opinion? I'm invited to a party Friday night, and all sorts of creative people will be there, including Ariel Dumont, the famous poet. Did you ever hear of him?"

I shook my head. "I haven't read much besides Walt Whitman and some Keats and Shelley, and one or two others in English class. I don't know any modern poets at all."

"Well, come along to the party and I'll introduce you."

"I'm a little shy around new people."

"It's time to get over that. Besides, I'll stay with you the whole time. Okay?"

"Okay," I said, feeling like I was entering the big time.

The people at the party were all painters and poets and theater people. I looked very smart in my new clothes, but I was afraid to say much because everyone was much older than I and sounded so sophisticated. They were a bohemian crowd, decked out in idiosyncrasies, which included more bracelets and kerchiefs and cigarette holders than I had ever seen in one place before.

One woman seemed to be holding court. She wore a black, pin-striped, double-breasted suit with padded shoulders. It was tailored like a man's suit, and it gracefully masked her curves. Where a man might have worn a necktie, she had tied a black silk kerchief. Beneath her white beret, her dark hair was cut in a severe bob and hung down straight to the bottom of her ears. Her features were handsome rather than pretty. Her gray eyes were clear, and her square jaw gave her a look of strength. In startling contrast to the dark lipstick and heavy mascara affected by most of the women around her, she wore no makeup, and she puffed on a long-stemmed white clay pipe from time to time. Chester saw me staring at her and took me over to introduce me to her.

"Danny. I'd like you to meet Minerva White. We all worship Minerva. She's one of the great artists of our generation. Her photographs are already hanging in the Museum of Modern Art."

"Fame has its drawbacks," she said in a throaty but pleasant voice. "Most of the companions one finds hanging in museums are dead people."

"Pay no attention to Minerva's false modesty, Danny," said Chester.

"How do you do, young man," she said, turning her attention to me. "Do you like to go to museums?"

"Yes, ma'am," I said softly.

"Speak up, boy. Nobody's going to bite you."

"Yes, ma'am," I repeated. "I went to my first museum this week, and I like them so far, anyway." I was intimidated by her importance, but somehow I sensed that I could trust her not to make fun of me.

"Are you Chester's new friend?"

I nodded.

"Speaking of friends, where's yours?" Chester asked.

"Here she comes now, with some drinks, I hope."

A short woman appeared from the crowd, carrying two cocktail glasses. She had a plain face with a sweet expression made oddly intense by a small, dark mole just above her nose, almost like a Hindu caste mark pleasantly punctuating her brow.

"Ah, there you are, my sweet," said Miss White.

"Ayuh. I had to fight my way through those ravenous beasts at the table," she said. And, turning to me, she added, "Who's this?"

"This is Daniel, Chester's friend."

"Oh, I see. Hello, Daniel. What a nice-looking young man you are! I bet the folks at home are proud of you," she said.

"Not especially," I said.

"Well never mind them, dear. Chester looks proud enough to make up for anyone else's failures."

"I've put my work aside while Danny's visiting," Chester said.

"Well, young love is different," Miss White said. "You don't take each other for granted the way we old timers do."

"Whoa, Minerva. We're not quite an item yet. We're just exploring."

"Don't wait too long," she counseled him. "This boy is ripe for plucking. I can see it in his eyes."

"You tell him, Miss White," I said. "Maybe he'll listen to a smart lady like you."

I felt as if she were really my friend. But other people were eager to talk to her, and Chester soon steered me away to another corner, where I was introduced to Ariel Dumont the poet. He was everything Minerva White was not. A purple cravat was tucked into his pink silk shirt, and he had a large ring on every one of his fingers but his thumbs. I thought I detected traces of rouge on his cheeks, but I couldn't be quite sure. I'd never seen a man in makeup before.

"Is this your young protégé?" he asked Chester. "He's not bad-looking, you old cradle robber, you." He turned to me. "Chester tells me you want to be a poet. Let me see your work. I can't bear to be kept in suspense."

I gave him my manuscript and he riffled through it, with only an occasional arching of his probably plucked eyebrows to let me know what he was thinking. He stopped only twice to read complete poems. When he was finished, he paused for a moment, and then he unleashed a torrent of criticism that still stings my ears all this time later.

"A few good images—'in agreement with the wind' and 'butterflies afire.' But so many archaic words. 'Abide' and 'long and long.' And '*imperturbe*'— what the hell does that mean? It sounds like a cheap copy of Whitman. Such coinages are just too cute for words." He stopped to snicker at his own cleverness. "And this: 'I sing the roots and the branches.' Dear boy, what century are you in? Haven't you read e. e. cummings or T. S. Eliot or Pound? Or even Jeffers? You write as if the modern era were still fifty years off. The only good thing I can say about your work is that at least every line doesn't rhyme. Chester, darling, why do you take up my precious time with such hopelessly juvenile amateurs?"

I was blushing and tongue-tied. Dumont had made a point of speaking loudly, and I was sure everyone had heard him. I wanted to crawl under the carpet. Then a throaty voice from behind me thundered, "Ariel Dumont, there is no reason to be such a bitch. Everyone knows a boy his age is just beginning. How great was your writing at his age—if you can remember that far back? I was nearly thirty before I sold a picture." It was Minerva White. She had taken my part twice in ten minutes now, and I adored her for it.

Chester joined the fray. "You jealous old queen. Why, if I'd gone to bed with you when you sniveled about your 'need to give yourself to a real man,' I bet you wouldn't be so mean!"

"Carry on all you want to, both of you," said Ariel Dumont superciliously. "That still won't make this brat into a poet."

"Go fuck yourself, Dumont! You're a half-baked poet and even less of a human being," said Minerva White. "Chester, promise me you'll bring this boy to lunch at my place tomorrow." She looked at me. "Will you come?"

I nodded silently, and Chester took me home to console me with chocolate ice cream and three good-night kisses.

The next day we went to a brownstone in the western part of Greenwich Village and climbed a flight of stone steps, where Minerva White greeted us at her door. This time she was wearing loose slacks and a small, dark green velvet vest over a pale green satin shirt with ballooning sleeves. She still carried her white clay pipe, using it like a wand to extend her gestures. She was the most interesting-looking person I had ever encountered, and I made sure to memorize every detail of her surroundings.

First she took us up to the top floor, to show us her studio. It was a large white space with a darkroom in the corner. Cameras on tripods stood in several places, and large, colored backdrop sheets hung from the walls. "Would you like me to take your picture?" she asked.

I was thrilled. "Would you? Golly, I've never had a professional photographer take my picture. Should I comb my hair? Where do you want me to stand? Should I say 'cheese'?"

She laughed deep in her throat and refused to let me tidy up. She took pictures of me sitting and standing and leaning against a wall, and she did the same with Chester. Then she took some shots of the two of us, sitting in chairs and staring into each other's eyes. I was surprised how easily my self-consciousness disappeared. It wasn't like the awkward pictures I had stiffly posed for at school. I felt like myself in front of her camera lens. I told her how impressed I was, but she said there was nothing unusual about it. That was her job.

Then she showed us around the house. The furniture was unremarkable, as if no pains had been taken to create a decorated look like Chester's apartment had. Instead, comfort was the keynote. There were large tables and big stuffed couches and chairs in an assortment of colors, but somehow everything went well with everything else, and I found the whole thing enchanting. What was unusual about the house was the walls. Almost every vertical surface was hung with photographs: wonderful images of faces and shadows and vegetables and flowers, each in a frame with barely any space between them, from floor to ceiling, as if they were engulfing the whole house. I was afraid to stand still too long, for fear that someone might a hang a picture on me.

I began to look at them closely. Many of the portraits were of the woman who had been with her at the party, portrayed in every imaginable mood and lit so that the shadows accented the planes of her cheeks and emphasized her eyes, making her plain face look beautiful.

Seeing me stare at one of them, Chester asked Miss White, "Where is she anyway?"

"She wanted very much to be here, but our friend Ada took sick at the Jersey shore this morning, and she had to run down there to help Louise take care of her."

"Your pictures are beautiful," I said, gushing with adolescent enthusiasm. "You have such a new way of seeing things. It makes me think about the things you photograph as if I'd never seen them before. I could look at these forever."

"I must ask you to stop. You'll make me blush, and if word got out that I was still capable of blushing, it would ruin my public image permanently.' "

I looked up to see if she was serious, but there was a big grin on her face. So I knew everything was all right, and I continued my inspection, going from room to room almost in a trance. "The light," I said. "How do you get things to glow like that?"

"Oh, I have my little tricks of the trade," she said. "You wouldn't ask a magician to tell you his secrets now, would you?"

"I guess not. Are you a magician?"

"I hope so."

Then I saw a picture of two luminous blossoms nestled against each other.

"I've seen this picture before," I said.

"Maybe in a magazine?" she suggested.

"No, back home, upstate. Miss Binder, our school librarian, had it in her parlor."

"I've been selling my pictures for years now. It's nice to think that they've reached the people in the hinterlands. What's the name of the town you come from?"

"Elysium," I said.

"How they love Greek upstate," she said. Chester laughed, but I didn't know what was so funny.

She took us downstairs to a warm kitchen, which opened onto a backyard garden where we had lunch under a chestnut tree.

"My creative skills don't extend as far as cooking," she said. "So I had this prepared at a restaurant around the corner. I hope you don't mind."

It was a delicious lunch of cold crabmeat salad. While we ate, she brought up the subject of the previous night's party, and my ears reddened at the very thought of it. "I don't want you to take old Dumont seriously," she said. "Promise me you'll go on writing. I can't tell you if you have talent, but I do know you have plenty of time to experiment and grow. If you're a real poet, you'll know it eventually, and never you mind what anyone else has to say. You just follow your own star and let the fools take care of themselves."

I promised to obey her advice, and when we were through and had said our good-byes, Chester took me to the Museum of Modern Art, where three of her photographs were hung: one of a tree bathed in mist, one of her friend's face with such a kind look in her eyes that she seemed to glow, and one of the same two blossoms I had noticed at lunch.

"I really admire her," I said to Chester as we left the museum. "You know, I never knew my mother."

He nodded sympathetically.

"I never even knew what she looked like. But I'd like to think she was something like Miss White. Do you suppose she would mind if I thought of her when I imagined my mother?"

"I'm sure she would be proud," he answered.

At the end of the afternoon, we went to see Miss Binder. She gave me some Walt Whitman books: some of his letters and early stories, his journal, *Specimen Days*, and a biography by Bliss Perry. They were intended as going-away presents, because Chester was taking me to his house on Long Island for my last week of vacation.

"Thanks so much for the books," I said. "I have so much studying to do. There are so many things I never knew about, back home. Now I'm starting to learn about sculpture and photography, too. That reminds me, do you remember the photograph of two flowers that you had on your parlor wall?"

"Yes, I still have it. It's an original by Minerva White."

"Where did you get it?" I asked.

She seemed to look at Chester rather than at me when she answered, "Miss Standish gave it to me for my birthday one year. Why?"

"Oh, it's just that I met Miss White yesterday, and I had lunch at her house today. She's swell. Did you know that the same picture is hanging in a museum?"

"Yes, I've seen it there. I treasure my copy of it. How lucky you were to meet such a great artist. You've been in town only two weeks and you're hobnobbing with celebrities already. Maybe you'll be a celebrity yourself someday, and then I can say I knew you before the world discovered you."

I didn't tell her what Ariel Dumont had said about my poetry, because I was afraid it would hurt her feelings almost as much as it had hurt mine. I was glad for her faith in my future, and I told her that I would do what I could to make her proud of me.

In the morning, we left for Long Island. The ride there was quiet, and I missed the excitement of the city even before we arrived at the shore. But the man I loved needed some time away from the crowds and the chaos, and it was more important to me to be with him than to explore more of the metropolis.

Chester's house was nestled in the dunes, with plenty of empty space between it and its neighbors. It didn't have any more rooms than his apartment in town, but it had a wide veranda where we could sit and look at the water. I immediately fell in love with the immensity of the ocean. For the first time I felt as if my mind were challenged. There was nothing to prevent it from expanding to fill the entire horizon. I liked to get up early to watch the sunrise, but Chester was a little too urban for such primitive pleasures. For the first time since I was with him, I noticed that he drank a considerable amount. Although he never seemed falling-down drunk, he sipped nearly half a bottle of bourbon every evening, and he slept until around noon each day.

On our second day there, when he finally emerged from the house rubbing his eyes, he found me romping in the surf without my bathing suit, hoping to tempt him even if the cold water shriveled my bait. In spite of the fact that no one could see us for a long stretch of empty beach, he insisted that I observe at least the minimal rules of propriety. I knew that there wasn't anything prudish about him. He was just doing his best to live up to our agreement, while I was doing my best to break it. I wondered if his drinking could be my fault, a way of curbing his desire.

He lay in the sun silently and spent some time alone with his modeling clay, making small studies for a sculpture he planned to work on when he got back to his studio, so I was left more to my own devices than I had been in the city. I swam and tried to read some of the books Miss Binder had given me. I wanted to work on some new poems, but in spite of the encouragement I had received from Minerva White, I was still too dispirited by Ariel Dumont's nastiness to produce much more than self-pity, and I put my work aside until I was in a better mood. I walked up long stretches of the beach, collecting pebbles and shells, and I arranged them as artfully as I could on tables and bookshelves. I collected wildflowers and reeds and composed elaborate bouquets to present to Chester until every room had two or three vases full, and Chester began to worry that the area would be stripped bare of vegetation and start to erode.

For the first few days the sand was clean and beautiful, except perhaps for some seaweed that had washed ashore. But one day hundreds or maybe thousands of alewives, small silver fish a little larger than sardines, lined the beach, cast up out of their element to die. Some still thrashed, desperately trying to breathe. I managed to toss a few back into the water, but there were far too many to save and I grew depressed. For several days the sand was littered with their rotting bodies, picked at by birds and insects, and I kept away from the beach.

I turned for companionship to my old friend Walt Whitman and began to read from the "Sea Drift" section of *Leaves of Grass* because it seemed like the most appropriate one for that place. The opening poem concerns a young boy who hears two birds singing on the beach, and when one of them disappears, the boy hears the remaining bird sing a mournful, solitary song, which gives him a glimpse of his own future:

Now in a moment I know what I am for, I awake . . .

Never more the cries of unsatisfied love be absent from me,
Never again leave me to be the peaceful child I was . . .

He asks the sea, whom he calls "the fierce old mother incessantly moaning," to give him a word of explanation:

> Whereto answering, the sea . . .
> Lisp'd to me the low and delicious word death,
> And again death, death, death, death . . .

I thought of all the dead fish when I read that, and it made me even sadder than I was already. I couldn't listen to the sound of the surf without hearing that word. I combed through the poem again, finding it more difficult than most, and eventually I found a note of hope for the boy, and of course for myself:

> My own songs awaked from that hour . . .

I understood that the boy learned from his experience with the birds and the sea that he would become a poet, but he knew that being a poet meant feeling the pain of life as well as the beauty. There was always a price to pay for understanding, I realized, and since I knew that I would always try to understand whatever I saw, I had to be willing to pay that price.

I walked a long way up the beach by myself, following the white line of the foam so I didn't have to worry about losing my way, and I lost myself in reveries of what my life would be like when I could leave home and be the master of my own fate. I would move to New York and live with Chester and become a famous poet and give parties of my own. My guests would be the brightest, most creative people in the world and would definitely not include Ariel Dumont. I could laugh now to think of how different my life turned out from what I imagined that summer day.

One evening, after lingering on the porch to watch the wide sky above the ocean fill with stars, and uselessly trying to imagine the vastness of space and time until the effort made me dizzy, I went upstairs to my room. I lay for a long while somewhere between waking and sleep, maybe in a dream, maybe not. I thought I heard the sound of air rushing past my ears, as if I were flying through space, but that made no sense. I felt as if the earth had dropped away beneath me, as if I were floating gently and aimlessly upward. The sensation was so real that I opened my eyes. And what I saw was myself, lying in the bed below me. I seemed to be floating somewhere near the ceiling in a body that looked like my own, except it was not made of flesh. It was almost transparent, gauzy-looking and luminous; to an onlooker I might have looked like a ghost. Terrified, I wondered if I had died and my soul had left my body.

Along with the fear there came motion, as if I had jumped back. When I was startled by the movement, my direction changed. I looked at the open window and found myself drawn toward it. Then I felt even more terror and I stopped, unwilling to leave the room where my body lay, for fear that if I were separated from it, I might never reenter it. Lines from the poem I had been reading flashed into my mind:

> Over the sterile sands and the fields beyond, where the child
> leaving his bed wander'd alone, bareheaded, barefoot . . .

Again, I felt myself drawn toward the open window. I looked through it, and suddenly I was outside the house. Trying to get back in, I looked into the windows. Behind one of them lay Chester, sleeping soundly in his bed. I tried to call to him, but I had no voice. Then I raised my vision toward the glittering sky and I began to rise. Afraid I would lose myself among all those stars, I looked quickly toward the long strip of pale sand bordering the ominously dark water. And suddenly I was on the beach.

I managed to "sit down" on the sand merely by thinking of sitting. I wasn't tired, but I was disoriented, and I wanted time to think. The dark waves rolled slowly up to the shore in cadence, the foam bubbling and hissing at the ocean's edge. I was afraid to think of the water for very long or to look in that direction, because to be drawn into the darkness might mean never to return. Beneath the sound of the surf, I could hear a low *thumping*, as if some distant bass drum were being solemnly struck. I thought the drum sound was especially strange, and couldn't imagine what might be causing it. It seemed to come from the very air: *thump . . . thump . . . thump*.

Then, from the corner of my eye I saw a tall, solitary figure, strolling calmly up the beach. He was clearly in no hurry. Occasionally he stopped to examine something at the water's edge, and now and then he stopped to look up at the stars. As he drew closer I could see that he wore a round-brimmed hat and a long white beard, and I recognized him at once. He looked just like the frontispiece in *Leaves of Grass*. It wasn't until he was almost upon me that he noticed me at all, but as soon as he saw me he was at my side. I never saw him take the final steps in my direction. He sat down next to me in the sand and with his glowing gray eyes looked straight into mine. Then he put a weightless arm around my shoulder. More words from his poem sprang into my mind:

> Throwing myself on the sand, confronting the waves,
> I, chanter of pains and joys, uniter of here and hereafter . . .

and lines from another of his poems as well:

> Kiss me my father,
> Touch me with your lips as I touch those I love . . .

I leaned my face close to his until our lips seemed to touch, but we passed through each other like two mists. There was no sensation except an inward feeling of great joy. Then the wraith before me slowly began to fade from sight. I couldn't bear to watch. Looking down, I saw that my own image was fading as well.

I awoke in my bed, looking up at the ceiling with a clear memory of what had happened. It was unlike any dream I had ever had. Excited, I ran to Chester's room and tried to wake him, so I could tell him what had happened and ask what it meant. But his bourbon had made it impossible to rouse him past semiconsciousness, and all I could get from him was a dull groan. I went back to my room, where I kept going over and over the details in my mind. The only thing that made no sense at all was the thumping sound of drums that I had heard in the background. Had it been the sound of my own heartbeat? It took me an hour to fall asleep. The next afternoon, when I calmly described my experience to Chester, I could tell by the way he humored me that he didn't believe a word of it.

That afternoon I wanted to write again. I sat down on the veranda in front of a fresh tablet of paper. It was a gray day and Chester sat there too, reading Marcel Proust. He looked dashing in his white flannels with a sweater knotted around his shoulders, and I couldn't have loved him more. But I had another love to commemorate. I wrote:

The Visitor

> Striding up the darkened beach,
> Out of time and out of place,
> Hearing seawhispers of death,
> I greet my other self with a kiss.
> Older than time.
> His footsteps are inside me.
>
> I have never been happier.
> One kiss offered,
> My father, my teacher, my love,
> Your arm around my shoulder only once.
> Then we fade into memory's mist,
> Everywhere, nowhere, now and then,
> Together beyond words,
> Beyond this life.

I was pleased with it, but I couldn't stop polishing it. I couldn't decide whether to put "together" on a separate line by itself or whether to change "inside me" or whether "seawhispers" should be two words, but playing with the sounds and watching how they affected meanings was sheer delight. I started to work on my next poem immediately.

Chester was impressed. "I'm proud of you," he said. "Not only because I think you have talent, but because you didn't let a little twerp like Ariel Dumont get you down. Why don't you spend this school year writing some more? If they turn out this good, I'll find some other people to show them to, and maybe we can even get some of them published."

I didn't know if I had too many like that in me, since I couldn't draw on many other experiences like the one which had inspired it, but at least I had something to look forward to as Chester drove me to New York to put me on the train back to Elysium. I said my farewells and thank-yous to Chester and suddenly gave him an embarrassed hug before I got onboard, hoping that anyone who saw us would think that he was my big brother.

When I arrived home, my father laid down the law. "If you're so ready to go traveling without my permission, then go and do it. As far as I'm concerned, I'm only responsible for you until you finish high school. Then you're on your own."

I withdrew into my own writing and reading while I was at home. I sat out at Martha's stone and wrote poems about the jar of dead fireflies from my boyhood, and about the split-rail fences along the path to town, and the apples in my father's orchard. There was material wherever I looked. I read the books about Whitman, adding whatever else I could get my hands on from the high school library. I learned about his boyhood in Brooklyn, his jobs as a printer's helper and as a teacher and editor and clerk. I already knew about his nursing of the wounded during the Civil War, but I learned more about his old age in Camden, New Jersey: poor but respected, and cared for by friends.

Most of the books about him painted him almost as a saint, declaiming poetry at the treetops and beyond the pleasures and pains of the flesh. But his journal, *Specimen Days*, showed me a glimpse of the real man, and I grew more determined to track down what traces I could of the truth.

One passage in *Specimen Days* made me blink with wonder. It was labeled "Sea-Shore Fancies" and in it Whitman says:

> There is a dream, a picture, that for years at intervals,
> (sometimes quite long ones, but surely again, in time,) has
> come noiselessly up before me, and I really believe,
> fiction as it is, has enter'd largely into my practical life—
> certainly into my writings, and shaped and color'd them.
> It is nothing more or less than a stretch of interminable
> white-brown sand, hard and smooth and broad, with the
> ocean perpetually, grandly, rolling in upon it, with slow-
> measured sweep, with rustle and hiss and foam, and many
> a thump as of low bass drums. This scene, this picture, I
> say, has risen before me at times for years. Sometimes I
> wake at night and can hear and see it plainly.

It was the same sound of low bass drums that I had heard in my vision! I knew then that something real had happened, but I still had no idea how to explain it. Whatever it might mean, I still had the realities of every day to face.

At school in my senior year, a scandal erupted when Mr. DeVito, my former English teacher, had to marry one of my classmates because he had gotten her pregnant. He wasn't forced to leave his job, but everyone in the school knew all about it and cruel jokes were written on all the boys' room walls. I was really amazed at how wrong I had been about him when I had assumed that his offer of friendship had stemmed from his being like me, and then I realized that in a way he *was* like me. Because he was having an affair that broke society's rules, and that made him different from the majority, too. But mainly he was a decent person who was simply trying to help someone in need. I went to see him one day, to congratulate him on his marriage and to offer my support and friendship even though I was no longer in his class. He didn't need any help, he told me, but he was really glad that I was coming into my own, and he was glad to be my friend.

I saw less of George Grimes, who now spent all his time with Bruno Todd, but I didn't miss his sour disposition anyway. Kelly and I helped with the collection of scrap metal to aid the British war effort, and we made plans for our lives after graduation. She would continue her search for the woman of her dreams in Syracuse and would travel until she had found her. I would leave for New York as soon as I was finished with school, to be with Chester.

I continued my writing and reading, paying as little attention as possible to the dreary homework assignments the teachers gave me and learning as much as I could about Walt Whitman on my own. My imagination was sparked by the book of letters, in which I could see the outlines of the relationship between the poet in his mid-forties and a twenty-one-year-old Confederate veteran named Peter Doyle, who had become a streetcar conductor in Washington, DC after the Civil War. They spent almost every day together, and when they had to be apart Walt wrote Pete the tenderest letters, especially when his young friend was suffering from a depressing barber's rash:

> My darling, if you are not well when I come back I will
> get a good room or two in some quiet place . . . and we
> will live together, & devote ourselves altogether to the
> job of curing you . . . & we would see that your mother
> should have a small sum every week to keep the pot a-
> boiling at home.

Most of their letters were filled with personal news and advice, like Chester's letters to me. But Walt's letters were more eloquent. The closings touched me most of all:

> Good night, my darling son—here is a kiss for you, dear
> boy—on the paper here—a good long one . . . I will

imagine you with your arm around my neck saying Good
night, Walt . . . Yours for life, dear Pete (& death the same)

There was a picture of the two men seated together, facing each other
with smiles and staring deeply into each other's eyes. In it, both of them
have their hats on, Walt his round-brimmed felt and Pete his derby. Walt's
arms are folded loosely across his chest. Pete has a kerchief in his jacket
pocket and a flower in his lapel. I stared at it for a long time, trying to read
their faces. Was it sex or love or amusement or embarrassment they shared?
I couldn't tell. I wanted badly to know what had really gone on between
them, but the picture could be read in many ways.

Late that fall, I received a package from Chester. In it was a collection of
photographs that Minerva White had given him to send to me. Each of them
was inscribed on the back: "For Daniel, With love, Minerva White, 1941."
There was one of me leaning against the wall of her studio, my arms folded
across my chest, and there was one of Chester laughing, and one of the two
of us seated across from each other, looking soulfully into each other's eyes.
Again I was astounded. The picture of Chester and me was posed almost
exactly like the picture of Walt Whitman and Peter Doyle that illustrated the
book of letters. We didn't have our hats on, but we sat facing each other and
staring with the same entranced expression into each other's eyes. In our
case, I was sure that it was love between us, so I hoped the same had been
true for Walt and Pete. I wondered if Minerva White knew something about
me that I myself didn't yet know, or if she really was a magician. I sent
Chester a thank-you note to give her, and in it I asked if she knew about the
picture of Whitman and Doyle. But I never received an answer, and I felt all
the more lonely after the reminder of the previous summer's joys.

On December seventh, I was in church with my father and Mrs. Warner
when the service was interrupted by a special announcement. The Japanese
had bombed Pearl Harbor. I had never heard of Pearl Harbor and I didn't
know what it would mean, but everyone was scared and angry, and by the
next day we were at war. I thought of all the beautiful young men who would
die, and I knew I had to do something to help them. But of course my first
job was to finish my final semester of school. At least the people I love are
safe, I thought, but I didn't know for how long that would continue to be
true.

A second package of photographs came in the early spring, and in it were
copies of the three pictures that hung in the Museum of Modern Art. I
couldn't believe my luck. I wrote a second thank-you note to Minerva White
and sent it via Chester, who explained in a letter that she was too busy to
reply, and that it was rare for her to interrupt her work to pay as much
attention to anyone as she had to me. But my father didn't even want to look
at the pictures. He refused to let me frame any of them, even when I
explained that they were good enough to be in museums.

His taste in art and morals became a little clearer to me that April. I had just finished helping him in the orchard one Saturday. He was still out among the trees when I returned and Mrs. Warner asked me to get a dish he had taken up to his room, because she needed it for dinner. While I was in the room, I noticed that the door to his walk-in closet had the key in its lock. Even though I had seen his keys lying in a bowl on his dresser, I had never known which was the key to that door. But I knew he had always kept the closet locked, and I had always wondered what he hid in there. I took a few minutes to open the door and look inside, and there I found a pile of magazines with pictures of partly clothed women and a few nudist publications with photographs of naked men and women together. So old Dad was an art collector himself—and a masturbator like me, to boot! In a way I was glad that in spite of his solitude he had some sort of outlet. I just couldn't understand why he wanted everyone else to feel guilty for their sexual desires when he had lusts of his own. After that, as soon as he was out of the house, I went up to his room and took the key from the bowl where he kept it. I went into the closet, where I could look at the men in the nudist magazines and play with myself. I had a few good sessions in there, but after about the third time, I must have been careless about the way I put back the pile of magazines because my father began to get suspicious.

The next time I opened the closet door, a pencil fell to the floor with a sharp tap. It had evidently been carefully placed in a leaning position against the inside of the door so that he would know if the door had been opened. I looked through the treasure trove, and when I had climaxed, I replaced the pencil carefully. I could outsmart him any day in the week, I thought. But the next time I went to the closet, I noticed a very thin thread tied across the edge of the door. To break it would have been a sure sign of guilt. So I kept away from there, not wanting any more trouble with him in my last two months at home. Besides, I had about worn out the thrill of those nudists, and I preferred to imagine the exciting things that Chester and I would do once we were together at last.

When June came, I began to get ready for graduation. The date I was really looking forward to was the twenty-eighth, when I could leave home. But on the morning of the fifteenth, my plans for the future collapsed. I received the only telegram of my life. It read:

DRAFTED. STOP. LEAVE GRAND CENTRAL JUNE 16, 3 P.M. STOP. SORRY NO TIME TO LET YOU KNOW. STOP. BETTER NOT TO MEET. STOP. PROMISE TO WRITE. STOP. PRAY FOR ME. STOP.

LOVE, CHESTER

I had to see him if I could. Of course my father was no help, and Mrs. Warner had no money. Finally I borrowed the train fare from Kelly's mother, and I left on the first train in the morning. I had a hell of a time even getting aboard because all the cars were full of servicemen on their way to be shipped out. For the first time the war became more than newspaper headlines to me. Despite the atmosphere of forced cheer and camaraderie that filled the train with songs and laughter, I could see the grim truth in the faces of these men on their way to battle.

We were delayed several times on the way to the city because so many trains were pulling out that day. By the time we made it to Grand Central, it was nearly four o'clock. I looked everywhere, but Chester had already gone, and I nearly wept with frustration.

Then I had to pull myself together. There was a three hour wait for the train back home, and I sat around in the waiting room surrounded by farewells and chaos and crying wives. I was one of them, but nobody knew it. I did my best to keep my feelings inside.

On one trip into the men's room, I stood next to a man in uniform who kept staring at me. I could see that his dick was hard, and when I stared back at him, he whispered, "Why don't you come into one of the stalls with me?" I wasn't above that sort of thing, even though I hadn't yet tried it, but with Chester maybe about to die to protect me, it just seemed too lewd. I just shook my head no.

I don't remember much about the ride back upstate. This train was also crowded with soldiers, and there were people sitting on duffel bags in the aisles. I managed to sleep anyway, too miserable to stay awake.

The last two weeks before graduation were busy with exams and rehearsals. I don't know how I got through them. If my father was glad about Chester, at least he had the good grace to hide it. Kelly did her best to console me, but she couldn't help. No one could help. My dreams were spoiled, maybe forever, and I needed a new plan. There was only one way I could think of to leave home now.

Two days after graduation, on my eighteenth birthday, I enlisted in the United States Army. When I told my father where I was going, he said, "Don't make me ashamed of you. Be a man."

PART II
DAN BLAKE

Beat! beat! drums!—blow! bugles! blow!
Make no parley—stop for no expostulation,
Mind not the timid—mind not the weeper or prayer,
Mind not the old man beseeching the young man,
Let not the child's voice be heard, nor the mother's entreaties,
Make even the trestles to shake the dead where they lie
   awaiting the hearses,
So strong you thump O terrible drums—so loud you bugles
   blow.

—Walt Whitman,
"Beat! Beat! Drums!"

CHAPTER FIVE

The induction center in Syracuse was crowded with hundreds of men of every description. Scattered among them there were more handsome young guys than I had seen in my whole life. At first I wondered if I could get through the day in my underwear without sporting an erection, which might earn me a black eye or a 4-F. But it turned out not to be too difficult, considering the dread we all felt.

Silently brooding or nervously chatting, all of us knew that this day meant the end of our individual freedoms for the duration, and that the war, which so far we had only seen in black-and-white newsreels and magazine photographs, would soon be at our feet in living color. Like most of the men, I kept my griefs and fears inside, but while they openly kidded each other about their adolescent lust, I kept mine hidden. I had practiced self-containment for years in my father's house, and I trusted that my stoic facade would remain impenetrable.

I kept my wrists rigid and my eyes at ankle height while I stood in line with the rest, and I spread my cheeks like a man (but perhaps a bit more hopefully) while the doctor inspected our assholes. I coughed like a man while he held my balls (but I wanted to say, "A little tighter, please, darling"), and I took my shots like a man, without a whimper, while some of the toughest-looking boys fainted dead away when they saw the needles (and me without my Flo Nightingale lamp!). Then it was time to be interviewed by the psychiatrist, and like any normal man with a guilty secret, I began to sweat.

I didn't want to lie, but I didn't know the penalties for telling the truth about my homosexual "tendencies." I figured it would mean rejection at best and imprisonment at worst, so I decided on selective honesty. I tried to be as cool as I could while the overworked doctor was busily filling out forms without looking up. He was mumbling questions so fast that I could barely hear most of them, let alone answer fully.

"Any history of mental illness?"

"No." (Well, there is a minor aberration or two.)

"Anyone in your family?"

"No." (But maybe you should check out my dad.)

"What about girls?"

"Girls, sir?" (Whatever do you mean?)

"Girls. Do you like 'em?"

"Sure." (Some of my best friends . . .)

"Next!"

It wasn't quite so easy when I found myself in a barracks outside San Francisco with forty-seven other recruits shitting, showering, and shucking their underwear in front of me. I kept my voice to a low growl and stiffened my motions so I could go undetected. Being butch is only a matter of mannerisms, and I was as good an actor as the next guy.

There was so much to do during basic training that my sex life was limited to the most perfunctory masturbation, under the coarse woolen army blanket after lights out. I wasn't the only self-indulger, judging by the rustling and panting that I could hear in the large, darkened room. But the other guys had to rely on fading memories of girls back home or the Betty Grable pin-ups in their foot lockers, while I had a hundred fresh mental snapshots of them to jerk off to. I was glad they couldn't see into the privacy of my mind. They might have felt exploited, or gotten mad, or—who knows?—maybe even fallen in love. Anyway, after long hours of squirming under barbed wire and climbing barricades and endless drill formations, there wasn't much energy left for sex, and most of what there was went right back into the training. Any desires that still remained were taken care of with cold showers. When I think of all that raw male sexuality going to waste, I could cry. If it were harnessed, the energy could have lit up Chicago! But the army wanted to keep our sexual instincts repressed, and I did too—for different reasons, of course. I even got to enjoy the calisthenics after a while. My body toned up nicely, and by the end of basic training I was hard and muscular, and I looked pretty spiffy in my new uniform.

I spent my first weekend pass exploring the steep hills of San Francisco and enjoying the beautiful views. But I wound up sitting alone in a bar with one drunk and two heavily made-up hookers, who were complaining loudly about how the shortage of nylon stockings had forced them to draw eyebrow pencil seams up the backs of their legs. When they couldn't make any headway with me, they tried the drunk, and I went to a John Garfield movie, where I had one of the most memorable but unsatisfying sexual experiences of my life.

I sat in the back of the theater's balcony because it was less crowded. Soon after the movie's credits had ended, I became aware that a man who was sitting one seat away from me had been watching me. I didn't think much of it, but when I casually put my arm around the back of the chair between us—for reasons of comfort only, I swear—his hand touched mine, and our two hands began caressing. Within a few minutes he moved into the empty seat between us, and we spent the rest of the movie fondling each other as discreetly as we could. It was all foreplay. Neither of us had an orgasm (at least, I know I didn't), but there seemed to be a nice gentleness and affection between us, and I assumed we would get together after the film was over (although I wouldn't have minded staying to see it again, since I hadn't paid any attention to it). But as soon as the film ended, before the house lights came on, he bolted from his seat and was out the door.

I ran after him, but I couldn't find him in the crowd. I could have been standing right next to him, but I wouldn't have known it because, in spite of the intimacy we had shared for almost two hours, I had no idea what his face looked like. I have fucked with some guys and forgotten them the next day, but I have never forgotten this guy. What we did together was tantalizing, and what we never got to do will always be perfect in my imagination. Sometimes I wonder what his reasons were. Maybe he looked like Boris Karloff's mummy and didn't want to be seen in the light. Maybe he was a stage three syphilitic and was doing me a favor. Maybe he was afraid his mother would find out—or his sergeant. Maybe he knew me and was embarrassed. I'll never be sure why he fled, but that shadowy stranger will always have a special corner in my heart.

For the most part my sex life had been a big zero up to that point in my life, and I was starting to get a little depressed about it. After all, I figured, I only had maybe seventy or seventy-five years on this planet—if the war didn't shorten it to nineteen—and I had already wasted almost one-third of my allotted time preparing myself and chasing a rainbow named Chester. This was my big chance to make up for lost time. War may have its drawbacks, but it's a hell of a lot easier to get laid when everybody's humming "There's No Tomorrow" as they get dressed for a date.

Try though I did in the streets and bars of San Francisco, the place I finally made contact was right on the base. His name was Jerry Tuft, and his blue eyes seemed to follow me wherever I went until I was almost sure something good was going on. He stared at me in the shower and during calisthenics and while we were in line at the mess hall. You can't be too cautious in front of a thousand hungry men whose opinions you can't trust, so I kept my distance. But when we were assigned to kitchen duty together, I finally decided to take a chance and break the ice. What the hell, I figured, even if I get into a fight, it's in a good cause. And with Hitler and Tojo waiting in the wings, it was now or maybe never.

We sat facing the same mountain of potatoes, and we talked as we peeled. As the stack of parings grew higher, so did our hard-ons.

"Your name's Jerry, right?"

"Right. It used to be Jerome back home. You're Dan, right?"

"Right. They used to call me Daniel, but now it's Dan."

"Were you drafted?"

"Nope, enlisted."

"Me, too. I just had to get out of Billings, Montana somehow. Besides, there's a war to fight."

"Me, too. I had to get out of Elysium, New York."

"Pretty lonely back home?" he asked.

"Yeah, unless you got a girl or something." (Something with muscular arms and a hairy chest.)

"Yeah."

"Do you have one?" I inquired.

"One what?"

"A girlfriend." (Or something.)

"Nope."

"Me neither." (Since you can't count Chester.)

"Oh."

"Didn't find the right one?" I asked. (Weren't there any willing men in Billings?)

"I don't want to settle down yet."

"Playing the field?" (Or the men's rooms?)

"Something like that."

After a while it didn't matter who said which lines. The real dialogue was taking place between our eyes, and it was clear that we both had the same thing on our minds. But I still didn't know how to get it into words and, even more important, how to get it into bed. Finally he saved me the trouble.

"I've been watching you in the barracks."

"I know."

"You watch the other guys a lot."

"Maybe I want to learn how to do things right."

"Maybe you think some of them are sort of . . . attractive?"

"I sure do."

"Me too."

"I thought we'd never get around to the real subject," I said, and we both sat there, grinning like morons, with half-peeled potatoes in our hands.

"Meet me tomorrow morning after mail call?"

"You bet."

The next morning we met as agreed. He had a package of chocolate chip cookies from home, and we shared them.

"I know where there's an empty storeroom," he said when we were finished.

"Let's go," I said.

When we got to the storeroom, he turned toward me and we kissed. Then he groped my crotch suddenly, as if he had lost some pages from the foreplay section of his sex manual. But I wasn't much more experienced, and it felt really amorous to me.

"Gently," I said. "You don't want to damage the equipment, do you?"

"I never did this back in Billings."

He opened my fly and took my cock in his mouth, so excitedly that he scratched me with his teeth. Then he tried to take more than he could handle and he started to gag on it.

"Hold on," I said. "Let me go first. I'll show you how." I was going to teach him some techniques I had figured out while servicing Bruno, but there was no time.

"I already came," he said.

"Terrific," I said. This was getting frustrating.

We met again, of course. That time he was a little calmer, and soon we had a pretty steady thing going.

"Do you think what we're doing is perverted?" he asked me as we were buttoning our flies one afternoon.

"I'm sure there are plenty of guys who do this," I said. "They just don't talk about it."

"I thought I was the only one," he told me. "There aren't any others in Billings, at least not as far as I know."

"We didn't have a big selection back in Elysium, either," I said. "For a while I thought I was the only one too, but eventually I learned otherwise."

"I'm glad we found each other," he whispered.

"Me too."

"Does this mean we're going steady?" he asked.

"Jerry, I guess I should have told you, but I've got a boyfriend back home—well, somewhere in the service now."

"Oh," he said, not sounding too crushed. "Are there any others like us around here?"

"I don't know any personally, but I'm willing to bet they're out there somewhere. Maybe we can look them up together."

"Thanks, Dan," he said. "You're a real buddy."

"Don't mention it, Jerry," I said. "The search will be good for both of us."

At the next mail call, I received a letter from Chester.

London, Oct. 20, 1942

Dear Danny,

God knows where this letter will find you. When you didn't answer my letters to your father's place, I wrote to Reverend Friendly to get your address, and that's how I found out you'd enlisted. I wish I'd been there to stop you. By now you must know what army life is like. I just hope you don't land in a war zone. The Blitz is a nightmare come to life. Sometimes the whistle of bombs overhead is a nightly occurrence.

The only good thing I can think of is that at least we're in the same army and somewhere on the same planet. Jesus, Danny, I hope we both live through this. Wherever they send you, you know my thoughts are with you. And someday, God willing, we will be together again and keep certain promises we made long ago, and celebrate by painting the town red—or maybe shocking pink!

I've just reread what I've written so far, and it sounds a good deal more religious than my earlier letters, so that shows just how much of an effect the war has already had on me.

Ariel Dumont, you will be glad to hear, has showed up in London. He's in love with someone who's stationed here and is willing to follow this person into the jaws of death. I don't know if his beloved returns his affections, but there is something rather disarming about the whole drippy affair, and Ariel says it will be the source of great poetry. I'll let you know what happens, if I hear anything.

Meanwhile, take good care of yourself. If I thought anything had happened to you, I don't know what I'd do. And by the way, if you run across a chance for a good time, be sure to take it. Life is too shaky these days for needless self-sacrifice. I am the sorriest person that I didn't take you up on your offer back in New York.

Please write and let me know how you are. My address is on the envelope.

Forever,
Chester

I felt a little guilty about receiving Chester's letter with Jerry Tuft's taste still in my mouth. But I allowed his advice to ease my conscience, and I told myself that no matter where my cock ended up, my heart would still be Chester's. We had wanted each other too long now for there to be any serious interference from some newcomer.

A few weeks later when I met Jerry after mail call, he said, "Guess what, Dan! I met somebody who told me all about this bar in town where guys like us can go!" The next day he introduced me to a cute private named Hank from New Orleans, who had a lot to teach us both about the world.

On the first night of our next weekend pass, Hank took us into the city, to a bar called the Black Cat Café on Montgomery Street. Crossing its threshold was like walking into another dimension. It looked like any ordinary neighborhood bar, but it felt different somehow. The outside of the place was a simple stone veneer storefront with a big window and a pink awning. Inside there were a few dozen people, many of them in uniform. Men were drinking alone at the bar next to heterosexual couples, women sat in pairs at tables in the rear, small mixed clusters were gathered here and there. In spite of the uniforms, there was a bohemian feeling about the place that reminded me of the party I had been to in New York. When Jerry saw the way some of the men appraised him as he entered, he rushed into the room like a thirsty nomad hurrying to an oasis while fully expecting it to be a mirage. Hank and I went over to the bar and I bought him a drink.

"Has this place been here long?" I asked him.

"Just since the army took this many randy studs from all over the country and put 'em all in one place. Some of 'em are just bound and determined to be interested in each other. There's plenty of bars for the straight boys to go to, but our crowd has only this one. The other one—the Techau on Powell Street—closed years ago. Or, you might try the Biltmore Hotel. They're the only places in town y'all can let your hair down, in a manner of speakin'. Back in New Ahlins Ah never went no place unless it was a little like this. Why look fo' trouble?"

"I think it's just wonderful," I said. "I've had a few friends like us, and I've been to a bohemian party or two, but I've never seen a public place where we can go to meet each other and be ourselves. Wow! What's the world coming to?"

In about fifteen minutes, Jerry passed us on his way out the door with a handsome sailor. "See you guys tomorrow," he said with a wink.

A few minutes later, a young civilian swished up to Hank with a smile and said, "Hi, soldier, remember me?"

"Sure," said Hank. "But Ah ain't too good about names."

"Just call me Nellie, handsome," he cooed, waving a fluid wrist toward the back of the room. "If you want me, I'll be by the jukebox."

I envied that man his freedom, but I was afraid to let my artificial butch posture slip even in a place like this, for fear it would be irretrievable. As long as I was in uniform, I was determined to play my part. But I was glad for Hank when he said good-bye with an apologetic shrug of his shoulders and followed the guy into the crowd.

I stood there alone for a while, still too new in these surroundings to chance striking up a conversation with a stranger. I was happy just to be there. But it wasn't very long before another recruit, whose face looked vaguely familiar from the base, came up and bought me a beer. About ten minutes later, he asked me to spend the night in a hotel with him, and my career as a gay barfly was launched.

I awoke in the morning a little hungover, remembering that we'd put away a few drinks before mouthing each other to orgasm twice and then sleeping all tangled up together. My bedmate's memory wasn't quite so clear. "Boy, was I drunk last night," he said as we sorted out our olive drab underwear. "I must have passed out. I don't remember a thing."

That was the first time I heard that pathetic line, but it was immediately clear to me that the guy didn't want to remember certain things, so I decided not to remind him.

I was a little more careful about going to the Black Cat after that. Even though I could be dead in a matter of weeks, I still thought my sex should have a little meaning to it. It didn't have to be love necessarily, but I didn't want it to be forgotten before dawn, or it probably wasn't worth doing. Somehow I felt that if I cheapened myself, I would cheapen Chester too. On the other hand, I didn't let my scruples become an anchor. Instead I looked at it this way. These were frightened young boys facing a terrible unknown future, maybe even death. And if I could minister to their bodies and take their minds off their fears for a few minutes, then I was doing something good, even if they didn't want to remember it the next day. But I was just kidding myself. My compassion was probably just a convenient excuse for my own fear and lust, but it made me feel a hell of a lot better about what I was doing. Besides, the whole world had gone mad. Wouldn't I be some kind of fool to be the last holdout?

So I spent some of my free time pursuing sex, and some of it in the movies (without a repeat of the strange incident that had happened during the John Garfield movie), and I saved some of my time for my old friend Walt Whitman. I read his journal descriptions of the bedraggled troops marching back into Washington, DC after a Civil War battle, and the awful sight he saw when he went to find his wounded brother in Virginia:

> Out doors, at the foot of a tree, within ten yards of the
> front of the house, I notice a heap of amputated feet,
> legs, arms, hands, &c., a full load for a one-horse cart.
> Several dead bodies lie near, each cover'd with its brown
> woolen blanket. In the door-yard, towards the river, are
> fresh graves . . .

I had just learned that I was being shipped to the South Pacific as a stretcher bearer and emergency paramedic, and I knew that I would see sights just as bad as Walt had, if not worse. If the horror stories that had emerged from the fall of Bataan and Corregidor in the preceding few months were any indication, the Japanese were a formidable enemy who showed little mercy. They had already swept into China and Southeast Asia, and even though the British were holding the line in India, it looked at first like nothing would stop them, especially since they had destroyed so much of our war fleet at Pearl Harbor. But we had just begun to fight. General MacArthur was building up our forces in Australia, waiting for his chance to take back the Philippines.

Early in December, as soon as I had finished my hasty training in first aid and field hospital techniques, I was shipped to a small base on the coast of New Guinea. Jerry Tuft was shipped to the same base, but I don't know where Hank or any of the guys I had sex with ended up. I hope they made it through the war, and I hope that my brief moments with them had given them at least a small respite from their terror, if not a pleasant memory, as they had given me.

The Japs (that was the name then for those poster caricatures of yellow faces with buck teeth and thick-lensed glasses) had been trying to retake Guadalcanal, an island on which they had built an airstrip that we had taken from them. The reason they wanted it so badly was that they could use it as a base for attacking our installation on New Guinea. The Solomon Islands, which were scattered between New Guinea and Guadalcanal, were pretty hot with fighting, and we got the wounded cases at our field hospital. It was mass-produced horror, but even that wasn't as bad as picking up the poor guys in the field after an island had been shelled or where there had been ground combat. What I saw there made Walt Whitman's Civil War seem tame.

There were bodies incinerated into ash or lying askew like innocent rag dolls, their clothing all rumpled and bloodstained, or blasted into several pieces and scattered around the base of a scarred palm tree. It was enough to give me the dry heaves the first couple of times to see all that waste of beautiful young manhood. But the guys who actually brought me to tears were the ones we picked up. They were almost as bad as the corpses. We'd find an arm ten yards from its owner, who was unconscious or in shock, and boys whose eyes or noses were replaced with bloody holes. One guy had his crotch ripped out by a grenade and couldn't stop crying. I was glad we had enough time and equipment so that we didn't have to practice triage. I couldn't have chosen between the wounded and the dying. I loved all of them the same, and I wanted to take them into my arms, blood and all, and make them whole again. I wanted to offer them the kind of love and comfort Whitman had offered his wounded soldiers. I never forgot one of his letters to a soldier named Sawyer, in which he spoke of how much he wanted to devote himself to those boys:

> Lew is so good, so affectionate—when I came away, he reached up his face, I put my arm around him, and we gave each other a long kiss, half a minute long . . . Dear comrade, you must not forget me, for I never shall you. My love you have in life or death forever. I don't know how you feel about it, but it is the wish of my heart to have your friendship, and also that if you should come safe out of this war, we should come together again in some place where we could make our living, and be true comrades and never be separated while life lasts—and take Lew Brown too, and never separate from him . . .

All I could do was pull my boys together the best I was able and help to keep them that way until we could get back to base, and there I watched helplessly, good only for holding IV bottles and mopping up blood while medical science did what it could to counteract military science. I kept asking myself why we didn't use clay pigeons to keep score. Human bodies are so much harder to fix. The thought made me angry, and while I tried to turn my anger on the enemy in the Japanese gunboats and planes, it was dawning on me that history itself was the enemy, that I had to look this carnage right in the eye if I wanted to understand anything about the human condition, and through it to understand myself.

The fight for Guadalcanal had been going on since August. The Allies had actually delivered the decisive blow in November when an engagement with our navy cost our opponents fifteen of their best ships, but they weren't used to losing, and they refused to stop fighting. The skirmishes among the islands continued for months afterward.

We did have occasional lulls, though, and when Christmas came, everyone wanted to celebrate, even if we weren't a big enough base to draw the Hollywood entertainers who were visiting the troops that year. The guys didn't have much time, but they decided to put on their own show, and because nobody wanted to look at a bunch of dogfaces in sweaty olive drabs, they decided a little femininity would give the show some class, and they cooked up a drag act. In spite of my protests, I was one of the men chosen. I guess my butch routine hadn't disguised the fact that I was one of the most feminine guys on the base, not swishy or anything, just sort of gentle. We can't all be like King Kong, I told myself, but underneath I was terrified that everybody would see my secret and throw me to the Japs for an appetizer.

Most of the other guys in the act were all broad and hairy-chested, and the drag costumes of mop wigs and flour-sack tits and banana-leaf skirts looked ridiculous on them, so they could play their parts for belly laughs. But one other guy and I seemed to make everyone a little nervous, because no matter how silly we looked and how funny we tried to be, there was something real about us. His name was Doug Swanson and he was from Ohio. He was slim and blond and gentle, but he exuded a quiet kind of strength. He had a dignity about him that shone through his clownish costume and turned me on to him while we rehearsed our numbers.

Even though I looked ridiculous, I found there was something that came naturally to me dressing like a woman; so instead of camping it up, I just let some inner part of myself out to play. My number was "White Christmas," which was a new song that year, and I just stood there and sang it as if I meant it. Somehow it worked. Everybody got so sentimental that they forgot to razz me about my costume, and I got through it without any problems. But Doug had to sing "Life Upon the Wicked Stage" from *Showboat*, which is a chorus girl's complaint about her social life. Being so desperate for entertainment, the guys thought Doug was a riot, and they gave him the usual catcalls and sucking noises to show him what a success he was. That much was fine, but one poor guy got carried away with himself and yelled, "Hubba hubba! Lift up them leaves, honey, so we can see your twat!" Doug tried to play it like a demure virgin, and he held his hands modestly over his crotch. But the excited GI wasn't satisfied and jumped up on the stage to try to give Doug a kiss, thinking he would give his buddies a good laugh. Doug swung at him, but he missed, and the guy put his arms around him, much to everybody else's delight. Doug got all upset and pushed the guy away, and ran off the stage and into the edge of the jungle. I followed him because I thought I could calm him down, and besides, I kind of liked the guy.

I caught up with him at a small clearing. He had ripped off his wig and thrown it away, but I was still in my idiotic costume because we had planned to come out for a bow when all the numbers were over.

"Don't worry about what happened back there," I said, to console him. "It's just because you were such a good actress."

He looked ready to hit me, but he started to laugh. "Go fuck yourself," he said. "I can't hit a woman."

"Everybody knows you're a real man," I told him. "They were just having fun."

"No, I had this problem back in school because I'm skinny and blond. I never should have let them talk me into it."

"You didn't do anything wrong," I said, taking off my wig and helping him to untie the ropes that held the flour sacks on his chest." I guess I was a little desperate myself, having done without body contact for so long, and I mindlessly began to massage his shoulders. "You just need to relax," I said.

He let out a huge sigh, and I could feel the tension drain from his body. My massaging hands ranged in wider and wider circles, reaching to his sides, and almost without my control they moved to the front of his banana-leaf skirt and made as if to enter.

He put his hand over mine, gently but firmly. "Forget it," he said. "I can take it off myself."

"I just thought . . ." I tried to explain.

"I know what you were doing," he said, "and I'm just not interested. All right? I know what you think I am, but I'm not. I have a wife back in Ohio."

I turned my face away, embarrassed.

"No hard feelings," he said. "I guess we're all a little lonely so far from home."

"I guess we are," I said. "I'm sorry. I didn't mean anything by it but a compliment."

"Hey, we'll just forget about it. Okay? It's Christmas. Let's go back and celebrate."

I followed him back to the camp, determined not to let my mask slip again.

The next day I received another letter from Chester.

Somewhere in Tunisia, December 1, 1942

Dear Danny,

It's been so hectic here, I hardly have a minute to write. The North African campaign has been bloody, but we're determined to go all the way. Who knows where that will take us? There are rumors that when we've reached our objective, we'll be shipping out for the big one (as if this isn't big enough!), but of course all information is classified.

So far I'm okay, and I hope that you are the same. I think of you all the time. I haven't had much chance for diversion with the fighting so heavy and all, but I've taken my opportunities where I found them, and I hope you've been doing the same. No matter whom I'm with, I know where the real meaning is, and I hope the same remains true for you.

Speaking of which, poor Ariel Dumont was killed in the London Blitz. He was found in a hotel room with someone who was <u>not</u> the person he had come there to be with. He wasn't a very nice person, but a higher Judge will deal with him.

I have to go now, Danny. I pray God keeps you safe through all this hell. Never forget our promise. I certainly won't.

Love,
Chester

I didn't dwell on the fate of Ariel Dumont. I had seen enough death and, as much as I had disliked him, I couldn't let myself take pleasure in his ignominious end. On the other hand, I didn't waste any energy mourning either. He just became another statistic to me, one more loss for our side. I was more concerned about Chester, and I wrote a letter to him to let him know that I was all right and that I was praying for his safety, too. I think I understood why his letters were sounding more and more religious. Maybe it wasn't what Reverend Friendly would have called "praying," but I concentrated my good wishes on Chester's safety. And I let myself forget about the incident with Doug Swanson until a few days after the new year started. That was when the witch hunt began.

Jerry Tuft, the innocent kid from Billings, Montana, who had never had a sexual experience with a man until he met me in San Francisco, was caught on base with another soldier's dick in his mouth. A similar incident had happened a month earlier, and the officers made a vow to clean up the base before it became infested with perverts. Soon a bulletin was issued, urging all enlisted men with homosexual tendencies to report to the medical officer. I didn't feel especially flattered that my sex life had graduated from being a sin to being a sickness. And besides, I hadn't had one sexual experience since I'd been there, and I was damned if I was going to let myself be punished for my daydreams. I ignored the order like any sane person would do. Instead, I took the chance of visiting Jerry, and I found out that the brass had promised to go easy on him if he named any other perverts he knew in the service.

"I didn't mention you," he said.

"Thanks," I told him. "Maybe I can do you a favor someday."

There was nothing I could do to help him. Even the visit had cast suspicion on me, and I soon found myself standing in front of a major, who came right to the point.

"You know, Dan," he said, sitting on the edge of his desk and talking in a confidential hush, "there are rumors that some of the guys on base have been approached by ... ah ... queers ... perverts ... you know, for sex. Did Jerry Tuft ever approach you in that way?"

"No, sir," I replied. (We approached each other.)

"How come you were visiting him, then?"

"We were in basic together, sir, and I heard he was in some kind of trouble." (The exact nature of his crime slips my mind.)

"Certain kinds of trouble are like flypaper," he said. "Whoever gets involved gets stuck himself, if you know what I mean."

"Yes, sir." (But you've got nothing to stick me with, sir.)

"Are you sure that Tuft never approached you? Or that you never approached him?"

"Yes, sir." (And fuck you, too, sir.)

"If anything of the kind should happen, be sure to inform me. We want to clear all ineffective soldiers off this base. We've got a war to fight. I'll be keeping an eye on you from now on. Is that understood?"

"Yes, sir." (I'm going to act like a "real man" from now on, you son of a bitch, even if it kills me.)

"Dismissed."

I sweated through the next couple of days, wondering when the axe might hit my neck. When I heard Doug Swanson get called into the major's office, I steeled myself. But nothing happened, and I was careful to keep a low profile.

When I found myself working with Doug on a rescue mission, I took the chance to thank him. "I appreciate your not saying anything to the major about the incident after the Christmas show," I said.

"It wasn't any of his business," he said. "Anyway, nothing happened, did it?"

"What's going to happen to the guys who get picked up?" I asked.

"The major told me some of them would go to the psychiatric hospital in Brisbane. The rest will be kept in the stockade. Then they'll be shipped back to the States, where they'll get Section Eights—you know, 'blue discharges,' not honorable and not dishonorable."

"And not good for much else besides permanent trouble," I said. "Thanks for keeping quiet. I owe you."

"Forget it," he said. "Let's go pick up some bodies. Those are the guys who really need help."

I got my chance to pay Doug back sooner than I had anticipated. The battle for Guadalcanal was grinding down and our victory seemed assured. The brass wanted to secure as many of the islands in the area as possible, so we set up a makeshift hospital tent on one of them to establish our presence, and there we received the wounded, so we could care for them immediately. There was still fighting all around the area, but we were so busy trying to patch bodies that we paid no attention to the occasional shelling all around us. So as I stood there holding up a bottle of blood while Doug was loading the patient onto the operating table, it came as a complete surprise to me when I heard someone shouting in my ear: "The Japs are here!"

CHAPTER SIX

I looked up to see a Japanese soldier standing in the entrance to the tent. "*Yamero!*" he shouted, gesturing with the tip of his rifle to indicate that we should leave the patient alone and back up against the canvas. But Doug kept gently easing the wounded man onto the operating table, for fear that he would drop to the floor. For his insolence, the soldier in the doorway repeated his command and stuck his bayonet into Doug's thigh. The patient crashed to the floor, as did Doug, and the bottle of blood was pulled from my hand and crashed uselessly beside them. Everyone else in the tent backed up as the soldier had commanded, and when he barked, "*Soto e dero!*" and gestured toward the exit with his rifle, we marched out in single file. I pulled Doug to his feet and wrapped his arm around my shoulder, so I could support him.

"The patient . . ." he murmured.

"We have to leave him. There's no choice."

The Japanese glowered at us as we squeezed past him into the glaring sunlight, where a whole squad of his friends was waiting for us. As they herded us toward the prison ship, which was waiting for us at the beach, we heard gunfire erupt behind us. They were killing the patients in the hospital tent. I half carried Doug for fear that they would do the same to him, and he hobbled along as quickly as he could, his thigh still dripping blood. The guards forced us into the hold of the ship, which in spite of the glaring sun was midnight black. It was already crowded with the huddled bodies of other prisoners. Although we couldn't see their faces, they welcomed us into the fetid darkness with anonymous voices.

"Over here."

"My buddy's wounded," I said.

"Make room. Let him lie down."

I used my sense of touch to stanch Doug's bleeding with a crumpled handkerchief. I just pressed tightly against it until I could put together a makeshift dressing. Then I stood guard, to keep him from being trampled in the dark. I don't know how long the trip was—a few days probably, maybe a week. We had no night or day and no food or water, and we had to drink our own urine to stay alive. Surviving became our primary objective. Twice more the ship stopped to pick up prisoners until the hold was so packed that we could barely breathe the thickened air, and tempers grew short. Men were dying all around us, and we had to sit on their corpses because there was no other room. In spite of the horrendous stench, there were mutters about eating their flesh and drinking their blood, and we probably would have turned to that if the ship hadn't landed at last.

We were force-marched some twenty miles that seemed like a thousand. Doug's bleeding had stopped, but I still had to help him walk. We were a line of grimy zombies, staggering forward to keep alive. Whoever tried to run off the road was shot, and the rest of us were commanded to keep marching: "*Zen shin!*" Whoever couldn't make it on his own or with a buddy's help was left to die where he fell, until a sporadic trail of bodies lay stretched behind us. There was nothing to slake our thirst except a few artesian wells along the side of the road where we were allowed to pause hurriedly, and there was nothing to eat except for some rice wrapped in banana leaves, which the local island people threw to us from the edge of the jungle. If not for their help, I doubt that many of us would have survived.

When we arrived at the camp, Doug was barely mobile. We had to turn out our clothing for inspection, and I helped him. There wasn't much. The only personal item I had with me was my copy of *Leaves of Grass*, a little the worse for wear, but still readable.

I had kept it in the expandable side pocket of my combat pants and had felt it bumping comfortingly against my knee during the long march. That and Minerva White's six photographs were the only personal effects I had taken into the army with me. I had stashed the photographs in San Francisco, but I didn't want to be parted from the book. The only other book among the prisoners was somebody's pocket Bible, and I saw that the guard let him keep it when he explained what it was by making the sign of prayer with his hands. So I simply did the same thing, and the guard let me keep my Scriptures, too. Without it, I might have lost touch with the world of pleasant illusions we call reality.

They put Doug into the "hospital" along with several others. There were no medical facilities, and the place was little more than a bamboo enclosure that served as a waiting room for the dying. The rest of us were put into crude thatched huts housing two dozen men each. We were sent out on daily work details to clear the jungle underbrush so a road could be built across the island. The exhausting labor, the hundred-and-ten-degree heat, and the Martian insects were the least of our problems. Getting enough to eat was the main worry. It was a day-by-day struggle not to die. Our captors gave us a handful of rice, sometimes mixed with unidentifiable soggy, boiled vegetables, and a cup of weak tea twice a day. Our survival meant nothing to them. They held us in contempt since they did not believe that any surrender was honorable. If we could find any fruit or kill a small animal—

even a rat—in the jungle, we put it into our shirts and shared it back at camp, along with the occasional small bundles of cooked rice given to us by the islanders.

Whenever I had anything to share, I brought it to the window near Doug's hospital bed. He needed it more than I did.

"You're keeping me alive," he whispered.

"Don't be silly," I told him. "We've got plenty."

Almost nobody came out of the hospital alive, but I saw to it that Doug did. After a month or so he was walking almost like he used to, with only a slight limp. He and I became close buddies then, and we looked out for each other. We bunked together and we worked together. We talked together and we grew to trust each other and to rely on each other. Yet it still came as a surprise to me when one day he brought up the subject of our first private encounter.

"Do you remember what happened after the Christmas show?" he asked. (As if I could forget!)

I didn't answer, but he continued. "I was just thinking that if you still want to . . . I mean . . ."

"What are you saying?" I asked, a little miffed. "Did I finally earn it? Are you trying to pay me for services rendered? Or are you just horny, and any hole will do in a pinch?"

"I'm not horny. I don't think any of the guys have thought much about sex lately. I just wanted to express how I feel about you, and I thought that might be a way to do it. It's not my style, but I thought it was yours. I guess I don't know much about this kind of thing. I didn't mean to hurt your feelings."

"Don't mind me," I said. "I'm just edgy. I haven't thought too much about sex lately either. I guess we all turned it off for the duration. Besides, we'd probably need more nutrition just to work up hard-ons, not to mention the right music and lighting. I just don't know."

"Smart-ass," he said, and we went back to work.

I was kind of prepared for it when he started playing with himself in the bunk that night after the others were asleep. He must have known I was awake beside him, because once he got himself hard—which was no mean feat—he put his hand behind my neck and gently drew it toward his groin, where, as slowly and silently as I could, I sucked him nicely dry.

For me it was purely an act of the spirit. I had no romantic notions about Doug, so I had only my good will to help me ignore the deplorable condition of his body and the smell of his ragged clothes, which like my own had had only rainwater to keep them clean. He may not have been at his most alluring, and I may not have been hot to trot, but we were sealing our friendship the best way we knew how. And I knew that Chester, wherever he was, would have approved of our efforts.

When Tim Chaney, the guy in the next bunk, came up to me the next day, I could tell right away that he had been awake while I was blowing Doug. His eyes seemed to know me, and his jawbone was visibly twitching behind his black cheeks. There were only a few black men in the camp. They had served in segregated units, and although they weren't kept separate in the prisoners' huts, this was the first time I had talked with any of them.

"Didn't get too much sleep last night," he said.

"Me neither."

"Ah knows. It was you who waked me up. Ah didn't know you was queer."

"I didn't know you were so nosy."

"Now wait up, Dan. Ah didn't mean nothin' by dat. Dat's just the way we talks. Do y'all call it by another name? Is dat de problem?"

"No, I don't know any better word myself. 'Homosexual' is what the books call it. The boys in San Francisco say 'gay,' but neither one sounds right to me."

"Well, Dan, what y'all name it ain't exactly mah point. You see . . . let me put it like dis. Dey ain't no women 'roun' here, and it ain't like Ah'm zackly rarin' to go dese days, but Ah's had mah share of queer boys . . . ah, homo-whatchamacallits . . . back home. Don't get me wrong now. Mah main course usually poontang . . . ah . . . pussy. Dis sort of lak a side dish, y'understan'? But Ah wants to know if de damn thing still in workin' condition. Uh . . . dammit, man, dey ain't nuttin' but misery 'roun' here, and Ah jus' wants to feel somethin' good fo' one lousy minute. Ah don't care what y'all call it. Ah jus' wants me some. Do y'all read me?"

I nodded. "Tim, you don't understand. I . . . I'll talk to you about it tomorrow, okay? I've got to have some time to think." I wondered if he was trying to blackmail me into sex or something, but I didn't think so. He seemed like a decent guy, and he was just in pain. Who wasn't?

"No rush, man," he answered. "Lak Ah says, Ah ain't zackly feelin' lak no Don Juan." He gave me the first grin that I'd seen since I'd arrived there.

The next day, after explaining the situation to Doug, I told Tim that my answer was yes, and after dark we sneaked behind the latrine, where I sucked him off.

"Thanks a lot, man," he said. "Y'all don' know how bad Ah needed dat."

"My pleasure, Tim," I said, and it was. I felt good not so much because of the sex—although Tim was a damned sexy man. I felt good because I'd been able to help out. It was the Christian spirit in me, I suppose.

But when Tim added, "Ah've got dis pal in de nex' barracks name o' Mel . . ." I wondered how much stamina my good spirit had. Before we were finished, I was servicing seven different guys on a semi-regular basis, earning my way straight to cocksucker heaven (or at least that was the direction I hoped my efforts would take me). And although the guys weren't as attractive as the men back in basic training had been, I wasn't exactly having a terrible time of it.

This state of affairs lasted for the next two months or so. We kept track of the days with notches carved on a pole inside our hut, and it was about six months into our stay when I was kneeling in front of Mel with his dick in my mouth just before dawn, feeling perfectly safe there in back of the latrine (which had become a regular spot for my rendezvous), when suddenly a bright light shone in my face. A voice yelled, ordering us to stop, and I felt a boot in my ribs that knocked the wind out of me. There was a lot of angry yelling in Japanese, and then Mel was dragged off to one of the solitary confinement cages, which were no more than small pits in the ground, where the prisoner barely had room to crouch and couldn't stretch out fully in any direction; the most a man could do was semi-stand, so he could look through a slit at everyone's feet. His guards yelled at him to get in: "*Naka e haire!*"

My captors started to drag me in the same direction, then apparently changed their minds and took me to the center of the compound where a stake had been fixed, for flogging anyone who was caught breaking rules. They tethered me to its base by my wrists. When the sun was above the horizon and the prisoners were lined up to be marched out to do the day's work, the guards walked up behind me, and one of them smacked my head with a club. Everything went black for a minute, but I didn't pass out. I just lay there, wishing I could die. Someone pulled on the tether, forcing me to my knees. Then one of them pushed my head into the dirt with his boot on the back of my neck. My pants were ripped away, and my ankles were pulled apart by two soldiers. Another guard knelt behind me, and after a few blind pokes, shoved a wooden club straight into my virgin ass.

I screamed. The pain was bad, made worse because I had kept my sphincter clenched against the assault. When I opened my eyes, all I could see were black boots and khaki-covered knees. I didn't want to look up because I knew all the prisoners were watching. "*Okama!*" one of the guards contemptuously called me—"Faggot!" And he spat on the side of my face.

After my tormentors were finished and they had marched the other prisoners off to work, another guard, whom I had never seen before, cut me loose. At first I shrank from him, but he treated me gently, removing the club carefully, with no hint of roughness, and I began to relax. I was almost touched by the look of compassion in his eyes until I reminded myself that he was the enemy. I didn't know what to make of it. He washed my head with cool water, calling me *tomodachi* or "friend," and he gave me some rice and tea, urging me to eat with whispers of "*Tabete.*" Then he took me over to one of the solitary confinement cages, with a lot of shoulder shrugging and apologetic-looking smiles. Opening the top, he said softly, "*Haite, haite,*" gesturing for me to get in.

I spent the next week in that cage. The pain only lasted for the first day. After that I was mostly numb. In the beginning I kept trying to peer through the slit, as if by tracking the comings and goings of feet I could participate in the world of the living. I had only two visits. Once a banana leaf full of rice was nudged through the slit, and Doug's voice whispered, "We won't let you die, Dan." Another time the top was opened, and the same guard who had taken me there left me more tea and a large portion of rice, which I ate a little at a time, not knowing when there would be more.

I dozed only in fits and starts, never quite fully asleep, and so weary that I was never quite fully awake either. The stink of my waste on the floor of the cage exhausted my sense of repulsion, and my sense of smell grew numb along with my joints. I couldn't see very much through the slit, and whatever sounds I heard were muffled. I lost track of the passing days and nights and stopped relating to the outside world. Except for the occasional passage of the soldiers' shiny boots and the prisoners' rag-wrapped feet, I knew nothing of the world. I lived completely inside my own befogged brain, deprived of definable sensation, alone with my memories and my imagination, both of which were playing games with me.

I felt as if I were in a haze, detached from time and space. All I could think of was that I wanted to remove myself from the horror I had been experiencing and to replace it with warm feelings of safety and love. Cautiously I willed my consciousness to rise without moving my body, and I felt myself floating. In my mind's eye, I could see above the treetops to the water, which lay dark and glistening beneath the starry sky. Then, following my dream, I was speeding over the softly rolling waves to a familiar beach a lifetime away, where for a moment I had once seen a gentle, white-bearded poet walking on the sand. He was there when I arrived, sitting at the edge of the restless sea. I felt soothingly warmed and glad just to be with him. He would protect me. It was as if he understood my every thought, as if he saw the same pictures in his mind as I did in my own, and there was no need for words between us. The love-light gleamed in his fatherly gray eyes as he nodded at me. I smiled. Although we were far from the nearest orchard, my nostrils were suddenly flooded with the rich scent of apple trees just before harvest, and I glowed with a feeling of innocence and peace. Somehow I knew that I would be all right, and I relaxed.

When I awoke, my mind was clearer and my captivity seemed less difficult. To keep my mind off my own life, I passed my time trying to imagine what Walt's life had felt like to him. Had his love of other men caused him as much grief as mine? How had he experienced their touch? Did he enter their bodies? Did they enter his? Did he feel that it made him any less manly? To keep sane, I arranged my thoughts and questions into a letter, knowing that I could never send it.

– Arnie Kantrowitz –

Somewhere in the South Pacific, 1943

Dear Walt,

I don't know if you can hear me, but it really doesn't matter. What matters is that I tell you how much you have meant to me from the first moment when I met you through your words. I wish you could know me as well as I think I know you. I like to think we would be great friends, maybe even lovers. I feel that we are attached in some supernatural way. Don't think me presumptuous, but even though I know I'll never be as great a poet as you, I feel almost as if I were your reincarnation! I'm sure many of your followers have felt as close, but I know that I can trust you not to laugh at me when I confide such things in you.

It's because I feel so bound to you that I can't stop wondering about you. Maybe you can help me with some questions. I am only asking because I love you, and I think you are the only one who can help me to understand why I am being punished.

How can it be evil to make love to other men? I know that some people say it is, but it feels so good to touch the skin of another man, to caress his flesh with my lips and tongue, to watch him become aroused at my ministrations and to help him reach his orgasm, drinking in his essence and making him part of myself. It feels like a way to show him my approval and my love, and it makes me glad to know that I can make his soul feel as ecstatic as his body does. If my conscience is the guide, I do not see how this can possibly be bad. And yet I'm told it is.

Beyond that, there is some mysterious connection between loving men and creating poems. I don't know how to describe it, but I feel sure that you know what I mean. If I were to stop making love to men, at least with my soul if not with my body, I think I would not be able to write poems. I think I might die.

Should I refuse to do what I was born to do? Should I deny myself and other men the solace we can offer each other? What did you do? I need to know, more than ever before. Help me, please.

Love,
Dan

I dozed on and off as I composed the letter, so I don't know if it took me hours or even days to write it. It didn't matter. What mattered was staying sane and keeping alive. Other questions and ideas floated through my mind

115

in no discernible order. I wondered whether—without the benefit of touch—two souls could find an ecstasy that paralleled the ecstasy of physical union, and if I might ever find such ecstasy with Walt. I put my hands on my genitals and tried to arouse myself thinking of him, but there was no reaction. I tried to make up poems, but I kept on forgetting the beginnings while I imagined the ends.

When the top of the cage was suddenly opened, the daylight nearly blinded me. I was so numb and dazed that I don't know who took me from there, but I woke up at last in the hospital. The walls were only six feet high, with a long, glassless window covered by an awning of low-hanging thatched eaves, which kept us in shadows all day, futilely pursuing a breath of cooler air. I knew I was in death's waiting room, and only a brief, furtive visit from Doug to the window near my bed could convince me otherwise.

"You're going to make it," he said, and he gave me an overripe mango.

"If you say so."

I was out of there by the end of the week. My only pants had been ruined, so the first thing I did was to improvise a loincloth out of a dead soldier's shirt, something like an Indian dhoti. I didn't look any more bizarre than the others, who wore an array of homemade costumes composed of rearranged tatters and rags which wouldn't have won any high-fashion awards, but which preserved the last shreds of our dignity. None of the prisoners wanted to raise the subject of my sexual services again. Our primary rule was never to do anything that might bring harm to a fellow prisoner.

A day or two after I had returned to work in the jungle, I was standing behind a large tree, shaking myself off after taking a long piss, when I suddenly realized I wasn't alone. The Japanese guard who had tried to be nice to me was moving steadily toward me, his eyes locked on my privates. I didn't know what to do, so I started stuffing myself back into my loincloth, which required some fancy rewrapping, and I hadn't finished before he was upon me and had taken my balls in his hand. He hefted them appreciatively and smiled at me. "*Anata wa kirei da,*" he said: "You are beautiful." I didn't reply. "*Anata ga suki da,*" he continued: "I like you." Then he took his penis out of his pants and offered it to me, still holding on to my genitals. I did nothing. Finally, he leaned over and took my dick in his mouth. I didn't move. I couldn't hit him and risk his anger. He sucked furiously. I'm not sure whether it was because of patriotism or terror or malnutrition, but I couldn't get a hard-on. He stood up, and staring at my exposed crotch, he pumped his cock real hard with his hand until he came. I rearranged myself and turned to go, but he leaned over and kissed me on the cheek while he was still stuffing himself back into his pants.

As he turned to leave, the commander of the work detail stepped from behind a tree. From the glower in his eyes, I knew he had seen everything. "*Uragirimono! Okama!*" the commander hissed: "Traitor! Faggot!" He barked questions and commands at the crestfallen soldier in staccato syllables, and the answers came in a murmur, with bowed head. Suddenly my guard grabbed his own rifle, which he had leaned against the tree, ran a few yards into the undergrowth, and plunged his bayonet into his own belly. It was an act of mad desperation, not the proper ritual disembowelment of hara-kiri. He lay there, writhing in his self-inflicted pain, his life blood pouring out onto the ground. The officer ignored his suffering contemptuously and just stood there watching. I wanted to comfort the dying man, at least to cradle his head in my arms, but I didn't dare to move a muscle. When the officer noticed me still standing there, he slapped my face with the back of his white-gloved hand and gestured me back to work. That was the last I had to do with sex for the next two years, until I was released.

As always, I turned to *Leaves of Grass* for comfort, and as always it inspired me.

> Beautiful that war, and all its deeds of carnage, must in time
>   be utterly lost;
> That the hands of the sisters Death and Night, incessantly
>   softly wash again, and ever again, this soil'd world:
> . . . For my enemy is dead—a man divine as myself is dead;
> I look where he lies, white-faced and still, in the coffin—I
>   draw near;
> I bend down and touch lightly with my lips the white face in
>   the coffin.

I knew then that I wanted to write again. But I had nothing to write with, so I contrived a pen out of a large thorn, and for ink I used berry juice strained carefully through a rag into a tin cup. I was stuck for paper, so I had to write my poems in the margins of *Leaves of Grass*, entwining my verses with Whitman's and nestling my words among his. I like to think Walt would have forgiven me the trespass, considering the circumstances. I wrote:

> Walt Whitman, how I want your arms
> around me, your eyes inside me knowing
> life and your penis pouring comfort
> like your words to tell me
> I am not alone in such strange peace.
> I remember clearly what you said, old
> beauty, old man, through all the agony
> in your bright eyes, so much
> I was wanting to say I love you
> while I live, for the brightness hovers
> everywhere, making me insufferably glad.

As I lost myself in writing, I transcended my surroundings and time and place meant nothing to me. I could have been sitting in hell itself and ignored it while I was writing. So my little makeshift pen became mightier than the enemy's sword. And I survived my imprisonment, slowly and painstakingly filling in the empty spaces in Walt Whitman's book.

The next two years passed this way, divided between work in the jungle and absorption in poetry. We prisoners grew weaker and thinner until all we had to live on was hope, but there was little news to sustain that. We lived in a vacuum, fighting despair. For all we knew the enemy was winning the war, but we held on anyway. Many of us died, including Mel, who had been caught *in flagrante delicto* with me, and it was tempting to envy them. But those who managed to keep living were determined to make it through to the end of the war somehow. I had discovered the will to live through my writing, and others had their own sources of inspiration—whether it was seeing their families back home or getting revenge on our captors or simply finding out what other tricks History had up her sleeve. And we all helped each other to survive the best we could.

At the beginning of July 1945, as the Japanese were retreating from the Philippines, we were herded into another prison ship and confined in a dark hold for several days until we landed in Japan, luckily nowhere near the atomic blasts that were detonated in Hiroshima and Nagasaki that August. We were held in a small camp until the surrender, waiting. Hope was beginning to mount as we saw our captors' faces growing grimmer and more tight-lipped with each day. Other camps were leafleted by air to let them know help was on the way, but our camp was too remote for that. It wasn't until American soldiers walked through our gate that we learned we had won the war. Then we all went wild and used the last of our strength singing and praying and crying and celebrating.

It took quite a while before we could eat more than a handful of the food our liberators brought us, but eventually we were fed and washed and clothed in uniforms, and we began to look like human beings again. It wasn't until late September that we finally set sail for San Francisco. I hoped we were coming back to a new world, that all the death had taught us that war would no longer be an acceptable way to solve problems. If not, what had all the pain and misery been for? I've never found the answer to that question.

I said good-bye to Doug at the base in San Francisco. He introduced me to his wife, Donna, who was blonde and pretty and shy.

"We've got to get back to Ohio," Doug said.

"I'll miss you," I said.

"I wouldn't be here if it weren't for you," he told me. "I'll never forget that."

"If you're ever in Ohio . . ." Donna offered.

"Sure," I said.

"No," Doug insisted. "We mean it."

"I know," I replied. "We'll see."

My own discharge was delayed, so I waited. I thought I would head for New York, to find Chester. There didn't seem much point in going back to my father. But before I left, a letter from my high school friend Kelly Barrett reached me. It had been knocking around various post offices for a year. I opened it with trembling fingers, suddenly in touch with a past that seemed several lifetimes ago:

January 30, 1944

Dear Danny,

It's been so long since anyone's heard from you. I hope that you are alive somewhere and that this letter finds you well although I'm sorry it has to bring bad news.

I just learned that Chester Stewart was killed in action last September at Salerno in Italy. His battalion landed there during the invasion, and he was one of the many who didn't make it to shore. Our newsreels showed some of the action, and the water was dark with blood and thick with our boys' bodies. Many were never found. People were fainting and crying in the movie theater. I'm sorry I don't have any more information, but I thought you'd want to know. I'm so sorry, Danny dear. I know how much you cared for Chester. So many people are mourning so many dead just now. There are gold stars in many of the windows in Elysium. But somehow we must all pick ourselves up and so on.

My mom has been very sick this year. It's cancer, and the doctors don't expect her to last more than another month or two. I'm going to stay with her until the end. But I've decided that, once she's gone, I'll be heading for the big city, where I hope I can find my own life at last. I don't know exactly where I'll be. I haven't made any formal plans yet. But we'll find each other somehow, I hope.

One last item. You remember Reverend Friendly, the minister, don't you? He was caught in a motel having sex with a sailor, and there was one hell of a scandal. Of course he was dismissed by the church elders, but that's not the worst of his problems. His wife left him soon afterward, for a traveling lingerie salesman. I'm not sure who took the kids or what became of Friendly. What a pity for all that poor family.

I'm sorry to have no cheerful news to send you, Danny. Maybe next time things will be better. Wherever you are, come home safe. I pray that I'll be seeing you.

Love,
Kelly

I suppose I wasn't really surprised. It had been too much to expect that Chester and I would both make it safely through the war. Besides, who knew what changes might have been wrought by the years of separation and bitter experience? All I knew was that my love for him was still intact, but it would never be consummated. I refused to weep, angry at whoever ran this universe for the cruelty and suffering that were everywhere. I tried to console myself at Land's End, where I spent an afternoon alone with my copy of *Leaves of Grass*. It seemed to be the only constant in a world gone mad with change. I found some lines from Whitman to help me mourn:

> . . . I made my way,
> Found you in death so cold dear comrade, found your body son
> of responding kisses, (never again on earth responding,) . . .
> Passing sweet hours, immortal and mystic hours with you
> dearest comrade—not a tear, not a word,
> Vigil of silence, love and death, vigil for you my son and my
> soldier . . .

But the soldier in Whitman's poem had at least died on land. I couldn't even visit the place where Chester was. I riffled through the pages again.

> And if the corpse of any one I love, or if my own corpse, be duly
> render'd to powder and pour'd in the sea, I shall be satisfied;
> Or if it be distributed to the winds, I shall be satisfied.

I looked out to sea, trying to imagine my way around the globe, sea connected to sea, water to water, down to the tip of South America, around into the South Atlantic, up the west coast of Africa to the Strait of Gibraltar and into the Mediterranean, where somewhere Chester's body lay, surrounded by miles of open sea. It cheered me to think that even in death, he had that special extra space around himself, only now the space was so vast that no one could find him in it. I tried to leave my grief there beside the ocean. It was too heavy to carry with me, so I looked for something a little more uplifting. After all, at least the war was over, wasn't it?

> War, sorrow, suffering gone—the rank earth purged—
> nothing but joy left!
> The ocean filled with joy—the atmosphere all joy!
> Joy! Joy! in freedom, worship, love! joy in the ecstasy of life!
> Enough to merely be, enough to breathe!
> Joy! Joy! all over joy!

But this time I couldn't buy Walt's message. The last thing I could feel was joy. Chester was at peace, but I was not. And to make matters worse, I had discovered that even the magic of *Leaves of Grass* had its limitations. Only then did I begin to cry bitter tears.

I finally found out why my separation from the army had been delayed, when I received my discharge papers. Instead of an honorable discharge, I had been given a "blue discharge," a Section Eight, which was neither honorable nor dishonorable. It didn't take much imagination to conclude that someone had told what had happened to me in the POW camp. The discharge didn't say anything specific about my offense, only that I was not eligible for re-enlistment or reinduction or an appeal of the decision.

At first I was furious that all my pains could be rewarded with such a slap in the face, but I didn't know what to do with my anger. Maybe it wouldn't matter much after all, I thought. It didn't seem so bad. Honorably or not, I was out of the army, and I could be my own man and do whatever I wanted to do. All I had to decide was what that was.

I spent some time hanging around San Francisco, living on my back pay from the army and trying to figure out what to do with myself. The first thing I did was to pick up my packet of Minerva White's photographs, which I had left with an acquaintance. Those pictures and my copy of *Leaves of Grass* traveled with me after that, and only extreme circumstances made me part with any of them. The pictures of Chester were painful to look at in the beginning, but eventually there was something magical about them. However I've changed, Chester has never grown any older. He's remained as wise and handsome as he seemed to my adolescent eyes, and our relationship has never suffered from foolish fights or wrinkled thighs. It's one of the few perfect things I have known.

Although I rented a furnished room, the Black Cat Café became my temporary home. I spent most of my evenings there, learning how to be a civilian again. It took me a little while to get back into the sexual world, but I did meet a couple of guys there who helped me prove I was still alive in bed. I even managed to let someone enter my ass, even though I was a little paranoid about the intrusion, having been deflowered so painfully. Eventually I just learned to relax and welcome the moment of penetration, but it has never been my favorite activity since it almost always makes me think back to the prison camp. I had some good times at the Black Cat, yet I didn't want to hang around there endlessly. It was like a long stopover at an oasis. But I still had to travel across the desert.

I thought about getting myself some education. Berkeley was the best school in the area, and I applied for admission, hoping to let the government pay my expenses through the GI Bill of Rights, which entitled me to a free ride for a while. I felt like I had paid my fare in the war, and now the United States owed me at least that much. I did get a dollar a day extra pay for my time in the POW camp, but the work had certainly been worth a hell of a lot more than those wages, and a college education could not only pay me in full, but provide me with some kind of a future.

That was how I discovered that I was in limbo. Berkeley accepted me without any problem. My grades from Valley High weren't all A's, but they were respectable enough. My discharge papers were not, however. It seems that a blue discharge didn't count when it came to collecting the benefits that every GI was entitled to, and I knew I'd never get decent paying work when I presented my papers with a little "H" marked in the corner like a scarlet letter. In spite of being born and bred in America, and in spite of the years of misery I had suffered through in the name of my country, the government still thought of me as an alien, and I was condemned to a life in exile from the system. But as angry as that treatment made me, I still couldn't think of any country I'd rather live in. Blue discharge or not, I was still an American. So I decided to take my chances and hit the road. As soon as I had made that decision, I took the next bus out of town.

CHAPTER SEVEN

The first place I landed was Seattle, Washington. It was sort of a poor man's San Francisco, whose hilly streets were covered with less elegant architecture. After an hour of wandering aimlessly around the downtown area near the bus station, I bought a copy of *The Intelligencer* and answered three want ads for jobs—as an office clerk, a salesman, and a medical lab assistant—but in each case my army papers stood in the way. "We have too many men with honorable discharges looking for work," was the standard reply. Eventually, hungry and dispirited, I stopped at a place called Gus's Diner for something to eat. It wasn't much of a place, but I was trying to conserve my money because I didn't know how long it would have to last.

I ordered a sandwich and coffee from the guy behind the counter, but before he had a chance to bring them to me, an argument started between two patrons a few stools away from me. Although they both looked like derelicts, the odds were uneven. One of them was about my size, and the other one was almost small enough to be a midget. The short one was accusing the taller guy of stealing a doughnut from the cake platter on the counter and dunking it in the little man's coffee. I had seen him do it, but I hadn't said anything because I'd thought they were buddies.

"I'm a diabetic," the midget yelled, as if he'd suffered one indignity too many. "Now there's sugar in my coffee, you creep!" Ignoring the difference in their size, he pushed the taller guy away, and the thief landed in my lap. He wasn't looking for a fight. He seemed more pathetic than mean.

I grabbed him. "I think you ought to pay for your doughnut and leave," I said quietly.

"I don't have any money," he whined.

"Then here's a doughnut for you to eat outside," I said, taking one from the tray. "Put this on my tab," I told the counterman.

The thief grabbed the donut and scurried toward the door, glad to be off the hook, and the counterman poured the indignant midget a fresh cup of coffee. He drank it without saying a word to me, as if I had owed him a favor.

When the counterman brought my sandwich, he said to me, "That was a pretty good way to handle the situation."

"I know what it's like to need a buck," I said. "But at least I'm not that bad off."

"You need a job?" he asked.

"Sure do," I said.

"Talk to me after you finish eating."

The job was washing dishes. It wasn't a position with a great future, but at least I wasn't asked about my discharge papers. Besides, the food wasn't as greasy as it is in some diners, so I figured the dishes wouldn't be all that hard to wash.

The guy who owned the place was named Gus Gainer. He was a burly middle-aged man with thick eyebrows and big arms, but he had a gentle look in his eyes. He and his wife, Mary, a plain, soft-spoken woman, were decent people. They took a liking to me and kind of adopted me, even giving me a room behind the diner to live in, and pretty soon I was learning to help with the short order cooking and then working behind the counter.

Watching how people eat, I learned a few things about the public. Some people don't even taste their food, and some make their whole day depend on it. The crowd who patronized Gus's was the original Skid Row crew: hopeless vagrants who panhandled the price of a meal, perpetually out-of-work lumberjacks, and dozens of displaced Indians, many of them alcoholic. Although there was occasional violence among this brotherhood of the dispossessed, on the whole they weren't such a bad bunch. I didn't mix with them overly much, preferring to keep to myself, but Gus and Mary tried to look after them as if they were all big children. That was the way Gus and Mary were with everybody. I guess it was because they didn't have kids of their own.

They did have a twenty-year-old niece, though. Her name was Laura. She was almost morbidly quiet, but kind of likably sweet-tempered. Her looks were ordinary, and she didn't do a lot to enhance them. Her hair, which was the color that dye companies call "mousy brown," hung limply down to her shoulders when she didn't have it tied back with a white ribbon. She dressed pretty simply, usually in muted-colored skirts and blouses, and while she wasn't exactly a scarecrow, she wasn't what you'd call a sweater girl either. The one thing that most appealed to me about her was her green eyes. There was a sad look in them, almost as if she expected everyone to treat her badly and had forgiven them before they did anything. I didn't think she was a masochist or anything like that, just a good Christian soul who always kept her other cheek turned. I could tell she'd been through some bad experiences, but she didn't like to talk about herself too much.

I didn't talk too much about my personal life either, so we got along just fine. Sometimes Laura helped out in the diner, peeling potatoes in the kitchen or waiting on tables quietly and efficiently. Once or twice customers were rude to her because they weren't happy with the food they'd ordered, and when that happened, Gus or I would go over to straighten things out. She always looked grateful to have been rescued from even the mildest confrontation. On one occasion a customer said something lewd to her, and she got so upset that she accidentally dropped a plate of pork chops and mashed potatoes in his lap. I was over there in a flash.

"What happened?" I asked her.

"She threw that food at me," the customer charged. "All I did was give her a compliment." He was a mean-looking guy, but luckily he had a puny build.

"He said he wanted to touch my bosom," Laura said. "I was scared. I didn't throw the food at him. It slipped. "

"I think you might find what you're looking for somewhere else," I told the customer, helping him to his feet.

"I ought to charge you for the cleaning bill," he grumbled.

"It'll make up for the price of your meal. Anything else?" I said, and he left.

Laura and I became closer after that. Gus and Mary liked me, so they were glad to see us hanging out together and did everything they could to encourage us, like giving me time off to take her to the movies and inviting me to be her escort at church socials. I didn't have anything better to do. I had put my sex life on hold for a while since I didn't know where to scout up any willing men and I didn't have much interest in haunting the men's room in the local train station. The fact is, I was glad to take a breather for a while until I had a better sense of my own direction.

Soon I was spending more and more time alone with Laura. She had her own rented room, and her aunt and uncle trusted her and didn't keep special track of her comings and goings. She could visit my room at the diner or I could visit her room, and nobody seemed to take much notice.

One night we were at her place talking about our favorite movies. Laura mentioned loving Bette Davis in *Now, Voyager*. I liked the idea that the title was taken from one of Whitman's poems, and I was trying to share some of my enthusiasm for poetry with Laura by reciting some of his lines:

"Now Voyager depart, (much, much for thee is yet in store,)
Often enough hast thou adventur'd o'er the seas . . .
But now obey thy cherish'd secret wish,
Embrace thy friends, leave all in order . . .
Depart upon thy endless cruise old Sailor."

"That's nice," she said. "But what does it have to do with the movie?"

"Beats me," I said, and we both laughed.

"No, really," she insisted. "I bet you do know. I bet you know more than you tell anybody."

"Don't we all?" I said.

"Won't you tell me?" she persisted.

"Well, the movie is about somebody who travels in search of a better self, somebody who goes through a lot of changes."

"Is that what the poem's about?"

"Partly, but it's really about dying. That's the final voyage for the old Sailor, the soul. It's one of Whitman's old age poems."

"That's sad, but nice," she said.

"I think so too."

"But it isn't what touched me about the movie," she continued. "Oh, I was impressed by all the changing Bette Davis went through. I really like her, don't you?" I nodded. "But what I really liked was the way her lover sacrificed his own happiness for his daughter's. He seemed like such a good man."

"Even though he was having an affair outside his marriage?" I asked.

"Well, we never got to know the wife, so we couldn't feel too sorry for her. Yes, he was good even in spite of his flaws. I could respect him."

"Is that what your father was like?"

She grew silent.

"Did I say something wrong?"

It took her a couple of minutes to answer. "We haven't told each other a lot about our private lives, but I think I know you well enough to trust you now. If I tell you my story, will you promise not to discuss it with Gus and Mary? I don't want them to know I told you about it."

"I'm pretty good at not discussing things," I said.

"My father wasn't a bad man," she said. "Maybe he was kind of sick. I mean, in his mind. My mother died when I was born, and he was pretty lonely, I guess. We lived outside of town. He was a farmer."

"What kind?"

"Apples."

"No kidding! My father raised apples too. And I never knew my mother either, not even a picture. My father told me she died when I was very young."

"That is a coincidence," she said. "Maybe that's why we understand each other so well. Anyway, my father never went out much. He devoted himself to raising me, and I'm grateful for that, but there was something wrong . . ."

"With his mind?"

"Well, he wasn't crazy or anything like that. I just think he was . . . well . . . *too* attached to me. Do you know what I mean?"

"I think so," I said, "but you tell me."

"I'm not sure if I can."

"You mean sexually?"

She nodded. "It happened a few times, when I was fifteen. I knew there was something wrong with it, but he made me promise not to tell. Then I found out I was pregnant, and I didn't know what to do. I couldn't have my own father's baby. He felt awful about it. He started drinking a lot. Then he took me for an abortion. I was real sick for a while after, but I got better eventually."

"And your father?"

"He got worse. He kept on drinking. He kept saying he was a sinner who was damned to hell for all eternity. I didn't know what to tell him. He was probably right, but I didn't want to make him feel any worse than he already did. I really think he couldn't help himself. He probably wanted to be a good father, and I believe that he really loved me in his own way. Maybe too strongly, but he did love me."

She was starting to cry by now, so I put my arm around her shoulder and we sat there, side by side, for a time without saying anything. Finally, when she was calmer, I asked, "What finally became of your father?"

"He killed himself. He locked himself in the garage and turned on the car. I found him in the morning on my way to school. It was awful."

"It must have been. So, Gus and Mary took you in?"

"They've been swell to me. I really owe them my life. I wanted to die too."

"And have you had any boyfriends since then? Closer to your own age?"

"Gus and Mary sent me to a convent school to finish my education. I met a few nice girls there, but you're the first real friend I've made since I graduated," she said, and she kissed me on the cheek.

I took her in my arms and the next thing I knew, I was kissing her. I don't know if she'd ever thought about sex between us, but I certainly hadn't. I considered telling her that the evening was over, but she seemed so trusting and needy—so available—that I stayed where I was and kissed her again. It didn't seem half bad. I'd gone without physical contact for months, and I needed the affection as badly as she did. So when she took my head and brought it to her chest, I didn't object. Instead, I opened the buttons of her blouse and slid my hand inside.

Her breast felt soft and warm under the brassiere. I couldn't help but go on. She removed her blouse, and I fumbled with the hook of her bra until she brushed me away with a soft laugh and undid it herself. Then I kissed her pliant flesh, and when her nipples grew erect, so did I.

I entered her right there on the daybed, without stopping to unfold it. I was afraid to lose the momentum that had begun. She was so gentle, so yielding. My equipment worked fine as I penetrated her, and she was so accepting, so eager for more, that I just kept going without anxiety. But when my orgasm came, I felt a sense of relief, not only of the physical pressure, but of the years of dread that I couldn't fuck a woman even if I wanted to.

I wasn't as passionate with Laura as I've been with some guys, but there was a real warmth between us, kind of a mutual comfort. The only thing that scared me was that I felt something like a father to her myself. She just seemed to need to be close to somebody so badly—and to tell the truth, so did I. But aside from feeling sorry for her, I really did like her. She was a fine person.

We slept together only a few times in the next couple of months. Even without burning lust, we managed to satisfy each other, and the comfort we offered each other was enough for me. I'm not sure if she felt the same way. We never talked about love.

One evening, soon after the first time we had sex, she invited me over to her place for a surprise dinner. When I saw the plate of apples piled high as a centerpiece, I knew I was in trouble. Sure enough, the first dish was apple soup. It was followed by a course of apple fritters with a side dish of applesauce, and dessert was Apple Brown Betty. The drink, of course, was apple cider.

"I know it isn't exactly a balanced meal," Laura said half apologetically. "But I thought it might make you feel at home."

"Oh it does," I said, gritting my teeth. "It makes me feel right at home. It brings back all kinds of memories, too."

I did my best to eat as much as was necessary not to offend her, but with each bite visions of my father's stern face and Martha's tombstone and the orchard clouded pink with springtime danced behind my eyes. Then I thought of Chester. I grew more silent as the meal progressed.

Seeing my half-eaten portions as she cleared the table, Laura said, "You didn't like it. I'm sorry. I thought it would be a treat."

"I guess I had enough apples to last me a lifetime when I was a kid."

"I know what you mean, " she said. "We ate apples all the time, too. I should have realized. I'll never serve you another apple again. Do you forgive me?"

"Of course," I said. "It was very thoughtful of you. Really it was." I kissed her forehead. "You're all the sweetness I need." I almost gagged on the cloying words, but I knew she wanted to hear them.

During our evenings together we talked about our interests and our pasts, but I never matched her intimate secret about her father with a revelation about my feelings for men. I didn't think she could handle it. And the stories I told her about the war were carefully censored. Without mentioning Chester, I told her about my trip to New York City and my visit to Minerva White. I even showed her some of the photographs Miss White had sent me, the ones of the luminous flowers, the fogbound tree, and the face of her friend.

"These are exquisite," she remarked. "I never realized that a photograph could be a work of art."

"They're museum pieces," I boasted. "There are very few copies. That makes them worth more and more as time goes by."

"You should keep these in a safe place," she advised. "You should cherish them."

"I do," I assured her.

At the end of the summer, she started acting funny. I knew something was wrong, but she wouldn't tell me what it was until she was good and ready. A couple of weeks went by like that, and then one evening after we had closed the diner, she asked me to walk her home. I noticed that she had borrowed her aunt's favorite maroon topper whose black Persian lamb cuffs added a sober weight to its sleeves, so I knew she had something important to say.

"I have to tell you something," she began.

"Am I going to like this?" I asked, trying to keep the tone light.

"I'm not sure," she said. "I'm pregnant."

I didn't answer her. I had all I could do to keep walking at her side without bolting. I tried to digest the information calmly. This woman was carrying a child I had fathered. Me, a father? It was too ridiculous. I wasn't cut out to be a father. I kept my eyes on the ground, and we must have walked two more blocks before I answered.

"Are you positive?"

"I waited to tell you until the doctor said it was definite."

"What do you want to do about it?" I asked, hoping she had some plan.

"One thing is certain. I'm not going to have another abortion, no matter what. I just couldn't face myself if I did."

"Does that mean we have to get married?"

"No. I've thought it out carefully. I don't want to trap you into anything. If you do want to get married, then I'm willing to think about it, but in any case I'm prepared to have the baby and raise it. I can handle it by myself. Gus and Mary will help me."

"Did you tell them before you told me?"

"I told Mary. I was too nervous to keep it to myself."

"What did she say?"

"She wasn't too surprised. She and Gus know we've been seeing each other alone. They're not *that* innocent."

"Did she say anything about marriage?"

"It was the first thing she mentioned, but I wouldn't let her talk about it. I told her that was between you and me."

"And she settled for that?"

"She said it was in God's hands, but she would love me whatever happened. She told me that she'd never leave me alone after all I'd been through."

"There's no end to her decency," I said.

"I'm lucky to have her."

"What are we going to do? I mean, do you think we should get married?"

"I told you, not if you don't want to."

"I want to do the right thing."

"Danny, there are lots of right things."

She smiled. Her eyes were full of warmth and trust, and I knew that whatever I decided, she wouldn't hate me for it.

I left her at her doorstep and went to a bar to think about my situation over a double scotch. I wasn't accustomed to sex with consequences. Sex had always been a private matter between my partner and me, with no commitment beyond orgasm. With Laura I had been in a new situation, and I had allowed myself to behave as I had in the past, without regard to the future. Like it or not, I had put myself in a different world with different rules when I had embraced her, and even if I had been acting out of compassion rather than lust, there was no excuse. I now had to pay the consequences prescribed by her world.

I ordered another double scotch. Even knowing about Laura's all-too-good reasons not to have an abortion, I had acted on a spontaneous whim, without even giving a passing thought to buying a condom or figuring out some kind of protection. I had planted my seed in her, and she had been too timid to protest. I had never even thought about ejaculating my semen as planting a seed before, only as the end of sex. But it wasn't an end; it was a beginning. Now there was a new life happening, and it was my responsibility. I was about to be a father, so I ought to be a husband too. Me, the head of a family? How could I bear such a load? How could I live with myself if I didn't?

I ordered a refill. I liked Laura, but I certainly wasn't in love with her. She wasn't the mate I wanted and I wasn't the husband she needed. How could I get married and live somebody else's life? I wouldn't last a year. That wouldn't be fair to either of us. The only advantage would be to give the baby my name. On the other hand, I would be a real heel to leave Laura in the lurch when it was my fault that she needed me.

I drank so much scotch in the course of those deliberations that I passed out with my forehead flat on the bar. I think the bartender helped me get a taxi—I'm not sure. But somehow or other I got home. In the morning, with a major hangover headache and a flannel tongue, I went to see Laura and I told her that I wanted to marry her.

"Are you really sure?" she asked.

I nodded, feeling the pain surge in my head.

"Well, if it's what you really want," she said.

Don't press me, I thought.

"I'll do my best to be a good wife to you and to make you happy," she promised.

Happy? What does happy have to do with it? I thought. But aloud, I said, "I know you will, and I'll do my best to make you proud of me." I kissed her on the lips, but there wasn't the slightest flicker of warmth in my groin. I felt more like her brother than her fiancé.

We were married before a justice of the peace. I had bought a blue serge suit for the occasion, and Laura wore a beige suit that looked suspiciously snug to me although she couldn't have been showing any belly that early. The suit was her something new. A cameo that her mother had worn was the something old. She had borrowed a handkerchief from Mary and she wore pale blue underwear. She carried a small bouquet of pink sweetheart roses. Gus and Mary stood beside us, he looking sober and she quietly dabbing her eyes and sniffling into a tissue. When the justice of the peace gave the signal, I put Laura's mother's gold band on her finger. I didn't wear a wedding ring.

Gus gave me a week off with pay and lent me his Studebaker for our honeymoon. To save money, we avoided hotels and went on a camping trip to Olympic National Park, in the northwesternmost corner of the continental United States. After I carried our supplies through a couple of miles of winding trails, we pitched our tent (another loan from Gus and Mary) on the shore of the Pacific, where, with some instructions from Laura, I made a reasonable facsimile of a campfire and, after watching the sun set over the water, we spent our evening huddled quietly together, warmed by the glowing embers.

Our wedding night was less than either of us might have hoped. It wasn't too comfortable in the tent. The hard ground was damp and cold at night, and our blankets provided a minimum of warmth and less softness. Laura had brought a new negligee for the occasion, and its silky smoothness seemed absurd against the rough woolen blankets and the coarse canvas environment of the tent. I caressed her hair with my hand and kissed her gently on the lips, and she moaned softly. I put my hand into her moist crotch and rubbed her until she seemed eager. Then I mounted her—and nothing happened. I couldn't get it up. All I could think of was her pregnancy, and I was afraid to hurt her.

"Let me help," she whispered, and she bent and fondled my penis.

"Kiss it," I whispered, and she obeyed.

Then she opened her mouth and it slipped in. At first I was surprised. Then I closed my eyes and let myself be engulfed by her warmth. She was clumsy and inexperienced, but it felt good nonetheless. It brought back memories of Jerry Tuft at the San Francisco army base, and as I thought of him, I eventually got hard. Finally I managed to enter her. I pushed and pumped, kissing and stroking her all the while, until she thrashed and groaned so loudly that I was sure she was having an orgasm. Then I thrashed and groaned along with her and pretended I was coming. But when I pulled out I was still stiff, and I doubt if I convinced her. When I was sure she was asleep, I left the tent and masturbated in the woods.

In the morning, as she was making flapjacks over the campfire, she said, "Was it good for you last night?"

I nodded. "Great," I said.

"I was worried if you weren't a little nervous, being a new bridegroom and all."

"Why should I be nervous?" I said. "I'm fine."

"I just wanted to remind you that I can't get pregnant again while I'm already expecting," she said, the color rising to her cheeks.

I laughed. "I know that," I said. "Don't worry. I'm right where I want to be."

"I hope so," she said. "I do love you, Danny."

"And I love you," I answered.

We spent our days exploring the area. The ocean was made more beautiful by huge, craggy rocks that jutted from it vertically, as they do in Japanese paintings. At its edge was a hushed pine forest bathed in mists, where tiny green saplings emerged from the huge decomposing trunks of fallen trees and reached toward the light in an eternal cycle of living and dying that I found comforting. On one of our walks we unexpectedly found ourselves on a precipice, which suddenly dropped hundreds of feet to reveal the ocean below, lapping at the base of the cliff as if it were a puddle licking at a titan's toes. The natural beauty was soothing to both of us, and our cares began to recede into the background. Soon I found myself able to function better sexually, and even if my heart wasn't fully in it, at least I didn't have to go through the process of faking it every night.

When we got back to town, our sex life quickly settled into once-or-twice-a-week encounters. I was as apt to say "Not tonight dear, I have a headache" as she was. She had her pregnancy as an excuse, and I had my financial worries. With a loan from Gus, we had set ourselves up in a small third-floor furnished apartment in a frame house a short walk from Gus and Mary's place. We had a living room, bedroom, and kitchen for forty-nine dollars a month, and Laura did her best to cheer it up with homemade curtains and inexpensive knickknacks.

She continued working as a waitress for as long as she could, and I spent my spare time looking for some work that would make me more money than I was earning at the diner. But in spite of all my applications at aircraft factories and insurance offices, and in spite of all my legitimate family needs, my blue discharge was still working against me. The only job I seemed eligible for was working in an apple orchard, which paid a little more than I was making at Gus's Diner, but I rejected that job as a matter of principle. So I stayed behind the counter at Gus's place and considered myself lucky. After a few months Laura stopped working, but with my taking on longer hours and thanks to a thoughtful raise from Gus, our finances were still manageable.

One evening, when I was working late, a slim young man with long, shiny black hair came in. He was wearing a tapered western shirt and a snug pair of jeans that were molded perfectly to his body. He ordered a cup of coffee and a piece of pie, and I could feel his eyes trained on me as I served them to him. Not frightened by his inspection, I met his measured gaze with my own, staring into his dark eyes without wavering. Judging by his high cheekbones and coppery complexion, I guessed that he had Indian blood. Whatever he was, he was damned attractive. He smiled at me, revealing a set of startlingly white teeth, and I smiled right back. No conversation passed between us, but I could feel his eyes on me as I went about my business. When he was finished, he put his money on the counter, gave me a curt nod, which I returned, and left.

Gus had left an hour earlier, so I worked alone as I cleaned up the counter and got ready to close. I kept thinking about the young guy. I felt a stirring in my groin. It had been a long time since I'd had sex with another man, and the idea seemed to grip me like an iron-jawed clamp. Images of the men I'd known flashed before me, and I concentrated on parts of their bodies: the back of one's neck, the shoulders of another, the heavily dangling genitals of a third. I cupped my crotch in my hand then let it go. Horny or not, I was a married man now.

When I left the diner, the young man was leaning against a car out front. He smiled at me, and I walked over to him.

"Finished up for the night?" he asked.

I nodded.

"Warm weather."

"Yeah," I said.

"What're you up to?"

"Nothing much, just heading home."

"Want some company?"

"Not at my place. I'm married."

"Shit, so am I," he said, and we both grinned.

"But you do want company," he persisted.

"Sure."

"What about a hotel?"

"Can't afford it."

"Shit," he said. "I like the way you look."

"Same here," I answered.

We stood there without saying anything for a minute or more. Finally he said, "I have an idea. Come with me." He took me to a nearby parking lot and we went into the back, behind the last row of cars. Ignoring the light drizzle, which was the usual climate in Seattle, he put his arms around me, and I encircled him with mine. Then he reached down and started to undo my pants.

Just then three people walked into the lot and headed for the car just behind the one where we were. I hastily closed my pants, and the two of us fled around the corner.

"Whew," he said. "That was a close call."

"I can't afford to get caught at this," I said.

"Do you think I can?"

"What should we do?"

"Come with me."

He stopped at a drugstore and bought a large paper shopping bag. Then we walked a few blocks to the railroad terminal and we went into the men's room, where the traffic was light. "Got a nickel?" he asked.

I gave it to him and he used it to open the door on one of the stalls. He sat down on the toilet, placed the open shopping bag in front of him, and motioned to me to step inside it.

"Are you kidding?" I said.

"Trust me. It works," he answered, gesturing toward the bag. "Hurry and close the door before somebody sees us."

I stepped into the bag and closed the door, and he opened my pants and took out my cock. He stroked it admiringly for a moment and then began to suck it eagerly. Somebody came into the men's room at that point, so we stopped what we were doing and waited silently. When the visitor had finished pissing and farting and washing his hands and cursing because there were no paper towels, he left, and we went back to work.

I shot my load quickly and easily, and then my partner gestured that we should trade places, which we did with a minimum of rattling and a lot of stifled giggles. When his feet were inside the bag, I opened his fly and took out his slim, hard dick. It was only in my mouth for a minute or so when he surrendered his load. I stood up and we embraced each other. Suddenly we exchanged one passionate kiss and tasted our own semen on each other's tongue. Then he stepped out of the bag, and we both got out of there.

Outside, he said, "Whew, what a relief!"

"I'll say," I responded.

"What's your name, man?"

"Dan," I said.

"I'm Ron," he answered. "Ron Barefoot."

"Dan Blake," I said, feeling guilty that I had hedged about giving him my last name.

"See you around, Dan," Ron said, and he walked off.

I stopped inside the terminal to buy some daisies, and then I went right home to Laura. "For the mother-to-be," I said grandly as I presented them to her. "Sorry I'm late, dear. Slow customer just at closing time."

"You're so good to me, darling," she said.

134

A few days later, I went to the farmers' market on Pike Street to buy some vegetables for the diner. I was poking around the corn and potatoes when for some reason I looked up. And there was Ron, standing behind the vegetable stall.

"Hi!" I said, breaking into a grin. But he didn't answer.

Looking at me as if he'd never seen me before, he said to a short, dark-haired woman behind him, "Maria, take care of the customer."

I bought the vegetables I'd picked out and left as soon as I could. From then on when I shopped at the Pike Street Market, I avoided their stall.

A week later, Ron came to the diner before closing time. There was another customer, so we couldn't talk as he finished the pie and coffee I served him. But he was waiting outside again when I had closed up.

"I just wanted to apologize, Dan," he said. "That was my wife. I didn't want to have to explain where I knew you from."

"I understood that," I said.

"I just didn't want you to be mad."

"I'm not mad."

"Maybe we can get together again sometime."

"Maybe."

"Do you want to do it now?"

"Can't," I said. "I'm expected home."

"Maybe some other time, then."

"Sure, some other time."

He never came back to the diner, so that other time never happened. But a floodgate had been opened, and I found myself thinking about sex with men all the time. I eyed the guys who came into the diner, hoping for some response, but there was none. Soon I found myself stopping by the men's room at the terminal after work. At first I was very cautious, afraid that the vice squad was watching the place, but after a while I became quite brazen and I met quite a few men there. We never exchanged names, though. We just went about our business and disappeared into the night. There were one or two regular habitués whom I noticed there, time and again, but I never spoke to them and I never had sex with them. We regarded one another as competition. It wasn't my idea of a lovely time, but it was a much-needed safety valve.

As far as I know, Laura never suspected that I had a secret life. She remained as sweet and loyal as ever while I watched her belly balloon with our child. As nice as she was, I began to resent her for her very goodness, which I knew I didn't deserve. But I always did my best not to let her see that. I was relieved when we could stop having sex because of her ungainliness. She was especially afraid because of the abortion she'd had. Once she whispered to me, "Just because I can't do it doesn't mean you should have to do without. Do you want to go to a prostitute or something?"

I shook my head no. "I'm a married man," I said.

She looked relieved. "I guess I was just testing you. It's just that I feel so ugly with this big belly."

"Don't talk that way," I said. "You're more beautiful than ever."

The next night I went back to the men's room.

It went on that way for a long time. I did all the things expectant fathers are supposed to do. I massaged Laura's aching back. I went out late at night to find butter pecan ice cream and a can of sardines for her. I reached for the phone every time she said she felt a pain, and she reminded me apologetically that there were several weeks to go.

Finally it was the real thing. I was asleep beside her when her water broke unexpectedly at 2 a.m. She had been feeling symptoms for hours, but she didn't want to disturb me until she was sure. "You work hard enough all day," she reminded me through gritted teeth. "You need your sleep."

I borrowed Gus's Studebaker and drove her gingerly to the hospital. I even remembered to take some towels, a ball of twine, and a pair of scissors, in case she gave birth before we got there. "Scream if you need to. The windows are shut," I advised her, but she sat there stoically without making a sound.

I got her into the maternity ward, where I found everyone else's calm demeanor nerve-racking. Then came five hours of waiting. Gus and Mary arrived sometime in the middle of it, and they tried to keep me calm while I paced and fidgeted. I don't know what they were thinking, but I was thinking that I wanted to be someplace else at that moment—the men's room at the railroad terminal, the Black Cat Café in San Francisco, anywhere.

At 7:30 in the morning my son was born, and I went home to get some sleep. That afternoon, I splurged on a dozen red roses, and I went to the hospital to visit my family. Laura looked tired but happy. She held the baby in her arms as he suckled at her breast.

"Are you okay?" I asked.

"Just a little tired."

"And the baby?"

"He's fine. I checked, and he has all his fingers and toes."

"Good."

"Let's call him Daniel," she said.

"How about Gus?" I tried.

"That can be his middle name."

"Hello, Daniel Gus Blake," I said, touching his tiny head. He ignored me and just kept right on having his lunch.

When I left the hospital, I knew what I had to do. I had seen this through as far as I could, but I couldn't take it for the rest of my life. I wasn't making enough money to support a family anyway. I had to look out for myself before I could look out for anybody else. I knew that Gus and Mary would look after Laura and the baby. I didn't want a son—not under these circumstances, anyway. And I certainly didn't want a wife, no matter how sweet she was. I didn't know what I wanted. I only knew what I didn't want. I didn't want to be an unwilling husband and father. I was damned if I would do to my child what my father had done to me. I had already seen what misery that could lead to. I didn't feel like much of a man that night. I didn't feel like much of a human being.

I put all the money I had—about a thousand dollars—in an envelope and left it where she would find it. I enclosed a note, saying:

> Dear Laura,
>
> You don't deserve this kind of treatment, but I'm no good for you. I can't explain why. I know the money will come in useful. I wish it could be more, but it's all I've got. Thank Gus and Mary for being so good to me. I just can't face them right now. I know you'll be a good mother to our child. God bless you. Please try to forgive me.
>
> > Good-bye.
> > Dan

As I packed my few things, I came across Minerva White's photographs. Without a second thought, I removed the picture of the mist-shrouded tree and added to Minerva White's signature on the back: "For Laura, With Love, Dan, 1946." I left it under the note. I packed my few things and left in the night without seeing anybody. I guess that was the lousiest thing I've ever done in my life, but I just didn't have any other answer.

I started walking east on the highway, hoping to hitch a ride. I thought of the appropriate lines from *Leaves of Grass* as I walked:

> Afoot and light-hearted I take to the open road,
> Healthy, free, the world before me,
> The long brown path before me leading wherever I choose.

Of course I was anything but light-hearted, but I was healthy and free, and the world, for better or worse, was before me.

PART III
DANNY BLAKE

From this hour I ordain myself loos'd of limits and imaginary
    lines,
Going where I list, my own master total and absolute,
Listening to others, considering well what they say
Pausing, searching, receiving, contemplating,
Gently, but with undeniable will, divesting myself of the
    holds that would hold me.

(Still here I carry my old delicious burdens,
I carry them, men and women, I carry them with me
    wherever I go,
I swear it is impossible for me to get rid of them . . .)
                    —Walt Whitman,
                    "Song of the Open Road"

CHAPTER EIGHT

Hitching rides was fairly easy after a little practice. For a few days I slowly made my way east with a series of short lifts from a variety of men. Even when they weren't especially good-looking, sitting next to them reawakened my long buried lust, but I was afraid to do anything about it because I was in new territory where I didn't know the rules. Soon I began to think about little besides sex, even when we were discussing such unerotic subjects as the weather, the war, and the local landscape. Several of them tried to talk about sports, the standard medium of discussion between men who don't know each other, but I told them I'd been too busy working to keep track of baseball that summer.

One driver was so attractive to me that I almost blew my cover and asked him outright for sex. His name was Chuck, and he picked me up in a Mack truck carrying a load of potatoes from southern Idaho to Missoula, Montana. We were perched high above the roadway in the cab of his truck, and I watched with pleasure as his strong arms maneuvered the large, horizontal steering wheel with casual expertise. He was wearing cowboy boots, jeans, and a T-shirt damp with his perspiration. As he raised his thick forearm to wipe the sweat from his brow, his rich, manly aroma filled the air around him, and I drank it in thirstily, wishing I could nestle my head against his chest and let his appealing scent overwhelm me. Instead, I allowed myself only sidelong glances at his attractive sunburned face, which was accented with a small blond mustache.

When he talked about how much he missed his girl and needed a little relief, I played dumb, afraid he might be innocently sharing his real feelings or maybe even setting some sort of trap because I had somehow inadvertently telegraphed my secret lust. So I just sat there, aching with want, and didn't say a word about what was really on my mind. I just tried to keep talking about the "Big Sky Country" country we were riding through, which wasn't easy since the reason for its nickname is that there's nothing at ground level to discuss but emptiness.

Chuck finally let me out just before reaching his destination. I felt as frustrated as a diabetic in a chocolate shop, but I breathed a sigh of relief because I hadn't given myself away. Yet almost as soon as I got down from the truck I was sorry that I hadn't risked his anger and possibly earned a moment of illicit ecstasy. I still think of Chuck the same way I remember that faceless guy I played handsies with at the John Garfield movie in San Francisco. Some things that don't happen are more memorable than some that do.

I began to realize how little I really understood about being different in America. And—although I knew I'd have to be on my guard at all times—I decided that if I were going to let fear rule my life, I'd never be happy. It wasn't until years later that I heard about the reputation truckers have for rutting with their riders. I was so naive that I might as well have stayed back on the farm.

From Missoula I got a ride all the way to Madison, Wisconsin. The driver was twice my age, somewhere in his late forties. He was slim and balding, with thin lips that he kept pursed, as if he expected to disapprove of whatever he heard next. He wore round, horn-rimmed glasses and a tweed sport coat and corduroy pants, even though Labor Day was still a week off and it was around eighty degrees. He looked me over carefully before he unlocked the door of his battered old Plymouth, which went well with his ratty sport coat, I thought.

"Sorry for the delay," he said. "It's not easy to judge strangers. I wouldn't want to choose the wrong man."

"You'll be safe with me," I said.

"I imagine so," he answered, offering his rather unconvincing version of a warm smile.

We introduced ourselves. His name was Willard Stevenson. He was an English professor at the University of Wisconsin.

"What do you do for a living?" he asked. "I don't suppose a good-looking young man like you is a professional wanderer."

"At the moment, that's exactly what I am," I answered.

"Are you escaping from a lurid past?"

"Let's just say I'm sort of between positions right now."

"You're capable of more than one position, judging from the looks of you," he said. It was hard to tell for sure, but I could swear he was leering at me behind his glasses.

I played it straight. "I'm not sure where I'm heading," I said. "I guess I won't know till I get there. And I'll take the first position that feels right."

"Many positions feel right," he said. "But some of them feel just wonderful." He snickered at his own cleverness.

"We are talking about employment, aren't we?" I asked.

"I'm not offering you a salary, if that's what you mean," he answered.

"What are you offering?"

"We seem to be getting a bit ahead of ourselves," he said. "Listen, I'm going to have to stop soon for supper, and then I'll have to look for a motel for the night."

"My finances are pretty low," I said. "In fact, I'm about broke."

"I'm not surprised," he replied. "But I like your company. I'm prepared to treat you to dinner and a night's lodging. How does that sound?"

"That's really nice of you, Professor Stevenson," I said. "I guess I don't have any choice but to say yes. I'm glad I ran into you."

"I'm glad, too, but not as glad as I'm going to be. Oh, and call me Willard."

I didn't press him for his meaning.

We stopped at a roadside café outside of Billings. I remembered that Jerry Tuft, my buddy who'd been imprisoned on sexual charges by the army medics, came from Billings, and I thought I would look him up if I got the chance.

The other café patrons were two retired-looking cowboys with weather-beaten faces, and a stern-faced Indian who looked resigned to his solitude. The whole place was decorated in saddles, lassoes, and steer horns. It looked like it had been waiting too long for a movie company to use it as a set, and dry rot was about to set in.

We ate our food with little conversation. Willard provided us with a bottle of California wine and attacked his liver with gusto, and I did the best I could with my bone-dry pork chops. He looked at me coquettishly over the rim of his wineglass, his amorous eyes utterly out of place in his pinched face.

"Do you read much?" he asked me.

"I enjoy reading—poetry mostly."

"Who's your favorite poet?"

"Walt Whitman."

"What do you like of his?"

"Almost everything. I memorize lots of it."

"Recite something."

Something about Willard made me think of my father and the orchard at home, so I chose these lines to recite.

"Smile O voluptuous cool-breath'd earth!
Earth of the slumbering and liquid trees!
Earth of departed sunset—earth of the mountains misty-topt! . . .
Far-swooping elbow'd earth—rich apple-blossom'd earth!
Smile, for your lover comes."

Willard looked surprised. "That's extraordinary! But tell me about it later," he said. "I don't want to think of you as a poetry lover tonight."

When he signed up for our motel room, I waited in the car. "Right this way to the theater," he said enigmatically, as he emerged from the office.

I wasn't surprised to find that the room had a double bed. It was a dreary place with water stains on the dull gray wallpaper beneath the window. If there had ever been a discernible pattern on it, it couldn't be made out now.

The furniture was Salvation Army modern: one chair, one dresser, one nightstand, one lamp, and the bed. But Willard acted as if he were in the palace at Versailles, sweeping about the room grandly like a duchess in heat.

I didn't say anything while we took our showers and slipped into the bed, both in our underwear. It took about fourteen seconds before I felt his hot breath on my shoulder and his hand edging over my hip.

"Just getting comfortable," he said.

"Suit yourself," I answered.

In short order we were engaged in foreplay. After a prolonged bout of kissing, he excused himself, and I lay there watching my erection wilt while he disappeared into the bathroom with his suitcase. When he emerged a few minutes later, he was wearing a dress and high heels and a flowing blonde wig.

I had to bite my pillow. He was outdoing Veronica Lake. His wig tumbled seductively over one eye, and a slash of scarlet lipstick covered his lips, which were still pursed. He looked far too elegant for the drab setting we were in. "Okay, big boy," he said. "Let's get down to some serious sex."

What the hell, I thought. I rose from the bed and took him by the waist and kissed him hard. It occurred to me that I had never kissed a mouth covered with lipstick before. Kelly and Laura had both dressed without its benefits. This "woman" certainly didn't bring either of them to mind. The kiss tasted waxy and smelled of perfume.

I was surprised again to discover black lace panties beneath Willard's dress, but by then I was beyond being shocked and just went about my business with great dispatch. Actually, it wasn't half bad. He wasn't pretty, but his technique, like his outfit, was pretty imaginative, and it wasn't long before we took each other's semen in our mouths.

In the morning, while Willard was still asleep, I went to a phone booth. The slim directory had three listings under Tuft. I tried the first.

"Hello," a flat-sounding woman's voice answered. Strangely, it reminded me of Mrs. Warner.

"Is there a Jerry Tuft there?"

"Who? Jerry?"

"Yes."

"Uh, that's Tom's boy. You have the wrong number."

One of the other listings read "Tuft, Thomas," so I called that. A man's voice answered.

"Hello."

"Good morning," I said. "Is Jerry Tuft there?"

There was a long silence. Then he asked, "Who is this?"

"I'm an old army buddy of his and I was just passing through town, so I thought I'd look him up."

"Jerry's not here."

"Will he be back soon?"

"No, he won't."

"Can I call him where he is?"

"Sorry, no."

"Is he all right?"

There was another pause.

"Were you his friend?"

"Yes."

"Jerry's in a veterans' hospital, down in Texas."

"Oh. Was he wounded?"

"He was hurt real bad. He had been in a hospital in Australia—I don't know for what—and the place was hit by a bomb. Mister, you don't want to see him. He's a paraplegic in a wheelchair—broke his back. And his face was hit by shrapnel. He can only see a little out of one eye, and he can't hear at all. He don't want no visitors. I been there twice, but it ain't no use."

I caught my breath, remembering Jerry's innocence and exuberance when we had made love, and his shattered optimism when the army had made an example of him for giving pleasure to some other soldier. He hadn't even understood what he'd done wrong. I tried to imagine Jerry as the broken form described by the voice on the phone, but it was too painful. I wanted to remember him as I'd first known him.

"I'm sorry to tell you like this," the voice said, with a kindlier tone. "Is there anything else?"

"Are you his father?"

"His brother."

"I'm sorry to hear the news. Is there anything I can do?"

"I don't think so. Thanks."

"Thank you," I said. "I didn't mean to bother you."

"That's okay," he said. "'Bye."

"Good-bye."

When I got back to the motel room, Veronica Lake was still in bed, with lipstick smeared across her chin and her blonde hair lying in a tangled heap on the floor. "Come to Mama, big boy," she said. "I thought you'd run away."

"I just went for a walk," I said, sinking slowly onto the mattress.

After breakfast, as Willard and I continued our ride, he looked as sedate as ever in his tweed jacket. He explained to me that he spent his summers in San Francisco, where he could "be himself." In Madison, of course, he had to be much more restrained. It wouldn't do for a college professor to run around dressed like Veronica Lake, not even if he were a female.

"We can't live our fantasies all the time," I said, with an understanding look.

"I suspect you have greater depth than I first imagined. What college did you go to?"

"None," I said. "My education was interrupted by the war."

"I'm impressed," he said. "You have a good deal of native intelligence. Don't you want to go to college?"

"I suppose so. It can't hurt, anyway."

"Enough of your rah-rah enthusiasm," he said. "College is hard work, but it might be just the thing for you."

"I can't afford it," I said. "I was accepted at Berkeley after I was separated from the army, but I have a blue discharge, because the army found out I'd had sex with another prisoner of war—maybe not as elaborately as we did it last night, but enough to get me in trouble. Anyway, I can't get the government to pay for my tuition, not with my Section Eight."

"I see." He was quiet for some minutes, and then he said, "I have a proposal for you. First, I liked what we did last night. Did you?"

"Sure," I said. "It was fun." I hoped I sounded more enthusiastic than I felt.

"I'd like to do it some more, in the privacy of my own home."

"Okay."

"I mean, on a regular basis."

"But I don't have a way to support myself."

"You don't have to."

"What happened? Did I win a contest?"

"You might say that. Listen. You can be a student at the university where I teach. If I say you're my nephew and you're living with me, your tuition will be nearly free. I assume you won't have any trouble with the entrance requirements if you were accepted at Berkeley."

"But what will I live on?" I asked.

"I can take care of that. There's plenty of room in my house for both of us, especially if we sleep in the same bed. Uh . . . of course we'll say you're sleeping in the spare room. And I can afford food and clothes for you. Let's consider it a fulfillment of my urge to be a parent. That way we both benefit. What do you say?"

Oh great, I thought. Now I've got Veronica Lake for a father. I'm batting a thousand when it comes to parents. On the other hand, it's a terrific offer. What do I have to lose? Certainly not my virginity. But does this make me some kind of prostitute? Oh fuck, it's a living, isn't it? What the hell. "Sure," I said. "Sounds great." I turned to him with a warm smile, realizing as I offered it that it was the first of many less than sincere gestures I'd have to make in my new position as hired "nephew."

"Of course. I'll expect you to keep the house clean for me, too. Do you think you can handle that?"

"I'll manage," I said. "A deal's a deal."

He spread his lips into a thin smile. "I knew I'd found the right man as soon as I opened the car door to let you in," he said.

Madison was beautiful in early autumn. The leaves were just beginning to yellow around the lake, and the neatly spaced rows of frame houses stood waiting for an early winter. Willard's house was small but comfortable: two bedrooms and a study upstairs, and a living room, dining room, and kitchen downstairs. All were done in somber-colored tweeds and leathers suitable to the academic life, but they made a rather prim setting for the midnight forays of Veronica Lake. I managed to take the incongruity in stride since I'd already learned never to judge things by their appearances.

With a lot of special delivery postage for my high school records and some favors by the dean of admissions for the distinguished Professor Stevenson, I was accepted for the fall semester. I ignored the freshman beanies and the fraternity hazings, although I admit I had to stifle some curiosity about the pornographic rituals of hell week. But I was damned lucky to be there, the way I figured it, so I concentrated on my one chance to get an education.

My classes were not exactly inspiring. The freshman English teacher, Professor Haggerty, had an ill-fitting glass eye that dripped constant tears, so that he kept a handkerchief always at the ready and looked as if he were emotionally overcome by whatever we were discussing, even the dullest student papers. We struggled to compose our assigned essays, addressing truly pressing topics like, "Is a word a symbol or a sign?" and "Define justice." But it was good exercise in logic, I suppose, and I liked it better than my other courses. The professor seemed to expect a good deal from me, aware that I was the "nephew" of his colleague, but that worked in my favor because it made me try all the harder. Whatever the quality of my work, the comment was, "Good, but you can do better." I usually received a polite A- or B+, and the tears kept streaming down my instructor's cheek, which made it hard to figure out what he really thought of me.

Professor Gambio, the biology teacher, had a facial tic that made her lips keep twitching, so that she always seemed to be smiling at inappropriate moments. After a few humiliating attempts to smile back at her, I quickly learned to ignore her expression. The complex categorizations of phylum, class, genus, and species seemed marvelous to me, but although I reproduced the whole system verbatim on the final exam, I can't remember any of it now. What I do remember is one comment she made about weeds. "There is no such thing as a weed," she said. "The term 'weed' is merely a social classification for a plant that is not desired in someone's garden. To a biologist, all plants are equal." Of course her smile kept flickering as she said it, whatever that meant, but I liked the democratic spirit of biology, and it gave me some insight into Whitman's choice of the common grass as his symbol.

The art history teacher, Professor Bollinger, showed slides every day, so most of our course was taught in a darkened room, and several of my classmates used the opportunity to catch up on their sleep. But I was fascinated—by the art, not by his dull, droning lectures. He was a very feminine man with hands that fluttered in the air as he spoke. He was intent on defining all the "isms" of art history and memorizing the birth and death dates of all the major artists. But I was more concerned with Michelangelo's gorgeous anatomies and trying to understand the cubists, whose paintings reminded me of Chester's collection and my boyhood dreams. The memories actually brought tears to my eyes one day. When the lights came on, the professor was beaming at me. I guess he thought I was overcome by the beauty. I let him believe whatever made him happy.

Keeping house for Willard and keeping up with my classes and homework assignments took up most of my days, but making love to Willard's version of Veronica Lake—which, as time passed seemed to me more and more like a bad imitation of Mae West—did not use up all my sexual energy. For that, I discovered the men's room in the basement of the college library. Whenever I had a chance, I spent an hour there.

The place was a college in itself. Nervous guys dropped in for quick and guilty blow jobs, and a lot of offers were scrawled on the walls. I tried to show up at the times that were written, but nobody ever seemed to keep those dates. Most of the action took place between the stalls, where a "glory hole" had been carved in the partition. You could see what your neighbor had in his lap and whether he was playing with it, and if the mood was right, one of you could stick himself through the hole in the partition to be greedily gobbled up by the stranger on the other side. I didn't make any attempt to meet any of the guys I had anonymous sex with. It was more convenient to keep that part of my life at a distance, since I didn't want to create any problems at home.

I did get friendly with one guy in my English class, but there was nothing sexual about our relationship, at least not on his part. His name was David Halpin. He was pretty good-looking, short and wiry with a mop of dark, curly hair that I wouldn't have minded running my fingers through. I didn't get to talk to him until Professor Haggerty assigned an essay on "The Value of Poetry" and asked the two of us to stay after class when the papers had been returned.

"I was concerned about the originality of your work," he told us. "Almost everyone in the class approached the problem in a general sense, discussing the humanizing impact poetry can have on an industrialized culture. But both of you responded personally about the role of poetry in your own lives, and both of you cite Walt Whitman as a major influence in your lives. I'm not convinced that you didn't collaborate on this. Your words are different, but your ideas are strikingly similar."

David and I both looked surprised. "We've never even met outside of class," I explained.

"I learned about Whitman in high school," David said. "I just felt connected to him, and that's what influence poetry has had on me."

"I've been reading Whitman since I was a boy," I explained. "The librarian at my grammar school gave me a copy of *Leaves of Grass* as a gift. It's always been a very important book for me."

"I suppose I'm worrying unduly," the professor said, wiping his dripping eye with his sodden handkerchief. "You two boys have always written competent papers with sufficient originality. I imagine such a coincidence is possible. But I'll be paying special attention to your work for the rest of the semester. Be sure this kind of 'accidental similarity' doesn't happen again. Do we understand each other?"

"Yes, Professor," I said. "But it really was a coincidence."

David nodded. We left the room together, and when we got into the hall, he said, "Do you want to have a cup of coffee in the student lounge?"

"Why not?" I said. "We can read each other's papers."

Despite the English professor's fears, David's paper seemed considerably different from mine. He had concentrated on Whitman as the poet of America, emphasizing his democratic ideals and his patriotism. I had had his spirituality and sexuality in mind, although I'd purposely kept the latter somewhat vague. David could see it, however.

"I don't know what the professor was talking about," he said when we'd finished reading. "It's almost as if we were writing about two different men."

"Maybe that's what's so good about Whitman," I said. "He's all things to all people."

"I wonder what he was to himself," David mused.

"Maybe just a masquerader," I suggested.

"I'd rather think he was sincere."

"Me too. Maybe he was a sincere masquerader."

"I guess all of us wear masks in one way or another," he said.

I wondered what he meant by that. Could he be sending me some sort of signal? I hoped so. "I guess we'll have to try to find the mask beneath the mask," I said.

"Do you think he was as patriotic as his poems make him seem?" David asked, ignoring my innuendo.

"I think he wanted the Union to remain intact," I answered. "I think he loved America for its promise."

"But I wonder if he would have fought for it—not just nursed the wounded, but actually picked up a gun."

"I've wondered the same thing," I said. "I wonder if he didn't theoretically turn everything into some form of good, sort of defining the bad right out of existence. With that kind of attitude, how could he want to fight? He even nursed the Confederate wounded. How could he have killed them, even if the country's survival depended on it?"

"Interesting," he said. "It's hard for our heroes to live up to all our ideals."

"As hard as it is for us to live up to our own, I suppose. I wrote a poem about Whitman confronting our own time. It's called 'Walt Whitman in World War II.'"

"I'd like to read it sometime," David said.

"I hope you're not just being polite," I answered. "I happen to have a copy with me."

I pulled it out of my briefcase.

Walt Whitman in World War II

Walt Whitman shook
like a leaf in World War II.
The terror alone enthralled him,
taught him the enormity of fear,
the world exploding all around
and no sure place to set a foot,
the necessity of murder, and
the necessity of forgiving.
He dressed himself in khaki
and rode in a Sherman tank.
He made adequate lists of atrocities.
He loved to fancy himself a Jew in Auschwitz,
which caused him great mystic pain and ecstasy.
He imagined he would never survive
the war and the bitterness that was its fruit.
It strained his faith to think
that the heights of goodness and joy
could equal these depths of terror and sorrow.
But he did survive.

He changed, of course, but he survived.
He crops up everywhere, like welcome weeds.
He reminds us to love war;
it is a chance to strive.
Style is the only matter in times like these,
when the spirit quivers
and applauds the wisdom of all struggle.
The Holocaust was a university of horror and hate,
and Walt Whitman loved its lessons.
World War II was just fine with him,
and so was every destruction that followed it,

one after another,
down to the last dead toad,
in which he discovered quintillions of joys.

"Hey," said David, "I really like that."

"Thanks," I said modestly. I was actually very proud of it. "I'm not sure if it's quite finished," I continued. "I haven't showed it to anyone else yet."

"Let me look at it," he said. He took the page and studied it for a while. Finally he said, "There's just one word that bothers me a little. Are you sure you mean 'style'?"

"Let me think about it," I answered. "That word's been bothering me too." I thought for a moment then crossed out "style" and wrote in "fear." I showed the page to David.

"That's much better," he said. " 'Fear is the only matter in times like these.' I like that. It even echoes Roosevelt." He adopted a gruff, nasal voice. *"The only thing we have to fear is fear itself."*

"The only thing we have to fear is style," I said. "No, the only thing we have to fear is Professor Haggerty." Then we both laughed out loud.

"Do you want to see one of my poems?" David asked.

"Sure," I said. "I'd be glad to."

"I just happen to have one with me too," he said, smiling. "You'll be surprised. It's on a subject similar to yours."

I read his poem gladly, but I was a little disappointed when I found that it rhymed in an old-fashioned way. It went something like this.

To Walt Whitman

Walt Whitman, where were you
When the drums were beating for World War II?
Did you smile our spirit to see
As America marched off to victory?
And were you proud at our banners unfurled
As we went out to save the world?
Wherever you are did you somehow know
That we would vanquish the Axis foe
And smash the Nazi and Japanese powers
So the freedom you loved would still be ours?

I could see several crossings out and replacements of "Axis" and "foe" and "powers," so I knew he'd worked hard at it. Of course I didn't much like it, but I remembered Ariel Dumont and how terrible his lack of charity toward my early efforts had made me feel, and I was determined not to be cruel.

David's brow knit while I was reading, and he said, "It's nowhere near as good as yours, but I'm just getting started writing poems. Can you tell me how to improve it?"

I was embarrassed, so I fished for something nice to say.

"It's a challenging subject."

"But your poem goes much deeper," he said admiringly.

"Maybe because yours is all a series of questions, so there's no room left for your answers, or the reader's," I suggested.

"I didn't think of that," he said. "I was thinking that yours sounds much more like a poem, even though mine rhymes and yours doesn't."

"Maybe you should take a clue from old Walt himself," I counseled. "He didn't use rhyme. He was one of the first to abandon it."

"Of course," said David. "Free verse. My high school teacher told us about that. Why didn't I remember it? I feel a little ridiculous."

"Don't be silly," I said. "You have to start somewhere."

"You've helped me a lot," he said. "I think I have some new ideas, so I can try it again. Thanks for being so generous. I don't think the poem deserves it."

"But you do," I said.

He flashed me a disconcerted look, but it quickly settled into a smile, which I returned.

After that we were friends, and we had coffee and conversation regularly after class. Dave was a sweet guy from a small town in northern Wisconsin, where his father was a hardware distributor. He was younger than I and had little direct experience with the war, except that his older brother had been killed in the Battle of the Bulge. He didn't know what his major would be, but he thought he might like to open a small business in his hometown and raise a family there. I think he may have been part Jewish, but I never asked. If he didn't volunteer that sort of information, I figured it was none of my business.

I told him about my background in the orchards of New York State and my experiences in the war, but I didn't volunteer anything about my sex life or my blue discharge. I said that I'd worked for a while in Seattle and that I had had a girl there, but I didn't mention why I'd left. As far as Dave knew, I really was Willard Stevenson's nephew, and I saw no reason to tell him otherwise or to explain how I was paying for my tuition.

I showed my Whitman poem to Willard one evening, but his response was not as admiring as David's. "An interesting conceit," he observed grudgingly. "But what makes you think Whitman would identify with people like the Jews—or even with the troops, for that matter? He probably would have nursed the wounded as he did in the Civil War. This wasn't one of your homework assignments, was it?"

"No, I wrote it on my own."

"Perhaps you'd better concentrate on your assigned work. That's the best way to get an education," he advised, pursing his lips with a faintly imperious air.

"But what about the moral questions raised by the war?" I persisted. "What would a peaceful person like Whitman do when faced with a monstrous threat like Hitler's?"

"Who knows? Probably get a job as a conscientious objector, cleaning hospital floors—which reminds me, did you clean out the cellar as I asked you to?"

"Yes, I did it before I went to class," I answered, trying not to sound sullen.

"Good, then come here and kiss me," he said, pursing his lips more intensely than usual.

Kissing Willard grew less and less amusing as time went on. It wasn't just a matter of boredom; it was a matter of integrity. The more I got to know him, the less I liked him. He had his good side, of course. After all, he was living up to a generous offer, but with each passing week it became more of a business arrangement and less of a relationship.

He didn't put on his drag very often after the first few months. I guess its shock value had worn off, or maybe it had just lost its point. Instead, he tended to order sex whenever he was in the mood, as if he were ordering a banana split from a soda jerk. He had no particular interest in what my mood might be or what else I might be busy with. Sometimes he would interrupt my schoolwork, and sometimes he would interrupt a household task he himself had assigned me. So I would have to stay up late to finish the task, which he still wanted done immediately. Then I'd be groggy in class the next day. The thing I hated most was when he would rudely awaken me out of a sound sleep. He wouldn't stroke me gently until I woke up. He would just shake my shoulder and expect me to be all ready to play.

Even when he eventually let me fuck him it was plain work, and although I resented being treated like a whore, that's what I was, wasn't I, when you come right down to it? So I didn't dare voice my resentments, because I didn't want to jeopardize my situation. I'd have to pay my way somehow, and this wasn't as bad a job as most.

I'm sure Willard sensed my discomfort and even took advantage of it in a sadistic way. Real sadomasochism never entered our bedroom life. Although he was willing to play elegantly at being Veronica Lake, Willard was too prim to act out his deeper feelings in the bedroom, where they might have been safely contained. Instead, he played unpleasant little power games with me, ordering me around at his convenience, so I would be reminded constantly that I was his inferior and he had the upper hand. Eventually, I became as good at hiding my resentment at home as I had been at hiding my sexuality on my father's farm. I was becoming quite an actor.

153

But when I was with Dave, I wanted more and more to be honest. I needed to let out my real feelings somewhere, and our friendship had grown so close that I didn't want to keep such major secrets from him. Besides, I was attracted to him. And who knew? Maybe the feeling was mutual. Maybe he could be homosexual too. After all, I told myself, he's sensitive and he does like poetry. So lost was I in my own train of thought that it came as a shock to me when Dave told me he had a date with a sophomore girl from our English class who had an available roommate. "How about a double date?" he offered.

"Sure," I said, without giving myself a chance to think of the consequences. I knew Willard wouldn't mind my absence for an evening, and I figured it would be a way to share an experience with Dave.

That Saturday night, we went to a movie with the two girls. Dave's date was a cute blonde named Beverly, whom I'd never paid any attention to in class, except to notice that her observations were pretty accurate whenever the professor asked a question. She had a good mind for analyzing other students' papers. My date had short, black hair and wore glasses. Her name was Marjorie. She was very quiet when it came to ideas, but she giggled frequently, in a shrill tone that set my teeth on edge. I hoped Beverly didn't think that Marjorie was a suitable girl for someone like me. I was sure she had arranged the date out of pity or as some kind of favor, or maybe she thought being seen in contrast to someone like that would make her look better to Dave.

I can't remember what the movie was. I spent most of it wondering what was going on between Dave and Beverly. He and I sat between the two girls, and I spent more time concentrating on the proximity of his thigh to my own than I spent being aware of Marjorie's shoulder, around which I had obligatorily draped my arm. I couldn't tell if Dave was aware of the pressure of my thigh or not. His attention seemed to be divided between the movie and Beverly's shoulder, which he cradled solicitously in his arm. Once or twice I heard her squeal softly and shift in her seat, and I imagined that he had let his fingers inadvertently graze her breast or, worse, that he had intentionally felt her up. I found myself growing angry, first at Beverly for intruding on my relationship with Dave, then at Dave for not seeing my interest in him, then at poor, innocent Marjorie for being poor, innocent Marjorie, and for giggling so much and for needing to be escorted home.

Jealousy was not a pleasant experience. When the movie was over, we stopped for ice cream at the local sweet shop, and I hardly joined in the conversation. Marjorie was quiet anyway, so that left Dave and Beverly to do the talking. They did so while looking into each other's eyes, so the silence between Marjorie and me grew all the louder, punctuated by the occasional sound of her annoying giggles. I paid devoted attention to my ice cream, eating tiny tastes from the tip of the long-handled spoon and watching the rest melt into a vanilla puddle, wishing I could be alone with Dave to explain to him how I felt and how good I could make him feel, wishing that Marjorie and Beverly would decide to go home by themselves, wishing that I were someone else, leading some other life.

When Dave suggested that we all go park out by the lake, I said I had some studying to do—a likely story on a Saturday night. I didn't think I could stand watching him in action with Beverly, and I certainly wasn't interested in amusing Marjorie in the backseat. She seemed equally uninterested. Who knows? Maybe she was a lesbian.

Dave dropped Marjorie and me off at her dorm and said in a casual way that he'd see me soon. I said a curt good night to Marjorie at her door without even attempting the standard good-night kiss. She didn't giggle then. She was probably wondering what she'd done wrong. Then I walked home, blowing great puffs of frosty breath into the clear night air and angrily kicking the snow with the tip of my shoe.

After the next few English classes, Dave left with Beverly as soon as the bell rang, so we didn't have our usual chance to talk over coffee. Finally I managed to find him alone and ask him if something was wrong.

"Nope," he said. "I've been spending some time with Beverly. That's all."

"Hey, did you get into her pants yet?" I asked, trying to sound butch but coming off as belligerent.

"What do you mean by that?"

"Just being friendly, you know, man to man," I answered, attempting a broad wink.

"Listen, man, I respect Beverly," Dave said. "In fact, I think she's something kind of special. So don't talk about her like she's some kind of tramp or something. All right?"

"Sure, Dave. I was just being friendly, that's all."

"Okay, let's just let it go. Hey, did you see Marjorie since Saturday night?"

"Ah . . . no. I don't think we hit it off especially well. I mean, she's a nice girl and all, just not my type."

"Who is your type?" he asked.

"You'd be surprised," I said, trying to ignore the implications of his question.

"Maybe," he said, trying to ignore the implications of my answer.

I tried to rescue our closeness. "Have you read anything by our favorite poet lately?"

"Haven't had time," he said absently.

"Listen to this," I offered. "I've been dwelling on it lately.

  'Passing stranger! you do not know how longingly I look upon you,

. . . your body has become not yours only nor left my body
    mine only,
You give me pleasure of your eyes, flesh, face, as we pass,
    you take of my beard, breast, hands, in return,
I am not to speak to you, I am to think of you when I sit
    alone or wake at night alone,
I am to wait, I do not doubt I am to meet you again,
I am to see to it that I do not lose you.'

Isn't that nice?"

"Actually, I think it's kind of weird, to get that involved with someone you don't even know," said Dave.

"But that's the beauty of it. He loves everybody."

"I'm not sure that's such a great idea," he said cautiously.

"Why not?" I pressed.

"All that business about beard and breast. It's not just spiritual love he's talking about, you know. It sounds suspiciously physical to me."

"What's suspicious about it? That's the same feeling that gave him so much sympathy for the young soldiers who died in the Civil War and for the wounded ones he nursed. Isn't that the source of the patriotism that you admire? Isn't it his love for all mankind that makes him great?"

"For a man to love mankind in a pure way, okay. But this guy doesn't sound so pure to me."

"Does that invalidate his poetry?"

"It might," he said.

We just left it at that. I didn't want to drive him to the point of saying something that would separate us.

I tried to spend more time at home with Willard, but he was busy marking his papers and preparing his classes and only had time for me late at night. So when I was finished with my household chores and homework, I drifted into the men's room at the library a little more frequently, just to help the time go by—or so I told myself. Waiting for potential sex partners, I spent more and more time sitting in my stall like a spider waiting in its web. I silently recited lines from Whitman or counted to one hundred in French just to help the time pass. And I masturbated almost continuously while I was there, stopping just short of orgasm in the hope that a man to share it with would appear at any moment.

Occasionally someone would enter the next stall, and I would wait for sounds of bathroom activity. If there were none after a reasonable time, I'd put my eye to the hole in the partition, to see if there were any action going on. I had a couple of minimal encounters that way, but nothing I'd call hot sex. It was mostly looking and playing with myself. If anyone was bold enough to put his dick through the hole, we were both so nervous that even though I sucked as hard as I could, we rarely made it to climax before someone else came in and we rushed back to our seats, trying to act normal. Sometimes, despite three or four interruptions, we would actually finish our business. But more often than not, my partner would get cold feet, zip up, and disappear, leaving me to begin the wait for an encounter all over again.

Once, some guy got me all aroused and ready to ejaculate when someone else entered the bathroom. My partner vanished, and I was left stranded at the peak of passion. The new person came into the stall my partner had abandoned and proceeded to arrange himself on the toilet seat. I was so hot that I didn't bother to wait for him to show any signs of sexual interest. I just stuck my tongue right through the hole, thinking that would simplify matters. While I sat there with my face glued to the partition and my tongue wagging up and down irresistibly, or so I assumed, the newcomer rose and left his stall to stand in front of mine. Now I was really excited, thinking we would go beyond anonymous sex through a hole in the wall. Here was someone I could actually touch, maybe even hold. Who knows? We might even go back to his dorm room together and have a wild time. I opened the stall door expectantly. Instead of finding an erect cock waiting, I found that my would-be paramour's pants were closed. Disappointed, I looked up to his face.

It was Dave!

I tried to shut the door immediately, just to give myself time to think, but he prevented it from closing all the way. So I let it swing open slowly, without any further effort at concealment. I just sat there with my pants around my ankles and my dick rapidly going limp. I can't imagine what the expression on my face looked like, but Dave's was dark and stormy.

"Queer?" He spat the word at me.

"Dave," I pleaded. "Wait. You don't understand."

"I understand plenty, you pansy. I understand it all now. If you were anybody else, I'd punch you right in the fucking mouth. Just keep away from me, do you hear? And that goes for your creepy friend Walt Whitman, too."

CHAPTER NINE

I couldn't tell Willard what had happened. If he knew that I had been caught playing around in the library men's room, he'd not only have infidelity to hold over my head, but he'd consider me a threat to his own secrecy. So I just kept the incident to myself and hoped Dave would, too.

As far as I could tell, Dave didn't tell anyone about it, but I did imagine that Beverly was giving me an odd look on one or two occasions in class. I made no attempt to communicate with Dave, and I was unwilling to expose myself to further danger by going back to the library men's room. So I satisfied myself with the lackluster sex that Willard offered, never revealing that I was anything less than delighted with it, and I rededicated myself to my studies.

The spring semester went by quietly and I finished my freshman year with pretty good grades. In the summer, Willard made his annual trip to San Francisco, but he never offered to take me along. Instead, I was left behind as house sitter. So I took a summer course in American history, to get a jump on my sophomore year. I didn't find the classes especially congenial or stimulating. They were taught by Professor Hartsdale, whose left eye was bulging out of its socket. It might have been caused by a tumor or something, but it made him look as if he were addicted to peeping through keyholes. I didn't meet anyone to pal around with in class, so I had plenty of time to myself. But I didn't mind. I was glad just to relax. Of course I turned to *Leaves of Grass* to pass the time. I spent my idle hours imitating Walt:

> I lean and loafe at my ease observing a spear of summer
> grass.

There was a mystery in that simple blade of grass, some intention of Walt's that I knew I hadn't quite grasped. But I was in no hurry to find out. The process of contemplation was a pleasure in itself. One thing that was obvious about it, however, was its length. It was already the middle of July, and I hadn't bothered to mow the lawn once, so I decided to get to work. That was when I met Harold.

I was struggling to push the lawn mower through the impenetrable thicket. My T-shirt was jammed in my back pocket, so I could sweat freely and get a little sun on my bony shoulders. I must have looked pretty good, though, because I noticed that Harold walked around the block three times as if he were lost—which he was, but emotionally, not geographically. The third time he passed, I stopped working and leaned on the lawn mower.

"Looking for something, fella?" I asked as he scurried by, noticeably trying to look inconspicuous. He was tall, slim, and angular, with pale skin which was lent color by the shock of strawberry blond hair that fell continuously over his blue eyes, causing him to toss his head so frequently that you'd think it was coming loose from his long neck. His small chin and large nose made it impossible for him to be handsome, but he wasn't homely either. Or maybe I should say his lost look gave him a kind of appeal that made me want to take care of him.

He looked up suddenly, as if he'd been startled while lost in thought, but I knew better than that. "Um, do you think I could have a glass of water?" he said. "It's pretty hot."

"I guess so. Sure, why not?" I said, taking my T-shirt from my pocket and wiping my forehead with it. I figured he'd like that. I'd always considered my manner pretty gentle, but next to Harold I felt like Humphrey Bogart. I kind of enjoyed that idea. "How about some lemonade?" I offered. "I've got a pitcher-full in the icebox."

"That'd be swell," he said, looking both relieved and intensely interested.

I brought out the pitcher with the glass, and we sat on the front steps while he drank from the glass. I drank straight from the pitcher, with chunks of lemon and ice bumping against my upper lip. I figured he'd like that too, and he did. So did I. Somehow he brought out the male animal in me. He watched me admiringly, and I ate it right up.

"What's your name?" he asked.

"Dan," I said. "Dan Blake. Yours?"

"Harold Fisher," he answered.

"How come you came up the same street three times, Harold?"

I expected him to blush, but he didn't. "I'm looking for a room to rent. I'm taking a summer course and I was staying in the dorm, but I don't want to stay there anymore. It's too noisy."

I could see that he wasn't telling the whole truth, but I guessed it would be unwise to press him for certain details until he was ready to share them. "What kind of course are you taking?"

"Art history."

"With Professor Bollinger?"

He nodded.

"I had him in my freshman year. A little weird, isn't he?"

"What do you mean by that?" I could see Harold putting on his armor. I guessed that he felt that Professor Bollinger's affectations were equal to his own.

"Oh, it's just that he's a little fussy and self-important," I said hastily. "But underneath that I guess he's not such a bad guy. We're all a little weird in our own ways, aren't we?"

Harold looked appreciative about that. Even if it was rather slim consolation, it must have inspired his confidence because he volunteered more of his story. "I guess I must seem a little weird, too—to some people. The guys in the dorm tease me about it."

"Why? Didn't they like your clothes or something?"

"My clothes? What's wrong with my clothes? No, they said I take too many showers."

"You can't be too clean," I offered. "After all, cleanliness is next to . . ."

"They said I was watching them." He looked into my eyes, to see what effect his confession would have.

I didn't even blink. "What's wrong with watching guys?" I asked. "They're pretty nice to look at. I used to watch the guys shower when I was in the army. Lots of men like to look at other men. You were watching me mow the lawn, for example, weren't you?"

Instead of answering my question, he said, "Do you have a room I could rent? I can afford twelve dollars a week. I could get my stuff and be back in an hour."

"This isn't really my house," I said. He looked crestfallen. "But it's sort of mine until the end of August," I added. "Maybe we can arrange something temporarily. Why not?"

Harold moved in that evening with a suitcase, an easel, and his box of paints. As he tried to get it all up the staircase, refusing help, both the suitcase and the paintbox flew open, and a spectrum of silk scarves, bold rings, and intricate bracelets was scattered down the stairs in colorful disarray, mixed with items from a more traditional campus wardrobe—saddle shoes, V-necked sweaters, and cuffed slacks—all punctuated with crumpled tubes of burnt sienna, yellow ocher, and cobalt blue, as well as a pickup-sticks arrangement of paintbrushes. Harold looked as if he were about to cry.

"Having a rough day?" I inquired.

Instead of crying, he began to laugh. I joined in for a bit, but he didn't stop when I did. He laughed so hard it started to sound a little maniacal, and I was wondering what I'd gotten myself into. Then his laughter changed to tears. And, still wondering whether he were fully sane, I sat beside him and, almost without wanting to, put my arm around his heaving shoulder until he was calm. We picked up his belongings together and put them in his room, which was really supposed to be my room, but I had continued to sleep in Willard's bed while he was away.

Over supper, Harold told me more about himself. He was from a small town called Speed, in Indiana. He'd never been happy there, not for a minute. He had tried to put up a butch front, but his feminine manners had always showed through. Even when he wasn't talking, people would imagine that whatever he wasn't saying had a lisp to it. As he told me his story, I agreed with them. I could never be sure what it was: the delicate angle at which he held his wrist or the jewelry he piled on—adding tasteful ring to tasteful bracelet to tasteful tiepin (without benefit of tie) until the sum total was beyond taste. Or the wounded look in his yearning eyes, which said, "You're going to reject me, aren't you?"

His boyhood in Speed had been torture, he said. He had been tormented not only by his schoolmates but by his family too, because of his affected airs. "It's as if I were born on the wrong planet—some sort of cosmic accident," he said with duchess-like flourishes of his bejeweled hands. "I mean, it's nothing I can help. I just do what comes naturally to me."

"But most of the time you try to keep it hidden, for safety's sake?" I suggested.

"Exactly," he said. "But that ploy doesn't work very well. I'm still pretty obvious, I guess. My parents never came right out and said they thought I was queer, but I knew my father was embarrassed by what he called my 'sissified ways.' And my mother always seemed to pity me, as if I were deformed or something. Mainly I just went about my own business and spent time with them only when I had to."

"My family wasn't very different," I said. "I spent quite a lot of time alone, too."

His eyes brightened for a moment. Then they dimmed as he continued his story. "I didn't have any friends at all. I just drew pictures by myself most of the time, mainly sketches of beautiful ladies in elegant evening gowns. But my mother periodically destroyed them. She never said a word about them, just threw them out like trash—or maybe she was hiding them from my father. I don't know who she was protecting, me or him. I tried to hide them, but she always found them and threw them away. So now there's nothing left. I think they both were really relieved when I left home for school. And I was, too."

I just nodded, hoping that my eyes conveyed my understanding. He was probably pouring out his heart for the first time, and I didn't want to interrupt the flow. "What happened when you got to school?" I prompted.

"It was worse. They didn't say anything about my art or my clothes, although they gave me plenty of odd looks. It was my eyes they hated. Not only did they accuse me of being queer, they were starting to gang up on me. They threatened to strip me and toss me out of a window. But how could I help myself? I'd never seen so many half-naked men before. I had an excuse to keep out of the gym in high school—a heart murmur."

"I bet you wanted to reach right out and touch them. I know I always had to restrain myself from doing that. Those guys should consider it a compliment, but instead they think it's a threat to their manhood."

"I didn't even dream of actually touching them. I only want to look at what's beautiful. What's the crime in that?"

"No crime. 'Beauty is in the eye of the beholder,' as they say, but the beholder's going to get a black eye if he finds his beauty in the wrong place. So 'When in Rome . . .' Wait a minute. Why should I resort to clichés? I bet there's something on the subject in my favorite book. Hold on."

I fetched *Leaves of Grass* from the living room and riffled through the pages. "I know what I'm looking for," I said. "I just want to get the words right. Ah, here it is.

> 'The expression of a well-made man appears not only in his
>   face,
> It is in his limbs and joints also, it is curiously in the joints of
>   his hips and wrists,
> It is in his walk, the carriage of his neck, the flex of his waist
>   and knees, dress does not hide him,
> The strong sweet quality he has strikes through the cotton
>   and broadcloth,
> To see him pass conveys as much as the best poem, perhaps
>   more,
> You linger to see his back, and the back of his neck and
>   shoulder-side.' "

"Wow!" said Harold. "That's it! That's exactly it! Who wrote that—Emily Dickinson or somebody?"

I smiled. "No, Harold. A man wrote it: Walt Whitman, America's greatest poet. Now aren't you glad you came to college?"

"I might learn something after all," he said. "I didn't expect to find this. I was just trying to escape from Indiana."

"You've done enough escaping for one day, don't you think, Harold? It's time for bed now." To make him feel welcome, I planted a kiss on his forehead.

He looked up at me trustingly. "Can I sleep in your bed tonight?" he asked.

"Somehow I think that was your idea in the first place," I said.

"From the first time I came down the block," he answered. "Or at least from the second time. Let me quote you something that will explain why.

> 'Among the men and women the multitude,
> I perceive one picking me out by secret and divine signs,
> Acknowledging none else, not parent, wife, husband, brother,
>   child, any nearer than I am,

163

Some are baffled, but that one is not——that one knows me.

'Ah lover and perfect equal,
I meant that you should discover me so by faint indirections.
And I when I meet you mean to discover you by the like in
     you.'

You see," he continued, "I knew who you were from the start."

I sputtered, genuinely shocked. "Why, you know Walt Whitman as well as I do! And here you've been letting me ramble on like a fool, quoting what you already knew. You lied to me!"

"I didn't actually lie," Harold said. "I was just seeing who you are."

"What about who you are?" I demanded.

"Let's just say I am a woman of many mysteries," he answered, with a faint trace of Marlene Dietrich's accent, lowering his eyelids seductively. "Can we go to bed now?"

I followed him up the stairs, appreciating the shape of his ass, to which I'm sure he added an extra sway for my benefit.

Harold may have been well-versed in poetry, but he was illiterate in the bedroom. He had lots of ideas about what he wanted to do, but being a virgin he wasn't sure which ones would work. He wanted to coerce me into taking charge, and at the same time he was eager to initiate each action. So we rolled back and forth, wrestling for control, with neither man winning until I let out a laugh and just stopped.

"Now Harold, let's take this one step at a time—very slowly," I suggested. "We don't have to get it all done in five minutes."

"I'm sorry. Maybe I was too eager. Why don't you show me what to do?"

"The way I showed you Walt Whitman? Are you sure you don't already know all this?"

"I'm sure," he said. "I just didn't want you to think I was unwilling or anything. I didn't want you to be disappointed."

"You're about as unwilling as Genghis Khan was about Asia. You don't have to conquer me. You've already got me in bed. All you have to do now is relax and enjoy it."

"Okay," he said. "Easy does it."

I made love to him slowly and carefully, using my tongue and my fingers and showing him how to do the same. Neither one of us attempted penetration. His orgasm came quickly, accompanied by a long scream, which might have been either joy or anguish. I couldn't tell which, and I hoped the neighbors couldn't either. My own climax came more slowly and quietly. Then we both fell asleep, exhausted.

In the morning, I found Harold in the kitchen. He seemed down in the dumps. "What's the matter?" I asked. "I hoped you might feel a bit more celebratory."

"Nothing's the matter. Well, it just wasn't quite what I'd expected. That's all."

"Didn't you like it?"

"Of course I liked it. I really did. I loved it. But here we are back in plain old reality again. I thought everything would be changed somehow. But I still have to go to class today, and I still have the same problems to deal with at home." He tossed his head, causing his strawberry hair to fly.

"Harold, if there were no valleys, there would be no thrill to mountain climbing. If you lived on the mountaintop, that would eventually be as boring as the valley."

"I know. It's just that I wanted to transcend—to break through to some new dimension. Don't think I'm crazy, but maybe I actually did. Not just sexually, but emotionally. Dan, what do you feel about me?"

"I hardly know, Harold. We just met yesterday. I like you, I guess."

"I think I'm in love with you, Dan," he said.

I paused for a minute, so I could figure out what to say. I was certainly not in love with Harold. I was just desperate for a little physical contact. But he was so vulnerable that I was afraid the truth would destroy him. I didn't want that kind of power over him. I was just trying to be helpful. I thought of that old Chinese expression that said once you save someone's life, you're responsible for it. I hadn't actually saved Harold, and I didn't want any obligation to him. Then I wondered what kind of man I was becoming. I hadn't wanted any obligation to Laura, either. I wasn't very proud of myself, but I didn't have much choice.

"Harold," I said calmly, "Do you know whose house this is? Everyone thinks Professor Stevenson is my uncle, but he's not. He's my lover. You're the only person I've told this to, and I know you'll keep it a secret. Willard and I have sex with each other—in the same bed that you and I slept in. We've been together for a year now, but he's away on a trip for the summer. That's the only reason I could let you stay here."

"Do you love him?" Harold asked.

"I told you Harold, we're lovers."

"That means you have sex. But do you love each other?"

"Harold, it's more complicated than that. We have an arrangement."

"If you don't love him then you're free to love me. Say it. Say you love me."

"Harold, you're not being rational."

"The heart has its reasons . . ."

"Harold, I . . . I don't love anyone right now—not Willard, not you, not anyone. I can't tell you why."

"Then there's still hope for me."

"I didn't say that, Harold. I'm not about to change my life right now."

"Someday you'll see that you do love me, Dan. I can wait."

165

"Harold, don't be so melodramatic. You sound like Mary Noble, Backstage Wife."

"That's not a bad show, is it? Do you listen to the radio much? We could listen together."

"Harold, you're late for class, aren't you?"

"What does time matter when you're in love?"

I threw a dishrag at him. "Get going," I said without rancor.

"Okay," he said. "But I'll be back. I have a future now."

Harold's passion would have to wait, I decided. I had work to do. There was a term paper due for my American history course in a week, and I hadn't done a thing about it. I decided to use the Civil War period as my subject, and finally I narrowed it down to "Images of Abraham Lincoln." My point was to show the human side of the national icon Lincoln had become. I included some of the traditional anecdotes about young Abe studying by firelight in a log cabin and walking miles to return a penny, and how much he loved his "angel of a mother."

On the next page I quoted statements from his debates with Stephen Douglas, which showed that Lincoln was a racist at heart, in spite of his signing of the Emancipation Proclamation and his belief that Negroes (as we called them then) were as entitled as whites to life, liberty, and the pursuit of happiness:

> I am not, nor ever have been, in favor of . . . making voters
> or jurors of Negroes, nor of qualifying them to hold office,
> nor to intermarry with white people . . . there is a physical
> difference between the white and black races . . . [I] am in
> favor of the race to which I belong having the superior
> position.

As for Lincoln's personal life, I mentioned the stories of his wife, Mary Todd Lincoln, dancing madly naked on the White House lawn, and Lincoln's affair with Anne Rutledge.

Finally, I quoted some passages from Walt Whitman's journals showing how Lincoln was idolized in life. Whitman describes encountering him in the streets of Washington:

> (I never see that man without feeling that he is one to become
> personally attach'd to, for his combination of purest, heartiest
> tenderness, and native western form of manliness.)

As I read on, I began to realize that Walt had actually had a crush on Lincoln:

> His face & manner have an expression & are inexpressibly
> sweet—one hand on his friend's shoulder, the other holds his
> hand. I love the President personally.

Especially after he was assassinated, Whitman saw Lincoln as a larger-than-life figure:

"The tragic splendor of his death, purging, illuminating all, throws round his form, his head, an aureole that will remain and will grow brighter through time, while history lives, and love of country lasts.

Whitman mourned Lincoln for the rest of his life. His love was the source of his great elegy, "When Lilacs Last in the Dooryard Bloom'd," in which the poet likens himself to a solitary bird singing a dirge:

O how shall I warble myself for the dead one there I loved?
And how shall I deck my song for the large sweet soul that
    has gone?
And what shall my perfume be for the grave of him I love?

As I wrote about how the clumsiness of "O Captain! My Captain!" failed to convey any of the poet's real grief, which was that of an unrequited lover, I smiled to myself, thinking of Miss Standish standing over us in the one-room schoolhouse back in Elysium, and I wondered if she had understood that and been unable to say so. I finished the Whitman section with a record of his lifelong dedication to his beloved president, shown in the Lincoln lectures he delivered in his old age. My closing statement was that to his countrymen. Lincoln was both less and more than he seemed to be, which is the nature of our heroes and idols, whose lives we appropriate for our own purposes. When I handed the paper in, I expected it would be received as the work of a good scholar and an original thinker. Instead, it came back with the following comment:

"D+ for your diligence and imagination, the only things that save you from failure. This paper is full of apocryphal stories and speculation rather than valid history. It is an insult to the president who is its subject and to the nation whose history we are studying—and especially to our most patriotic poet, whose opinions you not only distort for your own purposes, but rely upon too heavily for a balanced examination. A view of history through such a distorted lens is not true scholarship. It is defamation."

I tried to discuss these issues with my professor, but he refused to see me or any of the other students, stating in a note on his closed office door that the grades were final and any appeals would have to be made through the appropriate college-wide committee. In spite of the university's liberal reputation, I doubted that I had any better chance of a fair hearing at the appeals committee, given the nature of my subject. So, even though I was angry, I let the subject drop. I received a C in the course.

"You were skating on thin ice with that one," Harold counseled when I told him all about it.

"We're all on thin ice when it comes to the truth, my dear," I answered.

Harold and I had been having regular sex, which had grown more competent if not more impassioned on my part. While I had worked on my term paper, he had been painting strange pictures of yearning magenta eyes alluringly hidden behind blue veils. I told him they were very nice, but he would have to start packing them up. "Willard will be home at the end of the week. I'm afraid you'll have to find other accommodations very soon."

By the end of the week, Harold had grudgingly moved back to the dormitory. His ominous parting words were, "You're not finished with me yet, you know. A love like mine will not be destroyed by a little distance."

"I have other obligations, Harold," I said.

"Just tell me that we can still meet now and then whenever it's possible. Let me have at least that much to live on." He gave his strawberry hair a toss for punctuation. A tragic look was burning in his eyes.

"If it's possible," I agreed. "But I doubt that we can see each other very often."

"At least there's hope," he said. "That will sustain me while I'm living in hell." Something about him reminded me of Greta Garbo, but I wasn't sure what movie it was. He certainly didn't want to be alone, and I felt sorry for him as he trudged down the street burdened with his suitcase, easel, and paintbox. I knew life would not be very easy for him at the dorm, but what could I do?

Willard arrived the following day. His lips were pursed as he inspected the premises for signs of inattention. I'd made sure that everything was perfect. There was no trace of Harold's presence left. I'd combed the house twice, looking for anything that his ardor might have inspired him to leave behind in order to arouse Willard's suspicions. I'd dusted the furniture and washed the floors and the windows as well. I'd mowed the lawn and trimmed the privet hedge. I even had supper ready—a stew.

I could see the white gloves in Willard's eyes as they scanned the mantel, but I was confident that the house would pass inspection. He went from room to room as if he couldn't believe they were all equally tidy, but they were. Of course he pretended that he was just getting reacquainted with his beloved home. "It's so good to be back among familiar things," he kept exclaiming as he admired his own books and pictures and bric-a-brac. I assumed I was included in the inventory because he never once said how good it was to see me after three months' separation.

"Okay," he said as he concluded his inspection tour. "Let's bring in the luggage."

Great, I thought. The accommodations are clean enough to receive the sacred luggage.

"Be careful with it though. I have a surprise packed in it. "

How sweet, I thought. He's brought me a present. I forgave him his failure to be glad to see me, and we took his things upstairs. As he opened his drawer to find room for his belongings, we saw Harold's most flamboyant scarf—a cerise creation with gold threads running through it— lying extravagantly across Willard's mixed collection of lace panties and boxer shorts.

"What's this?" he said, somewhat disdainfully.

"Just a little welcome-home present," I lied, grateful for my presence of mind. "I thought you might like to wear it in the evenings."

"Sweet of you . . . thanks," he said with the slightest sneer in his voice. "It's lovely. I'm not sure it will go with my new things, though. Let's have supper."

We left the unpacking for later. Over dinner I asked him how his trip had been.

"Divine, as always," he said with a dreamy look in his eye.

"I sort of miss San Francisco a bit," I said. "More stew?"

"Yes, thanks. I know how you feel. You can be so free there."

Of course San Francisco wasn't then the gay capital it became later, but it was a lot more exciting than Madison could ever hope to be, and Willard felt relatively free there because he was far away from the people he worked with and from his "real" life. I wondered if he or I could ever feel really free anywhere, but I didn't inject that into the conversation. I wanted to start off the autumn with a positive evening.

After supper, Willard said, "And now it's time for us. I bet you thought I'd forgotten about that, didn't you?"

"I hoped you didn't," I said, trying to sound convincingly flirtatious.

"You clean up the supper dishes, and I'll get ready. Okay?"

I nodded and went right to work. I could hear him shuffling about upstairs as he unpacked. I wondered what he'd brought me. A book? A sweater? A knickknack from Chinatown? Soon I was finished with the dishes and I sat in the living room, waiting for the big surprise.

After half an hour of tissue paper rustling and suitcase slamming, Willard descended the stairs with a heavy clank of high-heeled shoes. He entered the living room with a flourish, turning around to make the flared bottom of his dress swirl while teetering only slightly on his sparkling white pumps, as if he were a mildly tipsy debutante. He was all in white—a clinging satin evening gown with shoulder straps, long gloves, and a chiffon kerchief in his hand. His lips were painted in a Cupid's bow, and a beauty mark accented the side of his chin. He wore a short wig waved in blaringly bleached blonde.

"How do you like it, big boy?" he asked.

Oh terrific, I thought. Good-bye, Veronica Lake. Hello, Jean Harlow.

"It's great," I said. "Beautiful."

"Okay lover boy, now you can kiss me," Professor Stevenson replied. "But try not to smudge my lipstick."

In spite of all the accoutrements, our lovemaking was as uninspired as usual. Absence had done little to make our hearts grow fonder, but we were both still satisfied with our arrangement. The interlude with Harold hadn't encouraged me to leave Willard, and Willard's annual trip to San Francisco was a self-contained voyage to never-never land, from which he returned to the reality of Madison as if awakening from a dream. I wouldn't have been at all surprised if he'd showed up with a replacement "nephew" for next semester, but since he hadn't found one, I would continue to do.

The next day, as he was settling into his syllabus preparations, I showed him my Lincoln term paper and the hostile comments on it.

"You must be out of your mind!" he said angrily.

"Why?" I inquired. "Are the ideas so preposterous?"

"Perhaps not," he answered, "but the idea of presenting them certainly is—especially to an ass like Hartsdale, the Mussolini of the history department. You're going to get yourself in a lot of trouble if you deal with subjects like this. You're almost begging the faculty to find out what you are—and worse, to find out about me. I'll let it slide this time, but if you want to stay here, you must promise me you won't deal with this subject again. Some stones are better left unturned."

"But what if these ideas are true?"

"What if they are?" he said. "That doesn't mean they have to be flung in America's face."

The next morning when I went to the back porch and opened the small wooden box which the milkman used for his deliveries, I found a note nestled among the tall, bulbous bottlenecks, where the cream had separated from the milk.

"I must see you," it read. "I'm desperate. Be at the library at 2 p.m., near the poetry corner. H."

I met him there as directed. He looked red-eyed and miserable.

"First of all, Harold, you can't leave notes there," I began, ignoring his condition. "What if Willard had opened the milk box?"

"What if I had died?" he said.

"What are you talking about? Did anyone attack you?"

"No," he said. "It's a different group from the summer school gang, so they don't know me or my reputation. Almost nobody's arrived yet for the fall semester, but I'm being so careful with my eyes that I look only at the floor. I hardly even know what the walls look like and I'm afraid to take a shower, except at six a.m. To make matters worse, I have to spend a few days back home in Indiana." He started to hum "The Banks of the Wabash" with a cruelly sardonic tone. But soon he was sniffling, and then the tears began. "I can't stand my life," he said. "I don't know if I can go on without you."

"Harold, we only spent a few weeks together. Be fair now. I told you the situation from the beginning. You mustn't depend on me so much. You have to learn to rely on yourself. Besides, I'm sure another Mr. Right will show up in your life soon. Meanwhile, I'll still see you when I can."

"Terrific," he said. "All I have to look forward to is the promise of nothing. I might as well be dead."

"Don't talk nonsense. You have your whole life ahead of you. Maybe you'll be a famous painter someday."

"Not according to Professor Bollinger. He said he likes me as a person, but it would be unkind to pretend that I had any talent."

"Maybe he was comparing you to Rembrandt or Michelangelo."

"What's wrong with that? If I were any good, I'd be able to stand such comparisons."

"If you expect too much of yourself, you won't appreciate what good you do produce. Why don't you give yourself a chance to grow up first?"

"Okay, but it's the last chance I'm giving myself, and if you won't see me, I won't come back to school at all."

"Come back to school, Harold. You don't want to stay in Speed, Indiana for the rest of your life, do you?"

"Not unless it's a short life," he said. "I couldn't take much more of that. I can barely stand it here. I don't belong anywhere. Oh, why was I born so weird? Why couldn't I just be an ordinary person?"

The tears were streaming down his face. I took him in my arms to comfort him, grateful that there was no one in that corner of the library to see us.

"My roommate hasn't arrived for the fall yet," he said, drying his eyes. "Will you come back to my dorm room with me?"

"I can only stay a little while," I said.

"I only need a little while," he said. "I come fast, remember?"

We had a brief, unamusing session in Harold's room. He was so eager to bind me to him that he overdid every gesture, and I was worried about getting back to Willard without arousing suspicion. Neither one of us had an orgasm. I was actually relieved that the imminent arrival of Harold's roommate would make his room unusable for such trysts, but of course I felt like a louse, knowing how needy Harold was.

He left for Indiana that evening, but he was back two days later. This time he telephoned the house.

"Harold, you cannot call me here. It's absolutely out of the question. Luckily Willard is out, but if you threaten my situation here, I won't see you at all. Is that clear?"

"I had an awful time," he said. "I just needed to tell somebody. Who can I talk to?"

"Oh all right. Meet me in the quadrangle," I said somewhat testily. "But I can't stay long. I have to get ready for classes."

The first autumn breezes were chilling the air as I walked to the campus. Harold sat on a bench wearing a school jacket enhanced with a paisley scarf. He had a dull look in his eyes.

"All right, what happened?" I asked,

"Nothing," he said. "Absolutely nothing."

"So what's the problem?"

"That's the problem. They hardly even talked to me. Two days of silence, as if I were a total stranger. Finally, at supper last night, my mother said, 'Harold, if you're going to wear those scarves indoors and out, maybe it would be better if you didn't visit home quite so often. You're becoming an embarrassment to us, son.' My father didn't say a word, but I could tell she was speaking for him. There was no point in discussing anything. I left on the first train in the morning. I didn't even say good-bye. Dan, you're all I've got in the world now."

"Harold, don't you think you might compromise a bit? If it's the scarves that bother them so much, maybe you could do without them, just for a weekend visit now and then."

"It isn't the scarves and we all know it. It's me that's the problem. There's no point in going back there."

"At least they're sending you through school. That's worth something."

"Sure," he said bitterly. "An educated weirdo is worth more than an uneducated one, but neither one is welcome in Indiana."

"The hell with Indiana, then. Get a degree and the world will be your oyster."

"Do you think clichés will solve all my problems? You always seem to have one ready," he said caustically.

I remained silent. The truth was I didn't have anything much better to offer him.

He took my silence for anger. "Don't be mad at me, Dan. I need a friend now. That's all."

"Okay, Harold. We'll think of something. First let's get started with the semester, okay? We'll figure out a plan later on."

"Don't worry, you won't have to take care of me," he said. "Just talk to me now and then."

"Of course," I answered, trying to sound warm. "We'll get together between classes."

"We can get together Mondays, Wednesdays, and Fridays at two," he said. "I signed up for the literature class you did."

"Great," I said halfheartedly. "Mondays, Wednesdays, and Fridays at two."

CHAPTER TEN

Mondays, Wednesdays, and Fridays at 2 looked like an all-out horror show to me. Harold wasn't the only problem in the class. David Halpin, whom I didn't trust to keep silent about our men's room encounter, sat right behind me with his girlfriend Beverly, both icily ignoring me. I did the same for them. I tried to switch into one of the other sections of English, but they were all full, and without this course my entire schedule would have fallen apart. So I gritted my teeth and continued along, consoling myself with the fact that Walt Whitman's "Song of Myself" was featured in the syllabus.

The instructor was a thick-waisted man with a dull wit. His name was Professor Morgan, and he was noted on campus for wearing the same green plaid bow tie and the same gray, V-necked sweater beneath the same drab tweed jacket throughout the entire semester. Early on, there was some minor speculation in the class about whether he ever had any of the ensemble dry-cleaned, but as the semester progressed, the growing dinginess of his wardrobe put a stop to that. The only thing animated about his appearance was his eyebrows. Beneath a bald head, his lackluster eyes, set in an expressionless face, were topped by bushy brows that seemed to rise and fall of their own accord, regardless of the subject under discussion. They lent an element of surprise to his otherwise static body. His pudgy-fingered hands remained still, often folded, as he sat behind his desk and spoke in a dry monotone about the tradition of spirituality in Western literature. My efforts to keep awake reminded me of how I had tried to keep conscious during Reverend Friendly's Sunday sermons back in Elysium. I almost found myself missing my father's elbow poking into my ribs, and for a day or two I considered writing a letter home just to find out how the old buzzard was doing. But I held firm until the feeling eased and soon it left of its own accord, like a brief cold snap in summer.

The first months of the semester went by without much trouble. Professor Morgan droned on and on about the Bible, Greek tragedy, and Dante's *Divine Comedy* while all of us did our best to listen. David and Beverly continued to keep their distance, which was fine with me. For the first few weeks, Harold waited to meet me after each class, his flamboyant scarves and rings always in startling contrast to the rest of his clothes. I did have coffee with him a few times, but I made a point of being cool to him, and I didn't pick up any of his hints about finding a place where we could have sex.

After several weeks had gone by, our meetings after class grew shorter and shorter. I sensed that he was distracted and hoped that he had developed some new interest, maybe even found a new object on whom to shower his intense affections. Eventually he didn't bother to wait for me, and when we did encounter each other our conversation was a lot lighter and less melodramatic. Not wanting to be any more involved with him than I had to be, I didn't press for an explanation, but greeted the new development with a sigh of relief and secret thanks to whoever it was who had taken him off my hands.

That year, the Kinsey Report came out and developed into a best seller. Reading it made me want to cheer. I almost wanted to stop Harold in the hall to tell him the comforting news that 50 percent of white American men admitted responding erotically to other men, but I decided to let him do his own research. I wasn't too surprised to learn that 37 percent of American men had had at least one homosexual experience after adolescence and that one out of eight were predominantly homosexual for at least three years, including the 4 percent who were exclusively homosexual. But the numbers were a little higher than even I had imagined.

The rest of America was shocked and indignant to be awakened from their illusions by these truths, and altogether outraged to learn that fully half of the nation's husbands had cheated on their wives and 95 percent had broken one law or another in pursuit of their sexual gratification. I memorized these statistics, so that I could recite them to myself if ever I felt alone in the world.

Willard was less excited about the news than I was, and cautioned me. "Don't think this is a license to blab about us. No one is going to hold us in any higher regard because there are more of us than they had thought there were. In fact, they'll probably see our kind as a greater threat than ever. Don't forget that what we do is still a crime. They can still fire me, or put us both in jail, or worse." I contented myself with him sexually, afraid to be caught with my pants down once again in the library men's room. It was sort of a dry time for me, but I decided that it was more important to have this chance at education than to play around. There would be plenty of time for that later, I hoped.

Once a week or so, Willard continued to don his extravagant drag. Most of our sex took place without it now, but there was something inside him that emerged periodically and wouldn't rest unless he was a glamour queen, and it made no difference to me. In fact it eventually seemed to be an unexceptional part of our household routine, almost as if we had a part-time boarder who dropped in now and then.

One night at the end of October, I was in the basement repainting the kitchen chairs. I'd been there for almost an hour when I heard a frantic rapping at the cellar window. My first thought was that it was Harold engaged in one of his desperate melodramas, but when I went to the window, which was covered with years of grime—due, I admit, to my imperfect housekeeping—it was Willard's angry face I saw. "Let me in," he said urgently through gritted teeth. "I'm locked out."

I went to the front door and didn't see him for a moment, so I waited. "Willard?" I called.

Finally I heard him coming around the side of the house, "Oh shit," he was saying, obviously for my benefit, "this boy is hopeless."

As he was scurrying across the front yard, I could see why he was so upset. He was wearing his Jean Harlow gown, but without benefit of wig or makeup. Just at that moment a carload of students pulled up, evidently heading to a party in a house across the street with a row of jack-o'-lanterns on its front steps. Willard tried to turn back to the driveway, then changed his mind and charged for the front porch. But it was too late.

"Hi, Professor Stevenson," a voice rang out. "Happy Halloween!"

"Happy Halloween," Willard said, in a tone that would have been more suitable to saying "Drop dead." And he brushed past me like a broomless witch, and collapsed on the living room sofa. I had all I could do to keep from laughing out loud as I called out, to no one in particular, "Happy Halloween?"

"Will you close that fucking door!" Willard snapped.

"But, Miss Harlow, you can't abandon your public," I said, trying to keep it light.

"I can abandon my fucking public, and I can abandon you too if you don't watch out," he said, his eyes glowering above his tightly pursed lips.

"Oh Willard, take it easy. There's no harm done. Surely even you can see the humor in the situation."

"Didn't you hear me calling you?" he asked.

"No, I can't hear you when I'm in the cellar."

"I was getting dressed . . . for the holiday," he said, as if he had to convince me of anything. "I'd bought a new lipstick, but I'd left it in the car, and I needed you to get it for me. It was too much trouble to get out of this damned outfit and back into it, so I thought I could slip into the garage without being seen. But the door locked behind me, and I didn't have my keys."

"No wonder—you have no pockets," I said.

Willard was not amused. "If I'd had my hair and face on, I might not have been recognized," he grumbled. "But of course you have to put the gown on first, so the makeup doesn't smear."

"It isn't easy being beautiful," I sighed.

"You'd better be grateful I am beautiful," he said coyly. "You wouldn't want Frankenstein to fuck you, would you?"

"Why not?" I quipped. "It's Halloween."

"And damned lucky it is, too," he said, dropping his coy tone. "If I got caught dressed like this any other day of the year, we might both be out of a job. Now hurry up and finish painting those chairs while I finish painting my face. But first make me a double scotch and soda. I need to calm down."

As we headed toward Thanksgiving, I started working on my term paper for Introduction to Literature. It was the only one that really interested me. My other courses were required subjects: physics and math—sheer drudgery for me. But in the English course, I could write about my favorite topic once more. In spite of the reception that my Lincoln essay had received, I decided to base my paper on the significance of Whitman's sexuality from the evidence in his letters, diaries, and textual revisions. It was the only subject I could get truly interested in. I figured I simply wouldn't show it to Willard since there was no reason to upset him.

Luckily the college library had some of the information I needed, and I was already familiar with the rest. All I had to do was put it together in the right way. I called the finished product:

THE REAL WALT WHITMAN

From evidence in Walt Whitman's journals and letters as well as his poems, we know that his sexual taste ran to young men and that there were many in his life. As a Brooklyn schoolboy he concealed his bookishness from the loafers he was attracted to at the docks. When he was a teenager teaching other teenagers in a one-room schoolhouse on Long Island, he boarded with his pupils' families, often sleeping in the attic with the sons. On at least one occasion he was asked to leave by an angry father. There is an old building still called the "Sodom School" in Southold, where he once taught. According to one account, he was denounced as a sodomite from the pulpit and tarred and feathered. But that is difficult to believe, considering that not even a veiled reference to such a trauma ever found its way into his writing.

In his early twenties, Walt wrote a series of short stories, which seem to reveal his youthful fantasies. "The Child and the Profligate" is the story of a widow's son named Charles, who is harassed by a drunken sailor in a tavern until a man named Langton comes to his aid and takes him to bed for the night. Whitman described the man lying next to the boy:

... he folded his arms around him, and, while he
slept, the boy's cheek rested on his bosom. Fair

were those two creatures in their unconscious beauty—glorious, but yet how differently glorious!

Later in the story, Whitman creatively passed judgment on the scene:

> With one of the brightest and earliest rays of the warm sun, a gentle angel entered his apartment, and hovering over the sleepers on invisible wings looked down with a pleasant smile and blessed them.

In the published edition of the story, Whitman drops this entire scene, and Langton merely arranges for Charles to sleep in another room at the inn. Walt may have removed the angel scene for artistic purposes, since it is rather far-fetched, but his deletions were just as likely inspired by his desire to keep his homoerotic portrait secret.

Whitman left behind a great many erasures and crossings out that show meanings altered for sound effects and structural purposes as well as for the sake of prudence. The most famous instance is the 1860 poem "Once I Pass'd Through a Populous City," which was apparently written about his trip to New Orleans in 1848, when he was twenty-eight years old. The original manuscript read, in part:

> But now of all that city I remember only a man who wandered with me there, for love of me, Day by day and night by night we were together. All else has long been forgotten by me—I remember only one rude and ignorant man who, when I departed, long and long held me by the hand, with silent lip, sad and tremulous.

In the published version, the man became "that woman who passionately clung to me." Such a change was not likely made for the sake of poetic rhythm. It was more likely made to disguise the poet's true experience, a homosexual relationship.

In his "Calamus" poems, he wrote of being in love:

> For an athlete is enamour'd of me, and I of him, But toward him there is something fierce and terrible in me eligible to burst forth, I dare not tell it in words, not even in these songs.

But he also described himself as someone:
  Who knew too well the sick, sick dread lest the one
  he lov'd might secretly be indifferent to him . . .

And finally he wrote of his disappointment:
  Hours continuing long, sore and heavy-hearted,
  Hours of the dusk, when I withdraw to a
  lonesome and unfrequented spot, seating myself,
  leaning my face in my hands . . .
  Hours discouraged, distracted—for the one I
  cannot content myself without, soon I saw him
  content himself without me;
  . . . (I am ashamed—but it is useless—I am what
  I am;)
  Hours of my torment—I wonder if other men
  ever have the like, out of the like feelings?
  Is there even one other like me—distracted—his
  friend, his lover, lost to him?

The artist in him, however, was more concerned with creating an idealized self-portrait than with revealing the true depth of his grief. So he removed that poem from the book and left instead a more positive, but less revealing, statement:
  (I loved a certain person ardently and my love
      was not return'd,
  Yet out of that I have written these songs.)

Walt spent the early years of the Civil War in Brooklyn, where he recorded in his diaries several incidents of picking up young men and taking them home "to sleep," even though they lived nearby:
  Saturday night Mike Ellis . . . took him home to
  150 37th Street . . . Dan'l Spencer . . . slept with
  me Sept 3d . . . Theodore M. Carr . . . came to
  the house with me . . . David Wilson—night of
  Oct 11, '62, walking up from Middagh—slept
  with me . . . October 9, 1863, Jerry Taylor . . .
  slept with me last night weather soft, cool
  enough, warm enough, heavenly.

Later in the Civil War Whitman was in Washington, DC, where he nursed the wounded of both sides, several of whom he grew romantically attached to, as witnessed by this letter to one of them:

> ... if you get these lines, my dear, darling
> comrade, and any thing should go wrong, so that
> we do not meet again, here on earth, it seems to
> me, (the way I feel now,) that my soul could
> never be entirely happy, even in the world to
> come, without you, dear comrade.

Early in 1865, when he was forty-five years old, Walt met
Peter Doyle, a twenty-one-year-old veteran of the Confederate
army who was working as a tram conductor. Here is Doyle's
account of their meeting:

> ... the storm was awful. Walt had his blanket—
> it was thrown round his shoulders—he seemed
> like an old sea-captain. He was the only
> passenger, it was a lonely night, so I thought I
> would go in and talk with him. Something in me
> made me do it and something in him drew me
> that way. He used to say there was something in
> me had the same effect on him. Anyway, I went
> into the car. We were familiar at once—I put my
> hand on his knee—we understood. He did not
> get out at the end of the trip—in fact went all the
> way back with me.

Soon they were fast friends and became daily companions
for the next seven years, enjoying long walks along the
Potomac while Whitman brought the barely literate young
man bunches of flowers and taught him about history and
astronomy and poetry. They didn't separate until 1873, when
Whitman suffered a major stroke and moved to Camden, New
Jersey to live with his brother. Nonetheless, Walt and Pete
wrote to each other sporadically for years and managed to visit
each other on a few occasions.

At the age of fifty-seven, Whitman had begun to recuperate
from his stroke. He was preparing the American centennial
edition of his poems when he encountered the young printer's
assistant Harry Stafford, who was then about eighteen years
old. Harry was moody and insecure and glad to have a mentor,
and soon Walt was visiting the farm where Harry's parents
lived. There he rediscovered the joys of nature, which helped
his recuperation along to the point where he could frolic with
his young companion. One of Walt's friends wrote that "they
cut up like two boys and annoyed me sometimes." And when
another friend invited Walt to visit him in New York State,

Walt wrote him that he would be accompanied by "my (adopted) son" and continued, "My nephew and I when traveling always share the same room together and the same bed." Their letters reveal that theirs was a stormy relationship, but despite their quarrels and despite the fact that Stafford eventually got married, the relationship between the poet and the young man was clearly a homosexual one.

While he conducted his relationship with Stafford, Walt also developed close relationships with John H. Johnston, Jr., the son of a Philadelphia artist, and with Albert Johnston, the son of a New York jeweler, as well as with Ed Cattell, a farmhand who worked for Harry Stafford's parents. In his semi-literate style, Cattell wrote:

> Would love to see you once moor for it seems an age Since i last met With you down at the pond and a lovely time we had of it to old man . . . i love you Walt and Know that my love is returned so i will Close

Apparently Walt was afraid that Harry might discover this liaison, for he responded from his Camden home:

> Do not call to see me any more at the Stafford family, & do not call there at all any more. Dont ask me why—I will explain to you when we meet. . . . I want you to keep this to yourself, & not mention it nor this letter to any one . . . & as to Harry you know how I love him. Ed you too have my unalterable love, & always shall have. I want you to come up here and see me.

When his sexual activities grew limited, Walt kept in his daybooks lists of young men he had encountered, including descriptions and biographical data. The following example is only one-half of such a list:

> Percy Ives, Mrs. Legget's grandson, age 16, a student intends to be an artist—lives bachelor's hall fashion in Philadelphia—reads Emerson, Carlyle, &c. March 1—driver I gave gloves—big, young, blonde Wm Powers/ boy 10 or 11, Eddy Rice newsboy, Ferry, Phila/ young new driver, sandy, Elias/ Clark Hilton extra conductor on 105 Market st.—I came down with (age 23 or '4) April 23 '81/ Wm Gibbs, umbrella maker . . . (age 20) / Wm Mosslander, paper hanging, on

> Federal St. above 5th—age 20—(on the boat
> April 23 evening) is a nephew of Delacour/
> druggist/ Sammy Cox boy, 17 or 18—Dick
> Davis's nephew—butter & cheese business in
> market stand—ice cream . . .

In an interview several years after he attended Whitman's funeral and more than twenty years after their separation, Peter Doyle said that he had kept Walt's old raglan overcoat:

> I now and then put it on, lay down, think I am in
> the old times. Then he is with me again. It's the
> only thing I kept amongst many old things.
> When I get it on and stretch out on the old sofa
> I am very well contented . . . I do not for a
> minute lose the old man. He is always near by.

Doyle's comment sounds more like the reminiscence of a lover than of a friend. Although there is no tangible proof, it seems probable that there was a sexual relationship between the two men.

Whatever men he may have known, the greatest love of Whitman's life was the figure he spoke to in his poems: "The great Camerado, the lover true for whom I pine," who was not only lover, but God, mentor, friend, and inspirational muse to the poet. No matter what physical sex happened between Walt and his comrades, his primary love was spiritual. Walt's Camerado is the soul of the universe, which he saw in the eyes of all the men he ever loved.

Whitman's homosexuality is the basis of his well-known spirituality and his widely applauded patriotism. All three themes come together in his poetry:

> I will plant companionship thick as trees along
>   all the rivers of America . . .
> I will make inseparable cities with their arms
>   about each other's necks,
>   By the love of comrades,
>   By the manly love of comrades.

The fact that America's favorite poet was homosexual does not limit the value of his poetry, but it does enrich our understanding of his vision. Without his appreciation of the affection possible between men, Whitman's poetry would lack the inspiration that makes it great.

I handed my masterpiece in on the Monday after Thanksgiving. The subject was a little controversial, I knew, but I was sure that the rich scholarship would overcome any misgivings on Professor Morgan's part. It had to be a better paper than he'd seen in years of teaching sophomore English. I could hardly wait until he returned it. Maybe it would be even better than an A. Maybe it would earn an A+.

Harold came up to me after class. He looked strangely pale. There was something different about him, but I wasn't sure what it was at first. Then I realized that he wasn't wearing his usual silk scarf and jewelry. On him, ordinary clothing without accessories had the look of sackcloth and ashes. "Can I talk to you?" he pleaded.

"Sure," I said, allowing the glow of achievement I felt about my term paper to extend to charitable feelings toward Harold. "Do you want to go for coffee?"

"Coffee, yes, coffee," Harold replied, as if coffee would be the answer to all his earthly problems.

We left the campus and went to a little coffee shop in town.

"Did you have a nice Thanksgiving?" I asked.

"The worst one of my life," he said. "I told my parents that I'm in love with a man—oh, it isn't you. I've met someone else."

I gave no voice to my relief. "What did your parents say?"

"They disowned me," he said, beginning to sniffle. Soon he was weeping audibly. After several moments, he regained control of himself and continued. "They told me not to come home anymore unless I was willing to live like a normal person. They said they wouldn't pay my tuition at school. They don't want anything to do with me." He heaved a great sigh.

"Well, maybe it's for the best," I consoled him. "Now you're free to live your life your own way."

"But I don't even know how to make a living," he whispered. "How can I survive?"

"What about this man you're in love with?" I asked. "Can't he help out a little?"

"Just because I'm in love with him doesn't mean he's in love with me," he answered, tossing his strawberry hair from his forehead.

"Are you actually having a relationship? Are you sleeping together?"

"When and where we can. He lives in a rooming house. We can't go there. And I live in the dorm. We can only use my room when my roommate's away and the halls are completely clear, so he can sneak in— which is practically never."

"Who is he?"

"I'd rather not say. I promised I wouldn't use his name."

"Well, at any rate, your tuition's already paid for this semester. That gives you a little time to think."

"It's only a few weeks until Christmas. Then what?"

"Maybe you can get a part-time job to help you get through school. If that doesn't work out, you could always take a leave and work until you've saved enough money to come back. You're in a tight situation, but it isn't the end of the world."

"I'm not so sure," he said, so softly that I could scarcely hear his words.

"Things will look better in the morning. You'll see."

"You've always been good with the clichés," he said. "You don't really care what happens to me."

"Harold, I do care about you, in my way. I just can't take charge of your whole life. I'm not doing all that well with my own."

"At least you're getting the help you need," he said accusingly.

"Well, maybe you'll get the help you need, too. At least ask your lover. You can do that much for yourself."

"Thanks for nothing," Harold said with resignation.

"Well, I'd help you if I could," I said, feeling guilty and resenting him for wanting me to.

"I know you would," he said, changing his tone. "I didn't mean to accuse you of anything. I know I have to look after myself. I'll manage somehow."

"That's the spirit," I said, glad to be off the hook and ashamed because I was glad. I left the coffee shop a few minutes later.

The next time I saw him we were in class, discussing "Song of Myself" by Walt Whitman. Professor Morgan sat immobile at his desk. Aside from his mouth, only his syncopated eyebrows were in motion as he spoke of Whitman's spiritual nature. "Whitman goes as far as to make love to his own soul," he said, quoting these lines:

I mind how we lay in June, such a transparent summer
    morning,
You settled your head athwart my hips, and gently turned
    over upon me,
And parted the shirt from my bosom-bone, and plunged your
    tongue to my bare-stript heart,
And reached till you felt my beard, and reached till you held
    my feet.

"Are you sure that he's only describing spiritual love?" asked Harold in a quiet voice. It was one of the only times he had volunteered an opinion in class, so even people who ordinarily paid little attention were listening.

"What do you mean?" asked Professor Morgan.

"It sounds awfully . . . sexual to me," Harold said. "If you figure out that position, one's head across the hips of another face downward, it seems that what's going on is—what's the word for it?—fellatio."

The other students gasped and tittered. Several even laughed out loud. Professor Morgan's eyebrows helplessly raised themselves several consecutive times, as if they had lost their moorings. He cleared his throat. "Whitman begins this section with the words, 'I believe in you my soul.' Therefore, the entire passage is addressed to his soul. So it is his soul that embraces his supine form, 'Song of Myself' is a spiritual poem, not a lascivious one."

Harold didn't answer. He shrank in his seat.

"Excuse me, Professor," I said, breaking the uncomfortable silence after several moments had passed. "Whitman says, when he addresses his soul, 'The other I am must not abase itself to you, and you must not be abased to the other.' Isn't 'the other' his body? And isn't he saying that body and soul are equal?"

"Perhaps that is part of his statement," Morgan said with a slight harrumph. "But you might also note that the two equals form a cross in the position the poet describes."

"I'd say it was more of a T than a cross. Besides, Whitman wasn't what you'd call a Christian, was he?"

The professor's brows lowered sternly. "He was a disciple of Emersonian transcendentalism. A pantheist."

"Then why would he form a cross?" I asked.

"You speak with considerable expertise for a sophomore. How would you read the passage?" he asked, gloating.

Without lowering my eyes to the text, keeping my gaze fixed on Morgan's face, I said, "I would connect it with what comes afterward:

'Swiftly arose and spread around me the peace and
    knowledge that pass all the argument of the earth,
And I know that the hand of God is the promise of my own,
And I know that the spirit of God is the brother of my own,
And that all the men ever born are also my brothers, and the
    women my sisters and lovers,
And that a kelson of the creation is love . . .'

I think the first passage is a sexual one, and it isn't clear that he's talking to his soul, because he shifts his pronouns in several places in his poems. What is clear is that the sexual experience is what gives rise to the spiritual feeling. Making love to a man who is the same as he is opens his awareness to the sameness of all creation."

Professor Morgan sat quietly thinking for several minutes, and the class remained hushed in expectation. Finally he said, "There is no way to prove what a dead poet had in his mind when he wrote. Perhaps we can sum up all this confusion with another line from the same poem: 'Do I contradict myself? Very well then I contradict myself, (I am large, I contain multitudes.)'"

Then David raised his hand.

"Yes, Mr. Halpin," the professor said with an exhausted air.

"I don't think we should be reading this sort of thing in class in the first place," David said. "It's immoral. It's almost pornographic. It gives people wrong ideas."

"That conclusion is exactly the one I had hoped you would not draw. There is no concrete evidence that Whitman had any real sexual contact, and although he was accused of lewdness in his own more prudish century, I think I can demonstrate to your satisfaction that his spiritual interests completely supplanted his physical drives. If anything, he worshiped an ancient Egyptian 'life force,' which inhibited carnal extravagance. Let us turn to another part of the poem then, one less susceptible to misinterpretation, and perhaps we can get this discussion back on a more scholarly and spiritual plane, which is what I believe the poet intended in the first place. Look at this line:

'I am an acme of things accomplish'd, and I an encloser of
    things to be.'

Surely you don't find immoral sex in that line, Mr. Fisher?" He was addressing Harold, who remained silent. "Mr. Blake?"

"No, sir," I replied.

"Mr. Halpin?"

"No, sir, but I do see a large ego."

"Very well then, let us continue," Professor Morgan said. "Whitman is often accused of egotism; however, the word 'I' is used to represent not just himself but all humanity, indeed all creation. With that in mind, we can see that the statement is a spiritual one. Are there any questions?"

There were none, so he folded his pudgy hands and returned his eyebrows to their resting place. Then, content that education had been accomplished, he went on with his lecture.

At the end of that week my term paper was returned. It had no mark on it, only the following comment:

No grade. In spite of the appearance of scholarship, this paper is based on speculation, closer to unsavory gossip than to literary analysis. Even if your conclusions were true, they are irrelevant. What bearing can they have on our interpretation of Whitman's work? Also, you refer to the poet as "Walt," which is an inappropriate form—unless, of course, you are personally acquainted with him.

I was furious. After class I waited until the others had left, so I could talk to Morgan. He gathered his lecture notes hurriedly, as if to signify that he had urgent business elsewhere, but I stood between him and the door.

"Professor," I said, "I have to tell you that I disagree with your comments on my paper."

"I assumed that you would, Mr. Blake. However, it is my job to teach you the art of scholarship, not to encourage you in gossip mongering."

"I accept your label of my work as 'speculation,' but I certainly think there was enough evidence presented to take it beyond mere gossip. I wasn't simply name-calling, you know. I don't presume to judge Whitman's sexuality—or anyone's. It's just that I believe that the poet's life should not be divorced from the poetry, and the poet's sexuality should not be divorced from his life. In this case, I think it helps us to understand the truth."

"Perhaps you are not aware of the New Criticism, Mr. Blake," he said, his eyebrows held sternly at half-mast. "In the mid-twentieth century, we are more interested in what is written on the page than in what did or did not transpire in the author's bedroom."

"I guess we're never going to agree on this," I said. "Is there anything I can do to get my grade?"

"Well, you might submit a substitute for this paper. I don't do this for everyone, but I am willing to read a second essay if you are willing to write one. I think that's a fair offer. And I think you will have learned a valuable lesson from the experience."

I was learning a valuable lesson all right, but it wasn't the one he thought it was. I tried not to sound sarcastic. "Suppose I write about Whitman's spirituality?" I suggested. "That ought to be a more acceptable topic."

"Yes. But it, too, is a rather nebulous area, you know."

"I have an idea about that passage from 'Song of Myself' that we discussed earlier this week—you know, the one where body and soul communicate? Do you know what 'astral projection' is? I've been reading about it."

"Well," he said, pompously clearing his throat and letting his eyebrows go loose, "perhaps I'll learn something new."

"Perhaps you will," I said sweetly.

I said nothing to Willard about my essay or Morgan's reception of it, for fear that he would get angry. I had no one to share my problem with, so I just set about writing my new paper. I cut my other classes and was busy for days at the library assembling citations for the information, which I was already familiar with. I worked late into the nights at the writing, putting a Turkish towel under the typewriter to muffle its sound so that Willard could sleep. He didn't bother me since he was busy himself marking his own students' term papers. I thought my new essay was more speculative than the first one, but matters of the spirit are even more intimate than matters of the flesh, and who can prove what's true and what isn't? I called my new paper:

WALT WHITMAN: THE MYSTIC AWARENESS

Walt Whitman subscribed to the world view known as transcendentalism, which Ralph Waldo Emerson popularized, based on his readings from Hinduism, Taoism, and Buddhism. According to the transcendentalists, the individual identity is part of a universal "oversoul" to which it returns at death, much as a bucket of water may be taken from the ocean, have a temporary separate identity, and then be returned to the ocean, becoming indistinguishable from the rest once more. The oversoul includes not only all people, but all of nature, both living and non-living. More than any other subscriber to transcendentalism, Whitman was able to speak with the voice of the universe in his poems, expressing an extraordinary sense of unity with the cosmos.

What is the source of the poet's special vision? One of Whitman's disciples, Dr. Richard Maurice Bucke, wrote a book called *Cosmic Consciousness*, a term which describes the ability to experience directly the unity of all creation. Bucke believed that Whitman exhibited that sensibility in the same way that Jesus and Buddha did, and considered those who manifest such awareness to be a superior order of beings.

A good deal of controversy rages over whether Whitman had a specific "mystical experience" that permanently altered his consciousness and gave rise to his remarkable poetry. Some critics believe his writing was mediocre and showed little promise until his early thirties, when he published the first edition of *Leaves of Grass* and suddenly emerged as a noteworthy poet. Dr. Bucke, who visited and corresponded with Whitman at length about this subject, believes that Whitman experienced a mystical illumination on a June morning in 1853 or 1854. William James, author of *The Varieties of Religious Experience*, cites Section 5 of "Song of Myself," in which the poet addresses his soul as a lover and then describes a sense of religious ecstasy. James finds this passage "a classical expression of this type of sporadic mystical experience."

Exactly what type of experience might Whitman have had? It was spontaneous, it dealt with a separation of body and spirit, and it gave rise to a sense of well-being and universal unity. One experience recorded in the annals of mysticism has all these traits. It is an experience of disembodiment called "astral projection," in which the individual's consciousness separates itself from the physical body and floats above it, encased in a sheer, luminous duplicate of the physical body, which is connected to it by a "non-physical" cord and is able to move, independent of gravity, at the direction of will power.

This "astral body" is described in the literature of a mystical sect called the Theosophists, founded by H. P. Blavatsky in the late nineteenth century, whose members subscribe to the same concept of pantheistic-universal brotherhood that Whitman described in his poetry. According to William Q. Judge, in *The Ocean of Theosophy*:

> The astral body is made of matter of very fine texture as compared with the visible body, and has a great tensile strength, so that it changes but little during a lifetime, while the physical alters every moment . . . but at the same time possesses an elasticity permitting its extension to a considerable distance . . . The matter of which it is composed is electrical and magnetic in its essence . . .

Whitman's poetry has many images which might refer to an astral body, for example:

> If I worship any particular thing, it shall be
> some of the spread of my body,
> Translucent mould of me, it shall be you!

He refers to the experience of separation from the physical body in some instances:

> That shadow my likeness that goes to and fro
> seeking a livelihood, chattering, chaffering,
> How often I find myself standing and looking
> at it where it flits . . .

and:

> . . . affectionate, haughty, electrical,
> I and this mystery here we stand.

and:

> As I walk'd with that electric self . . .

Finally, the experience of projecting the astral body is described:

> I project myself—also I return.

It is also possible that the "Camerado" Whitman often refers to as a companion is his own astral body. So when Whitman describes his soul turning over on his body in a sexual act, he may be describing sex with his astral self, which led to a spiritual awakening.

Whether Whitman had this specific experience cannot be proved with concrete evidence. What can be shown is that something in his consciousness led him to separate his body from his spirit and to identify one with the other. In doing so, he became seen as a sexual pervert and a religious prophet. He may have been neither or both. But he was certainly a great poet, one who created a body of literature that relates the physical and astral planes of existence in a way that no one had done before.

When I was finished, I felt that I had done a good job. If that wasn't scholarship enough, I thought, then fuck sophomore English. In fact, fuck school altogether.

I had hoped for a little praise before showing it to Professor Morgan, whose reaction I expected to be negative, but since Willard was at work the morning that I finished, I couldn't show it to him. That was probably just as well, I realized. Willard probably wouldn't have liked it either.

I headed for class without showing it to anyone. When I arrived, I thought I was in the wrong room. Professor Morgan wasn't in front of the class. In his place stood a frail-looking elderly man with rimless spectacles. I looked around, feeling that missing nearly a week of classes had turned me into Rip Van Winkle awaking to a world he couldn't fathom. Then I saw David Halpin, sitting in the front row, and several other faces I recognized. So I sat down.

"Good afternoon," the strange teacher began. "My name is Professor Birdwell. Professor Morgan was called away suddenly, and I will be finishing the semester with you. Can someone tell me what you've been discussing up to now?"

After class, I went up to the new professor to find out what had happened. He was no help. I took my term paper with me and turned to leave. David Halpin was standing in the hall, surrounded by a bunch of students eager to get the dirt.

"It happened last night," he was telling them. "I'm on the same floor as Harold Fisher. You know—that weird guy with the reddish blond hair and the fancy scarves and rings?" One of the guys wet his pinky and drew it daintily across his eyebrow to describe Harold, and the others laughed in recognition. I winced. "They started arguing at about one in the morning."

"Who?" someone asked.

"It was Morgan. I could recognize his voice. He was fighting with Harold."

"What was he doing in the dorm?" someone else inquired. Various voices chimed in.

"Beats me. I think Harold's roommate caught them."

"Maybe Morgan was tutoring Harold."

"In what? Cornholing?"

"What's cornholing?"

"*Shhh.* I'll tell you later."

"So, what happened?"

David continued. "Finally, a lot of guys woke up. Morgan was trying to sneak down the stairs, but everybody saw him. The word is that the dean of faculty gave him his walking papers this morning."

"Just like that?"

"What else would you do with a pervert?"

"What about Harold?" I asked.

"You'd better go look for him, if you're so interested," David said. "He ran out of the dorm last night, and nobody's seen him since."

I went out to find Harold, but I hardly knew where to begin. The streets were icy and the air was thick with snow. I looked around the dormitory, the library, and the coffee shop we had visited, but there wasn't a trace. Finally, I just began to wander around the town.

I arrived at the lakefront just in time to see the men carrying his body onto the shore. Evidently he'd run out onto the frozen lake during the night and fallen through the thin ice. No one knew whether he'd gone there on purpose, but I was sure he had. He'd had nowhere to go and no one to turn to. His face was blue-gray and frozen in a bizarre grimace. His shock of strawberry blond hair was rigidly plastered to his forehead. Icicles dripped from his hair, from his eyelids, even from his fingertips. He looked like a hideous sculpture of the ghost of winter. Grief-stricken and ashamed, I turned away.

When I got back to the house, Willard was there with his lips sternly pursed. "Did you hear about Morgan?" he asked.

"Yes, it was all over school."

"Things are going to get pretty bleak around here for a while."

"They just found his boyfriend's body in the lake," I told him.

"Did you know him?"

"He was in my class."

"Too bad."

"What now?" I asked.

"I'm afraid, Danny," he said.

I looked at him. The statement was so unlike him. His face seemed ashen. There were tears in his eyes.

"Hold me," he said, with a pleading tone in his voice.

I held him.

"You know, I may not always show it, but I really do care for you," he said.

"I guess we've gotten pretty used to each other," I said. "I care for you too."

"That's why this hurts me so much," he said, sniffling.

"What does?"

"That I have to ask you to leave."

I released him and stepped back to look at him.

"I can't help it," he whimpered. "Don't blame me. They'll be watching all of us now. If our situation is discovered, it will cost me my job."

"It's costing me mine," I said.

"I'll give you some money. We'll keep in touch. Maybe later you can come back. When all this is forgotten."

"It won't be forgotten," I said.

"Do you hate me?"

"No, Willard, I don't hate you. It's probably better this way. I'll leave first thing in the morning, okay?"

"I knew you'd understand."

"Yes, I understand."

That night I packed a suitcase with my clothes, my two term papers, my copy of *Leaves of Grass*, and Minerva White's photographs. I left soon after it was light. I was halfway to the train station before I realized it was Christmas Day.

PART IV
DELL BLAKE

Prais'd be the fathomless universe,
For life and joy, and for objects and knowledge curious.
And for love, sweet love—but praise! praise! praise!
For the sure-enwinding arms of cool-enfolding death.

—Walt Whitman,
"When Lilacs Last in the Dooryard Bloom'd"

CHAPTER ELEVEN

The railroad station was closed when I arrived, so I sat huddled in the cold for an hour, trying not to think about Willard and Harold or about my future. I had no idea where I was going, but the schedule said the next train was heading southward in the middle of the afternoon, and that was as good a direction as any, I decided. I bundled my coat around me and did my best to keep warm.

Suddenly a voice cut sharply through the wintry air. "You waitin' fo' de train, honey?"

I looked up to see a bosomy black woman in a short fur shrug, raccoon probably, with squared shoulders. Her knee-length black satin skirt was so tight that she had to mince rather than walk, and her ankle-high overshoes were not sufficient for the deep snow. Only net stockings covered her bronze legs. Her hair was the improbable color of copper wire and seemed ablaze in the December morning sunlight. Her eyes revealed nothing about her, but she had a friendly smile, broadly outlined in magenta lipstick.

I nodded. "But the next train's not for quite a while."

"Not fo' hours," she said. "You gonna sit out here in de cold all dat time?"

"I have no place else to go."

"Me neither," she said. "Ain't it a bitch?"

"Sure is," I agreed.

"Merry Christmas anyways," she said. "Mah name Maisie Dot—Maisie Dot McCoy."

"Dan Blake," I answered. "Merry Christmas, Maisie Dot."

She sat down next to me, cuddling close for warmth without asking if it was all right. I didn't mind. I needed the warmth as much as she did.

"Ah was jus' passin' through here las' night," she said. "A gentleman asked me to keep him company, but Ah waked up all by mah lonesome. He didn't even be nice enough to leave me none o' mah money. Some Christmas present."

"I kind of got kicked out of where I was living," I told her. "That's a nice present too."

"Well, de hell wit' it. Let's jus' make de best of it. Where y'all headin'?"

"I'm not sure. How about you?"

197

"Ah's goin' to Chicago, honey. Gonna set myself up someplace warm fo' de rest o' de winter."

"Sounds smart," I said.

"Listen, you wouldn't be wantin' to rent a room fo' a couple hours? You knows, to kill a little time? Ah can make you feel real good, make you forget your worries."

"I don't think so, Maisie Dot," I said.

"A little short on cash?"

"No, that's not it. I have a little."

"Don't you think Maisie Dot be pretty 'nuff?"

"Sure I do. You're real pretty. I'm just not in the mood. That's all."

"Ah guess Ah can understan' dat. Holiday spirit got you down, right?"

"Something like that."

She sat up straight and backed off a few inches. She looked at me for a while. I tried to return her cool, appraising gaze, but my eyes dropped several times. Then she spoke. "Ah knows what it be," she said. "Y'all don' really go in much fo' de womans, does you?"

"Sure I do," I lied. "I like women just fine. But I told you, I'm just not in the mood."

"Listen, chile. It all right wit' me if you don' want a nice warm woman's body in yo' bed wit' you. Ah meets mo' den enough men who does. Ah's jus' tryin' to work up mah carfare to Chicago, dat's all."

I raised my coat collar up around my cheeks a little higher and tried to snuggle into its warmth. I guess I was sulking a little at being identified as queer so easily. Maisie Dot just sat there, a foot away, fiddling with her black gloves. I noticed that the seam of one of them was ripped at the base of the thumb.

Finally I spoke. "Okay," I said. "You were right. I don't go out much with women. I just didn't like the idea of my personal business being out in the open so fast."

"Dat's okay, chile," she said. And she slid toward me again, snuggling close for my warmth. "It don' make no nevermind to me if you likes de boys or de girls. I was jus' doin' mah job. Know what Ah means?"

I nodded.

"Fact is, Ah had me mo'n a few womans in mah bed ova de yeahs," she said. "Can't say a man's any better'n a woman at makin' me feel good—jus' different. Queer boys has been some o' mah best friends. Ah ain't got nothin' against 'em. Girl can't make no livin' off 'em, is all."

I relaxed. "I'm not exactly sure I'm queer, not for good anyway. I have been to bed with women—a couple of them, in fact."

"It don' make no nevermind. De main thing be if you a good man, and Ah can tell you is. Now how 'bout buyin' Maisie Dot some breakfast? Ah knows where dere a diner open not too far from here."

"Okay. I guess I need something to eat myself."

We trudged through the calf-high snow to a little eatery that looked as if it had never seen better days and never would. I ordered a cup of coffee and a sweet roll, and Maisie Dot ordered bacon and eggs with hashed brown potatoes, coffee, and a side of buttered toast. She watched me as we ate, as if she were afraid to let me out of her sight.

When I came back from a trip to the men's room, I could see that my suitcase was in a different place from where I'd left it, and I wondered whether she'd opened it.

Seeing me notice the suitcase, she said, "Oh, Ah moved yo' satchel, honey. Where it be now, it help to block de draft comin' in from de front do'. Mah legs was gettin' cold. Mus' be ten below zero out dere."

She proceeded to wipe her mouth with a napkin, which looked like a wounded soldier's bandage when it was covered with her rich magenta lipstick. Then she began to reapply her makeup, which proved to be a major undertaking.

"Girl got to be lookin' good if she be wantin' to make a livin'," she said as she noticed me watching her.

When she was finished, she walked over to the counterman. "You wouldn't be interested in a li'l company dis col' Christmas Day now, would you, hon?"

"I'm working, lady," he said gruffly.

"Ain't no harm in tryin', is dere?" She had turned back to me, so it wasn't clear which one of us she was talking to. The rest of the diner was empty. She sat down at the table and deposited her elbow on it, then placed her chin in her open palm. Her nail polish shone ruby red in the light from the window. "Now how'm Ah gonna get me to Chicago?" she asked the air.

I don't know what prompted me, embarrassment maybe, but after a brief silence, I said, "Listen, Maisie Dot, I can lend you carfare to Chicago. It's not so much. I can afford it."

Her eyes lit up beneath her mascara-laden lids. "Whah, Danny, dat bein' a real gentleman. Ah thanks you. At least somebody 'roun' here gots de Christmas spirit. Waiter, Ah'll have me some apple pah wit' mah coffee, if you don' mind."

Watching her eat the apple pie reminded me of Christmases back in Elysium. Mrs. Warner had been especially proud of her pies—Dutch apple, French apple, and apple crumb. Then I thought of Laura's apple dinner in Seattle, and depression settled around my head and shoulders like a heavy woolen blanket without warmth "What de matter, honey? Got de holiday blues?" asked Maisie Dot through a mouthful of pie.

"I guess so," I mumbled. "It's hard not to."

"Too bad dere ain't nobody wantin' a little cheerin' up from Maisie Dot dis chilly Christmas Day. It jus' de thing to take a man's mind off his troubles."

Within half an hour we found ourselves in the lobby of a sleazy hotel near the railroad station. It promised no cheer at all, not even when the dour clerk in the threadbare sweater welcomed Maisie Dot. "Back so soon? And with luggage this time, I see," he said, eyeing my suitcase like a prize.

"It too cold out dere for waitin'," she said. "We needs to keep us warm, an' dis be de onliest place open 'roun' here."

The clerk gave us the key to a dreary room with rickety furniture and dingy wallpaper punctuated with clusters of faded flowers. Whatever colors the decor had started out to be seemed to have given up, and everything looked the same dingy tone. I plopped myself down on the bed, which groaned its acceptance of my weight.

Maisie Dot began a careful removal of her clothes, one article after another dangling from her thumb and forefinger before she dropped it to the cracked linoleum. Her act was calculated to excite me, but of course it only depressed me more.

When she was down to her slip, she turned to me and said, "Now, Ah knows you been nice 'bout breakfast and promisin' me mah train fare an' all dat, but dis here's work for me, understan'? And Ah gots to ask for mah pay up front. Dis be de same room where de man cheated me las' night."

"How much?" I said, trying to sound sympathetic.

"Ten," she said. "Holiday special."

I wondered how much her non-holiday price was, but I didn't ask. I took a ten dollar bill from my wallet, which I carefully replaced in the side pocket of my pants. She tucked the two bills in her beaded purse and said, "Might as well take off yo' clothes and get comfortable, honey. We's got a long wait."

I stripped down to my underwear, and she got down to her lace panties, leaving her large-cupped bra on the floor beside the bed. "Here," she said, taking my hand and putting it to her brown tipped breast, "hold dis, it'll keep yo' hand warm."

I held her breast gingerly. Then I moved my hand from one nipple to the other. I put my arms around her and kissed her, gently at first then deeply on the mouth. We rocked back and forth together. Then she put her hand into my underwear and cupped my balls. "Seem pretty quiet down here," she said.

She moved her head quickly to my groin, opening the buttons of my boxer shorts and engulfing my cock with her lips in the same gesture. I could feel the softness and the wet warmth, but I didn't feel any excitement. I was more anxious than bored. I was remembering my sexual failure with Kelly Barrett back in high school and wondering what had become of her, whether she had found a woman to love. Then I started to think of Laura, who represented my total experience of sexual success with women. I wondered if I should try to contact her to ask after our son, but I didn't think I could face her, not even on the telephone.

Maisie Dot raised her head. "No good, huh? Well, it don' make no nevermind to me. De main thing be to get warm." She lay down beside me and we held each other tightly. I could see her magenta lipstick all over my cock, making it look like a stalk of limp rhubarb. We lay there like that for almost an hour.

When we got to the train station, we still had to wait for another hour before the afternoon train to Chicago showed up. Once we were onboard, we relaxed into our seats and watched the snow-covered fields and towns slip by the window. We had lunch in the dining car, my treat again. I took out *Leaves of Grass* to read, and Maisie Dot, bored to the point of large yawns, began to read over my shoulder. Ever the missionary for Walt Whitman, I turned to an appropriate poem:

To a Common Prostitute

Be composed—be at ease with me—I am Walt Whitman,
    liberal and lusty as Nature,
Not till the sun excludes you do I exclude you,
Not till the waters refuse to glisten for you and the leaves to
    rustle for you, do my words refuse to glisten and rustle
    for you.

My girl I appoint with you an appointment, and I charge you
    that you make preparation to be worthy to meet me,
And I charge you that you be patient and perfect till I come.

Till then I salute you with a significant look that you do not
    forget me.

"Why you pick dat book to read?" asked Maisie Dot suspiciously.
"I thought you might like it. This is my favorite book of poems."
"What make you think Ah'd like dis particular page? Is you sayin' dat Ah's common? What dat mean anyhow?"
"It means ordinary."
"An' dat be what you thinks Ah is—ordinary?"
"No, Maisie Dot, you're not ordinary. You're quite exceptional."
"Dat be good, huh?"
"Yes."
"What dat business be 'bout de water glistenin'?"
"He's saying that you deserve as much as anybody else does."
"Not mo'?"
"Well, at least as much. Not less, anyhow."

"Ah guess dat be okay. How 'bout dis line?" she asked, putting her crimson fingernail on the word *appointment*. "He tryin' to make a date?"

I nodded.

"Den why don't he jus' come right out and say so?"

"He did."

"Well, maybe he did," she conceded. "But he ain't gonna get away wit' chargin' her. He de customer. He gots to do de payin'."

I laughed. "This poem is almost a hundred years old, so the language is a little different. When he says 'charge' he means to give instructions. He's just telling her to get dressed up and put on her makeup."

"Don' she know dat bah herself? What kinda ho' she be? An' look at dat *Be patient till Ah comes*. Is dat because he take an extra long time to shoot out his load or somethin'?"

"I hope not. He just means that she should wait for him."

"Don' he 'spect her to make a livin' in de meantime? If he was shoppin' at de grocery, he wouldn't 'spect de grocer not to sell nothin' until he decide to show up, right? Dat ain't no way to run no business."

"You're right," I said. "He probably wasn't looking at it that way."

"Prob'ly think he doin' her some big favor. Lotta white men look at it dat way. Look at dat: he givin' her a *significant look*. What dat supposed to be? If she smart, she better ask fo' cash, not no 'significant look.' Can't pay de rent wit' no significant looks."

"You really know your stuff," I said. "He probably didn't really have much experience with hookers."

"Den maybe he a li'l bit queer, like you."

"Maybe. Is that bad?"

"Don' make no nevermind to me."

"He just wanted to say that prostitutes are the same as everyone else," I explained. "He meant well."

"Dat ain't no big deal," she said.

"I guess not. To tell you the truth, he makes out like he's being honest, but when he talks to women, he doesn't sound very real to me. Let me get your opinion. You sure did a good job on that last poem." I riffled through some pages until I found what I was looking for. "Listen to this.

" 'It is I, you women, I make my way,
I am stern, acrid, large, undissuadable, but I love you,
I do not hurt you any more than is necessary for you,
I pour the stuff to start sons and daughters fit for these
　　　States, I press with slow rude muscle,
I brace myself effectually, I listen to no entreaties,
I dare not withdraw till I deposit what has so long
　　　accumulated within me.'

"Well, what do you think?"

"What does Ah think 'bout what?"

"Did you think that sounded sexy?"

"Is you kiddin' me?"

"No."

"Lemme see dat."

I showed her the book and she fussed over the passage, trying to make sense out of it, silently mouthing the words and pointing back and forth with her bright fingernail. Finally she said, "Dis be some heavy bullshit."

"Why do you say that?"

"Firs' of all, a man be tryin' to get some woman in bed, he talk plain English. Know what Ah means? He don' say, 'Ah am stern.' He say, 'Lah down, bitch, Ah's gonna fuck you.' "

I laughed with delight. "Go on," I urged.

"Beside dat, what kinda man use words his woman ain't gonna understan'? What dat mean: 'acrid'?"

"Strong. Or sharp-smelling."

"Den maybe he better take himself a bath. And what dis: 'undis . . .'?"

"Undissuadable. That means she can't stop him."

"Den I guess dat bath don' make no nevermind. Anyway, she sure ain' gonna be turned on bah dis baloney."

"Actually, he's writing this to all women, not just to one."

"Den he better write a powerful lot mo'. Dis crap ain't gonna get even one woman on her back, let alone all of us."

"You're absolutely right," I said. "Now let's take a look at one more."

"Okay," she said. "But jus' one. Dis stuff wearin' me out. Ah gots to get me some beauty sleep."

"Here it is." I read to her:

> " 'O to draw you to me, to plant on you for the first time the
> lips of a determin'd man . . .
>
> To have the gag remov'd from one's mouth!
> To have the feeling to-day or any day I am sufficient as I am . . .
>
> To drive free! to love free! to dash reckless and dangerous!
> To court destruction with taunts, with invitations!
> To ascend, to leap to the heavens of the love indicated to me!
> To rise thither with my inebriate soul!
> To be lost if it must be so!'

"How's that?" I asked. "Better?"

"A little," she said. "But Ah can tell y'all one thing. Dat guy better have a powerful lotta money if he really 'spectin to get laid. His talk ain't gonna do him much good."

"But was it sexier than the first one I read to you?"

"Not much. But he sure sound mo' excited, Ah could see dat. Is he talkin' to de same womans here?"

"He doesn't say. Personally, I think he's talking to a man in this one. He's saying he doesn't care anymore what the world thinks about two men making love. He just wants to be himself."

"Well, dat mo' like it anyways. What dat 'bout 'inebriate'?"

"That means drunk."

"Well, dat good. Ah could understan' what he talkin 'bout a li'l better if he drunk."

"Well, he wasn't much of a drinker."

"Man, what y'all wastin' yo' time fo'? Dis guy don' know what he talkin' 'bout nohow."

"But he lived in a different century."

"Den what y'all wastin' mah time fo'? Ah's tired." She turned on her side and ended the literary discussion.

As the late afternoon settled into dusk, we lowered the backs of our seats to take a nap. I fell asleep quickly, but I woke a short time later when I felt a hand in my lap. I thought Maisie Dot was trying to test my interest again, maybe to make another few dollars. But the hand rested for a moment and then continued toward my pocket. I waited until it had reached its goal, then I grabbed her wrist. "Didn't I give you enough today? Do you have to steal the rest?"

She didn't look especially ashamed, only annoyed at having been caught. "Ah can't help it," she said. "Ah ain't got nothin', and you said yo'self dat you gots enough. When we lands in Chicago, you prob'ly be goin' off someplace, and Ah gots to make out fo' mahself."

"I have no place to go," I explained. "That's all the money I have in the world."

"How's Ah supposed to know dat? Listen, don' be mad at me. You been nice to me. Maybe we can help each other out."

"Why?" I said with a surly tone. "Do you need a pimp?"

"Ah knows a nice house on de South Side," she said, ignoring my hostility. "Maybe we could both get work there."

"No thanks, my body's not for sale," I said superciliously, thinking at the same time that I'd just left exactly that sort of employment with Willard.

She laughed. "Dat ain't what Ah means. Sometimes de madam be needin' somebody to take care o' de towels and sheets an' like dat. Ain't no harm in tryin'."

I relaxed. "Maybe you're right," I said. "It is the middle of winter and I don't have any better offers."

We got into Chicago that night. The stores in the Loop were closed for the holiday, so I didn't have much of an impression of the downtown shopping area as we passed through on the El. After a short ride, we climbed down the stairs from the El station and walked a few slippery blocks through the snow. Eventually we arrived at a brownstone house in what seemed to be a dignified neighborhood. From inside, sultry music poured out into the stillness of the snowy street. Maisie Dot climbed the flight of stairs that composed half the building's front, and rang the bell.

A tall, elegant blonde woman answered. She wore a V-necked, maroon velvet gown with long sleeves and carried a cigarette holder. Maisie Dot spoke quietly to her for a minute or two, then stepped aside so the woman could look down the stairs at me. They talked for another minute, and then Maisie Dot signaled me to join her. I carried my suitcase up the stairs. "Dis here Miss Wanda," Maisie Dot said. "She goin' to be our boss."

"My name's . . . Dell," I said. Maisie Dot looked at me with an arched eyebrow, but she didn't say anything. Aliases are pretty common in her line of work.

"Come into my office," Wanda answered, ushering us inside.

We stepped past a parlor where I could see several women in various stages of undress and several respectable-looking men. Wanda's office was a small room off the downstairs kitchen. It was less opulent-looking than the other rooms we had passed, more severe and businesslike.

"Ah hear dis be a nice place," Maisie Dot said appreciatively.

"You know my rules, Maisie Dot. They're the same as they were in the other place you worked for me. You get forty-five percent and tips, plus room and board. The house gets the rest. If we catch you stealing, you're out. Okay?"

Maisie Dot nodded.

"Go up to the first room on the second floor and wash up. You'll find a dressing gown there. Put it on and come down to the parlor. You can start right now."

Maisie Dot left.

"Now, Dell, where are you from?"

"I was born back East. I've moved around since the war. Haven't settled down yet."

"Maisie Dot says you're queer. Is that true?"

"It wasn't her business to discuss that," I said.

"I don't care what you are, mister. The fact is it's easier on the house if you're not interested in messing with the merchandise. Keeps things more on a business footing."

"I'll be all business," I assured her.

"Good. Your duties are simple. You take care of laundering the sheets and towels. We have a machine in the basement. You clean out the rooms after each use or after the girls wake up, and bring in fresh supplies. In the late afternoons you can run errands to the market and the drugstore, or sometimes help fetch items from the dry cleaner or a dress shop. You work nights, except for Mondays and Tuesdays. You're off from the time you finish cleaning up until mid-afternoon. Think you can handle that?"

"I think so."

"Can you cook?"

"A little."

"Good. Then you can help with the meals once in a while. Our cook is a little less than dependable, but I keep her around because I owe her. Let's see, is there anything else?"

"Uh . . . I hate to bring it up, but how about salary?"

"Sorry. Seventy-five a week plus room and board. Okay?"

"Okay."

"One more thing. You on drugs or anything like that?"

"No."

"You sure?" She looked me in the eye, as if she were assessing my pupils.

"Um, sure."

"Good. Keep it that way. Some of the girls may need their fix to keep going, but your help is useless if you're high all the time."

"You don't have to worry about me."

"I hope not. Okay, come with me. I'll show you where you sleep. The last guy may have left it a mess. He walked out last week, and it's been miserable here since then."

I wondered why he'd left, but I decided not to ask. Wanda showed me to my room, which was on the other side of the kitchen. It wasn't much more than a cubbyhole, but it had a door, so I could have some privacy. I went right to work after depositing my suitcase, and it wasn't until the next morning that I had a chance to lie down and think about where I had landed. Without an honorable discharge, I still couldn't expect to find much in the way of legitimate employment. Eventually military service might not be such a major item on employment questionnaires.

Meanwhile, even though this wasn't my idea of a career, it would have to do until something better came along.

It wasn't hard to learn the chores. Once the girls got to know me, they gave me tips on how to satisfy Miss Wanda without doing more work than necessary. They were a pretty tough bunch if somebody crossed them. One of the johns was even knifed while I was at work, but Miss Wanda kept him quiet about it by threatening to tell his wife about the kinky tastes he came there to satisfy. The girls were more than willing to be friendly with me, though. They treated me almost as if I were the team mascot. I guess I brought out the mother love in them, what little there was of it.

My favorites, aside from Maisie Dot, were Tina, a flaming redhead with a bright smile and a steely glance, who loved to talk about her tricks; Gretchen, a blonde with a faint whisper of a European accent, who specialized in unusual sexual requests; and Aurora, who was of uncertain extraction, an attractive mix of several racial strains, who was completely dense but sincerely nice, at least when she wasn't at work. The four of us hung out together when we were off.

At first the winter kept us indoors most of the time. Since I had a reasonable amount of free time during the days, I found myself playing lots of checkers and 500 rummy. I checked books out of the local public library and caught up on my reading of some of the poets Ariel Dumont had once accused me of not being familiar with. I had a little trouble with T. S. Eliot since I didn't always know what he was referring to, but Dylan Thomas's virtuosity with words and e. e. cummings's typographical fireworks and William Carlos Williams's simplicity all appealed to me a lot. Of course none of them could replace Walt Whitman in my affections or esteem, but I welcomed them as new "friends" nonetheless.

I tried to share some of my love of poetry with the girls, but they weren't especially excited by it. They preferred to think me a little weird and to forgive me for my eccentricity. Even after I gave up hope of interesting them in the other poets, I still kept trying to reach out to them about Walt. I thought a good place to start might be the poem I had shown Maisie Dot on the train, but when I went to look it up, I was appalled to discover that the page was missing from the book. It had been ripped out so neatly that if I hadn't been looking for it in particular, years might have passed before I noticed that it was gone.

I ran angrily out of my room to find Maisie Dot. She was working at the moment, but I didn't let that stop me. I burst into her room to find her in bed, beneath a fat middle-aged man who was happily pumping away, oblivious of everything except the feeling in his groin. Behind his back, I held up the open book to Maisie Dot, mouthing the words, "Did you rip out this page from my book?"

"Later, honey," she said.

"What?" her customer asked.

"Ain't nothin' greater," she said.

"What are you talking about?" he asked.

"Yo' fuckin', big boy."

"Shut up and do your work," he said.

She waved her hand at me, and I left quietly. But I was back as soon as her john left. "Did you rip out this page?" I repeated.

"Uh-uh," she said, shaking her head.

"Then who did?"

"How de fuck does Ah know? Ah done showed it to a couple of de girls is all Ah remembers."

"Which ones?"

"Tina, Aurora . . . oh, yeah—and Miss Gretchen too."

I went to Tina's room. I opened her door to find her on her knees in front of a portly old man who was naked except for his black silk socks, which were held up by red garters. "Did you rip out this page?" I mouthed behind his back. She tried to talk, but her mouth was full, so I left.

There was a "Do Not Disturb" sign on Gretchen's doorknob, but I ignored it. I found Gretchen dressed in leather with a whip in her hands. Her customer was tied to the bed and blindfolded, so he couldn't see me. "Did you rip out this page from my book?" I mouthed silently. Her only answer was a flick of the whip in my direction.

Aurora was sitting on her customer's face, so he couldn't see me either. I repeated my question to her, again silently. She just shook her head and then her shoulders and her hips, causing her john to give a muffled squeal of delight. I wasn't sure if she'd answered my question or not.

I decided to save my investigation for the next morning, when things were a little less hectic. I went to sleep mad, but as soon as I woke up I went into the kitchen, where the four of them were having their coffee. I opened my book to the violated place—and the missing page, slightly crumpled but none the worse for wear, fluttered to the floor at my feet.

The four women all looked at me innocently, their eight eyelashes batting in unison. "Who did this?" I demanded.

None of them said a word.

"If anyone touches this book again, there'll be a murder here," I said sternly.

Then Maisie Dot cracked a smile, and soon all five of us burst into gales of laughter that went on for twenty minutes, as they traded stories of my interrogations the night before. They were right: I was ridiculous. But I still cherished my *Leaves of Grass*. So I Scotch-taped the page back in the book the best I could and put it in a safe place, where no one else could find it.

As the weather grew warmer, Chicago became our afternoon playground. When I had no errands to run, the five of us wandered around town, window-shopping in the Loop and enjoying the dismayed stares of middle-class matrons at the sexy clothes the girls liked to sport. They considered their apparel to be something like a form of advertising, even though none of them was a streetwalker at that time.

Maisie Dot and company relished the attention, of course, flaunting their legs through the high slits in their ultra-tight skirts and furiously batting their heavily mascaraed lashes. They often stopped to apply—with as much ostentation as possible—another layer of powder and rouge onto the inch of makeup they already wore.

Occasionally someone, usually an older woman, would mutter something at one of the girls like, "Whore! You shouldn't be allowed to parade around like that in public." Such a comment would usually be greeted with a response from one of the girls like, "We can't all get a big house in the suburbs for giving away our cunts now, can we, honey? Somebody's got to make an honest living around here." There would generally be a lot of harrumphing and snorting on both sides after such an exchange, but there was never any kind of violence, at least not while I was around, and we just wandered the city as freely as if we were visitors from another dimension, invulnerable to the morals of the local wives and the hypocrisy of their husbands.

More than once we ran into a familiar john out with his wife. Good business manners forbade any sign of recognition, but every once in a while Tina or Gretchen would start winking and tossing sassy expressions to a man she knew, and he would scurry away down the street, as if to protect his wife from such outrage, while we knew he was secretly heaving a sigh of relief. If they wanted to enjoy their next night at Miss Wanda's, they had to let us alone, even if their silence meant accepting an occasional tongue-lashing from their wives. They wouldn't put us down in public unless circumstances forced them to. And they never complained when they showed up at the house the next time, either. They were usually too horny for that. In our company, they liked to keep their minds on baser things than Sunday school morality, and we were all too willing to oblige.

In the summer we could go outside of town to Riverview Amusement Park, where our high spirits were less out of place. We rode on the largest roller coaster, the Bobs, sticking our legs precariously out of the cars and screaming and laughing raucously. We played the games of skill on the midway, throwing darts at balloons and baseballs at stacks of painted wooden bottles, and occasionally winning kewpie dolls and stuffed panda bears and such, which the girls added to the clutter in their working bedrooms.

Our favorite midway game involved dropping a series of metal discs onto a bright red heart painted on a plain white board. The object was to cover the red completely, but few people seemed able to do it. The two guys who ran the stand were named Moe and George. Moe was short and stubby, while George was taller and weighed about 350 pounds. Both of them kept cigars in their mouths at all times. Actually, they were pretty sweet guys, and it was hard to think of them as hucksters. But when they demonstrated the proper technique of concealment, they would wipe away the metal discs so quickly that you couldn't be sure the red heart had truly been covered. Whenever they checked the players' boards, however, they searched diligently for even a pin dot of red and would count the game lost if one minuscule trace of color could be found. Somehow they could always find a way to undo my efforts. No matter how much I practiced the art of dropping the discs, no matter how painstakingly I tried to conceal the last bit of color, some tiny speck of the heart showed through, and after dozens of tries, I finally decided that I was just no good at this game.

Aurora, on the other hand, fancied herself better at the game than most players, and she kept on trying. One day, after countless failures at covering the red heart, she grew frustrated and started to scream accusations at Moe and George, claiming that they were cheating. Quite a crowd gathered to see the show, as if the real amusement everyone had come to see was this spectacle of a thickly painted woman in tight, sexy clothes yelling obscenities at two nervous guys with cigars wagging like metronomes in their mouths. We finally calmed Aurora down, but she demanded a slow demonstration of a successful game. Both Moe and George tried it at the same time. They were really sweating over their work because if they failed, their credibility would be lost and their livelihood along with it. Finally, after several tries, both of them proved it could be done—although it would clearly take a lot of practice. They gave Aurora a brass ashtray anyway, just to show they had no hard feelings. Hard feelings were the last thing they should have, I thought, since Aurora's little scene had made them the midway's most popular game of the hour.

While the crowd lined up to try their skill, Gretchen and Maisie Dot managed to pick up two guys who had been cheering them on. They disappeared for a little overtime work, probably at some hotel in town. Tina, Aurora, and I ate pink cotton candy to celebrate our high spirits, getting it stuck all over our faces, so another round of makeup application was required. While the girls were in the ladies' room, I went to the men's room to wash my face, and I found myself lingering longer than I had to, aroused by the casually exposed maleness I could see at the urinals reflected in the mirror.

It had been some months since my last sexual encounter. Working in a whorehouse had been stimulating, but the men who patronized Miss Wanda's were there to meet women, not to meet me. I had actually tried to come on to one or two of them, but they had complained to Miss Wanda, who had warned me rudely that I should stick to my appointed job and let the girls take care of the real business. I followed her instructions, but I wished I knew of a male brothel where I could satisfy some of my needs.

I sighed into the mirror over the washbasin, thinking that I had to find some way to connect with men again, maybe at some bar in town. At that moment, I noticed a tall, blond, good-looking guy who had been standing at a urinal without peeing for what seemed like a long time. I watched him in the mirror as I continued to dry my hands on a paper towel until there was nothing left of the towel except wet shreds. The man cleared his throat as if to draw my attention. I looked around to see if he meant me, and then I realized that the traffic had diminished and the place was empty, except for the two of us. He cleared his throat again, so I thought I'd check him out. I wanted at least a chance at a good lay, but I was so horny, I would have been thrilled with just one good grope of his hot meat.

I casually sauntered over to the urinal next to his, which was enough of a signal of my interest, considering that a long row of unused porcelain receptacles stood waiting like silent witnesses. I pulled out my cock as if to piss, and he turned toward me showing me eight inches of hard penis with the head just peering coyly out from its long sheath of foreskin. I was entranced. I reached out and cupped his warm, hairy balls in my hand.

"Feels good," I murmured, and looked him in the eye. He nodded his head approvingly.

I bent over and put the head of his cock in my mouth, slipping the foreskin back with my taut lips. Then I heard his voice.

"Vice squad," he said. "You're under arrest."

CHAPTER TWELVE

During my trial, which was mercifully brief, I sat stiffly in my chair, feeling like a heretic facing the Spanish Inquisition. Miss Wanda had gotten me a lawyer, but she couldn't do any more than that. She needed all her connections just to keep her own place open. The lawyer, who was no Clarence Darrow, advised me to plead guilty and throw myself on the mercy of the court, since the judge was usually harsh on unrepentant "degenerates" and believed that entrapment was a good idea to root out social misfits.

I could see that his honor was a real fun lover, scowling up there on the bench in his puritanical black robe. Although I doubt that the colorful presence and jangling bracelets of Maisie Dot, Tina, Gretchen, and Aurora in the audience did much to help my cause in his eyes, I appreciated their moral support nonetheless, especially when the judge called me "a menace to social order" and "a threat to the American family." My father would have appreciated that, I thought. But in spite of what the judge said, I didn't feel ashamed of doing what came naturally to me. I had expected that my contribution to the war effort might at least win me a little leniency, but when my less-than-honorable discharge was revealed, the judge said I was "a disgrace to the army" in which I had served. The basic message was that he didn't approve of me. Well, the feeling was mutual, let me assure you, but I didn't think it would help my cause to tell him so. He sentenced me to six months in prison.

Miss Wanda let me store my stuff at her place, but aside from that and the half-assed moron of a lawyer she provided, I was left to my own devices. Somehow I had to find the wherewithal to face the second incarceration of my life.

I arrived at Cook County Jail on a cold autumn day. I was numb during the perfunctory medical exam, the photographing and fingerprinting and the issuing of a coarse, dark gray uniform. Nor did I pay attention to the tiers of barred cells my guard led me past as I was being ushered to my new home. It wasn't until I heard the unforgettable sound of the cell door closing behind me that I woke up to a new reality.

I was totally alone. I stared at the gray walls of the cell, minutely examining the flawed texture of the plaster and trying to imagine pictures where there were none. I paced up and down like a tiger in a zoo, six short paces from front to back and three from side to side, again and again. There was no window in the back wall, against which stood a small sink and a lidless toilet, both composed of cracked porcelain with rust-colored stains, and there was nothing but a blank wall to be seen through the twenty-one bars that formed the front. My bed was a thin mattress on a perforated metal shelf suspended from the side wall by a thick chain. An identical bunk hung above it, and of course I managed to bump my head as I sat down.

For hours I sat there, trying to think of ways to cope, but in spite of myself I started to cry, muffling my tears in the thin pillow I had been provided as a mockery of comfort. I couldn't even allow myself any good, healthy sobbing because I could hear the distant voices of other inmates, and I was afraid that if they heard me crying they would type me as a weakling and that could lead me into trouble later on. I didn't know exactly how the system worked, but I knew that there was a pecking order in most prisons and that it couldn't do me any good to be at the bottom of the list.

I wanted to escape into a little sex, but I didn't feel at all horny. Besides, I was afraid to masturbate because my solitude didn't even have the virtue of privacy, and I was afraid that some guard would pass by and see me. Somehow I needed to lift myself outside of this hole, at least spiritually if not physically. I remembered back to the cage in the Japanese prison camp and how I had survived there, and I thought that maybe my old friend Walt Whitman could help as he had before.

I lay down on the bunk. Closing my eyes, I tried to imagine a long, empty beach. I pictured myself sitting there alone, waiting for a bearded poet to come striding toward me. I tried to hear the sound of the surf and remember the smells of the salt air. But I couldn't. It had been years since I'd actually seen the seashore. I tried to concentrate. I tried to relax. Nothing worked. Then I just lay there, waiting to leave my body spontaneously as I had long before. But I felt leaden. I squeezed my mind as hard as I could, until I saw stars blinking on and off behind my eyelids. But nothing happened beyond that, and I knew I wasn't going anywhere.

Then I riffled through the pages of *Leaves of Grass* in my mind, glad I had memorized so much of it since I didn't even have the comfort of the book in my possession. The lines that seemed most appropriate were these.

> . . . I am possess'd!
> Embody all presences outlaw'd or suffering,
> See myself in prison shaped like another man,
> And feel the dull unintermitted pain.

For me the keepers of convicts shoulder their carbines and
keep watch,
It is I let out in the morning and barr'd at night.

Not a mutineer walks handcuff'd to jail but I am handcuff'd
to him and walk by his side . . .

It was as if Walt were trying to be with me even though I couldn't reach him, but for all his good intentions, I couldn't feel his presence. Maybe if I composed a letter to him, as I had earlier, I could get my mind off my own troubles.

Chicago, October 1949

Dear Walt,

Is this what you were afraid of? Is this why you covered your tracks so carefully, leaving only "faint clews and indirections" for those who came after you to find—why you changed the pronouns in your poems and burned certain letters and papers of yours more than once, and used a secret code even in your diaries? Did you think they would find you out and lock you in a tiny cell to protect themselves from you, that they would reject your loving poems and render your life's work meaningless?

A soul as bright as yours couldn't have been frightened. You were the personification of good. Did you doubt that? In spite of all the affirmation in your poems, were you secretly ashamed of your desires? Didn't you truly believe that the joining of bodies is a union of souls? You must have made love to the bodies of other men. Otherwise you couldn't have known how good and right it is. But outside of your poems, you refused to say so. If you had been able to, then my own life would make so much more sense.

You know I am not angry with you. We all have our limitations, and even if you couldn't be perfect, you are still my hero. Maybe we are forced to be secretive just to survive, but that doesn't mean we're not brave. No matter how much they punish me for being what I am, they won't convince me that my love for you—for all men—is anything but beautiful and good. I know that you understand me, even if no one else does. I know that when everything else turns against me, that you will remain my guide and my sustenance. After all, you are my "Camerado."

Love always,
Dell

Distracting myself with thoughts of Walt helped a little bit, but I knew I needed still more strength to get through the ordeal ahead. Finally, I found myself praying to God. It had been many years since I'd even tried that, and I didn't remember the words I'd heard in Reverend Friendly's Sunday school. So I just invented my own. It's hard to recall them exactly now. I know I didn't pray for some miraculous release from bondage, but for the means to endure my captivity. I prayed for God to be my friend. At last, exhausted, I fell asleep.

Eventually, somebody brought me a tray of tasteless food. I spent the night alone in the cell, alternately sleeping and waking from bad dreams to lie there thinking. It wasn't until the next day that I was introduced to the prison routine. We were awakened at 6 a.m., to wash. Breakfast was at 7 a.m. I was assigned to work all morning and part of the afternoon in the infirmary, thanks to my medical corps experience in the army. Work was interrupted by lunch at noon, and after 5 p.m. I was on my own. I could spend an hour in the yard if the weather was good. Except for supper, at 6 p.m., the rest of the evening was spent in my cell.

After a couple of days, I figured out how to masturbate while listening for the sounds of approaching footsteps. I summoned up images from the past: Adam Witherspoon in the orchard; Bruno Todd in the high school locker room; Chester in the bedroom of his Greenwich Village apartment; Chuck, the truck driver I'd hitched a ride with on my trip away from Seattle; Willard lying on his belly, waiting for me; Harold in Willard's bed; the soldiers showering in the barracks during basic training; glimpses of the other inmates I'd noticed during the day. For the first weeks, those shadowy memories were the only company I had in my cell.

In the dining hall, the yard, and the infirmary, I tried to keep my shoulders square and my gaze steady, walking in a manner I hoped would be seen as tough. Mostly I kept to myself, but I did meet a couple of guys to talk to. One was named Louie Pellegrino. Louie had a head of lustrous, thick black hair, which, along with the sparkling brown eyes set in his swarthy-but-not-quite-handsome face, made him resemble the dashing hero in a paperback romance novel, at least if the light wasn't too bright. But Louie wasn't exactly the dashing sort. He was a slightly effeminate, short guy in his early twenties, who always had an unfiltered cigarette dangling from his mouth, even when he was talking fast. The only time his butt briefly left his lips was when he had to pick off a wet piece of tobacco, an operation which he performed delicately, with his pinky raised.

I was Louie's assistant in the infirmary. He was a slapdash worker who didn't do too well in the precision department. Whatever he was counting out or measuring usually ended up being too much or too little, and I often had to redo his work. But I didn't mind. It wasn't like I had anything better to do with myself. There was usually free time left over between assignments, and Louie would always offer me a cigarette, even though I had told him several times that I didn't smoke.

"Ah simply don't know what Ah'd do without you, Dell," he said with an obviously phony Southern-belle accent, soon after we'd met. "Ah just don't know how Ah manage to get so many things wrong. Just careless, Ah guess." He batted his eyelashes.

"It's no big problem," I said.

He returned to his normal abuse of English. "Not as long as I have you here to check up on me, it ain't. We make a pretty good team, don't you think? Hmm?"

I watched him to see if his face showed what he was getting at. He looked as if he'd just delivered a challenge and was waiting for some proof of his assumptions.

"The work's not hard," I answered noncommittally.

"Not when we do it together," he said coyly.

"As long as it's just work you're talking about."

"Don't try to fool me," he said superciliously. "I know a sister when I see one."

"What do you mean?"

"I mean you're a cocksucker just like I am, so don't try to fake any Mr. Butch routine with me."

"I'm not faking anything. I'm just being myself. And what if I am what you say? That doesn't mean I have to go around advertising it. I just want to do my time and get the hell out of here."

"Me too," he said. "I didn't mean anythin' by what I said. I just wanted to make sure you were real. Friends?"

"Sure—for the duration," I said.

"Thank God you ain't one of them fickle queens. Most of them don't want such a long-term commitment."

"How long are you in for?" I inquired.

"Two years, but don't ask me what for. It ain't polite."

"I'm in for being myself," I said.

"A sex charge? Jesus, don't tell nobody. It could get you into some bum situations."

"I wasn't exactly planning to announce it at lunch."

"You're cute," he said. "Why don't you call me Lulu?"

"Suppose we make it Lou," I offered. "That might be safer around here." It ended up staying Louie, because that was what felt most comfortable.

The other guy I met was named Fred. He was a tall, lean black man with a handsome face that was marred by a scar which ran from his forehead to his cheek, across the bridge of his nose. Fred sat next to me during meals.

"Where y'all workin' at?" he asked in a friendly tone.

"Infirmary," I said, clipping my answers because I didn't want everybody at the long table to know my business.

"Ah gots de laundry. Ain't so bad."

"Infirmary's pretty soft, I guess. Could be worse."

"You punkin' fo' anybody yet?" he asked.

"What's that?"

"If you don't know, you be findin' out soon enough, boy," he said. "But don't worry. Ah ain't after you. Ah gots mah own old man to satisfy."

I wanted to get off this topic, but a guy across from us had overheard our discussion and intruded with, "I hope this isn't a private conversation, gentlemen."

"It private as far as you concerned," Fred said. "Why don't you button it up, Flapjaw? Get fucked."

"You think it can't be arranged?" Flapjaw said.

"Y'all already done yo' worst, so Ah don't gotta take no mo' shit from you."

"You'll take what I give you, punk. Nigger thinks he's got some choices. The only choice you got is whether to swallow it."

Fred started to his feet, ready for a fight, but the guy on the other side of him and I restrained him for his own sake. All of us were hoping to avoid the notice of the guards, who were just waiting for a reason to pacify the lot of us.

Fred sank back into his place on the bench, resigned. "Ah's all right," he whispered. "Y'all can let go of mah arm."

Flapjaw snickered. "We'll finish our discussion later," he said to me.

It wasn't until that afternoon out in the yard that Fred explained what had been going on. "Flapjaw," whose real name was Duke, was a kind of pimp, who got paid in cigarettes and favors to procure younger or smaller guys for the horny older or bigger men who could afford his services. Fred had been one of his victims, and there was nothing he could do about it.

"Ah ain't no queer," he said to me through tight lips, "but once Duke gets ahold of yo' ass, you ain't got nothin' to say 'bout it no mo'. Best try to keep away from him, is mah advice."

"I surely will," I said. "Thanks for the tip." I didn't bother to mention my own sexual proclivities.

Louie wasn't surprised to hear the story. "Happens all the time," he said, through the portion of his lips that weren't engaged holding his cigarette butt. "I'd gladly put myself up for sale, but everybody already knows that I'm used merchandise."

"Don't tell me they only marry virgins," I said.

"Hah! Of course not. But they don't pay Duke if they can have what they want for the askin'. Duke specializes in convincin' guys to work for him. He broke Fred's arms. Fred lost his cherry while he was wearing two casts and

218

couldn't do nothin' about what was goin' on behind him. Better not let Duke get too close to you if you're tryin' to stay pure."

"It's a little late to be pure," I said. "But I would like some say in the choice of partners."

"This ain't no residential hotel for young ladies, honey. If you want some say in the matter, you'd better have some way to back it up."

I started doing exercises in my cell that night, but I knew that no amount of physical strength would make the difference. I just did my best to stay out of Duke's way, hoping he would forget about me.

I did okay for the next few weeks, keeping to myself except for some occasional communication with Louie and Fred. The evenings in the cell were the worst part. My exercises took up my time and did a little for my biceps. They were beginning to bore me, but I continued anyway. Aside from making myself the referee of cockroach races, there was little else to do.

After I had been there for thirty days, I was told I had a visitor. I couldn't imagine who it might be, but the mere idea of some contact with another reality made me feel so grateful that I was ready to kiss the feet of whoever had been kind enough to remember me. It turned out to be Aurora. She looked like a face from home, even though Miss Wanda's house had scarcely been anybody's idea of a family hearth.

"I thought I'd check in and see how you were doing," she said in the artificially demure tone that had made her a hit with Miss Wanda's clientele.

"I can't tell you how good you look to me," I said.

"You don't look so bad yourself, hon, considering where you are."

"Oh, I've been working out a little, just to pass the time."

"Great. Well, I brought you something else to pass the time with." She held up a package wrapped in brown paper.

"Thanks, Aurora. I appreciate it."

"Actually, it was Maisie Dot's idea. Before she left, she made me promise to bring it to you."

"Where'd she go?"

"Who knows? Her pants get itchy every once in a while and she takes off. Maybe she'll be back one of these days, maybe not. She said to tell you good-bye."

"I'll miss her," I said.

"Looks like our old gang is just falling apart," she said.

"At least you're still here."

"Well, I may be going too."

"I guess Maisie Dot's not the only one with itchy pants."

"Well, you don't have to make it sound like we got the crabs, honey. A girl just likes a little change of scenery. You know, even a hooker needs to look at a different ceiling now and then."

"I wish I could have a change of scenery. I've got nothing to look at but a blank wall."

"Maybe these will help, Dell," she said, pointing to the envelope. There was no way to pass it through the wire barrier that separated us, so she held it up until a guard came along and took it from her.

"Thanks a million, Aurora. Whatever's in it, I'm sure I'll love it. The main thing is that you cared enough to come."

"Just don't take this gig too hard," she said. "Stay as sweet as you were."

"Do you suppose I can just pick up where I left off, once I get out of here?"

"I guess not," she said. "Miss Wanda's is closed now. The cops upped their monthly payment because some politician was leaning on them, and she refused to pay. That's really why we're all leaving. I wasn't going to tell you because I figure you're depressed enough in here, but what the hell. It would be worse if you found out by just going there and finding nobody home."

"Yeah," I said glumly. "I appreciate your coming to tell me."

"Well, good luck, hon. I have to go now. Train to catch."

She stood and made a quick turn and a clean exit. Through the grill I watched her go, until she disappeared behind the iron door at the end of the long visitors' table. Well, maybe I wouldn't have decided to go back to Miss Wanda's when this was over anyway, I thought. Maybe I had to do something a little better with myself than pick up dirty laundry when other people's sex was over. But now I had nothing at all to look forward to.

The guard met me at the end of the prisoner's table before I went through the iron door on my side. He handed me the package, with the wrapping ripped open and loosely crumpled.

"Here's your stuff," he said. "It's okay. Passed inspection."

"What? There was no file in it?" I said, trying to sound surprised rather than sarcastic. He gave me a dirty look.

The package contained the things most valuable to me: my copy of *Leaves of Grass*, my term papers, and the envelope of Minerva White's photographs. The cheap suitcase that I had left at Miss Wanda's had contained nothing else but clothes. They didn't compose much of a wardrobe, which was just as well since I knew I had no chance of ever seeing them again.

I took the stuff back to my cell. After supper that night, I decided to decorate the place minimally with just the photograph of Chester, which I mounted on the wall across from my bunk, where I could see it while lying down. It reminded me that there had once been someone who would always remain purer and more perfect than any of the other people I had since encountered in the world. I spent a long time staring at the remaining four pictures: myself as a boy, Chester and me together, the two luminous blossoms, and the face of Minerva White's friend. Then I gently replaced them in their envelope, which I carefully slid between my mattress and the board beneath it.

At last, I opened *Leaves of Grass* at random. Tears came to my eyes as I read.

> Love, that is all the earth to lovers—love, that mocks time
>   and space,
> Love, that is day and night—love, that is sun and moon and
>   stars,
> Love, that is crimson, sumptuous, sick with perfume,
> No other words but words of love, no other thought but
>   love.

Chester's picture fairly shone at me from the wall a few feet from my face. I stared at it and wondered: what had become of the boy who had once won his love? How had I ended up so far from where I had begun? Where was the love in my life? It hadn't come from my father or from anyone since Chester had died, with the possible exception of Laura, who might easily have been confusing love with need. It hadn't come from Willard or from poor Harold, God rest his soul. Both of them had used me for their own purposes as much as I had used them. It hadn't come from the breezy friendship of Maisie Dot and the girls at Miss Wanda's. And the future looked no more promising than the past. It was hard to believe that anything worthwhile would be in store for me upon my release. Maybe it would be better if I were never released, I thought. But I certainly didn't want to spend any longer than I had to in this hole. Maybe I could just close my eyes and make it all go away.

A strange assortment of things from different moments of my life whirled before my closed eyes: the apple blossoms in spring, the jar of dead fireflies, Martha's gravestone, Chester's yellow roadster, the fringed lamp in Miss Binder's living room, Kelly in the boys' room, Miss Standish at the sweater counter in Saks Fifth Avenue, Minerva White's studio, the train station after Chester had gone, the man I'd stroked but never seen in the theater in San Francisco, the Black Cat Café, Jerry Tuft in the stockade, Doug Swanson bringing me food in the prison camp, the Japanese soldier who had killed himself, mourning Chester at Land's End, the angry midget in Gus's Diner in Seattle, Laura's apple dinner, Willard caught in the yard dressed as Jean Harlow, Harold's frozen body dragged from the lake, Maisie Dot's net stockings in the snow, the game of cover-the-heart at Riverview Park. None of it made any sense. I couldn't even cry about it. I just wanted to leave it all behind me. I lay there in that state of mind without sleeping for most of the night.

Shortly before dawn, or so I assumed without a view of the night sky, I rose wearily from my bed. I removed my pants slowly and climbed to the upper bunk, where I knew I could reach a pipe that projected from the wall near the ceiling of the cell. I wrapped one trouser leg around the pipe, knotting it securely, and knotted the other leg around my neck as tightly as I could. Then I sat on the edge of the bunk and waited for the strength to jump off. I don't know how long I waited, maybe half an hour. I tried to think of reasons to stay alive, but there were none. I tried to think of reasons to die, but there were none of those either. It simply didn't seem to matter anymore. For a while I thought I'd sit at the edge and let God decide whether to push me off. Finally the thought of my father floated into my mind. I could almost feel his elbow in my ribs, as if we were at a Sunday sermon. I tried to remember his face. It was tight-lipped and stern, and he said not a word. I looked through the darkness to where I knew Chester's picture hung. Then I pushed myself off the edge of the bunk, into oblivion.

The only sound I heard was that of the trousers' seam ripping. I landed on my feet, standing there foolishly with my ripped pants still around my neck. There was nothing I could do but untie the knot from my throat, sink down on my bunk, and fall asleep.

I awoke a short while later when the lights were turned on, and got up to prepare for my day as if nothing had happened. My only problem was getting dressed. As I untied my trouser leg from the ceiling pipe, I found that the seat was ripped wide open. Since there was no choice, I just put them on and brazened it out. At breakfast I arranged with Fred to sneak me a fresh pair from the laundry. He didn't ask me how I'd ripped them, but he gave me a sympathetic look that said he assumed however I'd done it, it hadn't been much fun.

I wandered through the next couple of days in a fog, not much caring where I was or what I was doing. If I could stumble like that through all the days of my life, I thought, someday it would be over, one way or another. That was all that mattered. I hated my past and my present, and I dreaded my future. So I dealt with things on a smaller scale—things like anticipating breakfast and arranging the bottles in the infirmary.

It was Louie who brought me out of my funk. He showed up at the infirmary looking more like a patient than an aide. Both his eyes were blackened, and his lips were so puffy and split that he couldn't manage to keep his customary cigarette butt dangling from them and had to hold it in his hand. I could see him wince whenever he took a drag from it.

"What the hell happened to you?" I asked.

"I fell when I was gettin' out of my limousine at the opera," he said painfully.

"Be serious."

"I can't. If I get serious I'll start to cry, and I don't want to give them the satisfaction."

"What happened?"

"I got raped," he said.

"By Duke's boys?"

He nodded.

"The bastards. What can we do about it?"

"Nothin'."

"Not even tell the guards?"

"Are you kiddin'? That would only make things worse. Just help me put a little peroxide on these cuts."

He tried not to grimace as I dressed his wounds the best I could, but I could see that he was in serious pain. "Is there anything else that hurts?" I asked. "You know, inside you?"

"Only a broken heart," he muttered. And then, caught by his own wit, he started to laugh, and then began to cough hard, until I was really afraid for him. I put my arm around his shoulder and held him until the racking spasms subsided.

"Thanks," he said. "I needed that."

"Listen, I'd really like to help you," I said. "Are you sure there's nothing I can do?"

"Just be my friend," he said.

"Of course," I said.

Eventually he told me how they'd cornered him in the shower room. Five guys had assaulted him and dunked his head into the toilet bowl when he refused to service them. When he finally capitulated, they all took turns fucking his mouth and ass until he was unconscious. Duke had chosen them for the hit squad, as a repayment for favors they'd done him. Louie had made the mistake of punking for the man of his choice, and Duke was making it clear that he was the one who would decide who got to fuck whom around here. To defy him was to become his next victim, but he didn't even need that much excuse. All a guy needed was to be vulnerable in some way— physically slighter or the least bit more attractive than most of the other men—and Duke considered him fair game.

"Were the guys at least good-looking?" I asked, trying to cheer him up.

"If you think this was any kind of fun, forget it," Louie said. "It never even felt like sex, just violence."

"I'm sorry," I said. "I didn't mean it."

"Fred told me he heard from the guy he punks for that you're probably next," he said. "I wouldn't look forward to it if I was you."

"I'm not afraid of them. If I'm going to be next, whether I help you fight or not, then I might as well help you," I said angrily. But I wasn't sure if I really felt brave enough to confront those guys. I was just trying to make Louie feel a little more secure.

"Forget it," he said. "I ain't fightin' nobody. I just want to finish my time and get out of here alive. You'd better save your strength. You're probably gonna need it."

Two days later, I had a cellmate. His name was Carlos. His dark looks were craggily handsome, and he took over immediately. "I'm takin' the bottom bunk," he said. "You move to the top."

It didn't seem worth arguing about, so I took my book and my envelope of pictures and moved them to the top bunk.

"Who's that supposed to be, your boyfriend or somethin'?" he said, gesturing with his chin toward the photograph of Chester I had stuck on the wall.

I didn't answer.

He stood up and looked me square in the eye. "Get this straight," he said. "When I ask you somethin', you better answer right away, like you mean it." He slapped me hard on the cheek. "Got it?"

My hand rose involuntarily to where he had slapped me. In shock, I nodded.

"That's a little better," he said. "Now, who's this guy?"

"A friend of mine."

He snatched the picture from the wall and ripped it into a dozen small pieces. "I'm your old man now, punk. I paid Duke plenty to get me transferred into this cell, and I want my money's worth. Got it?"

I stared in disbelief at the pieces of Chester's picture as they drifted to the floor. I was furious, but I didn't know how to express my anger without inviting more violence. As I kept myself under control, my grief overwhelmed my anger. "He was my friend," I said quietly. "He died in the war." I started to weep softly, and my shoulders shook.

Carlos gave me a funny look. Then he hopped up to the top bunk and sat beside me. He put his arm around me. "Listen, kid, I didn't mean nothin' by it. You just gotta know who's the boss around here, right? Hey, you treat me right and I'll treat you right. Is it a deal? You gonna cooperate or what?"

I didn't know if I hated him or if I was grateful to him, but I had no choice in the matter. I nodded and wiped away my tears. "I'll cooperate," I said.

"That's a good boy. You can start by suckin' me off. Get on it." He opened his pants to reveal an already hard cock.

As I serviced him, my old lusts returned full force in spite of myself, and my head bobbed eagerly up and down in his groin. I didn't know what to think. I resented him and I was attracted to him at the same time. He wasn't much good in the foreplay department, but he certainly excited me. The confusion almost made me want to laugh, which made me feel guilty when I remembered what I'd been crying about only moments earlier. Trying to block out everything but the task before me, I worked at keeping my lips taut and my throat open, and soon my efforts were rewarded with a mouthful of semen.

"You better swallow all of it," Carlos said. "Don't waste none of it. You spit it out, and I'll make you lick it off the floor."

I swallowed. "You didn't have to tell me that," I said.

"You're gonna be all right," he said, and he hopped down to lie on his bunk and smoke a cigarette.

While Carlos watched with an emotionless gaze, I picked up the pieces of Chester's photograph. They were too small to save, so I threw them in the toilet and flushed them away, trying not to think of the sweetness and generosity that was disappearing with them. I consoled myself with the knowledge that I still had an image of him in Minerva White's photograph of the two of us, which remained in the envelope under my mattress.

Carlos and I got along all right after that—as long as I continued to do what he said. I didn't much like his macho manner when we weren't having sex, but he remained equally gruff in and out of bed, never giving a thought to satisfying my needs. So I gave him what he wanted, and he let me alone to give myself the pleasure that I wanted. If he heard me masturbating in my bunk after he was finished with me, he never let on. It wasn't exactly the relationship of my dreams, but I wasn't sure I had ever been suited for a cottage with a picket fence in the first place—and besides, I wasn't in a position to be choosy, was I?

The next time I went to work at the infirmary, Louie seemed to know more than I did about what had happened.

"I hear you set up housekeepin' with Carlos," he said grimly.

"Word gets around fast."

"When you're sleepin' with Duke, it does."

"You mean Duke was saving you for himself?"

He nodded. "But that gang rape almost ruined the merchandise. Some courtship."

"I hope your old man treats you a little more gently in bed than my gorilla does," I said.

"Are you kiddin'?" he asked with a smirk. "Look at Duke's track record. I'm lucky I get any time to heal between bouts. Let's face it, honey. We're just so much meat to these guys. They don't give a shit about us or our feelin's. They're just lookin' for a hot hole to dump their juice in."

"Alas," I sighed, waving my hand like a Victorian fan. "It's the white woman's burden."

"It's every woman's burden, honey, and don't you forget it."

"I suppose if you know so much about my new husband, then you know how much he paid for me."

"I do," he said, "but I ain't tellin'. I wouldn't want to hurt your feelin's."

"Bitch," I said. And we both laughed, in spite of it all.

The truth was that I did begin to like Carlos, even to fall a little bit in love with him. Once he saw that I would cooperate, he eased up a bit, and there were moments that he was almost gentle with me. But he always kept the upper hand and he never showed any sign of caring about my pleasure, only his own. Our sexual activity was pretty static. I sucked him and he fucked me. Carlos was not an imaginative man. He just wanted to get his rocks off.

He never spoke about his life outside of jail. I couldn't even find out what he had been sentenced for or how much time he was serving. Our conversation dealt only with the life inside the prison. I wondered what kind of work he did aside from his life of crime. For all I knew, he could have been a mailman or a mass murderer, or both. Left to my own devices, I imagined that he was a truck driver. I pictured him driving a rig like the one which had picked me up outside of Seattle, and I pictured myself riding the road beside him, smelling his manly aroma and yearning for his soul.

It went on like that for four months. I kept my fantasies to myself, of course, but I had even begun to hope that we might have some kind of life together outside this awful place, maybe an apartment where I could keep house for him and make him feel happy in his way. After all, I had no other future to look forward to, and I was getting out in a matter of weeks— actually a matter of four weeks, three days, and six hours. I had kept scrupulous track of the time. But one afternoon I returned to the cell after working at the infirmary to find Carlos packing all his things together.

"What's this?" I said cavalierly. "I thought I was supposed to do the housekeeping around here."

"Time's up," he said. "I'm gettin' out today."

"But what about me?" I said, before I had a chance to think.

"What about you? Don't worry. Duke'll find you somebody else to punk for."

I managed not to lose my composure. "Sure. It's just that I was getting kind of used to you. That's all."

"Listen, kid, I'm goin' back to the real world, back to my old lady. Got it? You been okay while I was in here. You cooperated just fine. I got no complaints. You got no complaints. Now, once I get out of here, I don't want to hear about you again. Never. Got it?"

"I got it," I said, and I hopped up to my bunk to watch him finish packing.

In a few minutes the guard came for him. "So long, kid," was his only farewell. I didn't bother to move my stuff back to the lower bunk. He'd probably been right about Duke finding a replacement for him, I thought.

"What did you expect, hearts and flowers?" said Louie when I met him in the yard and told him what had happened.

226

"I don't know. A polite thank you, maybe, or a diamond bracelet to remember him by," I said. The truth was that I would have loved a photograph of Carlos—or a lock of his hair or even a pair of his old undershorts. But I wasn't about to share that intimacy, not even with Louie.

"At least you're gettin' out on good behavior soon," said Louie. "You won't even have to be on parole. That ought to be some consolation."

Fred was walking past us as Louie said this. "Yo' time almost up?" he asked me.

I nodded. "About a month left."

"Lucky son of a bitch," Fred said. "Ah gots me another year mo' to go in here."

"I got a little more than that," Louie said.

"So why ain't you lookin' happy?" Fred asked me.

"Oh, her old man just moved out and she's got the blues," Louie told him.

"Don't be callin' him *her*," Fred warned him. "It ain't no joke. Listen, Dan, you best consider yo'self lucky he gone. Mah old man threatened to give me another scar to cross dis one, and he ain't kiddin'. If Ah don't do everything he tell me to, Ah's gonna have a big 'X' right across mah face. Ah can't take no more of dis shit."

"Fred, just cooperate. The main thing is survival. Remember that," I told him.

"Yeah, survival," said Fred. "De price a li'l steep, if y'all ask me. Even wit'out mo' of a scar, how is Ah gonna face mahself in de mirror when Ah gets out of here?"

"It could be worse," I said.

"Fuck dat shit, man. It could be better, too. Ain't dat right? Yo' old man left, and you be complainin' about it? Man, you well off, and you doesn't even know it."

I was too embarrassed to answer him.

When I got back to my cell, it seemed emptier than it had before Carlos had arrived. Now, in his absence, I felt as if I had lost my most intimate companion, even though it hadn't been a mutual relationship. I pulled out my copy of *Leaves of Grass* and thumbed through it for something familiar to comfort myself, and I eventually came across these lines.

> I will write the evangel-poem of comrades and of love,
> For who but I should understand love with all its sorrow and
>   joy?
> And who but I should be the poet of comrades?

I let the book fall closed and lay down on my bunk, but I couldn't rest. I got up and paced the cell, front to back, time and again, until I realized that I was only making things worse. What did Walt know about how I felt? He was talking about some ideal world that I had never had more than a glimpse of. I felt more confined than ever. I couldn't stop thinking of Carlos. Even the coldness he had offered me had been better than nothing. I wanted to get him out of my system, to exorcise the thought of him. He was only a man, I kept thinking, only a man. The words kept turning around in my mind. Finally, I took out a pencil and paper and wrote them down. After much crossing out and transposing, I held the first poem I had completed in a very long time.

Only a Man

He was no perfect being, only a man,
Mysterious and rudely passionate,
But by his very bones
And by the flesh that from those bones
Grew into grace for all the world to see,
And by the liquids of that flesh
And by the hairs that from it grew
I loved him,
And by the smoke of his warm breath
And by the countless dreams he left in me
For a remembrance
Once his touch had gone.

I wrote a number of poems in the next few weeks. I became so engrossed in selecting and arranging my words that the time flew quickly by, and before I had even prepared myself to face my return to freedom, I was released back into the world.

CHAPTER THIRTEEN

I had no idea where to go or what to do when I was released, but I had enough money to last for a couple of weeks. So I got myself a room in the Sheridan Plaza, a hotel in the center of Chicago notable only for its fading gentility. The lobby was appointed with the traditional potted palms, whose leaves needed dusting. I sat there by myself for a couple of hours, trying to figure out what to do next. Picking up where I could from the last place I had left off seemed like the most likely plan. There was no going back to Miss Wanda's brothel, so I decided to call Willard in Madison and see if he had any ideas. I went up to my room.

When I dialed his number, a woman's voice answered.

"Is this the Stevenson residence?" I asked.

"Yes," she said.

"Is Willard there?"

"No, he's in class right now. May I ask who's calling?" Her voice sounded sweet, but falsely melodious.

"An old friend. When will he be in?"

"I'm not certain."

"Who is this I'm talking to?"

"This is Mrs. Stevenson."

"His mother?"

"His wife. Would you like to leave a message?"

Willard married? He must have thought it was the only way to play it safe. Immediately, I imagined him going to bed in his white satin Jean Harlow gown. What would his wife wear? Flannel pajamas? Overalls? I almost laughed out loud. I stared at the image of my own face in the slim mirror on the closet door, as if it would give me an answer. It must have been quite a while before I remembered the phone. "No message, thanks," I said. But there was no one on the other end of the line, only a dial tone.

I considered tracing my steps a little further back. What was Laura doing now? What had become of her child? I saw my face screw into a wince in the mirror as I remembered that it was my child as well. Should I interfere in their lives after all this time? Did I have anything to offer them? Not without an income. Not even with an income. Still, I wondered how they were, and if she had forgiven me. I got as far as lifting the phone from its cradle and asking for long-distance information, but I hung up before the operator even came on. The kid probably didn't even know about me. There was nothing I could give them except pain. It was kinder to forget about them.

I certainly wasn't going to call up Elysium, New York. What would I say? "Hi, Dad! Remember me? I forgot to come home after the war, but I'm out of jail now, and I wondered if you were in the mood for a visit"? I didn't feel like visiting him.   I didn't want to know how he was. And I certainly didn't want him to know how I was. I didn't want to give the old bastard the satisfaction.

There was no point in sitting around in the hotel room, so I went out for a walk, hoping that some fresh air would help me to think. I wandered into Lincoln Park, oblivious of the snow that covered the ground. There was only one other person in sight. He looked at me steadily, perhaps hungrily, but I ignored him. Then I made my way to Lake Shore Drive and stood at the edge of Lake Michigan watching the chunks of ice collide until I could no longer stand the cold. Finally, I went back to the hotel and took a nap.

It was late in the evening when I awoke. After a supper of unidentifiable "casserole special" in a little place called only "Restaurant" on a pale blue neon sign that hung over its door, I decided to check out a gay bar that Louie had told me about. What the hell, I told myself, it's Friday night, isn't it?

Following Louie's detailed instructions, I made my way to the unmarked entrance, which was in an alley off a downtown side street. It felt like following a treasure map. The place itself wasn't so bad, but it was much less energetic than the Black Cat in San Francisco had been during the war. In the soft pink lighting I could see about two dozen men, almost all of them in V-necked sweaters, strung out along the mirrored bar and sitting at the few tables that lined the opposite wall. There were one or two hushed conversations going on among them, but most of the guys stood or sat silently by themselves, as if waiting to be discovered. I ordered a scotch and soda and explored the place with my eyes, trying to decide if I would be brave enough to approach anyone. Although no one moved as much as an eyelid, I had the distinct feeling that I was being carefully scrutinized the entire time I stood there, as if a hidden tribe of islanders were observing me from the foliage that lined the alien shore where I had landed.

I was so lost in my own fantasy that I was startled to find myself interrupted not by a warning arrow, but by the sound of a friendly voice.

"You're new around here, aren't you?"

I nodded, noticing that he was pretty cute. He had curly blond hair, and he wore the sleeves of his powder-blue V-necked sweater pushed up nearly to his elbows.

"Care for a drink?" he asked.

"I already have one," I said apologetically.

"Then let me get the next round, okay?"

"Sure," I said.

We talked for almost half an hour—I don't remember about what, exactly. My primary interest was in ascertaining whether he was going to arrest me. His was probably the same. Eventually, he seemed satisfied that I wasn't a cop, and he asked if I wanted to go somewhere with him.

"Yeah, I think so," I said, hoping that my judgment of him was correct. If he was a cop, he was a great actor.

"But it can't be my place, because I live with my family," he said. "Don't worry; I'm not jailbait," he added. "I just moved back home, because I'm between jobs."

So I invited him back to the hotel. The night clerk didn't seem any more interested in our arrival than the dusty potted palms which stood on pointless sentinel duty in the lobby. We entered my room quietly, and within a minute we were out of our clothes and in each other's arms. We made love for an hour or two, passionately, in as many positions as we could devise. It was mutual and giving and a hell of a lot more human than what Carlos had offered me in our cell. When we had both had our second orgasm, he rose quietly from the bed and, after a brief moment in the bathroom, he put on his clothes, gently kissed me good-bye, and left. "Thanks," was all he said. It wasn't until I awoke in the morning that I realized I didn't even know his name.

I couldn't afford to spend too many days doing the same thing aimlessly, so I decided to leave town and try my fortune elsewhere. A change of place might give me a fresh start. I bought one change of clothes and went to the bus station. I decided to go as far as three dollars would take me. That would leave me enough to find shelter and food for a few days, a week if I stretched it. By then I hoped I would have a job.

At the bus station, I decided to continue heading eastward. That had been my general direction since I'd left Seattle, and I saw no particular reason to change course. The next state was Indiana, and as I looked over the possibilities within my price range, I noticed the town of Speed. That was where Harold Fisher had come from. Without thinking any further, I moved my sights south as well as east. I was going to visit Harold's parents! I didn't have the faintest idea why, but it felt good to have some sort of plan. And who knew? Maybe some sort of life would suggest itself once I got there.

The bus ride took the better part of the day. For most of the time I sat next to two chatty nuns who were on their way back to Indiana after visiting a convent in Illinois where they both had blood sisters. They wanted to know all about me. But somehow I thought that the real story wouldn't be to their taste, so I invented a completely artificial past, something about working in my brother's hardware store while his wife had a baby. The two of them beamed. I didn't claim to be a Catholic, though, because I was afraid to be confronted with their catechism or something, and if they caught me lying, I'd never convince them that I was the nice boy they thought I was. But I really was a nice boy, wasn't I? Could I help it if my history couldn't live up to their expectations?

I arrived in Speed in the early evening. I was the only one to get off the bus. The depot was merely the front of a newspaper store on the main drag, and I couldn't find anything like a hotel nearby. I guess there weren't too many folks interested in staying over to see the sights of Speed. When I looked up Fisher in the phone book, I found four of them, and naturally the one I wanted was the fourth one I tried.

"Hello," came a quiet voice at the other end.

"Mrs. Fisher?"

"Yes."

"You don't know me. My name is Dell . . . uh . . . Daniel Blake. I was a friend of Harold's in Madison."

I heard a sharp intake of breath, but she said nothing.

"I was just passing through town, so I thought I'd say hello," I continued lamely.

"Of course, Daniel," she said slowly, clearly betraying her efforts at remaining composed. "I believe I remember Harold mentioning you. It's only that I was so startled. It's been over a year now."

"I'm sorry, Mrs. Fisher. I just thought it would be a nice thing to do."

"And I'm glad you did. You were right to call. Um, we'll be sitting down to supper soon. Won't you join us?"

I couldn't tell if she was being sincere, but I didn't have any other options, so I agreed. "But I don't have a car," I added.

"That's no problem. We're only a short walk from the bus stop." She gave me the directions. "By the time you get here, dinner will be on the table."

I arrived at a small, white, one-family house with a picket fence. The lawn was covered with snow, but it was easy to imagine a flower garden blooming there in the summer. A thin, worn-looking woman answered the door, wiping her hands on her apron. "You must be Daniel," she said, smiling warmly.

"Yes, ma'am," I answered.

"Well, come on in, son." At this point, I was not heartened by the "son." Any fantasy I might have entertained of finding a life there seemed ridiculous. Their own son hadn't found a life there.

A hollow-cheeked man appeared behind her. He was closely shaved, but nonetheless had a permanent five-o'clock shadow darkening his jaw. It gave him a slightly sinister air. "Clay," Mrs. Fisher said, "look who's here. A friend of Harold's."

232

"Your name Drake?" he asked. Even from that distance, I could smell alcohol on his breath.

"Blake," I said. We shook hands with his wife between us. His grip was surprisingly mild—not the nutcracker handshake I had anticipated.

Mrs. Fisher stepped aside, and I entered a small, drab living room. Everything was tidy and just short of threadbare. Nothing in the room commanded attention except for a large wood cross above the mantelpiece. No particular taste was discernible, only the desire to be ordinary.

"Would you like to clean up before dinner?" my hostess asked.

"I would. It's been a pretty long trip."

I changed into my other suit of clothes in the bathroom, imagining all the while that I could hear them furiously whispering and grumbling. But I couldn't make out anything they were saying.

When I came downstairs, Mr. Fisher was fixing himself a drink. "Care to join me?" he said. I shook my head. I wanted to keep a clear mind.

Mrs. Fisher and I had Coca-Cola with our meal, but Mr. Fisher continued drinking his neat gin or vodka. Somehow I knew that his wife was hoping I'd think it was water. Our dinner was a pot roast with carrots and spinach. Everything had clearly been stretched from two portions to three. The meat had been cut up into tiny pieces to make it look like more, and there were tiny portions of the vegetables, the smallest amounts on Mrs. Fisher's plate. I felt embarrassed, but her efforts at making me welcome reassured me a little.

"Where did you travel from?" she asked while we ate.

"From Chicago, ma'am."

"Oh my, that's quite a trip. Do you have family there?"

"Only my brother. He runs a hardware store. I was helping out while his wife had a baby."

"That's nice," she said. "Isn't that nice, Clay?"

Mr. Fisher grunted a grudging approval. "Very, very nice," he answered. His speech was beginning to sound a little thick.

"How well did you know Harold, Daniel?" his wife asked quickly, as if to curtail the bad manners she feared her husband might imminently display.

I must have blushed. It took me a minute to think of an appropriate answer, and I played with my spinach to give myself time. Finally I said, "We went to school together. We were friends."

"Well, at least you don't wear none of them fancy scarves like a damned queer," he grumbled. "Harold said lots of the boys there wear 'em, but I knew he was lyin'."

"Clay," Mrs. Fisher cautioned. "You promised."

Mr. Fisher returned to his supper, and we finished the rest of the main course in awkward silence.

"Mrs. Fisher," I said over coffee, "I just wanted to tell you one thing. Harold may have been confused, but he was still young. He was a good person, and a talented one. I think he would have grown into a fine man. I only wish I could have done more to help him. I'll always feel bad about that. I'll miss him. I just wanted you to know."

"His mother misses him too," Mr. Fisher muttered into his nearly empty glass. "That makes two of you," he added, chuckling to himself at his cleverness.

"Clay, that's twice," said Mrs. Fisher, revealing a strength that her sweet manner had belied. "You know you miss Harold. You certainly cried hard enough at his funeral." She turned to me. "I'm sorry, Daniel. It's just that Mr. Fisher gets forgetful now and then."

I nodded to show that I understood. Mr. Fisher grew quiet. He finished his coffee and went upstairs. On his way, he stopped in the living room to pour a new drink. From the staircase, he tossed back a final insult. "See what he wants from us, Millie. Maybe he wants our blessing. Hah!"

Ignoring him, Mrs. Fisher went on. "Thank you for what you said, Daniel. It helps me. I've asked the good Lord where I went wrong. I do want to understand why this terrible thing happened. But it helps me to know that a nice young man like you was Harold's friend. Would you like me to remember you in my prayers, Daniel?"

"That would be very nice, ma'am. Thank you. And thanks for the good meal."

"You're quite welcome. And, Daniel, don't you pay any mind to Mr. Fisher's comments. He means well. It's just that he feels so awful about what happened to Harold. I pray that God will help him to emerge from the darkness he's wandering in—help him to carry his burden as we all must."

She bowed her head as she spoke, and I didn't know if she was actually praying at the moment or simply telling me what she prayed about. So I said only, "Yes, ma'am."

"You're welcome to stay the night if you like," she offered. "I still keep Harold's old room made up."

I could tell that her offer was sincere, but I couldn't wait to get out of there. "That's very kind of you," I said. "But I do have to be somewhere tomorrow." She didn't press me. Instead, she simply nodded with a sad look in her eyes and saw me to the door. As I passed the front of the house, I could see her through the window, climbing slowly up the stairs to where her husband sat drinking away his memories.

I walked back to the bus stop and waited for the next bus, pacing back and forth and trying not to think about the past. For a while I thumbed through *Leaves of Grass* by the dim light of the streetlamp, looking for something to cheer myself up. I ended up playing a little game and looking for passages about mothers and fathers. I finally settled on this one as the most applicable.

> The mother at home quietly placing the dishes on the supper-
> table,
> The mother with mild words, clean her cap and gown, a
> wholesome odor falling off her person and clothes as she
> walks by,
> The father, strong, self-sufficient, manly, mean, anger'd,
> unjust,
> The blow, the quick loud word . . .

It sounded like all of us, Walt and Harold and I, had had the same kinds of parents. Our fathers were certainly all cut from the same cloth, anyway. I could only guess about my own mother, but I liked to think that she had been like that: mild and clean and wholesome. Maybe the theories that were fashionable at that time were true after all, I thought, the ones that said it was all the parents' fault. But they were probably wrong. There have been dozens of theories since then—everything from genes to hormones to role models to psychological immaturity to arbitrary choice to rebelliousness to nature's way of creating built-in babysitters. So today, after all that research, nobody knows how people become homosexual, any more than they know how people become heterosexual. But what difference does it make? We are what we are, I decided back then—and, like the rest of humanity, all we can do is to lead the best lives we can.

The bus didn't come until well after dawn. I was so frozen I didn't care where it was going. I just gave the driver a five dollar bill, and he gave me a ticket. I fell asleep immediately and didn't wake up until we were just outside of Cincinnati. Something about Cincinnati rang a bell. I thought for several minutes before I remembered. My army buddy Doug Swanson was from Ohio! I remembered saying good-bye to him and his wife, and their inviting me to visit them if I was ever in the neighborhood. What was her name? Gloria? Hardly. Linda? No. Donna? That was it: Donna. But I wasn't sure if it was Cincinnati they were from. I was pretty sure it was a city that began with a C, but in Ohio that's no big help.

Nonetheless, I got off the bus in Cincinnati and did a little detective work. With the aid of several phone books and a nice operator, I finally located a Douglas J. Swanson in Columbus, and I called the number. A woman answered.

"Is this Donna Swanson?" I asked.

"Yes."

"You probably won't remember me. My name is Dan Blake. We met only once, in San Francisco. I was Doug's friend."

"I'm not sure," she confessed. "It was so hectic there. I met so many people."

"I was in the prison camp with him."

She stopped for a moment. "Oh yes. Dan. I remember. Doug mentioned you many times. He said you saved his life. I'm sure he'll want to talk to you, but he's at work right now. Where are you calling from?"

"I'm on the road, actually. I'm in Cincinnati right now."

"Are you passing through Columbus?"

"I could."

"It's not very far. Listen, why don't you come here tonight? I'll make a nice dinner. I'm sure Doug will be thrilled to see you."

"If you're sure it's no bother," I said.

"Don't be silly. Why, Doug wouldn't be here at all if it weren't for you. It's the least we can do."

I arrived in Columbus in the late afternoon and made my way to their address, which turned out to be the second story of a three-family frame house. Doug wasn't home yet, and Donna seemed flustered when she greeted me at the door of their apartment. She wore her blonde hair in a simple, short haircut, and her plain face wasn't covered with makeup despite her slightly rough complexion. She looked about eight months pregnant under her navy blue maternity dress, which was unadorned with any jewelry or fancy trimmings. Her appearance reminded me of Laura, but I did my best to put that thought out of my mind.

"Dan? Hi," she said. "I called Doug at work and he said to put out the red carpet for you. I want you to make yourself right at home."

She led me into the living room, where we could hear the sound of a child crying in the back of the apartment.

"Oh, that's Doug Junior," she said apologetically. "He doesn't like to be left alone for a moment. I'll be right back."

I glanced around the room, which looked as plain and trim as Donna did. I could tell it had just been painstakingly cleaned. The faint smell of furniture polish still hung in the air. The carpet and the sofa and the single club chair were all done in dusty rose, as were the walls. I have nothing against dusty rose, but it seemed a bit difficult to breathe in all that monochromatic, dull pink. There were a few decorative pieces: one or two glass ashtrays, prints of Gainsborough's *Blue Boy* and Reynolds's *Age of Innocence* above the sofa, and a framed wedding picture of Donna and Doug on a mahogany side table. On the coffee table rested a neat stack of magazines—*Reader's Digest*, several issues of *Family Circle* (the one they sell in supermarkets), and the latest issues of *Life*, *Look*, and the *Saturday Evening Post*—all carefully arranged in order of size. In the corner stood a large wood cabinet, which housed a small television screen. I was impressed, having had little contact with television up to that point. It had become quite popular in the previous few years, but I hadn't had the chance to stay anywhere that was furnished with a set.

Donna returned, carrying a little boy about two years old with jelly smeared on his face. He was rubbing his grimy fist into his mouth, and his nose was running. He was just gasping away his crying fit and settling down against his mother's breast, where she held him close.

"He's a holy terror," she said, and then added encouragingly, "but he's going to be a good boy tonight, aren't you sweetheart?"

"He looks like his daddy," I observed.

"Do you think so?" she said. "Some people say he has my nose."

"He's a good-looking little boy, in any case."

She smiled with satisfied pride. "We're hoping for a girl this time."

"That would be ideal," I said.

"Yes," she answered. "But we'll take whatever the good Lord sends us. Oh my! I'm forgetting my manners. Would you care for a drink?"

"Scotch and soda, if you have it."

Her brow furrowed. "I know there's some scotch, but I'm not sure if we have any club soda. I could run out and get some, if you like. Or I think there's some Seven Up. Do people drink scotch and Seven Up?"

"Scotch and water will be fine," I said.

She looked relieved. "Would you mind keeping an eye on Dougie while I fix it?" she said. And without waiting for a reply, she deposited the little boy on my lap and left the room. Having had little experience with children, I looked at him as if he had just landed from outer space. He must have sensed my discomfort because he began to fret and cry immediately, and all the dandling and cooing I could muster had no effect except to make him cry all the harder. I'm sure there was a sheet of sweat on my brow as I tried to hold him close to my chest the way his mother had, but he just kept crying and I just kept perspiring.

Just then I heard a man's voice say "Dan?" and I looked up to see Doug with a salesman's sample case in one hand and his suit jacket in the other. His necktie was loosened and his hat was set far back on his head. He looked oddly worried as he dropped his case and rushed over to rescue his son from my lap.

"Are you okay?" he asked.

I wasn't sure whether he meant the baby or me, so I said, "We're doing fine."

"How are you, Dan?" he asked, so I assumed it was his son he had been worried about. I wondered if he thought I was a child molester.

"I'm okay," I said. I was waiting to see if he inspected the baby for any signs of damage. But of course the boy had stopped crying as soon as his daddy had picked him up, and Doug didn't do anything out of the ordinary, so I decided not to give way to my foolish fears. Donna appeared with my drink in a blue aluminum glass and handed it to me. It tasted metallic. She kissed Doug's cheek and said, "Hi, honey. Glad you're back early. Here, let me take the baby."

"What brings you to Ohio?" Doug asked as he was being relieved of his son.

My paranoid interpretation of that question was: How long are you going to impose yourself on us? I answered, "Just passing through."

"On your way to where?"

"Uh, actually, I'm not sure."

"Where are you coming from?"

"Chicago. My sister-in-law just had a baby, and I was helping out my brother in his hardware store for a while." I had told this lie so often that it was beginning to sound like the truth to me, but I stuck with it because somehow I didn't think Doug would appreciate my tales of Miss Wanda's brothel and the Cook County Jail. "Before that I went to college for a while, but I dropped out."

"Hey, I don't remember you saying anything about having a brother. So now you're an uncle, huh? Congratulations! And a college man, too! I never had a chance to go. I've been too busy showing my samples to storekeepers. Melmac dishes—plastic to you. Never chip, never break. I've got to do something to keep the meat and potatoes on the table. The family's getting bigger, but I'm sure you could figure that out."

"Congratulations yourself," I said. "You've got a beautiful family."

"So what line did you say you were in? Hardware?"

"Uh, yeah, hardware," I said.

"Supper's about ready," said Donna. "Why don't you boys wash up? You can catch up on old times while we eat."

Supper was served on chartreuse and dusty-rose Melmac dishes, which made strange, dull, *clacking* sounds whenever they were struck with the stainless steel flatware. There was a roast chicken, neatly cut up, with canned string beans and french-fried potatoes.

"It's delicious," I assured Donna.

"There's baked apple for dessert," she said sweetly.

"If I knew you were comin', I'd've baked a cake," Doug sang to the tune of a popular song of the day.

"Baked apple sounds just fine," I said, determined to keep a smile on my face throughout dessert in spite of my opinion of apples.

"Life is sure different now," Doug observed.

"I remember when we were thrilled to get some rice for supper," I said.

"Thank God that's over," he answered. Donna got up to do the dishes.

"Do you ever think back to those days in the camp?" I asked.

He looked at me oddly. "Not often," he answered. "It isn't exactly my favorite memory."

"Mine either," I said. "But going through something like that makes you grateful for everything else."

"I guess so," he said. "At least we have a little bit of say in what becomes of us now. I never want to be incarcerated again, for any reason."

"Neither do I," I said, thinking back to Cook County Jail.

"Listen, let's not drag up painful memories. Hey! Milton Berle's on tonight. Did you ever see him?"

I shook my head no.

"You'll get a kick out of this guy. He's a riot."

After Donna put Doug Junior to sleep, the three of us settled down to watch television. Doug and Donna sat together on the dusty-rose sofa, and I sat in the dusty-rose club chair. The little screen glowed with the Texaco service station men singing about how much they would do for your car. Then a guy in a derby pushed up the sleeves of his loud sport jacket and made a pitch to sell cans of motor oil. Finally Milton Berle came out, wearing a big, flowered dress with padded tits and ass and a mile-wide slash of lipstick on his mouth, and camped all over the stage. He looked nothing like Willard in drag, I thought. Then I thought back to Doug, dressed in banana leaves and flour sacks for the Christmas show, and my awkward attempt at seducing him. Thoughts of having sex with him in the prison camp wandered into my mind, and soon I was remembering the punishments I had endured for my efforts. Meanwhile, Doug and Donna were both laughing hysterically, with tears rolling down their cheeks as a little guy with a giant powder puff came out and dusted whoever had the misfortune to say the word "makeup." Some of the gags were pretty funny, I admit, but much of my own laughter was polite, and I felt myself nodding off before the show had ended. I had had a rough night in Indiana.

After he shut off the television, Doug said, "So you don't know where you're headed next?"

"My plans are pretty loose," I answered.

"Dan, you have to stay here with us until you're settled. I won't take no for an answer. It's the least I can do after all you did for me during the war. I'm sorry there's only the couch to sleep on."

"Please stay," Donna added.

"Well, just for tonight, okay?" I replied. "And it's only because I don't have a better offer. You guys have enough on your hands without me. Listen, Doug. You don't owe me anything for what I did during the war. You did as much for me."

"But you did it first," he said, and he put his arm around my shoulder. I wanted him to leave it there, but he released it and went to get the linens, so I could go to sleep.

Donna made up the couch, apologizing the whole while for not having a spare room. Meanwhile, Doug and I sat eyeing each other rather uncomfortably. I don't know what was on his mind. Maybe fear that I would sneak into his son's room and steal his virginity. Maybe he was remembering the camp. But on my mind was the old desire for him. It wasn't a driving passion, it was just that he was such a sweet guy. I wished I had someone to depend on the way his family depended on him. I wished my life were more organized than it was. I didn't need to be rich. I just needed to have some direction. I just needed someone to love. Hiding my needs was starting to become difficult. It was a relief when we all turned in for the night.

In spite of how tired I was, I lay in the darkened living room for hours, listening for sounds, imagining again and again that I could hear Doug stirring. I waited for him to come to me, to abandon his sleeping wife for just one hour and to reassure me that our past connection had meant something. But there was only silence and the faint sound of snoring. Finally, I jerked off into a handkerchief and fell sound asleep.

By the time I awoke, it was mid-morning and sunlight was streaming into the room. I could hear Donna stirring in the kitchen. I straightened the couch the best I could and went into the bathroom to splash some water in my face. In the kitchen I found her feeding Doug Junior in his high chair.

"Guess I slept pretty late," I said apologetically. "What time is it?"

"Ten-thirty. You must have been tired from your trip."

"Where's Doug?"

"He had to leave for work. He said to let you sleep as long as you wanted, and to make sure to say good morning for him."

"Good morning," I said.

"Want some breakfast? I kept some bacon and eggs warm for you."

While I ate, I tried to think what I would do next. All I could think of was to get on another bus and keep on going. I didn't want to intrude on Doug's life for any longer than I had to. There was really nothing between us except a nightmare we both wanted to forget.

At noon the phone rang. It was Doug. "Dan? Listen, I have good news for you. I have a friend in Cleveland who has a hardware supply store. My company supplies dishes to him. Anyway, to make a long story short, he's got a position open, but you have to get there before seven p.m. or it will go to somebody else. I hope it's okay. It's the best I could do on such short notice."

"Wow," I said. "It's more than okay. It's better than I've been able to do for myself. Thanks a lot."

He gave me the address. "Hey, I get up there every once in a while on my route," he said. "Maybe we can have lunch sometime."

"Sure," I said. "We'll have lunch."

We said good-bye.

I got my stuff together and thanked Donna for her hospitality. As I was leaving, I patted Doug Junior on the head in farewell; but he started to cry again, so I backed off. I took a taxi to the bus station and caught the next bus to Cleveland.

The trip took a few hours, and I spent it thinking over what had just happened. I couldn't decide if Doug had purposely found me a spot in another city because he didn't want me nearby to embarrass him about what we'd done in the prisoner-of-war camp, or if he didn't want me near his little boy, for fear I'd find a way to pervert him. Maybe I was just being too sensitive, and he'd simply done the best he could. I really was grateful to him. What the hell? Cleveland was better than no place, I figured.

When I got off the bus in Cleveland, it was getting dark. From the look of things, it wasn't very inviting. There was just a drabness about it that turned me off. It didn't feel like a small town, and it didn't feel like a big city. A city like Chicago can look drab too, but at least it has the promise of excitement, and here and there a touch of architectural splendor. From a map I had bought in the bus terminal, I knew that Cleveland was situated on Lake Erie, but as I looked around, it seemed like even a lake wouldn't help. The truth is that there wasn't so much wrong with Cleveland that isn't wrong with a lot of other places. I just didn't want to be there. I didn't want to be under obligation to Doug, and I didn't want him to feel responsible for me. I liked him too much for that.

Nonetheless, for lack of an alternative, I dutifully made my way to the address he had given me. I arrived at 6:30 and stood across the street from Acme Hardware. It was in a rundown neighborhood of small factories. Large vans and trucks were parked along the streets, and between them dirt and litter clogged the gutters. I stood there for a few minutes, trying to decide whether to cross the street in spite of it all. And then I started to laugh. For the first time that day, I realized that I didn't know a thing about hardware—at least not beyond hammering a nail to hang a picture or replacing a burned-out light bulb or a worn-out washer in the sink. I had gotten so embroiled in the story I'd made up that I had forgotten it was a lie. I wouldn't last an hour at that job. There was no point in even going inside. I simply turned and went back to the bus station.

It was getting late, and I was tired of traveling, so after an inexpensive meal, I rented a room in a fleabag near the terminal. I sat there for an hour, staring at the cracked linoleum floor and listening to strange rustling sounds in the walls that I thought might be the sound of rats, but I certainly didn't want to find out for sure. I counted my money. There was just enough to make another short trip and to support myself for a few days. Then I'd be flat broke. I decided to head for the next city eastward in the morning. According to the map, that was Pittsburgh.

Unable to afford even a movie for entertainment, I fell back on my old companion, *Leaves of Grass*. Thinking of Doug's protectiveness toward his little boy, I thumbed through the pages looking for passages about fathers (aside from the unpleasant one I'd read in Indiana). The first one I found was:

> The father holds his grown or ungrown son in his arms with
> measureless love, and the son holds the father in his arms
> with measureless love.

Charmed by that portrait and feeling sentimental, I kept on looking, and I found a second one:

> I knew a man, a common farmer, the father of five sons . . .
> This man was of wonderful vigor, calmness, beauty of person . . .

Then I did something stupid. I decided to call home. Maybe I had been taken in by what I'd been reading. Maybe it was the influence of being with Doug's family. Maybe it was because I had tried everything else I could think of. At any rate, I went down to the pay phone in the dingy lobby and, after ascertaining how much it would cost to call New York State and getting a fistful of coins, I asked the long-distance operator for the number in Elysium. I remembered it without even trying. It rang several times, and then my father's voice answered.

"Hello," he said.

I found that I couldn't speak. If I could, I don't know what I would have said, but it didn't matter because no words would come out anyway. I just stood there.

"Hello?" he repeated. "Hello?"

I started to cry softly, hoping the desk clerk wouldn't hear me.

"What is this, some darnfool joke or something?" he said, and slammed down the receiver.

I just stood there with the dead phone dangling from my hand, until the desk clerk came and gently took it from me.

"You okay, pal?" he asked. "Bad news?"

"I'm fine," I told him, and I went upstairs to my room. There was one other passage I wanted to find in *Leaves of Grass*.

> I throw myself on your breast my father,
> I cling to you so that you cannot unloose me,
> I hold you so firm till you answer me something.

I fell asleep immediately with all my clothes on and the book open on my chest. I didn't care about the rats or the linoleum or anything. Tomorrow I would be somewhere else.

CHAPTER FOURTEEN

I arrived in Pittsburgh the next afternoon. At first glance it seemed no more inviting to me than Cleveland had, but without additional carfare, I was there for better or worse. The money I had would last me for no more than two days. So I took the cheapest room I could find at the YMCA, and after a parsimonious meal at a downtown diner, I bought a *Pittsburgh Gazette*, so I could spend the evening going through the want ads.

I didn't know what heading to look under. "Hardware" was definitely out. "Brothel attendant" wasn't listed. "Diner Assistant" wasn't, either. What else did my experience fit me for? "Student and Kept Man" wasn't too helpful. "Inmate" and "Prisoner of War" held little promise. "Medical Aide" might be a useful category, but if I said my experience had been in the military, I'd probably have had to produce an honorable discharge. So I scratched that. The best I could do was go through the ads alphabetically and hope to find something suitable.

I went through every single ad and finally circled four that looked promising—or at least less impossible than the rest. One was for a position as a waiter. (I practiced balancing a glass of water on a phone book held on the outspread fingertips of one hand, and as it tumbled to the floor, I envisioned plates of food falling gracefully onto the diners' shoulders; but I kept at it, and eventually I got the hang of it.) Another advertiser was looking for a gas station attendant. (I pictured myself in a bow tie and a neatly pressed uniform with no oil smudges, like the singing Texaco men on the Milton Berle show.) A third one was for a clerk in a grocery store. (I imagined I would become a noble Lady Bountiful, distributing life's necessities to the masses.) And the last ad I marked was for a job as an assistant in an antique shop. (The only information I had about antiques was that they were old and useless and likely to be dirty, but I figured I could pick up the details later.)

The next day I went out early in the morning. The position as waiter was in a posh-looking restaurant with lace curtains and a French wine list. A snooty maître d' with a tiny, waxed mustache looked me up and down disdainfully, and before I could even tell him about my valuable experience in Gus's Diner, he informed me that the waiter's job had already been taken.

I was glad I wouldn't have to work under him. There were two other applicants for the gas station attendant's job, and both of them already had experience, so I lost. I didn't see a single bow tie in the place, and judging by the grease smeared all over the interviewer's coveralls and embedded under his fingernails, I wouldn't have had much to sing about. So much for Milton Berle. The job as grocery clerk was intended for a teenager who wanted to deliver boxes of food on a bicycle part-time after school, and when I offered to do it anyway, the manager told me the starting salary, which wouldn't even pay for my room at the Y, and I slinked out quietly. The downtrodden masses would have to be fed without my help. That left the antique shop. The ad read: "Antiques / Presentable young man wanted to assist shopkeeper with stock, sales, etc. / Inquire at Auld Appointments, Edwin Gable Roe, Prop." It gave both an address across town from where I was and a phone number. Sensing a need for formal propriety and not wanting to make a long trip in vain, I called to make an appointment to see Mr. Roe, Prop.

The phone was answered with a somewhat elegant "Hello," containing five or six melodious syllables.

"Is this Mr. Roe?" I asked.

"It is, indeed. May I be of service?"

"I think we might have this backward," I answered. "The question is whether *I* can be of service. I'm answering the advertisement you placed in the *Gazette*."

"Oh yes, of course. How silly of me. I do tend to forget sometimes. I'm not used to placing advertisements, you know."

I noticed that he stressed the second syllable instead of the third when he said "advertisements," and I found myself nodding politely, even though he couldn't see me over the phone.

"Have you had any experience with antique merchandising?" he continued.

"None whatsoever, I'm afraid," I replied, sensing that it would please the old buzzard if I emulated his polished phrasing.

"Then why did you choose my advertisement to reply to?"

"I'm not quite sure, actually. It just seemed rather . . . friendly." I put a bit of accent on the "friendly," hoping that he was as queer as his voice implied he was and that he could tell by my tone that I was, too.

"Well, I did try to place a businesslike statement," he said with a small sigh. "But I suppose I can't help sounding friendly. It is my nature, you know."

"I'm glad to hear that," I said.

"Ahem. Do you think you might like to be educated about antiques?"

"Oh yes. I've always been fond of them," I lied. "And I hope you'll see that I learn very quickly."

"You sound like an ambitious young man. Are you presentable, as the advertisement states?"

"I like to think so."

"Well, perhaps I'd better see for myself. Would you like to stop in so I can meet you?"

"I would be happy to."

"And what, may I ask, is your name?"

"Dell Blake, sir."

"Very well, Dell. Suppose you come by this afternoon."

"Yes, sir."

As I hung up the phone, I felt that I was putting down a Dickens novel. Mr. Roe was certainly in the right business, I decided. He sounded as antique as his merchandise. I had a quick lunch and took a bus across the Monongahela River to the South Side, an area that looked as if it had never been any grander than proletarian, with minimal middle-class pretensions. I got off the bus at Arlington Avenue, following the directions I'd gotten at the Y, and, after asking several people who had never heard of the place, I finally found the shop. It was under an ornately lettered sign reading exactly as the ad had: AULD APPOINTMENTS, EDWIN GABLE ROE, PROP. The facade had an air of faded elegance about it, which suggested that it was merely by a slight error that it had found itself in this particular neighborhood, but that it would deign to be the arbiter of local tastes nonetheless. *Noblesse oblige*, I thought.

Dusty-looking velvet curtains of olive drab trimmed in faded gold fringe served to frame the window display, which consisted of a rickety-looking wood chair supporting a large, sporadically fringed satin pillow that said something about Niagara Falls; a threadbare, embroidered footstool large enough for only one normal foot; and a spindly table covered with a yellowed lace doily dripping over the edges because it was far too large for its surface, upon which sat a pair of scratched crystal candlesticks, several ashtrays, one or two miniature pictures on tiny easels, and some ornate paperweights. In chaotic clusters around the central pieces was an assemblage of odd, unrelated items: an enameled chamber pot with a bouquet of formerly pink rosebuds painted on its cracked lid; an extravagant inkstand with a dusty, balding plume emerging from its top; several chipped china vases and pitchers and plates, hand-painted with landscapes and maidens' faces; a few old bottles and pipes and canes; an iron dog, which I guessed was intended to be a doorstop; and some corroded-looking baskets and bowls and rusting candy tins. Swell, I thought, and opened the front door, which caused a small bell somewhere above my head to tinkle gently.

A short, old man with a wrinkled, cherubic face and a gracefully held head of carefully arranged white hair sat on a stool behind the counter. In spite of the fact that the sweater he was wearing looked as antique and moth-eaten as his merchandise, his bearing was aristocratic. He carried a silver-handled black cane, which proved to be not a decorative touch but a necessity since he leaned upon it heavily when he rose to greet me. "Yes?" he said. "May I assist you?" He smiled graciously, which caused his puffy cheeks to quiver.

"I spoke to you on the telephone. I'm here to answer the advertisement?" I don't know why, but I turned my statement into a question, and of course I accented the *ver* in "advertisement."

"Oh yes, of course. What was your name again? Dill?"

"Dell. Dell Blake, sir."

"Oh please, there's no need for formality. You may call me Mr. Roe."

"Yes, Mr. Roe."

"That's better. Now, Dull ... Wait, don't tell me ... Dell. Now, Dell, you said you have no experience with antiques. What makes you think you'd like to work in a shop like this?"

I looked around, and realized that nothing could make me want to work there except the imminent threat of starvation. "I'm new in town," I said truthfully. "I thought I might want to settle here, at least for a while, and I need work to sustain myself. When I looked at the want ads in the paper, yours caught my eye. It's the first one I answered." There was no point in being too truthful, I figured.

"That's good. You said on the phone that you're fond of antiques. Can you explain what you mean by that?"

"Well ... ah ... I've always respected old things, although I can't tell one from another, to be honest. The truth is that it's mostly nineteenth-century literature that I like—especially Walt Whitman—and I'd like to learn about the objects that surrounded him." I was relieved to be telling at least part of the truth. I was pretty pleased with my on-the-spot invention, and I hoped that the reference to Whitman would appeal to his presumably homosexual sensibility.

"Well, I suppose your interest in literature is admirable," he said with a hesitant air. "But Walt Whitman? Don't you find his writings rather crude?"

"Crude, sir?"

"Yes. When I went to school, Whitman was considered somewhat shocking, you know."

"Oh yes, I know what you mean. Well, I suppose some of his physical references might be considered rough-hewn. But, you know, there is a strong spiritual side to his writing which attracts me, and a patriotic side as well."

"Well, I suppose the main thing is your literary interest. *De gustibus non disputandum est* and all that."

"Sir?"

"You may as well call me Edwin. You know, 'You can't argue about taste' and that sort of thing."

"Oh, no, sir . . . Mr. Roe . . . Edwin."

"That's better. Now, Doll . . . I mean Dell, I want to be honest with you as well. I've run that advertisement for a week now, and you're the first person to answer it. I suppose we're lucky to find one another. Have you had lunch yet?"

"Yes, I have."

"Well, I have not. I generally close the shop about now for an hour and go home for my afternoon meal. Why don't you join me? Perhaps you'd like a cup of tea while I dine."

I didn't know if that meant that I was being hired or if I were still being interviewed, but it seemed impolite to ask about anything as crude as salary. So I simply said, "Yes, that would be very nice." Then I wondered if this were some elaborate ploy to get me into his lair so he could have his way with my firm young flesh. What difference does it make? I asked myself. Have you had any better offers today?

He went to the front of the shop and carefully turned the yellowed sign which hung in the doorway, so that the side reading "Closed" faced outward. Then he slowly drew down the fringed shade that covered the door's glass pane, and he locked the door in two places. His movements seemed like a kind of ritual.

Didn't he say we were going to his house? I thought. But our destination became clear to me when he walked to the back of the shop and elegantly drew aside a heavy brocade curtain, from whose faded iridescent folds small clouds of dust puffed forth, and, gesturing me inside with his silver-handled walking stick, he said, "Welcome to my home."

There were three rooms behind the shop: a sitting room, bedroom, and kitchen. As he showed me around, he referred to them as the "parlor," the "sleeping chamber," and the "scullery." He established me on the divan in the parlor while he went into the scullery to prepare his lunch with a great deal of clinking and clattering. I took the opportunity to look around. There was so much clutter that it was difficult to tell the parlor from the antique shop. Dusty bric-a-brac filled every available surface. Some of it might have been attractive or even valuable, but it was difficult to sort it out with the eye. The walls were covered with gilt-framed old paintings hung so closely that the edges of their frames touched. Most of them were portraits of heroic male figures, I noticed. And a closer look at the clutter revealed that many of the sculptured pieces were dark bronze statuettes of handsome males. I felt like I was drowning in a sea of artistic musculature, and I remember thinking that I could imagine worse fates.

The one thing that didn't seem to fit into its surroundings was a three-foot statue of the Virgin Mary. It stood alone in a corner on a small pedestal, with a small votive candle burning at its feet. It couldn't have been a part of the artistic collection since it was the kind of icon that one could buy by the dozen; so it was clear that Edwin was a devout Catholic.

Stately, plump Edwin Gable Roe emerged from his scullery with a silver tray in his hands. He set the tray down with great care and ceremoniously lifted and replaced an elaborately embroidered tea cozy to reveal a flowered china teapot, next to which stood a matching sugar bowl, creamer, and two cups and saucers. Two miniature silver spoons lay parallel to each other alongside the cups. I noticed that their stems had been crafted into tiny soldiers on whose uniforms the buttons could be clearly seen. The tray also featured a crystal plate of watercress sandwiches with the crusts neatly trimmed, and two small beige napkins with lace trim. "I thought you might relent and join me for a bite," my host said graciously. Then he settled himself into a wingback chair and sighed contentedly.

After a moment he remembered himself and, like a duchess called to duty, removed the tea cozy, carefully swayed the pot several times, first to one side and then the other, and finally poured the tea without spilling a drop.

"One lump or two?" he asked sweetly.

"One, please."

I watched his measured movements as he used tiny silver tongs to place a lump of sugar gently into each cup. He added a bit of cream to one of them, held the tilted cream pitcher poised above the other, and looked at me with a raised eyebrow, at which I nodded my head once, as if by custom. With a precise movement of his wrist he added a bit of cream to the second cup and proffered it to me. "Please help yourself to the sandwiches," he said, and to be polite I took one. It looked a little silly, but it didn't taste bad at all.

"Now . . ." He seemed lost.

"Dell," I reminded him.

"Of course, Dell," he said and paused, as if he were really fixing it in his memory this time. He began again. "Now, Dell, what do you see before you?"

"A very agreeable lunch," I said, surprised at my own vocabulary.

"I mean the service on which it appears."

Then I realized that I was getting my first lesson. "Well," I speculated, "the tray looks like silver."

"Where do you think it's from?"

I looked at it more carefully. It wasn't like some silver trays I'd seen. Willard had one from Belgium that was very ornately engraved with elaborately curlicued handles. This one was rather plain, with no etching and squared handles. I made a guess. "America?"

"Excellent," he responded. "You are a promising pupil. Actually, this piece is from the workshop of Paul Revere, about 1770."

I acted very impressed. "Really? It must be worth a good deal."

He beamed his assent. Then a look of concern flitted across his brow, and he remarked. "These pieces are easily traceable, you know, so there's little point in anyone trying to abscond with them."

"You don't have to worry, Edwin. I'm not a thief."

He relaxed a little. Then he went on. "And the tea service?"

It was made of fluted white china with delicate yellow blossoms and sprays of tiny green leaves wreathing each piece. Again I guessed. Where would they make a big deal out of a teapot? "English?" I suggested.

"Wonderful. When?"

The only thing English I could think of at the moment was Queen Victoria.

"Nineteenth century?"

"Excellent. Very early, of course—circa 1810. Are you sure you have no training in this field?"

"None. I was just lucky."

"Lucky, indeed. Young man, you have the job. How does sixty dollars a week sound to you?"

It didn't sound great, considering that I'd made more at Miss Wanda's. But I assumed that a brothel could afford to pay more than an antique shop, and for the moment, a steady sixty dollars coming in every week would help keep me alive, even though it wouldn't be in high style.

I must have hesitated while I was thinking, because the old man quickly added, "Of course after a while, a raise is possible."

"It sounds just fine," I said, smiling. "When do I start?"

"Why, right now, my boy."

When he had put away the dishes, we went back into the shop and, while he sat quietly on his stool, I unlocked the door and turned the sign around to read "Open." Then I suggested, "Maybe I could begin by cleaning up."

"There's a feather duster behind the portiere," he said, his cheeks aquiver as he nodded toward the brocade curtain.

I spent the afternoon dusting the shop and sneezing. Edwin eventually retired into his sitting room, perhaps to avoid the dust, or maybe to take a nap. He didn't emerge again until it was nearly 5 p.m. "Closing time," he said. Not one customer had come into the shop all afternoon.

I went back to the YMCA for the night. Old Edwin had been an honorable gentleman. He had made no move to seduce me. But sex was on my mind nonetheless. As I headed toward the shower, I noticed someone going into a doorway that had been left ajar.

There was the muffled sound of conversation, which I thought strange because I knew all the rooms were singles. Then the door closed.

In the shower, I relaxed under the hot water, letting the dust of Auld Appointments and the exhaustion of a day's work wash down the drain. I soaped myself and washed my hair, and only when I was rinsing off did I realize that I was being watched. I looked across to the shower stall opposite mine in time to see its occupant quickly avert his gaze. I knew that gesture, having used it enough times myself in high school gym class and in the army barracks. The guy wasn't bad-looking, about my height with brown hair plastered to his skull by the shower water and a nice set of equipment hanging beneath his midriff, which was slightly thickened by food or beer and lightly covered with hair. I kept on rinsing myself for longer than was necessary and paid extra attention to my genitals while I kept checking to see if he was watching, which he was. Then I stepped out of the shower and slowly toweled myself off, giving him ample opportunity to check my merchandise as he stepped from his stall and, following my lead, toweled himself dry at the same pace. When I was done, I said, "Hi."

"Hi," he said.

We left the shower room, carrying our toiletries and wearing only our towels wrapped around our waists. He walked a few steps in front of me, his well-padded buttocks moving invitingly beneath the white terry cloth, and I wanted to reach out to touch them, but of course I didn't dare. Periodically, he looked over his shoulder to see if I were still following, and each time he did so, our eyes met. Soon he slowed down, and I slowed behind him. Even though I was almost sure he wanted me to wait as he fiddled with his room key, I had to keep moving, because I had no legitimate excuse to stop. He kept looking around as I moved past him, and we smiled at each other. But we couldn't say anything without taking the chance of being overheard. Finally he got his door open, and waited until I turned around again to meet his eyes before he entered, leaving his door ajar. I turned in my tracks and walked slowly past his room—and when I arrived at his door, he was standing just inside, beckoning with his finger. He ushered me inside and quickly shut the door. "My name is Martin," he said.

"I'm Dell."

"Are you a friend of Dorothy?" he asked.

"Who's Dorothy?"

"Never mind," he said. "Why did you come in here?"

"Um . . . You seemed like you might like some company."

"What did you have in mind?" he inquired.

"Whatever you like."

"Good," he replied, and he took off his towel to reveal a respectable erection. Then he reached over and removed my towel. Before I could say anything, he was on his knees before me. After a few minutes of greedy attention to my groin, he stood and drew me toward his bed.

Once there, we cuddled together, rubbing our bodies against each other. He felt as good as the nameless man from the Chicago bar had felt. Had that been only a couple of days earlier? It seemed like months. I nuzzled Martin's cheek, and he moaned. But as I moved my lips to cover his, he said, "Uh-uh. I don't kiss on the first date."

"Why not?" I asked.

"Let's not get personal," he said.

"How much more personal can we get?"

"I mean, let's keep it just sex. Okay?"

"If you say so," I said, disappointed.

We kept it just sex, as he suggested, but one thing I really like is kissing, and his reluctance to do so put a damper on the whole procedure for me. When we had finished, he made an elaborate display of stretching and yawning. Then he said, "I have to get home now."

"Didn't you take a room for the night?" I asked, mystified.

"I paid for the night, but I can only stay for the evening. I told the desk clerk that I only needed it for a short nap. I have to get back to my folks. They don't know about the seamy side of my life."

"Thanks a lot," I retorted.

"Don't take it personally," he said. "It's just the way I feel about this kind of stuff in general."

"Then why do it?"

"Because I have to," he answered. "Why do you do it?"

"I guess because I have to, too, but I like it."

"Don't you think it's a little sleazy?" he asked.

"Do you know any better way?"

"Of course. We could marry good women and raise families, like we're supposed to."

"I tried marriage," I told him, "and it didn't work. You don't really want to get married."

"This is a sickness," he said. "I can't help myself. Why should I inflict my mental illness on some innocent woman?"

"Why should you inflict it on some innocent man?"

"You mean on you?" He raised his eyebrows. "You're not so innocent. You're just as perverted as I am."

"Maybe," I said. "Anyway, I have to get up early for work in the morning, so I'd better get to bed . . . I mean, to sleep."

"Okay."

"But before I go, what was that business you asked me about Dorothy's friend when I came in?"

"You know . . . Dorothy, from *The Wizard of Oz*. Don't you like Judy Garland?"

"Sure, I guess so," I said.

251

"Well it's just the way gay boys identify each other," he explained.

"Oh. You mean like a secret code? Well, in that case, I'm a friend of Dorothy."

"Welcome to fantasy land. Good night now . . . and thanks," he said in a conciliatory tone.

"Good night, Martin."

He looked a little annoyed that I had remembered his name.

When I went back to my own room, I kept thinking about him. I felt as if I had met him before. I knew that was impossible, yet there was something familiar about his tone that insistently reminded me of someone. It wasn't until an hour later that I remembered who it was. He reminded me of George Grimes, my unhappy gay friend back in high school. I had introduced him to Bruno Todd, the contemptuous brute who'd paid for tutoring with sex, because I thought their personalities would fit well together. As I drifted off to sleep, I wondered what had become of them.

I awoke in the middle of the night, all confused. It took me a few moments to recognize the strange environment as my room at the YMCA, but I was still disoriented. I had just had a dream.

George and Bruno were in an antique shop covered with cobwebs, which was also a classroom. George was trying to kiss Bruno, who kept pulling his head away, saying, "If you love me, you won't try to kiss me. Do you love me?"—which only made George try all the harder. George was also Edwin, and Bruno turned into Willard Stevenson and back. So sometimes George was trying to kiss Willard, and Edwin was trying to kiss Bruno. But the action and the dialogue remained the same. Then, while my new friend Martin held me up, I was writing the words in lipstick on the stone wall of a shower stall: "If you love me, you won't try to kiss me."

I soon found an inexpensive apartment not far from Auld Appointments. It was very small—one room with a daybed and a Pullman kitchen. The only window opened on a detailed view of a brick wall, and I usually kept the shade drawn so that the place wouldn't remind me of my cell in Cook County Jail. It certainly wasn't my idea of gracious living. But it was all mine, and I told myself that it was home, at least until something better came along.

One of the first things I did, once I had an address, was to write to Louie in jail:

February 7, 1950

Dear Louie,

I don't know if you'll be surprised to hear from me so soon, but I just wanted you to know where I am. I've settled in Pittsburgh, Pa., of all places! Don't ask me how I got here, it just happened. I'm working in an antique shop, dusting knickknacks for a sweet but confused old man. (I'm sure he's one of us, but we haven't had a chance to talk about such lofty matters yet.)

I have had a couple of encounters since I've been out, but nothing to write home about. If I run into any real excitement, I'll be sure to tell you. I just wanted to let you know you're not missing anything special out here. I hope you get my drift. At least I don't have lugs like Duke doing my picking for me— although so far his taste has proved better than mine! Did anybody ever mention hearing from Carlos?

How are you and Fred doing? I can't say I want to be where you are, right now, but I do miss you guys. Funny, isn't it? You two are as close as any friends I've got. I wish I could do you some good. Anyway, if you want to write to me, the address is on the envelope.

I know you're not one for highfalutin stuff like poetry, but if you don't mind, I'll leave you with a few lines from my favorite poet, Walt Whitman:

> ". . . though the live-oak glistens there in Louisiana
>   solitary in a wide flat space,
> Uttering joyous leaves all its life without a friend a lover
>   near,
> I know very well I could not."

Sincerely yours,
Dell Blake

In a week I received Louie's answer:

February 12, 1950

Dear Dell,

Its real good to hear from you! I didnt think you would want to remember youre old buddies in the pen. Please forgive my bad spelling and penmenship. It was never my strong point in school. I hope it aint to hard on youre educated eyes. Thanks for sending me some poetry. Im pretty sure I get what it says and it makes me feel kind of proud.

Dell, Im sorry to have some bad news for you. Two days after you got sprung Fred got into a big fight with Duke, and was killed. Stabbed. Duke is in solitary now and will go to trial soon. Its a dam shame if you ask me. Fred was one of the few descent guys in this joint. Now that you and him are both gone, Im the only guy I like here. Ecxept for my old man that is, sort of. I hope poor Fred rests in peace, he didnt deserve what he got, thats for sure.

I have a new partner working with me in the infirmery now. His name is Jake and hes nothing like you or me, if you know what I mean. Hes a real jerk and a bore and thanks to him I have to do all the double checking on the counting and everything because if anything hes worse then I am at it!

I asked around and nobody knows anything about Carlos. Ill keep trying.

You asked if you could do me some good. Well buddy you can, if you dont mind that is. I hate to ask you but I aint got much choice. Do you think you could send me a fin or even a sawbuck maybe? Its for cigarets. You know I cant go on for long without a butt between my lips (if theres nothing else handy, that is, ha ha!) Keep in touch, okay? I hope to see you again when I get out of here.

Youre good friend,
Louie

Hearing about Fred really depressed me. He was an innocent victim if ever I heard of one. Who knows what his life might have been like if he didn't have so much bad luck? I wrote back to Louie and sent him five dollars, which was all I could afford. But we kept in touch from then on, and whenever I could spare a little, I sent it to him.

In the following months I worked conscientiously at the antique shop. Edwin seemed to welcome my company, but as gracious as he was, he was not forthcoming about his personal life. I dropped as many "beads" and "hairpins" as I could, but no matter how many hints I let loose about my sexual identity, he remained politely oblivious and kept our relationship on a professional basis, treating me like a prize pupil and considering himself my mentor at the university of antiques. But even though I grew to like him and I'm sure he felt the same way, we never became real friends or equals because he always hid behind his wall of civility.

Once in a rare while, one of his few friends would drop in to visit him. They were all men in their late sixties or early seventies, and they were all excessively well-groomed. One wore a trim, waxed mustache, and two of them had an unnatural touch of blue in their smoothly combed white hair. All of them wore vested suits and ties, usually with obviously costly tiepins and cuff links or a well-crafted watch chain or boutonniere to accent their fastidiousness. Edwin always greeted them with a little cry of surprise, which set his cheeks aquiver. Although it was clear that he had known his friends for many years, he invariably addressed them with cordial politeness and introduced them to me formally.

"Mr. Hastings, this is my assistant, Mr. Blake. Mr. Blake, Mr. Hastings."

"How do you do?" his friends would say to me, and then they would turn to my employer and add something like, "What an attractive young man. You've done well for yourself, Edwin," as if they were discussing a new piece of furniture.

"How do you do?" I would reply, and then Edwin would escort them through the brocade curtain and into his parlor for an hour of tea and conversation, leaving me to tend the shop and wonder if they ever relaxed their etiquette when they were alone.

I discovered some places to cruise for sex—the railroad yards and Mellon Square and Dithridge Street in the university area, and a bar or two. But if I mentioned any of them, Edwin acted as if I were a tourist describing the local sights, and dismissed my innuendos with a graceful wave of the hand and the suggestion that I might like to visit Mount Washington and ride up the incline on the motorized chair. If I suggested that I found the Monongahela Valley steelworkers attractive, he would change the subject to his collection of bronze male nudes and keep his responses on an artistic footing. If I asked about whom I might encounter at night in the heart of town at Point State Park, where the Ohio, Allegheny, and Monongahela Rivers all meet, he would say, "I always found the confluence of the three rivers quite lovely at night, with the lights of the city tracing their routes."

There was little to do at work since there were almost no customers. Often, I wondered how Edwin paid his rent. I assumed he had some other source of income and that the shop was only a way of keeping himself busy. But he didn't give it much of his time, since every afternoon he would disappear and spend longer and longer periods lost in the back apartment while I took care of business. When I had finished cleaning all the merchandise and learning a few things about it, I redoubled my efforts to improve the shop's appearance.

One afternoon I decided to surprise him by redoing the window. I removed a lot of the clutter and left behind only a few of the better pieces, which I arranged so that the entire display looked as nearly as possible like an actual room of a century earlier. He was delighted with the result. And so, apparently, were the neighbors, because business actually picked up a little. Edwin seemed to take no notice that the shop's income was improving. He did, however, raise my salary by ten dollars a week.

Emboldened by my success, I decided to reorganize the inventory, so we could locate things when we wanted them. Little by little, imperceptibly at first, I placed the silver with the silver, the china with the china, and so on, and then I arranged them according to the period when they were made, consolidating what Edwin had taught me and the information in several antiques catalogues that he kept behind the counter. He remained blind to the changes around him until one day when he tried to find something and couldn't.

"Oh dear, Dall!" he called, still having occasional trouble with my name. "I hope you didn't sell the green cloisonné bowl that was here. I did so fancy it."

"It's Dell, Edwin, remember? And the bowl is over here now, with the other enamelware."

"Dell, yes, Dell," he said, with his brow scrunched up in an effort to fix my name behind it once and for all. "With what other enamelware?"

"I found these other pieces, on the bottom shelf behind the counter, and I thought I'd arrange them together."

"Let me see," he said, coming over to where I was. "Why, I haven't seen those pieces in years! And there they are, all in a row. How clever of you!"

"Thank you," I said, as if he had patted my head.

"But how will we ever find them if we need them? Shouldn't you put everything back where it belongs now?"

"If you want me to, I will," I answered. "But this arrangement ought to make it easier to find things. All you have to remember is where each type of item is located."

"I suppose you're right," he said. "It does look awfully orderly. More businesslike."

"Maybe this new look will even attract a few of the rich ladies from Squirrel Hill, and you'll have some new customers."

"Perhaps," he said. "But then I'd have to order new stock to replace it, and I did so like the things I already had. Besides, I used to know where everything was. Couldn't we let the ladies from Squirrel Hill shop at Kaufmann's Department Store? Or Horne's?"

"I'll put everything back, if you like."

"Well, maybe . . . No, I suppose we should try this new system. It's just that it looks so serious."

"Am I fired?" I asked.

"Of course not, Dill . . . Wait, don't tell me . . . Dell. Why, you're the best employee I've ever had." He paused for a moment to reflect, then added, "Of course, you're also the first."

Both of us laughed at that, but I sensed that he was really relieved soon afterward, when it was closing time and he could have his domain back to himself.

One evening at about that time, I was cruising in Mellon Square when I saw a familiar figure. It was Martin, the man I'd met at the YMCA. I turned the corner to avoid him, but when I came around again there he was, cruising me just as eagerly as he had in the shower room.

"Hello, Martin," I said.

"Oh, I didn't recognize you at first," he answered. "I'm sorry, but I've forgotten your name."

"Dell," I reminded him. "Do you remember where we met?"

"Of course," he said. "At the Y. I don't go out that often."

"Well, it's nice to know that we're still attracted to each other," I said, trying to sound friendly.

"I don't usually see the same person more than once."

"Then I'm all the more flattered," I said.

"Do you have someplace to go?" he asked.

"You certainly don't waste words, do you?"

"I don't see why we shouldn't get right to the point," he said huffily.

"What's the point?" I asked.

"I want to suck your cock."

"How shocking! It must be love," I said, hoping to relax him.

"I think I have to go now," he said.

"Don't be silly. I was only kidding," I explained.

"Oh."

"But I do have one question," I said.

"What?" He sounded impatient.

"Do you kiss on the second date?"

"Why is kissing so important to you?" he asked.

"Let's just say I'm an old-fashioned guy."

"Well, I associate kissing with love," he asserted.

"Then I guess you're the old-fashioned guy," I said. "Do you associate sex with love?"

"Rarely. Maybe in marriage."

"You have a very high opinion of married life," I said.

"Listen, do you have someplace to go or not?" he asked.

"I gather that you're still living at home with your family."

"Naturally," he said. "I'm a bachelor."

"Well, I guess we can go to my apartment," I offered. "But only if you'll promise to kiss me."

"Oh all right, if you're going to make such a big deal about it," he grumbled.

"That's the spirit," I said.

We went back to my tiny apartment, and this time Martin let me kiss him. He tried to keep his lips closed at first, but I eventually pried my tongue between them. It wasn't exactly a satisfying experience. I didn't much like the feeling that I was coercing an unwilling victim. But when we got down to the fundamentals, Martin was pretty skilled at sucking my cock. And he seemed to enjoy having his own tended to, even if he was unwilling to say so.

When we were finished, he got up to go as he had the first time.

"You're welcome to stay the night," I said, trying to be a good host.

He looked at my narrow daybed, which was barely wide enough for one, and said, "Thanks, but I have to get back to my family. My mother worries."

"Isn't that sweet." My tone sounded more sarcastic than I had intended it to.

"I think so," he replied. He narrowed his eyes.

"Don't get upset," I said. "I'm just jealous. I never even knew my mother."

"Did she die when you were born?" he asked, sounding suddenly compassionate.

"Something like that. I never got the story quite clear."

"That's strange," he said. He waited to see if I would volunteer an explanation.

"Isn't it strange for a grown man to rush home to his mother?" I asked.

"Not in my neighborhood," he answered. "If you don't have a wife to look after you, it's your mother's responsibility—and my mom takes her work seriously."

"Is it because of her that you're so afraid of getting involved?"

"Who said I was afraid? I'm just not ready." He folded his arms across his chest defiantly.

"I see."

"Are you inviting me to get involved with you?" he asked.

"I'm not in love with you, if that's what you mean," I said. "I just happen to be free, and walking the streets can get to be a bore."

"I'll say. And it isn't safe anymore, either."

"You mean you get beat up?" I asked.

"Well, not me personally, but I have heard of it happening," he explained. "That wasn't what I meant, though."

"What did you mean, then?"

"Haven't you been reading the papers?" he asked.

"Oh, you mean that guy in Washington. What's his name?"

"Senator McCarthy is no *what's his name*," he said. "He's really dangerous. Did you read where he has a list of homosexuals working in the State Department? He wants to go after us."

"You don't work in the State Department, do you?"

"No, I work in a bakery. That's not the point," he said. "Once they start a witch hunt, nobody knows where it'll end. If you're smart, you'll watch your ass."

"I'd rather watch yours," I said.

"Thanks." He smiled briefly. "But listen to what I'm telling you. I wouldn't blab to everybody about my private affairs if I were you."

"Are you trying to protect me or yourself?" I asked.

"Both of us," he said. "Don't be an idiot."

"Martin, would you like to visit me again?"

"I might," he said cautiously.

"There's one condition, though."

"What?"

"You have to tell me your last name," I said.

"First tell me yours."

"Blake."

He waited a full minute before he responded.

"My name is Martin Gale. Maybe you know my cousin Dorothy, in the Emerald City?"

"Yes, I'm a friend of hers," I said. "And don't worry. You're not under arrest."

"That's a relief. My last name really is Gale, though."

"How about next Wednesday night?"

"That's my mother's bridge night," he said. "I have to help her serve."

"Thursday?" I suggested.

"I guess that'll be okay."

So we started seeing each other on a fairly regular basis. Neither one of us ever referred to it as a relationship. We were just a convenience for each other in an inconvenient world.

One Sunday in late spring, when I went out to get the morning paper, I passed Auld Appointments just as Edwin emerged and locked the door from outside. Curious, because I'd never actually seen him leave the premises before, I stopped and waited. He was surprised to see me standing there when he turned to leave.

"Dill," he said. "What are you doing here? Isn't this Sunday?"

I had stopped correcting him about my name because I knew it was useless. "I'm just out getting the paper," I said.

"And I'm on my way to services. Why don't you walk with me?"

"I'd be proud to accompany you, sir," I replied, hoping my exaggerated courtier's manners wouldn't offend him. "You look very natty today, if I may say so."

He was wearing a black suit whose cut was out of date. It had been carefully preserved, however, and the trouser creases were razor sharp. A black pearl stickpin accented his subtly striped tie, and a white carnation blossomed in his lapel. The faint blush that covered his flabby cheeks made me wonder whether his normally pallid complexion had been enhanced with a touch of rouge. Covering his white hair at a slight tilt was a black fedora. He leaned heavily on his silver-handled walking stick as we moved along the sidewalk, and when we came to each corner, he took my arm as well.

Edwin seemed delighted with my appreciation of his sartorial efforts, and he became even friendlier than usual. "Why don't you come to services with me?" he asked.

"Church? But I'm not a Catholic," I said, remembering the statue of the Virgin I'd seen in his parlor. "In fact, I'm not particularly religious at all. Besides, I'm not dressed properly. I don't even own a suit."

"I find attending church a great comfort," he said, ignoring my excuses. "I never miss a Sunday."

"I had some bad experiences in church when I was younger."

"That may not be the fault of Our Lord, but of man's imperfection."

"Probably, but I don't see why I need to be in church to communicate with . . . whatever it is I communicate with."

"But Dull, church provides order and structure and continuity to one's religious experience. It is a center."

I remained silent. I didn't want to prolong the discussion.

"I hope I haven't offended you," he said. "I suppose I can't help being a bit of a missionary."

"You haven't offended me at all," I answered. "I'm glad to learn a little more about your interests."

"If I promise not to proselytize anymore, will you walk with me the rest of the way?" he asked, leaning especially heavily on my arm. "It's only two more blocks, and I'd like you to meet Father James. He's an old friend of mine."

"Of course," I said. And we slowly made our way down the avenue, like a frail old lady and a boy scout earning a merit badge.

Our conversation flagged, and I kept my mind occupied with lines from "Song of Myself":

> Why should I pray? why should I venerate and be
> ceremonious? . . .
>
> Divine am I inside and out, and I make holy whatever I
> touch or am touch'd from,
> The scent of these arm-pits aroma finer than prayer,
> This head more than churches, bibles, and all the creeds.

I didn't share my thoughts with Edwin, however. I didn't want to show disrespect for his beliefs. Our differences were likely to be vast. And, after all, the man was my boss.

We arrived at the stone church building along with several groups of parishioners, most of them older women with kerchiefs on their heads. All of them made their way up the flight of stone steps, at whose top stood a man in a priest's cassock, greeting them by name. His face was old, but still remarkably handsome. "That's Father James," Edwin whispered reverently.

I helped Edwin up the stairs. He had to stop twice to rest before he reached the top. Father James reached down to help him up the final few steps. "Good morning, Eddie," he said. "You're looking quite dapper today."

"But not very spry, I'm afraid, Father."

"And who is this with you?"

"This is my young shop assistant, the one I told you about," he said. "Father James, meet . . ." I could see him concentrating hard to get my name right, and I was just about to intervene when he said, "Dell Blake." I was impressed, although I couldn't help wondering if he had hit upon the right vowel in my name through memory or chance.

"Hello, Dell," Father James said warmly. "I hope you'll be staying with us for Mass."

"Not this morning, I'm afraid. I have another commitment."

"You're welcome any time," he said. "Thank you for seeing Eddie here safely." He took Edwin's arm and escorted him to the church door, where he delivered him into the care of an usher. Turning back to me, he added, "Take good care of him, Dell. He's not as strong as he used to be, you know."

"I'll do my best, Father," I assured him.

"I'm sure you will," he said. "Good morning."

After that, I met Edwin every Sunday morning and escorted him to church. Sometimes I even came back at the end of Mass and escorted him back to his shop. Even though I never went past the top of the stone staircase and into the building to attend services, Father James was unfailingly cordial. Once as I turned to leave, he said to me, "I don't know what you consider yourself, Dell, but I suspect you're a good Christian at heart."

One Sunday morning, Edwin didn't appear on time. I waited for about ten minutes, and then, worried about him, I used the key he had given me and entered the shop. The little bell jangled softly above my head. "Edwin?" I called. There was no answer.

I went to the back of the store and swept aside the brocade curtain. There were no puffs of dust now; I had seen to that with a vacuum cleaner. The scullery was empty. I peeked into the bed chamber, half expecting to find him asleep, or even dead, in his bed. But the room was empty. Then I tried the parlor. "Edwin," I called again.

Behind the statue of the Virgin, a brocade curtain stirred. It matched the drape over the entrance to his apartment, and I had thought it was only a decorative backdrop. But when Edwin emerged from behind it, all dressed for church, I realized that there was another room back there. I knew the building pretty well by then, and I was sure there couldn't be space for much more than a large walk-in closet. Edwin was all flustered. "Oh my goodness," he said. "Are you here already, Doll? I must have lost track of time. Or maybe I dozed off in there. I've been doing that lately. Are we late?"

"Not yet," I answered.

He turned and pulled a long key chain from his pocket. Then he carefully locked the door behind him and arranged the brocade curtain in front of it.

Stepping gingerly so as not to disturb the Virgin's statue, he came toward me, stumbling. "My walking stick," he muttered. "Now where did I . . . ?"

"Here it is," I said. It was lying across a chair, which stood beside the corner where the statue presided.

Edwin looked at me gratefully, and with a reassured sigh he took my arm. We arrived at the church just as Father James was turning to go inside. "I was worried that you weren't coming, Eddie. That's not like you," he chided.

"I'm sorry, Father. I'll try not to let it happen again."

Father James nodded to me as he took Edwin's arm and personally led him inside.

The months in Pittsburgh passed with a growing sense of quiet regularity. My life wasn't exciting, but there was a comfortable predictability about it.

One afternoon that fall, I got a call from Martin Gale, which was a rare event. We had drifted into a once-a-week date at my apartment and our sex had become somewhat monotonous, but it was still safer and easier than cruising the streets.

"Can I see you this afternoon?" he asked.

"To what do I owe this pleasure?" I said. "Are you having a sudden attack of the hornies?" I didn't mind if he was. I had been planning to see a movie, but it could certainly wait. A little spontaneity was just what our sex life needed.

"I have to talk to you," he said.

"Sure," I answered. "What time?"

At exactly 3:30 p.m., as we had planned, Martin arrived. I had done my best to arrange my little room for our sexual encounter, with drawn window shades and lighted candles and even a bottle of wine I'd been saving for just such an emergency. I was hoping that my efforts would brighten up what had diminished into a dreary routine.

When he entered, he said, "I can't stay long."

"Then I guess we'd better get right down to business as usual," I said, reaching for his crotch.

"Not today," he said. "Let's talk."

"Okay."

"I don't exactly know where to start. In the first place, Dell, I want you to know I do like you."

Uh-oh, I thought. This isn't going to be pleasant.

"But you're not the only man I've been seeing," he continued.

I nodded my understanding.

"I mean, we didn't have any formal arrangement or anything, did we?"

I shook my head from side to side, noticing his use of the past tense.

"Well," he continued, "this other person I've been seeing—let's just call him X—I care for him quite a bit."

I waited.

"I think he really cares for me, too, but I guess that's not the point."

I do hope there is a point, I thought.

"Well, anyway, to make a long story short . . ."

It's too late for that already, I thought.

"I'm really in love with X, but he's not around too often. He works in Washington. Oh, maybe I shouldn't have said that. Anyway, he has a government job, but now he's afraid he's going to be investigated by Senator McCarthy. He's afraid they'll call him a security risk and make a big deal out of it. So he's planning to quit his job and go up to Canada for a while. And, well . . . he wants me to go with him."

"What about your mother?" I asked, nobly putting my own lack of interest aside.

"She's the real problem. I don't know what to tell her. If I was something other than a bakery worker, I could blame it on my work. But I doubt that she'll believe me if I tell her that a bakery in Toronto has made me an offer."

"You could say you have a chance to get into some other kind of business."

"That's not such a bad idea—and then I could withdraw some of my savings and tell her it's for an investment. Yeah. Thanks, Dell. I knew you'd understand."

"Think nothing of it," I said cheerfully.

"Are you sure you're not mad at me?"

"Only a little disappointed," I said, lying charitably. "I'll get over it." The truth was that I didn't much care one way or the other. Martin could be replaced without too much trouble.

"I just didn't want to go away without saying good-bye," he said wistfully.

"That's very nice of you, Martin."

"I'll keep in touch, Dell. I really will," he said.

He left as quickly as he'd arrived, and as I blew out the candles, I thought: He won't keep in touch.

I was right. I never heard from him again.

CHAPTER FIFTEEN

I spent most of the following winter and spring alone. When I was in the shop, Edwin spent more and more time in his private quarters. I didn't have too much luck meeting anyone around town with the exception of an occasional stranger for sex, and since my tiny apartment felt crowded with just myself and the new TV set I had bought, I rarely invited anyone home. I did add an orange striped tomcat to my household, though. I met him in the street one evening when I was leaving the shop. He looked cold and hungry, so I stopped to pet him. Since I felt the same way as he did at the moment, I took him home and treated him to a can of tuna fish. After that we were best friends, and he curled himself into a ball in my lap and went to sleep. I called him Calamus, in honor of Whitman's cycle of poems. Even though I was glad of his presence, I still didn't have anyone to talk to. I didn't mind my own company, though. I used the time to read some more about Whitman and to write some poems of my own, born from the inactivity in my life. Here's an example.

Ephemera

I live with passing beauty:
the patterns of daylight sliding across the floor,
a glimpse of an orange and its shadow
precisely poised in an earthenware bowl,
the sleeping cat's shuddering paw,
stirrings of passion,
and many vases of cut, bright flowers,
radio music briefly silvering the air,
gentle aromas breathed and gone,
the fleeting desire in a stranger's eye,
occasional moments of passion,
fading flowers in a vase,
brief sentences spoken and forgotten,
the deliciousness of dinner at the lips,

pursued by a fragile glass of wine,

swift memories of passion,

brittle ghosts of flowers,

far too many flowers to suit good taste.

I called them my "Stillness Poems." There were about twelve of them. They may look simple, but each one took endless amounts of revising and word juggling before it was finished, and to this day I keep wanting to change them. When I had finished writing the one you've just read, I looked around at the aesthetic disappointment of my furnished apartment. There weren't really lots of flowers, only one ceramic vase of dried purple statice, which had long ago faded to an ugly shade of gray-lavender. Without a second thought, I threw the whole bunch in the garbage. I surveyed the walls, which held a year-old cardboard calendar from a Chinese restaurant with a picture of the heavily made-up face of a smiling woman wearing a red hat, from whose crown hung an array of gold tassels; a warped print of Rembrandt's *The Night Watch* in an unfinished wood frame without glass; and a mirror with a central patch of black freckles and a small crack in its corner, framed in chipped gilt. I took the three atrocities down and stored them beside the refrigerator.

The next day I asked Edwin where I could find some picture frames, and he sent me to Kaufmann's Department Store, where I bought plain white mats and simple black frames for the four remaining photographs that Minerva White had sent me: the two luminous blossoms; my face at seventeen; Chester and I looking into each other's eyes; and the face of Miss White's friend with its clear, intent gaze beneath the mole that separated her eyebrows. I showed Edwin what I had wrought, and he found them very handsome.

"Are you redecorating your apartment, Doll?" he asked.

"Only enough to make it mine."

"Then wait. I think I have something for you." He started to hunt in every corner of the shop. "I'm afraid I'll never understand this filing system of yours," he said.

"I can still change it back," I suggested.

"How? Even I can't remember where everything used to be."

I didn't answer. There were days when I was surprised that he remembered his own name.

"Now let me see," he continued, having organized his search into a shelf-by-shelf survey, which was impeded by his heavy reliance on his walking stick. "Oh dear, I do hope it hasn't been sold. Ah, here it is. What a strange location to find it in!"

He presented me with the green cloisonné bowl he'd been unable to find once before. "Oh, thank you," I said. "It's really beautiful. It'll look just right on my coffee table."

Edwin smiled happily at my appreciation, giving his head a slight toss, which set his cheeks aquiver. I did like the bowl. It was pretty if not practical, and as a gift it was a vast improvement over the Edwardian gold stickpin he had given me for Christmas (which lay idle in my dresser drawer, waiting for the vagaries of fashion to resurrect the cravat). The cloisonné bowl and the photographs, on the other hand, would not only dress up the room a bit, but would make it a little more mine.

After trying thirteen other, less successful arrangements, I placed three of the pictures above my daybed—with the two portraits on either side of the photograph of Chester and me—and I hung the picture of the blossoms on a separate wall. I put the bowl on the coffee table, unintentionally disturbing Calamus, who had been using it as a chaise longue. I picked him up and stroked his fur while he gave an unconcerned yawn, and then I sat back to enjoy my private domain. It wasn't a magnificent mansion, I knew, but at least I had earned it myself. I didn't feel especially attached to the place, nor to Pittsburgh as a whole. But I had grown to feel an attachment to old Edwin, and that was enough motivation to stay put in that first nest of my own for a while.

That spring I met another man, with whom I had sex several times. His name was Paul, and he was a drama student at the University of Pittsburgh. Our encounters were pleasant, but the sex was less than inspired, and I don't remember the man so much as a new book he showed to me. It was called *The Homosexual in America* by Donald Webster Cory.

"Is this like the Kinsey Report?" I asked him. "Is it another statistical study about one man out of eight being gay?"

"It's more about how those one in eight are treated by the other seven."

"Hmm," I said. "Sounds interesting."

"Want to borrow it?" he asked.

"Sure. Then I'll have a chance to see you again, when I return it."

"Flatterer," he said.

"You love it," I answered.

"I can't say I mind it."

I read the book and it opened my eyes. At last someone was daring to say that homosexuals are treated unfairly. Not only that, but the book argued that homosexuals were not just a criminal class of unrepentant sinners, but that they represent an actual minority group of human beings entitled to the full rights of life. One of its statements has stayed with me to this day:

> Until we are willing to speak out openly and frankly in defense
> of our activities, and to identify ourselves with the millions

      pursuing these activities, we are unlikely to find the attitudes
      of the world undergoing any significant change.

I was in a state of excitement when I returned the book to Paul. "Who is this guy?" I asked.

"Nobody knows," he answered. "There's a rumor that he's one of us and that he's using a false name."

"Then he's not willing to practice what he preaches about speaking out openly?"

"He is speaking out openly, but he'd probably lose his job if he signed his real name to it. Don't despair, though. I've heard from a friend of mine that there's an organization to promote tolerance of homosexuals, in California."

"Really? What's it called?"

"The Mattachine Society," he said.

"Mattachine?"

"It's an old term for the court jester, the one who told the truth to the king from behind a mask and used humor so he wouldn't be punished for it."

"That's pretty clever. Does that mean the court jesters were homosexuals?"

"Maybe," he said.

"Is 'Donald Webster Cory' a member?"

He shrugged his shoulders.

"So, what is this group going to do?" I asked.

"Some of the people in Mattachine would rather see homosexuality accepted as a kind of variation on human sexuality, not something to be punished as a crime. Others think that homosexuals represent a separate culture, and that we should invent our own rules to live by."

"I hope Senator McCarthy doesn't get hold of this," I said. "He'll call them communists."

"Some of them probably are," he told me. "But some homosexuals are pretty right-wing. The word is that McCarthy himself is gay."

I was shocked at the idea. "If he is, then that would mean we're our own worst enemy. What an awful thought."

"That's what Mattachine wants to change."

"Good luck to all of us," I said as I put on my coat.

Paul kissed me good-bye. "Yes," he said. "Good luck to us all."

As spring threatened to turn into a hot, sticky summer, the sooty buildings of Pittsburgh didn't look any lovelier than they did in the gray light of winter. Edwin began to talk about getting away.

"I'd love to go back to Monhegan once more," he said.

"Where is Monhegan?" I asked him.

"It's a little island off the coast of Maine," he said, with a dreamy look in his eyes. "It's lovely there, a simple place. They don't even have electricity."

"Sounds charming," I said, with a sarcastic edge to my tone.

"It is. There are cliffs above the rocky coast, pine forests, and country lanes. You'd love it."

"I can't afford a vacation," I said.

"I know," he answered. "I don't pay you nearly what you're worth to me. But I have a proposal. Suppose I paid you to come with me? It would be good for both of us to get away. You'd have some time to yourself. I know the idea of traveling with an old man doesn't sound like much fun, but to tell you the truth I'm a little nervous about going by myself. I've been feeling so frail lately that I might blow away in the breeze. I'm afraid I'm turning into one of my own antiques!"

"How could I refuse such a charming offer?" I said.

"Then you'll come?"

"It's better than spending the time in Pittsburgh."

"You mustn't think too harshly of Pittsburgh. It is our home, you know."

The thought chilled me. I certainly didn't want to spend the rest of my life there. I was suddenly reminded of the fact that I had no plans, that I was only staying in that dreary city out of loyalty to Edwin. I really had no life of my own. But I put those ideas away. They were too unpleasant to think about. Something would turn up. Something always did.

The next Sunday when I walked Edwin to church, he started talking to Father James as soon as he got to the top of the steps. "Dull is coming with me!"

"That's good, Eddie. You both need the rest, I'm sure." And, turning to me, he added, "I know you'll love Monhegan, Dell."

"That's right, it's Dell . . . *Dell*," Edwin reminded himself, but I knew it was futile.

"Have you been to Monhegan, Father James?" I asked, surprised. I couldn't imagine a priest going on such a vacation.

"Once, very long ago," he said, sighing almost imperceptibly. "It was before I took my vows."

I tried to imagine him as a young man. Beneath his whitening hair and creased brow, a pair of youthful blue eyes shone forth. And suddenly I could picture him on a long-ago beach, frolicking in some ancient surf in an old-fashioned woolen bathing suit.

"Eddie will need special looking after on such a trip," he cautioned me.

"Who's better at looking after him than I am?" I asked.

"No one, I suppose," he said, with another one of his nearly imperceptible sighs.

"Gentlemen, I thank you both for all your solicitude," Edwin interrupted. "But may I remind you that I am still in charge of myself? I just need someone to lean on now and then."

"Of course, Eddie," Father James said, the color rising to his cheeks. "We were just talking nonsense. Come inside now, it's almost time for Mass." As he turned to lead Edwin into the church, he winked at me, and I winked back.

Edwin and I left for Maine in mid-July. I had hoped we might fly directly there, but he didn't trust airplanes. And so I was treated to a view—through a combination of train and bus windows—of Pennsylvania, western New York State (far from Elysium, thank God), Vermont, and New Hampshire. It was my grand tour of New England. I got to see the Green Mountains and the White Mountains and several lovely lakes. We stopped in a few small towns and spent a little time browsing for antiques and sleeping in quiet inns, just to make the trip less arduous for Edwin.

He seemed elated whenever we found the places where he had stayed on some previous trip. If they were still operating, we were sure to stay overnight in them. More and more, Edwin's journey seemed like a voyage into his own memory, as if he were saying good-bye to his past.

Our penultimate stop was Portland, where we spent the night before going to Port Clyde, the town from which the Monhegan ferry left. Portland was a depressed city no more glamorous than Pittsburgh, and I couldn't imagine anyone wanting to vacation there. The only reason we had stopped was that Edwin had an old friend who lived there, and he wanted to look him up.

We registered at the Eastland Hotel and Edwin called his friend, who invited both of us over for dinner. But I decided that I'd rather have the evening to myself. I wanted to see a film that I'd noticed on the marquee of a theater on Congress Street. It was a Joan Crawford film called *Good-bye, My Fancy*. I had no idea what it was about, and I wasn't especially fond of Crawford, who had always seemed too tough for me to sympathize with, but I wanted to see the movie anyway because its title was taken from a Walt Whitman poem. So I put Edwin in a taxicab on the way to visit his friend. Then I had a quiet dinner alone in the hotel dining room, and I went to the movies.

I sat in the balcony, glad to be alone for a couple of hours. But as the lights were lowering, a tall, good-looking man rushed in and sat a seat away from mine. We were the only ones in that section of the theater. I proceeded to divide my attention between the film and him. The movie, of course, had nothing to do with Walt Whitman. It was a forgettable story about a Congresswoman who goes back to visit her alma mater in the Midwest and rekindles an old love affair. What I enjoyed most about it was Eve Arden, especially when she quipped: "I don't believe in looking at the past. I was born in Newark, New Jersey. Every time I go through on a train, I pull down the shade!" I felt the same way about Elysium, New York.

While I was watching the film, I glanced occasionally at the man who had sat near me. Once or twice I caught him glancing back at me, but when I tried to look his way a little longer, he suddenly turned his attention back to the movie. Before a quarter of it was over, I casually placed my hand on the back of the seat between us, only to discover that his arm had beaten me to it. "Excuse me," I mumbled, embarrassed, as I withdrew my arm. He moved his arm also. A short while later, I unconsciously rested my hand in the seat between us—and within seconds, I felt his hand descend on mine and cover it. Instead of flinching, I managed to keep still, and soon we were caressing each other's hands under cover of the comforting darkness.

When the film was almost over, I considered rushing out of the theater before the lights came up, so I could meet Edwin when he returned from his dinner. Suddenly I flashed back to the theater in San Francisco where someone had done just that to me and left me wondering about him forever. I didn't want to do that to someone else.

I didn't have time for much more speculation because my partner slid into the seat between us and put his hand possessively on my thigh. I kind of liked his interest, but I wasn't sure how I felt about his aggression. Then I decided that I liked that even better, and I slid down in my seat and relaxed while his hands moved freely all over me. Then he leaned over and whispered, "Want to go somewhere and finish this?" And he quickly stuck his tongue into my ear before sitting back in his seat.

"I'm just in town for the night," I said quietly.

"Too bad. Can we go to your hotel?"

"No. I'm traveling with someone."

"Your lover?" he asked.

"My boss," I replied.

"That's good," he said.

"It's okay, I guess."

"Want to come home with me for the night?"

"I don't know," I said. "What did you have in mind?"

"Passion."

"You said the magic word."

"Meet me downstairs," he said, almost as if it were an order.

"In the lobby?"

"No," he said. "I'll be recognized there. Meet me outside, in front of the closed liquor store next door."

"When?"

"Now," he said, and he got up and left.

I didn't care about the end of the movie, so I followed him. He was standing in front of the liquor store with his collar up, as if he were afraid to be noticed.

"Hi," I said. "Remember me?"

"I want to kiss you," he said. "But not here."

"I have to make a phone call," I said. "Then I'll be free."

"Make it from my house," he said, taking my arm and steering me toward his car, which turned out to be a large silver Cadillac El Dorado.

"Can we put the top down?" I asked with a childlike glee.

"I'd rather not be so visible," he said. "A lot of people know me here. But it's only a short ride."

I settled into the luxurious front seat, remembering an afternoon several lifetimes ago when Chester Stewart had given me a ride in his glamorous yellow roadster. I couldn't help asking myself: Is this man to be my next love? And I couldn't help answering myself right back, with a mental kick in the pants: Don't be such a romantic idiot! And for God's sake, don't fall in love because of a car!

"Tell me something," I inquired. "Did you sit near me in the balcony by accident?"

"I saw you downstairs in the lobby," he said, "and I followed you. Then I waited until the movie was about to start, so everyone else wouldn't notice where I was sitting."

"Thanks," I said. "That's just what I wanted to hear."

"I figured as much," he replied.

He drove steadily with a sense of assurance. In a few minutes we turned a corner and he said, "Here we are, Deering Street. Not quite the Western Prom, but it will do."

"Western Prom?" I inquired.

"The Western Promenade. It's the ritzy section of town, right near here."

"This is ritzy enough for me," I said as we left the Cadillac and entered a large, old brick house. I couldn't help noticing a sign near the door that read, "Gordon Thomas, M.D. Office Hours 10 a.m. to 12 noon and 2 p.m. to 5 p.m."

"Are you a doctor?" I asked.

"In my spare time."

"What do you do with the rest of your time?"

"I make love to good-looking young men like you," he said, putting his arm around my neck and drawing me to him for a long, passionate kiss. When we had finished, he took my hand and guided it to his crotch. "See what an effect you have on me?" he asked as I stroked a more than respectable erection through his linen pants.

"You have the same effect on me," I said, taking his hand and imitating his action against my own crotch. He started to undo the zipper of my pants, but I stopped him. "Before we go any further, I have to make a phone call, remember?"

"I'm sorry," he said. "There's a phone in the office, over there."

I had a chance to look at my surroundings then. We were in a living room furnished in real colonial pieces, not the cheap imitations they sell in most furniture stores. Edwin had taught me to recognize quality, and I could see that there were valuable antiques and originals all around the room. Across from a large, carpeted entrance hall was the office area. I entered the waiting room, which was done in molded plastic chairs and lush hanging plants, with several interesting modern paintings on the walls and a corner rack filled with European art magazines. There was a Danish modern receptionist's desk made of blond wood, on which I found the telephone. Before I picked it up, I looked through an open door to see a consultation room lined with an impressive array of fat medical volumes surrounding a large mahogany desk covered with a plate of glass, on which several small contemporary sculptures were displayed.

I got the number of the hotel from information and tried to call our room, but there was no answer. Edwin was probably still at his friend's house, and I was glad. I asked the desk clerk if I could leave a message. "Of course, sir," he said, with a trace of contempt in his tone. "The Eastland gladly accepts messages for its guests."

Gordon had followed me into the room and stood stroking his erection through his pants as I talked.

"Please tell Mr. Roe that I am visiting a friend and that I will be home a little later."

"Much later," Gordon mouthed silently. "Morning."

"Make that quite late," I amended the message.

"Anything else, sir?" the clerk said officiously. I caught myself worrying whether something in my voice had told him I was about to have sex with a man. Maybe he was suspicious about two men sharing a room. Maybe he hated homosexuals. Or maybe he was gay and thought I was cheating on my lover. Maybe he thought Edwin was my sugar daddy. Then I wondered: what am I feeling so guilty about? I haven't done anything wrong. Fuck him.

"That will be all, thank you," I said, trying to sound as arrogant as he did, and I hung up the phone.

Gordon was out of his jacket by that time. He took me by the hand and said, "You don't want to waste time having a drink first or anything like that, do you? You're welcome to one, if you want it."

"The only thing I want is you," I said, wondering if I had heard this dialogue on some radio soap opera years ago. I couldn't believe such words were issuing from my lips.

Gordon said no more. He led me to the staircase and up to his bedroom, where a large, canopied four-poster bed stood. It was covered with an elaborately ruffled, white organdy spread. Matching curtains gracefully crisscrossed the windows, and an ultra-thick rag rug covered the center of the floor. The room looked strangely soft for a man like Gordon. Then I noticed that a closet door was slightly ajar, and hanging inside I could see a row of women's frilly dresses. I gulped. Had I found another Willard?

"Are you a drag queen?" I asked.

"A what?" Gordon said, startled. "Am I a . . ." He started to laugh, falling back on the bed and rolling from side to side in his hysteria. Between paroxysms of laughter, he would start to repeat it again. "Am I a . . ." And the thought would set him laughing again until the tears were streaming down his cheeks. I stood bemused in the middle of the room.

Finally he regained his composure. "Come here," he said firmly. As I crossed the room, he stood and removed the bedspread with a single gesture. Then he opened his pants and sat back on the bed. "Take this in your mouth," he said with an air of command. I hastened to obey.

When I had sucked on his cock for a few minutes, he pulled it from my lips. "Come here," he said, lying back on the bed. I joined him, and he put his arm around me, so I could nestle against his muscular, hair-covered chest. I studied his face. He had a tapered, firm jaw, a sharp, aquiline nose that reminded me of a Roman sculpture, and dark blue, almost violet eyes. His hair was dark brown and combed directly back with a slight wave above his forehead and a precise part on one side. I couldn't be sure of his age, but he seemed to be in his mid-thirties. "Do you like the taste of my meat?" he asked.

"Mm-hmm. I sure do," I said, leaning over to start tasting it again. He braced me with his hand, preventing me from reaching it, which made me want it all the more.

"The clothes in the closet aren't mine," he said. "They're my wife's. She's away on vacation for the summer. Does that bother you?"

"I've been with married men before," I said. "Nothing bothers me."

"I have a son, too. He's sixteen. He's with his mother on Monhegan. "

"That's where I'm headed," I said.

"Good. It's a great place. Do you mind that I have a son not much younger than you?"

"More than ten years younger," I said.

"Does it bother you?"

"I told you, nothing bothers me."

"Then get back on that cock. What are you waiting for?" was his reply.

We spent the night cavorting in his bed, falling asleep and then waking up for more sex. He took control throughout, telling me what positions to take and deciding what we would do, which included an impressive variety of positions and sensations. I was having a wonderful time and I didn't want it to end. But eventually the morning light shone through the filmy, ruffled curtains, and he said, "I don't have to be in the office until ten, but the receptionist will be here at nine-forty-five. What time do you have to be back at the hotel?"

"I'm not sure. I guess I should be back before then."

"I would drive you, but it's too dangerous. I might be seen, and I'm not sure how to explain you . . . not even to myself."

"I know how to explain you," I said. "Great sex. But I guess you couldn't tell that to your patients."

"Can you imagine them letting me examine their naked bodies—or their children's—if they knew about me?"

"It would be their loss," I answered. "You did a terrific job of examining mine."

I wasn't sure if his red cheeks meant that he was blushing or heating up with more passion, but before I had time to decide, we were kissing again. And then he was entering me, and I was loving every minute of it.

When we had finished, he said, "Suppose I call you a cab and have him pick you up a block from here? Will that be okay?"

"Of course," I said. "But let's not separate until we have to." Then we were kissing again and clasping each other tightly, our combined form rocking back and forth on the bed.

When at last we said our good-byes, I was lost in a wonderful afterglow, and I knew there would be an enigmatic smile on my face for the rest of the day. But at the same time I was feeling more than a little miserable because there would be no more good times with this man. Don't be greedy, I told myself. It was a wonderful relationship while it lasted.

Edwin was a little put out when I arrived at the hotel at ten o'clock. "Where were you all night?" he asked. "I was worried about you being lost or hurt—or kidnapped or worse in a strange city."

"I was kidnapped," I said, "and I had a wonderful time. Didn't you get my message?"

"Yes, but it wasn't very explicit. Now we'll just have enough time to make our bus to Port Clyde. I hope you've eaten breakfast. I had mine in the room, thinking you would at least call."

"I'm sorry," I said. "It was thoughtless of me."

"It's just that I'm afraid I've grown to need you, Dall. I'd hate to lose you."

"Don't worry," I said. "You won't lose me." As I said that, I thought of the day I had left Laura.

We arrived in Port Clyde in plenty of time for the Monhegan ferry, and by evening we were settled on the island in a charmingly rustic hotel called the Trailing Yew. We had separate rooms next door to each other. The kerosene lamps on our nightstands took only a little getting used to, as did the flashlights which were needed to get to the bathroom at night.

In the morning, after a hearty breakfast in the hotel dining room, we set out on a walk. Edwin seemed to know exactly where he wanted to go, so I let him lead the way. He moved more and more slowly and leaned quite heavily on his walking stick as well as my arm, and he paused for a rest every ten minutes or so. Finally we reached an open meadow filled with lupines—tall wildflowers that ranged from deep purple to bright white—and surrounded by pine trees. There was a large rock near the center of the clearing, and we sat on it.

"All those years gone by, and yet everything looks just the same," he said with a sigh. He seemed lost in a reverie for a few minutes.

I said nothing. Knowing how private a person he was, I assumed he would be unhappy if he were aware that I was observing him. Then he moved his lips silently. He seemed to be forming the words, "Until death us do part," but I couldn't be certain.

Realizing suddenly that I was there, he shook his head as if to clear his mind, which set his cheeks quivering. He offered me an explanation.

"I know you think my life is an empty one, Dill, but it wasn't always what you see. Once there was a very special person, whom I adored. We came here together, and it was the most beautiful experience I ever had. It was perfection."

That was more than he had ever told me about his personal life, and I knew he might feel as if he were betraying his own trust by sharing even that much, so I said, "I'm glad to know that you were happy, Edwin. And I'm very interested in anything you want to tell me, but I won't ask you any questions."

He nodded his understanding, looking grateful and sighing with relief, and he volunteered no further information.

We wandered down to Lobster Cove and inspected the rusty hulk of a wrecked ship that lay on its side near the shoreline. The water lapped steadily at its edges, as if it intended to reclaim its prize eventually, no matter how many years it might take. I wandered around, picking up some pieces of gnarled driftwood and looking out to sea, where the water slapped over an ancient rock that Edwin told me was called the Washerwoman, and I felt more at peace with myself than I had for years.

In the afternoon Edwin took a nap, and I went walking by myself. Eventually I came to a place that I loved. It was a stone cliff called Burnt Head, towering high above the sea. At its base, far below, the water incessantly beat itself into a froth against a row of rocks. Just over the cliff's edge I found a small niche, and I climbed carefully down into it and nestled there, listening to the wind and feeling that here was a spot on the planet that was my very own, a precarious place, but one where I could feel secure.

Soon my thoughts drifted back to another place where I had once felt safe. The image of a gravestone rose in my mind, a simple marker with the word "Martha" surrounded by a plain circle. And, unable to help myself, I began to wonder what had become of my father after I'd left, and if Mrs. Warner was still dutifully seeing to his needs. Feeling an unpleasant chill, I managed to escape from those unpleasant thoughts by willing my memory back to Martha's stone, where once again I could invent stories about who she had been and why her grave was so different from the others.

By the time I snapped back into the present, the sun was halfway down in the afternoon sky. I didn't think I had fallen asleep, but somehow several hours had passed without my being aware of them. I wasn't sure what time it was, but it didn't matter. After all, this was supposed to be a vacation. So I wandered down through the pine forest on my way back to the hotel.

Still lost in thought, composing a poem in my head, I wandered among the giant trees, enjoying the softness of the carpet of rust-colored pine needles beneath my feet and the rich pine fragrance that filled the air. Suddenly, a tall figure in white stepped from behind a tree. "Remember me?" he asked.

"Gordon!" I said. "What are you doing here?"

"When you said you were heading for Monhegan, I thought I would too. It was time to check on how my family's vacation was proceeding, anyway. They're doing fine, so I went for a walk. When I saw you coming down the trail, I hid. Did you like my surprise?"

"I'm so glad you came," I whispered.

"Then get over here and show me you mean it," he said, in that certain tone whose commands I didn't think I could ever willfully disobey.

I went over to where he was, and he took my hand and put it in his crotch, where I could feel his flaccid penis rising in response to my touch. He put his hands on my shoulders and showed me with their pressure that he wanted me to kneel. I knelt. He opened his zipper slowly, and with tantalizing deliberateness pulled his cock out from the folds of his underwear. I was ecstatic. I took it in my mouth right there in the open, savoring the thrill of possible discovery until I could drink his semen and be done.

"Can I come to your room later?" he asked.

"Whenever you want to," I said, and told him where it was.

Edwin was still asleep when I returned, but I woke him in time for supper. In the hotel's dining room, we sat at one end of a long communal table, surrounded by the pleasant chatter of the guests. All the places were set with bowls of creamy New England clam chowder, and in the center was a line of platters heaped high with boiled lobsters, potato salad, and sweet corn. At the other end of the table sat Gordon with a well-coiffed, red-haired woman in a dress that managed to be both suitable for the country and chic at the same time. She appeared to be about Gordon's age and, unlike some women, had done nothing to make herself seem younger. Her attractive, even-featured face was carefully made-up but not self-consciously glamorous. Beside them sat a young man who looked exactly like Gordon must have looked twenty years earlier. The three of them did not join in the general chatter, nor did they talk much to each other beyond requests for salt or butter. Instead, they paid close attention to their food. At our end of the table, Edwin and I did the same. All five of us, I suspected, were lost in our own thoughts.

Gordon did not greet me, except for a questioning look in his eyes, which I assumed to be asking whether the presence of his wife and son bothered me, or perhaps he was wondering what time he might come to my room. I did not nod at him, but kept a pleasant expression on my face, which my fellow diners were free to read however they wished.

After dinner, Edwin and I sat in the community room of an outbuilding called the Sea Gull, where someone was playing popular folk tunes on an old, decrepit organ, and we listened to a dozen or so of the guests singing along. Their singing was more convivial than tuneful, but they exuded a generous energy, and I could see that it was a tonic for Edwin, who seemed happier than I could remember having seen him before. At last, when it was time for bed, I saw him first to the bathroom and then to his room, and I went to my own room to wait.

I didn't have to wait more than an hour before there was a soft knock on the door. I opened it and Gordon hurried in. "I can only stay a few minutes," he said. "If Renee—that's my wife—if she wakes up and finds me gone, I'll have trouble explaining a prolonged absence."

I kissed him softly, to show that it was all right with me, and he took my face in his hands and kissed me very hard. Then he took me to the bed and lowered me quickly to it. He undid my pants and lowered them to my ankles. Not even stopping to remove them, he opened his own pants and entered my body with his already hard cock. In a short time we were done, and he rose, kissed me, and washed himself off, using the bowl and pitcher that stood on the dresser. He inspected himself in the mirror, kissed me once more, and left. The entire encounter had taken no more than ten minutes, and I hadn't said a single word.

For the next week, this state of affairs continued. I spent my afternoons and evenings with Edwin, and whenever Gordon could arrange to get away, I gladly made myself available to him. Our sex stayed as passionate as it had been on the first night, perhaps because it was forbidden. I had never enjoyed myself so much, so mutually and repeatedly, with one man, and I knew I was hopelessly in love. When the week neared its end, he told me, "I have to go back to Portland tomorrow. I can't leave my practice indefinitely."

"I wish you didn't have to go," I said.

Seeing my crestfallen face, he said, "This week has meant a lot to me. How can we see each other again?"

"I don't know," I said. "I promised Edwin I wouldn't leave him, and he seems to need me more each day. He's not well, I just know it. I'd never forgive myself if I abandoned him and something awful happened to him."

"I admire you for that," Gordon said. "But I can't say it will be easy to live with. Is there any chance you can visit Portland again soon?"

"I'll try to figure out a way," I said.

"I want you to come live there," he told me, with the same authoritative tone with which he could command me to cross a room and suck his cock. I wondered if he could command me to cross several states to do it. Of course he could, I decided immediately, and he wants to, but he wouldn't ask me to abandon Edwin, and I'm grateful to him for that.

"I want to be near you," I said. "But right now I can't be. Maybe in the future."

"How soon?"

"As soon as I can. I'll have to figure out how to support myself too, you know."

"Don't worry about that. I'll arrange to take you on as an assistant."

"Well, I was in the medical corps in the army," I offered.

"Fantastic," he said. "Listen, here's my address. We'll have to be discreet, but do you promise to keep in touch?"

"Of course," I said. "There isn't anything I want more."

"I'll be thinking of you every day. My cock will be waiting for you. I won't touch anyone else until you come back—except for Renee, that is."

I didn't know whether to believe his pledge, and I didn't stop to notice how absurd it was. All I heard was the heartfelt tone with which he made his promise. There were stars in my eyes, but they soon were replaced by tears when the door closed behind him. I didn't know if I could figure out a way to get to Portland, but I was damned well going to try.

The next week on Monhegan with Edwin was tame and boring. We visited the Ice Pond to inspect the old ice factory; we went to the seal ledges and watched the seals. And we rested. When he was asleep, I spent a good deal of time by myself, writing love poems to Gordon and ripping them up because they weren't good enough to capture what I was feeling. The more I tried to write about him, the more I realized that I really knew him only sexually, and that the rest of his life and his character were a mystery to me.

I studied his wife and son from a distance, but I made a point of not getting too close to them and of remaining as inconspicuous as possible, hoping they wouldn't remember my face. I envied them their knowledge of Gordon as a husband and father. I envied the trusting looks I knew his son must have given him, because I wanted those looks to be in my eyes. And I envied his wife's vagina for all the times it had received Gordon's cock, because I wanted those moments to be mine as well. I wondered if she had used her mouth on him as I had and if she had licked every part of his body as I wanted to do at that very moment. Did she miss him as much as I did, or was she foolish enough to take him for granted? Could he satisfy her sexually if his real interest was in someone else? Would she get out of our way if she knew about us? This way lies madness, I told myself finally, and I forced myself to think of something else.

When it was time for Edwin and me to leave the island, I was relieved. We made the trip back with no excursions, stopping only to rest, and we were there in three days. As we left Penn Station, Pittsburgh had never looked drearier. It was no worse looking than Portland, but the memory of Portland was made beautiful to me by the thought of Gordon. I was so lost in dreams and desires that I found it difficult to pay attention to my surroundings.

Edwin looked exhausted when I left him at Auld Appointments. I helped him to take his suitcases inside, and he disappeared into his parlor—probably into his secret closet, I thought. Father James had volunteered to look after Calamus, and I went to the church to fetch him. As he handed the cat to me, the priest said, "How is Eddie? Did the trip tire him out?"

"He's moving very slowly," I said, adding silently to myself: almost as if he's grinding to a halt. But to Father James, I said only, "We did have a wonderful time, though."

"I knew you would," he answered. "I prayed for you both." I thanked him for his prayers and for taking care of the cat, and then I went back to my own apartment, which seemed all the lonelier now, even with Calamus at my side.

I wrote a letter to Gordon and marked it "Personal." Then I tore it up. Hoping that his wife and son were still away, I called his number.

"I want you here," he reminded me. "I want you where I can tell you to take me in your mouth. I want you where I can look after you."

"I'll be there as soon as I can," I promised.

We arranged that he would rent a post office box and call me with an address that I could write to since calling his house was too risky. And, satisfied that I could keep in touch with him and that he would call me at least once a week, I returned to my life in the antique shop.

Edwin didn't complain very much, but sensing that he wasn't well, I enlisted the help of Father James to prevail upon him to see a doctor.

"It's his heart," the doctor said. "It's very weak and could give out at any time. He mustn't be allowed to move around any more than necessary, and he must avoid stress." That meant that Edwin spent nearly all his time in his parlor and I took over the running of the shop, at which I proved reasonably skillful, if the receipts were any indication. Edwin didn't seem too interested in the shop's profits and even less interested in replenishing the stock, so my real purpose in improving the business was to see if I could do it.

Things went on this way for several months. I kept in touch with Gordon, who began to share more of himself with me, confiding that he was worried about his son Sean's lack of manliness and was afraid that he might have influenced the boy psychologically, or perhaps even biologically, to be queer. I thought his fatherly concern was endearing, but I wondered what it said about his self-respect, if he thought that the worst thing that could happen to his son was to be like him.

I didn't go cruising for sex because it seemed like too much trouble for too little reward, and I knew no one would satisfy me while I was thinking of Gordon. So I spent my time at home, writing poetry and watching TV. I especially enjoyed the old movies on *The Late Show*.

I was watching *Captains Courageous* one night when the phone rang. I turned down the sound, hoping it was Gordon, but it was Father James. "Can you come to the shop right away?" he said. "I think Eddie has just had a heart attack."

I raced over there and arrived just as the ambulance was pulling up. Father James was inside, cradling Edwin's head in his arms. I got inside too, and the attendants closed the ambulance door behind us and began to work on Edwin's prostrate form.

"You know that I phone to check on him now and then?" Father James said to me through the wail of the siren. I nodded. He was evidently trying to include every detail to get the story clear in his own mind, or perhaps he was trying to distract himself from the sight of Edwin's body being subjected to the feverish ministrations of the attendants. "I was talking to him when he started making these funny noises, and when I asked what was the matter, there was no answer. I rushed right here and found him on the floor, unconscious. First I called the ambulance. Then I called you. While you were on the way over, I performed the last rites . . . just in case. I pray to God that I was wrong."

"Let's see what happens at the hospital," I suggested.

When we arrived, Edwin was taken to the emergency room. After a long wait, the doctor came out to speak to us. "Are you related to Mr. Roe?" he asked.

"We're his friends," I said.

"I'm his priest," Father James said. "Is he going to die?"

"Not yet, Father. He's had an attack that will keep him in bed for a while, but if he's careful, he'll pull through . . . for now."

Edwin was in the hospital for a few weeks. Father James and I visited every evening, and I kept the shop open every day and reported to Edwin about its progress. Finally, the doctors said that he could go home, but that he would have to limit his physical activity. I wondered how much more he could limit himself. I shopped for his food and ran his business, and he sat alone in his cluttered rooms, probably thinking about the past.

About two weeks after his return from the hospital, I was in the shop when a customer asked about a silver Revere tray. I knew that Edwin had one in the back, but I didn't know if he'd part with it. When I went into the back, I couldn't find him anywhere. His bed was unmade, but empty. The scullery table had a half-full teacup on it, and there was no one in the parlor. I called Edwin's name, but there was no answer. I stuck my head out through the brocade-curtained doorway and told the customer that she would have to try again at another time. I knew where Edwin must be.

Returning to the empty parlor, I stepped behind the statue of the Virgin and swept aside the brocade drape. The door to the secret closet was locked. I knocked on it and called Edwin's name loudly, but there was no answer. Maybe I had missed him in my rapid search. I checked the sleeping chamber again, even looking under the bed, in case he had fallen there. I checked the bathroom too, but he was nowhere to be found. Finally, with a sense of doom, I returned to the secret closet in the parlor. Using an antique poker that was nestled in the corner (despite the fact that the room had no fireplace), I broke through the thin paneling on the door. There was a light on inside! I reached in and unlocked the bolt.

Edwin was there, slumped in a chair, which, along with a small desk— the sort used by eighteenth-century French ladies for their correspondence— nearly filled the space. I shook his shoulder, but there was no response. So I went back into the parlor and called the hospital for an ambulance, just in case. Then I returned to his closet.

Clutched in his hand was a letter, evidently taken from a small pile on the desk. The faded purple ribbon that had been used to tie the bundle together lay open, its length punctuated by constricted areas where the knot had been tied. I gently removed the letter from his hand and, overwhelmed by curiosity, I read it. It was dated some fifty-six years earlier.

Lyme, Connecticut
11 June 1896

My dearest E,

Although it is unbearably difficult to say so, this must be my final letter. You know that I have made my decision, and that it is irrevocable. I leave for the seminary tomorrow. It will be best this way, sparing us and those we love from further torture. Then the feelings we share will be pure in the sight of God, and perhaps our sins will be forgiven.

I could not leave, however, without a word of farewell, without telling you in writing that you have meant more to me than any other human being. No matter where our destinies take us or how far apart we are, know that I will love you always. I will remember you as you were in the meadow on Monhegan— full of hope and love, gentler and more beautiful than any man can be expected to be. Who would not have loved such a one? Next to God you shall retain the foremost place in my heart forever—before my parents, before my superiors, before anyone. This I pledge to you until death us do part.

God bless you,

J.

Tears filled my eyes as I read and understood what Edwin's life had been about. A quick glance showed that the other letters were in the same script, so without invading Edwin's cherished privacy any further, I returned the letter to the pile and retied the ribbon around the bundle and put it in my pocket.

Before the ambulance arrived, I called Father James. "It's Edwin," I told him gently. "I think he's gone." I could hear him weeping softly through the phone. When he was finished I told him the details of how I had found the body, but I didn't mention the bundle of letters. I didn't know what to do with it.

A nephew—Edwin's only living relative—was located. "I understand you were very helpful to my uncle," he said to me. "I just wanted to show you my appreciation." He gave me an envelope with twenty-five dollars in it.

The funeral took place a few days later. Father James officiated at the Mass. Aside from the nephew and myself, only three old friends of Edwin's were there. I recognized them from their visits to Edwin's living quarters. Each of them was elegantly attired in a black suit accented with tasteful jewelry. Edwin would have been proud, I thought.

As Father James intoned his Latin prayers at the graveside, I decided I would rather hear some hopeful thoughts of the eternal renewal of nature. So I thought of some lines from Whitman, to commemorate Edwin's passing in my own way.

> Again the deathless grass, so noiseless soft and green,
> Again the blood-red roses blooming . . .

When the service was over, I paid perfunctory respects to the nephew and went to the side of Father James, whose brow was furrowed with grief. "Is there anything I can do?" I asked.

"I'll be all right," he said. "Eddie was my oldest friend. We were boys together in Connecticut, you know."

"I think I have something that belongs to you," I said, and I pulled the packet of letters from my pocket.

He recognized them immediately. "Where did you find these?"

"He was reading one of them when he died."

Father James began to cry. When he had regained his composure, he asked, "Did you read them?"

"Only one of them," I answered. "So I would know what to do with them."

He nodded. "When I was assigned to this parish many years ago, he followed me here," he said. "We've been together since, but at the distance prescribed by our church."

I nodded. "I'm truly sorry, Father. He was a lovely man. I loved him too, you know."

"I know you did, and he loved you, though he may not have shown it. He was worried about you, about your future. He confided that in me. Do you have plans, Dell?"

"You don't have to worry, Father James. I know where I'm going."

"Good luck, then," he said, "and God bless you."

That night I wrote to Gordon and told him what had happened, and to expect me before the week was out. The next day I dismantled my apartment, keeping only *Leaves of Grass*, Minerva White's pictures, my own writings, the cloisonné bowl Edwin had given me, and of course Calamus the cat, in a new traveling case. The day afterward I was on the train to Portland.

PART V
DELLA BLAKE

I too . . .
Was call'd by my nighest name by clear loud voices of young
    men as they saw me approaching or passing,
Felt their arms on my neck as I stood, or the negligent leaning
    of their flesh against me as I sat,
Saw many I loved in the street or ferry-boat or public
    assembly, yet never told them a word . . .

—Walt Whitman,
"Crossing Brooklyn Ferry"

CHAPTER SIXTEEN

I arrived in Portland in the evening, hoping that Gordon would meet me at the train station, but he wasn't there. When I called his number, a woman's voice answered.

"Is Dr. Thomas there?" I asked.

"I'm sorry, he's not available right now. May I take a message?"

"I'm not sure."

"Is it some sort of medical problem?"

"Is this his wife?"

"Yes."

"My name is Dell. I'm going to be his new assistant."

"Oh, yes. Dell. I'm Renee Thomas. Gordon mentioned you to me. He's actually at the bus station, seeing Merle off. Merle was your predecessor. Where are you?"

"At the train station."

"Do you know how to get here?"

"I'm afraid I don't."

"Well, you can find a taxi at the station, I'm sure. Do you know the address?"

"Yes."

"Fine. Then I'll see you in ten minutes or so."

I didn't feel so wonderful having cost some poor woman her job, and I hoped that Merle had some other work to go to, but Gordon hadn't mentioned to me that the position had been filled. I consoled myself with the thought that at least he cared enough about me to disrupt someone else's life as well as his own household.

Gordon's wife greeted me at the front door, looking more elegant than she had on Monhegan. She wore a long-sleeved, powder-blue crepe blouse with a single strand of pearls at her throat and a slim, charcoal-gray woolen skirt. "I see you made it in one piece," she said. I nodded. "Good. Then I may as well show you to your room. You're a nice-looking young man."

"Thank you."

"Gordon always has such good taste in assistants."

Her tone sounded as though she might have meant her comment to be sarcastic. But I couldn't be sure, so I didn't respond. I assumed we were heading toward the staircase to go up to the second floor, but she led me to the back of the first floor, where we passed the door of a small room, evidently intended for a maid.

"This room belongs to Carlotta, our housekeeper," she said. "She's off tonight, so your room hasn't been cleaned out since Merle left. I hope you don't mind. She'll get to it tomorrow."

"That's no problem," I said.

Then she led me to the cellar stairs. As we went down, I remembered my tiny room at Miss Wanda's and hoped that I would do better here. I was pleasantly surprised. The basement was finished as a kind of den, and off to the side was a bedroom which turned out to be larger than Carlotta's. It was neatly appointed, with a simple walnut dresser and a three-quarter-size bed with a vinyl-covered Hollywood headboard in an unfortunate shade of pumpkin orange. The bed was stripped, but a clean, folded sheet was lying on the mattress, and a blanket lay crumpled on a nearby easy chair. I was glad to see that there was a small table with a lamp on it that I could use as a writing desk, even if the lamp's base was composed of a chartreuse ceramic panther.

"I'm sure this will be fine," I told her.

"Good," she said. "When Gordon comes home, I'll tell him that you're here. Good night, now."

After I set up a litter box and a feeding dish for Calamus in the adjoining bathroom and let him out to explore his new downstairs domain, I decided to make the bed and unpack my things, so I could go to sleep early. I was tired from my trip. As I opened the dresser drawers in order to empty my suitcase, I found a few strange items: a crumpled jockstrap, a pair of ripped boxer shorts, a nearly empty tube of lubricating jelly, and a pair of men's sunglasses with a crack in the left lens. Maybe Merle's boyfriend had visited her in her room, I thought. I put the things in the wastebasket under the desk, and I unpacked my clothes. I put my Minerva White photographs out, ready to be hung, and I placed Edwin's cloisonné bowl on the dresser. Then I lay down to rest.

It was dark, and I don't know how long I had been sleeping when I awoke, realizing that someone was in the room with me.

"Gordon?" I whispered.

"Come over here," Gordon's voice commanded, and I got out of the bed and crossed to where he stood. Touching him, I could feel that he was wearing an open bathrobe with nothing under it. He put his hand on the top of my head and slowly and steadily pushed until I was on my knees. I sucked his cock until he came. Then he lifted me up by my armpits, kissed me hard, turned, and left the room without another word. That mysterious scene made me so excited that I couldn't wait until I was back in bed before I started stroking myself, and I shot my load across the carpet. Then I went to bed and slept soundly for the rest of the night.

In the morning, I joined the family for breakfast. Renee presided graciously in a white, quilted floor-length housecoat while the housekeeper quietly and efficiently served French toast and sausages. Carlotta was an attractive, short, slim Hispanic woman in her twenties who wore a sober gray dress with a white collar that had the artificial look of a uniform without quite being one. It didn't go with the twinkle in her eye and her ready smile, and I was sure it had been Renee's idea. Gordon, looking handsomer than ever, wore a well-fashioned blue suit and a dignified tie. He looked like an ambassador.

"Did you have a good trip, Dell?" he asked paternally.

"Yes. I enjoy looking out of train windows."

"It's beautiful country, isn't it?" he said.

I nodded.

"Maple syrup?" Renee said.

The conversation stayed at that level of intimacy until Sean arrived, bounding into the room while pulling his sweater over his head. "Sorry," he mumbled, and slid into his place.

"Sean, in the future, make more of an effort to be at the table on time," Gordon said.

"I was up late doing homework," Sean complained.

"Say 'Good morning' first, Sean," Renee counseled. "This is Dell. He's going to be your father's new assistant."

Sean looked at me appraisingly, then grudgingly stuck his hand across the table for me to shake.

"Nice to meet you," I said, but he ignored me.

"He really was up late, dear," Renee said to Gordon. "I saw the light burning in his room when I went to bed at midnight. Did Merle get off all right?"

Gordon smiled. "Yes," he said.

Sean sulked.

"Burning the midnight oil?" I said to Sean in my best big-brotherly tone. "I did the same thing when I was in school. Maybe I can help out with your homework sometime. What are you studying?"

The three of them looked at me as if I were a leaf of lettuce that had suddenly wilted. Renee said, "Sean is an honor student. He doesn't need anyone's help."

Sean smirked.

Gordon said, "Enough of this amusement. It's time to get to work. Tell Carlotta to bring my coffee into the office. Come on, Dell. I'll show you what to do."

In the office, Gordon was completely professional. Not only would his patients have no inkling of what had gone on between us the night before, but I was tempted to forget it myself. He showed me my duties, which consisted of such things as weighing people, measuring children's height, taking blood samples and labeling them to be picked up by the laboratory's messenger, finding the right file for the patient whose appointment was next and putting it in the examination room, keeping the file up to date by painstakingly typing Gordon's nearly indecipherable notes, and cleaning the examination room between patients.

There was a receptionist named Miss Hawser in the office who took care of making appointments and sending bills. She was a stern-faced woman in her fifties, a mechanically efficient worker who had no compassion for the patients' countless ills, and no interest whatsoever in her fellow employee. Our relationship was conducted in terse requests, questions, and replies, and we knew nothing about each other's lives.

"She's really a lot of fun to work with," I said of her to Gordon.

"Is that a trace of sarcasm I hear in your innocent voice, boy?" he said to me.

"Just a trace," I said.

"Don't be too hard on Hawser. She's as queer as you are, but her lady friend has Parkinson's disease, and Hawser has to support them both."

I felt sorry for her after I heard that, and I tried to be a little friendlier. But she wasn't interested, so when I was in the office, I went about my duties and kept to myself. Aside from her, I didn't mind the job at all. It wasn't difficult and I learned it pretty quickly. If I wasn't chatting with Hawser (no one seemed to use "Miss" in front of her name), I occasionally had a chance to chat with the patients as I took their blood or installed them in the examination room. Most of them were older working people or young mothers with children in tow. But occasionally a strapping specimen of manhood in his prime would show up, and I would be more courteous than a greedy maître d' and linger as long as I could, in case he might need help changing his clothes—which in most cases eventually earned me a quizzically raised eyebrow, clearly indicating: Don't even think about it.

I didn't think I was being disloyal to Gordon by being interested in other men's bodies. After all, I didn't actually have sex with them. Gordon was the one I wanted—especially when we were in the same room with other people and I couldn't say what was on my mind, which grew to be an exquisite torture. It wasn't that Gordon wasn't enough for me, but he was busy most of the time, either with his work or with his wife, and if I needed any attention, I had to wait for those rare times when he could steal a few moments for us to be alone. When he did appear, our sexual experiences continued to be brief, but hot. One time he appeared with a tube of lubricating jelly for me to keep in my room, and after that, whenever there was time, he would fuck my ass until I purred. Unfortunately most of the sessions were too brief for that, so I had to content myself with quickly servicing him by mouth, and who could complain about that? On the whole, I was glad I was there.

In the extra time I had, although I kept my distance from Renee (who seemed to live in a world of shopping and beauty salons and bridge games), I tried to be a little friendlier with Sean. After all, he was as close to my age as Gordon was, even if it was in the other direction. At first he wanted no part of me, but as time passed, he relented and allowed me to sue for *his* friendship.

"Sean, why don't you like me?" I asked him directly one time when we were alone in the house. He had been listening to Rachmaninoff's Piano Concerto No. 2 on the phonograph, and I had quietly joined him, waiting until it was over before I asked my question.

"I don't dislike you," he answered.

"That doesn't answer my question."

"What's to like?" he said.

"Thanks."

"I didn't mean that the way it sounded," he explained.

"Maybe it's because I was friendly with Merle."

"Believe me," I said, "I didn't know I was taking somebody else's job. Do you miss her?"

He paused for a moment, then said, "Merle is also a man's name, you know."

"Merle is a man?" I said, flabbergasted. Of course. That explained the jockstrap and the sunglasses—and the empty tube of lubricant.

"Yes, Merle is a man, and yes, I do miss him."

"I'm sorry," I said.

"It's not your fault."

"Were you good friends?" I asked.

"Very."

"I see."

"I doubt that," he said, opening a magazine.

I didn't pursue the subject, although I couldn't help wondering exactly what Merle's relationship to Sean had been. I was more certain about my predecessor's relationship to Gordon.

The next time I was with Gordon, I didn't wait for him to start our sex before I said, "Tell me about Merle."

"What about him?"

"Did you have sex with him?" I asked.

"Why is that your business?"

"It isn't," I said. "I just wanted to know."

"Yes, I did," he said emotionlessly.

"Did you love him?" I continued.

"No."

I was dying to ask him if he loved me, but I didn't dare. What if he answered with the same curt "No"? Instead, I asked, "When did you meet him?"

"Right after you went back to Portland."

"Oh," I said, crestfallen.

"Listen, Dell, don't work yourself up about it. I know I promised to be faithful—except for Renee—but I just ran into him. He was here and you were there. What was I supposed to do? Besides, I got rid of him when you were ready to come here, didn't I? Doesn't that prove my intentions were honorable?"

"I guess so," I said.

"You guess so, or you know so?"

"I know so."

"Good. Now get down on the bed and spread your legs."

That time he entered me without any preliminaries and fucked me harder and faster than ever before. When he rose from my exhausted body, he said, "Now don't be late for work in the morning," and he left. He didn't come to my room for a week after that, and I wondered if I were being punished for my curiosity. I kept myself busy with other things.

My correspondence with Louie had continued all the time I had been in Pittsburgh. When I was settled in Portland, I wrote to him in Chicago again, to tell him what had been happening with Gordon and to make sure he had my new address. He wrote back.

Dec. 8, 1951

Dear Dell (Im still not used to youre new name),

Im real glad to hear from you as always buddy. I was sorry to hear about youre friend Edwin. He sounded like a nice old gent, and Im sure you did youre best for him. Dont feel to bad we all have to go sometime so they say and he had a pretty long life anyways. Now look at you—the doctors other wife (I sure hope he dont read youre mail!) Im truely happy for you Dell. Thanks for the dough you sent me I realy needed it. This time I have some good news for a change. Im getting sprung on good behavior like you! No parole! Can you believe it after all this time? Halaluyah! I sure aint gonna miss Duke and his kind. (He is in Joliet for life now for Freds murder. To bad. If anyone ever deserved the death penilty its Duke. I hate that bastard as you can tell.)

Anyway the main reason I wanted to write you is so that we dont lose touch. You may not believe this Dell buddy but even thogh we only knew each other a short time in person, I feel closer to you than anybody and I hope we can stay friends. Do you aggree? I guess you do or you woudnt of sent me letters and money in the first place. Thanks again. Im gonna be on the road for awhile, but Im planing to end up not to far from where you are in Provincetown Mass or P-Town as we call it. Theres lots of our kind of fellas there (wink) and lots of good times. I got a friend named Dominick to stay with, and Im thinking of going into the (dont laugh now) beauty parlor profesion eventualy! Can you picture me a hair burner? Ha! Anyway buddy I will let you know my adress as soon as I have one and I hope you will be able to come visit me there someday. In the meantime please keep in touch.

Youre good friend,
Louie

PS I apologize again for my bad spelling. I hope it dont come between us, especially with you being a poet and all!

In my spare time, I reread my favorite passages from *Leaves of Grass*. I tried to share them with Gordon by copying out several of my favorites and presenting them to him. He kept promising to read them, but he never seemed to find the time, and I finally accepted that he simply wasn't interested in all the same things I was. Too bad, I told myself, he might have enjoyed it. But that's the way most people are about poetry. It's worse than castor oil. I finally decided that it didn't matter if we cared about different things as long as we cared about each other.

Sean, on the other hand, seemed genuinely interested when I quoted Whitman. "Let me hear that line again," he said, and I recited.

" 'O you whom I often and silently come where you are that
    I may be with you,
As I walk by your side or sit near, or remain in the same
    room with you,
Little you know the subtle electric fire that for your sake is
    playing within me.' "

"That's neat," he said. "I never read Whitman before."

"He's my favorite," I said.

"He seems to know a lot about secret love."

"Yes," I said warily. "He loved . . . in an unusual way."

"What do you mean 'unusual'?"

For a moment I thought I heard Gordon's footsteps. Then I realized that I was just feeling my own heart beating faster with fear. "Let's talk about it another time," I said.

He frowned. "I'm not a baby, you know."

"I know."

"Then why won't you tell me?" he asked.

"Your father probably wouldn't like it."

His tone grew petulant. "Oh, what does he know?"

"More than you think," I said.

"I hope not," he said worriedly. "Okay, if you won't tell me, can I guess?"

"Guess what?" I was beginning to get nervous.

"About Whitman's unusual love," he said. "Was it for another man?"

"Yes," I replied, caught off guard by his boldness.

"I thought so. There's just something about it. Dell, can I tell you something?"

"Of course."

"Do you promise not to tell anybody—especially Dad?"

I could see that his appeal was earnest. "I promise."

"Those lines you just quoted. I think that describes the way I felt about Merle," he confessed.

All I could say was, "Oh."

"You won't tell my father?"

"No," I assured him. "You can trust me."

"Is that why you like those lines?" he continued.

"What do you mean?" I asked, doubting that I sounded innocent.

"Have you ever felt that way about someone?"

"I may have," I said. I hated to use subterfuge, remembering how badly I had once needed the reassurance of someone older and wiser.

He persisted. "Was it a man?"

"What's the difference?"

"Just wondering," he said quietly. "Never mind."

"Sean, will you tell me something now?"

"What?"

"Did you do anything about your feelings for Merle?"

"Like what?" His smile was all innocence, but he couldn't hide the truth in his eyes.

"You know." I gave him time to consider his answer.

"All right," he said, his shoulders dropping. "Yes, I did. Does that make you happy?"

"It doesn't make me unhappy."

"You still won't tell my father?" he pleaded.

"I won't tell. Don't worry."

"Maybe I shouldn't have told you."

"It's okay," I said soothingly.

"You're sure?"

"I'm sure. Your secret is safe with me."

"Okay then. Dell?"

"What?" I said softly.

"Did you ever do anything about your feelings?"

I couldn't lie when he was so vulnerable. "Yes," I replied.

He looked both confident and trusting. "It was a man, wasn't it?" he asked.

"Yes."

"Was it . . ."

"I think we shouldn't discuss this any further, or we might both be sorry," I said.

"Okay," he replied. "There's one more thing, though."

"What?" I said with a sigh.

"I think we can be friends now."

Sean wasn't the only one I became friendlier with that winter. Carlotta, the housekeeper, and I found ourselves together now and then, and we enjoyed each other's company. I hung around in the kitchen sometimes while she was cooking or cleaning up, and occasionally I even helped her. Aside from that she kept to herself most of the time, a dark-eyed woman of mystery.

"Where do you go on your day off?" I asked her one time. She answered in her soft-spoken, sibilant Spanish accent:

"I veesit my brother Diego. His work ees near here."

"Where is the rest of your family?"

"Some are in New York. Some are still in Puerto Rico. We are helping to bring them to the mainland."

"How many of you are there?"

"Nine, plus my parents and my old grandmother."

"How did you end up in Maine? Am I asking too many questions?"

"Ees awright. Diego first got his job through a friend, and here he meet Dr. Thomas. And you? How deed you come to Maine?" she asked me.

"I met Gordon while I was traveling here."

"Dr. Thomas ees a generous man," she said.

"Yes," I said. We both looked at each other as if each of us was waiting for the other to add something more about our employer. But neither of us did.

"You do not go out very much. Do you have lady friend?" she asked me.

"No," I answered. "Is that an invitation?" I don't know what made me say it, since sleeping with Carlotta was the farthest thing from my mind.

She looked slightly alarmed and shook her head in a barely noticeable "no." But I assured her with a big grin that I was only kidding, and then she looked relieved.

"Do you have a boyfriend?" I countered.

"Maybe," she said.

"What does 'maybe' mean?"

"I see someone, but we are not engaged," she explained.

"Do you love him?"

"Maybe." She smiled shyly.

"Are you sleeping together?"

She looked at me, shocked, and didn't answer.

"I'm sorry," I said. "It's none of my business."

"Among my people, eet ees important for a woman to remain, how do you say . . ."

"Chaste?"

She still looked confused.

"Virgin?" I tried.

"*Si*, virgin," she said, blushing.

I didn't ask her any more.

One evening that spring when no one else was home, Sean asked if I would help him carry some books up to his room. I had seen the second floor only fleetingly since the first night Gordon had brought me home. Sean's lair was down the hall from Gordon and Renee's colonial bedroom. It was painted a pale blue and furnished with simply tailored pieces in several darker shades of blue. Small, framed reproductions of paintings by Picasso, Chagall, Van Gogh, and Gauguin filled the walls that weren't occupied by tall bookshelves containing a haphazard array of volumes and papers. There were none of the football pennants or provocative pictures of women that usually graced the walls of boys his age. I had time to notice only a few of the book titles: Hemingway's *The Sun Also Rises*, Fitzgerald's *Tender Is the Night*, and Salinger's *The Catcher in the Rye*—respectable reading for a young student.

When we had put down the pile of books, Sean invited me to sit down, gesturing toward a navy blue corduroy club chair in the corner. I sat.

"How about a drink?" he asked, gesturing with his chin toward a small table on which there was a tray with a bottle of scotch and two glasses, next to a small bowl of ice. I doubted that the arrangement was part of the usual decor.

"I see you were expecting me," I said.

"I invited you, didn't I?"

"To help carry books."

"Don't be difficult," he said. "We're here now, so what's the difference?"

Feeling that I had been set up, I said, "I'll skip the drink, thanks." When he didn't respond, I added, "Won't your father be mad about his scotch?"

"He won't notice."

"So what did you want to talk about?" I asked.

"Us," he said.

"What about us?"

"You're really going to make me do all the work, aren't you?" he asked, leaning back against the corduroy bolster that cushioned the wall behind his bed. He put one foot up on the bedspread and casually—so casually that I could swear that he'd rehearsed the gesture—allowed his hand to drop between his legs, where it drew attention to an impressive basket of genitalia beneath his trousers.

"I'm not trying to make you work," I said. "I just wanted to be your friend."

"Merle was my friend."

"I'm not Merle. "

"Maybe you'll be even better than Merle." He delicately scratched his balls. "After all, we are birds of a feather, aren't we?"

"Sean," I said, "I really like you. Really I do. But not in that way. You're a handsome boy. I appreciate your interest in me. I'm flattered by it. But I just don't think it's a good idea for me to get involved with my boss's son, especially not since I could get thrown in jail for it. I've already been in jail, and I have no intention of going back if I can help it."

"You were in jail?" he said with an interest keen enough to make him forget his efforts at seduction. "Where? What for?"

"It was a couple of years ago, in Chicago. It happened because I was foolish enough to forget where I was, and I let my lust overcome my reason."

"What was it like?" he asked eagerly.

"I don't want to talk about it."

"Wow! It must have been exciting."

"Don't glamorize it, Sean. It was no fun. And I'd appreciate it if you didn't mention it to your parents. We'll keep each other's secrets, okay?"

"Okay." He nodded his head.

"Great," I said, standing up. "I've got to go downstairs to feed Calamus now. We'll talk again sometime."

His eyes sparkled seductively. "We'll do more than that if I can help it."

"I wish you would put such ideas out of your mind," I said firmly.

"I can't," he replied. "I might be falling in love."

I remembered how desperately I had wanted Chester when I was Sean's age, and I started to go over to him, wanting to put my arm around his shoulder—to show him that I understood and that I wasn't rejecting him as a person, that only his youth and the fact that he was Gordon's son were stopping me. But I stopped myself, afraid that it would get out of hand in one way or another, afraid that we'd either end up in bed, victimized by my compassion, or that I'd somehow let slip that I was having sex with his father, and I knew that Gordon would never forgive me for that.

"For your own sake, I hope you're wrong about your feelings, Sean," I said. "I can't tell you why, but I'm not the right man for you. I really do like you, though, and I want to be your friend—nothing more. I'm going downstairs now."

"Good night, then," he said sullenly.

When I finally got to know Renee a little better, things weren't much different, although they were a bit more subtle. She and Gordon went out separately quite often. It was all very amiable. He'd be busy with meetings or socializing with other doctors, and she would see her own friends at cocktail parties, or visit with the other doctors' wives. Sometimes she would ask me up to her bedroom when she was getting ready for an evening out. The scent of her expensive perfume was so heavy it was almost visible. It would hang about the room like smog, and I was sure that I'd reek of the stuff myself when I left. Usually she'd ask me to do up the back of one of her elegant, long-sleeved party dresses. "Sean is studying, and I hate to make Carlotta climb the stairs just for this," she'd explain. "The poor thing has enough to take care of as it is."

One time when I arrived, she didn't have her dress on yet. She was wearing a blue satin robe that slid sinuously over her skin as she moved. "Pour yourself a glass of sherry," she said. "I'd like to talk to you." She indicated a crystal decanter that stood on her dresser. I poured a minuscule amount into a tiny glass and sat nervously on a chair. She established herself on her chaise longue like Camille getting herself ready for some heartache, and began to talk.

"You're in a strange position," she said, "living so closely with our family."

"What do you mean?" I asked casually. Did she suspect something about Gordon and me?

"I'm sure you know more than you let on. You're such a quiet one." She brought her knee up closer to her torso, and the satin robe slid off her leg. She readjusted it carefully, smoothing it over her calf and watching to see if I were admiring her. I was looking at the pink pearl polish on her carefully manicured fingernails.

"It's just that we haven't had much chance to talk," I explained.

"Well, this is our chance, isn't it?" She didn't sound very enthusiastic, so I assumed something other than this conversation was on her mind.

"Sure," I answered. It was her party. She'd get around to the real agenda in her own good time.

"I really wanted to ask you about Sean," she said. She braced her shoulders back, so that the front of her robe separated to reveal more of her cleavage, and she left it that way.

I felt as if she were measuring my responses. Was she testing me? Did she suspect something about me?

"You've had plenty of opportunity to be around Sean," she continued. I could feel small beads of perspiration forming on my upper lip. "Do you think he's . . . normally masculine?"

"He's okay," I said, hoping to buy some time.

"I admire his interest in art and literature," she went on. "But I'm not sure it's all quite healthy."

"Why not?" I asked.

"There's just something too soft about him. Have you noticed it?"

"All boys can't be tough guys," I said. "What's wrong with being cultured?"

"Then you don't think that there's anything wrong with him?"

"I doubt it," I replied.

"That's a relief," she said, stretching out her arm and admiring her pink nail polish. "He doesn't seem to socialize much, and I just thought there's something . . . well, morbid about his hanging around the house so much. It makes me so tense. Dell, do you think you could do me a favor?"

"Of course," I said warily.

"Could you come over here and massage the back of my neck? I can just feel the tension building up there. It's so tight."

I crossed over to where she was sitting, noticing that as I neared she moved her legs so that the satin robe revealed them both up to the middle of her thighs. She didn't bother to rearrange it. I massaged her neck as gingerly as I could, feeling no arousal whatsoever, wondering if she were laying some kind of elaborate trap for me, or if she were as unaware of her seductive moves as she appeared to be.

"That feels much better," she said.

I stood there, afraid to move either closer to her or farther away.

"Maybe Sean doesn't go out because he's got something to keep him at home," she said.

She thinks it's me, I thought. How can I prove otherwise?

"Maybe he's sleeping with Carlotta," she continued. "Have you seen or heard anything?"

"Nothing," I said, relieved. "I think he's just a quiet kid. And I've talked with Carlotta. She's a very serious young woman. I don't think she'd do anything like that."

"Don't be naive," she said. "Carlotta's from the Caribbean. They all screw like rabbits. Pardon my French."

"I don't think she's like that."

"We're all like that," she said.

"I don't know what you mean."

"Maybe you don't, but you will. Thanks for the chat. Let's do it again sometime." She stood up, and I headed toward the door.

"Just don't think I don't know what's going on around here," she added.

"I never thought that," I assured her, suppressing a laugh.

I didn't report the incident to Gordon because I didn't know what to make of it, and nothing had actually happened. I wasn't sure Gordon would have cared, anyway. He seemed less and less interested in what I had to say, as well as in my sex. I began to feel that his trips to my room, which were growing more infrequent all the time, were becoming a matter of obligation rather than lust. But I didn't know how to keep him excited. I was still as aroused by him as ever. In fact, the less interested he grew, the more interested I became. I made myself as available to him as I could. I obeyed his every command without reservation. Maybe if I had played a little harder to get, it would have kept him interested, but he already knew that he could have me whenever he wanted to. Short of pretending to have a headache, there wasn't much I could do. So he came and went as rarely as he pleased, sometimes only once or twice a month, and I just put up with his erratic schedule the best I could, turning to the pleasures of my own hand more and more often, no longer afraid to waste my sexual energy in case he should suddenly decide to appear.

In the summer of 1952, Gordon rented a house in Ogunquit, a resort community about an hour's drive south of Portland. I had hoped that he would send Renee and Sean there, maybe even with Carlotta to tend to their needs, leaving me alone with him in the house. But he sent me along with the three of them for a month, telling me, "The change will do you good." I didn't know whether to feel grateful or insulted.

Ogunquit was a small, charming town of seaside cottages. Our house was airy and pretty, but it didn't accommodate the four of us very comfortably. Only Calamus was happy as he went about his feline business in the neighboring yards. The rest of us felt cramped. It wasn't the size of the small rooms that bothered us; it was their closeness. The house had only one story, and all the bedrooms opened onto the cozy living room. Sean's room was right next to mine. I could sense his sexual heat through the wall that divided us, but he didn't dare make a move in plain view of his mother. Renee's room was on the other side of mine, and I felt as if I were under her surveillance, even when her door was closed. Carlotta's tiny maid's room was off the kitchen. She seemed to need companionship more than ever, but I didn't feel as comfortable hanging around and chatting with her while Renee was so near. I didn't want the boss's wife to think that the housekeeper wasn't paying attention to her job, besides which Carlotta and I couldn't discuss personal subjects without being easily overheard through the cardboard walls. As a result, we all went our separate ways. Sean escaped to the beach, Renee lost herself in a pile of historical romance novels, Carlotta hid out in the kitchen, and I went for walks.

A mile-long path aptly called Marginal Way connected Ogunquit to Perkins Cove, a summer artist's colony, which was full of idiosyncratic individualists. A person's sexual eccentricities were not so likely to be noticed there, I felt— not that I was advertising my proclivities—and I walked the length of Marginal Way many times, to get away from the tensions in the Ogunquit house.

Several small galleries sold the works of the artists who had studios nearby, and after visiting each of them a few times, I preferred to walk outside of town along the beach. There I found an artist—an attractive man of about forty with a handsome, sun-leathered face—painting vague pastel seascapes that had a pleasing aura of mystery about them. I enjoyed watching him at work, and his concentration seemed so deep that I was sure he wasn't even aware of my presence. But I was wrong. On the third afternoon that I watched him, he suddenly turned and asked, "What do you like best—the ocean, the art, or the artist?"

"All three, I guess," I replied.

"Fair enough," he said. "My name's Elliot."

"Dell."

"Do you swim, Dell?"

"Sure," I said. "But it's been a while. Anyway, isn't it too cold?"

"Only for sissies. Come on," he invited, laying aside his brushes and stripping off the denim shirt he wore above his bathing suit as he headed toward the water.

I joined him and we frolicked in the icy water for a few minutes, splashing and squealing like two little boys. When we emerged, he said, "We'd better go back to my place to dry off."

He collected his easel and supplies, and I followed him back to his studio, where we had a shower. He offered me a gin and tonic, which I accepted. Then he sat down next to me on the couch, and we started to talk.

"From around here?" he inquired.

"I'm from Portland, right now. Before that I lived in lots of places across the country. New York State, originally."

"I've lived down east all my life," he said. "So I guess I take living in Maine for granted. But I still find it beautiful enough to capture on canvas. What makes you watch me paint?"

"I enjoy it," I answered.

"Are you an *artistic* type of person?" His emphasis on "artistic" made it sound erotic.

"I write some poetry," I said.

"About what?"

I didn't give him any help. "About everything, I guess. Nature. Love. That kind of thing."

"What kind of love?" he pursued.

I was starting to enjoy his game. "How many kinds are there?"

"Oh, there are several," he said with a little smile. "Who's your favorite poet?"

"Walt Whitman."

He raised his eyebrows. "I see. That's very interesting."

"Who's your favorite painter?" I asked, trying to make the conversation sound less like a one-way interrogation.

"I am," he said. "I hope that doesn't sound immodest."

I shook my head.

"Sometimes I think you might be watching me, not the painting," he said.

"Maybe. You're part of the scenery."

"An important part?" he asked hopefully.

"I think so."

He slid over next to me and put his hand on my knee. "Are you sure about that?"

"I thought we were discussing art," I said.

"We are," he answered, looking searchingly into my eyes. Then he leaned over and, bracing the back of my head with his hand, he kissed me on the lips.

Unable to help myself, I returned his kiss. It felt so good that I didn't want to stop, but eventually I pulled back. "I shouldn't be here," I said.

"Why not? Afraid to be kissed by another man?"

"It isn't that," I explained. "I like being kissed by a man. I especially like being kissed by you. But that's the problem. I belong to somebody else."

"Belong?"

"He's not only my lover," I told him. "He's my boss."

"But he doesn't own you."

"I love him," I said.

"I see." He took his hand from the back of my head.

"But he's married," I continued.

"Then he's not faithful to you."

"He is except for his wife," I explained. "But I'm completely faithful to him. That's the deal."

"It doesn't sound fair to me," he said.

"What does fairness have to do with it?"

"That's up to you," he said. "Don't you ever slip, just a little?"

"I don't usually get the chance."

"You have the chance now." He stroked his basket suggestively.

I watched him and felt a stirring in my groin. I put my hand down to my own basket and rubbed lightly. There was an instant reaction.

"You can't say you don't want to," he commented, looking at the growing mound in my crotch.

"I do want to," I said, forcibly breaking my concentration. "But I can't. It wouldn't be right."

"I had to find a moralist," he said, with a disgusted tone.

"I'm sorry, Elliot. I didn't mean to lead you on or anything."

"Like hell you didn't, you cock teaser. You practically begged me to come on to you, sitting there like a spider watching me, day after day."

"I'm sorry," I whispered. "I'd better go."

"That sounds like a good idea," he said coldly.

All the way back to Ogunquit I asked myself if I were crazy for passing up such a good offer. The guy was handsome and willing, and nobody ever needed to know about it. I was obeying my conscience while Gordon was scarcely even aware of my existence any longer. He'd probably sent me here just to get me out of his way—for what purpose I wasn't sure, but I could guess. Still, if I ever hoped to arouse his interest in me again it wouldn't help if I spent all my sexual energy elsewhere. On the other hand, what else was I going to do with it?

Sean, of course, had an answer for me. If anyone in the neighborhood could be called a spider, he was the most likely candidate. He had been waiting in ambush, just biding his time until his mother was out of the house. Finally, a few days later, she left for Portland. "I just have to get back to the city for a couple of days," she said. "I have some unfinished business to attend to."

The day she left, Sean stopped going to the beach and started hanging around the house. I was home a good deal of the time as well, having lost much of my incentive for walking to Perkins Cove. Sean wore nothing but a pair of skimpy gym shorts, and he took every opportunity to sit in a chair opposite me. Then he would casually raise his leg, and his plump balls would fall out. "Excuse me," he would say while ostentatiously stuffing them back into the leg of his shorts, from which they were sure to emerge again within moments.

I can't say I minded the show. After all, Sean was a good-looking young man in his prime. Seventeen can be such a succulent age. But I did my level best to ignore him. His response was to accelerate his efforts, inventing reasons to brush his crotch against my shoulder as I sat in a chair, or leaving his bedroom door open so I could "accidentally" catch him changing. He must have stood there with his shorts in his hand for twenty minutes at a time waiting for me to pass by. I was as flattered by his efforts as I had been by Elliot's, but I was equally frustrated by both of them. The man I really wanted was in Portland with his wife.

Knowing that his mother would return any day only made Sean's efforts more frantic. Finally he walked into my room naked while I was in my bed, and he played with his erection while he buried his head in my blanket-covered crotch, nearly sobbing, "I want you so badly, Dell. Please don't say no."

Our grand scene was interrupted by a small shriek and a crash in the doorway, which Sean had forgotten to shut in his eagerness. Carlotta had been passing by, just in time to see him climb onto my bed. She had been carrying a lamp into the kitchen for cleaning, and it lay broken at her feet.

Sean starting sobbing in earnest then. He ran past her and back into his room, blushing and clutching his wilting genitals in his hands. Carlotta retreated into her kitchen.

I rose from my bed, put on a robe, and first went to Sean's room. "Don't say anything," I told him. "I'll talk to Carlotta. But you'd better lie low for a while. And don't give her any more evidence." He nodded weakly, his shoulders shuddering with fear.

I found Carlotta in the kitchen. "Don't be upset about the lamp," I said. "I'll take the blame for it."

"Ees not your fault," she whispered. She seemed utterly confused by what she had seen. She had no way to interpret it or to deal with it.

"It wasn't what you thought," I said.

"No?"

"First of all, what do you think was going on?"

"I think Mr. Sean ees *maricon*. Maybe you too. I do not know."

"Sean is just young and confused. He needed to talk to somebody, and he came to my room."

"He wore no clothes." She was blushing.

"He was undressed in his room, and he got upset about something. Men don't need to cover themselves in front of each other the way they do in front of a woman."

"He had his head against your body."

"He needed me to comfort him."

"He wass holding his own . . . He wass hard."

"Maybe he just got carried away. Didn't you ever do anything you weren't supposed to?"

She blushed all over again. "*Si*," she said, and she started to weep softly.

"Carlotta, is there anything you want to tell me? Remember, I'm your friend."

"I cannot talk about it," she said.

"Is it serious?"

"*Si*, very serious."

"Can I help you in some way?"

"I do not think so. *Gracias*."

"Let me know if there's anything I can do."

She nodded.

"Would you promise me something, Carlotta?"

"What ees it?"

"Promise me you won't tell Dr. and Mrs. Thomas about Sean. They wouldn't understand, and it would only cause all of them pain. Will you promise me that?"

She was silent for a moment. Then she said, "*Sí*."

"Thanks, Carlotta. You're doing the right thing. Remember, if you need my help, just ask me. And don't worry about the lamp. I'll take care of it."

"*Gracias*," she said, and she returned to her soft weeping. I held her for a few moments. Then I helped her to dry her eyes, kissed her on the forehead, and went back to my room to think.

Renee returned the following day to a household sobered by fear. She, on the other hand, was not even slightly sober. Even if someone did tell her what had been going on in her absence, she would have been too blurry to understand it. On her first night back, she called me into her room. She was lying on the bed with a glass in her hand. Without her makeup she looked haggard and drawn. There were circles under her eyes and she seemed half asleep.

"Want some sherry?" she asked.

I shook my head.

"How about some gin then? I'm having some. See?" She held up her glass, which had no trace of ice or mixer, just straight warm gin.

I shook my head again.

"Puritan. Probably think you're holier than I am."

I didn't answer, amazed at her willingness to reveal this hidden side of herself. She downed her gin in one gulp and unsteadily poured herself another. Then she downed that as well.

"Maybe you should take it easy," I suggested.

"I am taking it easy," she said. "What the hell do you know?"

"I know you're unhappy about something."

"Well, thank you, Dr. Freud. It's so nice to have a genius around the house." She tried to pour another drink, slopping half of it onto her bed as she held it out to me. "Sure you won't join me?"

"No, thanks," I said.

She started to pout. Then a devilish expression came over her face, and she said, "How about a fix then, honey?" She laughed as she opened her nightstand drawer to reveal a hypodermic syringe, a length of rubber tubing, a spoon, a candle, and several glassine packets of white powder. "Bet you didn't know that about old Renee."

I was shocked, but I tried to hide it. "No, I didn't. Are you all right?"

"Tell me the truth, Dell," she said, closing the drawer, bracing her shoulders, and patting her still tidy hairdo. "Do you think I'm an attractive woman?"

"Of course you are," I replied. "You're very striking."

"Striking? What does that mean—that I wear too much makeup or something?"

"It means you're very elegant-looking," I said diplomatically.

"The hell with elegant. Am I sexy?" she demanded.

"Sure, but in a ladylike way."

"I guess I don't look so ladylike tonight, do I?" she said, wobbling her head on her neck as if she had tried to give it an arrogant toss.

"Is something the matter?" I asked.

She started to laugh, but it turned into a cough. When it had subsided, she said, "Of course there's something the matter, you fool. Do you think I'd make such a display of myself if nothing was the matter?"

"I don't know," I answered truthfully.

"Now don't you turn bastard on me. I've had enough of that in my life already. Come here and sit down." She patted the bed next to her. She was wearing the same blue satin robe she'd worn the last time she'd called me into her room to ask about Sean, and once again it fell open to reveal her thighs. I sat down gingerly on the edge of the bed.

"Do you really think I'm sexy?" she continued. I could tell that she wasn't trying to be coy.

"Yes," I said.

"Then why don't you ever try to put the make on me?"

"You're Gordon's wife."

"I wish he were as aware of that fact."

I was afraid to unleash more of her grief and anger, but I had to say something. "Did you have a bad time back in Portland?" I asked.

"I had no time at all," she said. "The bastard hasn't got five minutes to spend with his own wife." She started crying, lost in a boozy haze of self-pity. "He doesn't love me anymore."

"Don't say that," I offered. "I'm sure Gordon cares a great deal about you."

"Oh, what the fuck do you know? You're just a kid. Oops, pardon my French."

"He told me he loves you," I said.

"That's more than he's told me lately. Look at what's becoming of me, stuck out here on the edge of the world waiting for something—anything— to happen. Do you know I read every one of those damned books twice?" she asked, pointing at a stack of romance novels.

"That's what a vacation is for," I said.

"Oh bullshit," she retorted. "A vacation is for fun and parties. Wanna have a party?"

"I don't think you're feeling well enough," I counseled.

"Fuck you. And don't pardon my French. I'm feeling fine. I'm just a little high is all. You didn't know that I got high every night, did you? Nobody knows, not even Carlotta. I have to drag myself to the next door neighbor's garbage can to hide the evidence from my own maid. Some glamorous life."

"You just need some rest, Renee."

"Rest is the last thing I need, honey. What I need is to get laid. Pardon my English. Ha, ha, ha! Oops, sorry." She had spit up some saliva on the lapel of her robe. She made a great fuss of wiping herself clean with a tissue and readjusting herself, but a dark, wet spot remained on the blue satin lapel. When she raised her hand to touch it mournfully, her satin sleeve slid away, and for the first time I could see the rows of tiny needle marks along her arm. Then she looked at me with reddened eyes. She leaned forward as if to kiss me, and I leaned back out of her reach involuntarily. "Please?" she said pitiably, and she reached for my crotch. I stood up.

"You don't want to do something you'll be sorry for in the morning. I'm going to bed now. I'll send Carlotta in to put you to bed."

"Coward!" she spat at me. "You know you want me. You're just afraid of your almighty boss. Well, he doesn't care what's happening here. He's not even planning to drop in for a visit. He's too busy fucking around with his new girlfriend!"

"You're just upset," I said calmly. "I'm going to bed now."

"It's your loss," she said, and she passed out on her pillow.

As I left the room, I could see Carlotta standing in the doorway of the kitchen, wide-eyed with alarm. Sean was in the living room, slumped in a chair, his face buried in his hands. I patted his head gently as I passed his chair. Then I went to the kitchen and asked Carlotta to help put Mrs. Thomas into bed.

In the morning, no one mentioned the scene of the night before. We all pretended it hadn't happened, and we went back to our individual escapes, not wanting to endanger our secrets with any conversation that might lead to one of several risky topics. Sean went to the beach, Carlotta stayed in the kitchen, Renee reread one of her novels again, and I walked to Perkins Cove. Along the way I was plagued by the question: If Gordon isn't having sex with Renee, and he isn't having sex with me, then just who is the bastard fucking?

When I arrived at the Cove, Elliot was painting on the beach, just as I'd first seen him. His tan face looked as attractive as ever, and I sat on my customary rock and watched him for an hour. I was ready for him now. There didn't seem much point in being faithful to Gordon. But Elliot didn't look in my direction or say anything to me. He just acted as if I weren't there. After a while, a blond young man came walking up the beach toward him. They waved at each other, and when the young man arrived at the easel, they both took off their shirts and ran into the water to play. I turned away from the ocean and followed Marginal Way back to Ogunquit.

CHAPTER SEVENTEEN

Our return to Portland put everyone into a depression. Renee put her impenetrable makeup back on and kept her image intact, but she stayed in her own room more and more. Carlotta almost never came out of the kitchen except to clean the house, which she did silently. Sean returned to school, but he was subdued and frightened, waiting for the axe to fall. And I returned to my job without enthusiasm since it meant spending the day with the grim-faced receptionist Hawser and the increasingly distant Gordon. I went about my office duties with as little involvement as possible. It was a living and no more.

I tried going out now and then, but aside from our neurotic household, Portland seemed to offer even fewer opportunities for sexual encounters than Pittsburgh had. Maybe it was due to my mood more than to Portland's, but I wound up spending most of my evenings in my room alone. At night I wrote poems about blood and marrow and asthma and cramps and children who couldn't walk. I had stopped waiting for Gordon to visit my room. I think he would have been glad to be rid of me, but he was probably afraid I would vengefully tell his wife about our affair. He didn't know me very well. I wouldn't have done anything like that—not out of respect for Gordon, but out of pity for poor Renee. She had troubles enough of her own.

Aside from her drug habit, Sean was her greatest problem. His fear turned to resentment, which he started to express with more and more flamboyantly feminine gestures. His jewelry was a little too gaudy, his shirts a little too loud, and his wrists a little too limp. But his eyes didn't have the twinkle that went with such clowning. Instead, they looked wounded and angry. Finally Renee insisted that he see a psychiatrist or leave home. He chose the psychiatrist.

He came to talk to me after his third session. "I wanted to apologize for that scene at the house in Ogunquit," he said. "It was a turning point for me. I went farther than I ever intended to."

"It wasn't your fault," I consoled him. "You were under a lot of pressure."

"The therapist is helping me to see that," he said. "He's trying to show me that it's only a phase I'm going through. He says I'm not really queer. I'm just mad at my father."

I stopped to think. There was good reason to be mad at Gordon, I reflected, but what did that have to do with Sean's loving men? On the other hand, I thought, I had been mad at my father and I loved men. Maybe the doctor did know something. After all, he was supposed to be the expert. Finally I spoke, cautiously.

"Your father probably means well," I said. "We all have our limitations."

"That's what the doctor said. He thinks my mother was overprotective and that's what drove my father away. He says if I can just control my urges, they'll turn in a healthier direction—to girls—and I'll grow out of all this."

"I guess it's worth a try," I told him, hating myself for saying it. Whatever might be the source of his loving men, I knew Sean wasn't going to change. I just didn't want to sabotage whatever effort he was making. He was too close to the edge, and that might drive him over it. I didn't have anything to replace his psychotherapy, and I didn't want Sean to end up at the bottom of a lake like Harold Fisher.

I tried to speak to Gordon about it one time, when Hawser had gone on an errand and we were alone in the office. "Gordon, I know it isn't my place to say this, but your son needs you," I said. As soon as I said it, I was flooded with guilt about my own son a continent away. What if he needed me? How could I help him? Gordon brought me back to the present.

"I don't think you should interfere in my family's private business," he said coldly.

This was the first opportunity in months I'd had to talk intimately with him, and I knew I had to take a chance. "What went wrong between us?" I asked. "Why did you stop coming to my room?"

"It was beginning to get repetitious," he replied.

"I would have changed. Why didn't you tell me?"

"It wasn't worth it. Anyway, it was too late. I had already lost interest."

"Do you want me to leave?" I asked.

"It doesn't matter to me," he said.

"Then I'll stay—until I can think of something better to do."

"Fine," he said.

"But I meant what I said about Sean. A little kindness from you would go a long way. I hope you don't blame yourself if his sexual desires turn out like your own. Whatever he is, he needs your love and support."

"Mind your own business, Dell," he said. "I mean that." The discussion was closed.

In the early fall, Carlotta's secret was revealed. She was pregnant. "I am so ashamed," she confided to me in the kitchen. "You muss promise not to tell anyone else. Ees secret. Like Mr. Sean's secret."

"I won't tell anyone. I don't judge you," I assured her. "I'm certainly still your friend. But I thought that being a virgin was so important to you."

Tears streamed from her eyes. "Ees important," she said. "I wass a fool."

"What are you going to do?"

"My brother Diego hass arranged for me to marry the boy I wass dating. He doss not know. My parents do not know. Only Diego knows, and now you."

"What about the father? Why doesn't he marry you?"

She buried her face in the crook of her arm on the tabletop and wailed. "I deed not even tell heem. He ees married to someone else. What could he do? I weel not have an abortion. That ees a worse seen than the one I have already commeeted."

Suddenly I knew what had happened. "Was it Gordon? Dr. Thomas?" I asked.

She raised her tear-wet face from her arm and said, wide-eyed with fear, "You muss not tell heem. I do not want heem to know. Promise me."

"I think you're being foolish. He could do something for you, at least give you some money. But if it's so important to you, I promise I won't say anything. Can I help you in some way?"

"You help me by telling no one," she said, and she kissed me on the cheek.

Carlotta left soon afterward and returned to Puerto Rico. She was replaced by Mrs. Trump, who was about as warm as Hawser the receptionist. I had lost a friend. Renee and Sean weren't happy about Mrs. Trump either, but Gordon insisted that an efficient housekeeper was what our home needed. At least he's not about to seduce her, I thought. She looks like Abraham Lincoln, and that's not Gordon's type.

I couldn't help wondering who was his type. If he was no longer interested in me and he no longer bothered to mollify Renee, and he offered no affection to Sean, and he no longer had Carlotta for sexual release, where was his libido investing its energy?

That winter, I thought for a moment that I had the answer. It was a cold night in January, and I was snuggling with Calamus under my blankets in my darkened room, when I heard the door open quietly. A shadowy figure entered my room and stood there, watching the bed and making no sound. At last, I thought, he's come back. And I left the warmth of my blankets to seek the heat between Gordon's thighs.

I knelt before him without saying a word, undid his pajamas, and surrounded his dick with my hot mouth. It felt wonderful. I licked up and down, waiting for the usual stern commands, but none came. I sucked at his balls. The longer I silently worked at giving him pleasure, the surer I was that something was wrong. There was something different about him. It had been a long time, but he couldn't have changed that much. I took my head away from his groin and I stood up to turn on the light. There, standing in the middle of my room with his pajamas around his ankles, was Sean! His erection stood straight out and a look of oblivion veiled his face. I wondered if he were walking in his sleep.

"Sean?" I whispered.

"I . . . I couldn't help myself," he said with a moan. And he began to cry, in great, gasping sobs.

I went to him and held him close. "It's all right," I said. "Everything's going to be all right."

He reached slowly toward my groin, and I made no move to stop him. I drew him toward the bed, where we lay down and I held him. Then I let him do what he wanted. I needed the relief as much as he did.

When we were finished, he nestled against my chest. "I love you, Dell," he said.

"No you don't, Sean. You need me. There's a difference."

He changed the topic. "Thanks for letting me stay."

"My pleasure," I replied.

"I won't bother you again."

"What are you going to do?" I asked. "Are you going to tell your therapist about this?"

"I have to. But I won't tell him who you are. I'll tell him I slipped and had sex with a man, but I'll make up a story about the circumstances. I don't want you to lose your job."

"Thanks," I said.

"Dell?" he whispered.

"What?"

"Does my father know about you?"

"You mean, does he know that I'm gay?" I asked.

"Yes."

I paused for a moment. Telling Sean might make him suspect Gordon, and if that happened, it might destroy all of us. "No," I said. "Your father doesn't know."

"Thanks," he said, and snuggled against me once more. Then he got up, rearranged his pajamas, and went back to his room.

The next week he told me he was going to undergo a new kind of treatment. "It's called aversion therapy," he said, "and the doctor says it's definitely going to make me change. Don't expect me back in your room . . . I hope."

Soon after Sean began his new treatments, Renee started on me again. When Gordon was out, which was the case almost every evening now, she called me up to her room. I could see from her heavy-lidded eyes that she was high again, but she had done her best to hide the evidence. She didn't offer me sherry and she wasn't drinking her gin. "Have you changed your mind?" she asked in a husky voice.

"About what?" I asked.

"Don't play games with me, Dell. You know what I'm talking about."

"I haven't changed my mind."

She stood up a little shakily and opened her robe to show me her naked body. "Are you sure?" she asked. I was beginning to realize that her invitation wasn't the product of her unsatisfied lust. She really didn't seem horny at all. Her drugs had probably calmed her sexual desires.

"You don't really want me," I said. "You're just testing me, aren't you?"

"No, you moron. I'm testing myself—and I'm failing. Now get out of here. You're embarrassing me."

"No hard feelings, Renee? Okay?"

"Hard feelings my ass. I know you don't go out, and you must be getting it someplace, you bastard." A light of recognition dawned in her dulled eyes. "Wait a minute. What a fool I've been. Of course. All I had to do was put two and two together."

I waited for the axe to fall. It didn't matter whether she'd guessed about Gordon or Sean. Either one would be enough to ruin me. But she said nothing. "What are you talking about?" I finally asked.

"Never mind," she said. "I want to discuss this with my husband first." She sank onto the bed and fumbled with the door of her nightstand. When she finally got it open, I could see a half-full bottle of gin inside. I turned and left the room.

The next day, Gordon took me aside. "What's been going on between you and Renee?" he asked sternly.

"Nothing. Why?"

"She says you were trying to get into her pants."

"You should know better than that, Gordon."

"I suppose so," he said. "But she also said you were responsible for Carlotta's leaving."

"What do you mean?" I asked.

"Dell, was Carlotta pregnant when she left here?"

I didn't break my promise to keep silent. "How should I know?" I said.

"Renee thinks she was. She thinks you did it."

"And what do you think?" I asked, wondering where he got his nerve.

"I don't know," he replied.

"I think you do, but there's no point in worrying about it now," I said. "She's gone back home, and she's married."

"Renee said I ought to fire you."

"Is that what you're going to do?"

"No," he said. "You didn't do anything wrong."

I was sure that his real reason for not firing me was his fear that I'd tell Renee about us. I wondered if he'd feel I was so innocent if he knew about me and Sean.

I felt even worse about Sean when he told me what his aversion therapy was like. "It's awful," he said. "They strap me in a chair and they attach electrodes to my skin. Then they show me slides of naked women and men. When I'm looking at a naked woman, I get a pleasant feeling like a massage. But when I'm looking at a man, the electrodes give me a shock, and I have to vomit."

"I see," I said. "So you'll seek women because you associate them with pleasure and avoid men because you associate them with pain. Is it working?"

"Not yet," he said. "But I really want it to. I can't take too much more of this treatment. I hate it."

"That's one way to convince you," I said.

"Don't be cruel to me, Dell. I couldn't take that from you. You know, these treatments might not be such a bad idea for someone like you."

"No, thanks," I said. "I'll just live with the illness. I like it better than the cure."

Renee, it turned out, was more distrustful of Gordon than ever, and his decision not to fire me must have served only to fuel her suspicions. Finally, in the late spring, she took matters into her own hands and blew the lid right off our household.

The first thing I heard about it was when Mrs. Trump came to my room. Her calm facade had slipped, and she looked terrified. "Dell, do you think you can do anything? They're having a terrible fight. I'm not used to this sort of behavior. I'm afraid they'll kill each other."

"Who's having a fight?" I asked her.

"Dr. and Mrs. Thomas, up in their room."

I went to the first floor. We could hear them clearly from there.

"You bastard," Renee was yelling. "A wife wasn't enough for you. You needed a lover on the side—and a queer one, to boot!"

"You'd never satisfy any man," Gordon charged. "You're in too much of a stupor from that goddamned needle you're always poking in your arm."

"I'm not in any stupor right now," she screamed. "And I won't be in a stupor tomorrow when I see my lawyer." The sound of breaking china clattered through the house.

"Don't you throw things at me," he yelled. "I'll stop your dope supply, and then we'll see how nasty you'll be."

"Go ahead and stop it, you rat!" Another crash echoed through the halls. "I wouldn't have needed any junk in the first place if it weren't for you! I can go to that place in Kentucky and dry out. I'm going to pull my life back together again."

314

"You won't dry out," he said. "You don't have the guts to face life as it is."

"Not as it is!" she yelled. "Not with a queer for a husband. I'm going to face life as a decent person again. This whole town is going to know about you now, you louse."

"Tell whoever you want, bitch. At least I'll be rid of you."

"You'll be rid of more than me, you creep. You'll be rid of your career and your son, too! No wonder Sean has to go to a psychiatrist. Look what he's got for a father. A fruit! A fairy! You queer! Get out! Get out! I curse the day I married you! Get out of my sight!" There was another crash. The bedroom door opened and Gordon, his cheeks red with fury, came bounding down the stairs and out the front door without even looking at us.

"Where is Sean?" I asked Mrs. Trump.

"He's at his therapy session."

"Don't tell him about all this when he comes home, okay? Let me talk to him."

"You needn't worry. I'd rather not discuss this with anyone."

I went up and knocked on Renee's door. "Are you all right?" I asked her.

"No."

"Can I come in?" I asked.

"No." She spoke quietly. "I don't want to see anyone. I don't want to be disturbed. I'm going to sleep. Good night."

"Good night, then," I said.

I waited in the hallway until Sean came home. As soon as he opened the door, I took him aside. "Sean, before you go upstairs, I thought I should warn you. There's been a terrible fight."

"Who was it?" he asked.

"Your parents."

"They've fought before," he said.

"Not like this," I told him.

"Are they all right?"

"I don't think there's been any physical harm," I said. "But there's been plenty of emotional damage."

"What happened?" he asked.

"I don't think it's my place to tell you."

"Dell, that's cruel."

"I'm sorry, Sean. I just wanted to alert you to watch out for trouble."

"I'll have to ask them myself, then," he said. "Are they home?"

"Your father went out," I explained. "Your mother's home, but she doesn't want to be disturbed."

"Sounds like a typical evening on Deering Street to me," he quipped. But there was no humor in his eyes.

"I'm sorry," I said.

"Yeah, well, thanks anyway. I'm going up to see my mother."

He climbed the stairs with slow deliberation, as if he were using the time to steel himself for the scene ahead. I waited at the bottom of the staircase, not wanting to eavesdrop, but wanting to be available in case help was needed. Sean knocked on the door. "Go away," answered Renee's muffled voice.

"It's Sean," he said. "Let me in, Mother." He knocked again, then he waited a few moments and knocked once more. The door finally opened.

"What happened between you and Dad tonight?"

"I told your father that I know the truth about him."

"What truth?" Sean asked.

"That he's been unfaithful to me," she said.

"Does that surprise you?"

I heard the sound of a slap.

"That's right, Mother. Take it out on me. I'm not going through enough misery, am I?"

"Oh God, Sean. I didn't mean it. I'm sorry." She started to cry.

"It's all right," he said. "I don't blame you. Now, what happened? Start from the beginning."

She sniffled away her tears. "You know that your father's been acting strangely for the last year or so, don't you? Staying out late and all that?"

"Yes."

"Well, I couldn't stand it anymore, so I finally hired a detective to follow him."

"And?"

"And I got his report today. Sean, your father's a . . . Do you remember Merle?"

"Of course," he replied.

"Well, the detective followed your father to an apartment near the waterfront, on Fore Street."

"You mean those warehouses in the red-light district?"

"Yes," she said. "Your father went inside, and that's were Merle was. Evidently Daddy had set him up in a place there."

"You mean he's been living there all along?" Sean asked. "Merle never left town? Then why didn't we ever run into him?"

"I don't know. Maybe he was careful about where he went. I don't have any business in that neighborhood. Do you?"

"Of course not," he said. "So, what happened?"

"The detective saw them . . . I can't explain this. I'll have to show you the pictures he took. Just a minute. Ah, here they are."

Sean let out a horrifying scream. There was a crash. "Calm down, baby," Renee said. "You still have Mother."

I raced up the stairs. Sean had thrown himself to the floor and had knocked over a china pitcher in the process. Shiny shards of it surrounded him, some of them with hand-painted flowers on them. I went toward him, but he picked one of them up and threatened me with it. "Don't come near me," he growled, "either of you."

"Honey, I'm your mother. I love you," Renee said.

"You don't love anything but your needle," he yelled. "Merle was the one who loved me, and my own father took him away from me! My father is a . . ." He started to cry.

Renee started to cry, too. I moved closer, trying to calm them both.

"And you," Sean yelled at me, still crying. "You were Merle's replacement. You were the reason Merle had to leave. Did my father fuck you, too? Was he as good in bed as I was?" He started to gurgle in his throat, and couldn't say any more.

Renee slumped downward, as if she had imploded. I stood there paralyzed. Sean raised the china shard in his hand, ready to plunge it into his own face. Suddenly a hand grabbed his wrist and stopped him. It was Mrs. Trump.

"I'm sorry to intrude on a private moment," she said, "but it sounded as if things were getting out of hand." The absurd incongruity of her calm manner wasn't lost on me, but I was too horrified to laugh. Sean dropped the piece of china and sat there, looking numb. The three of us were so spent that Mrs. Trump had no difficulty in taking control. "I think it would be best if we all went to our rooms to rest," she said. "This discussion might be more productive if it were continued in the morning, when everyone is feeling a bit less excited." She escorted Renee to her bed and helped her to lie down. Then she took Sean to his room and did the same for him. I went down to the first floor by myself.

"What should we do?" I asked when she had come downstairs.

"Go to bed," she ordered. "That's what I'm planning to do."

I went downstairs, but I couldn't fall asleep. Instead I packed my things—my photographs and my poetry manuscripts, my copy of *Leaves of Grass*, my bowl and my clothes—and I got Calamus ready to travel. Then I called Louie at the number he had given me in Provincetown.

"Louie," I said. "It's Dell."

"Darlin', how are you?"

"Terrible."

"What's the matter?" he asked.

"It's a long story," I said. "I can't tell you now. Things are falling apart here."

"Where are you?"

"I'm in Portland, but I have to get out of here soon. Can I come and visit you? You said I'd be welcome anytime."

"Fabulous!" he said. "We'll have a wonderful time. You'll love Dominick. I told him all about you, and he's dyin' to meet you. When will you be here?"

"Tomorrow sometime. I'll let you know."

"Fab. I'll meet you. Call me."

"Louie?"

"What, dear?"

"Thank God for you."

"Don't be silly, darlin'," he said. "What are jail mates for? Ta-ta."

I felt a shiver of joy as I hung up the phone. The reality I was living in had turned so horrible that I couldn't wait to be somewhere else. The brightness in Louie's voice had been like a ray of light in a dungeon after months of darkness. I went right to sleep.

In the morning, I went up to the office to see if Gordon had returned. Hawser was at her usual post as if nothing were wrong, and several patients—an old woman with a bad cough, accompanied by her confused husband; a sniveling child being comforted by his weary mother; a pregnant young woman—were sitting in the waiting room.

"Is he in?" I asked Hawser. She nodded.

I went back to Gordon's office. He sat at his desk doing nothing, perhaps trying to find the strength to get through the day.

"Gordon?" I said. "I hope I'm not interrupting."

"No," he replied without looking at me. "What is it?"

"I couldn't help hearing what Renee was saying last night."

He looked up. "So?"

"We're in trouble. I think it would be best if I left." I continued meeting his gaze.

"Do you really want to go?" he asked.

"I think it would be best," I said. "I just wanted to say good-bye."

"Do I owe you any money?"

"No," I told him. "I just got paid yesterday."

"Well, I'm sure you could use this," he said, taking out his wallet and handing me two hundred dollars. "It will help you get settled."

"Thanks," I said. "I appreciate it. I'll miss you, Gordon."

"You may not believe this, Dell, but I'll miss you, too. I did mean well, you know."

"I know," I said.

Just then Renee burst into the room. "Gordon," she said, "you have to do something. It's Sean."

"What's the matter?"

"I can't get him out of bed. He's awake. His eyes are open, but he won't move. He's in a catatonic trance or something. Help him."

"Calm down. Now, what happened?"

318

Then she noticed me for the first time. "What is he doing here?" she asked Gordon.

"Don't start, Renee."

"I don't have to start. Sean knows all about you and Merle, and he knows all about you and Dell, too."

Gordon groaned.

"And I have more news for you, mister sex pervert. Dell and Sean have been to bed with each other, too."

Gordon's eyes lit up with fury, and he stood up with his hands raised, as if to reach for my throat. But Renee stopped him. "Never mind about him now. Sean's in trouble. Call an ambulance."

While Gordon dialed for help, she said to me coolly, "You'd better go, Dell. There's no place for you here anymore."

"Renee, let me explain."

"It doesn't matter anymore," she said. "Just go."

I looked at Gordon, who had calmed down. He was waiting for someone to answer his call. He just nodded at me, defeated. I turned and left the office without looking back at them. As I passed through the waiting room, I noticed that all of the patients were sitting there with their mouths agape. Hawser was poised in mid-gesture with a filing card in her hand, as if she couldn't decide whether to file it or to flee.

I got my things from downstairs and put Calamus into his box. Then I called a taxi to take me to the train station. As I put down the phone, I heard the ambulance pull up, and I heard Gordon say, "He'll be all right, Renee. Stop crying." Then I heard the doors of the ambulance slam, and it pulled away with a screech. When I got to the front door, I turned to look back at the house before I left. There was no one to say good-bye to, so I went outside quietly, to wait for the cab.

When I arrived in Boston it was early evening and I was depressed. I caught the last ferry across the bay to Provincetown. Louie met me at the dock. He looked wonderful, slightly tan and carefully coiffed, his hair a good deal redder than I remembered it. He wore black Bermuda shorts and a bright aquamarine boatneck Jersey with three-quarter sleeves. His customary cigarette dangled from his lips, but he delicately removed it to kiss my cheek. A balding, middle-aged man was with him.

"Dom, this is my sister, Miss Della," Louie said. I glared at him to caution against feminizing my name, but he remained as nonchalant as before, and continued, "Dell, this is Dominick, my sweetie." Dominick wore an open Hawaiian shirt, which framed his hairy beer belly, and a pair of dark-rimmed sunglasses, which looked especially sinister at night. He took my suitcase, and we headed toward the car.

"We got a fabulous little honeymoon cottage on Standish Street," Louie said. "And you're welcome to the guest room for the whole summer. Ain't he, sweetie?"

"Sure," Dominick replied. "Plenty a room. No problem."

"Ain't Dom adorable, Dell? And he's so generous to his sweetie, too, sharing his house with her sisters. I know you two boys are going to get along real well—but not too well, I hope. If you go near each other. I'll scratch all four of your eyes out."

"You're such a jealous cunt," Dominick said. I assumed he was kidding, but I couldn't be sure.

"I love it when you talk dirty, sweetie."

"Lulu's my all-time favorite pussy," Dom announced over his shoulder. "I wouldn't mess wid nobody else for no money."

"That's my sweetie," Louie said. "Ain't she some hunk of man?"

I thought I might gag in the backseat of the white Cadillac, but I watched the lighted windows of Commercial Street's crafts and jewelry shops instead. The sidewalks were crowded with tourists, even though it was still early in the season, and it looked like I might actually relax and enjoy myself for a change.

"Speakin' of pussy," Louie added, "I see you brought yours along. Hi, kitty! What's her name?"

"*His* name is Calamus," I said.

"She's cute. She'll like it here."

I could see I was going to have a pronoun problem. But I decided not to take any gender references literally, and to act like myself, no matter what I was called.

We parked in front of a small house and Louie escorted me inside. He showed me a small bedroom with maple furniture and a pink chenille bedspread. A pink plaster-of-Paris ballerina hung from a cheap wrought-iron grill on the flowered wallpaper, and the lamp shade wore a pink bow. "Isn't it cute?" he said.

"Very cute," I agreed.

"Feed the cat and dump your stuff, and we'll dish for a while. Dom has to go out, so we can take a walk, and that'll give us a chance to catch up."

"Sounds great," I said.

"So, what happened up in Maine?" he asked as we left the house. "You sounded terrible on the phone."

"Oh, I was in love with a married man, but that was the least of it." I told him the whole story, and he listened without shock, as if I were telling him about a visit to grandma's house. I liked that. "What about you?" I said. "You seem totally different from the guy I knew in Chicago. You even sound different from your own letters."

"Well, a girl can't exactly let her hair down in Cook County Jail, and you remember how they used to read our mail. Here I can be myself a little more. I mean, the cops hassle us once in a while, especially if we get too raucous, and the straight boys punch somebody out now and then, but it's still better than where we came from. The main difference is that here we can be sisters instead of buddies."

"Amen to that," I said, giving up any hope of being called Dell that summer. "What about Dominick? What's his story?"

"He's a sweetie most of the time, but he can be a pain in the ass too. He comes from a Cosa Nostra family."

"Cosa Nostra?"

"Mafia to you, dear. Anyway, they pay him to stay away from home, so he don't embarrass his father, the godfather. He's sort of like a fairy prince in exile."

"I know how he feels," I said. "I don't talk to my family either."

"Dominick talks to his family. His mother calls him here on Tuesdays. But if his father ever found out, he'd be dead meat. The old man thinks he's protectin' the old lady. Go figure."

"I'll try not to answer the phone on Tuesdays. What about your family? You never told me about them."

"That's right. Next topic."

"Sorry, I didn't mean to pry."

"Don't be silly. My life is an open book. It's just that most of the pages have been erased."

"So what do you do, just keep house?"

"I wish. No, dear heart, I ain't no lady of leisure. I work for a livin'. I'm a hair burner at the Pink Poodle Beauty Salon on Commercial Street, on Thursdays, Fridays, and Saturdays. The rest of the week is yours."

"I didn't mean to be a burden to you. I just wanted a place to escape to."

"Honey, I'm only too glad to have the company. Dominick's out on secret business half the time and unconscious most of the rest of the time. I mean, I love him and all of that, but he's more fun in bed than in the parlor, if you know what I mean."

"Well, thanks, Louie. You're a lifesaver."

"Don't be silly, Miss Della. I owe you."

"You don't owe me anything."

"I want to, then. Okay?"

"Okay," I agreed.

Life with Louie and Dom was easygoing for most of the summer. I was feeling blue and I needed a rest, so I spent lots of time at the beach getting tan. I went for long walks along the water's edge, thinking of Gordon and Carlos and Chester and my father, and of the hopelessness of love. And of course I thought of Walt. As I looked at the bubbles bursting at the edge of the surf, lines from one of his "Sea Drift" poems floated through my mind:

See, from my dead lips the ooze exuding at last,
See, the prismatic colors glistening and rolling . . .

But eventually my depression started to ease, and I enjoyed watching the men who were showing off their tans and cramming their assets into the skimpiest bathing suits that were legal.

On good afternoons I would meet one of them and strike up a brief and meaningless conversation, in which we didn't learn any more about each other than whether we were both interested in some fun. Then, pretending we were innocent children of nature, we would retreat to the dunes for a hurried sexual encounter, inhibited only by the fear of being discovered, which enhanced the moment's thrill.

In the evenings, Louie and I went to a bar called the Ace of Spades, where lots of gay pansies mixed with the straight hollyhocks. It was a dark, crowded place, filled with handsome men and a sprinkling of eager women, all with tans to set off their white smiles. Everyone wore bright summer colors and chatted noisily. But beneath all the frenzy of the hunt for mates, the place had a mellow air. The piano player, Bert, never played anything written after 1940, so we heard lots of romantic, in-the-mood music, instead of the loud, thumping rock 'n' roll which was starting to catch on elsewhere. Bert would sit there drinking a glass of gin between songs, and every time a regular would walk in, he'd play a special theme. Half of the men were devoted Judy Garland fans, and three or four people (including Louie) chose "Over the Rainbow" as their theme. Mine was "It Might as Well Be Spring." I don't know why. I guess I had always liked the melody, but now even the lyrics seemed to suit my mood, especially the line about feeling "so gay in a melancholy way."

I wasn't accustomed to the brazen manner in which the Ace of Spades practically advertised its true nature, but I loved it. Its matchbooks read "The Gayest Spot in Town." Although the straight boys who also hung out there were likely to punch a guy in the mouth if he tried to get too friendly, I met my share of queers and sometimes even got to spend the whole night with them in their hotel rooms. In spite of myself, I had to admit I was having a ball.

Louie and I spent so much time hanging out at the Ace of Spades that by August Dominick started to get jealous. Every morning he'd try to pump me to find out where Louie had been the night before, and with whom and for how long. I stayed as friendly as possible, but I told him that I didn't want to mix in and that he ought to ask Louie. I could swear he was shooting me menacing looks from behind his ever-present sunglasses, but Dom wasn't about to be open enough to look at me eye to eye. I learned what I needed to know about him from Louie, and from the loud discussions that wafted through the thin plasterboard walls like bad cooking odors.

"I'm home in time to give you what you really want from me, ain't I?" Louie demanded in return to Dom's nagging questions.

"You'd damn well better be, you cunt, or you'll be out of here on your cute little ass. You and your fairy friend wit' you."

I lay in my bed wondering how any guy who was having an affair with Louie Pellegrino could imagine that he was straighter than I was. I guess he needed the lie to maintain his version of self-respect. At least I'm man enough to face what I am, I thought, drawing my smugness around me like a protective blanket so I could fall asleep.

"Who the fuck does she think she is?" Louie demanded of me the next morning. "She don't own me." And to prove that he was an independent person, he stayed out longer and longer. Finally, when a friend of his offered him a room right next door to the Ace of Spades, he said yes. "I'll show her who owns me and who don't," he said to me of Dom. "She needs me more than I need her."

It was the tail end of the summer when the two of us and the cat moved into a cramped room that was little more than a wall-to-wall mattress and a closet, where I stored my clothes and my few possessions. Calamus managed by living partly indoors and partly outdoors. We heard the sounds of the Ace of Spades every night, since our room actually abutted the bar and we shared a common wall with it (the one at the head of our bed). It was easier to spend all our time in the bar instead of listening to it in the room, so we became daily as well as nightly habitués. "We won't be here for long," Louie assured me. "I just want to show that mug that I can get along without him."

"Sure," I said. "This is fine. Maybe I ought to think about where to head next, though."

"Don't be silly, darlin'. It's still summer," he said. "Besides, we're buddies, ain't we, and sisters to boot?"

"Absolutely," I said, and I meant it.

"Fine, then let's see about gettin' ourselves laid."

At first we took turns with the bedroom. One of us would go into the Ace of Spades and fish out a trick, and while he was carrying on in the room, the other one would be lining up a bedmate for the next shift.

After a few days, Louie said to me. "You won't believe this, Miss Thing, but I think we just struck gold. Did you notice that last guy I was with?"

I shook my head no.

"Well, hold your bloomers, honey. No, scratch that. Let 'em loose. That guy was gorgeous, and hung like Seabiscuit, to boot. That's what I call him, Seabiscuit, but his real name is Rupert."

"I'm very happy for you, Louie, but what's the big deal? Is Seabiscuit coming back?"

"You're missin' the whole point, dummy. Rupert is in the British navy—and that's their ship, the *HMS St Austell Bay*, anchored off the coast. It's a frigate," he added and giggled.

"So?" I said.

"So we're gonna frig it! Rupert asked me if I might be willin' to entertain some of his shipmates tonight. You see, half the crew gets off one night, and half the crew for the next night, and they alternate like that all week long."

"You mean half the crew of a frigate" (I chuckled to myself) "is coming here tonight?"

"Well, let's not exaggerate. More like half a dozen."

"And they're all gay?"

"No, stupid, that's the best part. They're all straight, or so they say, but they've been at sea for months, and they're all eager to stick their big dicks into the first open hole they come across."

"And that's where we come in?" I asked. "Servicing the British navy?"

"I knew you'd get the point eventually. You may be slow, but you're not altogether hopeless."

"Thanks a lot," I said. "Coming from you that's a real compliment. Now tell me, genius, where are we going to put all those willing young men? Stack them up on the veranda?"

"Don't be such a difficult twat, Mary. We'll think of something. They can take turns, and some of them can wait in the bar. We might lose a few to the ladies in there, but somebody's got to handle the overflow. Listen, are my seams straight? Oh God, I must be in heaven. Is it okay, then?"

"I guess so," I said. "What the fuck."

"That's the spirit, sweetheart. I knew you'd see it my way. Oh, this is gonna be fabulous, just fabulous! Now let's decorate the place for the occasion."

I groaned. "You mean veils and pillows like a harem, or what?"

"Nope. Simple understatement. I asked Rupert for somethin' very British. You know, to inspire the boys? And he sent me this picture of Sir Winston Churchill, no less. Who's he, their queen?"

"The Prime Minister, I think."

"I was only kiddin'. I ain't totally ignorant, you know. We'll hang Miss Churchill right over here." He swept a boring picture of a whaling ship off the wall and in one continuous gesture slid it under the bed. He hung the picture of Churchill and stood back to see if it was properly centered. Then he plumped a pillow two or three times, stood back to admire his handiwork, and said, "Ready!" He tossed himself on the bed and spread his legs. "Wait. There's one more thing. We're gonna need some stamina, so take this."

"What is it?"

"A benny—Benzedrine. It'll keep you goin' all night long."

"Are you sure it's safe?"

"Honey, I practically live on 'em. Trust me."

I took one and, after half an hour or so, my head was rushing like a locomotive. "Wow," I said.

"Like it?" asked Louie.

"I love it, but I have so much energy, I can't sit still."

"Then try this," Louie said, fishing in his bag for some papers and a packet of what looked like oregano, and rolling it into a misshapen cigarette.

"What's that?" I asked.

"Tea."

"Tea?"

"You know, tea. Mary Jane. Oh God, Miss Della, you are out of touch. It's marijuana. You smoke it and you feel good. Here."

"I never heard of it before, honest."

"Not that way, dummy. Hold it in your lungs as long as you can."

I did a good deal of coughing, but I managed to follow his instructions. I was scared for a moment, remembering what drugs had done to Renee, but this had nothing to with needles. Soon I felt light-headed, and it eased the rush of the benny. "This is going to be great," I said dubiously. And it was.

About a dozen men showed up that night. They wore snug white pants that hugged their buns and light blue jackets with gold buttons, and those cute little English sailor caps that had the name of the ship on the hatbands, right across their adorable foreheads, and little tails of ribbon hanging down in the back. We threw all modesty to the wind, and the two of us just stayed in bed alongside each other, servicing stud after stud. One thing I have to say about those British boys. They treated us like real ladies. They were nice and polite about sharing us and taking turns with us, and they were remarkably loyal, too. All of them returned on their next night off, and I don't think we lost a single one of them to the girls in the Ace of Spades, although I can't be sure because I was far too busy to keep count. They appreciated us, too, for showing them a good time, Yankee style. They brought us little presents from the ship, and they brought us take-out food from the local restaurants—to keep our energy up—and we fucked and sucked that crew of handsome sailors all day and all night for a week. It was as close to paradise as I ever expect to get, but by the end of the week I was slightly out of my mind. All I could think of was sex.

I did have a flash of responsibility, on Thursday or Friday. "Aren't you supposed to be at the Pink Poodle around now?" I asked Louie, when we were catching our breath between gigs.

"Oh, fuck them miserable bitches, honey. Let 'em shave their ugly old heads if they want to look better. Miss Lulu is occ-u-pied." The next two sailors came in then, and we were much too busy helping them to unbutton their many buttons to continue any reasonable discourse on the subjects of misogyny and responsibility.

Eventually the last day of the *HMS St Austell Bay*'s stay arrived, and our horny crew bid us a heartfelt farewell. One of them gave Louie a telescope, so we could watch the ship return to sea. He played the scene to the hilt, bringing a large printed kerchief to the porch with him so he could alternately use it to dab at his tears and to wave farewell to the boys. As the ship sailed out of sight, Louie stood there like the brave, loyal heroine he was, looking through the telescope and waving the kerchief until suddenly he said, "Wait a minute. What's that? La Heine de la . . . Miss Della, it's a French ship, and I just know it's full of delicious sailors! Quick, take down Churchill and find a picture of De Gaulle! *Vive la France!*"

We laughed for an hour over that, but we never got a chance to see what the French boys were like. Two grim-faced goons showed up that evening, asking for Lulu. "That's me," Louie volunteered. "What can we do for you boys?"

"I got a message for you from Dominick."

"Yeah? Is he ready for me to come back yet?" Louie said, winking at me to show he'd proved his point about his right to independence.

The goon punched Louie right in the eye and knocked him to the floor. I rushed over to help him, but the other guy held me back. "This message ain't for you. It's for Lulu. But you can listen in if you want."

Louie didn't try to fight back. He knew it was useless. He just tried to protect himself the best he could. The beating only lasted a couple of minutes, but it was effective. "The message is this," the goon said to Louie's crumpled form when he had finished. "You're through here. Get your ass out of P-Town, you cheap hoor, and don't come crawlin' back."

The two of them left, not even bothering to look over their shoulders. I went over to Louie, to help him up. His face was a mess.

"I told you he loved me," he groaned, smiling in spite of his pain, and he passed out.

I called a doctor, who patched him up. There was no major damage, although his face looked like it had been inspecting the underside of a moving Sherman tank. After the doctor was finished, there remained a few bandaged cuts and bruises, and a grossly swollen black eye, into which I had to put salve twice a day, holding back my urge to vomit, so Louie wouldn't get upset. We didn't go out of the room, except to buy food.

When Louie called up the Pink Poodle, he was informed that he was no longer employed there. I could hear the manager's voice shrieking at him over the phone, even though I was sitting across the room.

"They're friends of Dominick's," Louie explained. "I guess we better take his advice and get out of here. Where do you think we should go next?"

"How about New York City?" I suggested. "I once had a good time there, a long while back."

"New York it is," he said.

A few days later, Louie got hold of a used car. "Where did you get the money for this?" I asked, surprised.

"A girl has to set aside something for a rainy day, don't she?" he explained. "And if I ain't mistaken, it's pourin'."

We packed up our few things and put them in the trunk, and in no time we were on the road to New York. As we left Cape Cod, we started to talk about our pasts, possibly because it was time to start considering our futures.

"I'm from Illinois," Louie told me. "My father walked out on us when I was eleven. We been poor since I can remember, livin' on welfare mostly, and on some sewin' my mom took in. She thinks homosexuality is the work of the devil, or possibly the communists or the Jews. I ain't seen her in four or five years."

"I'm from New York State," I told him. "I never knew my mother, and my father is an apple farmer who would get along just fine with your mother."

"So, you became a sex offender just to show him a thing or two, huh?"

"No," I answered, "because I'm a hopeless cock hound, even when the cock belongs to the vice squad. By the way, you never did tell me what got you into Cook County Jail."

"Stealin' cars," he said. "I was embarrassed to tell you it wasn't a sex crime. A girl has a reputation to keep up."

I smiled nervously and tried to take a look in the rearview mirror, to see if the cops were following us.

"Don't be nervous," Louie said. "I bought this heap. It's legit. The registration is in the glove compartment, if you don't believe me. Honest."

"I believe you," I said. "I don't have to see it."

"Honey, the only mistakes I make twice have to do with men. I'm a fool for a hairy chest and a big dick. But no Oldsmobile is ever gonna get me in trouble again. No, sir. Now relax."

"I am relaxed."

"Fabulous," he said. "Now look in my bag and find me my sunglasses. I don't want Miss Lulu's East Coast fans to see her black eye. They might think she hangs out with the wrong kind of people. Oh, and pass me one of those bennies. We have a long drive ahead."

CHAPTER EIGHTEEN

The trip to New York took the better part of the day. Louie turned out to be a great traveling companion. As soon as his benny took effect, he began rattling off a long commentary on the many tricks he'd had sex with, vengefully detailing Dominick's bedroom idiosyncrasies. He discussed his contempt for the self-righteous straight world and the competitive gay world alike (because neither of them wanted to know the truth about themselves) and he bemoaned the dullness of the small cities we were passing and gushed about the wonders in store for us in the "Big Apple" (a nickname that I never used because it left a bad taste in my mouth). From most people that much chatter might have been intolerable, but from Louie it was delightfully funny, and I never even suggested turning on the car radio.

As much as I enjoyed Louie's company, I still didn't feel totally safe about the car because I didn't want any more trouble with the law. When he stopped to go into the men's room at a gas station in Rhode Island, I thought I should take his advice and check to see whether his registration for the car actually was in the glove compartment. But as I reached my hand toward the knob, I stopped myself, deciding that it would be better to trust him. As it turned out, we weren't arrested for car theft, so either the cops were inefficient or maybe he did buy the car legitimately.

We arrived in New York City at dusk. As we rode down the Henry Hudson Parkway, the lights of the tall buildings were just beginning to sparkle above us in the lavender air, but once we were in Manhattan proper, the sky no longer mattered. There was too much distraction on the ground. People crowded the sidewalks and the streets were filled with noisy traffic. The place was charged with the same energy that I remembered from my visit with Chester a dozen years earlier, and it had the same magic aura about it.

My mind helplessly summoned up memories of Chester: that special clear space he always had around him, his handsome smile, the warmth in his eyes. I remembered how he had looked at art galleries; at the theater; at Saks Fifth Avenue, where Miss Standish had stood behind the sweater counter; at the library, where Miss Binder had worked; at Minerva White's house while she had taken photographs of us. I knew that the New York I was encountering now would be a different place from the one I had seen then. Chester had told me that New York never stayed the same for very long. It thrived on change. It ate the latest fashions and ideas and stars for breakfast and was out looking for new ones by dinnertime. I wondered how differently I would see things with twelve years of experience added to my vision. I got so lost in memories and speculations that I didn't see the car in front of us until Louie smacked right into it.

"What the fuck was that?" Louie said, jarred out of his monologue, which had gone on without me for several miles. "Oh God, I didn't even see it."

It was a maroon Hudson coupe, out of which the driver, a burly-looking man with a red beard, emerged and stood there looking at the dent in his front fender.

"Where did you come from?" Louie asked him. The man started cursing, so Louie tried to calm him down, explaining that nobody had been hurt and the cars were only slightly damaged, with dents that might even give them a touch of character.

The other person who emerged from the car was a slim Asian man who looked a few years younger than I was. He stared at me as if he were challenging me to begin a conversation.

I stared right back. He came over to talk to me. "How you doing?" he said with an Asiatic lilt.

"Okay, under the circumstances."

"Nobody got hurt," he said. "The damage rooks minor. I sink it's gonna be okay."

"I guess so," I said.

"Where you from? I see you got outta-state prates."

"We just came in from Massachusetts," I said.

"Visiting?"

"I guess so. I'm not sure."

"It's exciting city. You gonna rike it. You been here before?"

"A long time ago."

"Been to Greenwich Village?"

I nodded.

"Strange people there, you sink so?"

I knew he was "dropping hairpins" to let me know he was gay, so I dropped a few of my own.

"They're not so strange when you understand them," I said.

"You staying wit' friends?"

I shook my head no.

"What hoterr you stay in?" he asked.

"I don't know yet."

330

"Too bad," he said. "I sought sometime we might have cup o' coffee togezzer, maybe."

"That would be nice," I replied. But I wasn't really sure how nice it would be. He was the first Japanese I'd met since the war, and even though I couldn't blame him personally for what I'd gone through, I didn't want to be reminded of the prison camp, especially not of the gay soldier who had died because he'd wanted sex with me. Besides, I didn't know what the red-bearded man would think about his friend's meeting me. "Isn't there someplace I can reach you?" I asked.

"I rive wit' him," he said, gesturing with his head toward the man with the beard. "He get suspicious when somebody not Japanese caw me up."

"Maybe I'll run into you somewhere, then."

"Maybe. Try Faisan d'Or on Sixth Avenue, near Fifty-Third Street. You rook it up. Sometimes I wait there."

"Faisan d'Or?"

"You know, French 'Go'den Pheasant.' Few praces on East Side have names rike dat: Brue Parrot, Pink Framingo, Swan. People call dem 'bird circuit.' Rotta gay boys go to dem."

"Cute," I said. "I'll try to do that. What's your name?"

"Yoshioka Amakazo. You caw me Yoshi. What's yours?"

"Dell Blake. Nice to meet you, Yoshi." Then I gave him the Japanese equivalent of 'How do you do?': '*Hajimemashite?*' "

He looked at me with surprise, but there was no time to ask where I had learned Japanese because the two drivers had finished their discussion and were heading toward us. "See you, Dehr Brake. I hope soon." He winked at me then turned to join his companion. Louie and I went back to our car.

As soon as we closed the doors, Louie said, "Oh Mary, what the fuck was that? A tornado or a steamroller?"

"No," I said. "It was our welcome to New York. Are you all right?"

"I need an aspirin," he said.

We settled ourselves at the counter in a nearby drugstore and Louie ordered an Alka-Seltzer. When he had downed it, I asked, "What did that guy say to you?"

"He told me they didn't have any insurance, and I told him I didn't have any either. So we decided there wasn't no point in carryin' on, and we decided to fix our own dents."

"Sounds like a wise idea."

"And where were you while all this was goin' on?" he asked.

"The other guy was trying to pick me up," I told him.

"The Chink? I didn't know you were a rice queen."

"First of all, he's Japanese," I said. "And even if he were Chinese, that's no reason to call him names—or me, either. I am not a rice queen. I just think this guy is cute."

Unruffled by my vocabulary lesson, he went on.

"You don't waste no time, do you, Miss Thing? Can't you at least wait to unpack?"

I shook my head. "He said he hangs out at Faisan d'Or. Can we go there this week?"

"Why not?" he said. "We can spend a week or two havin' a ball. Then Miss Lulu has to see about gettin' a job in some beauty parlor. I am an artiste, you know."

"Not behind the wheel of a car, you're not."

"You'd better be good, or I won't be your chauffeur anymore," Louie cautioned.

"I'll be good."

"Well, don't be too good, honey. We don't want to overdo it."

"There's just no satisfying you, is there?" I asked.

"That doesn't mean you should stop tryin'."

"Bitch."

"Cunt."

"I really love you, Louie."

"I know, sweetie. I really love you, too. Now let's find ourselves a pile of hay to hit. This benny's wearin' off, and I gotta rest these tired ol' bones."

We took a room in the Chelsea Hotel on Twenty-Third Street. It was a big old building with rows of cast-iron balconies that might have been looking out at Mardi Gras on Bourbon Street. The place was full of writers, musicians, and painters who rented by the month.

"Will there be anything else?" the desk clerk asked when we had finished registering.

"Yes, there will . . . unless you're busy later, darlin'," Louie said, removing his sunglasses and batting his bruised eyelids like Scarlett O'Hara in heat.

The homely desk clerk didn't look either interested or annoyed. He didn't even look up. That's one of the things I like about New York. Nobody gives a damn. We went upstairs to our room and, except for letting Calamus out of his box and feeding him, we didn't bother to unpack. We just went right to sleep.

In the morning we had a greasy breakfast in a local beanery. Over dishwater coffee, Louie said, "Now that we're here, what would you like to do most, Miss Della?"

"You're not going to like it," I said. "It means more traveling."

"Slave driver. Where is it now? Mexico City?"

"Not quite that far. Camden, New Jersey."

"Camden, New Jersey? Who the fuck goes to Camden, New Jersey? That ain't no place for a reigning queen. The only thing that place is famous for is bein' dead."

"There's something there that I want to see," I said.

"What could there possibly be to see in Camden? Your grandfather's grave?"

"Close," I explained. "Walt Whitman's grave—and the house where he lived."

"Walt Whitman? Who was she? Your first trick?"

"I wish. He's my favorite poet."

"Oh, I remember. The one you were always carrying on about. Honey, what good is it gonna do you to visit a dead man? Don't you have enough trouble putting up with the ones whose so-called hearts are still beatin'?"

"It's important to me," I said. "You asked what I wanted to do most."

"God, you really mean it, don't you? Well, okay then. What the hell. I ain't exactly got a book full of appointments for today. But it must be a long ride, so we better leave right now, before I change my mind. Hand me my bag, sweetie. I'm gonna need another benny for this one."

It took us the rest of the morning and the better part of the afternoon to get down New Jersey's old highways to Camden, which turned out to be right near Philadelphia. The town looked like it could use a face-lift. Drab, shabby frame buildings crowded against each other, competing for the title of "Most Likely to Collapse."

"Is this what you wanted to see? America the beautiful?" Louie asked. "We shoulda brought a bucket of paint to spruce up the joint."

"I'm sure it looked a little better three-quarters of a century ago," I said.

"We all looked a little better then, honey. Now, what's the address?"

"Three-twenty-eight Mickle Street," I said with certainty.

"Sounds real charmin'," Louie said.

We drove around looking for Mickle Street, which from what I'd read was a small, quiet lane. It turned out to be a major boulevard.

"I guess they've widened the street," I commented.

"Probably the only improvement around here since the Civil War," Louie answered.

We parked the car. Outside the door of number 328 was a block of stone, which I knew Walt had used for getting into the buggy his friends had given him when he was old and feeble. He had had a series of male nurses to look after him and drive him everywhere. What lucky kids they were, I thought, imagining myself escorting the handsome old man around town.

A neatly tailored black woman answered the door. "Come in, gentlemen," she said. "May I help you?"

"I just want to look around, if that's all right. I'm a fan of Mr. Whitman's."

"Many of us are," she said. "Help yourself, but please don't touch anything. We're trying to preserve it. I'll be in the back room if you should need me." She retreated into a little office that had been fashioned at the back of the first floor, and Louie and I began to explore.

"I bet he didn't even have a radio back then," Louie said. "What did he do for fun?"

"He wrote poems," I answered.

My attention was immediately drawn to a handwritten notice in a plain brown wood frame hanging on the wall in the foyer. It was Dr. McAlister's notice of Walt's death that had been posted on the door on March 26, 1892. I read the simple, somber announcement as far as "He continued to grow worse and died at 6:43 p.m. The end came peacefully. He was conscious until the last." Then my eyes filled with tears, and I couldn't read any more.

"Jesus," Louie said. "The guy died over sixty years ago. You'd think you'd be over it by now."

"Don't laugh at me, Louie," I replied. "We all have our soft spots."

"Not me," he said. "Woman of steel, here."

"Sure," I answered. "Steel with a black eye."

"Oh, that? I wear that just to look vulnerable. The boys go in for it. Cute, don't you think?" He tried to wink, but failed.

I smiled. When he saw that he had pulled me out of my mood, he said, "Let's look around and get outta here. This place gives me the willies."

I could see that the furniture was not all the same stuff that had been photographed during Whitman's life. There were some new additions, some empty spaces, and some original pieces: glass-doored bookcases, wicker chairs with strings stretched from arm to arm to prevent wanton twentieth-century sitting, and assorted pictures and busts, which had been given to the aging poet as gifts. On the mantel was an old clock whose painted cherries had been picked off by a pet parrot. The villain had been stuffed and stood on display next to the evidence of his crime. I liked that, but I was most impressed by seeing the battered old hat Whitman had actually worn. I wanted more than anything to put it on my head, to see if I would look or feel anything like him. But it was kept locked away in a glass case like a sacred relic and I couldn't even stroke it with my fingertips, except in my imagination.

The house seemed small and cramped by modern standards. We made our way up a narrow staircase to the second floor where the bedrooms were. One room was for Walt's male nurse and the other was the old man's. I stopped at the doorway to his room. The decor was bare, almost spartan, although I knew that during his life it had been heaped helter-skelter with piles of articles and manuscripts and books. In the center stood a plain single bed with a square wooden headboard and footboard made by Walt's carpenter father. It was covered by a simple white spread. Beneath the bed was a large, round metal pan, which had been used when he was given sponge baths in his final months. I knew it was the bed where he had died. I sat down gingerly, hoping the springs wouldn't creak and alert the guardian downstairs. Suddenly I found myself cold and depressed, and I began to shiver.

What was I going to do with my life now, I wondered. My summer of escape was over and I had made no plans. At least Louie could find a job as a hairdresser. But how could I earn a living? Where could I go next? I hadn't written anything for months, and I wondered whether I would ever start writing again. I felt as desperately lost and helpless as I ever had before, and I wished I could feel the fatherly warmth that the old poet had offered his young friends. If only I could spend a few moments with him, I thought. I needed him more than ever. I wanted his advice, the reassurance of his arm around my shoulder, or at least the comfort of his glance.

I looked across the room to an old wicker chair that stood in a dark corner, and I concentrated my imagination as hard as I could, trying to force myself to see what I so badly wanted to see. I don't even know if my eyes were open or closed. But finally I thought I could make out a vaguely glowing mist shimmering in the afternoon shadows. I willed it to grow clearer and clearer, until I could recognize Walt's familiar form. His suit and vest were comfortably rumpled, as they were in my favorite photograph, and he held one knee across the other casually, allowing his leg to dangle freely, as if he were relaxing after a pleasant stroll. His round hat was cocked back on his head and his beard framed his face like a cloudy white aura. His penetrating gray eyes were radiant with love, and his gaze was steady.

"Walt . . ." I started to say. But my vision silenced me with a wave of his hand. Then he uncrossed his legs and rose, ignoring the protective string that stretched from one armrest of his chair to the other. He began to move toward the bed, his beaming eyes locked to mine. Frightened by my own success, I backed up, and as he came closer I lay down, feeling the old mattress yield to my body as once it had yielded to his.

As he approached the side of the bed, I raised my shoulders and reached my arms up, wanting his embrace, not knowing or caring whether I would find passion or solace or death in his arms. At last he stood next to me. I could see his lips moving as if he were speaking, but as hard as I tried, I couldn't hear any sounds. His form hovered above mine, drawing closer. When he reached out, I couldn't feel his touch, yet I grew strangely excited. It seemed as if he were passing right through me, exhilarating me as he went. But all I felt in his wake was a sure peace spreading inside me and filling me. It was as if I were hearing his lines from "Song of Myself":

> This is the press of a bashful hand, this is the float and odor
> of hair,
> This is the touch of my lips to yours, this is the murmur of
> yearning . . .
> Do you guess I have some intricate purpose?
> Well I have . . .

I suddenly relaxed my concentration and fell back on the pillow, exhausted.

"Dell, we gotta get outta here," Louie said, startling me from my reverie. "This place is drivin' you cuckoo bananas. You should see yourself. You look really fried. Are you okay?"

I let him help me to my feet and escort me downstairs. By the time we got to the bottom, I was back in reality. "Good-bye, ma'am," I called to the caretaker from the front doorway.

"Come again," she invited melodiously, probably eager for the company. I wondered how many people made this pilgrimage to Camden in a year, and whether it had affected any of them the way it had me.

"Can we get back to the city now?" Louie asked, once we had settled in the car.

"There's just one more thing. I promise it'll be short," I said.

"What is it now?" Louie asked, sounding exasperated, although I knew he didn't really mind.

"Harleigh Cemetery," I said. "He's buried there."

"Great," Louie said. "This fuckin' state has everythin' you could want: bad roads, lousy architecture, a depressin' old poet's house, and now a cemetery. Which way?"

I consulted a brochure I had found in the house. "Left, I think."

We found the cemetery without too much trouble. It was a little more work to find the grave, but we did. It was in a mausoleum with Walt's name carved over the door. Whitman had designed it himself, I knew, and he was buried there along with half-a-dozen other members of his family. When I entered the tomb, I learned that he wasn't actually "buried" at all, since all the coffins were raised above the floor. I found myself looking at two rows of doors, behind each of which was a coffin's end. I was disappointed. Some of my favorite lines were among the final verses of "Song of Myself":

> I bequeath myself to the dirt to grow from the grass I love,
> If you want me again look for me under your boot-soles.

"Nothing is ever what it's supposed to be," I muttered.

"Nope, nothin'," Louie agreed, on general principles.

The only perfection is death, I thought, and I whispered to myself some other lines from the poem:

> My rendezvous is appointed, it is certain,
> The Lord will be there and wait till I come on perfect terms,
> The great Camerado, the lover true for whom I pine will be
>   there.

"Louie," I said aloud. "I have to leave something, some token to say I was here."

"Like what? A callin' card?"

"Something like that."

"Maybe we can have some printed up. Do you want raised or flat print?"

I could see he was getting annoyed, so I searched through my pockets for some token I could leave. The only thing I could find was a cherry-flavored sour ball covered in cellophane. I unwrapped it and put the small bright red sphere on the soil near the entrance to the tomb. "Well, at least it's something," I said. Then, seeing how its garish color intruded on the serenity of the place, I changed my mind. "No, it's all wrong."

I wandered a little distance from the tomb while Louie waited for me. Finally I found what I wanted: a clump of white asters. I picked three of them, feeling like a thief. I wrapped them in a piece of green ribbon that I kept in my pocket to fiddle with when I was nervous. Finally I took out the pen and pad I always carried with me and wrote a note that inverted one of Whitman's lines to show that I was agreeing with it:

> Dear Walt,
> For every atom belonging to you as good belongs to me.
> Love,
> Dell

I tied the note to the flowers and brought them back to the tomb, where I showed them to Louie. "Very nice," he said unconvincingly, while giving me a worried look.

I left the flowers and the note on the floor of the tomb, beneath the door to Walt's coffin. "So long, Camerado," I whispered.

"We'd better get out of here before the guys in the white coats come for you, nutso," Louie said. "As far as I'm concerned, you're turnin' into a case, and I ain't in the mood to be no custodian."

"I'm okay. Really I am," I said. "It was just something I needed to do."

"Well, it's done. Now get in the car and let's go. I can't fuckin' breathe in this place."

We were back in the city by late evening, and we ended up having supper at the same greasy spoon where we'd had breakfast. "This caps a great day," Louie said acerbically, holding aloft a piece of dry, flaky halibut impaled on a dirty fork. "Let's do it again, real soon."

"It was one of the sweetest days of my life, and I'll never forget it," I said. "Even if you think I got a little weird. Thank you, Louie. I really mean it. Thanks a lot."

"Anything for a sister," he said. "But tomorrow it's my turn, and we'll do somethin' a little more normal, okay?"

"Okay," I said. "You're the expert on normal."

After sleeping late, we spent the next day walking around Greenwich Village. Although many of the shops had changed hands, the area didn't look remarkably different from the place Chester had introduced me to. But his old apartment was no longer recognizable because buildings had filled in the empty spaces on either side of it, and it no longer seemed special. Washington Square looked the same as ever, but Louie said that he'd heard it was a major gay cruising ground at night. "They call this the meat rack," he told me as we walked along its western edge. "We have to come back here some night."

"Isn't it dangerous?" I asked.

"You mean the law? Of course, darling, but every place that's gay is dangerous. We never know when the cops are gonna break in and muscle us up. I hear it has to do with local politics. Some people say they have a certain quota to fill. But what's the difference? We have to be where the boys are, no?"

"Not if it means another stretch in jail," I reminded him.

"You've got a point there, Miss Thing. What do you suggest?"

"Let's go to Faisan d'Or tonight."

"Now you're talkin'."

An ugly bruiser in sunglasses and a tuxedo sat on a stool just inside the doorway. "Looks like one of Miss Dominick's friends," Louie whispered in my ear. "Good evenin'," he said to the bruiser.

"Where do youse guys tink yer goin'?" the bruiser asked.

"Inside, of course. We're payin' customers," Louie said.

"Uh-uh. Nobody goes inside widout a jacket 'n' tie. Boss's orders." We were wearing neatly pressed sport shirts and slacks, but no jackets and ties.

"Can't we have just a little peek?" Louie said coyly.

"Uh-uh. Nobody goes inside . . ."

"I know," Louie finished for him, *"widout a jacket 'n' tie."*

"You bein' cute?" the bruiser asked, angry at the mockery of his pronunciation.

"I try. God knows I try," Louie said to him. Then, turning to me, he said, "Come on, Della. We'll take our trade elsewhere."

"You don't by any chance know someone named Yoshi?" I asked the bruiser.

"I don't know nobody," he said. "Youse guys better move it. Yer blockin' da door."

"Oh, terribly sorry," Louie said.

"You better watch it, buddy. Dis bulge in my pocket ain't no cigarette case." He started to rise from his stool, and we left in a hurry.

We went to a movie instead, and the next day we went shopping for clothes at Gimbel's. "We're gonna need these anyway," Louie proclaimed as he paid for a beige silk shantung jacket. "New York is a dressy town." I bought a dark blue linen jacket and a powder-blue tie.

That night we tried Faisan d'Or again. The same bruiser sat on his stool in the doorway, but he didn't seem to recognize us, and let us pass by without a challenge. "Do you think it's our new look that made him so friendly?" I asked.

"No, I think it's a weak memory," answered Louie. "But let's put all that behind us. We're here."

"Here" turned out to be a small supper club with a bar. The tables in the restaurant were mostly filled with straight couples, but sprinkled among them were tables with pairs and groups of fashionably dressed men. The customers at the bar were all male. We had a gin and tonic first. The homely, potbellied bartender, who looked like the doorman's brother, had obviously not been hired to enhance the understated decor. The other patrons at the bar watched us and one another with interest. Everyone behaved decorously on the surface, but their eyes revealed their true hunger for sex. Their conversation was composed of brassy sophistication: judgmental and full of snide innuendo, as if they were afraid to let down their guard for a moment. Men could make dates in such a place, but the tense atmosphere was neither sexual nor social. It was simply competitive. I couldn't imagine Yoshi in such an atmosphere. Everyone looked like an overly well-groomed refugee from the Middle West. Maybe I had the wrong place.

When we sat down to dinner, I understood why Yoshi had suggested Faisan d'Or. He was our waiter. He didn't say anything to indicate he knew me, perhaps afraid of the maître d', who was from the bruiser family that guarded the door and ran the bar. But his eyes glinted with recognition, and he gave a slight nod to say hello. Louie and I had a dinner of what they used to call "fairy food": veal chops with little paper panties and potatoes lyonnaise and slender asparagus spears sprinkled with slivered almonds. Dessert was lime sherbet in a graham shell.

"How adorable," I remarked.

"Don't be snotty now, dear," Louie said. "Learn how to eat like a civilized pansy."

"Listen, Louie, how am I going to make a date with this guy if he doesn't want to talk?"

"Use your imagination, dummy. Leave your name and number under the dessert plate. He'll get the message."

"But where can we go?"

"Will my sacrifices never end? Invite him to our room, of course. I'll go for a late-night promenade."

"You're a prince, Louie."

"A queen, and don't you forget it."

I left my name and our number at the Chelsea on a slip of paper under the plate, and sure enough Yoshi called at 1 a.m.

"Is this Dehr?" he asked.

"Yes. Yoshi?"

"Just got off work," he said. "Sorry I couldn't talk dere. Guys get fired for making out wit' customers. Waiters not supposed to be queer."

"Nobody's supposed to be," I answered. "It's just luck."

"Can I come over?"

"Sure, but what about your boyfriend?"

"He probabry sreeping. Gets up at six-sirty every morning. You arone?"

"I will be. For a while, anyway."

"Great. See you soon."

Louie disappeared into the night, and Yoshi showed up half an hour later. He was out of his clothes before he had crossed the room. We kissed slowly and deeply, and then we both waited. I got the feeling that each of us wanted the other to take charge, so we were at an impasse. Finally he made some simple expert moves to arouse me. We made love hard and fast. I barely had time to admire his silken skin with my fingertips before we were finished.

"What's the hurry?" I asked. "We probably can do it again."

"Got to get home so I can get some sreep," he said. "Got to be dere when he wake up."

"I see," I said. "Maybe another time?"

"Maybe." He nodded his head and gave a slight, curt bow from the waist.

"*Sayonara*, then," I said in farewell, and I complimented his beauty: "*Anata wa kireida.*"

"Where you rearn Japanese?" he asked.

"It's a long story," I told him.

He looked into my eyes. His glance and a barely perceptible nod told me that he understood it had something to do with the war.

"I don't speak Japanese," he said.

"Then how did you get your accent?"

"I copied it from my parents. They were born in Japan, but they've been here for forty years. Caucasians expect me to have an accent, so I produce one for them. It's easier."

"Don't you get enough of pretending to be what you're not when you're at work?" I asked.

"People still feel funny about the Japanese. If I act oriental, it helps them relax. But you don't seem to like it. You were in the Pacific during the war, weren't you?"

"Yes."

"I was in the army, too," he continued. "In Europe—a special unit of Japanese Americans."

My eyes widened. "I was in a Japanese POW camp for two years," I confided softly.

He nodded with recognition. "My parents were put in a camp in California for almost four years," he said. "Does that make us even?"

I didn't know how to answer him.

"None of this is our fault," he said, looking hard into my eyes. "It shouldn't come between us."

"You're right," I whispered. "It's too much baggage to carry around, anyway."

"So, I can call you again?"

"Yes," I said.

He left quickly and I lay back, unwillingly recalling moments from my years in the camp: Doug offering me his body in gratitude for my saving his life; Tim Chaney politely asking me to suck his cock, just so he could "feel somethin' good fo' one lousy minute" in that terrible place; the Japanese soldiers brutally jamming a club up my ass; my desperate letter to Walt Whitman from the underground cage; the yearning look in the guard's eyes as he reached toward my crotch; the "oof" sound that my suitor made as he plunged his bayonet into his belly. I felt a tear slide crookedly from the corner of my eye toward my ear before I turned over and mercifully fell asleep.

Yoshi did call back a couple of times, and we got together once more in the same fashion as the first time. It was diverting, but not exciting, and it summoned up too much past pain. The other times he called, I already had plans.

In the following days, I tried to find some of the people I had known in New York. Minerva White, I discovered, had moved to the Southwest. One person at the Museum of Modern Art said she was in Taos, New Mexico, and another said she was somewhere in Arizona. At any rate, she was no longer in New York. Nobody at Saks Fifth Avenue knew where Miss Standish was, so I went to the Forty-Second Street library. Just being there was an inspiration, and I promised myself that I would return for some reading. A friendly woman at the information desk told me sadly that Betsy Binder had died several years before, and that her friend was in a nursing home.

I found Miss Standish there. She was old and frail, hardly able to hear through her hearing aid and hardly able to see through her cataracts. "Do you remember me?" I said loudly. "I'm Daniel from Elysium."

"Daniel?" she inquired.

"Daniel Blake. I was your student."

"Yes," she said. "I remember. Helen Dell's boy."

"I wanted to say how sorry I was about Miss Binder."

"Yes," she said. "I'll be sure to tell Betsy."

Thinking she didn't understand, I shouted, "Is there anything I can do to help you?"

"Don't shout, Daniel. It isn't polite. You be a good boy and study hard."

"I will, Miss Standish."

"What's that?" she said.

"I said, 'Good-bye'."

"Good-bye, Daniel."

The next day I went back to the library, and I began to spend my afternoons there, reading more about Walt Whitman. They had a larger collection than any library I'd been to, and I really enjoyed myself, especially when I went through the volumes of his conversations recorded by Horace Traubel, who had loyally come to visit him in the house on Mickle Street every day for years. I read Walt's opinions and complaints and desires, which showed me quite a different man from the one who had spoken in his poems. He was not as cheerful, rugged, or healthy as he had always claimed to be. But while his flaws made him seem less perfect, they also made him seem more human, and of course I only loved him more. It was the next best thing to listening to the old man talking in person, and as I read, I felt transported into another world.

In the evenings, Louie and I explored gay New York. One night we went to Club 82 on East Fourth Street. Louie didn't tell me anything about it before we went, and I didn't see what was so wonderful about the glamorous woman with the long, red hair singing her sexy but not too tuneful rendition of "Temptation" until the end of the act, when she raised her long, red-fingernailed hand to her head and ripped off her wig. My mouth was agape. All I could think was that Willard Stevenson should have been there. Louie was laughing so hard that I thought he'd have a stroke. "You should see yourself, Miss Thing," he said. "You look like you saw a ghost!"

Another night he took me to the St. Marks Baths. It was a horrible, dank place, where the permanent sweat on the white-tiled walls was turning moldy green. Though it was mostly straight and mostly immigrants during the day, at night it was mostly gay. We each took a "room," which turned out to be a tiny cell with space enough for only a thin mattress on a flimsy cot. Since an open doorway might be seem to be an invitation to enter and have sex, the rule said that the doors had to be kept closed. But the rule wasn't always obeyed, and a few embarrassed men in short, white robes nervously stalked the hails and peered into the occasional cubicles whose doors were ajar. "If they're layin' face up, they wanna get sucked," Louie advised me. "And if they're layin' face down, you can fuck 'em." I could hardly see which way they were lying in the darkened rooms, and I decided I didn't especially want to do either one, so I sat on the cot in my room with the door slightly open and I waited while Louie prowled the hallways alone.

"Want some company?" a voice said from the doorway. I didn't answer. A figure came in and shut the door then kneeled before me, parted my robe, and took my cock in his mouth. I had trouble getting it up. After about five minutes of futile sucking the figure rose and said, "Maybe some other time. You must be tired." He left before I could say a word. After an hour, Louie returned, his lust completely satisfied (if I could judge by his high spirits), and we went back to the hotel.

"Did you have a good time there?" I asked.

"Let's just say I'd rather not sit down just now," he said. "I know it's tacky there, but what's a little disgust between friends?"

During our second week there, Louie surprised me with tickets to *Tea and Sympathy*, which had just opened on Broadway. We got dressed in our new clothes, had dinner at Lindy's, and joined the crowd under the marquee. "I don't know anything about this play," I said to Louie.

"Someone told me it's got a queer character," he said. "That's all you have to know about it." I was excited, having never seen a homosexual on the stage before. Aside from the high school performance I'd seen Kelly Barrett in, the few plays I'd been to were school productions of the standards by Ibsen and Chekhov. I had seen one road production of *A Streetcar Named Desire*, which I loved, but it had no gay characters except for one who was already dead, unless you wanted to consider Blanche DuBois a queer in drag, which didn't seem very gratifying to me.

As I watched the story of effeminate Tom Lee unfold, I found myself getting depressed. Tom was the only one at his college who didn't know what he was. Everyone else thought he was gay and hated him for it, except his housemaster's wife, Laura Reynolds, who wanted to save him from himself. As soon as I heard the name "Laura," I was transported back to Seattle, and I began wondering whether staying with Laura could have saved me from the pointless life I was now living. The actor who played Bill Reynolds, Tom Lee's angry housemaster, somehow reminded me of Gordon Thomas, and I started to think of young Sean in Portland, and wondering what had become of him. At the end of the play, when Laura Reynolds offered her body to Tom Lee to prove his manhood, I thought of Renee offering herself to me to prove that she was still attractive. I was so lost in the past that I had trouble paying attention to the play. But there wasn't a single good memory in the bunch, and I felt like shit as we left the theater.

"Well, sweetie, what did you think of our little drama?" Louie asked, when we were having a drink at an after-theater club on Forty-Sixth Street.

"I don't know. It just depressed me."

"Why?"

"Look at how everybody tortured that poor gay kid—even the people who wanted to help him."

"How do you know he was queer?" Louie asked.

"What do you mean? He sewed buttons. He liked longhair music. He couldn't get it up for the local hooker. He was dropping beads all over the place."

"Don't be too sure," Louie said. "I used to know some straight boys that I coulda swore were queer. You know, the skinny types with limp wrists who get all excited about movie stars the way I do? But they turned out to be as straight as celery stalks. You can't always tell."

"So what was the play about?" I asked.

"It was about what other people think. What the kid really is doesn't matter."

"But I thought you said there was a homosexual."

"Honey, didn't you check out that housemaster, Miss Bill? Now that was a closet case if ever there was one. Why do you think he was so mad at poor little Tom? The kid reminded him of what he was hiding in himself."

"You should have been a theater critic, or at least a psychologist," I commented.

"Mary, I'm a hair burner. That's just as good, believe me. Now, where should we go from here? What do you say we get laid?"

"Why not?" I said. "Maybe the fleet is in."

"Forget it, Della," he replied. "We'll never have it as good as it was that week in P-Town. How about us changin' our clothes and driftin' down to Greenwich Village?"

"Do you think it's safe?" I asked.

"You mean the vice squad? I don't care if it's safe or not. I need me some fresh meat."

"Oh Miss Lulu, how you do talk!" I said. He loved it when I camped, and I was trying to get out of my blue mood.

"Good, then it's set. Waiter, check please!"

Back at the hotel, we took off our good clothes and changed into sport clothes. Then we took a cab down to the Village. First we went to Lenny's Hideaway, a downstairs bar off Sheridan Square. It was full of well-manicured men staring at each other. The jukebox played songs from *Kiss Me, Kate* and *South Pacific*, and some of the men sang along while I thought that if they knew what the South Pacific had really been like during the war, they wouldn't have much to sing about. Then we went to Mary's on Eighth Street. It seemed very cruisy, but after an hour neither one of us had made out, so we drifted down the street to Washington Square, which this late at night was a different place from the one we had seen in the daylight.

Shadowy figures drifted up and down the sidewalk inspecting the male merchandise, which had arrayed itself on the fence that lined the park. We separated, so we could concentrate on our cruising. I walked past the men who sat on the railings, watching with an expert appraiser's interest as they took lurid drags on their cigarettes or suggestively stroked their baskets.

It was a hot show, and I put away my bad mood as I relaxed and began to enjoy it, strolling back and forth for about twenty minutes. Once a squad car cruised by and everyone on the rack sprang into motion, pretending to be going somewhere. But as soon as the police had passed, we all resumed our casual air.

Then my heart started to beat a little faster when I saw two good-looking young punks, both eyeing me. They were standing on the corner, their heads together in close consultation. It was a warm night for the beginning of October, and they were wearing only T-shirts and black chinos. One of them had his cigarette pack rolled up in the sleeve of his shirt, which, along with the carefully arranged curl of hair that jutted out over his forehead, gave him the look of a young hood. The other one had a short crew cut, which made him look like a military type. I didn't want to appear too eager, so I looked at them hard and long, to show I was definitely interested, and then I walked a little way past them and leaned against the railing.

After a couple of minutes, they turned and sauntered past. The one with the crew cut gave me a curt nod, which I returned, and the two of them stopped in front of me.

"Nice night," said the one with the curl.

"Yes, it is," I agreed.

"What are you lookin' for?" asked the crew cut.

"Just out enjoying the weather," I said.

"Yeah, we are too. Ain't we, Mike?" said the curl. "Oh, by the way, he's Mike and I'm Joe. We didn't get your name."

"Hi, Mike. Hi, Joe. I'm Dell," I said.

"Dell," Joe repeated. "Ain't that a nice name?"

"Sure is," said Mike. "Kinda pretty, almost like Della."

"So, what did you say you were up to, Dell?" Joe asked.

"Nothing much, just out walking."

"Nice night for walkin'," said Joe.

"You already said that," said Mike.

"Oh yeah. Must be your turn, Mike."

"Nice night," said Mike, and the two of them laughed.

I was beginning to get a weird feeling about them, but they were both so sexy I couldn't pull myself away.

"Let's cut the shit," said Joe. "You live around here, uh . . . what's your name again? Don't tell me. Oh yeah—Della. No, Dell." He pronounced it a little too carefully, just to tease me.

I blushed. "I'm staying at a hotel on Twenty-Third Street."

"Yeah? You from out of town?" asked Mike.

"Mm-hmm," I said.

"Where from?"

"All over. Provincetown was the last place."

"Oh, a gypsy boy, eh? We like gypsy boys. Don't we, Joe?"

"Oh yeah. Gypsy boys are real sweet," said Joe. "So, whadda ya say?"

"To what?" I asked.

"Wanna go to your hotel?"

"Well, I have a roommate, but he's here. Let me ask him, and I'll be right back. Okay?"

I had a funny feeling about the two of them, but I figured maybe Louie would join us and it would be okay. The guys were incredibly sexy, and I hated to lose them. I walked up the block a little way and then I saw him walking toward me, with a tall, dark-haired young man wearing a baseball jacket.

"Dell, I'm glad I found you," Louie said. "This is Marvin. We're going back to his place. The hotel room is all yours. See you in the morning, love."

"Have a good time," I said. I turned around to find that Mike and Joe had followed me.

"Guess we're all set then," Mike said. "Taxi!"

They sat on either side of me in the cab, each one with a hand on my knees, as if I were a prize they didn't want to lose. When we pulled up in front of the hotel, they made no effort to pay the fare. So I paid it myself and gave the driver a big tip, to show what a sport I was. We arrived at the room a few minutes later and I ushered them in, saying, "Make yourselves comfortable, gentlemen." Calamus hid himself discreetly under the bed.

"Why don't you take your clothes off first, gypsy boy?" Joe suggested, and I complied with the request, trying to do a provocatively slow striptease and at the same time hurrying, so we could get down to the action.

Once I was naked, I felt a little silly, since the two of them were still fully dressed. "Aren't you going to join me?" I invited.

"Oh yeah, sweetmeat, we're gonna join you," Mike said, pulling something from his pocket. I heard a click, and suddenly a switchblade knife was staring me in the face. "Now, where's your travelin' money, queer?" he said.

"What?" I said, confused.

"Don't play dumb, you little fairy," he said. He kept the knife to my throat and maneuvered around behind me, grabbing my wrist and pulling my arm into a hammerlock. "Okay, Joe, convince him," he said.

Joe punched me in the gut with his fist, which knocked the wind right out of me. I heaved and gasped for long moments, afraid I was never going to catch my breath and that I would die. The two of them waited while I buckled and thrashed. Finally, after what seemed like an impossibly long time without air, I was able to suck in a lifesaving breath, which I drank down gratefully. When I was breathing normally again, Mike said, "That was just the beginning, fruitcake. Now, where do you keep the money?"

"We don't have much money," I tried to explain. Joe cut my explanation short by punching me in the face a few times. I tried to knee him in the groin, but he caught me and did it to me instead. I passed out.

When I came to, I found myself tied to the bed with my arms above my head. Some cloth had been stuffed in my mouth and tied fast. My right eye was throbbing, and I could feel warm blood running from my nose. My whole face and my groin were electric with pain. Mike and Joe were going through the suitcases. I could see them toss aside Minerva White's photographs, and I heard the glass on one of them crack. They took all my money and the cloisonné bowl Edwin had given me. They also took all of Louie's money and his beautician's tools, as well as his supply of bennies and marijuana. Then they went to the closet and took out our new jackets. Each of them tried one on, and they admired each other. "Yep," said Mike. "It looks just right. I think you should take it."

"Sold," said Joe, and they both laughed.

They were stuffing all their loot into my suitcase and getting ready to go when Mike said, "Wait a minute. We oughta give the little faggot his money's worth. Whadda ya say, Joe?"

They put down their new acquisitions and stood over me on either side of the bed, moving as if they had rehearsed their choreography before. Both of them opened their pants and stroked themselves to erections. A few minutes later, they were ready to shoot. "Aim for his eye," Mike said. "Let him see what real men are made of."

The last thing I saw was the gism spurting from the head of Joe's cock. Then I heard them gather their loot, shut the light, and go down the hall, whistling and laughing. I lay there for the rest of the night, trying not to think, but I couldn't help myself. I couldn't see in the dark, but I probably couldn't have seen anything even if the light were on, since one eye was swollen shut and the other was clotted with semen, which I could also feel drying on my forehead and cheeks. I did my best to clear my eye by rubbing it against my shoulder, but I could still feel it ache. Maybe I would go blind and never have to see reality again. I felt so degraded that I wanted to die right there. How could I face Louie and explain all this to him? There was no way to find Mike and Joe. I knew I couldn't go to the cops. They'd probably just tell me that I'd gotten what I deserved. For all I knew, Mike and Joe were off-duty cops themselves. No, that was probably silly. But I could bet their names weren't Mike and Joe. I was stupid for going with them. I was humiliated for being attracted to them. Why didn't I have the wisdom of Walt Whitman? Had he ever hated himself as I did now? To pass the silent time, I searched through my memory for verses that showed that he had, and I finally remembered some from "Crossing Brooklyn Ferry":

It is not upon you alone the dark patches fall,
The dark threw its patches down upon me also,
The best I had done seem'd to me blank and suspicious . . .
I am he who knew what it was to be evil,
I too knitted the old knot of contrariety,

347

Blabb'd, blush'd, resented, lied, stole, grudg'd,
Had guile, anger, lust, hot wishes I dared not speak,
Was wayward, vain, greedy, shallow, sly, cowardly, malignant,
The wolf, the snake, the hog, not wanting in me,
The cheating look, the frivolous word, the adulterous wish,
    not wanting,
Refusals, hates, postponements, meanness, laziness, none of
    these wanting . . .

At least he had his bad moments too, I thought. But the idea gave me little comfort. Walt was dead and his bad moments were over. Why wasn't I dead with him? How could I go on? The last line of *Tea and Sympathy* kept flashing through my mind: "Years from now, when you speak of this—and you will—be kind." In the middle of my pain, I laughed bitterly.

In the morning, Louie opened the door and said, "What the fuck? I didn't know you were into S and M, Miss Della!"

I couldn't see him, and I couldn't answer through my gag, but he soon had me untied. "What the hell happened here?" he asked. "The place looks like Kansas the day Dorothy left. I hope at least you had a good time."

"It isn't funny," I said, rubbing my wrists. "We've been robbed."

"We'll deal with that second," he said. "First, are you all right?" I'll always be grateful to him for that.

He got me washed off and patched up without having to take me to the hospital. Lots of warm water got the dried semen out of my eye, whose vision wasn't destroyed, although the ache lasted for a day or so. We used the ointment that was left over from treating his black eye to treat mine. "Too bad mine faded so soon," he said. "We'd look like the Gold Dust Twins."

"No, the Dolly Sisters," I said, trying to lighten up, but failing.

Once I was back together again, he said, "Okay, that's item number one. Now let's take inventory."

"There's nothing left," I said. "They took all our money, our new clothes, and your tools and drugs to boot."

He looked serious for a minute. Then he saw that I was on the verge of tears. "Oh well," he said. "Easy come, easy go. At least it's all replaceable."

"I'll never forget you for this," I said.

"Honey, are you kidding? You won't have a chance to forget me. I ain't goin' nowhere without you. Do you think you're the first queen to pick up some rough trade and end up black-and-blue? Don't you think Miss Lulu's had her share of that too?"

Then I did begin to cry. All of my hurt and anger and humiliation came pouring out, and Louie held me. When I was finished, he said, "Well, now that we've got that out of your system, let's figure out what to do next. It looks like I better check out the want ads. Lucky I had my wallet with me. We have enough money to last us a few days, until I can find some work."

He bought some breakfast and brought it up to the room with the newspaper, and while we ate, he checked out the ads for beauticians. "I won't have trouble finding somethin'," he said. "There are lots of ads. Thank God beauty parlors are a basic necessity. We'll be back on our feet in no time."

He went out to look for work and I stayed in bed to recuperate. At the end of the day, he came back with some take-out food from a luncheonette and announced, "Ta-da. Presenting Monsieur Louis of Chez Femmes! And now, would madame care for a taste of chateaubriand, *non*?" He whipped a meat loaf sandwich on a roll out of the brown paper bag and presented it with a flourish. "*Voilà!* And all the trimmings to go with it—meaning ketchup—plus a cream soda for dessert."

"Oh, thank you, Monsieur Louis," I said, through sore, stiffened lips. "It's just what I wanted. Did you really find a job so fast?"

"A hundred a week plus tips," he said. "And all the henna I can rinse."

"When do you start?"

"Tomorrow. By this time next week, we'll be eating chateaubriand for real."

"I owe you for this, Lulu."

"Don't be silly, sugar. It'll even out."

The next day he went to work and I lay in the hotel room, trying to concentrate on healing. I had to figure out how I could make a living too, once I was presentable again. I looked through the want ads for an idea. There were no ads for doctor's assistants or antique shop clerks. Slowly the realization that I was completely unskilled began to settle in. I remembered that every time that I had gone to work, I had started from scratch. Edwin had really hired me as a companion, and Gordon had really hired me for sex. I couldn't expect poor Louie to support me for long, and I didn't know where to turn. My life up to that point had produced absolutely nothing besides a collection of unhappy memories, and my future looked grimmer than my past. I sank into a depression even deeper than the one I had been in on the night of the robbery.

My dark mood went on for the next two days. I tried to keep it from Louie, who was so busy with news of his new job that he didn't realize how quiet I had grown. When he was asleep at night, I lay in the bed and tried to make my breathing so shallow that it would stop altogether. When he was gone during the day, I sat in the darkened room trying not to think, or at least confining my thoughts to Walt Whitman, whose "Crossing Brooklyn Ferry" kept sliding into my consciousness. In it, he stands on the ferry from Manhattan to Brooklyn and speaks to the men and women of the future.

I too many and many a time cross'd the river of old . . .

– Song of Myself –

Saw the reflection of the summer sky in the water,
Had my eyes dazzled by the shimmering track of beams,
Look'd at the fine centrifugal spokes of light round the shape
    of my head in the sunlit water . . .
I too lived, Brooklyn of ample hills was mine,
I too walk'd the streets of Manhattan island, and bathed in
    the waters around it . . .

I don't know what force drove me out after three days in the dark hotel room. I only knew that I had to see the harbor for myself, to see the spokes of light around the shape of my head in the sunlit water as Walt had seen them. The next morning after Louie left for work, I put on the clothes the thieves had left me and looked in the mirror for the first time. With my black eye bulging out and my bruises just fading from purple to green, I looked like Quasimodo on a bad day. I turned away and went to the door.

Downstairs, I expected people to shrink from the sight of me. But although one or two looked at me curiously, most people didn't seem to notice anything out of the ordinary. Consulting my tourist map, I turned southward and walked for miles. Then I turned east and walked until I saw it: the Brooklyn Bridge, tall and majestic and old and sturdy and comforting. I decided to walk across it on the pedestrian footpath, so I could look down into the water. The cool breezes of mid-October soothed my sore skin as I walked, reciting Whitman's verses to myself in a whisper.

When I reached the center, I simply climbed over the railing and got to the edge. Then I worked my way up one of the many slim supporting cables until I had reached the gigantic cable that swooped in a gracefully spread arc from one of the bridge's towers to the other. I climbed atop the cable and stood there facing seaward, with the harbor spread out before me, and I chanted in my loudest voice: "Diverge, fine spokes of light, from the shape of my head, or any one's head, in the sunlit water!" And I continued reciting the lines of Walt's poem.

Soon I heard commotion behind me. Horns were blaring and people were shouting. It sounded like a traffic jam. As I turned to look, I lost my balance and slipped—but I managed not to fall all the way off. I was afraid to look down at the water behind me, and I clung to the cable with my hands and tried several times to get my body back on it until I succeeded. At first I lay the length of my body along it, afraid to get up, but finally I was able to sit up and then stand again. A burst of applause came from behind me. But I was afraid to turn around and look, in case the same thing happened again.

"Jump!" someone yelled, and I froze.

A moment later, a siren penetrated the air, and then a car's brakes screeched. A loud voice came over a bullhorn: "This is the police! You are illegally trespassing on city property. Come down immediately!" I stayed

350

where I was, shouting my recitation aloud: "It avails not, time nor place—distance avails not, / I am with you, you men and women of a generation, or ever so many generations hence."

At that point I realized that someone was climbing toward me from my right. I turned and saw that it was a cop. The crowd cheered him on. I continued: "Just as you feel when you look on the river and sky, so I felt, / Just as any of you is one of a living crowd, I was one of a crowd."

"Now, stay calm," the cop said, as he reached the cable that supported me.

"I'm perfectly calm," I said. "Why shouldn't I be calm?" And I went on with the incantation of Walt's words.

"Just as you are refresh'd by the gladness of the river and the bright flow, I was refresh'd . . ."

I looked down into the water, so I could see my face surrounded by spokes of light, and I gasped. Far below me, there was indeed a face amid radiating spokes of light, an old face with sparkling eyes and a great, white beard floating outward from his chin. I recognized my beloved Walt immediately and leaned forward, so I could kiss his lips. Just then I felt a hand grab my left ankle, and I was trapped. There had been two cops climbing up. The other one had reached me, and they both held on to me.

"It's all right, buddy. You're safe now," one of them said. "What's your name?"

"Walt Whitman," I answered, and I passed out.

When I woke up, I was in a gray hospital ward, dressed in gray pajamas. A man sat in the bed next to mine, opening and closing his gray seersucker bathrobe. "Where are we?" I asked him.

"Bellevue, silly. Don't you even know what hospital you're in?"

"Thanks," I said.

I spent the next thirty days there, eating tasteless food with a spoon because they didn't trust me with a knife. "Stabbing is not my style," I tried to explain.

"Eat your food before it gets cold," was the answer.

There was nothing to do all day except sit and stare or listen to the other men's stories. Three of the patients in my ward were alcoholics drying out from sprees on the Bowery. One was a retarded boy. He didn't seem crazy, but no one could explain why he was in the ward. There were two paranoids, one pursued by small purple creatures from another dimension and the other waiting for the FBI to break in and take him away to be questioned. We had one autistic case, who sat in a corner and said nothing, ever, and one case of split personality, who held conversations with himself in three different voices, day and night. One other man had tried suicide. His wrists were thickly bandaged and he had a dull look in his eyes. He did not wish to discuss his problems. The guards and nurses treated us all equally—with contempt. Nothing we said to them was taken seriously because we were supposedly mad and they were supposedly sane, and they obviously relished the power that gave them over us.

The doctor saw each of the patients for a few minutes, once a day. "Why did you try to jump from there?" he asked me.

"I just wanted to see the view," I said.

"Don't be flip, or we'll keep you here."

"I feel like a failure at life," I said.

"That's no reason to die," he commented.

"Can you think of a better one?" I asked.

After three days, Louie showed up, his face ashen. "Honey, this place is worse than Cook County. What made you do it?"

"I was depressed," I said.

"Why didn't you tell me?"

"I didn't want to be a burden," I explained. "You've already done too much for me."

"You helped me when I needed it," he answered simply.

"It wasn't the same thing," I replied.

"So, who's weighing? Listen, are you gonna be all right?"

"I guess so. How long can they keep me here?"

"A month, for observation. Then they have to let you out. You're not dangerous, are you?"

"Louie, I'm not crazy, just depressed."

"Don't get excited," he said. "I was just checking. Listen, don't worry about the cat. I'm taking care of her."

"Thank you."

"Honey, if you want my advice, this city ain't where you oughta be right now. My boss has a place in San Francisco, and he wants me to go there to work. If I'm good, he says I'll become the manager in a year. Should we go?"

"Why not?"

Louie came every other evening for the next few weeks. Between his visits, I tried to think about what I wanted to do when I got out. I finally decided I wanted to write a book. I wanted to bring Walt Whitman to the twentieth century, maybe rewrite *Leaves of Grass* in twentieth-century language. The next day I realized how ridiculous an idea that was. Walt's poetry was doing fine on its own. So I started again. I decided I would write a biography of him, telling the long-buried truth about his sexuality. The next day I knew that was out of the question. I didn't want to be a scholar. So I decided I would write a novel about his life, showing what he was really like as a person—at least what he seemed like from my point of view, which was as good as anyone else's version. I spent the rest of my time thinking of ideas about what parts of his life to include and how to dramatize them. It kept me busy enough not to go mad.

When my time was up, the doctor said, "You're going home tomorrow. Do you think you can you handle it?"

"Am I cured?" I asked.

"Are you going to try to jump off the Brooklyn Bridge again?"

"No," I declared.

"Then I guess you're cured," he said. "Get out of here."

Louie met me at the gate with a suitcase and Calamus in his traveling box, and we took a cab right from the hospital to the airport, to catch our flight to San Francisco.

PART VI
D. D. BLAKE

This poem drooping shy and unseen that I always carry, and
    that all men carry,
(Know once for all, avow'd on purpose, wherever are men
    like me, are our lusty lurking masculine poems.)

—Walt Whitman,
"Spontaneous Me"

CHAPTER NINETEEN

I t didn't take us long to set ourselves up in San Francisco. Louie went to work at Chez Femmes West, and we shared an apartment near Buena Vista Park until I could support a place of my own. I found a job in an antique shop, but the owner was a supercilious type, and I didn't last long. Then I used my experience at Gus's Diner in Seattle as a basis for looking in the ads. Within a week, I found a job as a waiter at a nightclub in North Beach, and a few weeks after that I was in an apartment of my own, near my job.

My apartment was small, but comfortable: a living room, bedroom, and kitchen on the second floor of an old Victorian frame house, which had been subdivided. I loved the big old windows looking out on the street, especially when fog rolled across the bay and gentled the edges of the city with its mist. Then I felt secure. I don't know what possessed me—maybe it was just the first real chance that I had to express my own taste—but I started with Minerva White's pictures, and eventually I had all the walls covered with framed photographs, some of which I bought and some of which I cut out from magazines. The effect reminded me of Miss White's studio back in New York, where all the walls had been covered with her photographs. They weren't meant to be a fashionable decor; they were just what I wanted to look at. Calamus also felt right at home there. He usually curled himself up to sleep on the wide windowsill, and he and I were very happy when we were at home together, almost like a normal family.

My job, however, was on the other side of the looking glass. The Finocchio Club was not your usual sort of nightspot. Like the Club 82 in New York, it featured drag performers, who entertained a large tourist crowd. The place opened in 1936 and was still popular. I was only a waiter at first, but I got to know some of the performers of the day and to like them. The best ones were truly feminine and looked better in drag than they did out of it, since they were more convincing as women than they were as men. The greatest drag stars—like T. C. Jones (who appeared on *The Ed Sullivan Show*) and Charles Pierce (who later achieved a national reputation, with his fabulous Bette Davis and Tallulah Bankhead impersonations)—

appeared at other clubs. The stars with top billing at Finocchio's were Lucian, who looked like Joan Blondell playing her own mother, and Ray Francis and John Lonas, "The Two Old Bags from Oakland," who looked like they had stepped out of a Toulouse-Lautrec poster.

I was friendlier with the lesser lights, like Robin Starling, who dressed in simple gowns and sang unadorned ballads in such a beautiful, throaty woman's voice that people stopped caring what he wore and just wanted to hear him sing. Robin was the only performer who wore women's clothes to go home in after the show. There was a rumor that he had been to Denmark for a sex-change operation and that he was really a woman now, but no one could verify it since he—or she—was very modest and changed costumes in a private dressing room. I was fascinated by the idea of a woman who had once been a man, but I never had enough nerve to ask outright and, like the rest of Robin's fans, I was left to figure it out for myself.

Robin's mystery was unique at Finocchio's. None of the fans had any questions about the gender of my other favorite, Francis Frances. No matter how many feathers and sequins adorned his costume, he looked like the butchest woman I ever saw. But he did a marvelously funny imitation of Mae West, and he compensated for his minor singing and dancing talent with lots of makeup and enthusiasm. The more absurd he looked, the more we loved him.

The dancers were also men in drag, but they were a little less artistic than the main performers and were present mostly to add a colorful backdrop and to fill in during costume changes. I had been working there for almost a year when Hilary, one of the dancers, who had been very nice about filling in for me as a waiter when I was ill, sprained his ankle backstage. "I can't miss any more performances or I'll be fired," he told me. "Someone has to go on for me."

"Who?" I asked.

"You," he said.

"Me? You've got to be kidding."

"I was never more serious. If I lose this job, I can't finish school, and my career as an architect goes down the drain."

"But I don't know anything about the costume."

"I'll get you into the costume," he assured me.

"I don't know the steps," I said, desperate for any excuse.

"It doesn't take Eleanor Powell to kick first the left foot and then the right," he said. "This isn't the Radio City Rockettes, you know."

He was right. I'd seen the show, and a wooden leg would have been no barrier to performing those steps. I had no more excuses, and I did owe him a favor.

"Okay then," I said. "But just this once."

"Oh I promise: just this once."

It took almost an hour to make me up. First he shaved my armpits and legs, including the edges of my pubic hair so that it wouldn't show through the leg holes of my costume. I snorted my disapproval, but to no avail. Then he gave my face a close shave and applied an inch of foundation, followed by clouds of powder. After he won the battle over whether to tweeze my eyebrows, he applied heavy streaks of eyebrow pencil and much too much rouge and eye shadow, which no one would notice above the ultra-thick black eyelashes that he had affixed to my lids. Next he waxed my mouth with enough lipstick to coat the Golden Gate Bridge. I wondered how women could put up with living behind such a mask every day. My face yearned for a bar of soap.

"I can't possibly pass as a woman," I said, "even behind all this crap."

"Don't be silly," he replied. "With an amber gel on the spotlight, all things are possible."

He helped me into the costume, a showgirl's tight bodysuit, which required that I tuck my balls up into their sockets and tape my dick between my legs. Then he stuffed me into a concoction of pink velvet with bugle beads, sequins, and feathers sprouting from improbable places, and he packed extra foam rubber into the bodice to fill out my breasts. Finally he crowned his creation with a wavy red wig. He stood back to admire his handiwork. He leaned forward and added a large beauty mark to my right cheek, just beneath the outer corner of my eye, then leaned back again.

"*Voilà*," he announced. "Presenting Miss Dell Blake."

I looked in the mirror. To my surprise, in spite of all the excess makeup and the overdone trimmings, I didn't look half bad. In fact I was almost pretty—if you go in for big-boned women. "What a construction," I said. "I think you've already earned your architect's degree!"

I made it through the evening's performances with no problem beyond a few mistimed kicks. At first I felt ridiculous, trying to wriggle and strut like a chorus girl, but after I was onstage for a few minutes and I heard the applause, I actually began to enjoy it—and I kicked and pranced with an enthusiasm that made some of the more jaded dancers work a little harder than usual, just to keep up.

"You were great," Hilary said with a big grin when I came offstage.

"Ah, my adoring public," I said, graciously tendering the back of my hand for his kiss. "Thank you, thank you, everyone."

"You weren't that good," he said. "Give me back my wig."

I remained a waiter, but every once in a while in the next few years I allowed myself to be shanghaied into being a substitute, or even to dance for the run of a show. When I was asked how I wanted my name listed on the program, I wasn't sure.

"How about plain Dell Blake?" Mrs. Finocchio suggested.

"No, I want something more mysterious."

"What about Della?"

"No, that's not intriguing. Wait a minute—I know! I'll be D. D. Blake. Let my admirers figure it out."

"Fine," she said, shrugging her shoulders at the silly pretentions of a chorus boy.

It's just for a laugh, I told myself. But the truth is that I was really a little stagestruck. I rather liked thinking of myself as a career woman.

Louie, on the other hand, had become quite a homebody, often cooking dinner for me and several other guests. He had a new boyfriend, named Roger, a handsome black mathematics major from Berkeley, and when I knew I was going to appear, I would alert Louie, and he and Roger would come by and watch me strut my stuff.

I expected them to be the only people I knew in the audience, but one night, while I was strutting and kicking, I thought I saw someone I knew sitting at a ringside table. I had to squint to see past the stage lights, but after several tours around the performance area, I was sure. It was Willard Stevenson. His lips were pursed, as always, and he was dressed in a dark suit and tie. Beside him sat a plain-looking woman with horn-rimmed glasses, wearing a gray cotton dress set off by a string of pink plastic pop-it beads. Her hair was cropped in a straight line just below her earringless ears. I couldn't watch them talking with each other because both of them seemed absorbed in the show, but although they were at a dime-sized table, they managed to sit slightly apart, like an old married couple who are beyond sexual enthusiasm. So I assumed that she was his wife, the woman I had spoken to on the phone from Chicago. I tried to dance as close to the table as I could without destroying the choreography, hoping that Willard might recognize me, but he seemed completely oblivious of my efforts. When the show was over and I had taken off my makeup, he was already gone. I wondered if he was as content with his masquerade of a happily married man as he had been with his masquerade as my uncle, or if he even cared. He probably wasn't really satisfied with either role. I tried to imagine what his life might have been like if he could live as he really wanted to. But a person as frightened as Willard probably never even entertained such fantasies.

Not all homosexuals were as frightened as he. In January 1953, some members of the Mattachine Society had begun publishing *One* magazine, to spread the word that we deserved the right to self-respect and freedom from harassment. That wasn't enough to stop either the self-hatred or the harassment, of course. In some cases it only intensified them. Journalists were no help. Some of them openly wrote about us as a pernicious threat to society, and some of them attacked the Mattachine Society as a Communist front. But even if it was, I thought, at least someone was brave enough to say that we were human beings, and I was glad of that.

In December 1954, Senator McCarthy was censured by the United States Senate, and his ugly little game was over at last. The House Un-American Activities Committee's atmosphere of red-baiting and fear mongering, the witch-hunting of homosexuals, and the blacklisting of left-wing writers all began to evaporate, and everyone was able to breathe a little more freely for a while.

I continued to write poems in my spare time. Since I worked at the club most evenings, I often spent my afternoons writing at one of North Beach's cafés, surrounded by the local literary circle—the crowds of black-sweatered beatniks who sat around looking fashionably depressed. At first I didn't feel like I belonged with them, because I was gay, and I wondered how they would react if they saw me onstage around the corner at Finocchio's. But they were interested in poetry, and I needed to exercise that side of myself as well. I was estranged from mainstream society for different reasons than they were, but all of us were nonconformists in our way, and their disillusioned rebelliousness was an influence on me. Here's an example of what I was writing then.

Night Song for Mister
I am an aberration
lurking in the alleyway
where the junkies piss
behind the blue jazz bar,
where you come, Mister,
when you are high enough to feel
like sucking in the night.

I am an error of creation;
Mister, will you love my mal-
formed beautiful body
twisted burly shoulders
stunted shapely legs
stifled yearning soul,
my blind Walt Whitman eyes
that pour hopeless love
into the screaming
terrified night?

My heart stopped long ago.
What good is a heart
in the chest
of a whore faggot cocksucker pig?
You would have to love corpses to love me:
Mister, will you put your splendid manhood
in my rotting mouth

anyway?
What the hell, Mister,
just for the fun of it,
will you love me
just for to-
night?

Of course that wasn't the way I felt about myself. It was my statement about the way society wanted me to feel. I was afraid to show that poem to people, for fear of being misunderstood. Then, in a club called The Place, I discovered that I wasn't the only homosexual in the crowd. Poets like Robin Blaser, Jack Spicer, and Robert Duncan met at The Place daily and talked about other, more famous gay poets like Hart Crane, Federico Garcia Lorca, and Arthur Rimbaud. I went right to the library to catch up on my reading. Then I went back to The Place, to listen some more. They talked about our contemporaries, Frank O'Hara and Allen Ginsberg. There was a whole gay side to the beat generation, and I had known nothing about it. I was encouraged enough to begin sending out my less explicit poems to some small literary magazines—and, to my amazement, several of them were actually published! After I saw my words in print, I walked around with a new dignity. I was an author now.

At Lawrence Ferlinghetti's City Lights bookstore, where I spent a good deal of time browsing—partly to see if anyone actually bought the magazines my poems were in—I saw an announcement that Ginsberg was going to read at the Six Gallery. It meant taking a night off from work, but I went to hear him read his new poem "Howl." I sat in back of the room while this unpretentious-looking Jewish boy with dark curly hair and thick eyeglasses prefaced his poem with a line from Whitman: "Unscrew the locks from the doors! Unscrew the doors themselves from their jambs!" Then he began reading:

"I saw the best minds of my generation destroyed by
    madness, starving hysterical naked,
dragging themselves through the negro streets at dawn
    looking for an angry fix . . ."

He went on to describe his mother's hospitalization for madness, and to sing the praises of homosexuality not only as an earthly delight, but even as something sacred. The audience was electrified, and I was stunned. Not only were there other gay poets, but there were soul mates out there. There was a future!

The next day at The Place, Ginsberg's reading was all that anyone wanted to discuss.

"It's a landmark," said one voice.

"It's a continuation of the Whitman tradition," said another.

"Speaking of the Whitman tradition," said a third, "did you hear the story Ginsberg tells, that he had sex with Neal Cassady, who had sex with Gavin Arthur, President Chester Alan Arthur's grandson? Arthur had sex with Edward Carpenter, the English socialist, back in 1923, and Carpenter told him he had had sex with old Walt Whitman himself, when he visited America in 1877 and again in 1884. Isn't that cool? They're really passing along the old man's touch."

I was fascinated with that bit of literary gossip, and it didn't take me long to hatch a plan. I would find Ginsberg and seduce him, and through him I would inherit the touch that could be traced back from him to Arthur, to Carpenter, and to Whitman. It was as close as I could get to making love to Walt himself. It was my sacred duty!

My plan was made easier when I found out that Ginsberg frequented my old hangout on Montgomery Street, the Black Cat Café. On my next night off, I went right there, ready for action. The place was jumping. By that time it had become a popular hangout for everybody. Flamboyant gays and businessmen and longshoremen all gathered around to talk and have fun while a honky-tonk piano competed with dozens of boisterous conversations. Ginsberg wasn't there the first few times I went, so I tried again and again, and eventually I saw him. He was with friends, but I walked right over.

"Aren't you Allen Ginsberg?" I asked.

"Yes," he said.

"I really liked your reading at the Six Gallery a few weeks ago."

"Hey, man," he said. "That's really cool. I appreciate your telling me. Thanks a lot."

"Can I buy you a drink?"

"Uh, I'm already with someone."

"Oh, maybe some other time," I said, embarrassed.

"Right," he said, and turned back to his friends.

I felt ridiculous. I wandered out of the bar and down to Polk Street, where I had a couple of drinks in another gay bar. From there I found my way to the "meat rack" at Market Street and Powell in San Francisco's downtown, Tenderloin, and I picked up a hustler and paid him five dollars to let me suck him off. That was as close as I came to sleeping with Walt Whitman outside of my own fantasies.

A year later, when "Howl" came out in print, the police seized the book and put it on trial for obscenity. Eventually it was cleared, but the trial made it a best seller, and even more people read it than would have if the cops hadn't been so stupid in the first place.

In spite of his relationship with his new boyfriend Roger, Louie wasn't faring much better than I was. He came over to my apartment, to complain over a cup of jasmine tea, one Sunday afternoon.

"It just isn't working out right," he said, past his ever-present cigarette butt.

"Aren't you having good sex anymore?" I asked.

"Of course, Della. I always have good sex. It isn't that."

"Why, then? Because you're a hairdresser and he wants to be a math teacher?"

He shook his head.

I tried another tack. "Doesn't he want to be queer anymore? Is he afraid his family will find out?"

"That's not the problem," Louie said.

"Then what is, for God's sake?"

"It's because I'm white!"

"Surely he noticed that when he started seeing you," I said. "Or maybe one time in bed it caught his attention?" I started to laugh.

"It isn't funny, Della. You know all the trouble that's been going on in the South? About segregation in the schools and civil rights for Negroes?"

"Of course. Do you think I don't read the papers? But I thought the aim was integration."

"It is. But the more Roger sees on TV, the angrier he gets about the way whites treat blacks. He says he always knew it was bad, but it's gettin' worse, and it doesn't matter that some of us are trying to help. He feels like a traitor to his people when he's with me."

"Maybe you could go to a genealogist and see if there's a Negro in your family tree somewhere," I suggested cavalierly.

"Thanks a lot, but I don't have a family tree. I don't even have anyone to ask." He stubbed out his cigarette.

"I thought you said your mother lives in Illinois."

"The truth is that my father died when I was eleven and my mother died five years ago. She did take in sewin', just like I told you. She wasn't a bad woman. She did her best for me and I loved her for it, but she could never understand what my life was about."

I wasn't surprised to learn that his earlier stories weren't quite true. By then I had learned that Louie had a somewhat sporadic relationship with reality. "You don't have to talk about it if you don't want to," I said.

"It's okay, honey. There ain't nothin' more to talk about anyway. Now, what am I gonna do about Roger?"

"Why don't you let things take their own course? You're still the same person you were when he fell in love with you."

"But he ain't the same person I fell in love with. He's changin'. Why can't anythin' in my life be normal?"

"Because you're so exceptional, sweetie. Normal just isn't good enough for you."

"Oh Miss Della, you're the one I truly love."

"I know that, Lulu. We'll stick together, you and me."

"That's a deal."

To cheer Louie up, I took him to the Black Cat, where on Sunday afternoons there was an act to rival Finocchio's show. But, unlike the performances at Finocchio's, which were tailored to the straight tourists' tastes, this one was just for us. It was a kind of camp parody of grand opera, starring a flamboyant drag queen named José Sarria, who did his act on a stage improvised from wood planks supported by cases of beer. What made it special was that it was political. Instead of portraying Carmen struggling with the Spanish police, he would turn her into a homosexual struggling with the vice squad.

The law was coming down heavily on us during this period. San Francisco was famous for being tolerant of artistic bohemian types, and had drawn a pretty large homosexual population by that time. The bars were the only places where we could gather and feel like a community, and most of them paid off the cops. But the Black Cat was something special. Not only did it draw the biggest crowds, but its owner refused to pay off the cops, which got him into trouble with the politicians.

The city was alarmed about how open we were becoming, and then the California legislature passed a statute that gave the Alcoholic Beverage Control Board the right to revoke the liquor license of any place that served as a "resort for homosexuals." Then the guardians of the law began to harass the Black Cat in earnest. The vice squad would infiltrate the crowds of two hundred or so that came to see the shows, trying to make everyone feel like a dangerous criminal, and agents from the Alcoholic Beverage Control Department would park their squad cars outside, where we could see them writing down the names of people they recognized.

The owner of the bar did what he could to fight back in the courts, and the people in the bar fought back by refusing to budge. At the end of his performances, José Sarria had us all stand and sing, "God save us nelly queens" (instead of "My country 'tis of thee"), which was a way of defying the law and saying that we are human beings who deserve to be treated with respect. I had the strange thought that I wished my father could see me, as I stood there with my arm around Louie's shoulder singing for freedom that Sunday.

The newspapers were full of homosexuality at that time. At the end of 1955, three men were arrested in Boise, Idaho for having sex with teenaged boys, and a major witch hunt began. Innocent gay men fled from Idaho like wartime refugees, but over a thousand were hauled in for questioning and pressured into betraying their friends. The trial went on for well over a year, and people were doing their best to lie low until the terror was over.

I didn't have a steady boyfriend during those years. Once in a while I did meet someone sexy and we'd see each other for a few weeks or a couple of months, but nothing permanent ever seemed to come of it. For one period, I was seeing both members of a couple named Hank and Henry. They were in their fifties and had been together for over thirty years, long enough so that they both needed a little variety now and then. I had met Hank on Polk Street and taken him to my place. When Henry heard about how much fun we'd had, he was a little jealous, so Hank took me to their apartment and introduced me to his lover. Then he left us alone, so Henry could seduce me too. On other occasions, the three of us all got in bed together and had a good time. But when it was over, they stayed together and I went home alone. I wasn't lonely, though. I had my friends, I had my job, I had my cat, and I had my writing.

To prepare for the book on Whitman that I had decided to write, I read biographies, commentary, and criticism about him. My favorite at the time was an essay called "Images of Walt Whitman" by Leslie Fiedler. Fiedler called Whitman the "artificer of 'sincerity'," and said that Walt's most important creation had not been *Leaves of Grass* but Walt Whitman. He showed that Walt had been an accomplished poseur, creating in turn the roles of dandy, nurse, laborer, mystic, patriot, and "good gray poet." He had worn carpenter's clothes, even though he had worked only as the bookkeeper for his father's construction company while his brothers had pounded the nails. His claim to be robust and hardy was a mask for a soft, unmuscular physique. The famous "barbaric yawp" that he sounded over the rooftops actually came from a gentle, civilized, scholarly poet. One of my favorite photographs showed Walt raising his hand with a butterfly fearlessly perched on his outstretched finger, to prove how attuned he was to nature. Fiedler pointed out that Walt was wearing a sweater in the picture, which meant it was too cold to be butterfly season—and besides, the picture had been taken indoors. So the butterfly was obviously a fake that had been attached to his finger.

The same must have been true about Walt's facade of liberated sexuality. Only a few scholars openly acknowledged Walt's homosexual nature without condemning him for it. Others kept finding new ways to hide the obvious truth. His critics had portrayed him variously over the years, as an asexual ascetic, an immature masturbator, an active heterosexual, a bisexual, and a homosexually inclined virgin. I was especially incensed when one book claimed that Walt had been a "mild bisexual." I'm still trying to figure out what that means.

None of Walt's intimates had ever seen him display any interest in the opposite sex, even though women were always pursuing him. When one of his readers had sent a note to him saying that she wanted to beget his child on a mountaintop, he had scrawled on the envelope "?insane asylum." But the most dramatic case was Anne Gilchrist, a widowed English literary critic who had fallen in love with his poetry and wanted to move her household, complete with her grown children, to America to be near him. She had written:

> It is a sweet & precious thing this love; it clings so close, so close to the Soul and Body, all so tenderly dear, so beautiful, so sacred . . . never yet has bride sprung into her husband's arms with the joy with which I would take thy hand & spring from the shore.

He kept trying to stall her.

> I do not approve your American trans-settlement . . . Don't do any thing toward such a move, nor resolve on it, nor indeed make any move at all in it, without further advice from me . . .

She had ignored his advice and come anyway, moving into a house in Philadelphia, as close as possible to his home in Camden. He had visited her and they had befriended each other. But there had been no passion, and after two years of trying, she had moved back to England, defeated.

The only woman he'd had a close relationship with was his mother, a semi-literate Quaker, who had never let the fact that she was unable to understand her son's poetry come between them. Although he hadn't gotten along with his father, Walt had never been able to do enough for his mother. He had made long trips to visit her and, when they'd been separated, they'd kept up a steady correspondence. While he had been recuperating from his stroke in Washington, DC, she had lain dying at his brother's house in New Jersey. Finally, he had got out of his sickbed and had arrived at her side three days before she'd died. He was the only one mentioned by name in her final note to her children, which read:

> farewell my beloved sons farewell i have lived beyond all comfort in this world dont mourn for me my beloved sons and daughters farewell my dear beloved Walter

After her death, Walt had been inconsolable. He had moved into the room where she had spent her final months and had gone into a long period of mourning. He couldn't have loved her more if he'd been Oedipus Rex himself. If Walt was bisexual, I decided, then I was the Wizard of Oz.

Once I had mulled over what I had read, I thought I should begin my writing, but I soon found that it was not going to be an easy job. At first I thought that I would write it in the voices of the people in his life, and I began with Anne Gilchrist describing what she felt as she dreamed of her beloved from afar. I quickly realized that I didn't know enough about her, or about most of the people who were familiar with Walt, and I would have to do as much research on each of them as I had already done on Walt in order to make their observations seem authentic.

That much work was out of the question. So I thought of casting the novel in the form of a secret journal, which would allow me to use Walt's voice to describe his personal experiences. It would be hard to believe that anyone would keep such a journal as a child, so I had to begin later in his life. I tried recording his response to Anne Gilchrist's arrival in Philadelphia, but the writing came out strangely flat. It took me quite a while to find out what was wrong with it, but eventually I understood that I couldn't feel comfortable writing Walt's thoughts in his own words. It would be like trespassing. Also it wouldn't be easy to have my characters talk to each other in somebody's journal. It would be my reporting of Walt's reporting of what somebody else had said.

So I tried it again, as if Walt were telling his own story to a friend. But that didn't work either. For one thing it sounded phony. Why would somebody tell someone else what he already knew? I also realized that the language would be a problem. It wouldn't be easy to write in an authentic nineteenth-century voice. If I wrote the way Walt did, or if I imitated the way he sounded in Horace Traubel's recorded conversations, it would sound artificial and be hard for a lot of modern readers to understand. If I modernized it, it would also sound wrong. Eventually I got frustrated and put everything away.

The next time I sat down, a few days later, I spent the whole day sharpening pencils and arranging pads and wondering if it was a good investment to buy a typewriter. Then I went for a walk around the block. By the end of the day, I hadn't written a word.

The following time, I decided to tell the story in my own voice and to use the third person, so I could avoid all the language problems. This time I didn't know what was wrong, but I just wasn't happy with it. If I knew little about Walt's secret thoughts, I knew even less about his friends' minds. Frustrated, I put the project away for a while, hoping to get a better fix on it eventually. Writing had turned out to be a lot harder than I had anticipated.

Over the next few years, I tried again and again, amassing over two dozen false beginnings. Something was wrong with each of them, but I never lost my faith in the idea itself. I felt I just wasn't ready yet.

Failing to write wasn't all I did during those years. I continued my waiter's job, earning enough money to support myself in decent fashion and to accumulate some savings for later on. My collection of framed photographs grew and grew until it filled the walls of all my rooms. Mostly I seemed attracted to pictures of interesting faces, but there were lots of sunset and moonrise pictures, lots of pictures of appealing men's bodies, both clothed and nude, and as many curiosities and special-effects photos as I could find. For example, a face composed of an arrangement of seashells on the sand, or a picture that could be seen as an image of two men or as a landscape, depending on how you looked at it. Calamus would lay coiled in my lap, asleep, as I looked at the pictures. We spent many peaceful nights alone in those rooms.

We were alone when I felt a sudden pain in my chest, penetrating through to my back. I could hardly breathe, and I fell to my knees, sure that I was having a heart attack. I lay there in agony, expecting to die and wondering how many days it would be before my body was discovered. Worrying about who would feed Calamus helped me to take my mind off the pain. Eventually it subsided, but the next day I went to a doctor, afraid that it could happen again.

"You have gallstones," he told me. "Your gallbladder will have to come out."

I got depressed immediately. I had never faced any illness more major than the flu before that, and now I was going to be cut open and left incomplete. I scheduled the surgery for a few weeks after that, eager to get it over with, because every night I was having horrible nightmares about my body splitting open and my intestines falling all over Finocchio's floor. Thank God that Louie was there to keep me calm.

I went into the hospital on a fall day, feeling as if I would never come out alive. As I was being wheeled into the operating room, I said to Louie, who was scurrying to keep up with the gurney, "I love you very much."

Tears filled his eyes. "Don't talk like that," he said. "You're gonna be fine." When I awoke after surgery, there were tubes running up my nose and down into my stomach, attaching me to some kind of suction machine. My body ached sorely and I was afraid to move, for fear of ripping open. Louie was at the side of the bed. "Well, the sleeping beauty is finally awake," he said. "The doctor said you're gonna be fine. But if you ask me, you look like shit."

"Thanks a lot," I mumbled past the tubing. "You don't look so hot yourself."

"It's my hair," he said. "I just can't seem to do a thing with it. Do you think I oughta bleach it or somethin'?"

"Bleach your ass," I said. "I feel awful."

"Well, Miss Thing's got her rudeness back. Now I know she's gonna be all right."

It took me some months before I could feel like myself again. I had developed a new sense of my body. I no longer took it for granted, because I knew it wouldn't last forever. My scar was seven inches long, and at first I didn't want to be seen without my shirt. But eventually it faded, and I was able to pick up my sex life where I had left off. I had decided that, for the present, I didn't want a permanent lover. I enjoyed variety too much, and I could easily find someone at the Black Cat or at the Church Street Baths, where I could rent a locker and prowl the halls for quick sex—or at The Ensign at the foot of Mission Street, where dozens of drinks stood waiting on the bar for their owners, who were all downstairs having an orgy with one ear cocked for the bartender's signal that the police had been sighted, so they could return to their drinks in time. There were fewer complications playing the field. Louie taught me that lesson. I saw him very often. His relationship with Roger had ended and he had taken up with a minister's son named Kenneth, who felt so guilty about being queer that he couldn't have an orgasm.

"I don't know what makes me hang out with this guy," Louie said through his cigarette butt one day.

"So find somebody else," I said, distracted.

"Thanks a lot for the help," he said.

"Oh Louie, I didn't mean anything by it. It's just that there are so many guys out there. Why bother with Kenneth and his problems?"

"I don't know," he said. "I kind of feel sorry for him, I guess."

"More likely you feel horny for him, and you won't be satisfied until he gives you his sperm."

"Give me a little more credit than that," he said.

"Maybe you love him?" I suggested.

"Maybe."

"You're not sure?" I asked.

"Listen, honey, I've been through an awful lot of men in my time. I'm not even sure what love means anymore."

"Do you love me?"

"Of course," he said. "But that's different. We're sisters."

"You know what love means," I answered.

He smiled.

Kenneth went back home to the Middle West after a while. He had decided to be a minister, like his dad. Louie tried to tell him what a mistake he was making, but he wouldn't listen. A year later Kenneth showed up back in town with a new boyfriend in tow.

"Good," said Louie. "Let somebody else enjoy the frustration for a while."

Louie also hung around with a twenty-five-year-old woman named Marlene who worked in the beauty parlor with him, and she became part of our circle. Marlene's face was pretty enough, except that her eyes were so deeply set in their sockets that her forehead became an overhang that kept them in shadow, and looking into them was a bit like looking into twin caverns. She had a sparkle in them, however, whenever Louie or I wisecracked, and we all liked to get stoned on marijuana together and laugh up a storm. Since she seemed to be permanently between boyfriends, Marlene often came with us to listen to progressive jazz or to hang out at the Black Cat.

"Do you really think you'll meet a guy for yourself there?" I asked her once.

"Who knows?" she said. "There are plenty of straight men there too, you know."

"Don't remind me," I said. "It makes the cruising more complicated."

"The kind of guy I'm looking for would probably hang out in a place like this. I couldn't stand anyone who was too square to enjoy it here. Besides, I really enjoy gay company. It's so refreshing."

"I know what you mean," I said. But I wasn't sure that I did.

When Louie and I were alone one time, I talked to him about Marlene. "Do you think she's secretly in love with you?" I asked.

"Could be," he said.

"Doesn't that bother you?"

"Why should it? She knows I'm queer."

"But what if she's really hoping you'll convert?"

"Then she's got a long wait, Mary. Listen, don't you worry about Marlene. She'd rather have fun with us than be married. She's a fruit fly. You know, a fag hag."

"I hate those terms," I said. "They're so undignified."

"Well, they're honest, honey. It don't mean I don't love her. It's just what she is."

"As long as she's happy," I said.

"Who's happy?" said Louie. He had just broken up with another boyfriend, an American Indian named Joe Eagle, who had dreams of being a movie star and had left for Hollywood. "If you want to know the truth, I'm gettin' tired of this burg."

"You don't mean that," I said.

"Well, maybe not," he replied. "But we been here a pretty long time now."

Louie and Marlene weren't the only friends I saw. I also became close with a woman named Cynthia Chin, who lived next door to my house. Cynthia was rare—a fat Chinese woman with shiny bangs hanging straight across her forehead and the rest of her hair pulled back into a bun. There were dimples in her cheeks when she smiled, which was often. She always wore loose, brocaded silk cheongsams in deliciously rich shades. I had seen her around for months, but hadn't spoken to her until one day when her shopping bag broke on the way back from the grocery, and I helped her carry the loose items up to her apartment. There were four dozen eggs among the wreckage, and I said, "I hope you like omelets. You have enough here for ten people." That's when she told me that she ran a brothel.

I dropped in every once in a while during the slow hours in the afternoon, and I felt right at home. It reminded me of Miss Wanda's house in Chicago. Eight women worked for Cynthia. She was all business with her employees, but she treated them fairly and they respected her. The girls enjoyed making a fuss over me, and served me tea and cookies. "I hope you don't mind that I'm not a paying customer," I said.

"You a refreshing change," Cynthia observed. "Gay boys are more gentlemen."

"Not when we're chasing ass," I said.

"Nobody gentleman then," she said.

"So, what's a nice girl like you doing in a place like this?" I asked.

"Why? Isn't this nice place?" she asked.

"Very nice. I was just wondering."

"I do the same you do in Finocchio. Make a living."

"I used to work in a place like this," I told her.

"Why you stop?"

"It's a long story."

"We all have long story. We should start here, not look backward."

"That's usually a good idea," I said. "But I wonder if it's really possible."

"You should come back to this business, maybe for gay boys. You make good money that way. I have friend in New York who does it."

"But I have a job."

"Don't you get tired?"

She was right. Waiting on tables was getting exhausting, and I hadn't appeared in a show for a long time. I continued to try my hand at writing occasionally, but I still hadn't found that magic sentence that would lead me into the rest of the novel, and I kept on putting it aside.

As time passed, I felt more and more like an authentic San Franciscan. In 1961, José Sarria, the comic opera star of the Black Cat, ran for a seat on San Francisco's Board of Supervisors and got 6,000 votes, including mine. Nobody ever expected him to win. The whole point was that he was able to run in spite of the fact that the gay bars were still being harassed and everybody knew his reputation as a flaming queen who performed at one of them. What José proved was that we were real people, even if we ourselves didn't think so. I had never been much interested in voting before then, but I've made it a point ever since. I'm often on the losing side, but at least I get to have my say.

Louie wasn't feeling as connected to the city as I was. He hadn't had a steady boyfriend in a while and he was getting more and more restless and depressed as the next couple of years passed by. The one thing that eventually lightened him up was Marlene's wedding plans.

It was a marriage made in the Black Cat. She and Louie and I had gone there, as we did often, and I had run into Hilary, the man who had first rigged me up in drag at Finocchio's. Hilary was no longer performing. He had graduated from school and was working as an architect for a large firm.

"If I want to get anywhere in my company, I have to put a picture of my wife and family on my desk," he said.

"Can't you fake it?" I asked.

"No. They expect to meet the little lady at company parties."

"I suppose they don't know about your past at Finocchio's?"

"Are you kidding? If they ever find out, I'll be out on my ass. As far as they know I'm a respectable citizen, except that I'm not married."

"But how can you stand being married? Aren't you gay?"

"Only part-time, my dear. I really enjoy sleeping with women too."

"Hilary, I'd like you to meet Marlene. Marlene, do you promise to love, honor, and . . ."

"I do," Marlene said, her eyes aglow.

Actually, it didn't happen quite like that, but it was almost as fast. Louie was the best man and hairdresser, and I was Marlene's attendant-at-large. "Always a bridesmaid," Louie complained, but he was really happy for Marlene. The wedding took place at a little church in San Mateo, and then we all came back to my place for the party. All our friends were there: the entire staff of the beauty parlor; Hilary's old friends from Finocchio (but no one from the architectural firm); even Cynthia Chin and several of her employees from next door. We all smoked lots of marijuana and drank lots of champagne and ate as much as we could of a ridiculously large, tilted wedding cake that the drag queen Robin Starling had made herself. By the time everyone left, I was in a complete stupor. I left the mess of soggy paper plates and trailing crepe paper and overflowing ashtrays, and passed out on the couch.

I awoke a couple of hours later to the sound of sirens and the flashing of a red light. Something smelled funny. It was smoke. Then I realized that there were flames growing in the windows! The curtains had caught fire from one of the chairs, where someone had probably left a smoldering cigarette. Half groggy, I jumped up. The flames had not yet reached the doorway, but it was only a matter of moments. I rushed to my desk and grabbed my copy of *Leaves of Grass* and my manuscripts of poetry and the notes for the novel, clutching them all to my chest. The flames were gobbling up picture after picture on my overdecorated walls, and I reached to save the four remaining Minerva White photographs. The heat was growing unbearable, and I couldn't stop coughing. There was no time to gather any clothes, so I ran for the door—pursued by a sheet of flame—and made it into the hallway. Then I heard a frightened meow, coming from the bedroom. Calamus! I dropped my salvaged items and tried to get back into the apartment. But it was too late. The ceiling collapsed and blocked my path. My eyes filling with tears, I gathered what I had saved and rushed down the stairs, where Cynthia Chin gathered me to her ample bosom, and I cried my eyes out for my poor little cat.

I moved to Louie's place until I could decide what to do next. Cynthia came over to see how I was doing, and we sat around Louie's kitchen table to discuss plans.

"Personally, I think we oughta blow this burg," said Louie. "I can be a hair burner anyplace. I need a change of scenery."

"Me, too," I said, depressed.

"Why don't you both go to New York?" Cynthia suggested. "My friend could start Dell in business like mine. Good business, you know."

Louie and I looked at each other, and we both shrugged our shoulders at the same time. A week later, we were on our way back to New York.

CHAPTER TWENTY

We landed in New York with enough money between us to live comfortably until we could set ourselves up in business. At first we stayed at a small hotel in midtown, but before either of us even looked for a place to live, I asked Louie to do me a special favor. We took a cab downtown and got out at the entrance to the Brooklyn Bridge.

"Now what?" Louie asked.

"Now we walk across it," I said.

"Don't tell me you're going to pull that shit again. I didn't fly three thousand miles to fish your body out of the river."

"I don't want to jump, silly. I just don't want to be afraid of this place anymore."

"Afraid of the bridge?"

"Afraid of the whole city."

"You know something, Miss Della? You're weird."

"Too weird for you, Lulu?"

"No, just weird. Which way do we go?"

We walked across the pedestrian footpath as I had done a decade earlier. A cool breeze from the river stroked our faces. I noticed that barbed wire had been strung along the top of the railing, probably to prevent people from doing the sort of thing I had done.

"Too bad they didn't put some of that across the railing of the Golden Gate," I mused.

"What're you talkin' about, hon?" Louie inquired.

"That barbed wire," I said, pointing to the barrier. "In San Francisco, jumping from the bridge is as popular a method for suicides as it is here."

"Swell," he said. "Maybe you guys should form a club."

"No, really," I continued. "I heard that nobody understands why suicides jump off the Golden Gate facing back toward the city instead of looking at the setting sun, but I figured it out."

"Okay, mastermind, I'll bite. But this story better have a good punch line. Why don't they face the sunset when they jump?"

"Because the walking path is on the side toward the city. They'd have to cross two lanes of traffic to get to the railing on the western side . . ."

". . . and they wouldn't want to get run over, right?" He groaned. "Oh, you are one sick queen, Miss Della. Can we finish up here? It's gettin' windy, and I don't want my hair to get messed up."

When we reached the center of the bridge, I walked to the edge and peered down into the East River. It was much farther away than I had remembered. I didn't expect to see a vision this time, but I thought at least I might see my reflection. What I saw was black water. There was no face visible in it, neither Walt's nor mine, and there were no spokes of radiant light, only murky wavelets driven by the wind and a small tugboat heading from Brooklyn toward New York Harbor. I took a deep breath and exhaled, making a *whooshing* sound. "Are you all right?" Louie asked.

"Yes. I'm fine, really fine."

"Great," he said. "Now let's get down to business."

Louie had decided to open his own beauty shop in Greenwich Village, and he immediately started looking for a space and some hairdressers and manicurists. I had decided to follow Cynthia's advice and set up a gay brothel, so I also needed a space and some employees. Eventually, Louie opened "Hairdos" on Bleecker Street and found an apartment nearby. And I used some money I had saved, plus a little I had borrowed from Cynthia Chin, to buy some furniture and rent a brownstone on a respectable-looking block of East Fifty-Second Street. I wanted my establishment to be a class act, not a cheap whorehouse.

I didn't want any more trouble with the law than I needed, so I made sure to avoid any underage "chicken." And I double-checked to see that the boys I hired to work for me were eighteen- to twenty-two-year-olds who had come to the city to be models or actors, and who needed the extra few bucks to see them through until they got rich and famous. I gave them a good split. Instead of the usual 50 percent for the house and 50 for the boy, I gave them 60 percent of what they earned, and I took 40 for the house.

I invested most of what I had in fixing up the place and paying off the proper authorities so they would look the other way. Cynthia's friend, a very fat, amiable guy named Sam, who wore an improbably large, curlicued handlebar mustache and lots of jewelry, put me in touch with the right people, and I soon had a good-looking collection of employees, set up in simply decorated bedrooms. With a few carefully phrased ads about escorts in the right magazines, I drew a clientele of middle-aged businessmen and professionals. The money was starting to come in, the customers were satisfied, the boys were making money, and I was content.

Aside from a few friends, the one thing I missed most about San Francisco was Mount Tamalpais, which was just outside of town. Louie and I had spent many afternoons there in the sunshine. He had usually napped while I had read. My favorite thing had been to take my shoes off and walk barefoot, remembering, as I felt the grass tickling the bottom of my feet, Walt's mystical love of it and the secret meanings he had gleaned from it:

> . . . now I see it is true, what I guess'd at,
> What I guess'd when I loaf'd on the grass . . .

Most of the grass in New York is imprisoned behind walls and fences, but I did go to Central Park as often as I could, and I removed my shoes and took long solitary walks. It was as close to nature as I could get, but unless I went there right after it had rained, the grass felt strangely dusty between my toes.

That was the fall when John F. Kennedy was shot. I had never paid much attention to presidents since Franklin Roosevelt, whom none of his successors had lived up to. But Kennedy had been the one with the most promise. I had even made a point of listening to his speeches, and I remembered the argument I had had with myself about trusting him during the Cuban missile crisis the year before, when I thought all of us were sure to be blown to hell by a nuclear war. When the news that he had been shot came over the radio, I didn't take it too seriously. Presidents were often the targets of foiled assassination attempts, and Kennedy was young and invincible. None of the johns kept their appointments that afternoon, so the boys and I sat around looking glum and playing gin rummy. I remember I was standing at the toilet peeing when one of them came in to wash his hands and said, "Did you hear that he died?"

"He what?" I asked incredulously.

He didn't need to answer.

I thought of the moment I'd heard Roosevelt was dead. It was in San Francisco, when I'd just returned from the prison camp. It was already old news by the time I heard it, and it was soon overshadowed by the letter about Chester's death. This loss of a president felt much worse.

Most of the boys went home when they heard what had happened, and I spent the weekend watching television—amazed when I saw the murder of Lee Harvey Oswald by Jack Ruby as it was actually happening, during a news report. I sat through the funeral, sniffling when Kennedy's little son saluted, and by the end of the day I was exhausted, in bed with a muscle spasm and a heating pad because nothing would ever seem safe anymore.

Somebody on television had the bad taste to read Whitman's poem on Lincoln's death, "O Captain! My Captain!" In school I had liked that one least, and I decided to do something about it. I chose some lines from "When Lilacs Last in the Dooryard Bloom'd," which was much more eloquent about Lincoln's death.

> . . . with the cities draped in black,
> . . . with the silent sea of faces and the unbared heads . . .
> With the tolling tolling bells' perpetual clang,

Here, coffin that slowly passes,
I give you my sprig of lilac . . .
For the sweetest, wisest soul of all my days and lands . . .

I sent it as a sympathy note to Jackie Kennedy, feeling better because at least I had made a gesture, no matter how small. I doubt that she ever saw it among the millions of condolences she must have received, but I did get a nice printed thank-you message a few weeks later.

Soon after the assassination I got myself a new cat, a black one with blue eyes, who had a Siamese pitched wail. I thought of naming him Calamus II, but I knew he could never replace my old friend, whom I still missed sorely. So I called my new pet Camerado, instead. He was a fearless little beggar, who wandered in and out of the rooms, occasionally frightening the customers by crawling out from under their beds and joining them with a yowl in the middle of their sex. But when I went to bed, he always slept at my feet, and I soon learned to love him for himself. My sense of peace was slowly restored. I was proud that I had been able to construct a workable new life with so little trouble, to make a home for myself and to provide employment for ambitious young men and pleasure for those in need of relief. Then one evening, about six months after I had opened, while the bedrooms were full and several men were nervously waiting their turn in the front room, there was suddenly a loud knock on the door. "Police!" a voice yelled. "Open up!"

The cops, claiming that they were looking for drugs, made sure to destroy all the furniture I had paid so much money for. The boys who worked for me were roughed up a little and warned not to come back. The customers were allowed to flee in terror, to save their reputations. And I had to pay a stiff fine, which drained most of what I had earned. But I luckily escaped imprisonment, since this was my first offense in New York State. Later I found out that the owner of a similar establishment nearby, which was funded by organized crime, didn't want the competition I offered and had threatened to expose the cops who were taking his bribes if they didn't stop taking mine and close down my operation. It was the free enterprise system at work.

The raid didn't scare me out of the business since I knew that most such operations were safe for long enough to be quite profitable. I had just planted myself in the wrong place. I had to start at square one again—but I didn't have as much money to set up the same sort of house. So I rented a floor in a converted brownstone building on West Forty-Seventh Street, in a neighborhood called Hell's Kitchen.

Sam told me that most male brothels in Hell's Kitchen got their boys from the Port Authority Bus Terminal as they arrived in the big city, freshly escaped from Smalltown, USA. I refused to do that, because runaway boys were usually only fifteen or sixteen even if they told you otherwise, and I didn't want to be the one to introduce them to "the life" (which is what we called prostitution). So I decided that I would "rescue" young men who were already hustling on the streets—if they were eighteen or over—and give them a warm, dry, indoor place to work at their chosen profession.

I met one or two boys by cruising the streets myself, and when I showed them the apartment I had fixed up and explained that I would give them a fair share of the money their work earned and not exploit them in any way, they were glad to tell their friends about the offer, so that it didn't take more than a few weeks to staff the place completely. And D.D. Blake—which is what I told them my name was, in order to avoid getting too personal—was back in business again.

There were times when it felt like I was running a kind of school as groups of them "graduated" out into the world and a new "class" would arrive to take their place. In spite of their toughness and bad backgrounds, they were a lovely bunch of boys in their way. Although all of them did claim to be eighteen, some were probably only seventeen. I tried to convince anyone who looked younger than that to go back where he came from and give home life another try. Few were older than twenty, since by that time they were usually ready to take off on their own.

The boys had their own ways of being individuals. One wore only blue. Another changed his name several times a week, as if he were trying identities on for size. A third couldn't stop looking in mirrors, even when he was talking to someone. It seemed as if he couldn't get over his own beauty, but I think he was trying to reassure himself that he was really there. They came in several colors, but most of them had similarly skinny torsos and arms with fledgling muscles, and all of them had the same needy look in their eyes, which they tried to hide behind a thin mask of bravado. I fed them as well as I could to put a little meat on their ribs, and I gave them as much love as I could, because I knew they would turn into totally hardened cynics without it.

The johns who came to have sex with them ranged in age from their mid-twenties to their mid-sixties. Most of them were furtive and nervous, as if they hated themselves for sinking into such degradation, and I tried to make sure that they didn't take their misery out on my boys. Some of them wore wedding bands or had rings of pale skin where they had removed them, which said that they had other lives to live and that this event was a moment in a different dimension. Some of them were homely or insecure and didn't know any other way to find the sex they needed. Some of them were good-looking enough, but had to pay for their sex so they could feel superior to their partners and not risk any emotional involvement. Most of them were small businessmen or office workers or teachers, I guessed. But on a couple of occasions the gentle, middle-aged men with mild eyes who politely asked the boys to beat them with belts turned out to be priests who were helplessly breaking their vows of celibacy. We had every imaginable type there, and most of them had the good time they were looking for without damaging the merchandise.

You may not believe this, but most of my own sex was still effected with my trusty right hand. I could meet men easily enough, but it didn't seem as urgent to me as it had when I was younger. I didn't generally have sex with the boys in the house myself. But occasionally, if the mood was right and there was some honest feeling between us, I did.

One boy I remember was named Curtis. He looked about eighteen years old, although he might have been younger. He had a dark-cocoa-brown complexion and a cute kind of toughness that made me want to soothe and cuddle him. When I asked him if that would be all right, he said, "Sho. What you gon' give me fo' it?"

"A kiss," I said.

"Dat ain't no big deal," he replied. "I already had me plenty o' dem."

"Do you want me to pay you?" I asked.

He nodded.

"But I'm the boss here," I said.

"Ain't nobody mah boss, D.D. Ah mah own boss."

"I just thought it might be a friendly thing to do. You know, just to feel good."

"D.D., just cause Ah works here don' mean Ah's queer. Ah just does dis fo' a livin' right now."

"Oh, I'm sorry," I said. "I thought the boys here liked what they were doing."

"Ah laks it all right," he told me. "You done had any complaints 'bout me from de customers?"

"No."

"So?"

"So, like you say, no big deal," I said. "I just thought we might make each other feel good. But I'd rather not pay for the privilege."

"Suit yo'self."

"Okay, forget I asked you."

"Okay den . . . D.D.?"

"Yes?"

"Maybe Ah come by yo' room later—if Ah ain't too busy. Jus' fo' a visit."

"Suit yourself."

"Now you got it. Ah be by later, hear?"

"Mm-hmm," I answered, pretending to be busy with my cooking. I knew Curtis was gay, but like a lot of the boys he didn't want to know it himself, and he certainly didn't want anybody else to know it. It was part of their front. To hear them tell it, they were all just making a living and not having any fun at their work. For all I knew, that was true in one or two cases. But almost all the boys were gay, whether they said so or not.

Late that night Curtis came to my room with a cocky air. I was already in bed. "You jus' like dem johns always sittin' in de parlor," he said, unzipping his pants. "Can't wait to get yo' hands on mah big, black dick."

"It's not your dick I wanted to see, Curtis. It's you."

"What you mean?" he asked, furrowing his brow but continuing to remove his pants.

"I just wanted to be with you, to be your friend. Now come over here."

"Jus' you 'member now—Ah don' do nothin'. Ah just gets done."

"I'll remember."

He sank heavily onto the bed and sat beside me, waiting.

"Okay, D.D. Now what?" he said.

I put my arm around his shoulder. "Just lie back and relax," I said, drawing him down beside me. I let him get comfortable, and then I started to massage his shoulders. After a while he turned face down so I could continue my work more effectively.

"Dat feel real good," he said into the pillow.

"My treat," I said. "There's no charge."

He laughed a little, but in a short time he began to snore softly. I turned out the lights and went to sleep beside him. A few hours later, I woke to find him snuggled in my arms and sucking his thumb. He opened his eyes, pulled out his thumb, and kissed me on the lips. I kissed him back. Then he slid down and started to suck my cock, which rose to the occasion.

"Y'all wanna fuck me?" he whispered.

"If that's what you want, Curtis."

"Yeah," he said softly. "Dat be okay."

I entered him slowly and carefully, even though I was sure I was not the first to do so. His body responded with excitement, thrashing hard against the bed while his anal sphincter held tight to my pumping cock. Finally I shot my load and slowly removed myself from him.

"What about you?" I asked.

"Ah already done come," he said, bringing my hand to the tip of his cock, where I could feel the slimy wetness as proof.

"Then let's go to sleep," I said.

Before he left my room the next afternoon, he said, "Don' you be tellin' nobody 'bout dis, 'cause Ah'll get you fo' sure if you do."

"I won't tell," I promised.

I had sex with Curtis once or twice after that, and we became friends. Once in a while we simply slept together without sex. He trusted me enough to tell me when somebody asked him to peddle drugs, and I cared enough about him to talk him out of it. When he finally left the house, it was to go to a job at a tree nursery in New Jersey.

I wish I had had as easy a time with Walt Whitman's sex life as I did with Curtis's. I tried again and again to work on my book, which I'd decided to call *Song of Myself,* after Walt's greatest poem. I thought I'd begin by describing his relationship with Peter Doyle, the young streetcar conductor, but that was where I got stuck.

What had actually happened between them? Of course there was no record left, other than veiled hints and oblique references, which could be read in several ways. It hadn't been a time when two men could casually have sex without giving it a second thought. Or had it been? They were certainly too close to be "just good friends." Of course they had had a father-son relationship, but that didn't preclude sex, not judging by some of the May-December gay couples I'd met. In fact, Curtis and I were about the same ages as Pete and Walt were when they fell in love.

I fervently hoped, for Walt's sake, that there had been lovely, hot, wild sex between the two of them every day of their relationship, but I doubted that there had been. Whatever had happened, I couldn't bring myself to open the door of Walt's bedroom and imagine America's greatest poet in bed with the cock of an eighteen-year-old trolley conductor in his mouth. It seemed sacrilegious, even if it had actually happened. I was all tied up in knots trying to figure out what to do next, and Walt's records were worse than no help.

For all his praises of love and the body, he sometimes sounded as tortured about his sex life as Martin Gale, the man I'd met in the Pittsburgh YMCA. The following notebook entry is the strangest passage Walt ever composed. It was evidently written after a fight with Pete, whom he cautiously referred to as "16.4"—a code that used "16" for Pete's first initial and "4" for the "D" in Doyle—as well as erasing the word "him" and covering it with "her":

July 15, 1870

Cheating, childish abandonment of myself, fancying what does not really exist in another, but is all the time in myself alone—utterly deluded & cheated by myself, & my own weakness—REMEMBER WHERE I AM MOST WEAK, & most lacking. Yet always preserve a kind spirit & demeanor to 16. BUT PURSUE HER NO MORE . . . It is IMPERATIVE, that I obviate & remove myself (& my orbit) at all hazards, from this incessant enormous & abnormal PERTURBATION . . . TO GIVE UP ABSOLUTELY & for good, from the present hour, this FEVERISH, FLUCTUATING, useless UNDIGNIFIED PURSUIT of 16.4 —too long, (much too long) persevered in,—so humiliating—It must come at last & had better come now—

(It cannot possibly be a success) LET THERE FROM THIS
HOUR BE NO FALTERING, NO GETTING at all
henceforth, (NOT ONCE, UNDER any circumstances)—
avoid seeing her, or meeting her, or any talk or explanations—
or ANY MEETING WHATEVER, FROM THIS HOUR
FORTH, FOR LIFE

I didn't know what to make of that. Was Pete totally unaware of Walt's
sexual interest, or was the subject something other than sex? I felt even less
able to render their private relationship in fiction than I had before, in spite
of the following letter of reconciliation, which Walt wrote to Pete about two
weeks later:

July 30, 1870

Pete, there was something in that hour from 10 to 11 o'clock
(parting though it was) that has left me pleasure & comfort
for good—I never dreamed that you made so much of having
me with you, nor that you could feel so downcast at losing
me. I foolishly thought it was all on the other side. But all I
will say further on the subject is, I now see clearly, that was all
wrong . . .

Had it all been a lover's quarrel? Probably, but what had it really been about?
I thought about it for quite a while and came up with over a dozen
possibilities. But I couldn't simply choose one as being any closer to reality
than all the others, so I decided to write about another part of his life.

This time I tried to describe the relationship he'd had with Harry
Stafford, the young printer's assistant he had met in New Jersey while
recuperating from his stroke. Harry was eighteen years old when they met
and Walt was fifty-seven. Harry was passionately involved with Walt, to the
point of wanting to dress like him. In one of his letters, he wrote, with an
occasional lapse of spelling:

I have been thinking of the suit of cloths which I am to have
like yours: I have had myself all pictured out with a suit of gray,
and a white slouch hat on about fifty times, since you spoke of
it; the fellows will call me Walt then. I will have to do
something great and good in honor of the name. What will it
be?

But Harry was also worried about having such a relationship:

I think of you where ever I have a moment to think, I don't
get much time to think about anyone for when I am not
thinking of my business I am thinking of what I am shielding.

I want to try and make a man of my-self, and do what is right
if I can do it.

Was Harry willing to announce their relationship by trying to dress like Walt,
and then did he grow afraid that everyone would think he was "unnatural"?
Was his sex life with Walt the thing he was shielding, and did he feel like less
of a man because of it? I knew that something had caused a good deal of
tension between them. Could it be that Walt had pursued Harry in vain, as
he might have pursued Pete? Whatever the source of their arguments, when
they made up, Harry could be very apologetic:

I have come up to ask your forgiveness . . . I know that it is
my falt and not yours. Can you forgive me and take me back
and love me the same I will try by the grace of God to do
better. I cannot give you up . . .

Your lovin but bad tempered,
Harry.

And Walt could be magnanimously forgiving:

Of the occasional ridiculous little storms & squalls of the past
I have quite discarded them from my memory—& I hope you
will too—the other recollections overtop them altogether, &
occupy the only permanent place in my heart—as a manly
loving friendship for you does also, & will while life lasts

Walt gave Harry a ring, which Harry returned several times, perhaps from a
fear of commitment to Walt or to a life that he was afraid to lead—or maybe
he was just being petulant:

I wish you would put the ring on my finger again, it seems to
me there is something that is wanting to compleete our
friendship when I am with you. I have tride to studdy it out
but cannot find out what it is. You know when you put it on
there was but one thing to part it from me and that was death.

What was the missing part of their relationship? Was it sex? Was Harry
afraid of his own nature or of Walt's? Was Walt honest with Harry about his
desires? Was he honest with himself? As the questions multiplied, I was
beginning to feel that the more I read about him the less I knew. He was
more than his words could say—that was the only thing I knew for sure.
Once more I put my book away and told myself that it takes time before a
book is ready to be born and I had to be patient. After all, Walt had spent
his whole life patiently producing nine different editions of *Leaves of Grass*
before he was satisfied.

While I was torturing myself with my literary career, poor Louie was
torturing himself with yet another love affair. He had taken up with a young

man named Wesley, who lived with his parents in Queens and saw Louie on the sly. Wesley worked as a librarian in a branch near his parents' home, and he came into Manhattan mostly on weekends. I had never warmed to him, always held at a distance by the strange look in his eyes, an odd combination of ardor and fear, which made him seem like a zealous rabbit. Louie, of course, imagined that he loved the man who was hiding beneath that superficial appearance. But the treatment he got for his efforts proved that Wesley's eyes didn't lie.

"He's drivin' me crazy," Louie complained over a cup of espresso at the Café Figaro, near his MacDougal Street apartment. "He keeps cancelin' our dates 'cause he's afraid his parents are gonna be suspicious. I never know if he's gonna show up or not. Do you know how many suppers I threw in the garbage can because of him?"

"So dump him," I said. "Frankly, Lulu, I think you can do better. I know you like your men a little weird, but he's beyond weird, if you ask me."

"Sure, it's easy for you to talk. You can have your pick of the boys in your little stable whenever you want. But it ain't so easy for me to keep startin' again. Maybe you haven't looked in the mirror lately, Mister Madam, but the two of us ain't gettin' any younger. Besides, I kind of like Wesley."

"Why?"

"Because he's weird."

We both laughed, and then I said, "Are you sure that's what you really want?"

"Let's put it this way, Della. It's what I got."

"It's your funeral," I said, and we raised our espresso cups in a mock toast to madness.

Things didn't stay that simple, of course. The next time I saw Louie— for lunch at Lindy's, near my place—he said, "Now I'm startin' to worry about Wesley. First he was afraid of his folks and now he's gettin' afraid of everythin' he sees."

"What do you mean?" I asked.

"Well, for example, he calls and tells me he can't see me last night. Then, an hour later, he shows up anyway. So I ask him what happened and he says, 'I was tryin' to throw them off the trail.' 'Throw who off what trail?' I ask him. And he says, 'I can't tell you.' 'Is it your folks?' I say. And he says, 'Yes, I think they hired somebody to follow me, maybe the FBI.' 'You can't hire the FBI to follow anybody you want,' I tell him. So he says, 'My father has connections, you know.' So I say, 'Are you sure they didn't follow you here?' And he says, 'I don't know.' Then he goes over to the window and looks between two slats in the blinds—you know, like they do in the Alan Ladd movies?—and he says, 'That might be them.' So, idiot that I am, I go over to look. And who is he pointin' at? The panhandler on the corner, this creep who's been standin' there like a cigar store Indian since I first moved in.

'That ain't the FBI,' I tell him. 'That's Reuben the panhandler.' So you know what he says? He says, 'You're one of them, ain't you?' "

"Is this for real?" I asked.

"Would I lie to a sister?"

"Lulu, the guy's a real case. What makes you stay with him?"

"He's a good lay," Louie said. And we both laughed so hard, we almost choked on our cream sodas.

"Seriously," I continued, when we had regained our composure. "He sounds like more trouble than you can handle."

"The truth is, he ain't even such a good lay," Louie confessed. "Even when we do have sex without any problems, he cries afterward, like he can't forgive himself for committin' such a sin."

"Sounds like a real party," I said. "You'd be better off coming up to see some of my boys."

"No offense, Miss D, but the day I have to pay for it is the day I pack it in. I have my pride too, you know."

"Not when it comes to Wesley, you don't."

He jarred his head back, as if he had been slapped. "Thanks, I needed that," he said, quoting a dozen B movies at once.

"You'll get worse than that if you don't take better care of yourself. There are no homes for fallen women, you know."

"Oh, I just love it when you're mean to me, you adorable bastard," he squealed.

A week or two later, we were having Sunday brunch downtown when Louie told me, "The nut job tried to kill me last night."

"Who? Wesley?"

"No, Mamie Eisenhower. Of course Wesley. Who else?"

I laughed so hard that I spilled some of my Bloody Mary. "Now look what you did to my shirt," I complained.

"Your shirt'll get worse than that if you don't listen. This is serious."

"Okay, what happened?"

"Well, he comes over to keep our date, only an hour late for a change, but he's actin' kinda strange."

"How could you tell?"

"Don't be a smart-ass. Anyway, he takes off his shirt, and I say, 'What about the pants, big boy? You can't have sex with your pants on, you know.' 'I have to keep them on,' he says. So, like a dummy, I ask, 'What for?' And he says, 'In case I have to get away fast.' 'Don't tell me it's the goddamned FBI again,' I say. And you know what he says? Get this. He says, 'No, it's the Jews.' "

Both of us started to laugh then. "You have great taste in men," I told him.

"Fuck you," he said, smiling. "Anyway, I had to keep from laughin' at him, 'cause he was dead serious. 'I don't want to upset you,' I tell him, 'but I'm gettin' kinda nervous about all this. So maybe you better go.' So then he says, 'I can't go. I have to hide here.' 'Hide here?' I say. 'You gotta be kiddin'.' 'No,' he says. 'I ain't kiddin'. And if you don't help me, they're gonna get you too.'"

The waiter interrupted the story, to clear the table and bring us our dessert.

"Go on," I said when we were alone again. "This is getting good."

"I'm glad you're enjoyin' yourself, sweetie. It sure wasn't my idea of a good time. Anyway, I say to him, 'Listen, honey, the Jews ain't after you. Why the fuck should the Jews care about you?' You'll love what he says next. Are you ready for this? He says, 'The Jews are after me because they know that I'm Jesus Christ, and they want to kill me.' Well, I have a lot of trouble keepin' a straight face. But I do, and I tell him, 'Wesley, if you're Jesus Christ, then I'm your mother the Virgin Mary, and I say it's time to go home to bed!' That's when he tries to kill me."

We both lost half our cappuccinos laughing then, and the waiter had to help us clean it up. But it was worth the embarrassment.

"So, what happened?" I asked, once order had been restored to the table.

"Oh, so I finally got you interested," he said. "Well, he grabs me by the throat and he starts chokin' me."

"Did he hurt you?"

"No, he's not strong enough. I just slap him in the face, and he lets go of my throat and starts to cry like a baby. So I calm him down the best I can, and I hand him his clothes and I say to him, 'Honey, take my advice. Go home and see a good headshrinker. You've got problems.' I mean, I feel sorry for the guy and all that, but I don't want to be his mother. I'm only lookin' to get laid. And when he gets to the door, I tell him, 'Here's some more advice. Don't come back here. I ain't gonna be home from now on.'"

"Good for you," I said.

"You don't think I was too mean, or anythin' like that?"

"Hell no. He's dangerous. If he comes back and you let him in, I'll send *you* to a shrink. I'm glad that Wesley's out of your hair. He was no good for you. But what are you going to do now?"

"I don't know about you, my dear," he said. "But as soon as we're finished with brunch, I'm goin' up to the Everard Baths, and I ain't comin' out till tomorrow. I still need to get laid."

I decided to go with him, so he wouldn't feel abandoned. We took a cab up to Twenty-Eighth Street and went into a decrepit-looking building. On the main floor we gave our money to a sour-faced clerk who sat in a cashier's cage across from a scummy-looking luncheonette. Upstairs, we hung our clothes in our little cubicles and joined the men in towels who were patrolling the hallways looking for an open doorway that might mean sex.

The management probably never had the floors washed, because within a few minutes the soles of our feet were black. Louie took me down to the basement, where there was a swimming pool filled with murky water, a steam room with slimy walls, a shower room with only half its nozzles in working order, and a little side room almost filled with a narrow table on which a fat guy gave massages to the customers. While Louie disappeared upstairs, I took a shower and visited the masseur, which made me feel relaxed and sexy. Then I walked the halls and finally met somebody, who gave me a blow job. I looked for Louie, but I couldn't find him, so I put on my clothes and left. My whole stay was no more than an hour. But the next time I spoke to Louie, I learned that he had kept his word and stayed the night. He had enjoyed himself so much that he went back once or twice a week for many years, saying that as a way to get sex, it sure beat dating a nutcase.

Another way Louie liked to get sex in the summertime was to take the train and the ferry out to Fire Island. There we could escape from the harsher realities of life, in a town called Cherry Grove that had been growing gayer and gayer since the 1920s, until it was over 90 percent gay and lesbian in the 1960s.

The Grove was built along boardwalks that substituted for sidewalks and held the community perched unrealistically above the land, as if the whole town planned to stay only a short while. It was full of cute little houses painted bright colors and given funny, sexy names like "The Pillows of Society" or "Spank You Very Much" or "Bottoms Up." I told Louie that if I ever built one, I would call it "The Object of My Erection." But I doubted that I ever would. The houses were as fragile as Fire Island itself, which was really little more than a successful sandbar, and any of the hurricanes that swept up the East Coast each autumn might blow away several roofs or entire homes, and seriously damage the delicate sand dunes on which the resort's existence depended.

In this precarious environment, the householders would hold elaborate parties with all the guests dressed in pink or black or white, or costumed in outrageous drag to go with some theme like "Dante's Inferno" or "The Body Beautiful" or "Tropical Paradise." We went to one called "Arabian Nights," both of us arrayed in sheer veils and shiny lamé pasha pants. The crowd was so large and so heavily costumed that there probably wasn't a spare feather, veil, or sequin available for fifty miles around. Everyone drank and danced far into the night, and then they changed into simpler clothes and went to the moonlit woods outside of town to hold large-scale orgies that spilled over onto the boardwalks, where they were politely ignored by the townsfolk.

388

The next night, when we went to the Sea Shack, the local bar, the contrast with all this freedom was overwhelming. It was like being reminded of reality in the middle of a lovely dream. With the exception of a few friendly women, all the customers were gay, but the management was so frightened of the local police, who occasionally raided the woods and arrested the fleeing orgiasts, that the law was enforced beyond the letter. Men were not allowed to touch one another, on penalty of being kicked out. While drinking they had to face the bar and while dancing they had to be accompanied by a woman. (I have often wondered what was going through the mind of the lone woman I saw dancing the Madison with a row of thirty men!) The strangest part was that, in spite of their numbers, no one complained about the situation. Instead, they accepted it as their due because they were queers.

During these years, gay organizations like Mattachine continued to do their work, proclaiming, in the face of public condemnation, that homosexuality was a healthy matter of natural preference, rather than a mental illness. In spite of the psychiatric profession's eagerness to treat people like Gordon's son, Sean, I knew that was true. It was all the pressure of fear and shame that drove people like Wesley over the brink, not being gay itself.

It was that year that I met Danny. One of my boys, Phil, had just "graduated" into a steady relationship with a john who wanted to support him. But before he left, he brought a friend to the house to apply for the position. My place had a good reputation with the boys on the street, and many of them were ready to fill any vacancy that occurred, so I could have my pick of the applicants. I had already interviewed two or three who hadn't seemed very promising, either because they were too sullen or too homely. But I could see at first glance that Danny's sandy hair, firm, square chin, and straight nose would make him popular with my clientele. Rather than sullen, he looked a little ill at ease, standing there with his hands in his pockets and his bony shoulders hunched as if against the winter cold, even though we were in a warm kitchen—a posture which only made him all the more appealing.

"D.D., this is Danny Oliver," Phil announced.

"Hi, Danny. You're a good-looking boy," I said. "Where did you find this one, Phil?"

"Times Square. Where else?" Phil said.

"Are you eighteen, Danny?" I asked, looking into his gray eyes. I thought there was something familiar-looking about them, but I wasn't sure what it could be. I knew better than to ask him about his background right off. Most of the boys didn't like to talk about their home lives until they felt comfortable with me.

He nodded. "I'm nineteen," he said.

"Well, you do look at least eighteen, so I'll take your word for it."

"Does that mean I can work here?" he asked.

"Had any experience?"

"Only on the streets," he said.

"Was it nasty?" I asked. I knew it was an odd question, and he just gave me a cool gaze instead of replying. "Never mind," I said. "We'll talk about that later. Are you good at sex?"

"Sure, real good. Wanna try me out?" he said, beaming with a surprisingly self-confident smile that utterly beguiled me.

"That's okay, you're hired," I said, casting my eyes down to the tabletop, because—for the first time since I had opened the place—I felt a little embarrassed and shy, almost like I was falling in love.

"When do I start?"

"Tonight, if you're ready," I said. "We have a lot of appointments scheduled and it's going to be busy around here. I'll show you to your room, okay?"

I took him to Phil's former room and showed him around. "Think you'll be comfortable here?" I asked.

"Sure," he said with a grin. "It's better than the Times Square flophouse I've been staying at." He tossed himself on the bed, fully clothed, and snuggled down to show how comfortable he was. I had an overwhelming urge to join him, but I didn't want to take advantage of my position. If anything happened between us—and I hoped that it would—I wanted it to be something we both wanted.

"You can take a nap until they arrive," I said. "And there's food in the kitchen if you want a snack."

"I'm not hungry," he replied. "I'll just snooze."

"I won't bother to tuck you in," I said. "You won't have much need for your blankets tonight."

"I'm fine, D.D. Hey, thanks for hiring me. I'll try to make you glad you did."

"I'm already glad," I said.

He smiled again—and I was lost. I couldn't take my mind off him for the entire evening. Several men went to his room and came out looking satisfied, and I found myself wondering, as I never had about any of the other boys, who had done what to whom, and how it had felt, and whether Danny was okay. At dawn, when the business was over and the boys were asleep on beds and couches all around the place, I tiptoed over to Danny's room and opened the door. He lay there sleeping, with a faint trace of his smile and a look of angelic innocence on his face. God help me, I thought. I'm in love.

The next afternoon, when everyone had slept off the night's work and had a good breakfast, I asked Danny if he wanted to go to the museum with me, so we could get to know each other a little better. "Sure," he said, grinning broadly.

I took him to the Museum of Modern Art, which I hadn't visited in quite a while, and we wandered through all the Picassos and Pollocks while I told him what little I knew about them and he listened as if he were glad to learn.

"Did you finish high school?" I asked.

"Yeah, but I didn't love it," he said.

"Bad grades?"

"Nope, good grades. Bad company." He said no more, and I didn't press him for details.

"What about college?" I asked.

"Can't afford it."

"Would you go if you could?"

"I guess so," he said with a shrug.

"What would you study?" I asked.

"You'll laugh if I tell you."

"No I won't," I said. "Try me."

"Well, I'm not sure, but I think I'd like to be a writer. Is that goofy or what?"

"No, it's not goofy," I said. "It's admirable." I was glad he didn't flash his smile then, or I would have kissed him right there.

We wandered through more of the museum, until we came to the photography section. "I want to show you something in here," I told him. And, after a little looking through the rearranged photographs, I found the Minerva White pictures.

"They're nice," he said. "I think I've seen one of them before, though— that one with the tree in the fog."

"Her pictures are reprinted in magazines now and then."

"Yeah, I guess that's where I must've seen it."

"I knew the photographer, you know. She invited me to lunch at her house once."

"No kidding," he said, with admiration in his eyes. "That must've been groovy. What was she like?"

"A great lady," I said. "Wise and generous and very talented. You would have liked her."

"I wish I could meet her," he said. "Where is she now?"

"I'm not sure. She was somewhere in the Southwest the last I heard, but I don't even know if she's still alive."

"I hope she is," he said.

"I do too," I replied. "Listen, why don't we blow this joint? Do you want to go to the movies? Radio City's not far from here."

"Oh wow," he said. "I've never been there."

We saw *Charade*, with Audrey Hepburn and Cary Grant. It was a caper movie involving a stolen diamond, but I don't remember anything about it. I was too busy paying attention to Danny's hand, which had found its way onto my knee and was as easy to ignore as a burning coal. Finally I put my arm around his shoulder, and he snuggled against me. We sat that way through the rest of the film and most of the stage show. He seemed to love the Rockettes' precision kicking, and I loved being able to show it to him. Afterward I bought him some dinner at a restaurant in Rockefeller Center, and we went home happy.

"I don't think you should work tonight," I said, once we were back at the house.

"But . . ."

"I'll pay you for your time, if that's what's bothering you," I said. "I'd like you all to myself tonight. Is that okay?"

"Sure," he said. And then a moment later he added, "D.D., you don't have to pay me."

"That's okay," I said. "I want to." The truth was that I didn't want to buy his services. I wanted him to want me, and I wanted to take care of him, and the real reason I had offered him the money was that I was afraid that it might not occur to him to think of me sexually. But I told myself that I was being conscious of the poverty that had put him in this position, and that I didn't want to cost him an evening's wages.

We went to my room instead of his, because it seemed a little less businesslike. I lay down on the bed fully dressed, and he lay beside me, snuggling in the crook of my arm as he had in the movie theater. Then I turned to him and we kissed—a long, delirious kiss. And then another and another, until I felt I needed air. When we finally stopped, he began to massage my shoulders, and then he slowly opened my shirt and my pants, kissing me all over, taking me in his mouth until I was hard, nuzzling beneath my balls until he found my ass, which he circled with his tongue until it opened and was ready. Then he stood and removed his own clothes while I watched him. His body was smooth except for his firm chest, which was covered with soft, blond hair. He held his beautiful genitals in his hands, and I sat up and kissed them, drawing his cock deep into my mouth, feeling it rise and stiffen until it more than filled my mouth and slid into my waiting throat. He pumped it several times and then slowly withdrew it. "Roll over, D.D.," he said. "I'm going to fuck you."

I rolled over without a second thought, and he mounted me, inserting his cock in my ass gently and slowly, pausing to give me time to open so I could accommodate him, then moving steadily deeper until he was all the way in. After several such strokes, he withdrew almost to the tip and said, "Turn back over carefully. Don't lose me." I did as I was told and he held on, keeping the tip of his cock inside me the whole time. When I was on my back, he raised my legs to his firm young shoulders and plunged himself in all the way to the hilt. Then he began pumping in earnest. I watched his gray eyes gazing steadily into mine, and when the drops of sweat fell from his forehead, I caught them on my tongue and swallowed them. That was when he smiled—and then I had my orgasm without touching myself, groaning and rolling my eyes upward while his shoulders shuddered with the tension, and I felt the pulsing of his cock while he shot his load very deep inside me, and at last relaxed.

"Wow," he said, still panting.

"The best," I said.

He started to smile. "Don't smile," I said, "or you'll get me started all over again."

He smiled anyway, and we started all over again. This time I fucked him, and he clung to me and moved with me as if his body had been made for mine. When we finished he lay beside me, humming contentedly to himself.

"Do you like me, D.D.?" he asked.

"Yes," I said. "I do. A lot."

"I thought so," he said. "I like you too."

In a few minutes we put out the lights and we both fell fast asleep. When we awoke, we lay side by side in the darkness.

"You were right," I said. "You are good at sex."

"I don't lie," he said.

"Does it bother you?" I asked him. "Being gay, I mean."

"No. I'm not really gay. I just do this for the bread. I have a girlfriend back home. Or I *had* one, anyway. I'd like to get back to her before too long."

"I see. Do you love her?"

"Sure, but that doesn't mean I don't like you."

"You mean you enjoy your work?"

"It means I enjoy you. But the work's not so bad, you know. It's nice to get paid for something that feels so good."

"Unless you have to do it when you don't want to."

"Does it bother you to be gay, D.D.?"

"To tell you the truth," I said, "I never thought about it much. It did at first, I guess, but only because some people where I came from made an ugly fuss about that sort of thing. It's not like I could help it, though. It's just how I've always been."

"Where did you come from originally?" he asked.

"Upstate. My father had an apple orchard there. I haven't been home in many years. I don't even know if he's still alive. How about you? Where are you from, Danny?"

"Washington."

"D.C.?"

"No," he said. "The state."

"Seattle?"

"No," he replied. "Tacoma. But I was born in Seattle."

"That's nice. What about your folks?"

"I never knew my dad. He died when I was young. My mom married again, though. That's when we moved to Tacoma, and my stepdad adopted me."

"Is your stepfather a nice man?" I asked.

"I don't like him."

"Do you like your mom?"

"She's okay," he said.

"Why did you leave home?" I continued.

"I had a part-time job in my uncle's diner. He wanted me to work there full-time when I graduated from high school, but I wanted something better."

Suddenly I felt a chill. I thought I knew what had drawn me to him, and why I loved him. He was so much like I had been at his age. I didn't dare to ask him if his middle name was Gus, or if his mother's name was Laura. I didn't want to know. Instead I said, "Danny?"

"What?"

"Just one more question. I can't see your face in the dark. Are you smiling?"

"I am now," he said, and he started to roll over on top of me.

"No, I wasn't asking for more sex," I said. "I just wanted to know."

"Are you okay?" he asked.

"I'm fine," I said. "Now, why don't we get some more sleep?"

"Sure," he said, and he snuggled against me trustingly.

I lay there frozen with panic. What if he really were my son? Did he know who I was? No—he wouldn't have gone to bed with me if he knew. I tried to decide if I would have acted out my fantasies and had sex with my father if he'd wanted to. But that had been different, because I'd lived in the same house with him for years. How had my son grown up? I thought back to Laura, to her trust and need and love, and I felt the tears well up in my eyes. All I had left her was the photograph of the tree in the mist that Danny somehow remembered. It was too late to be nice to her now, but it wasn't too late for Danny. What could I do for him? I couldn't tell him that I might be his father, not after what we'd just done, not after I'd let other men pay to have sex with him. Besides, he thought his father was dead, and it was just as well that he did. I spent the rest of the night thinking, and by morning I had a plan.

We awoke before the rest of the household and had breakfast. "Are you sure you don't want to go another round?" Danny asked. "I've got plenty of energy, you know. I'm still young. Oh, I didn't mean any offense by that, D.D. It's just that I know it's different for men at different ages."

"It was perfect as it was," I said. "I don't want to ruin it by trying to repeat it."

"You mean you don't want to have sex with me anymore?"

"I mean that I think you're very special—so special that I'm going to do one of the most difficult things I've ever had to do. I'm going to send you away."

"What?" he said. "I thought I had a good job here." Tears filled his eyes. "Did I do something wrong?"

"No, Danny, you didn't do anything wrong. Don't ever think that. You did everything perfectly. What I'm trying to say is that I think you're too good for a life like this. I think you deserve something better than this or working in a diner, and I want to give you a chance at it." I added a little lie: "I've done as much for other boys, and they've thanked me for it. That makes me happy. That's why I want to send you away from here, for your own good. Do you trust me?"

"Sure, D.D.," he replied, but he didn't offer me his smile.

"Then come here," I said.

He came to me, and I took him in my arms and held him close for a long time, until he relaxed. I kissed him on the forehead and said, "Come into my room. There are some things I want to give you."

I gave him a copy of *Leaves of Grass* that I had been using to read from, since my original copy was in danger of falling apart and I didn't want to lose all the poems and notes I had written in the margins. "This book is one of the most important things in my life. Promise me that you'll read from it a little each day until you've finished it, and then keep it with you. It helped me when times were bad, and it will do the same for you."

"Okay," he said.

I took a pen and wrote on the title page, beneath Walt Whitman's name: "For Danny. Always remember me with love. From D.D."

"Thanks," he said.

"I've underlined a passage in the first preface," I said. "I want you to take special note of it." I watched as he read.

> This is what you shall do: Love the earth and sun and the animals, despise riches, give alms to every one that asks, stand up for the stupid and crazy, devote your income and labor to others, hate tyrants, argue not concerning God, have patience and indulgence toward the people, take off your hat to nothing known or unknown or to any man or number of men, go freely with powerful uneducated persons and with the young and with the mothers of families, read these leaves in the open air every season of every year of your life, re-examine all you have

been told at school or church or in any book, dismiss whatever insults your own soul, and your very flesh shall be a great poem and have the richest fluency not only in its words but in the silent lines of its lips and face and between the lashes of your eyes and in every motion and joint of your body.

He looked up from it with shining eyes. "This is beautiful," he said. "I see what you mean. I will read it all. I promise."

"Good," I said. "Now I'm going to give you this picture." I handed him one of Minerva White's photographs. "This is a picture of me when I was a little younger than you are now. My hair was combed differently, but I looked a little like you when I was your age, didn't I?"

"A little," he said.

"This is the picture taken by Minerva White, the lady whose photographs we saw in the museum yesterday."

"I remember," he said. "You had lunch at her house."

"This isn't important because it's a picture of my face," I said. "It's worth a lot of money now, and if you sell it to an art dealer, you should make enough to pay for your first year's college tuition. Maybe more."

"I don't believe this," he said. "Why should you give me something so valuable?"

"I told you why," I replied. "It makes me happy to do this kind of thing. And if you send me proof that you are enrolled in a college, I'll do my best to help you with your tuition, if I can."

He kissed me then, and I kissed him back, without parting my lips.

"Now I'm going to make a reservation on a flight to the West Coast this afternoon. Okay? That's where you said you wanted to go—to see your girlfriend, right?"

"Right."

I made a reservation for Tacoma, and I got a taxi to take us to the bank and then to the airport. When we were there, I gave him a thousand dollars in cash. "If you're careful with this you won't have to hustle," I said. "It will keep you going until you get into school."

"How can I thank you?" he said.

"You can't, so don't even try," I answered. "Just try to make me glad I did this."

We hugged each other very closely for a few minutes, and then he smiled his wonderful smile. I didn't cry until he was gone.

I went back into the city depressed. Within a week I had closed my business. "The life" is fine for those who want it, but I didn't want to be a part of it anymore. A short time later, I found a job as a masseur in the basement of the Everard Baths.

CHAPTER TWENTY-ONE

"You must be crazy, givin' up a gold mine like that," Louie said as I was treating him to a massage at the baths. "I'm takin' you back to Bellevue. *Ow!* Don't rub so hard! I want the skin to last a few more years."

"Sorry. I'll be more careful. I just didn't want to run a whorehouse anymore," I explained. "I'm not saying there's anything wrong with people paying for sex. I just don't feel like being the salesman."

"But you ain't gonna make any money poundin' flesh in the tubs."

"I'll make enough," I said. "I don't need much. I feel better doing this."

"Okay, Miss D, it's your life. But don't come cryin' to me."

"Don't worry. I won't."

"Listen, do you need any money?" he said, turning serious. "I've got some extra."

"No, but thanks."

"Dell, I gotta say one thing. I don't believe Danny was your kid. Life don't work like that. You're just feelin' guilty about what happened almost twenty years ago."

"It doesn't matter," I said. "Let's forget about it."

"Well, I still think you're cuckoo bananas givin' up a good business for no reason. It must be all that damn poetry you're always readin'."

"Must be," I said. "Listen, my next customer's waiting outside."

"Okay, I'm goin' upstairs to get laid. Thanks for the massage."

"Sure. Thanks for the advice."

"Oh, go fuck yourself. That's my advice, sweetie. See you later."

"Don't play too hard now," I cautioned.

"Hah! What good is playin' with it if it ain't too hard?"

The crowd at the Everard was changing its look during those years. Some were protesting the militarism of the Vietnam War with their appearance, and others were just following the latest fashion. Their hair was growing longer and longer. Many of them wore beads and bracelets along with their towels, and their eyes had the beatific look of those who are "tripping their tits off." Drugs were everywhere. I dropped acid once with Louie, and then I bored him half to death by quoting Whitman for hours while savoring the "colors" of each line and insisting that he could see them if he opened his inner eye. Then I got undressed and left him sitting in a chair while I writhed against the coolness of my bedsheets. I had such a headache the next day that I didn't try the stuff again. But I was in the minority in the Everard. The given wisdom was that you couldn't fully enjoy a night at the baths without dropping acid or mescaline, preceded by alcohol and grass to help smooth your trip up, amyl nitrite to intensify the peak, and a quaalude or a Valium with a little more grass to help you settle back to earth.

More and more people were coming to the baths, either inspired by the hippy ethic of free love or attracted by the ready availability of abundant sex that made the conversations at the traditional bars and cruising grounds look like too much work. As the sound of the Beatles joined the standards piped into the pool area, "Make love, not war" was being practiced every few seconds by the patrons before they draped themselves onto my massage table in search of yet more relaxation.

If some of them got any more relaxed, I used to think, they'd have to be poured into pitchers for safekeeping. Even the mini-course in massage that I'd taken to prepare myself for my new job had proved unnecessary since most of the clientele lapsed into unconsciousness as soon as I began my work. I did the full job anyway, telling myself that their minds might not have known they were being massaged, but their bodies did.

Being in my mid-forties at that time, I wasn't too happy with the youth culture's motto, "Don't trust anyone over thirty," but the Everard's patrons—both young and old—put themselves in my hands and apparently enjoyed it. "That was far out. *Ciao,*" they would mumble blearily as they tipped me and stumbled toward the shower. I got a kick out of the way the nonconformists all nonconformed in exactly the same way. Louie used to complain, "I'm lockin' my door for good if one more guy leaves my room and says, 'You're a hot man. *Ciao.*' Don't nobody say 'good-bye' no more?"

I was really impressed and inspired and proud when the first homosexual and lesbian picket lines appeared, at Independence Hall in Philadelphia, on July 4, 1965. But when Louie and I went to see *The Boys in the Band* in 1968, I saw a different portrait of gay life. Suddenly we were plunged back a few years, into a world where everyone who was gay hated himself and had contempt for those like him. With the exception of the sharp-tongued quips of Emory, the play was a downer, but in one sense it was an up: It was true to at least some of life and, happy or not, it was the gayest play I'd ever seen. This was no *Tea and Sympathy*. It was as out of the closet as a play could get at that time.

In the middle of 1969, a lot more people began pouring out of their gay closets. I was helping Louie get over the death of his beloved Judy Garland when the cops pulled one of their customary raids on a gay bar called the Stonewall Inn. A bunch of drag queens finally decided they had taken enough shit, and for the first time they began fighting back. They threw things at the cops and almost set the place on fire. They rioted for three nights in a row. It was the talk of the gay world. The revolution had at last begun! Soon there were new gay political groups—the Gay Liberation Front and the Gay Activists Alliance—demonstrating in the streets, demanding equality and civil rights for gay people. Mostly, the new movement meant more customers on the massage table for me as gay life got looser and bolder than ever. But there was so much excitement in the air that eventually even I got political.

It was 1970 when I sat in on a meeting of the Gay Activists Alliance. I had gone there to bring them a word of cheer from Walt Whitman:

> Be not dishearten'd, affection shall solve the problems of
>   freedom yet,
> Those who love each other shall become invincible . . .
>
> You shall yet laugh to scorn the attacks of all the remainder
>   of the earth . . .
>
> It shall be customary in the houses and streets to see manly
>   affection . . .
> The dependence of Liberty shall be lovers,
> The continuance of Equality shall be comrades.
>
> These shall tie you and band you stronger than hoops of iron . . .

But I forgot all about giving it to them when I got absorbed in what they were saying. They were discussing whether to hold a demonstration in Times Square to protest police harassment of the hustlers who were working there. One of the organization's officers was Arnie Kantrowitz, a short guy with a shaved head, a big red mustache, and rose-colored glasses. He argued in favor of the demonstration, saying that prostitution could be an honorable profession if it were freed of coercion, exploitation, and drug addiction, and that if the gay movement was going to be part of the broader sexual revolution, it should support the rights of sex workers.

The idea of respectability for hustlers was so stunning to me that I went up to him to find out more about it. "Did you mean what you said about prostitution?" I asked.

"Sure," he said. "Why not?"

"I used to work in a whorehouse—more than one, in fact."

"Some gay liberationists argue that it's degrading, but that puts them in league with the conservatives who don't want to allow any lifestyle except the nuclear family," he said. "If prostitution were legal, even sexually transmitted diseases could be controlled."

"Where did you get all these ideas?" I asked. "Are they written down anywhere?"

"There's a great book called *Sisters Under the Skin*," he said. "It's by Kelly Barrett."

"Kelly Barrett?" I asked, wondering if it could be the same Kelly Barrett I had once known in Elysium. "Do you know her?"

"I've met her," he said. "Listen, I'd like to talk more, but I have six other people to talk to. Come back to another meeting, okay?" He turned to someone near me and said, "Did you hear about our proposed civil rights bill for New York City? It would protect gay people from being fired or kicked out of their apartments . . ."

I didn't think I wanted to go to a lot of meetings, but I did want to see the demonstration. And I certainly wanted to find a copy of *Sisters Under the Skin*, and talk to its author as well. I bought the book the next day and read it in one sitting. The author's photograph was artistically stylized with deep shadows, and I knew that the twenty-eight years since I had seen her would have wrought as many changes in her face as they had in mine, so it was hard to determine if it was a picture of the same Kelly I had known back in high school. I wrote a letter, asking if she were from upstate New York and telling her who I was, and I sent it to the publisher, hoping it would be forwarded.

Later that week at the demonstration, I saw that the facts had a way to go before they could catch up with the theories. Several hundred gay militants chanted and marched around Forty-Second Street with big placards demanding justice, thinking they would solve an ancient problem in one night. The hustlers were terrified by all the public exposure, and they shrank into the protective doorways with embarrassment and eventually fled from the street for fear of involvement. The activists marched downtown to Greenwich Village and rallied outside the Women's House of Detention. Somehow the angry inmates and the angry activists and a crowd of angry shoppers on nearby Eighth Street all got mixed together, and a riot developed. Bottles were breaking, cars were overturned, and people were running everywhere. I decided I had had enough liberation for one night and took the subway back uptown.

The next day, I got a phone call. "Is this Danny Blake?" a woman's voice asked.

"Yes."

"Are you from Elysium?"

"Yes."

"Oh, Danny," she said, starting to cry. "I thought you were dead all these years. It's Kelly."

"Kelly, it really is you! It's so good to hear your voice."

"I want to see you."

We arranged to meet for dinner at a Village restaurant the next night. When I arrived, she was already there. We had both changed, but we had no trouble recognizing each other. Her hair was cut short and there was a little gray in it. She still wore no lipstick, but her face was attractive without it. She was dressed in a blue work shirt and dungarees with construction-worker boots. As soon as I walked in, she rose from the table and came to greet me.

After a long, long hug and lots of sniffling, we sat down to talk.

"Did you ever get that last letter I sent you?" she asked.

"Yes. It was very painful for me to come out of the war and find that Chester didn't make it."

"He was a lovely man. At least you had him for a while."

"Not the way I wanted to. What fools we were to wait."

"What happened to you after that?"

"I didn't know where to contact you, so I couldn't answer your letter," I said. "There didn't seem much point in going back home, so I just began to wander." I told her the general outline of my experiences with Laura, Willard and Harold, Maisie Dot, Edwin, Gordon, and Louie. Then I told her about the book I was trying to write.

"My God, your life has been so full," she remarked.

"And yet empty at the same time," I replied. "Now tell me about yours."

"There's not a lot to tell," she said. "I haven't had as complicated a past as you. I came here right after my mother died, and a few months later I met Amber, my lover. We've been together since then. I work as a copy editor. In the last few years I've become politicized. I've been very active in GAA's Lesbian Liberation Committee, but now some members believe we need to be more radical—that we need to make our own way, independent of the women's movement and the gay men's movement. We may form our own group outside GAA."

"Does that mean we can't be friends?"

"Of course it doesn't. Just don't tell the other women in the group, though. They might not understand. Oh, and of course you know about my book."

"It's a very good book."

"Thanks, but I'm reconsidering some of the points. The movement isn't always clear on the subject of prostitution. Some people say it's capitalist exploitation, and some say it's victimization by male chauvinists. Others say it's sexual freedom."

"Like most things, it's probably what you make of it," I said. "Tell me something, if it's not too personal. Did you ever practice what you preach?"

"You mean, was I ever a whore? No, dear, I'm just an abstract theoretician. A lot of prostitutes are lesbians, so I was able to interview some of them, but I never had too much to do with their world."

"I ran a brothel for a while, but I gave it up."

"Why?"

"I'm still not sure. Maybe I thought I wouldn't want my own kid doing that."

"Haven't you heard about children's liberation?"

"Oh, give me a break," I said, and we both laughed. Then we started to reminisce about Valley High School: about the English teacher I'd been attracted to and the play in which I'd first seen Kelly; about the sour disposition of George Grimes, who had hated being gay; and about our adventure writing Bruno Todd's name on the boys' room wall.

"I wonder what became of them," she mused.

"We'll probably never find out," I speculated. "But at least we found each other."

"Yes," she said. "Thank God for that."

Before we left the restaurant, we arranged to see each other often, and she made me promise to come to the gay pride march a few weeks later, in order to celebrate the first anniversary of the Stonewall revolt.

I couldn't march with Kelly because she was a marshal, but I did say hello to her. I had asked Louie to march with me, but he had said, "What's the point of a bunch of faggots parading in the streets? They oughta be out havin' brunch." And I hadn't been able to convince him to give up a weekend on Fire Island just to demand his civil rights. So I marched alone. But I had a good time anyway, wandering among the exuberant crowds. The march started off with a few hundred people straggling up Sixth Avenue, but by the time it reached Central Park there were about ten thousand of us.

Most of the marchers were young and dressed in blue jeans, but a few wore more flamboyant costumes or dressed in drag. My favorite was Sam, Cynthia Chin's friend, who had helped me set up my business when I first arrived back in New York. He had covered his huge belly with a flowing white caftan. His handlebar mustache was waxed and curled more elegantly than ever, and he wore 15 pounds of gold chains and medallions around his neck and a large, jeweled ring on every finger. Behind him trailed half a dozen of the boys from his brothel, all without shirts to show off their skinny torsos in the June sunlight. The contingent caused some grumbling among the anti-prostitution faction, but that didn't bother Sam. The absurd crowning touch to his hyper-gay bit of street theater was a large political button reading *"How dare you presume I'm heterosexual."*

When we got to the park, I wandered among the throngs of happy people all relishing the historical moment they were creating. Glad faces were everywhere, and for a moment I thought of old Edwin Gable Roe back in Pittsburgh, and how he hadn't been allowed to live his life in the open as these young people were. I was so grateful to be part of the generation that could witness this change that I had tears in my eyes. But I wondered what Edwin would have thought of it. Would he have been frightened by it because it threatened the values by which he had been forced to live?

I was brought out of my reverie when I thought I recognized someone's face, and I rushed over to him before he could get lost in the crowd. "Sean?" I said. "Is it you?"

"Hey, Dell!" he said. "Wow! It's been such a long time."

"Seventeen years," I said, calculating the time quickly. "You look good— better than when I saw you last."

"Oh God, don't remind me. I was in awful shape back then. But I got over it with a little—more than a little—help, and everything's okay now. I'm working with gifted science students. Oh, Dell, this is my lover, Gary."

I shook hands with a tall, thin, long-haired man with gentle eyes. "Glad to meet you," I said. "When I last saw Sean, it didn't look like he had any future, let alone a happy one."

"How about you?" Sean said. "What have you been up to?"

"Oh, it's a long story. I've lived in a few places—San Francisco for a while. I've been working on some writing on and off, and I've had a few different jobs—nothing you could call a career."

"Well, it's great to see you," he said. "You're looking good."

"Sean, how's your father?"

"Oh, he and my mother were divorced soon after you left. She's remarried now and off drugs. She has two other kids. My dad is still working as a doctor in Maine, but he has a steady lover. You'd like him. His name is Ron."

"That's great," I said. "I'm glad to hear it. Please tell him I said hello. Okay?"

"I sure will," he said, and he and Gary turned to rejoin the celebration.

I went home that night more contented than I'd been in a long, long time. Soon afterward, I received a letter from Danny, the boy I'd sent away, and it made me even happier.

July 10, 1970

Dear D.D.,

I hope you can forgive me for taking so long to write to you, but I wanted to wait until I had something worth telling. First, I want to thank you for changing my life. It wouldn't have been as good if I hadn't met you. That much is for sure.

I know that a lot of kids who started out the way I did might have used what you gave them for a few good times and laughed at you, but I was so touched by your beautiful gesture that I did exactly what you advised me to. I sold the picture and used the money for my first year at the University of Washington, where I majored in English. I did so well that I won a scholarship for the next two years.

Then things changed. I met a guy named Jerome in one of my classes and we became lovers. You were right, of course— I was gay all the time, but afraid to face it. Jerome and I decided that we wanted to leave college and open a business together. So we've moved to San Francisco and we've recently opened a gay bookstore. Business is doing well, because the gay community is very active here. By the way, we call the shop Leaves of Grass. I can't tell you how much of an influence that book has had on my life, and I can't thank you enough for turning me on to it.

One last bit of good news: I did pursue the writing I told you about, and I produced a few dozen short stories. About half of them will be collected into a volume called *Doorways*, which I hope to get published. If I succeed, I'll be sure to send you one. I'm going to dedicate it to you.

Again, thank you for all the good you did me at that crucial moment in my life. I will never forget you for it. If there is ever anything I can do for you, please let me know, and in the meanwhile, let's keep in touch.

Sincerely yours,
Danny Oliver

I couldn't have been prouder if he'd been elected President.

The 1970s became a huge coming-out party for gay people. Although I turned fifty years old in 1974—celebrated very quietly over dinner with Louie—I remained sexually active, though not with as much energy as I had once had. When the slimy old St. Marks Baths was taken over by a new management and redecorated, Louie and I went there to check out the competition. The place was a sleek and elegant modern concoction, the opposite of the tacky old Everard. There was a hot tub and the floors were carpeted. But I didn't have a very good time. I couldn't seem to attract anyone. Finally, in desperation, I went to the darkened dormitory room where there was usually a sexual free-for-all, and I reached under someone's towel without being asked. He grabbed my wrist forcefully. "Why don't you leave the partying to the young folks, old man?" he said. I left the room, stunned. Then I gathered my things and left the bathhouse, without even bothering to find Louie.

He called the next day. "What happened to you?" he asked.

"I got depressed and I left. Some guy turned me down because I'm too old."

"Do you want me to bring your shawl over, Auntie Della?" he asked.

"This isn't funny, Lulu. I'm over the hill."

"What? You wouldn't know the hill if you were sittin' on it."

"I'll probably never sit on it again," I said.

404

"This sounds serious. Let's have brunch."

Over eggs sardou and mimosas, Louie tried to cheer me up. "Honey, there's a demand for every kind of person. What you need is to freshen up your act. You can't be an ingenue forever, but that don't mean you can't play character parts."

"Ingenue?" I said. "Where did you learn to talk like that?"

"I may be ignorant, but that don't mean I don't know nothin'," he said, wagging his shoulders with mock self-importance. "As it happens, I been sleepin' with an off-Broadway director, and he's been teachin' me a few things."

"A director?" I said. "Is it serious?"

"No, it ain't serious," he mimicked. "But it is nine inches long!"

"Slut," I said.

"You better believe it. Now let's see what we can do about makin' you one, too."

I got over my mood, of course. The world was changing around me, and if I wanted to stay part of it, I had to change with it. The hippy hair and beads of the 1960s gave way to the "clone" look of the '70s: short hair, clipped mustache, flannel shirts, Levi's button-fly jeans, and engineer's boots. As Louie put it: "Nelly is out. Macho is in. Now get over to that gym and buy yourself some muscles, girl."

The clothes and the haircut were easy enough, but the muscles took more work. I did go to the gym regularly for a while, which soon became now and then, and if my body didn't regain all the muscles I'd developed thirty years earlier in basic training, it did show a little improvement. Then Louie took me to a new place that was just what I needed. It was called the Mineshaft and it was hidden away in the Meatpacking District, near the Hudson River. Posted on the front door there was a dress code, which forbade cologne, dress pants, and the then-fashionable pullover shirts with the little alligator above the left tit. The look was "leather and western" or nothing. Once inside, some guys chose "nothing" by checking their clothes and walking around naked and ready for action, showing off their tattoos or the metal rings they had inserted through their nipples or their foreskins, or even their noses. Other guys wore only jockstraps or leather chaps that left their buns exposed to whoever wanted to play with them. I usually wore blue jeans and a flannel shirt with its sleeves rolled up and its front unbuttoned.

There were a couple of barrooms and several "play" rooms on two floors. The sexual style was sadomasochism, whose use of suffering to induce pleasure reminded me of the motto posted on the wall of the gym: "No Pain, No Gain." The sex wasn't all that different from what was being done at the Everard, but here it was done with the equipment necessary for professionals —slings for men to lie in while other men pushed fists into their asses, tubs for men to sit in while other men pissed on them, racks for men to be tied to while other men whipped them, and a stage where men could show off their sexual prowess while other men appreciated them. Although everyone seemed to be having a wonderful time, I was intimidated at first because the place was a little strong for my country-boy tastes. But I was becoming a new person, I reminded myself, so I figured I'd give it a try.

I joined a row of men standing against the wall in one of the back rooms and waited for my eyes to adjust to the gloom, so I could watch the proceedings and learn from them. In a few moments, I felt a hand on my basket, and then the fly of my jeans was being unbuttoned without my having to do a thing. Then there was a shadowy form kneeling before me, taking my cock in his mouth, stopping only to say, "Please, Daddy, twist my tits." *Daddy*, I thought—so that's who I am. "Please, Daddy," the voice repeated. I obliged happily, even when he said, "Harder, Daddy." It gave me a sense of power even while I knew I was doing it to please him. I liked it. And evidently he did too, so I did it until I came in his mouth. "Thank you, Daddy. I hope we meet again soon. I'll be here next Wednesday night," he said, after neatly licking me clean and rebuttoning my jeans.

"*Ciao*, man. Thanks," I growled with a deep voice, as I had heard the other men do. And my partner disappeared into the crowd

I was amazed. If most people had seen us having sex, they would have thought that I was an evil brute and he was a self-hating psycho. But I knew there had been warmth between us, and that he had controlled the entire scene. Even in the dark, I could see that S&M had a lot of new things to teach me about my body and my mind, and the first one was that I didn't need to be under thirty to be attractive to someone. In this world, I was still sexy and my years of experience were considered a prize.

"Did you have a good time, my sweet?" Louie asked as we left, making our way along the west end of Fourteenth Street where the meatpackers in their bloody white coats had already begun their predawn shift.

"What the fuck was that?" I asked, completely boggled.

"That, my dear, was the future."

"But Lulu, aren't you a little too femme for a place like this?"

"Oh honey, lots of nelly queens like me go there. It's really a short trip from feathers to leathers. Who's gonna know the difference, if you keep your mouth shut and just grunt once in a while? Don't we deserve a good time as well as the next guy? As long as we're willin' to play the game, that is. Besides, I didn't notice nobody mindin' how old you were. Did you, Daddy?"

"Was that you?" I gasped.

"Of course not, silly. I have better taste than that. I was just standin' next to you the whole time, to make sure you were enjoyin' yourself. Is that a smile I see?"

"For an illiterate, you're very wise, Lulu."

"I'll take that as a compliment. Now all I see is these ugly meatpackers hangin' up dead cows. Where the fuck can a lady find some breakfast around here?"

I continued going to the Mineshaft. And occasionally, when I had finished my work at the Everard, I went upstairs to join the fun. The people there were less fussy about how old a man was, if he knew how to treat them right. Sometimes I would just lie on the cot in my cubicle and listen to the sounds of men having sex in the rooms all around me. The partitions didn't go up to the ceiling, so there was only visual privacy. Any but the most quietly whispered conversations were in the public domain. Usually we heard one-liners such as, "Use me like a woman." But occasionally everyone on the entire floor would stop what they were doing and burst out laughing, if the dialogue was really sharp. My favorite was composed of two anonymous voices, one of them very butch:

"On your knees, slave. Do you want to suck my cock?"

"Don't just nod. Speak up."

"Yes."

"Louder."

"YES! "

"Yes, what?"

There was a hush as we waited for the ritual "Yes, Master," to signal the slave's submission. But first there was a pause.

Finally the slave shouted, "YES, MARY!" and amid the raucous laughter of dozens of eavesdroppers, the sharp slam of a door could be heard.

Sometimes I would take out my pad and write in the dim light of my room. I found that those places where the air was thick with other men's sexual fantasies seemed to charge my creativity, so I always took a pad with me to the baths and the Mineshaft, and even to the porno films I occasionally visited. The light was best at the baths though, and the incessant tinkle of the room keys that hung by elastic straps from everyone's wrists or ankles made a gently musical backdrop to my compositions, like the sound of wind chimes heard across a lake. I wrote this poem at the Everard:

Looking for Walt Whitman at the Baths

Where did you come from, Walt Whitman, old drifter,
old dreamer, old master,
old mentor, where are you from?
Where but inside me, musing and pregnant,
summoned out of the dark and the silence,
puddled in corners of motherless minds,
tingling with wonder, with warmth and with wisdom
and sorrowfully thinking your innocence lied?

And where are you now, Walt Whitman, old father,

old child, old brother,
old comrade, where are you now?
Where but inside me, singing your love songs,
tinkling and vague like wind chimes on water,
where could you be but in paradise buried,
here in a thousand bedrooms a day,
where men entice and comfort men,
encouraging, touching men with words,
with caring, with fingers, with licking and sucking
and fucking and finally fountains of sperm?

And where will you be, Walt Whitman, old husband,
old lover, old prophet,
old poet, where will you be
when the sun hangs dead at last in the sky?
Where but inside me, smiling sagely,
certain like childhood, like limitless fancy,
like music remembered,
like lust at sunrise,
where will you be?

Even if most of the encounters were anonymous, I had some touching experiences at the baths. Once, I began making love to a man's feet and slowly worked my way upward until I reached his head, which was covered with a Dynel toupee, dry and droopy and dead to the fingertips. I quietly slipped it off and kissed the top of his bald head. "There," I said. "Doesn't that feel better?"

"Oh thank you," he whispered. "I was so afraid."

Another time, as I passed an open doorway, I noticed that the light inside was brighter than usual, and that the man lying nude on the bed had only one leg. I found his honesty appealing, and I went inside and closed the door behind me. Then I leaned over and caressed his body—including his stump, which felt lumpy at the end where the amputation had healed. He scooted over on the cot to make room for me, and I lay down beside him and kissed his lips. Then I moved my head to his groin and put his cock in my mouth and sucked him until he came. I kissed him once more and stood up to adjust the towel around my waist, so I could leave.

"Please," he whispered.

I could see the pleading look in his eyes, and I knew how much he wanted me to stay. He was probably so used to being rejected that he was willing to accept as a lover anyone who was willing to touch him. I felt guilty, because I knew that it was charity that had drawn me to him and not lust, and I didn't want him to know that, but there was no alternative now.

"I'm sorry," I whispered, and I left.

I felt even worse the next day, when I discovered that he had given me a case of the crabs. I had had visits from body lice before, and I knew that a couple of applications of lotion and a lot of laundering of clothes and sheets would easily get rid of them. But the first time I had had the experience, I had felt crawly and itchy for a week afterward. My threshold of revulsion had gotten lower and lower, and within a few years my doctor had treated a dose of syphilis with penicillin, a case of venereal warts with a liquid that burned the lining of my rectum and kept me awake all night, and God knows how many colds. Of course I found some lines of Walt's to comfort me.

> This is the meal equally set . . .
> I will not have a single person slighted or left away,
> The kept-woman, sponger, thief, are hereby invited,
> The heavy-lipp'd slave is invited, the venerealee is invited . . .

It was awfully nice of him to invite me to dinner, I thought, sulking, but I bet he wouldn't want to go to bed with a "venerealee."

Whenever I had a communicable condition, I was always very careful to suspend my sexual activities until it was safe, but apparently all of my playmates weren't as careful. The general attitude was that the "clap doctor" could take care of anything, and diseases that had once decimated whole populations were now seen as petty annoyances. "Safety last" seemed to be everyone's motto.

On May 5, 1977, I was in the middle of giving a massage to an unconscious patron at the Everard when I heard a lot of shouting from upstairs. Thinking there had been a fight or something, I went on with my work, when suddenly I smelled smoke, and somebody shouted down from the main floor, "Fire!" I shook my client, but I couldn't get much more than a groggy groan from him. So I took his towel and dragged him to the stairway. We made it out to the street, where we joined a crowd of sixty or seventy men in towels, many of them coughing from the smoke, and a few dozen in street clothes who had been waiting to get rooms. Then the fire trucks roared up, and the firefighters began working furiously to extinguish the flames. They rescued a number of men from the building, but they didn't get all of them. In spite of the mouth-to-mouth resuscitation that the firemen, to our amazement, tried as a final desperate maneuver, nine men died in that fire. No one knew whether it had been started by faulty wiring or a carelessly smoking customer, but the sprinkler system wasn't in operating condition, probably because the landlord didn't care enough to check it out. Most of the building was heavily damaged and the place was closed for months. So I had to find a new job.

I ended up working at the Mineshaft, where I became a part-time bartender and janitor. The hours were even weirder than those at the baths because the place was open only from 11 p.m. to 8 a.m., so I stayed up all night and became a stranger to daylight for most of the week. Tending the bar was as much fun as it was work. The main room was more of a clubhouse than a sex room although many a man was fucked right on the pool table and many a cock was sucked right at the bar. The men in black leather and chains held conversations about anything—politics, motorcycle runs, or theater—and sometimes they forgot themselves and kept right on talking in the back rooms, which broke the concentration of those engaged in heavy sex until the management posted a sign saying: "Discussions of opera will be confined to the main barroom." Cleaning up the place at the end of the night was less of a pleasure. The bathtubs downstairs were not connected to any plumbing, so the floor was awash in urine by morning and had to be hosed down. Occasionally men went further than that, and I found myself cleaning up stray turds and considering the meaning of the human condition. Since I was working, I didn't get to participate in the revelry too often. But occasionally I made a date with one of the patrons, and then I played Daddy at home.

I was on my way home one rainy morning when I noticed a stoop-shouldered black cleaning woman in the doorway of a midtown office building, evidently waiting for a bus to take her home from work. I felt a kinship with her, since I had just mopped a floor too, and I smiled at her as I passed. Then I stopped in my tracks. Something seemed familiar about her face. I turned and looked at her. Her hair was graying under a shabby kerchief, which hung to the shoulders of her shapeless gray coat, and she carried a wrinkled paper shopping bag in which I could see her work clothes. I stared at her face for a moment. It was lined and careworn. Just then I could hear a bus coming up the street behind me, and I said to her quickly, "Excuse me, ma'am, but is your name Maisie Dot? Maisie Dot McCoy?"

She just stared at me blankly and started to move from the doorway.

"Would you mind if I gave you something?" I asked, and I pulled a twenty dollar bill out of my wallet.

She plucked it quickly from my fingers and mumbled, "Don' make no nevermind to me." And she scurried off to catch her bus.

I was almost sure she had been my friend from Chicago, and I checked that doorway every morning on my way home from work. But I never saw her again.

Home was a quiet place in those years. I had only Camerado the cat for company, and after a night out in the busy underground sex world, cuddling his furry body was more than enough. The two of us slept through the daylight hours after I got home from work, but he didn't complain and neither did I.

Eventually, I started to miss the daytime world, so when somebody offered me a job as a clerk in a back-room establishment called Manbooks on the Upper West Side, I accepted. The place was open twenty-four hours a day, but my shift was from 2 p.m. to 10 p.m., so I didn't feel as removed from the world of reality as I had at the Mineshaft. Instead I sat in a room full of giant rubber dildoes and sleazy porn magazines and took the admission fees as the customers entered the back room, where they watched endless loops of plotless porno movies in claustrophobic booths and had "fast food sex" on their way home from their respectable office jobs, leaving the floor covered with their slimy semen. It wasn't the most glamorous position I've held, and it made me feel a little sordid for the first time, but it did leave me some hours to try my hand at the Whitman novel again.

I read some more at the library in order to get myself started, and in the course of reading, I came across something that disturbed me deeply. A married homosexual critic from England named John Addington Symonds had written a carefully phrased question to Whitman, hoping for support from the man who had written such courageous poems:

> In your conception of comradeship, do you contemplate the possible intrusion of those semi-sexual emotions & actions which no doubt do occur between men? I do not ask, whether you approve of them, or regard them as a necessary part of the relation? But I should like much to know whether you are prepared to leave them to the inclinations & the conscience of the individuals concerned?

According to Horace Traubel's record of Walt's conversations, the letter had thrown old Walt into a snit. He had felt plagued and persecuted by Symonds, who had repeated his question in several other letters. Finally Walt had answered him:

> ... that the calamus part has even allow'd the possibility of such construction as mention'd is terrible—I am fain to hope the pages themselves are not to be even mention'd for such gratuitous and quite at the time entirely undream'd & unreck'd possibility of morbid inferences—wh' are disavow'd by me & seem damnable. Then one great difference between you and me, temperament & theory, is *restraint* ... My life, young manhood, mid-age, times South, &c: have all been jolly, bodily, and probably open to criticism—
>
> Tho' always unmarried I have had six children—two are dead—One living southern grandchild, fine boy, who writes to me occasionally. Circumstances connected with their benefit and fortune have separated me from intimate relations.
>
> I see I have written with haste & too great effusion—but let it stand.

411

I was thunderstruck! Was this my hero who had so openly proclaimed the beauty of love between men? Was it possible that I had been misreading an outdated turn of phrasing from a time when friendships were described in effusive language? Was all my feeling of kinship with Walt a self-delusion? I couldn't believe that he had so utterly denounced his true sexuality, and I became depressed.

A little more thought and a little more reading revealed how much Walt, the "artificer of 'sincerity,'" had falsified in his letter. No one had ever heard of the children he claimed to have fathered, and no letters from his "grandson" have ever been found. It's true that Walt had burned some of his papers, more than once, but Peter Doyle's letters had been among them. So it seems clear that he had been hiding his homosexuality, not the heterosexuality he had invented to baffle poor Symonds. Besides, Symonds himself had been married and had children even though he was homosexual, so he would have known that such a claim constituted no real proof.

Not only had Walt lied about the six children, but about his "times South," since he had been to New Orleans only once, for a few months. He even lied about having "written with haste," since he had composed at least two drafts of the letter. Had he lied about his youth being "jolly" and "bodily" as well? Was everything he had ever written a lie? Was *Leaves of Grass* actually a novel? I worked myself into such a maelstrom of emotions and questions, that the only thing that calmed me was finding the disillusioned assessment of Walt that Symonds published sometime later.

> No one who knows anything about Walt Whitman will for a moment doubt his candour and sincerity. Therefore, the man who wrote "Calamus," and preached the gospel of comradeship, entertains feelings at least as hostile to sexual inversion as any law-abiding humdrum Anglo-Saxon could desire.

The next day, I realized that no matter how much I read and no matter how much empathy I could feel for Walt, I couldn't ever truly know what it had been like to live in another time. He was my forebear, but I felt that the more I learned about him, the less I really knew him. Perhaps I had been trying to interpret his innocent nineteenth-century life through jaded twentieth-century eyes. After all, it wasn't a world that had places like the Everard or the Mineshaft or Manbooks, where you could have what you wanted just by reaching out and grabbing it.

Homosexuality must have been an entirely different experience in Walt's time. A century ago, American men who had sex with other men didn't even have a name for what they were. Walt had called it his "adhesive nature," a term for the inclination toward same-sex friendship taken from phrenology, the "science" of studying the bumps on the head to determine personality traits. Even if they enjoyed each other's company outside of the bedroom, nineteenth-century homosexuals hadn't yet developed an identity as a group, much less a sense of communal strength. They didn't see themselves as a category of humanity; they merely happened to perform certain sexual acts, which they knew they must be even more secretive about than most people were.

In spite of it all, I still felt close to Walt. I couldn't put aside a lifelong passion because of one letter. He must have had his reasons for lying. My guess was that he had been afraid that the truth about his sexuality would make his poetry seem less than universal and render him ineligible for the post of America's national bard. He wanted to be the "divine literatus," who would cure America of its inferiority complex about European culture and make a new religion of native literature. But I was only guessing. I could never be sure. Still, for better or worse, I knew I was somehow connected to him—not only through my reading of his words, but through the flow of history and our mutual perception of it—and I knew that we were a part of each other forever. To give myself more time to think, I decided to put the book aside yet again. I wasn't sure if I'd ever be able to write it.

At that time, the politics of twentieth-century homosexuality were moving onto the front pages of the news. When some communities passed civil rights ordinances to protect gay jobs and homes, religious fanatics began to denounce us openly, led by a singing orange juice saleslady named Anita Bryant. Their fulminations made it respectable to attack gay people in the press and in the streets. I kept in touch with Danny, and he kept me abreast of the gay political scene in San Francisco as it grew into a well-organized, potent force in which he played an active part. When Mayor George Moscone and the first openly gay city supervisor, Harvey Milk, were assassinated in 1979, he wrote a stirring description of the candlelight march to City Hall held by thousands of mourners, which moved me to tears. Later, when the assassin was given a sentence of only seven years, San Francisco erupted in violent rioting, and Danny was clubbed by an enraged policeman for setting a police car on fire. But he managed to get away and, after a week of recuperation, he was back in his now successful bookstore. I was very proud of him, and sent him a donation for his political group.

As gay politics grew more and more legitimate, in the early 1980s, the first rumblings of a new horror began to be felt. First one, then several, then many deaths from a strange new disease were reported. No one knew what it was, but the rumor was that it was passed on through sexual contact, which at first no one wanted to believe. We had all worked so hard to be free that it seemed impossible that our joy could be turned to ashes so quickly. Whispers went around to be careful, and I suspended my trips to the Mineshaft and the Everard. The crowd in the back room of Manbooks pretended not to hear at first, but men kept dying. The term "gay plague" began to appear, and the religious fanatics began to give the wrath of their God all the credit for it. A chill went through the gay community, and then fewer and fewer men appeared to play in the bookstore's back room. The disease was finally given the name AIDS.

I decided to wait it out, to see what was going to happen before I allowed myself to feel panic. Then it became more real for me when I read in the local gay newspaper that Sean Thomas, Gordon's son, had become a leader in the fight to save people with AIDS from discrimination after his lover Gary had been diagnosed and had been fired from his job. Sean had had to support him until he died. I sent a check to Sean's group to help, but it was too late. By the time I received the canceled check back from the bank the following month, I had learned that Sean was dead too. I sent a note of condolence to Gordon at his old address in Portland, but I never received a reply.

I had some time to myself at that point, since I had decided to quit my job at Manbooks and live on my savings for a while. The place stayed open with almost no clientele for the next year or two, and then, late in 1984, closed for lack of business. There was a great wave of anger and fear among gays when the city forcibly closed down the Mineshaft the following November, and then the Everard a few months later. Ugly editorials calling for harsher measures were met with angry demonstrations. But in spite of all the protests, the era of libertinism came to an end. Sex was repressed or driven underground, and my world became more like the nineteenth-century world that Walt Whitman had lived in. I was sorry to see it happen, but if people couldn't resist doing unsanitary things in those places, I was glad that they were closed. I couldn't live with the thought that by selling tickets to the orgy, I had been unwittingly helping to spread the disease. I wondered how many beautiful young men were dying or dead partly because of me, and I was haunted by the thought of the boys who had worked for me, and the men I'd served at the Mineshaft, and the men I'd admitted to the back room of Manbooks, and all the men I'd slept with at the Everard. What would become of them? And what would become of me? But I didn't waste time speculating. Instead, I got to work.

Since New York City was so slow in responding to the emergency with medical facilities, the community formed its own self-help group, called Gay Men's Health Crisis. I volunteered to become a "buddy" and to be responsible for a patient by visiting him and cleaning his apartment, doing his shopping, helping him to fill out medical and insurance forms, getting him to his doctor's appointments, and generally being his friend. My assigned patient was named Nathan. He had been an off-Broadway actor and, like most actors, he had little money between roles. When I met him, he hadn't worked for some months, and his medical bills had eaten up all his savings. So I did what I could to help.

Nathan had been stricken with Kaposi's sarcoma, a skin cancer that produced horrible purple spots on the skin and eventually did irreparable internal damage. From the pictures in the press clippings that he showed me, he had been a handsome, well-built young man. At the time I met him, he weighed 115 pounds and was covered with so many skin lesions that he looked like a blueberry muffin, although I never would have said such a thing to him. Instead I was as encouraging as I could be and told him that he was looking okay, and that I could see signs of improvement. He was grateful to hear such things, even if he knew I was lying.

Sometimes I didn't have to lie. I didn't have to say anything. I just spent the evening holding his hand and being with him, and when I got ready to go, he would whisper, "Thank you," and I would cry as soon as I was in the hall. Nathan had a few friends who helped with the chores and the visiting, but as time went on, he didn't want to be seen by the people who had known him. I was never sure whether it was because he was too vain or because he didn't want to put his friends through such a painful experience, and wanted them to remember him as he had been.

His family in South Carolina knew about his situation, but they kept their distance. His mother came to see him once, and he asked me to be there to help.

She wore tasteful and obviously costly clothes, and she showed a hint of reluctance to use the furniture, as if it might sully her outfit. Finally she sat in a chair next to his bed and said in a softly Southern accent, "Is theah anythin' that you need, Nathan?"

"I just need to be held, Mama," he said tearfully.

She just sat there, unable to touch him. Later, in the living room, she tried to explain herself to me.

"Ah do love mah boy," she said. "But ah'm afraid of bein' too neah him."

"You know that you can't catch AIDS from just touching him, don't you?" I said. "The doctors are sure about that. It's not easy to get. You would have to come into contact with the patient's blood. It can only be spread by sexual contact or by sharing contaminated hypodermic needles."

"Ah've been told that," she said. "Ah'm not quite convinced, but may Ah be frank with you?"

"Of course," I said, nodding.

"Evah since Nathan's illness revealed to me that he was ... um ... homosexual, oah gay, oah whatevah you people call yo'selves, Ah have been unable to stop feelin' that he is somehow alien to me. Ah hope you will believe that Ah have truly trahd to ovahcome such feelin's, but trah though Ah maht to ignoah mah distaste, Ah fahnd that Ah simply cannot deal with him. Ah know this must sound terrible to you, and Ah wish Ah could behave differently, but Ah simply cain't. It was a great effort even to come heah to see him. His father refused to come at all."

"I can't say I admire your feelings," I said. "But thank you for being honest with me."

"Ah do hope you will take good care of Nathan," she said, and she handed me a check for two hundred and fifty dollars. That won't even pay a month's rent, I thought. I had already spent nearly five times as much on her son.

Nathan also had two brothers and a sister, but none of them ever visited. I spoke to one of his brothers on the phone. "It's because we all have children at home," he explained when I asked why he hadn't come. "We've talked it ovah, of course, and weah afraid we might bring germs back with us. We have to considah ouah children's health first. You can understand that."

"But the doctors say it isn't spread that way," I said, patiently explaining once again about contact with blood and the transmission routes of sex and needles.

"We know all that," he said. "But we all feel that the doctahs can't be one hundred percent shuah, and weah not willin' to take that chance with ouah children's lahves."

By that time, famous people like the movie actor Rock Hudson had begun to die of AIDS, and the public responded with panic. In New York, parents heard that there was one child with AIDS somewhere in the giant school system, and they pulled their children out of classes and began to picket the schools. Gay people were being assaulted in the streets by teenage thugs who yelled, "Die, AIDS carrier!" People were losing their jobs. Landlords were kicking sick people out of their apartments and into the streets, and the city had no shelters for them. Editorials called for the tattooing of anyone who tested positive for antibodies to the virus, and politicians were seriously discussing a massive quarantine, a gathering of people that would outstrip the internment of Japanese Americans during World War II and begin to rival the concentration of European Jews into ghettos during the Holocaust.

Nathan never knew about any of this. He died on a Tuesday in October, 1985. He was twenty-eight years old. His friends held a memorial service three days later, which his parents did not attend. Instead they asked that he be cremated and that his ashes be sent home to them in an urn. I don't know how they were disposed of.

Two days after Nathan's service, I was having breakfast when the phone rang. It was Louie.

"Can you come over right away?" he said, coughing between his words. "I think I'm sick."

PART VII
DANIEL DELL BLAKE

O how can it be that the ground itself does not sicken? . . .
Are they not continually putting distemper'd corpses within
    you?
Is not every continent work'd over and over with sour dead? . . .

What chemistry!
That the winds are really not infectious,
That this is no cheat, this transparent green-wash of the sea
    which is so amorous after me,
That it is safe to allow it to lick my naked body all over with
    its tongues,
That it will not endanger me with the fevers that have
    deposited themselves in it,
That all is clean forever and forever . . .
That when I recline on the grass I do not catch any disease,
Though probably every spear of grass rises out of what was
    once a catching disease . . .

                          —Walt Whitman,
                          "This Compost"

CHAPTER TWENTY-TWO

I rushed over to Louie's apartment, where I found him with a raging fever. He had lost a noticeable amount of weight in the few weeks since I had seen him, and he couldn't stop coughing. The only thing I could do was call an ambulance to take him to the hospital, and hope the doctors could do something. The first hospital we went to wouldn't admit him. "Your friend looks like he has AIDS. We have more than our share of cases already. I'm sorry, but you'll have to go somewhere else," the doctor said, turning away. No amount of threatening and screaming on my part could change his mind. So we were forced to travel to another hospital on the East Side, where Louie was accepted. He was given a bronchoscopy, which showed that he had *Pneumocystis carinii* pneumonia, an opportunistic AIDS infection. They put him on a respirator in the intensive care unit, and we waited.

"If your friend pulls through this bout, we can hope for a year at best," the doctor said. This was before any of the life-prolonging drugs were released by the Food and Drug Administration, which wasn't in any particular hurry to save the lives of gay men and drug addicts.

"Can I stay with him?" I asked.

"There are three visiting periods a day in the intensive care ward," the doctor said. "You can come then. Believe me, we'll do all we can."

I felt a little better then. In the past, I had heard from too many friends about hospitals which would allow only blood relatives to visit the gravely ill, and of gay patients dying in the company of brothers or cousins whom they had never loved while being denied the right to see their chosen life mates. At least in that respect times had changed, thank God—or better yet, thank the gay liberation movement, I thought.

Several days passed, and I found myself having to attend to the technical details of Louie's life. Between visiting periods at the hospital, I went to his house and phoned his employees and found his health insurance policy and watered his plants. Then I went back to the hospital and filled out forms.

I didn't know whom to share my fears with, until I finally decided to call Kelly and tell her what was happening. She had met Louie in the early 1970s, and at first she had bristled at what she saw as the mockery of women in his use of female genders and names for men. But eventually they had warmed to each other, and as the ideological fervor of the early movement years had mellowed, they had begun to accept each other as they were. "Let me come over," she said, and she was at my house within an hour.

"I can't thank you enough for coming," I said.

"Hey," she said. "This is my war too."

"What about your lesbian separatism?" I asked.

"That was then. This is now. What can I do to help?"

She stayed with me that evening and took me out to dinner. She called every day to see how Louie was doing, and she came to the hospital twice to be with me. She was my friend when I needed one most.

Several of Louie's friends heard what had happened and came to the hospital to see if they could be helpful. Then we would sit there together, watching him fight for breath, our eyes filled with tears. I kept imagining that he would wake and say something sentimental like, "We had fun while it lasted, didn't we?" Or something outrageous like Oscar Wilde's legendary last words in a Paris hotel, "Either that wallpaper goes or I do." But he just lay there, heavily sedated so he wouldn't try to fight the respirator tubes, and we just sat there waiting and trying to hope.

After five days, it was over. He just stopped living. I saw it happen. One moment he was alive and the next he wasn't. It was that simple. The doctor was there, and he ordered the respirator turned off. Then he turned to me and said, "I'm sorry. We did the best we could."

I wanted to thank him, to tell him that I knew how hard he had tried. But I couldn't say anything at all. I just stood there. Then I turned and left. I went home and spent that afternoon and evening sitting in a chair. I didn't feed Camerado. I didn't turn on the lights. I just sat there, remembering. Finally I went to sleep.

The next day I had to deal with his funeral.

It was just like Louie to think he didn't need such things as a burial plot or a will because he was planning to live forever. I knew from things he had said that he had wanted a traditional burial, and I felt that keeping busy would be the best thing for me. So I called several undertakers to inquire about prices and procedures, only to discover that they didn't want to deal with him at all because he had died of AIDS. The fourth one was willing to deal with his body, but only if no embalming was involved—and he wanted his money up front.

I called Kelly for advice. "What am I going to do?" I asked. "The undertaker wants to be paid in advance."

"Is there anything you can hock, so you can give them a down payment?"

I thought for a while. I didn't own all that much, and little of it was worth considering, but I did have Minerva White's photographs. I looked at the three remaining pictures on the wall: the luminous white blossoms, the portrait of Chester and me, and the face of Miss White's friend. Without too much thought, I took the photograph of Miss White's friend off the wall. I don't know why I chose that one. Maybe it was because I loved the warmth in her eyes and I wanted to give Louie the comfort she had always offered me. It was hard to part with. Over the years I had looked at it again and again and I had grown to love everything about it, even the strange mole between her eyebrows. I held the photograph to my chest to say good-bye and cried before I parted with it. Of course I knew I was really crying for Louie, and I would gladly have given away all my pictures and everything I owned if I could bring him back. Kelly took the picture to a dealer while I went back to the hospital. Later that day she showed up with three thousand dollars in cash.

"It's the best I could do," she explained.

"It's great," I said. "Thanks."

I added some of my dwindling savings to it, and we buried him in a nice cemetery in New Jersey. Kelly came, and so did Louie's friends and the people who had worked in his shop. We didn't have a clergyman. Instead I thought I would say a few words. I wrote them down, knowing it wouldn't be easy to concentrate, and when the coffin had been lowered in the grave, I tried to speak. But I began to sob so hard that I couldn't say a word. Kelly took the paper from me, and read.

"Louis Pellegrino was my best friend. He always gave me generously of his love, his time, his money, and his loyalty, and he asked only my friendship in return. To some people he might have seemed a person of little consequence, but he was important to those whose lives he touched. To some people he might have seemed to be a simple man, but if he didn't go to many schools, he still learned many lessons, and in his own way he was wise. To some people he might have seemed a frivolous, undirected person, but to those who benefited from his presence, he lived a graceful life whose purposes were pleasure and beauty and love. He never did anyone any harm, and not too many of us can say that of ourselves. The world may not know it, but it will be poorer for his absence. I know that I will. Good-bye, Miss Lulu. Enjoy your rest. You earned it."

I took a spray of the lavender roses called "sterling silver," which had been his favorite flower, and I dropped them gently one by one into his grave, quoting a line from Whitman's elegy for Lincoln: "O Death, I cover you over with roses." Then I turned and left.

I was at loose ends after the funeral. I didn't have a job or much money. I wasn't old enough for Social Security, even if I were eligible, which I wasn't sure I would be. I was too old to wander around on my own. What I needed was a job, but it had to be something that would help confront the epidemic that was destroying my world. I had to feel that I was doing something useful. I owed that much to Louie and Nathan and Sean and a host of others, whom I'd mindlessly helped to expose themselves to the deadly virus.

Two weeks later I found just what I had been looking for. I started working as an office assistant to Neil King, M.D., whose practice was largely composed of people with AIDS. Dr. King was younger than I was by some ten years or so, somewhere in his early fifties. He had a chocolate-brown complexion, close-cropped steel-wool hair shot through with gray, and wise eyes over which he wore horn-rimmed glasses, which, along with his vested suits and inconspicuous neckties, gave him a faintly academic air. He spoke without a trace of Southern accent and sounded as if he had been raised in New England. But he came from Georgia and had gone to great pains, he told me, to polish his English so that he would have as few strikes against him as possible in the white man's medical world.

He wasn't a political radical, but he did have a strong sense of self-worth and a special compassion for members of minority groups, particularly the two to which he belonged, neither of which appreciated him. As a black man he was often considered an Uncle Tom by radical separatists, in spite of his special attempts to seek out black patients and to warn black leaders that in spite of their desire for a more acceptable community image, if they didn't want even greater numbers of their people to die, they needed to acknowledge that there were drug addicts and homosexuals and prostitutes among them. He told them what they didn't want to hear: that the disease was attacking them in numbers disproportionate to their percentage of the population, and that they had to confront the danger facing them as the gays had, with self-help groups that filled the gap created by government inattention. Even though he never denied his homosexual orientation, gay radicals considered him a closet case since he did little in the way of speech-making and demonstrating. Instead he warned his gay patients that they had to curb their desire for sexual excess and told gay leaders that they had to redouble their commitment to the fight for political equality as the blacks had, even in the face of setbacks and tokenism. In short, he was that much maligned creature, "a credit to both his communities."

"How old are you, Dell?" he had asked me when I was first interviewed.

"I'll be sixty-three next June, but I'm still an efficient worker."

"Why shouldn't you be?" he said. "Your age probably makes you all the more dependable."

"I think we're going to get along fine," I said.

"Why do you want to do this kind of work?"

"In the first place, I've had some experience working in a doctor's office, although it was quite a while ago. In the second place, I've lost too many friends, and I want to feel that I'm doing something to help, no matter how insignificant it is. In the third place . . . well, maybe there isn't a third place."

"How about you 'like to work with people'? Or you 'need to make a living'?"

"Yes, both of those are in third place."

"Can you start tomorrow at seven a.m.?" he asked.

"Sure," I said with a smile. "I'll be here."

My duties were much the same as those I had performed in Gordon Thomas's office in Portland. I arranged appointments and escorted patients and filled files with data and cleaned out examination rooms and took weight statistics and blood samples— the last with extreme caution, so that I wouldn't accidentally stick myself with a contaminated needle and expose myself to the virus.

Some of the patients were familiar to me as my massage patrons at the Everard, or as denizens of the Mineshaft whom I'd seen at their exotic play, or as customers who had stopped off on the way home from work for a quick sexual release in the back room of Manbooks. But the majority of them were men I didn't know, men who had led quiet lives, who hadn't had more than a few sexual partners. Most of them were good-looking, gentle-mannered, and intelligent, and most of them were frightened half to death, although they revealed their feelings in a multitude of ways, ranging from soft desperation to visible rage.

All of us by that time had become regular inspectors of our skin after each shower, hoping not to find the first lesion that marked us for death. And we had become suspicious listeners, demanding of every cough that it have a chest cold to explain itself. A sore throat or a headache or a fungus might be a danger sign, and people visited the doctor for any possible symptom, hoping to be called hypochondriacs and to be able to laugh at themselves with relief.

Soon after I started working with Neil, an olive-skinned man about forty years old appeared in the office. I thought he was the most attractive man I'd seen in years. His thick, dark hair and beard surrounded a strong-featured face with large, limpid brown eyes that promised understanding beneath dark, bushy brows, a prominent, well-formed nose, and plump, sensuous lips. I found myself wanting to kiss him hello, but instead I smiled and asked his name.

"Aaron Friedman," he replied. "I have an appointment."

"And what is the nature of your problem, Mr. Friedman?"

"I have a white patch in my mouth. It's probably thrush. I've already had lymphadenopathy and shingles."

"Take a seat. Dr. King will see you as soon as he's able."

He was the last patient of the day, and Dr. King was notorious for keeping his patients waiting for hours. He always meant well when his schedule was arranged, but somehow or other he got caught up in one case, or an emergency intervened, or a phone call from a colleague had to be answered, and whoever had the later appointments in the day could expect to wait for a very long time.

Aaron sat in his chair calmly, as if he were resigned to having an unpleasant experience, and he didn't pick up a magazine or pull out a crossword puzzle. He did nothing to entertain himself, and when I wasn't involved with one of the other patients, I did nothing but watch him. Very slowly, one by one, the long line of people who were ahead of him began to disappear into the farthest reaches of the office, behind a wooden door. But even though there were rumblings of complaint from people who had arrived only a short time before he had, he continued to wait calmly. After an hour and a half, when there were still five people ahead of him, he noticed the copy of *Leaves of Grass* that I kept on my desk.

"Do you mind if I look at your book?" he asked.

"My pleasure," I said.

He read through it for over an hour, remaining completely absorbed, turning the pages back and forth from poem to poem as if he were already familiar with them, sometimes nodding in agreement, sometimes shaking his head in dismay. I watched him as he read, wondering what was going on in his mind. But I was too polite to ask. Finally it was his turn to be examined, and he returned the book to me, and said simply, "Thank you."

"Did you enjoy it?" I asked.

"I always do," he said. "I must know half of it by heart already. I've been in love with Walt for years."

"I feel the same way about him," I said as I ushered him into the examination room. "Good luck with the exam."

"Thanks," he said. "I think I'll need it."

When he came out nearly half an hour later, everyone else was gone and I was closing the office for the day. He sat down for a moment, to collect himself before leaving.

"How did it go?" I inquired.

"I do have thrush," he said. "The doctor says it's not a good sign, but it's common among people with AIDS. It will pass."

"I hope so," I said.

"Thanks."

"Hey, would you like to have a cup of coffee?" I asked. "I know a little place near here where we could just talk. I have a feeling you could use it, and to tell you the truth I could too. By the way, my name's Dell. Actually, Daniel Dell Blake is the long form, but people call me Dell."

"Okay, Dell," he answered. "I don't have to be home for a while. My son is at my mother's house, and she'll give him supper."

"Are you married?" I asked.

"I was," he said. "But we were divorced when I came out of the closet."

After we had settled ourselves over a cup of coffee in a small Hungarian restaurant, we talked about Walt Whitman.

424

"I write poetry myself," he said. "And Walt's always been a model for me."

"I write poetry too," I said. "And the same is true for me."

"Do you suppose we're writing the same poems?"

"Not likely," I said. "I'm over twenty years older than you are."

"So what?" he said. "What does that have to do with the price of condoms in Greenwich Village?"

I looked up in surprise. Had he intended to make a sexual invitation? He had a twinkle in his eye, and I could see signs of welcome, but I had no way to know whether they were erotic or not.

"Would you like to read one of my poems?" he asked.

"Very much," I said.

He took a slender sheaf of papers from the portfolio he was carrying and, after thumbing through the pages, he handed me one. I read:

Instructions for Reading "Song of Myself"

1. Go swimming in it, don't just walk. (Fly, don't drown.)
2. Wear nothing except skin (shiny, perspired).
3. Think One from now on.
4. Check the mirror now and then:
     a. the pits of your arms (deep)
     b. the soles of your feet (high)
     c. the part of your body most central (core)
5. Get scared of a blade of grass, as if of God.
6. Fall in love with yourself. Who are you? A blade of grass?
7. One: looks, listens, smells, tastes, touches: One
8. Make very long lists of your own: add them up to the
     world you know. Start with your feet on the grass.
9. Answer back: Are you going to let Walt Whitman tell you
     what to think?
10. Get wet; let the sun dry you; get sunburned; jump in the
     water; swim; keep swimming; float.
11. Don't give up.
12. I (wanted to tell you) . . .

When I was finished, I looked up and said, "Will you marry me?"

He laughed, but he soon grew serious. "I would," he said. "But I have AIDS."

"So what?" I replied. "What does that have to do with the price of condoms in Greenwich Village?" And we both laughed. "Seriously," I continued. "What kind of work do you do?"

"I teach writing," he said. "I use that poem with my freshman class."

"Where do you teach?"

"In a branch of the City University in Queens. I also teach an advanced course in Whitman. My view of Whitman—the gay view, that is."

"Now about that marriage . . . Should we pick out a china pattern?"

Somehow I knew he wasn't really changing the subject when he asked, "Have you worked for Dr. King very long?"

"Only a couple of weeks," I said. "I've had what you call a 'checkered career.' I've lived in a number of places across the country—San Francisco, Seattle, Chicago, Pittsburgh, a few others—and I've had different kinds of jobs."

"I've been teaching since I got out of graduate school," he said.

"Why do you like Whitman?" I asked.

"His work coincides with the emergence of a gay identity. He wrote just at the point when enough people were gathering in America's cities for the gays among them to begin forming a subculture. But more than that, he expresses the spiritual side of the gay experience. He's a voice for freedom in spite of his own fears and limitations. He became a voice for the nation in spite of—or maybe because of—his being different. Besides all that, he's a damn fine poet."

"I think so too," I said. "I've been working on a book about him for years, but I haven't managed to get very far into it."

"Why not?" he asked.

"I'm not sure," I answered. "I think it's because I keep trying to understand what the world looked like through his eyes. But I live in a different time, with a different vision."

"There are differences, but there are similarities too," he commented.

"Even if there are, he's so hard to pin down with all his contradictions. He said himself he 'contains multitudes.' "

"I know what you mean," Aaron said, waxing enthusiastic. "For example, he was a great individualist, an exemplar of his era's ideals, but at the same time he was an American nationalist, and beyond that a universalist. He lived on all those levels at once. Today's world demands a global sensibility. If he were alive today, I'm sure he'd focus not just on America's place in the world, but on Earth, preparing to reach out to cultures beyond our solar system."

"Do you think he would be a gay liberationist?" I asked.

"Of course. If he could be an individualist and a national patriot at the same time, he could champion the rights of a group as well. One reason he could encompass the whole nation so easily was the size of the population. The whole country held millions of people then. It holds hundreds of millions now, with millions of gay people among them. Even though he wasn't much of a champion of political causes, if such a group had been defined in his day, I'm sure he would have been supportive. He singled them out instinctively anyway. Do you know 'Native Moments'?"

"I think I know the lines you mean," I said, quoting:

'I will play a part no longer, why should I exile myself
   from my companions?
O you shunn'd persons, I at least do not shun you,
I come forthwith in your midst, I will be your poet,
I will be more to you than to any of the rest.' "

"Exactly," he said. "You really do know your Whitman, don't you?"

"It's a labor of love," I said.

"Will you excuse me a minute?" he said. "I have to make a phone call."

While he was away from the table, I entertained myself with thoughts of what his body looked like under the loose sweater and corduroy pants he wore. He was a little shorter than I, and he seemed to have a slim, wiry build. I liked that. I imagined caressing his hard buttocks. Maybe I could offer him a massage, I thought.

When he returned, he said, "I just asked my mother if Alexander—that's my son—could stay the night. Would you like to come back to my place? I can make us some dinner."

"As it happens, I'm free tonight—and very willing."

"Good. Do you like fish? I can pick up some salmon steaks."

"That sounds great," I said.

"And there's some blueberry pie my mother baked. We can have that for dessert."

"I just knew it wouldn't be apple," I said. "I'd love some."

"What did you say about apple?"

"I was just being glad it wasn't apple pie," I explained. "I hate apples."

We ate by candlelight. I felt right at home in his apartment on the Upper West Side. It was lined with books and interesting pictures. The furniture was solid and comfortable, the colors were warm, and the food was delicious.

Over dinner, I asked him about his son.

"Alexander is eleven," he said. "He's had a rough time of it. I married his mother when I was still closeted, and he was born a year later. In the mid-seventies, I decided I was really gay and I didn't want to live a lie. She divorced me, and we had a long custody battle over Alexander. The court decided that we should share custody, but she wasn't too happy about that because she thought I was a bad influence. She eventually became a fanatic fundamentalist, a follower of one of those television evangelists . . ."

I interrupted his story. "What was her religion when you married her?"

"Presbyterian. But that wasn't important to me. Anyway, she refused to let him come back when it was time. I got a court injunction, so she disappeared with him. It took almost a year to locate them. Then the court granted me sole custody because she had been in contempt. That was six

427

years ago. Things are a little calmer now. She's remarried and has other children to look after."

"And Alexander's happy with you?"

"He wanted to stay with me in the first place. I had only let him stay with her because the court ordered it. He's a great kid. You'll like him."

"I'm sure I will," I said. But I wondered if that were true. I'd never had the chance to relate to someone that young.

Wandering around the rooms while Aaron cleared the dishes, I noticed a yellow star made of cloth with the word *Jood* in the center. It was on a backing of black velvet, framed in plain wood, and standing on a small easel. I brought it into the kitchen.

"What's this?" I asked.

"It was my grandmother's. At least it could have been," he said. "She was killed in Auschwitz."

"I'm sorry," I said.

"That's my other big passion," he told me. "I collect books and videotapes about the Holocaust. I'm fascinated by what happened to my Jewish and gay counterparts in the concentration camps, but not in a moribund way. I'm just trying to understand what it really says about human nature."

"You don't have to apologize," I said.

"Was I apologizing? I guess I was. I didn't realize it. So many people think it's distasteful or demented to be interested in a horror like that. But I'm concerned that it could happen again, this time with the focus on the gays. A lot of the early signs are present already: the talk of rounding up people for quarantine; tattooing; violent attacks in the street against a hated minority . . ."

"I know," I said. "I worry, too."

"I like you," he said.

"But I'm an old man," I answered.

"Only if you think you are. Besides, what's wrong with old men?"

"Nothing," I said, and I put my arms around him. We hugged, cheek to cheek, and held each other for several minutes. Then we kissed chastely on the lips and drew apart.

"I'm not sure how to behave," I said. "I've had plenty of experience, but it's been quite a while since the last one, and the rules are different now."

"Don't worry," he said. "I won't let us do anything that isn't safe."

He led me into the bedroom, where we stroked each other's faces gently. Then he began to remove my clothes. I followed suit and removed his. His body was just as I had imagined it, with a fine coat of hair covering his chest. We touched each other carefully all over. It was more sensual than any foreplay I could remember. Then I gave him that massage I had been thinking about, and he gave me one in return. When we were both relaxed, he began to kiss every part of me until I was hard. I did the same to him.

He stood back and looked at our two erections. "I'd really like to fuck you, Dell."

"I'd like that too. And I'd like to return the favor."

He reached into the nightstand drawer and pulled out two condoms. Each of us put one on the other's cock. He turned me over and played with my ass until it was ready. Then he entered me slowly and carefully and left his cock inside. "I like the warmth," he said.

"I like the hardness," I said.

He moved expertly and began to pump, pleasuring both of us that way for five minutes or so. Then he pulled out.

"Now you," he said.

I did the same things to him. When I was resting inside, I repeated his words. "I like the warmth," I said, and he repeated my reply.

After a few minutes of moving inside him, I withdrew.

I turned him over and took his balls in my mouth.

"That feels so good," he said.

The two of us sat facing each other, looking into each other's eyes.

"I'd like to suck your cock," he said, jerking on his own.

"I'd like to suck yours too, and I'd like to bury my face in your ass and stick my tongue inside."

"That would be hot," he said. "I'd like to lick up and down the crack of your ass before I fuck you."

"I'd like to lick the come from the tip of your cock."

"I'd like to swallow your hot load."

"I'd like to feel it shooting inside my hot ass."

"I'd like to tongue kiss you for hours."

"I'd like to sleep with my face in your sweaty crotch."

"Take off your rubber," he said, and he began to remove his as I removed mine. We stared into each other's eyes as we sat cross-legged, facing each other, jerking on our cocks. Then he moved closer until he could put his legs around me and our cocks were standing up together. We took turns jerking on both of them at once. I was holding them when he began to shoot his semen, and seeing it made me shoot my own. Then he took his hands and spread our mutual liquid all around both our groins, and we lay back and held each other and thought our separate thoughts for a while.

Eventually, he said, "What's your favorite line from Whitman?"

I recited my answer without having to stop and think: "I believe a leaf of grass is no less than the journey-work of the stars."

"Yes," he said softly. "A beautiful choice. I think it's my favorite too. It says it all. Maybe you can use it as a way into your book."

"There is no way into my book," I said.

"You should keep trying," he answered. "Do you know that there's a double meaning to the title *Leaves of Grass*?" He went on without waiting for an answer. "Printers used the term 'grass' to refer to trial pages that they threw out. That's why Whitman used the term 'leaves' instead of the usual word, 'blades.' It can refer either to the writer's discarded pages or to the countless units which together compose a single lawn. It's the small, insignificant creation that the entire universe is composed of: 'the good green grass, that delicate miracle the ever-recurring grass.' Do you know what I mean?"

I waited a very long time before I answered, lying absolutely still so my senses could have time to expand, until I was able to see the shadows that hung about the room, to hear the distant sounds of the city, to feel the wrinkled sheets beneath my back, to smell the mortal aroma of the man lying beside me, to taste the night. Then I said, "Yes, I understand."

"And the grass is something else, too," he continued. "In a burial ground, it's the resurrection of life growing out of the dead. Listen to this:

'In unseen essence and odor of surface and grass, centuries
   hence,
In blowing airs from the fields back again give me my
   darlings, give my immortal heroes,
Exhale me them centuries hence, breathe me their breath, let
   not an atom be lost . . .' "

Of course I thought of Louie in his grave. The memory was still painfully fresh, and my eyes brimmed over with tears.

"Thank you," I whispered.

Aaron held me and I held him, and we fell asleep in each other's arms.

The next day was my day off, and when I got home, I took out my manuscript again. I stared at it and thought, "I believe a leaf of grass is no less than the journey-work of the stars." And then I stared at it some more. What was it I wanted to say? Merely that Walt Whitman's sensibility was homosexual? I knew I could contradict the latest biographies that insisted that even if the poet were homosexual, either he didn't act on his feelings and merely fantasized about them, or they simply weren't important and had no bearing on interpreting his poems. But that dealt only with Walt's sexuality. What about his spirit?

Suddenly, without knowing why, I put on my coat and went to the library. I began at the beginning of the catalogue listings of books about Walt Whitman and worked my way slowly to the end. This time I was looking for something different. It took me two hours of looking, but I finally found what I needed. Four other novels about Walt Whitman had already been written. I sent for them to be brought to the reading room, and I spent the rest of the day going through them.

There were no revelations among them. All of them were decades old and showed the innocence of age. They paid homage to an American icon, the larger-than-life poet who declaimed lines from Shakespeare at the treetops, whose family loved him but didn't understand his poems, who befriended working men and soldiers out of altruism alone, who worked diligently at his craft and proclaimed his patriotism and hinted at mystical meanings just beyond one's understanding. They didn't present the impostor, most of whose siblings were mad or retarded or alcoholic, who anonymously wrote glowing reviews of his own book in order to promote himself, who was the prophet of sexual freedom yet lied about his own sexuality and nonetheless lighted the way for a later generation of his kind. Walt's words of caution echoed in my mind:

> When I read the book, the biography famous,
> And is this then (said I) what the author calls a man's life?
> And so will some one when I am dead and gone write my
> life?
> (As if any man really knew aught of my life,
> Why even I myself I often think know little or nothing of my
> real life,
> Only a few hints, a few diffused faint clews and indirections
> I seek for my own use to trace out here.)

I knew that each novel was a personal homage, revealing as much about its author as about the poet who was its subject. When I rose from the reading room table, I was undaunted by my predecessors. I knew that just as their books had expressed their visions, my book would express mine. But before I could do that I needed to define my vision. I needed to write about my own life before I could write about somebody else's. I felt a new sense of purpose rising. Maybe I wasn't a failure as a writer after all, I thought. Maybe I was only a late bloomer.

In that year, death kept intruding its eyeless face in my life, as if to remind me that there was only so much time to do my work. The day after I went to the library, my sweet little cat Camerado died. He was old and had been fading, and for some time I had become his nurse more than his companion. I had his remains cremated and went from the crematorium directly to the Brooklyn Bridge, where once I had seen Walt Whitman's face surrounded by radiant light. As I solemnly strewed Camerado's ashes into the water I wept, but I wasn't sad. Our relationship had been a full one, and it was complete. Then I went home to be alone.

In the weeks afterward, I heard that several other people I had known were dead of AIDS. One was Hilary, the drag performer turned architect, whose wedding to Marlene I had hosted in San Francisco. Their marriage had lasted for five years before he had quit his job and become openly gay.

Cynthia Chin had written her friend Sam and asked him to tell me the news. Sam was now retired as a male madam and had saved enough money to do what he wanted. He was a colorful figure at gay rallies and styled himself one of the first gay liberationists, calling himself the "Mayor of Greenwich Village"—and no one remembered enough about his career to challenge his credentials.

I also learned, from a man who had once worked in my brothel, that Curtis, the boy I'd had sex with, had died in New Jersey. He had stayed at the tree nursery for many years and had become the owner's lover. But eventually they had separated and Curtis had worked as a trainer in a gym. No one seemed to know anything more about his private life, except that he had gone home to his sister's house to die. Then Danny Oliver wrote me from San Francisco that his lover Jerome had died. He was planning to sell the bookstore, which contained too many painful memories, and move to the mountains of northern California, where he could devote himself to his writing.

I didn't know what to do with all this death. Grieving and sorrow threatened to become a full-time occupation, and I didn't want to let it linger. Finally, I decided that my mourning for them all would have to be condensed into a single act, and I resolved to visit Louie's grave. I took a bus to New Jersey and a taxi to the cemetery, where I found my way to the grave alone. I placed my tribute of sterling silver roses at the base of the simple tombstone that I had had erected, which said "Louis Pellegrino" with no dates, since I wasn't sure of the year he had been born. Then I thought of all the joy and nurture Louie had given me, and I began to miss him terribly. I stood there and cried for almost an hour, grieving for them all and for myself as well. Then I looked again at the letters of his name, carved plainly in the stone and surrounded by a simple circle, and my eyes widened. I remembered the word "Martha" carved on a similar stone years before, and I realized that I had ordered the design of Louie's stone in subconscious imitation of that memory. I sat down and leaned against it, and felt a strange comfort flow through me. Then I rose and returned home.

In my mailbox I found an envelope with Aaron's return address on it. Inside it was one of Whitman's most beautiful male love poems, in which the passion survives death itself:

> We two, how long we were fool'd,
> Now transmuted, we swiftly escape as Nature escapes,
> We are Nature, long have we been absent, but now we
> return,
> We become plants, trunks, foliage, roots, bark,
> We are bedded in the ground, we are rocks,
> We are oaks, we grow in the openings side by side,

We browse, we are two among the wild herds spontaneous as
    any,
We are two fishes swimming in the sea together,
We are what locust blossoms are, we drop scent around lanes
    mornings and evenings,
We are also the coarse smut of beasts, vegetables, minerals,
We are two predatory hawks, we soar above and look down,
We are two resplendent suns, we it is who balance ourselves
    orbic and stellar, we are as two comets,
We prowl fang'd and four-footed in the woods, we spring on
    prey,
We are two clouds forenoons and afternoons driving
    overhead,
We are seas mingling, we are two of those cheerful waves
    rolling over each other and interwetting each other,
We are what the atmosphere is, transparent, receptive,
    pervious, impervious,
We are snow, rain, cold, darkness, we are each product and
    influence of the globe,
We have circled and circled till we have arrived home again,
    we two,
We have voided all but freedom and all but our own joy.

Aaron couldn't have told me he loved me in a nicer way. He and I saw each other almost every day. His son Alexander was home most of the time, and we got along famously. The first time I met him, he said, "Are you Dad's new boyfriend?"

"I hope so," I answered.

"That's good," he replied. "Dad always has good taste in men."

"Alex!" cautioned his father. "You make me sound like I've had twenty lovers."

"He's had five," Alex said. "But you're the oldest."

"Is that bad?" Aaron asked him.

"Nope. It's probably good. Maybe you can teach him a few things."

"I think it's the other way around," I answered.

"Dad," Alexander said, changing the topic, "one of the kids called me a faggot in the school playground today."

"Are you one?" Aaron asked, without showing alarm.

"Nope," the boy replied. "You're not, either. You're gay, though."

"What did you do when he called you that?" I asked.

"I punched him."

"And what did he do?" I continued.

"He cried," Alexander said in a matter-of-fact tone. "What's for supper?"

"Roast chicken," Aaron said, and he smiled at me. "That's my son the avenger."

"Better that than your son the victim," I said.

I met Aaron's parents, a couple in their mid-seventies, who were eager to invite me to dinner soon after I had met their son. The three of us traveled to the northern part of the Bronx for the occasion. The Friedmans lived in a high-rise apartment house surrounded by parking lots. Aaron's father was short and rotund, with a bald head and rosy cheeks. He said very little, but I sensed a genuine feeling of warmth in him. He carried his open newspaper around, but never seemed to finish reading it. Mrs. Friedman was even shorter, and equally plump. Her short, gray hair had been neatly bobbed in a local beauty parlor, and she wore harlequin-style eyeglasses, which frequently rode down her large nose because their thick lenses were so heavy. She was constantly busy with something: preparing supper, hanging up coats, or smoothing her apron. At the same time she was constantly talking: encouraging us to eat the chopped liver and crackers she had put out as hors d'oeuvres, but reminding us to be sure to leave enough room for supper; worrying about the warmth of Aaron's clothes; asking me questions about my work; and making sure Alexander had done his homework. In anyone else such intense scrutiny might have seemed meddlesome and overbearing, but in her it was clearly nothing but love.

"Did you wash your hands, Alexi sweetheart?" she inquired.

"Yes, Grandma," he said with a groan.

"Pardon me. I was only asking. It's not because I'm worried you'll dirty my good napkins, you know."

"I know."

"Come here and give me a kiss," she said. He obliged as if it were a chore.

"Thank you, darling. I'm sorry to be so much trouble. Dell, is this boy gorgeous or what? Give me an honest opinion."

"He's gorgeous."

"Aaron, you should bring Dell here more often. He's got good taste. Do you like *cholent*, Dell?"

"I don't know," I said. "I never had it."

She clapped her hand to her cheek and rocked her head from side to side. "A grown man living in New York doesn't know Jewish food? This is shocking! Try it. You'll like it. It's beans and potato mashed with bits of meat. What could be bad?"

"It's very good," I said.

"You're not just being polite?"

"No. Really."

"Oh God, thank you," she said. "At my age that I should find a brand new customer is a blessing. I feel like a lecher who just met a virgin!"

"Ma!" Aaron warned.

"So you should be the only one in the family with a quick tongue? I'm sorry, Dell. I didn't mean to imply that you were a virgin."

"You're making it worse," Aaron said.

"So I'll start from scratch. Do you like *tsimmes*, Dell?"

"*Oy!*" said Aaron.

"I guess I am a virgin when it comes to such good food," I said.

"A lovely person," she said definitively. "Marry him quickly, Aaron, before he gets away. All right, don't look at me that way! I didn't mean a thing. Just the raving of an old woman. Look, look, I'm back in the kitchen already, minding my own business."

I went in and kissed her on the cheek. "I like you too," I said. "And I think I'll take your advice."

She looked around the stove through the door, to see if Aaron was listening, but he had gone to the bathroom. Then she whispered. "How is he, really? I don't think he looks so good. You have experience. You work with this in the doctor's office, no?"

"He's okay for the present," I said. "All we can do is wait and hope."

"Thank you for not running away from him," she said.

"Mrs. Friedman . . ."

"Esther," she interrupted. "And the quiet one with the newspaper is Sol."

"Esther, I couldn't run away from him if I wanted to. I love him. I only worry that I'm too old for him."

"Feh, nonsense! What you need is a little consciousness-raising about your age. I'm ten years older than you are, and I'm not too old for anything. If my Sol wasn't such a good man, I'd . . . well, never mind that."

I walked into the living room. Sol spoke to me while he held his newspaper open. "Tell me," he said. "You work in a doctor's office. You might know. How is he, really? I can take the truth."

A few weeks later, I moved my things to Aaron's apartment, and he and Alexander and I became a family—complete with visiting in-laws. We even had a little ceremony with a cake, one of Esther's mocha masterpieces. Each of us in turn read these lines from Whitman:

> Camerado, I give you my hand!
> I give you my love more precious than money,
> I give you myself before preaching or law;
> Will you give me yourself? will you come travel with me?
> Shall we stick by each other as long as we live?

After each of us spoke the words, the other said simply, "Yes." And then we embraced, while Esther and Sol yelled, "*Mazel tov!*" and Alexander said, "That's neat."

The next day I began to write this book. In the next few months, I used every spare moment when I wasn't at Dr. King's office or in Aaron's arms to work on it. The process went slowly. Much of the time away from the typewriter was spent remembering, which wasn't always a pleasant task. Sometimes old anger or guilt had to be felt all over again: when I thought of the Japanese prison camp, or Laura on her way to the hospital, or Harold's body being dragged from the lake in Madison, or Duke in the Cook County Jail. But I also got to live old pleasures again: when I wrote about Louie and the English sailors in Provincetown, or about listening to José Sarria at the Black Cat Café, or dancing in front of Willard at Finocchio's, or going to Riverview Amusement Park with Maisie Dot and the girls from Miss Wanda's house.

Aaron was as supportive as he could be. He listened to me read my rough drafts aloud, amazed at how much I had seen. "I feel like I've led such a sheltered life," he said.

"Maybe you're lucky," I answered.

That spring, New York City finally passed a law protecting gay people from discrimination in jobs and housing, after fifteen years of rejecting it. There had been a lot of editorials in the newspapers, some of them ugly threats of doom and some of them quiet appeals to reason. Supporters and opponents had marched in the streets, and tensions had run high. A great wave of exuberance swept through the gay community in the wake of the bill's passage. Everyone was eager to turn away from the epidemic for a moment to celebrate.

In June, Aaron and I marched together in the gay pride parade, accompanied by Alexander, Esther, and Sol. We walked part of the way with the Parents and Friends of Lesbians and Gays, which the Friedmans had belonged to for years, and part of the way with the People With AIDS Coalition. It was a happy day, full of sunshine and promise. But I cried when everyone stopped to release balloons in memory of those who had died of AIDS. I had brought six balloons—in memory of Louie, Sean, Gary, Curtis, Hilary, and Jerome—but I didn't cry only for them. I cried for fear that the next year there could be a seventh one, for Aaron.

A few days after the gay pride march, the United States Supreme Court decided, in *Bowers v. Hardwick*, that the states had the right to keep their sodomy laws on the books, which meant that Americans did not have the right to privacy in their own bedrooms. We were back on the streets that day, demonstrating our rage.

In the evening, Aaron told me he wanted to discuss something serious.

"I've made out my will," he said.

"Let's not be morbid," I replied.

"I'm not. I'm being practical. I've been relatively lucky with this thing so far, but that can't last too much longer."

"Okay," I said.

"Mom and Dad have their pensions and some investments, so they're all right. I want to leave whatever I have to you. It isn't much, but I want you to have it because I love you."

"You don't have to give me anything," I said.

"You didn't have to stay with me," he answered.

"Oh yes I did, and I don't want to be paid for it. I didn't do it because I was sorry for you. I did it because a year with you is worth ten years with an ordinary person."

"I wasn't thinking in terms of payment," he said. "I was thinking of Alexander. I want you to adopt him."

"Me?" I said. "A father?"

"Of course. Why not?"

"You know that I abandoned my own son in Seattle?"

"Dell, that was forty years ago. You're a different person now."

"Do you think it will be all right with Alexander?"

"He suggested it," Aaron said.

"Do you think he might be gay?" I asked.

"Beats me," he said. "Why don't we leave that up to him?"

"We don't have any choice in the matter," I replied.

"Will you love him any the less if he's straight?"

"Of course not."

"I knew that," Aaron said. "Now the problems as I see them are fourfold. First, you're gay. But gay people are being allowed to adopt more and more often."

"Will that stay the same after the Supreme Court's decision?"

"Sodomy is not a crime in New York State," he reminded me.

"No, it's just unsafe," I said.

"Second," he continued, ignoring my acerbic comment, "you're older than most adoptive parents. But my parents are too old to start such a commitment, and Alexander already loves you. I only hope his mother doesn't try to fight this. She's made no effort to keep in touch with Alexander, and she and her new husband probably won't want to add the child of a gay person with AIDS to their household."

"Let's pray they won't," I said.

"Let's not. Just promise me that if she tries to interfere, you'll fight for as long as it takes and that you'll go to the highest court you can until you get the law on your side. Two judges have voted against her fanaticism already, so it's not an impossible battle."

"I promise."

"Thanks, I knew you would. The third problem is that, being gay, you're at risk for AIDS."

"No," I said. "I tested negative for antibodies."

"That's great," he said. "Why didn't you tell me?"

"I didn't want to make you jealous."

"Very funny. The only problem remaining is your somewhat checkered past. No matter what theories we may have about prostitution, running a brothel full of teenage hustlers is not usually considered a great recommendation for parenthood."

"Aren't you going to ask me if I would sell Alexander into white slavery?"

"No," he said. "Not after what you did for young Danny. There's no reason that anyone should discover your past. You didn't pay taxes from the job at Miss Wanda's, or from the proceeds at your own place, did you?"

"No," I answered. "Only from my jobs at Gus's Diner in Seattle, at Edwin's antique shop, at Gordon's office in Portland, and right now at Dr. King's office."

"So, who's to know?"

"It's in my book," I said.

"This may be done before it's published."

"Don't say that, Aaron. You'll be around for a long time yet."

"Maybe," he said. "But just in case, I've decided what I'd like on my tombstone. Most people won't know what it means, but you and I will. He gave me a slip of paper with a few lines from one of Walt's poems:

> "Publish my name and hang up my picture as that of the
>   tenderest lover,
> The friend the lover's portrait, of whom his friend his lover
>   was fondest,
> Who was not proud of his songs, but of the measureless
>   ocean of love within him, and freely pour'd it forth."

That was the first time I got really depressed about Aaron's condition. Maybe I had been practicing some fancy form of denial up to that point, but after that discussion it was hard to pretend everything was going to be all right. I called Kelly to discuss the adoption, and she said, "I think it's a great idea. It'll be good for both you and the boy. I'm so much in favor of it that I'll even marry you if it'll help."

"Is this a proposal?" I asked.

"No, it's a capitulation to the system," she said. "But it's for a good cause."

I was almost finished with the first draft of *Song of Myself* by then. (I had decided at last to use the title for my Whitman novel, because so much of my own life story was about not writing that book.) But I had stopped writing again, because I didn't want to finish the final pages.

Then one morning, Aaron woke up and he couldn't get out of bed. His right side was paralyzed. I thought Aaron might have undergone something similar to Walt Whitman, who had been in the same condition after a massive stroke, but Dr. King diagnosed it as toxoplasmosis of the central nervous system, an AIDS-related disease. Aaron finally admitted that he had to stop working. He spent several weeks in the hospital, getting his strength back. Esther and Sol and Alexander and I were there every day to cheer him up. But he didn't regain mobility in his limbs. I took a leave from my job at Dr. King's office, so I could look after him. In order to have enough cash, I sold another of Minerva White's photographs. This time I had to choose between the picture of me and Chester and the one of the luminous white blossoms. I sold the one of me and Chester, perhaps to say that the past is over and that Aaron and I are the present. After all, I'm now nearly forty years older than Chester was when he died. He will always be much younger than Aaron is, and I'm far too old for him. We must finally let go of the past. Chester's memory will live in this book, along with the memory of everyone I've loved. So I am left with the photograph of the luminous blossoms. I've promised myself that I will part with it only if the survival of Alexander or me or my writing depends on it. Something about it has always gone to the very depth of my being, and I'd still like to find out what it is.

We brought Aaron home this morning, to see if he recovers and can go on for a while. In some cases, with treatment these symptoms are only temporary, and perhaps he will recover. We can only wait and hope. As I sat by his bed today, Aaron told me in his mumbled speech, caused by the partial paralysis of his face, to look in the nightstand drawer. There I found an envelope marked: "For Dell. Open when it's over." I put it in my pocket.

When it's my turn to sleep, Alexander takes my place and sits at his father's bedside. I have tried to prepare him for his father's death by telling him that, even though we do the best that we can, there are forces greater than our own to which we must bow. We are only here in the sunlight for a moment, yet we are very important. Each of us is no more than a leaf of grass, but each of us is no less than the journey-work of the stars.

EPILOGUE

I can't seem to stop writing *Song of Myself*, but a book, like a life, has to end somewhere. On the day that Aaron died, I opened the envelope he had given me. His last message, true to form, was by Walt Whitman:

Good-bye my Fancy!
Farewell dear mate, dear love!
I'm going away, I know not where,
Or to what fortune, or whether I may ever see you again,
So Good-bye my Fancy.

Now for my last—let me look back a moment;
The slower fainter ticking of the clock is in me,
Exit, nightfall, and soon the heart-thud stopping.

Long have we lived, joy'd, caress'd together;
Delightful!—now separation—Good-bye my Fancy.

One of the hardest things about losing Aaron, I realized at that moment, was that I wouldn't be able to share his love of Walt's poetry any longer. I decided that day to buy Alexander his own copy of *Leaves of Grass*.

As soon as we finished straightening up from Aaron's funeral, my son and I left for Elysium. Now I'm sitting on the northbound train, watching the Hudson River flow past, and Alexander is asleep in the seat beside me. I've finished the prologue, and I've decided to spend the rest of the time on the train taking notes for an ending.

After all these years, I'm finally going home. I told myself that I'm doing it for Alexander, but the real reason is that I'm feeling somewhat shell-shocked from the long siege of illness and death. And—even though I'm supposedly too old for that sort of thing—I want the solace of Martha's stone, that once served so well to soothe my childhood grief. Or maybe I just want to say a final farewell to my past before I start all over again. I wonder what I'll find there. I wonder if there will be even a trace left of anyone or anything I knew, and if it will even matter after all this time.

Reality is rarely kind enough to give a pleasant shape to things, so perhaps for the sake of symmetry I could end with my return home as I would like it to be . . .

Notes for an Ending

As we arrive in Elysium, I don't recognize the center of town, which has grown quite large. The houses on the outskirts look vaguely familiar, but it isn't until we arrive at the orchard on Orphean Hill that I feel the past gathering me into its folds. The door is opened by an old woman with a kind, strangely familiar face. I introduce myself and my son. "I am your aunt, Martha Blake," she says, with tears filling her eyes. "Come inside. Your father is sleeping. He's been ill."

"I didn't know I had an aunt," I tell her.

Alexander and I listen enrapt while she tells me her story over a cup of tea.

"When I was a young woman, I fell madly in love with another young woman, Helen Dell, who lived in the valley. We were lovers, body and soul. My brother, your father, was infuriated at how openly we went around together and ignored the company of men. So he tried to destroy our love—by accosting Helen when she was alone. He committed rape on her body. But he never touched her spirit, and our love did not falter.

She did, however, become pregnant, and when her father discovered her condition, he forced my brother at gunpoint to marry her, against the will of both of them. When her son— when you—were born, she deposited you with your father, and she and I ran off to New York City together, and left this life behind. My father, your grandfather, died of a stroke soon after I left. But before his death, he erected the tombstone with only my first name on it, to say to the world that for my sin I would be considered dead in his eyes, and that I didn't even deserve the family name. Of course I kept my name, but Helen changed her name to Minerva White, and became an illustrious photographer."

"You mean that Minerva White was my mother?"

"Yes. Didn't you ever wish it? Didn't you ever guess? We met you once, at a party in Greenwich Village when you were a boy. But we were afraid to reveal our identities, for fear of disrupting your life and alerting your father to Minerva's identity. It caused us great pain to keep silent. Later, when we tried to find you, we were told you had never returned from the war."

Only then do I realize why her face is familiar. It is the face in the photograph that my mother gave me, the photograph of her companion, Martha. There the mole sits, between her eyebrows, as evidence. I show her my mother's photograph of the luminous blossoms, and she weeps with understanding.

"Minerva and I moved to New Mexico," she continues, "where we lived happily for years while she photographed the desertscape and I wrote poetry. Recently, she died."

"Then I won't have a chance to speak to her."

"I decided to come home, to bring my life full circle. I found your father in a wheelchair. His legs had grown gangrenous with diabetes and had to be removed, so I decided to stay and take care of him."

"Why should you do this, after the way he treated you?"

"He is my brother, after all, and those things happened a long time ago."

"What became of Mrs. Warner?" I ask.

"She died several years ago. She choked on a chunk of apple and couldn't get her breath. Your father found her on the kitchen floor. Now he has suffered a heart attack, and he is near death too."

I look into his room, where he lies sleeping a heavy sleep. Rather than try to wake him, I decide to walk out to the cemetery, to give myself time to get my hearings and to digest Aunt Martha's story.

When Alexander and I reach the cemetery, I kneel before Martha's stone and weep for both my parents. Alexander watches in silent awe.

We return to the house and we go in to see my father, who has awakened. He is a tiny, shriveled creature who fills only a small part of his large bed. He can barely move his lips to say a word, even if he wants to. Martha introduces me, and his eyes widen and fill with tears. He tries to speak. I lean close.

"My son," he says, and he winces with pain. He is having another attack. Martha rushes to call the doctor. "Forgive," he whispers, but I can't tell for sure if he wants to forgive me, or if he wants me to forgive him.

"Don't try to talk, Father. Save your strength," I advise him. "We'll talk later, when you're well."

He tries to speak nonetheless. I am not sure what he is saying. It sounds like "All flesh is grass." In spite of all that we have never shared, I find myself crying and turn away, in order not to upset him further. Maybe I've seen too much illness and death to be unaffected, or maybe I'm growing more sentimental with age. Or maybe Aunt Martha is right and he is my father, after all. Whatever wounds there were have long since healed, and I have managed to forgive him at last.

When the doctor arrives, he makes my father comfortable, but he tells us that there is very little time left.

My son and I decide to stay in Elysium, at least until my father dies. During that time, I seek out remnants of my past and meet George Grimes, my high school friend, and Bruno Todd, my high school enemy, who are aging lovers. Even in their sixties, they continue to wear matching leather jackets and ride their motorcycle around the valley, with George's arms clutched tightly around Bruno's waist.

"I'm glad you've made your peace with being gay," I say to Bruno.

"We're just friends," Bruno says. George smiles.

"But everyone I asked about you said you were lovers," I confide.

"It's none of their business what we are," George says. "If people knew too much about us, they might be afraid of catching some disease or something. As long as we don't spell it out, they can think whatever they want."

"My father was Dell's lover," Alexander announces proudly. "But he died of AIDS."

"Alexander is my son now," I explain.

Bruno looks away, and George appears genuinely shocked. We promise to get together for dinner, but I doubt that we will find the time.

In looking for traces of Chester, I discover that I was the beneficiary of his will, which left me his home. Since they couldn't find me, the state took it over, but did nothing with it. A lawyer tells me that if I pay the back taxes, it will be mine. The house still stands and, after a brief look around, I realize that it would make a wonderful hospice for people with AIDS. Someday, I tell myself, the epidemic will be over, and there will be no more need for a hospice. Then maybe I can turn the place into a gay retirement home. When I return to tell Martha about my idea, she tells me she has been considering turning the family homestead into a Minerva White Museum once my father dies. We agree to help each other with our plans.

After another week, my father dies, and we bury him in the family plot.

With the help of a good lawyer, I am able to adopt Alexander legally. My book becomes a great success, and we are wealthy enough to set up both the hospice and the museum. My son Daniel reads my book in Washington and travels east for a reunion. He and Alexander become good friends. Aaron's parents, Esther and Sol, visit us frequently.

Many years later, I feel what Walt Whitman described:

Old age superbly rising! O welcome, ineffable
grace of dying days!

When it is finally time for me to die. Walt appears in a golden cloud to escort me to the next world, where Aaron and Louie and Chester are waiting for me.

And perhaps someday, a young writer of the twenty-first century will write a book about my literary career. I hope he won't have as much trouble trying to understand me as I had trying to understand Walt. I've tried to make myself clear, but who knows what obstacles history will erect between me and my future readers?

I certainly let myself get carried away, didn't I? I can just imagine what Aaron would have said about such a plot. "Sentimental and self-indulgent. If it were one of my students' papers, I would give it a D." He would be right, of course. Life simply isn't that neat. Maybe someday I'll make a novel out of that daydream, but for now I'll try a more realistic ending.

Notes for an Ending #2

I return to Elysium with Alexander to find that my father has been dead for years. Martha's stone is still there, but there has never been an answer to its mystery. All the people I knew in the valley are now gone. There was no point in going home again. We can't stay there. What would we do? Sit around and eat apple pie? My book contract has given me a modest sum, so I can choose what I want to do next. I ask Alexander if he wants to return to New York City or if he wants to take a guided tour of my America. If he agrees to travel, perhaps I'll try to find my son Daniel along the way. Then I'll settle down somewhere near Sol and Esther, and open an antique shop while Alexander finishes school. I hope we all live to see his graduation.

That sounds more plausible. But of course the only way to find out what really will happen is to wait until I get there. I'm just a little nervous, is all. Our stop is coming up soon and it's almost time to wake Alexander, who has managed to miss most of the beautiful view of New York State. But he's been through a lot in the last weeks and he needs his rest. Besides, I needed these hours alone so I could collect myself. I need to be ready to face both my past and my future.

What I've already learned on this trip is that I definitely want to keep writing. This book will have to end now, but I can start another one. Maybe, at long last, I can begin my book about Walt Whitman.